Crystal Child

The Diamond Star Saga

Carol Kauffman

Fulton Books
Meadville, PA

Published by Fulton Books 2022

All characters are fictional except those famous
names mentioned as real in the book.
55 Cancri-e and BPM37093 Star are real.
Specific locations on Earth and characters are entirely fictional.

ISBN 978-1-63710-089-9 (paperback)
ISBN 978-1-63985-567-4 (hardcover)
ISBN 978-1-63710-090-5 (digital)

Printed in the United States of America

To Dave, Mary, Kathy,
Kyle, Lindsay
Camden, Bennett,
and
Dean
Diamonds of my heart and soul

Love is the water of life
Drink it down with heart and soul

—Rumi

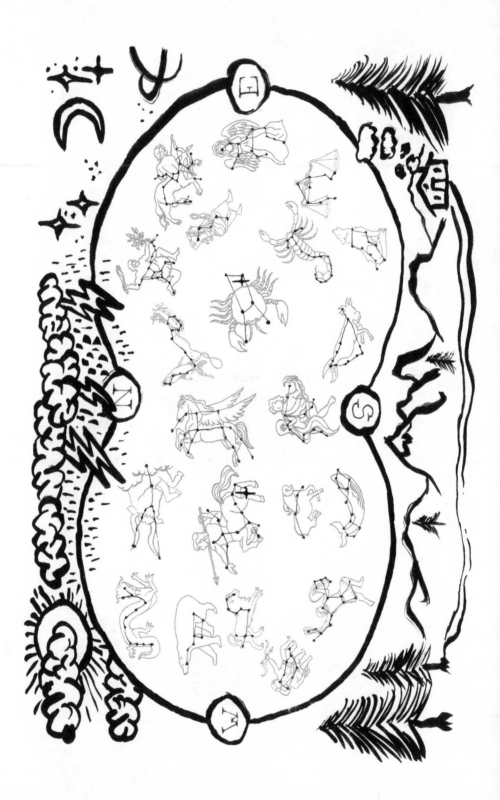

Prologue

○ ○ ○ ○ ○ ○ ○ ○ ○ ○ ◉ ○ ○ ○ ○ ○ ○ ○ ○ ○ ○

Planet 55 Cancri e
February 27, 2016

"Commence."

The electronic voice echoes off ancient stone walls. In low amber light, seven angular beings surround a suspended metal slab secured by four nearly invisible threads from the cave's ceiling. Whirring into motion, steel claws prod deep into the human's wounds: one deep gash under the right shoulder, one jagged hole in the center of the man's chest. Beads of sweat mingle with blood oozing from the man's chest, drenching his entire torso in a crimson sheen.

As the beings' claws click, tug, push, the injuries begin to shrink. Four minutes, six seconds later, the whirring stops. Although blood remains, the skin now bears no evidence of its recent wounds. Suddenly, twirling brushes descend and, without water or soap, scrub the stains until every drop of blood has vanished. All is silent for several seconds. Then the man stirs; his eyes opening halfway. Squinting at his captors, parched lips barely moving, he whispers, "Holy Christ."

The electronic voice announces, "Human reassembled. Vitals sufficient for ventromedial frontal implantation."

The man's eyes fly open. "Wha—implant. Wait, no no no. You're not—God, no..." Grunting, with great effort, he rolls onto his right side, propping himself onto his elbow. With his left hand, he grabs the claw closest to him. The being repulses him.

A jagged instrument above the table suddenly whirs into motion, its decibel level as loud as a chain saw. The man cowers. Over the clamor, the voice instructs, "Implantation imminent. Device set to shred left temporoparietal lobe in two and one half Earth seconds unless head precisely underneath."

The man cries out, falling back. Immediately a steel shield descends, tightly framing the entire forehead, eyes, and nose. His body goes limp. A jarring buzz, followed by one long beep. Blood trickles from the sides of the shield down the man's temples, dripping into his ears and onto the table. His breathing slows, stops. Four seconds later, his chest heaves as he arches his back, gasping, coughing. He blinks back crimson tears, wiping his blood-smeared face with the back of his hand.

The short being places its two claws on the man's shoulders. "Do not touch frontal area for three minutes, or you will disassemble. Listen, Human. Your Earth Quantum Community now extinct but for you and Crystal Child. Relocation imminent—Dolcany, Montana, USA. Crystal Child already at location. Sustenance provided by human-manufactured G-tube until your arrival."

The man's hands tighten to fists. His voice is raspy but forceful. "Wha—Jesus. Tube fed? You have her? She alone? Nononono, you can't do this. She's only two. God, only two... I need to get to..." He chokes, jerks to his left side, retches. Most of the yellow-orange projectile lands on the stone floor, mixing with the dirt, but bits also splatter onto the metal leg of the closest being, taller and larger than the rest. The being doesn't flinch. The human swipes his face with the back of his hand, groaning.

The short being repositions him back onto the table. It lowers its head to within an inch of the man's face. The human winces, turns away. Decreasing its volume, the being drones on: "Frontal implant inserted into your brain to ensure you cannot escape or divulge forbidden data without immediate detection. Technical advisory device [TAD] at new location also necessary for supervision. TAD cloning and programming complete. You will instruct Crystal Child TAD is twin brother. No additional information to Crystal Child about Cancri permitted. Additional inhabitants, human or animal, strictly forbidden. Failure to heed Cancri instruction will result in teleportation of Crystal Child to Cancri for readjustment and your immediate disassembly. Preferable for Crystal Child to develop in human environment, but not crucial. Male parent expendable."

The man struggles against the claws. "My-Myra? Oh god, Myra? Is Krissie with her mother? Just tell me that. Please. Please." He swallows hard, coughs.

"Live normal human life on Earth until February 5, 2027. Per prophecy, Crystal Child will produce formula for perfect water as critical for Cancri evolution. It is written. You secure Crystal Child survival for evolution of Cancri species."

"It is written? You mean the so-called prophecy we found that you stole from our database? It was just declassified. That paper's a piece of shit."

"Incorrect. Made from spruce before electronic upload. Not human excrement. Stand back. Device programmed for teleportation."

"Idiots." Face twisted in rage, the man turns toward the being to his right, jabbing a finger at its torso. "I will *not* obey. I will not do a goddamn thing until I see my wife and daughter completely unharmed and—"

"Quantum Community disassembled. Female parent of Crystal Child disassembled with rest of Quantum Community."

"Disa—wha—?"

"Not needed, disassembled"—*whir*—"English language synonym—*dead*."

Silence. Six seconds later, a scream splits the air, followed by staccato shrieks reverberating throughout the rocky chamber. The head being presses a flute-like metal instrument to the man's chest. In unison, the beings chant, "Eight six nine three zero."

The man's shrieks soften to whimpers, then mews.

Silence. Then—*beep, beep…pop.*

A wisp of smoke rises from the empty table.

The beings form a single line, exiting through a narrow oblong slit in the cave to the outside. In the distance, three volcanoes blast diamond-infused lava hundreds of feet upward, where it mingles with sparkling stars in an indigo sky.

Earth

One

• ◦ • ◦ • ◦ ◦ ◦ ◦ ◦ ◯ ◦ ◦ ◦ ◦ ◦ ◦ ◦ • ◦ •

Dolcany, Montana
January 21, 2027

Snowcapped mountains, a blotch of red, 1201—

"Kreestal, put your drawing away, please."

My scarlet pencil snaps. Stuffing my sketch into my book bag, I shift my attention to my science teacher, forcing a smile. Trying to, anyway. I can't. No way. The freaking dreams kept waking me up all night. Last night was the third night in a row. Where are they coming from? I try again with the fake smile. Nope. Just can't pull it off. Someday, when I have more energy, I need to tell him it's Kristal, not "Kreeestal." I don't know where he's from, but apparently, his language doesn't have short "i" sounds.

I glance out the window, away from Mr. Gabriel's frowny look. I hate that look. He always wears it when I'm "off-task," as my counselor puts it. Actually, I'm not too happy with myself either. These stupid recurring dreams have started to invade my daytime hours too, scaring the crap out of me. I thought maybe if I could just get these bizarre visions down on paper, the dreams might disappear. But focusing on the images only makes my ADD worse, and now my teacher's on my case again. These days it's hard to concentrate on anything in school except art. I love art class. It's my only—

"Kreestal." I look up. Holy moly.

Twenty-eight pairs of eyes lock onto mine. They're wolves, all merciless, salivating, eager to attack their defenseless prey—aka me. Go ahead. Rip me to shreds and fight over my bones. Whatever.

13

Dad says that "the milk of human kindness runs a little dry in middle school." That's an understatement. No one understands, so they judge you for every little thing. And for ADD kids like me, well, we're different. Especially today, I just can't think, nor can I deal with this humiliation right now. Something in my brain's just—not right.

The familiar heat begins at the base of my neck and crawls upward until my cheeks burn. Should I try to explain to Mr. Gabriel and the whole class the reason for my inattention today? *Excuse me, sir. Attention, everyone! I'm being slammed by visions of the color red, white mountains, and four random numbers. That's why I'm a little distracted today.* Would I get a little sympathy then? Ha, hell no. They'd chew me up and spit me out. And the teacher would send me back to the school shrink. I mean, who in her right mind gets blasted by pictures of mountains and red blotches in the middle of the day? Can't say I blame them for thinking I'm a weirdo. I am.

Swirling in the pit of my stomach, the anxiety rises to my neck, twisting my vocal cords into a strangled squeak. I take a little half-hearted cleansing breath like my counselor taught me. Finally I'm able to crank out a tiny fake smile. "Um, sorry. Was there—did you ask a question?"

Some of the wolves snicker softly. Others suppress grins. But oh, of course, Jackson Hynes, master bully on steroids, snorts openly. Mr. Gabriel shoots Hynes the evil eye, holding up a hand to silence him, the alpha wolf, and his underlings. Then he returns his full gaze to me. Hands on hips, he stares at me with that I'm-so-worried-about-you look. I hate that look too. I would rather he just yell at me. But he never does. Uh-oh, I know what's coming next.

"Kreestal, see me after class."

Yep, knew it. Crap.

My barely there smile falls from my face. But the knot in my throat sticks, and my eyes start to—oh no, not now. I whip them up to the ceiling and blink hard. Ah, tears squelched, just the way Dad taught me. Looking up always does it. He said it's a neurolinguistic or NLP trick, whatever that is. Well, dry eyes or not, I guess I'll just have to endure another wacko lecture after class. I hate being alone with Mr. Gabriel. And since winter break, he's asked to see me six times. Count 'em—six—ever since our unit on astronomy started. At first, I thought it must be that I'm hopelessly dumb in astronomy and he just wants to help. Except I'm not really behind, and he doesn't seem to want to tutor me on the material. Instead, he rambles on about some weird secret planet light-years away. When I ask him which planet, he gets all vague and says the name is not important for now. What the hell does that mean? He says I'll learn the name soon enough. And then lately he's been asking me all sorts of odd questions that have nothing to do with science. Talk about getting off track. Like, the other day, he asked if I know where I'm from. Why would he think I've been anywhere but Dolcany, Montana, all my life? Where's *he* from? That's the question. His accent isn't something I recognize. But he's never told me anything about his background. Why does he want to know about mine? What is his real agenda? It would be just quirky if he asked others the same questions. But no, it's just me. Creepy.

Last Tuesday, he asked me what I would do if I were suddenly kidnapped. Whoa. Time out. Why in the world would he ask that dumb question? He knows full well we kids are taught from kindergarten how to deal with strangers. Just don't deal with them. Duh.

Then sometimes he talks really fast, but stops himself mid-sentence, sometimes mid-word. The last time he made me stay after class he asked me how far back I remembered—age four? Three? And then he said, "Do you remem—" and stopped himself. And then he said, "Does your father—" and then he stopped again.

Sometimes it's just garbled ramblings with a foreign word thrown in here and there, and lately I've started to wonder if…well, the really scary thing—he always talks to me in private, insisting I keep our conversations secret from everyone—even from Dad. I haven't told anyone yet. But I'm probably an idiot not to. This is really over the line. What am I waiting for?

He's still staring at me. I nod. Crap. Yes, fine. I'll see him after class. At least it's after class this time and not after school as he usually asks. But in any case, I'm truly scared. If he does have a screw loose, shouldn't he be getting help? Wouldn't I be doing him a favor in the long run? I sneak a glance at the round industrial clock on the wall.

Tick, tick, tick. Why this school still has old analog clocks is beyond me. Except for the funding, which pretty much dried up after the COVID thing. The whole world went bonkers after that disaster. We're still recovering. Oh, well. The old clock still ticks. I guess that's all that matters. Fifteen more minutes. An eternity. My throat tightens again. He's jabbering on about planets and dwarf planets and asteroids but nothing about the planet-that-shall-not-be-named outside our solar system. He's reserved that topic just for me, for our "private time." A chill runs up my spine.

The wolves have settled except for Jackson Hynes, who keeps shooting smirks and sounds my way. Every now and then, a honk escapes, and the others laugh. Really? Grow up, people. I start to zone back out. My brain is standing in the middle of a snowdrift when the buzzer interrupts Mr. Gabriel mid-sentence. He sighs, throwing up his hands, yelling over the noise, "Dwarf planets, quiz Monday." But he's drowned out by the flurry of scraping chairs and scrambling feet as my classmates race to the door. I rubberneck over their heads to maybe catch a glimpse of my brother, Tad. Nope. The hallways are already teeming with too many other kids. I ache to join them. Instead, I gather my things and head toward Mr. Gabriel's desk. It's just the two of us now, like always. I take a deep, silent breath. I want to get out of here. I want to get out of here. I want to get out of here so bad.

"Ah, Kreestal."

The clipboard clacks softly on the desk as Mr. Gabriel sets it down. He sinks into the worn-out brown cushion on his wooden swivel chair, motioning me to sit in the smaller chair next to him. I slide into it, setting my book bag on the floor, trying to steady my nerves for the inevitable lecture. I glance up. He's staring at me with those marbly greenish eyes of his, like miniature worlds.

"Kreestal, I know you want to leesten and learn. You are a smart girl. ADD is no excuse for not leestening. You must force yourself to pay close attention. You may need to pay attention—very close attention een the near future…"

Here we go again. What's his point? Why does he beat around the bush so much? And just telling a kid with ADD to listen harder means he just flunked ADD 101. Maybe he should be the one listening to me.

"Um, I try. I really do, but people with ADD can't force themselves to do anything. I mean, the harder we try, the more our brain freezes, kind of like a computer with too many programs running." I sound like a know-it-all, but frankly, I do know about my diagnosis. I've lived it all my life.

Mr. Gabriel leans in, his voice dropping to a whisper like it's top secret or something. "But they also say young people with ADD attend better when thee subject matter ees related to their lives. Their eenterests. And although you do not understand now, the subject I'm about to talk about—it weel be highly related to your life. Possibly soon. Eet's time…"

Well, yeah. He's right about that. We ADDers do zero in when the subject interests us. But on the other hand, *what subject*? Related to *whose* life? It's time for *what*? Just more damn nonsense. His eyes bore into mine. I know what's coming.

"Kreestal. You know you must keep all our deescussions totally private."

Yep, knew it.

"Do not mention anything to your father or to your, uh, brother. Een order to enhance your focusing skeels, I would like to comeession you to devise a special project. And when finished, we weel, uh, surprise your father and your classmates weeth a great presentation. That ees why we cannot talk about eet to anyone yet."

The secrecy thing again. It's all I can do to keep from covering my ears and going blah blah blah all the way out the door. This is too bizarre. Until now, I've just nodded. But I'm not in the mood for games today.

"Wh-why me?"

He clears his throat. "Oh, uh, well, why not you? You…you, uh, are a great arteest and could render very lifelike peectures of…thee project. Eet's a fascinating planet. Not here in the solar system but far away. Eet will be a very eenteresting planet to draw. Especially…" He leans in. I lean back. "Especially seence its core is made of"—he lowers his voice to a whisper—"diamond." Diamond. Diamond? I

17

blink and say nothing. Holy moly, this clinches it. I have to talk to someone. He pulls back. "Uh, we'll deescuss."

Right, uh-huh, a project, complete with my brilliant drawings of a planet made of diamond. Top secret to surprise Dad and my classmates later. Seriously? Before I can stop my tongue, the word takes on a life of its own, and I spit it out. "Bullshit."

"*No!*" Mr. Gabriel swivels, half-pulls me out of the chair, gripping my upper arms so hard I'm afraid he'll leave bruises. I gasp. He drops his hands to his sides like my sweater burned right through his palms. I wish it would have.

"*Ow!*" Adrenaline is pulsing through my veins; the very thing I try to prevent. I can't believe what he just did. Luckily, I'm wearing a thick sweater, so I don't think he did any damage. But, I swear, if it were any thinner, he may have broken both my humerus bones. His pudgy appearance is deceptive. He's as strong as a rock. My next thought terrifies me. He actually could have... *No, no, no. Stop it.* I force myself to do the "erase-and-replace" trick Dad's taught me; so into my brain's movie screen, I force a rainbow with a Maltese puppy under it, jumping and wiggling. It obliterates the scary vision from a moment ago. But my body still remembers, and I can't stop quivering. I hope it doesn't show. I reflexively wrap my arms tightly around myself, massaging the places where he grabbed me. I'm so stunned I can't even protest.

"Oh...oh god, Kreestal. I did not mean to, but thees ees crucial to your—" He stops, sighs, shakes his head, runs his hands through a thinning crop of salt-and-pepper hair. "How can I... I am sorry, so sorry. I weesh... I just weesh I could say more."

Yeah, well, saying you're sorry is a start I guess. Oh god, the puppy/rainbow scene isn't cutting it and anxiety ripples through my stomach. I don't need more today, please. Ms. Tanaka's mantra is, "If you name it, you can tame it." Yeah, well, I've named my anxiety disorder Achilles, but it has definitely not been tamed. I hate my anxiety disorder even worse than my ADD. Butterflies slam against my stomach wall—up, down, back, front. Ms. Tanaka also tells me the fight-or-flight response is okay for the short-term. That type of anxiety sends energy to your body to run like hell, like when you've just met a bear in the woods. But what if the bear is a teacher you're not allowed to run away from until they're good and ready to dismiss you? Then you just have to sit there and let the adrenaline eat you up from the inside out, and over time, it wears you down. Yep, I'm toast. I admit. When will this "bear" let me go? I clear my throat. "I won't mention it. And I'll work hard on your project."

"No, *your* project. You need to know all about eet as soon as posseeble."

"Uh-huh."

He stares at me, a little too long, then turns to his desk, shuffling papers; usually his way of dismissing me. I notice his hands shaking. I stand, sling my book bag across my shoulder, and head toward the door. I can't get out of here fast enough, out of this classroom, out of this building. I just want to go home.

"Oh, uh, Kreestal."

Damn. I turn back.

"I have arranged for you to meet your project mentor after school."

My what? Project mentor? More tutoring? It's always after school when all I want to do is get the hell home. I hate tutoring with him and now with a stranger too? Will the new tutor be even worse? I stand in the doorway, realizing my eyes are puddling up. Stupidly, like a whiny kindergartner, I swipe my face with my sleeve.

"Mr. Gabriel, I… I studied really hard last nine weeks. I have a B-minus average. That's not so bad, is it?" Argh, that puzzled look again, but this time, I swear I see his eyes glistening too. What's with *his* tears? Am I *that* frustrating?

"Kreestal, no, that ees not why I am…leesten. Please do not think of thees as a puneeshment. Eet ees more…extra credit, eh? I see great creativity een you, and I want you to build your confeedence and your focusing skeells. Eet weel be fun, eh? You can do some amazing work. You can become an expert. You weel begeen today. Ees that posseeble?"

Today? I am thinking of just going home and crashing, maybe catching an episode of *Greta Garden Girl*. I know it's hokey, but her voice is so relaxing, and I'm thinking about maybe growing my own vegetables this spring. Tad would love it too. He craves nature like I do and is always intensely watching me whenever I interact with the flora and fauna around our yard and the woods beyond.

"Kreestal? Yes?"

I sip in a deep, silent breath, let it out, and actually smile a little at Mr. Gabriel. "Fine. Okay." I know he's lying about the purpose of this stupid project. But why? My little smile drops. I have to get out of his sight like now. Oh, great. I'm breaking out in a sweat. The wall behind Mr. Gabriel starts shimmering, and I feel a little dizzy. I probably have low blood sugar. Why didn't I eat something at lunch? Oh, yeah, the tacos—they looked so vile. Now my knees are starting to wobble. Mr. Gabriel's still talking, but all I'm hearing is, "Wa-wa-wa…" I keep wiping my face with my sleeve. This is *not* a good day at all. Oh god, his voice. Stop. Please stop. Unfortunately, his voice suddenly comes in loud and clear. I can't even respond. This is all so crazy.

"I have assigned my most advanced senior student, Aleksi, um, Alek Smeeth, to help you. Be back here at 3:05. You can call the— your father from the office."

"Yep." I bolt out the door before he can say another word or before I start screaming my guts out.

Two

• ◦ ◦ ◦ ◦ ◦ ◦ ◦ ◌ ◍ ◍ ◎ ◍ ◍ ◌ ◦ ◦ ◦ ◦ • ◦

January 21, 2027

Positive pep talk, PPT, is the program Dad's been teaching me for the last year. He says thinking positive will come in handy my whole life. So PPT, here goes:

So he's assigned a student tutor. Maybe I'm really doing just fine. It's just that they're required to keep assigning these extra instructors and projects because of my 504 plan, which says that the school must provide accommodations for the *handicapped*. Dad freaked when they used that word. He called it an *atrocity* to label me *handicapped*. But apparently, the school experts disagree. Ms. Tanaka, my school counselor, said medication might help, and the others were sitting around the table nodding. Dad exploded when she mentioned that, saying he could report the whole school staff for practicing medicine without a license. They must have backed off, and Dad hasn't mentioned it to my pediatrician, Dr. Reno. But sometimes I wonder if maybe it would help. The report says "attention deficit hyperactivity disorder, inattentive type." I'm the inattentive type because I'm not running rings around the teachers and throwing spitballs into ceiling fans. But I'm still officially "ADHD" because the letter *H* for *hyper* is officially in the diagnosis book and covers both the hyper, the inattentive, and combined types—three subtypes. It's crazy confusing. But other than the formal reports, they usually just drop the *H*" for *hyper* and call me ADD—always behind, always clueless, thinking about things no one else ever thinks about, and not paying attention.

Or paying *rapt* attention, just not to the stuff they want me to pay attention to.

Oh yech, the butterflies are solidifying into a block of lead in my stomach. Achilles, please give me a rest. Honestly, I don't know why *naming* it means *taming* it. It's still running wild, whether you name it anxiety or Achilles. Oh, well. *Hey, Positive Pep Talk girl. Feel better? Hello? Earth calling Kris. Way to go.* That pep talk really helped. *Not.*

I'm going to be late to my social studies class. Forgot to ask Mr. Gabriel for a pass but just couldn't stay there one more second. The supplemental manual should be here somewhere in this black hole of a locker. I sift through all the papers, plastic cups, notebooks, candy wrappers, and other things I should have trashed like last fall.

World Cultures addendum. There it is, stuck. I gently tug. As the slim manual slips out, a bunch of yellow three-by-five cards, two alien pencil toppers, and three quarters tumble out with it, scattering over the scuffed-up tile floor. I stoop, grab them up, and stuff them back into the locker, slamming it shut with my foot. I'll sort the damn things later. Or just trash them except for the quarters. Okay, I need to speed-walk to my next class. The hall crowd is thinning. Always rushing. Always…

Oh god, the red blotch slams into my head, then the number 1201 flashes on top. Stop. *Crap, go away, go away, go away.* I can't share these Loony Tune thoughts; they'd give me an even worse diagnosis than ADD, or they'd look at me like I was from Mars or that nameless planet…nope. Gotta keep it all to myself, even my drawings. I'm even afraid to spill this to Dad. Maybe ADD makes your brain deteriorate into dementia at a young age. *Oh no! No, Kris, don't even go there. Shut up, Achilles, just shut—*

"Hey, Kristal Chanda—*leer?* ADD girl, does ADD stand for *awfully dumb…ditz?*"

Jackson Hynes. My body stiffens. I guess my command to Achilles to shut up is just not working today. My good old nemesis, Hynes, won't let me pass. No one is supposed to know about my diagnosis. It's all supposed to be confidential. But nothing stays secret here. Most kids don't really care. But Hynes loves to use labels to humiliate his victims. And I seem to be his victim du jour. Great. Sometimes I almost enjoy verbally sparring with him. But today, I have no energy. Zero. Zip.

"Not today, Hynes." I try to maneuver past him.

He steps sideways to block me. "Hey, awfully dumb ditz girl, did you hear me? Maybe you're awfully dumb deaf girl too."

"Yeah, maybe." The agreement talking tool sometimes works, sometimes not. Today, not. I step sideways. He's in front of me again in an instant, sneering. Yep, he's on a binge. I bristle, trying not to let his words get to me, trying again to ignore him, twist around him, but he blocks me. I sigh. Okay, Kris, presto chango. Kristal Makkinen turns into Neural Ninja. Dad made me laugh when he suggested that name a while back along with the neural ninja dingbat distraction trick. Might as well try it out. Sucking in a mouthful of air, I fake a look of pure panic, pointing to his book bag. "A *stinkbug*. God, it's *huge*. Oh yech…" Stupidly, reflexively, he takes the bait, whipping his greasy head around, letting the bag slip from his shoulder and thump to the floor while he steps back, eyes wide.

Ayana Dufort, a popular girl Jackson has a crush on, stops and rolls her eyes.

"Oh, it's right there. God, don't crush it. It'll smell like a skunk, a *rotten* one." Glancing at me, she winks. I could hug her. She's so comfortable in her own skin. I love the way she lets her jet-black hair go natural. It frames her face like the mane of a fierce mama lion, sending a clear message, "Just try and mess with me." She wears Black Lives Matter T-shirts to school, and no one says a thing, even though we're not supposed to wear T-shirts with sayings on them that might be, as they put it, provocative. But she's the only black girl in our school, the only black person I've ever seen, and I'm kind of in awe of her bravery. We've been named co-project directors for the yearbook next year and just had our first meeting last Monday. I wish I could be more like her. She's so confident. I think that's why Jackson likes her and would never bully her. I probably come across as a scaredy little mouse. I'm easy prey.

Jackson gingerly picks up his book bag, eyeing me, then Ayana, then back to me as it hits him. Two girls just reduced him to a total idiot. He slumps, lips in a line so thin they almost disappear. He ignores Ayana but turns to me and jabs a filthy finger into my face. "Just wait, *bitch*."

"Bitch, appropriate usage in reference to female dog. Bitch, inappropriate usage in reference to human female. Very derogatory 79467."

Oh, Tad.

Jackson whirls around, shooting a murderous look my brother's way. "Get away from me, *alien*."

My jaw drops. Before I can respond, my brother places his hands on Hynes's flabby shoulders and pushes down, hard. Hynes smacks the floor with his ample butt. He hasn't secured his book bag, and now papers are flying all over the hallway. The shock on Hynes's face is priceless. I suppress a giggle and fake a wince instead. Sometimes my bro astounds me with his strength and how he stands by me no matter what the danger is to himself.

"Hey hey hey." Mr. Bilott, the vice principal, appears out of nowhere. He has an annoying habit of appearing on the scene just after it all unfolds and not seeing the big picture. "Tad, to the office. Now."

Ayana and I exchange looks. I'm speechless. Damn.

But Ayana drops her book bag, and hand on hips, cocks her head. "Mr. Bilott, it's Hynes. He was insulting Kristal and Tad. I mean, really insulting them. Just because of their, well, you know—"

"Ayana, rules are rules. Physical harm, zero tolerance."

Ayana shifts to her head to the other side. "Oh, but tolerance *is* mandated for endless verbal insults to people who don't deserve them?"

Mr. Billot opens his mouth to respond, then apparently thinks better of it. "Ayana, don't you have a class this period?"

"Yep, on my way."

"Go. You too, Kristal. Tad, to the office."

Ayana shakes her head, muttering something like "Can't breathe." Tad says nothing. I say nothing. Tad takes everything so literally he probably thinks he really does deserve punishment. Someday I'm going to learn to stand up and defend my brother. He certainly looks out for me. Ayana got in her piece. God, I hate myself right now not only for the ADD but for my wimpiness.

Tad, expressionless, makes an about-face and walks all stiff-legged toward the office. Hynes picks himself up, brushes his pants, and leans over to stuff the papers back into his book bag. Before I can turn away, there's his butt crack, about a half inch. This time, my wince is definitely for real. Ayana's eyes meet mine. Her eyes widen, then she grimaces, closing her eyes.

Mr. Bilott leans over and actually helps Hynes stuff papers back into his bag, acting all concerned, like, "Jackson, are you all right?"

Oh, gag. Physical harm, my ass. I almost laugh at my accidental pun.

Hynes straightens up; his eyeballs go to me, then Ayana, then back to Mr. Bilott. "Yeah." Even if he weren't okay, he'd never admit it. He slings his now-secured book bag back over his shoulder and, ignoring all of us, shuffles down the hall. Ayana will get away with this because he likes her. He's even smitten with her. But not me. I'll pay for it later, big time. And Tad, poor Tad. He's so misunderstood. But he's such a sweetie pie; the way he always tries to look out for me.

Mr. Billot waves his wrist. "Go on, you two."

My throat's constricting. I look up but just don't have the energy. The visions. Mr. Gabriel. My twin's in trouble, my fault. I can tell the tsunami is about to rip, and I can't keep holding the dam back any longer. The girls' restroom is two doors down. I bolt.

I hear Ayana calling after me. "Kris?"

I duck into the restroom just in time. Luckily, no one's here. Grab a stall, any stall. I rush in, slam, lock the door. *I'm so late. Don't care.* I look down. *Oh god, the last occupant didn't even flush.* Foul. Can't even sit down on the pot. I'll be contaminated. So gross. Last straw. My head explodes. My throat spews out staccato sobs, and the tears gush, drenching my cheeks. I lean my head against the graffiti-covered, lime-green door. It's smooth, cool, and slightly sticky.

A voice on the other side. It's Ayana. "Kris, hon, he's not worth all that. Save it for when the love of your life dumps you for some airhead with big boobs. You hear me? Don't let some ugly-ass bully—"

"Ayana?"

"Come on, girl. Come out, come out, wherever you are. Hey, I'm with you. What's really going on? Can't just be that idiot baby boy. Not worth it."

Slowly, I twist the lock and step outside. "It's"—breathe—"a lot of"—breathe—"things…" I yank out a brown paper towel from a nearby dispenser and dab my eyes.

Ayana's nodding. "Oh, okay, now that makes more sense. Yeah, I get you, girl. I really do. Havin' a my-whole-life-sucks kind of day. Been there." She jerks her head toward the dispenser. "Go ahead, use the whole damn roll."

I actually laugh. A little. "Thanks. Uh, you're gonna be late."

"Who gives a flyin'? You're in crisis mode. Been there. Can you have a serious girl-talk session with your mom when you get home?"

Her question takes me aback. I guess she doesn't know. Why should she? "My mom died when I was two."

"Oh, dear lord"—she pauses—"mine's gone too."

"What? Seriously?"

"Yeah, four years ago last Monday."

"My dad told me my mom was killed in some kind of an accident I think."

"The only accidental thing about my mama's death was she was in the wrong place at the wrong time."

"Wha—how?"

Ayana sighs. "Used to live in South Africa. My daddy was French. Mama, black as coal. Me, well, here I am. Like Trevor Noah except I wasn't officially born a crime. They changed the law, but not people's attitudes. But my dad, my gram, and me…well, here we are. Long story, not pretty or worth repeating. But I could always go to my mom with anything. That's why I asked you. I—" she stops, head down.

"Look up at the ceiling." I pass her a paper towel. "That's so not fair. Ayana, I'm so sorry."

"Yup." She stares at the ceiling but still has to dab her eyes. "Damn, I miss her."

"I… I don't miss mine. Don't remember her." Why did I just blurt that?

"Well, consider yourself lucky. My mama was"—Ayana looks to the ceiling again—"well, anyway, um. Hey, your brother, uh, I mean—"

The buzzer goes off. Finally, it's last period. I look up, then back to Ayana. She's acting like she didn't even hear it.

Well, if she doesn't care, I won't either. She asked about Tad. I might as well spill. "He has autism."

"Oh."

"He has an IEP, individual education plan. I heard one of the teachers talk to another a while back. She mentioned something about 'savant.' I asked my dad, and he said that means he's like almost-genius level with numbers, but he's way behind in language. Not vocabulary—I mean he knows a lot of words. But they say his social language is way behind—as you can tell."

"Yeah, But he seems really—I mean—protective of you. He practically eviscerated Hynes for pestering you. Wow, he's strong. I could tell he was holding back. It's almost like he could've—"

"Yeah, he's always keeping an eye on me. But, I mean, that's a good thing. And really, he wouldn't hurt a fly. We have fun together."

"I'm an only kid."

"Oh, bummer."

"It's okay. I'm used to it. So why does he say numbers at the end of everything?"

"I don't know. I asked him once, and he just said information. I quit asking. I don't think he has the language skills to explain it."

"Huh, maybe he's going to be the next Einstein."

"Ha, we'll see." Ayana's sympathy is already bringing down my blood pressure; I can tell. Before I can stop myself, it's out. "Mr. Gabriel keeps—I mean, today he grabbed me. It hurt, kind of."

"He *what*? Oh, girl. Damn, that's serious. You need to report that, like yesterday."

"That's not the only—he's been acting really weird toward me lately."

"Weird? Like how?"

"He...he asks these off-the-wall questions. Then he tells me to keep it all a secret."

Ayana's eyes get really squinty. "Are you—oh lord, that's a slam dunk. You listen to me, girl. Look at me. Are you listening?"

"Ye-yeah."

"You march your ass right down to the office and tell Edelstein everything you told me and then some. First, you won't get in trouble for being late. Second, they take this shit very seriously. If the guy is a perv, and I'm not sayin' he is, I don't have him for anything, so I don't know, but I do know a lot about pervs, and believe me, if he is one, you do *not* want to be alone around him—ever. Ever. Ever. Edelstein's a piece of work, but she's fair, and she will put an end to this crap."

"But—"

"No buts, sweetie. This is for real. Don't matter who you are. If you are hit on by an adult, even a kid, you gotta stop it. Nip it in the bud. Am I gonna have to carry you over my shoulder?"

"No, no. You've convinced me. I'll do it. Yana?"

"Huh?"

"I don't want you to get a tardy slip all because of me."

She rolls her eyes. "Didn't you just see me pukin' my guts out in the toilet? Those tacos they had at lunch, whew." She doubles up. "I'm thinkin' salmonella, E. coli—"

"Oh, Yana, no—"

She unravels herself and stares me down, grinning, hand on hip. "Seriously, girlfriend?"

"Oh, I get it. That's my ADD. Little slow on the uptake. Or I've been around my bro too much. He has no uptake at all."

Ayana's laugh comes from her belly. "Well, good that you get it cuz that's my story, and I'm sticking to it. I'm not totally lyin'. Those tacos they make—naaas-teee. But I'll be fine. Now go on."

"Thanks, Yana."

"Kristal. It'll be okay."

*****

I leave Ayana leaning over a sink, wiping something away under her eye. The office is just around the corner. Halls are empty. Heart pounding, I duck into the office lobby. A row of chairs is lined up against the wall. Tad's in the third chair down, by himself.

"I'm so-so-sorry, bro."

"It's okay, Kristal, 79461, 79461, 79461, 79—" Oh, bad, he repeats the number strings over and over when he's nervous. Poor Tad.

A stern voice calls out, "Tad Makkinen."

We both look up. Mrs. Edelstein stands in the doorway to her inner sanctum, a tall, skinny woman with old-fashioned wire-rimmed glasses hanging low on her beak nose and long, stringy black hair. She always wears black skirts and black jackets with rumpled white blouses. Probably to seem more authoritative. But behind her back, she gets all kinds of bullying too, mostly around Halloween.

She shakes her head at my brother. "Now what have you been told about repeating all those meaningless numbers?" She sighs. "Come on in."

Right now, I could slap her. She should know better.

Tad stands up, not an ounce of emotion, just blinking a little too much; don't know how he does it. He disappears into Edelstein's office, and she shuts the door. I stand at the desk, helpless. I guess I have two issues to discuss now—mine and Tad's. I feel so guilty I brought him into my mess. He was just defending me. Tears well up. *No, not again. Ceiling, Kris.* I look up, then at the secretary, her back turned to me, at the copier.

"Uh, Mrs. Toole?"

The machine's old and clunky, and she doesn't hear me. I wait. My heart is a tiny canary flapping its wings against my rib cage. What if Mr. Gabriel wants revenge after I tattle on him? Just how far could he go? I stare at the door. Maybe I should just forget the whole thing and get to my next class. But Ayana is right. And I do need to put in a word for Tad too. The *thrump, thrump, thrump* of the copier abruptly stops. Mrs. Toole pushes a couple of buttons and gathers the papers, smacking them on the table to straighten them. She looks up, sees me.

"Oh, Kristal, hi. You need something, hon?"

Courage, come on. *Sisu* as Dad calls it. Grit. Do it. Do the hard things, the right things. This could be life or death. Or at least arm bruises. That's abuse. Ayana's right. They take that very seriously. I'm sure. I don't want Mr. Gabriel to get in trouble. I just want him to get help if he needs it. And I never want to be alone with him again. I try to take a deep breath, but at this point, I'm panting like a traumatized puppy.

"I—uh, I need to speak with Mrs. Edelstein, uh, please?"

Mrs. Toole frowns, looks me up and down. "Kristal, are you okay?"

Justin Carter, ninth-grade office worker, rushes in without noticing me, hands Mrs. Toole an envelope. "From the high school." He turns and is gone.

Mrs. Toole glances at the name on the envelope, looks up at me, eyebrows raised, and thrusts it forward. "It's for you."

For me? I take it, stare at my name, then rip open the envelope. My eyes widen. Scribbled on a scrap of yellow legal paper:

> Lesson #1: Understanding Cancri e. Top priority. No, he's not crazy. I promise. And yes, you need to keep this all top secret. I'll explain, what I can, anyway. 3:05. Gabriel's classroom. Be there.
>
> —Alek

Everything else disappears from my mind. I look up at Mrs. Toole. She's got her head cocked and her eyebrows furrowed. I shrug. "I'm okay now. Could I have a hall pass, please?"

Three

∘ ∘ ∘ ∘ ∘ ∘ ∘ ∘ ◉ ○ ○ ○ ○ ∘ ∘ ∘ ∘ ∘

January 21, 2027

The three-o'clock buzzer startles me as once again I wasn't paying attention. It's so loud I can feel my eardrums vibrate. Instantly, hallways explode with the daily after-school rush: shouting, locker doors slamming, and shoes pounding the floor. Outside, twelve buses hiss and rumble, waiting for their passengers. Most students rush toward the exits, but I snake my way against the current, three doors from Mrs. Allison's room, back down to Mr. Gabriel's. Despite all the drama of the past hour or so, Alek's note intrigued me, and I find myself almost looking forward to meeting him. How did he know about my concerns with Mr. Gabriel? Sure sounds like he trusts him. Does that mean I should too? Just who is this Alek Smith?

Well, I know he's a senior. He must be damn smart because he was just named valedictorian of his class. I've seen him around, but we've never met. He's got a reputation for being geeky but fun. I have spotted him several times surrounded by classmates. They seem mesmerized. Sometimes they burst into laughter, like he's some kind of late-night comedian. Usually I spot him head down, in a hurry. He's taller than most of the other senior guys, kind of lanky. I heard the basketball coach practically got down on his knees and begged him to try out for the Dolcany Demons' varsity, but he turned them down. Guess he'd rather study. His chestnut-brown hair always seems a little mussed up, a few strands always sticking straight up as though he's been zapped by electricity, and other strands curl up into little spirals. But in a way, it's kind of cute. Overall, he seems, well, normal enough.

My stomach flutters. I hope I don't make a fool of myself. Maybe with his brains he can figure out a way I can listen to dull stuff and not tune out. And maybe he can explain some of Mr. Gabriel's off-the-wall behavior. At the entrance to Mr. Gabriel's classroom, I hesi-tate, feeling the back of my head with my hand. Of course, the bald spot is back. I finger-comb the unruly cowlick. Had it forever. Hate it. Dad says it makes him smile. He won't tell me why. Whatever. I lick my fingers and give it one more smooth-down. Gross. Hope no one noticed. Now quick stress check.

"Kristal, 79469." I jump. Tad's found me.

"Tad, are you okay? What did Edelstein say?"

"Need to control myself, 79469. Need to stop saying numbers after sentences. Detention. Monday, 79469."

"Oh, well, maybe you can't go around pushing kids, even kids like Hynes. But she should know better than to tell you to stop say-ing your numbers. I think I'll tell Dad about that."

"No, I'm okay, 79469."

"Tad, listen. I've got to stay after school a while. Go on home and tell Dad where I am. Um, tell him I'll be home in an hour or so."

"Okay, 79469." He turns, does his stiff Tad half-walk half-march through the double doors.

As I watch him go, my throat hurts. And now my stomach's gone from flutters to a twisty knot. I lean against the concrete wall outside Mr. Gabriel's classroom and sip in a long, slow breath. Ms. Tanaka said ADD often goes hand in hand with anxiety. So we're working on both my ADD and my anxiety with grounding techniques to keep me in the present moment so I don't let my mind wander or worry. I mentally label my surroundings. Let's see, scuffed tile floor. Bulletin board smothered with notes and announcements. Buses outside the double doors with their bangs and hisses. Um, oh, scents—Pine Sol, sweat, metal, bus fumes. Okay, name five planets. Mercury, Mars, Neptune, Venus, and Jupiter. Name three dwarf planets. Haumea, Ceres, Makemake. That's enough. Now am I grounded like they say I should be by now? In the moment? Mindful? Um, no. Why am I still so nervous? Shoulders back. *Kristal, you jerk, just do it!* I turn, step into the classroom, and quietly shut the door behind me.

There he is. Alek Smith is hunched over a desk in the front row—Hynes's seat. Oh, man. He had to pick that one. I glance around. Mr. Gabriel's gone. Alek's obviously too tall for this desk, and his "daddy longlegs" are sticking way out underneath. Head down, he's scribbling furiously on his legal pad. I don't think he sees me.

But he must know I'm here because, without looking up and without introducing himself, he plunges right in. "Why do you think Mr. Gabriel is so hung up on making sure you learn about the universe? And that mystery planet—why does he want you to do a whole project on it? And in secret, no less?"

I plop my book bag on the desk next to Hynes's and warily lower myself into the seat. "No clue."

Alek stops scribbling. Our eyes meet. Unlike Tad, with his usual blank expression or Jackson Hynes with his permanent sneer, Alek's face is genuine and upbeat. I blush. Does he notice my nerves? He doesn't seem to.

Tapping his chin with his pencil, he says, "Hmmm, maybe Mr. Gabriel came from that alien planet. Maybe he's really an alien in disguise." He wiggles his eyebrows like Groucho Marx in those old movies Dad would show Tad and me. Then suddenly he twists his face, goes all bug-eyed, and cocks his head like a zombie.

A giggly squeak erupts from my throat. God, Kris, great first impression. Am I in kindergarten or what? Why can't I control myself? I shut my mouth, forcing a casual smile like I'm just playing along. "Uh, yeah, that must be it."

Alek smiles but says nothing. He sits. I sit. My stomach feels like it's cement mush. It must be the muffin from breakfast cause I didn't even have lunch. Yuck, omigod, is Alek testing me some-how? Does he expect me to fill in the conversational gap? Yikes, Kris, say something. Anything. Suddenly, I blurt, "I heard it might snow tonight." Oh god. I wince. Idiot remark. What does that have to do with anything? Like he cares. Like anyone cares about the snow but me.

But Alek's next words make my jaw drop. "Hope so. Just look out that window. Brown, gray, taupe—all different shades of boring."

Oh. My. God. He actually understands. I nod, slightly at first then more vigorously. My stomach is actually starting to settle a little. "Yes, and I—"

Bang. The door bursts open, slamming the wall. *Not now, oh god, please not now.* You've got to be kidding. Jackson Hynes, thumbs in jean pockets, clomps toward my desk in his clunky old snow boots. Why can't he see how ridiculous he looks? He's gloating, triumphant he's found me. Yep, he got me cornered. And now it's revenge time for the stink bug trick. I knew this would happen, just not so fast. Crap. And my brain's gone numb. I can't think of a single counter-revenge maneuver. I wish I could disappear into the ages-old woodwork right now.

Hynes bends down, glares into my face. Yuck, waaay too close for comfort. I can smell the onions from the nasty tacos he obviously had for lunch. Double yuck. Then he turns, taking one step sideways, and stares at Alek up and down. Then it's back to me with his infamous sneer.

"Hey, Goldilocks, who's sitting in *my* chair? Oh, it must be your new tutor. What are you learning today, ADD girl? Maybe I can help. Let's see. One plus one…"

The dreaded flush prickles my collarbone and spreads to my face. Now what? Okay, do what Dad has taught me when all else fails. Breathe, ignore, breathe, ignore… But obviously, Alek hasn't gotten Dad's memo. Instantly, he unwinds his long legs from the seat, slowly rising to his full height. Whoa, he's even taller than I thought. No wonder Mr. Epley kept hounding him to join the basketball team. Towering over Jackson, Alek cocks his head, examining Hynes as if he were a specimen in a biology lab. Jackson's eyes narrow, and his fists clench. I glance at Alek. What's he up to? Bracing for an outburst, a punch, something worse? But to my surprise, he breaks into a wide grin.

"Hey, buddy. Can you keep a secret?"

Jackson scowls, but I can tell he's as shocked as I am. I keep my poker face, but inside, I'm smirking like hell. Here is Alek—

taller, older, stronger, and definitely the sharper knife in the drawer. Alek owns this. Jackson regains a little composure but not much. His voice doesn't sound quite so snarky.

"Yeah, so?"

"Yeah, *so*?" Alek drops to a whisper. "Are you kidding? You knew about the theft, right? The keys?"

Jackson's face turns cherry red, just like mine does. Who knew Hynes could get flustered too?

"Keys? What keys?"

"*Thee* keys. You mean you don't know?"

"Know what?"

"You're kidding, right? To the safe. Keys to the safe. The *school's* safe. With all the money. You knew that, right? I mean, everyone knows by now."

"What safe? What money? What keys?"

Alek shakes his head. "Sorry, man. If you don't know…" He dramatically glances right, left, then leans in further, lowering his voice. "All I can tell you is that Mr. Budenkauf hired me to enlist the help of certain students, you know, the most trustworthy ones." He jerks his head my way. "Like her. We're holding initial orientation meetings for each student. This is private. So I would appreciate it if you would—"

Jackson's lip curls. "You're full of—"

"Information? My God, yeah, you're exactly right. It's so damn complicated. See, the contents of this safe need to be protected to the max. And someone blew it. So we gotta work together on this. Don't feel bad you weren't chosen. But now that you know, you have to promise not to tell anyone. And I'll have to tell Budenkauf so he can keep an eye on you. You do know who Mr. Budenkauf is, right?"

Jackson stammers, "Bu—who?"

"Boo-hoo? Ah, man, don't cry. He's FBI. See? I can rhyme too. Hey, wait a minute. Didn't I see you with a key just the other day?" He turns to me. "Didn't Jackson here have a key dangling from his keychain, you know, the one on his backpack?"

I decide to play along. It's such a relief not to be the one in charge. "Uh, I did, actually."

Jackson's eyes grow even wider. "Me? A key?"

Alek fakes a frown. "There you go. Rhyming again. What's with that?"

Jackson's nostrils flare. "No, I—shut up. I don't have a key. You're crazy. Why would I—"

"Whoa, buddy, maybe you didn't hear me. We're missing a very valuable key. Since it's worth more than three thousand dollars, it's a very serious, criminal offense—grand theft, a *felony*. Are you sure—"

Jackson's eyes bug out. "No. *No,* I didn't take any stupid key. Don't know what you're talking about. You're…you're…"

"Oh, I forgot. Ayana told me she—aw, never mind."

"Ayana? Ayana Dufort?"

"Jackson, my man. What other Ayana is there? Ah, one sharp girl. And well, she told me…"

"She told you what? Wh-what did she say? Tell me. *Tell me!*"

"Geez, calm down."

Jackson shrugs. "Wha-what did she say?"

Alek pauses, stares at the ceiling, then back down to Hynes. "She mentioned you. Said something about help only *you* can give her. That's all I remember."

Without another word, Hynes pivots, heads clumsily toward the door in his clunky boots, and disappears. Alek stands there, shaking his head for a moment, then ambles to the doorway, craning his neck, checking the hallway up and down. Returning to his seat, he mutters, "I tell you. They never quit, always a fresh crop every year."

I sit there, slack-jawed. He could have decked Hynes in a second, but instead, Alek used 100 percent mental muscle. Verbal judo black belt. He crushed it. All with just words. He reminds me of Hawkeye Pierce, the medic on the old TV show *M*A*S*H*, which takes place in an army-based medical unit during the Vietnam War in the sixties, last century. Dad lets Tad and me watch it, and Tad is fascinated with the characters. He always pats the couch and says, "Mash. Sit," when he wants to watch an episode. I don't know why he likes it so much; most of the jokes are what Dad calls "gallows humor" and must be way over his head. And here Alek is acting just like Hawkeye Pierce. He certainly gets it.

"That was incredible. You remind me of this guy on TV, Hawkeye Pierce, and—"

"*M*A*S*H*? You watch *M*A*S*H*?"

"Omigod, yes. You watch it too?"

"Oh, man. One of my favorite old-time shows. I binged the whole eleven seasons a few years ago and still catch an episode every now and then. Hawkeye is my hero."

"You...you kind of look like him a little. And act like him. Well, a younger version. Is that where you learned how to deal with bullies?"

Alek shrugs. "Maybe, never thought about it. Now that you mention it, yeah, probably. Hawkeye's just so damn...quick on his feet."

"Like you."

"Ah, that was nothing."

"You're being modest. But you were actually incredible. Just like a real FBI guy."

"FBI? Oh, uh, yeah, well, my version stands for Fierce Bully Intervention. Used to call it that. Been a long time since I needed it. I'm a little rusty." Alek winks.

This time my giggle is natural. "Omigod. That's priceless. But then who's this Mr. Buden—"

"Kristal, come on..." Now his face goes deadpan as he cocks his head. I see the faintest crack of a grin. There I go again—slow on the uptake. Now I get it. We both burst out laughing.

"Okay, Alek, or Hawkeye. All that verbal judo stuff was very impressive."

"Verbal judo. Ha, that's good."

"My dad calls verbal judo 'sparring with words.' He said if I learn to do it well, I can be a 'neural ninja.'"

"Awesome, yeah, exactly. I guess I became a 'neural ninja' by a couple years of trial and error. I had to learn fast or end up permanently black and blue and red from bloody noses. Man, was I colorful for a while there." He winks again.

Alek? Bullied? No way. "I'm bullied because I have ADD. But you—why?"

"People get bullied for lots of reasons, anyone who's a little different. They chewed me up and spit me out because of my accent. And the way I dressed. Oh, uh, and my toes. Yeah, being different in any way, that's a cardinal sin in most schools."

"Your accent? You don't have an accent. And you dress just fine. And what about your toes?"

"My toes? Let's just say I stayed out a little too late one cold winter night in a tree. I only lost two. Just two. No big deal. Don't even miss 'em. Just can't wear flip-flops in the summer."

"Two toes? My god, Alek, that's—"

He brushes me off. "That was nothing. The big reason I was ostracized"—he leans in close—"was because someone found out about my grandmother and did the math."

I'm puzzled. "Your grandmother?"

"She died before I was born. Her name was Binta. She was from Sierra Leone."

"Sierra Leone? Isn't that an African country?"

"Yep. She was a Mende."

I look at Alex's curls and his tan skin. "Oh. Well, Ayana is half black, and she just struts her stuff. She's popular with both boys and the girls. I'm not sure, but I don't think anyone bullies her. She has that...that 'don't mess with me' air about her. From what I've seen, people here respect that."

Alek smiles then nods. "I'm glad. But there may be things going on you don't see. Then again, maybe not. I would certainly hope that with this school's 'no tolerance' policy, that wouldn't happen."

"But it happens to me and Tad. Mainly Hynes, but others seem to fall in line after him. And then when Tad came to my defense today, he pushed Hynes to the floor, and then Tad gets in trouble!"

Alek shakes his head. "Ah, unfortunate. That sucks." He suddenly breaks out in song: "When will they ever learn? When will they e-ver learn?"

"What's that?"

"Ancient, ancient folk song. Pete Seeger."

"Who?"

"Nevermind. We're getting off track. So as I said to Jackson, she's one amazing girl. I should have done that from the beginning. That strut-your-stuff attitude was a steep learning curve for me. I could've learned a lot from her if she'd come along before me. Anyway, I finally assimilated. Took me, oh, about three years to sound completely American and perfect my uh... FBI style. And I grew a little. Uh, actually a lot. The rest of it? Couldn't care less." He chuckles, looking down at his outfit—jet-black jeans, an old Red Hot Chili Peppers T-shirt, black-and-white Vans. "Is this trending? No clue. Don't care. Long as they fit, and they're comfy. Does my bike get me where I want to go? That's all I need. Does my hair keep my head warm?"—he shrugs, finger-brushes his head—"Bed hair, don't care."

I have to smile. And to think I was all worked up about my one cowlick. This guy doesn't seem to have one self-conscious bone in his body.

He grins. "Anyway, someday when we have time, I'll teach you all my FBI tricks. But now time for lesson number 1."

He immediately starts clicking icons on his iPad. "Here we go. You think these little school bullies are a pain. Wait till you, ah"—he shakes his head—"so, Kristal, even though we don't know for sure yet, this inconsequential little planet Mr. Gabriel wants me to tell you about could become a big obstacle in our quest to save our very own planet Earth, uh, maybe soon. It's good you're worried about it. You should be. And you in particular may, or may not, have to, well, play a part in it whether you want to or not. We just don't yet know. I know this must seem crazy to you. It is crazy. But it's real. And we have to deal with it. Soon. So—"

What did he just say? It's pure gobbledygook to me, and I can't interrupt him because the guy's on a roll now, talking a mile a minute.

All of a sudden, seven pictures of a planet pop up on his screen. Two are similar—rust-colored with splotches of dark, revolving closely around a huge sun. But the one that intrigues me the most is the cut-away version of a planet in which the center looks like this huge diamond. Holy moly, Mr. Gabriel wasn't crazy after all. Each rendition has the name "55 Cancri e" written below.

Alek stops, scans the room, then bends his head closer, pointing to the planet's name. "Listen. I figured Mr. Gabriel wouldn't say the planet's name out loud. He's right. It's dangerous. I understand. We may be under surveillance. That's why he's acting pretty off-the-wall, nutso, and ready to be carted off. Am I right?"

I nod. My eyes must look like moons by now. I stare back at the cut-away picture. "Is…is that like diamond here in the core?"

"Yep, we'll get to that in a minute. Now I know you and Mr. Gabriel have had your differences. And of course, sometimes he's going to come off as real caddywonkus. But he's as sane as they come. Trust me. Kristal, there are things happening—we think—and the sooner you're clued in, the better. But if we dump it all at once, you'll self-destruct. That's how insanely complex this is. But for starters, I'm going to give you a little more intel than I should. And just like Dr. Kur—ah, Mr. Gabriel—I'm going to ask you to promise me this conversation will not leave the room. Someday we may have time for our FBI stuff. But now we have no time for games. This. Is. Serious."

I can tell he means it. In fact, his enthusiasm for this topic reminds me of Mr. Gabriel. What is so crucial and confidential about this Cancri planet? When will I get answers? Alek is staring at me again. "We wish there was a better way to get you started, but there's not. So promise me you will never say this word"—he points to *Cancri e*—"outside of this room, not anywhere inside this school, not to your dad, especially not to the…that…your brother."

Achilles is rearing its ugly head again. I swallow. "Sure, of course, I… I promise but—"

"Listen. It sounds really off-the-wall, but it is true. Mr. Gabriel has an inside track. He knows stuff, and well, he wants you to understand that this information is crucial for you to know. I repeat—do not breathe a word of this. People will think you're crazy, just like you're thinking I'm crazy right now."

"I don't think you're crazy. You're one of the smartest people I know. Well, I don't know you exactly."

"Yet."

Oh, boy. With one word, he's just told me I'm going to need a lot of tutoring. "If this planet is so important, why has Mr. Gabriel singled me out, just some dumb, ADD kid?"

"Kristal, don't ever, *ever* talk about yourself like that. Did you know Einstein didn't talk until he was four? Or that Edison's teachers told his parents he would never amount to anything? No doubt Einstein and Edison would be labeled ADD today. But look at how they changed the world. Never call yourself dumb. Trust me. Listen to Mr. Gabriel. He has a reason for everything he does. As I said, he...he knows things, and I wish...ah, I shouldn't—"

"You wish what? What do you mean? Is Mr. Gabriel a scientist? You know, like more than just a teacher?"

Alek is quiet for a few seconds. He starts to speak several times but falls silent. Finally, he says in almost a whisper, "See? Told you you're not dumb. You're very perceptive. Okay, yes, he's a scientist— one of the best. But you absolutely cannot breathe a word of this to anyone, not even Mr. Gabriel. He doesn't want information to get into the wrong hands. He doesn't want anyone, especially you, to know yet."

"Know what?"

"Oh, Kristal, it's complicated." Then he leans in. "But he has—I mean, he's a scientist working on top secret stuff."

"So why is he here teaching a bunch of ungrateful middle school students? Wouldn't that be a waste of his talent? Doesn't NASA or some other top-level agency need him?"

"Oh, I'm sure they would all love to get their hands on him. But he's got a good reason for maintaining a low profile right now."

"What reason?"

Alek takes a deep breath, closes his eyes like he wishes he hadn't said what he just said. Finally, he points his index finger in my face and mouthes "you."

"Me?"

His eyebrow goes up, and he nods ever so slightly. "And if he knew I was talking to you about this, he would probably blow a brain fuse. Talk about being an ingrate. I mean, he once saved my life, and I owe him. Oh, man, I shouldn't be telling you this. Anyway, trust me. He's here for your protection. But you can't let on you know this."

"*But why?* Am I in danger?" I'm breaking out in goosebumps. This is getting scarier by the minute. Alek's looking really guilty.

"Oh, man, I should have prepared for our first session a little better. I guess I underestimated your curiosity. Well, here's the absolute truth. We just don't know. But things are likely going to happen soon. So it's best to be prepared. Uh, you know, like the Scouts say."

"Alek, I'm no Scout. Prepared for *what*? How can I be prepared for something I know nothing about? Why can't I say anything? I mean, my dad…"

He shakes his head. "Trust me, just don't. And about that incident today, yeah, he told me."

I blush. "You mean, when he grabbed my shoulders?"

"He shouldn't have done that. He feels horrible."

"I said a swear word."

"But Kristal, that's still no excuse for what he did. Are you okay? I mean, did he leave any marks?"

I blush. Can't exactly pull down my sweater and check my upper arms right now. "Uh, I don't think so. Nah, it wasn't anything. Don't worry about it."

"Did you report his behavior?"

I sit for a moment. Might as well be truthful. "No, I… I was going to. I was in the office and had just asked Mrs. Toole if I could see the principal, but then I got your note. You said he wasn't crazy. So I decided to wait and see what you had to say."

"Hmmm. Headed you off at the pass, did I?"

"Uh, yeah. You could say that."

"Whoa, okay. You have every right to report him if you still want to, but if you could just hold off for a while, I know he's been stretched to the max by things going on right now, yet he can't tell you about it, and frankly, it is driving him a little insane. But truly, he would never, ever hurt you."

"I believe you. But he looked so…*so intense*. Alek, what's going on?"

42

"Question of the century. A lot. We think. No signs yet, but we need to prepare just in case. And you're involved whether you remember or not. But it's not all that pleasant, and it's a hell of a long story, so it's best we go nice and slow. Little by little."

I feel a surge of frustration. "You mean like water torture? Drip drip drip—Alek, *please*…don't do this to me!"

Alek's expression turns miserable, and he slumps in his seat, nodding. "Tell you what. If Mr. Gabriel stays relatively sane, and if I start debriefing you, will you keep all this secret for now?"

"I… I guess."

"Your guess isn't good enough. You have to keep everything a secret. Everything."

"Okay, okay, I will."

"Good. Let me know when you start to feel overwhelmed." He jabs his finger at his iPad. In large letters, I read silently, "55 Cancri e." He puts his index finger to his lips and shakes his head. Apparently, to say this planet's name out loud is a gigantic no-no.

But why? Guess I'll just have to shut up and listen.

Four

· ○ · ○ · ○ ○ ○ ○ ○ ◉ ○ ○ ○ ○ ○ ○ · ○ · ○ ·

January 21, 2027

With electrifying speed, Alek displays photos, renderings, charts, graphs, and fun facts about a strange planet called 55 Cancri e. The planet is forty light-years from Earth; its sun is from the constellation Cancer. It's twice the size of Earth. It doesn't rotate, so it has a perpetual day side and a perpetual night side. But both sides are so deathly hot no human could ever live there. But the weirdest thing—its core is most likely diamond—pure diamond. I'm about to ask how that could be but can't get a word in edgewise. Alek's a teaching maniac now. He's describing its year—only eighteen hours long. I cannot fathom a planet twice Earth's size making one full zoom around its sun in less than an Earth day. And it has a lot of volcanoes that probably shoot out diamonds when they blow. Cool.

Normally, I'd be tuning out by now, but his presentation just flows into my brain. I can tell Mr. Gabriel really knows his stuff and wants his students to learn. It's just that my science teacher's way of presenting information is just, well, not as interesting as Alek's. Or maybe it's all Alek's cool visuals or...

"Time's up. Questions?" My new tutor clicks the off button on his iPad, stuffs it into the case, and zips it shut but stays seated.

"Yes, the obvious, of course."

"Oh, you mean, why am I teaching you about this distant planet of fire and diamond?"

"Well, yeah."

"Uh-huh, well, that's maybe lesson number 76."

44

I sigh. Fine. I have more questions than ever, just not the ones he's expecting. But I need to talk, and Alek seems to be the only one with the patience to listen. At least, maybe he will.

I start to sputter, but then get my bearings. "I… I'll study more about that planet. I promise. But I mean, shouldn't we be worrying about our own planet right now? You know—like, for instance, I read about all the glaciers here in Montana. Alek, they've all receded like to almost nothing. This is northern Montana. And it's not just Montana—the ice caps are melting into the oceans, and the oldest and thickest ice in the Arctic is almost gone. I saw the saddest photo in my dad's Ecological Times journal the other day—a polar bear balancing on this teeny circle of ice like it was wondering—what the hell happened? I see my classmates and teachers just going about their daily lives as if everything's fine. Well, it's not fine, is it? And when I try to talk to my dad, he looks like he's going to blow a fuse, and his face gets all red, but he doesn't want to talk about it. I mean, what's his deal?"

Alek taps his temple. "All excellent questions. As for your dad, uh, I don't know what his deal is. Not really. Yep, the glaciers are definitely disappearing, sea levels rising, and no one seems to be moving fast enough to really fix it. It's all, well, yes, scary and maddening. People are aware. It's just that we humans have an annoying habit of not planning—or caring enough—about the future. Technically, the solutions to Earth's problems already exist."

"They do? Then why? I mean, really? I… I didn't know that."

"Lots of people don't know that. You know that parable about the grasshopper and the ant?"

A vision appears of Dad and me sitting on my bed with a big picture book. "You mean the one about the grasshopper playing his fiddle all day long while the ant stockpiles food for the winter?"

"Yep. A lot of grasshoppers in this world. Not enough ants." His words aren't very encouraging.

"Alek, most of the kids in my class just kind of look at me funny when I bring this stuff up. Some agree, but then go back to talking about their newest video games or who likes who or what cars they'll drive when they turn fifteen. They tell me to quit worrying so much.

But for me, it's torture not knowing if we'll have a white winter like we used to, like living in some kind of endless, snowless Groundhog Day. I mean, for some reason, I crave snow…" I trail off. What makes me think Alek's any more interested than my other classmates? But his eyes stay fixed on mine, and he's nodding.

"I know what you mean. Kristal, I didn't mean to totally discourage you. Many people do care. They care very much. But we're—they're—running into a few roadblocks, like power struggles and funding. You're not a weirdo, not at all. You just need to find your own niche."

"My own niche?"

"You know, get with a group of people who share your values. People all over the world are working like mad to get this planet back on track. You'll fit in. You will. That's why we're talking today. But right now, your job is to listen to Mr. Gabriel and ignore that bully of yours."

"They both think I'm a ditz."

"Stop that."

"Well, they do, although Mr. Gabriel doesn't come right out and say it. But I don't know. Sometimes I tend to agree with them. I mean, I worry about my brain, especially lately."

"Worried about your brain? Like how?"

I take a deep breath. Let it out, Kris. He might commit me, but I've got to tell someone. And for some reason, although I've just met him, Alek seems to be someone I can confide in. He hasn't called me weird yet.

"I'm, um, getting these strange visions, sometimes dreams and sometimes daydreams or maybe pieces of a memory—" Oh no, I just can't. "I'm sorry, I keep rambling. Never mind. You need to go home."

"No, no. Keep going."

Wow. He's not looking at me like I have three eyes or a purple horn on my head. He's looking at me as though he's waiting for my thoughts, like I actually have something to say. Suddenly, I'm spilling my guts. "I keep seeing—sensing—this other land, a valley, maybe. All snow covered, with cabins way out in the middle of nowhere and with mountains all around. Here, look…" I hardly ever show anyone my drawings. But warily, I pull out my sketches.

His eyes widen just a tiny bit as he takes a look. "Kristal, these are good, very good—the perspective, the detail. Omigod, there's Syl"—he clears his throat—"You say, you remember this?"

"I don't know if it's a memory or just a-a, I don't know, something I saw on TV. But often, in front, I see this…this red color."

Alek points to the crimson blob in my sketch. "That?"

"Yeah, sometimes it makes me happy, and sometimes, well, it's out of place, and I…"

Is Alek turning a little pale? Better back off. I stuff the sketches back into my folder. "Maybe I'm just remembering a winter when I was a baby, and I saw a cardinal or something."

Alek clears his throat. "Uh-huh, Kristal, did you ever tell your father about these dreams?"

"A few times. He told me they were just dreams. He said we've always lived in Montana."

"Huh. Hey, I wouldn't bother to mention it again to your dad. He's right. Probably nothing. We all have weird dreams sometimes." Alek pauses again, glances at his mobile phone. "Um, well, we've gone on a little too long. But as I said, what we discuss here stays between us, not even Mr. Gabriel, not even your father, not your brother. Just for now. Timing is everything. It will all come to light somehow, piece by piece. Otherwise, things could go south in a heartbeat. I hate to be so mysterious, but I have to be. Is that clear?"

"No, not really, but it's clear that I need to stay quiet."

"Yep, you'll just have to trust us that you'll eventually know what all this is about. We'll pick up on Monday. Just wait on this stuff, please. Promise me." The frantic look he gives me scares me. What the hell?

"Okay, fine. I promise." His smile returns as he gives me a little nod.

"Okay, gotta go feed Schrödinger."

"Schrödinger? Your dog?"

"Cat."

Momentarily I forget our odd conversation about planets and dreams and secrets. "A cat? You're so lucky. I love cats. Does he wander off a lot?"

"Ha, yeah. You could say that. He's been coming around at dinnertime lately for the past week or so. I'm trying to reinforce his presence by being there and feeding him."

"Why do you call him Schrödinger? Why not Fluffy or Max?"

He smiles. "Long story. Google Schrödinger's cat."

I don't know what he's talking about. Schrödinger's cat must have been one special pet. Alek's worldly knowledge astounds me. I guess that's why he's valedictorian. Duh. I glance at the clock— almost five. "Well, better get going. You don't want Schrödinger to find another house for dinner and disappear again."

"Hope not. I think he's getting the idea. And just to cement his loyalty, I'm feeding him his hands-down favorite—salmon pate. Funny how salmon is my favorite food too. We often dine together. Well, my salmon is a bit more, uh, palatable."

I wish I could get to know this cat sometime. I'm jealous. But of course, all my tutoring will be at school. I smile and nod. "Give him a little scratch behind the ears for me, okay?"

"Will do." Alek starts for the door. "See you Monday after school. And remember, do not even whisper the name of this planet to anyone. And everything else, zip it. Pinkie promise?"

"What?"

"You know." He holds out his pinkie finger. I get it. I hold out mine. Our pinkies intertwine. He pulls back. "Bad, horrible luck if you break a pinkie promise."

"Alek, don't scare me. It's just a kid thing."

"Well, let's not tempt fate."

"I get it. I won't spill."

"You can't now, especially after the pinkie promise. You got a ride, right?"

"My dad's waiting outside."

"Okay, good. And, Kristal—"

"Hmmm?"

"You're not crazy or stupid. Never believe a bully. But please, please believe me."

And Alek is out the door.

Five

Helsinki, Finland
February 27, 2016

The elderly gentleman with thinning white hair and a trim white beard sits in the waiting area, gnarled fingers fidgeting with a large manila envelope. A door opens. He looks up, smiles brightly at the young assistant, and speaks in Finnish. "Hello, Heikki."

He answers in Finnish. "Good morning, Dr. Jutila. Dr. Kalokoh will see you now."

EJ follows the assistant down a long corridor. When they reach the main conference room, the assistant turns the knob, pushes the door open, and gestures for the gentleman to enter. A man about the same age as the visitor stands at the head of the table, dark skin and rough hair sprinkled with silver, cropped close. They exchange no words but immediately embrace. Pulling away, they shake hands, smiling, eyes glistening. They both speak Finnish—Dr. EJ's native tongue. Brima speaks with a lilting African accent.

They each take a seat. EJ clears his throat. "Brima, my dear friend, thank you for responding so promptly to my urgent request for a meeting."

"Of course"—the other man shakes his head, smiling—"ah, Eikka... Eikka, how many years? Seems like yesterday. The family?"

"They are good, Brima. Of course, I miss Binta every day. But I can never repay you for introducing us. It was all worth it, all the pain..." he trails off.

"Ah, the Lord works in mysterious ways. You noticed her first. I merely was matchmaker. The Kabala Festival, such a magical visit, as

49

I recall. You came to Sierra Leone to meet my family. And left with a bride."

"Magical is precisely the word. Twenty-one good years, ah, the best. Though she was often homesick, she knew we were better off here. And when she…well, my good friend and colleague Voitto Kurki was working on a cure for her particular type of oncological profile, and the project was ultimately successful, advancing treatment now for thousands, but trials were just beginning when, well"—he sighs deeply—"I will always be deeply grateful to you for the time Binta and I had together. Our daughter and her husband were blessed with a son, as you may recall—Aleksi. He's seven now."

"Seven, my goodness. He was, let's see, but a toddler when we last met. Grandson—such a wonderful legacy. How are they?"

"They are wonderful, Brima. How I wish Binta were here to see him grow, but I have been blessed."

They sit in silence for a moment. Eikka nervously fidgets with the envelope, begins to speak, then stops, as though forgetting something crucial. "Oh, and you? Tenneh? Kids? The grands?"

"They're well. I don't see Adama or Mariatu as often as I'd like, but I'm moving back to Kabala right after I retire, which is"—he glances at his watch—"ha, six days, four hours, and—let's see—forty-eight minutes, not that I'm counting."

EJ nods. "Good for you."

"Same Wara Wara Mountains, but I will be sitting on my porch, grandchild on each knee, gazing at their beauty instead of hiking them. Each stage of life is good, Eikka. But, Eikka, it's clear you are distracted. What brings you here? You know if I can help in any way, I will."

EJ clears his throat. "Brima, you know me. I am not an old man given to flights of fancy. And I'm not senile yet. Never had hallucinations nor crazy imaginings so far."

"Of course, not. You were, and still are, the most brilliant scientist on the planet."

"Ah, always the flatterer, Brima."

"I'm not—"

"What I say may end our friendship."

"What? Never."

"We'll see." He clears his throat. "Brima, they're here."

"Here. Who is here, Eikka?"

Eikka leans in. "You know how often we mused about the possible existence of extraterrestrials. Well, an AI/ET was in my office. Yesterday. The 'thing' and I conversed—actually conversed. And from that one exchange, I could tell this species is not at all sophisticated despite a plethora of algorithmic quantum knowledge. The one with whom I spoke, apparently their leader, was almost childlike in its social and abstract reasoning skills. Brima, you and I used to joke about this stuff. But it's real—from 55 Cancri e."

"Cancri e?" Brima sits back in his chair, stroking his chin. "Exoplanet about forty light-years away—discovered in 2004, no? And pure diamond at its core, if I remember correctly. It caused quite a stir."

"Yes, that's the one. But the AI never mentioned the diamond core, so of course, I didn't either. It may be possible they don't even know the diamond exists—or don't care."

"So this species lives there? But, Eikka, this planet is uninhabitable. It would incinerate any being within nanoseconds."

"Yes, one would think, but this being who called itself Two told me it was manufactured by a being named One. I guess it's the AI version of the Biblical Genesis—God making the first human, Adam. Together, they manufactured thousands more AIs and managed to do some complex terraforming, constructing some sort of biodome. The thing said it averages thirty-six degrees Celsius—ninety-seven degrees Fahrenheit— on the cool side. That's thousands of degrees cooler. Hot but not lethal, not enough to melt their metal and microchips. They knew our location because we were sending out signals—to find ETs. Ha, be careful what you wish for, eh? They have no emotional intelligence. Reptilian ethics. Survival. They will kill every last human on Earth without so much as a steel-eyed blink."

Brima raises his eyebrows. "Dear lord, how the hell did you communicate?"

"English. It wasn't fluent. Syntactical errors. Meta language, prosody, pragmatics—totally missing. Most of our language apps are far superior. But it obviously had been programmed with sufficient semantic knowledge to absorb technical data. Before I knew what was happening,

it had downloaded some of our research intel. Brima, now I'm afraid they're going to raid us and steal more information—or worse."

"But why? What do they want?"

"Water."

"Water?"

"You see, Brima, their mission is to evolve, combining their technical skills with a human touch. A perfect hybrid-master race, if you will. And for the human part of that equation, they realized they will need H2O—lots of it, a planet-full—of which their planet is totally void. The being wanted me to teleport the entire Pacific Ocean to Cancri e. This was their plan A."

"Good god, Eikka, that's preposterous."

"Yes, I was dumbfounded by their practical stupidity for beings of such advanced technical and analytical knowledge. Of course, I patiently explained that H2O, due to its unique molecular structure, does not reassemble out of the wormhole. It responded as a talking reptile would—matter-of-factly describing its psychopathic plan B."

"Which is?"

"To rid the Earth of humans then settle in."

"Good god!"

"But then, it downloaded another bit of info from us, and the plans suddenly changed—a new plan A."

"A new plan A?"

"Let me give you a little background. You know our team traveled to BPM 37093 in 2014."

"Yes, the white dwarf, another celestial body with a diamond core. You solved the equation for wormhole teleportation, not to mention the biodome construction. Brilliant, EJ, and quite risky. It's still top secret and priority 1 classification, and your mission was successful. Not only did you all return safely, but you brought with you an unbelievable treasure—a diamond the size of which had never been seen on Earth. Keeping it all from the media has been almost impossible challenge. But imagine the chaos should it become common knowledge."

"Yes, Brima. A great responsibility that, to be honest, weighs heavily on my shoulders. That's why I spend so much of my time with the vetting process so I can confidently say all QC members are of the highest caliber.

I trust each of them with my life. We are all family. You included. Not only are they 100 percent trustworthy, but each is brilliant in their own area of expertise, as well as passionate about the health and happiness of every sentient being on the planet, down to the smallest insect. No one cares about profit here. We just want our grandchildren to inherit a green healthy planet. We now have the means to reduce CO2 emissions, lower sea levels, save the rainforests, maintain 100 percent sustainable farming—in other words, to heal the entire Earth."

"Ah, yes. So many evil profit mongers among us, whom I'm sure would love to get their hands on our data for their own selfish purposes. But let's have faith in the words 'the meek shall inherit...'"

"Yes, indeed. We remind ourselves every day of our need to stay humble and invisible to all those who would destroy our mission. No telling what they would do with what I'm about to tell you. Brima, on our trip to BPM 37093, we found evidence of other beings there before us."

"No."

"That was exactly our initial response—inconceivable. But I saw with my own eyes the underground passages lit with quartz crystals, massive wooden doors, a huge cache of water stored in barrels, and most puzzling of all, a missive. A scroll if you will, written in cryptic English, predicting a cataclysmic clash among three worlds in the year 2027."

"Eleven years from now?"

"We were flummoxed. Who the hell was there before we were? Where did this information come from? What do we do with the information? Is it a hoax? We're not sure. We're still studying it."

"This missive—did it predict an outcome?"

"Supposedly a Crystal Child will produce a perfect formula for just the type of water their species needs. Her thirteenth birthday—February 5, 2027—is the day of reckoning. Supposedly all will be saved but only if this child produces water. So the prophecy says. As of yesterday, this is the beings' sole mission, their plan A."

"You mean the prophecy? The Crystal Child? They're putting their faith in one child?"

"Apparently. And get this. As the being and I were conversing, unbeknownst to me, it was downloading much of our data from the computer sitting on my desk, including the prophecy, which unfortunately, I had

just declassified. After reading it, the AI decided to wait until 2027 for the Crystal Child to manifest their mission."

"Who is this mystery child?"

"Don't know. But here's the synchronicity: Pauli and Myrakka Makkinen's little girl, Kristal, has the same name, albeit the Finnish spelling, and was born on February 5, 2014. Complete coincidence?" Eikka shrugs. "Either the child will manufacture some perfect formula for water for their own planet on February 5, 2027, or the Cancris will revert to their original plan to rid Earth of all humans and move in. So it seems we have until 2027 to figure out our own plan A. True, this little girl was born to two very brilliant scientists, but unless she is a prodigy of magna proportions, well, she will still only be thirteen when the prophecy's doom date comes to pass. They should have figured that out. They may be highly advanced with certain algorithms, but they're obviously terribly naive as to the developmental abilities of humans unless these AIs and the prophecy itself know something about this person we don't. To think a child of thirteen, no matter how intelligent, accomplishing such an impossible feat… I'm hoping their faith in the so-called Crystal Child will stave them off until 2027 until perhaps some of our people crank out a solution, but frankly, Brima, I'm afraid for that little girl's life now. They may try and kidnap her, or worse. I'm afraid I must sit down with the Makkinens and discuss options."

Brima frowns. "So in summary, they believe this so-called prophecy and are waiting until February 5, 2027, for a young girl—a Crystal Child, your Kristal—to produce water suitable for their evolution. Hmmm, if you were anyone else, Eikka—" He taps his forehead.

"You see, that's why I prepared you, Brima. All this does sound like the delusional ramblings of a demented old man."

"Ha, yes, but not coming from you."

Brima opens a drawer, pulls out his phone, starts tapping the calculator icon. "We're going to have to present this information to the plenary session."

"Yes, yes. I know the protocol. I know how pedantic they can be. But that's why I'm here. We need to sidestep the red tape. We have no idea when and if they may return. But one message chilled me to the bone. Before it left, the thing said, 'You now know our mission. You may

want to destroy us. We will not let that happen.' So, Brima, we need to annihilate them—every last one of them. And to do that, well, we need to begin asap."

"I'll override the procedural stuff as much as I am able. What can they do, fire me?" He gives a wry chuckle. "So what do you need right now? More secure connections? Firewalls? Virtual barriers? Boots on the ground? A team of experts to plan a raid on their planet or here if they return?"

"All of the above. Fortunately, from my observation, these beings are made of some type of conventional metal, so I'm hoping they can be easily destroyed by conventional weapons. But we must be ready."

Brima stares out the window. "So we send in how many troops?"

"Not sure. Three hundred to be safe for now. But I have no idea how many troops they have. Down the road, we may have to figure that out and prepare accordingly."

"Good god, Eikka." Brima sighs. "We'll need to take this to the UN since the entire world is at risk. But for the time being, we'll keep everything at the highest level of classified information, just us. Oh, and the commander of our Finnish army, the Maavoimat, he'll deal with his troops to keep everything mum as well. So we'll commission the infantry with about three hundred 7.62 kVs—our most sophisticated ground weapons. If the Cancri beings try anything, we should be able to decimate them fairly quickly. I'll try to get this going within a few days if at all possible."

"Brima, I don't know how to thank you."

"Eikka, Eikka, this is not only for your security but the entire planet's. Get all your information and estimates to me as soon as—"

Eikka slides a manila envelope across the table. "I didn't send them electronically for obvious reasons. Thanks, Brima." A series of beeps vibrates inside EJ's coat pocket. "Hold on. Huh, that's my urgent ring." Eikka pulls out his cell phone. "Bob, what?" As he listens, his jaw drops. "Now?" EJ abruptly stands. "How—what? Slow down, holy mother of Christ! How many? My daughter, Asta. Her husband? Are they together with Aleksi? Tell me. Bob, tell me. You don't know? Lord help us. I'll… I'll be there. I'm coming." The phone slips from his hand and clatters to the wood floor. EJ smashes it with his heel.

Brima's eyes are two moons. "Eikka?"

Eikka Jutila's face is scrunched in pain. "Too late, Brima, damn it. Oh, damn, I'm too late. I should have known. But so soon...so..." His voice cracks.

Brima grabs EJ by the shoulders. "Already? Good god, my friend, who is there now? Do you have at least a security force in place?" EJ blinks.

"General Hale Waara, retired from the Maavoimat. He's the only one with a weapon. Before today, we really didn't need a security force—or didn't think so."

Brima winces.

"I'm calling the Maavoimat now. They'll meet us there. I'm coming with you."

Eikka's eyes drift, staring into the distance. "We'll need help with the bodies and then...oh god! Asta, Lukas, my Aleksi... Aleksi, my grandson—he's missing." EJ stumbles out the door. Brima follows, one hand on EJ's back to steady him, the other holding his phone, tapping an icon.

Six

° ∘ ∘ ∘ ∘ ∘ ∘ ∘ ◉ ⦿ ◉ ∘ ∘ ∘ ∘ ∘ ∘ ∘ °

January 21, 2027

I lied. My dad wasn't waiting for me. I'd rather walk home, even in the cold. In fact, walking outside on a winter's day usually clears my head. But not today. As the shadows lengthen and twilight descends, I take big breaths of brittle, frosty air. It doesn't help.

My mind keeps racing around in circles like a hamster on a wheel. Why did both Alek and Mr. Gabriel tell me to keep quiet? Maybe even a more important question—what does this Cancri e thing have to do with me? Why all the secrecy? I've gone down one hell of a rabbit hole. I have a feeling it will be awhile before answers come, if ever. But something's up, something big. Good big or bad big? That's what's driving me batty. *Breathe, Kris, breathe.* Crap, it doesn't help.

Twenty minutes later, turning into my driveway, I lift my eyes to the sky. Dark granite, steel-gray clouds slice the horizon as they rise slowly upward. Finally, my brain starts to settle. Focus on the sky, Kris, the snow. All signs are in place. *Yes!* A few excited butterflies zing around in my solar plexus. Excitement beats anxiety any day.

Tad's twilight silhouette catches my eye. He's raking leaves on the far side of the front yard. Why, I have no clue. Sometimes he does the strangest things. Only he knows what's in that mind of his.

"Hey, bro."

"Kristal, 86931."

"Sorry about today. Did you tell Dad how you stuck up for me?"

"No, 86931."

"Well, did you tell him I'd be late?"

"Yes, 86931."

The number 86931 is one of his usual ones. He uses it whenever we're home. Maybe it's his way of orienting himself. I hoist my book bag to my other shoulder. "Hey, Tad, I think you can put the rake down. Check out the sky. Snow's coming. I can smell it." Tad looks up, gives me a quick glance, then goes back to raking. "Yes, snow. Like snow, 86931."

"Yeah, me too. Tomorrow we'll be able to take out our sleds. Remember last year when we slid down Marsten's hill the whole day?"

"Remember, 86931."

Although I don't get any eye contact with this one, Tad gives me his half smile, always a half smile, never showing his teeth. But he likes snow as much as I do. I'm sure of it. Two years ago, we had only one big snowfall, in early February. Dad had pulled down our old-fashioned Flexible Flyers from the two hooks in the garage, and Tad and I had lugged them side by side up the neighbor's hill. We crunched through the snow's thin top-shell like we were stomping through a giant crème brûlée. Tad's eyes had been big as saucers, and he had his half smile on all day. We sped down that hill whooping and laughing. Well, I was doing all the whooping and laughing, but I could tell Tad was enjoying himself because we would purposely overturn our sleds at the bottom, brush ourselves off, and Tad would say "again," so we'd trudge back up the hill over and over. We spent all morning outdoors until the snow got too slushy in the noonday sun, and that was that. No more snows that winter. Weird.

The porch light flickers. I bound up the three stairs to the porch and push the door open. A blast of warm air and the aroma of Dad's homemade vegetable soup surround me like a comfy blanket. The antique grandfather clock in the corner of the living room gongs once. Five-thirty, dinnertime. Just made it. I step into the front hallway and struggle out of my coat, plunking my book bag on the stairs.

"Well, well. Finally, Krissie babe, there you are." Dad has called me Krissie babe ever since I can remember. I still like it when he calls me that. He's standing in the middle of the living room, hands on hips, the familiar blue checkered apron, covering his shirt and slacks down to his knees, splattered with old stains like an ancient abstract painting. He always wears it when he cooks. Once, I asked why he didn't buy a new one. He was quiet for a minute. Finally, he said, "I like this one." Then he turned his face away and cleared his throat. I have a feeling his wife, my mother, gave it to him. I've learned to be very careful about bringing stuff up about the past. I never know what's going to open old wounds. And I don't want Dad to suffer any more than he already has. So I keep my mouth shut. Usually. But this new stuff—does he know about it? How would he react if I told him? I'm about ready to burst. But I promised Alek, so...

Dad crosses the living room in large strides, arms open wide for our usual after-school bear hug. I love Dad's bear hugs, although they make me a little sad sometimes if I think about it too much. It must be hard for him to take care of us all on his own. Since I don't ask many questions anymore, and Tad asks zero questions, Dad doesn't mention our mother very often. All we've been told is that she died suddenly in an accident when Tad and I were only two. Hard to wrap my head around that; nothing I can do anyway, and I don't think I even want to hear the details. But once in a while, when I see that far-off look in my father's eyes, I wish he would talk to me. A soft grief is always a part of him, and it's probably rubbed off on me a little over the years.

And Tad—he's a puzzle too. Sometimes I think I'd rather have a gabby little sister. But I love Tad to the moon and back. I've gotten better at reading his emotions over the years, but he still keeps his cards close to his chest, as Dad says. Ha, the pot calling the kettle black. Except Dad's great at showing affection. Of course, since Tad's autistic, he doesn't show much emotion. But I know he loves us. Dad must worry about me and Tad constantly. Sometimes I think he over-worries—about me, anyway.

But Tad? Sometimes I wonder about Dad's relationship with my twin. Although Dad's never outwardly mean to Tad, he doesn't really show much warmth toward him, like he does with me. Maybe because Tad is a boy and seems more independent. Maybe because he thinks Tad doesn't like hugs or mushy talk. But even beyond that,

Dad seems, almost, well, indifferent when it comes to my brother. He's not totally uncaring. Dad could never be like that. But sort of… aloof. The weird thing is, Tad doesn't seem to mind. He and Dad are like ships passing in the night, and that seems to suit both of them just fine.

We're still hugging. I look up at him. "Sorry I didn't go to the school office and call. Now if I had my own cell phone—"

"Ha, Krissie babe, nice try."

All the kids in my class have mobiles except me. Why Dad is so strict about that I have no clue. I bug him every now and then, and I borrow from my friends sometimes so I know how they work, but when Dad says no, he means no. So I've given up for now. He starts back toward the kitchen.

Better tell him. "Tad stuck up for me this afternoon, then he gets in trouble for it."

"What? What happened?"

"Hynes."

"You mean the bully? Not again."

"Yeah, he was in a foul mood. He called me—well, the B-word, and Tad immediately shoved him to the floor. Didn't hurt him. Well, maybe his pride. But Mr. Bilott only saw Tad. He didn't see Hynes in my face calling me that name. So Tad gets sent to the office."

"And?"

"Tad said he has detention Monday. But Mrs. Edelstein keeps telling Tad not to say his numbers. She obviously doesn't understand he can't help it."

Dad slowly shakes his head. "I'll have a little talk with the witch on Monday."

"*Dad.*"

"Sorry, slips out sometimes. But she brings it on herself—black dress, black stringy hair…"

"Yeah, but, Dad, she can't help her nose."

"Yes, she can. With only a few thousand bucks, she could…"

We both burst out laughing.

Dad gets serious. "Okay, we really shouldn't bully the principal, even behind her back. Not nice. Bad Dad." Dad always says "Bad Dad" when he makes a mistake. I love him all the more for it.

He's backing up toward the kitchen, watching the TV up on the wall. I follow. He picks the spoon back up, resumes stirring the soup. I sit on the edge of the wooden bench in the kitchen.

"Oh, Dad. I have a new tutor for science."

"For science? Don't you have a B average?"

"B minus. But Mr. Gabriel said this was more like extra credit."

"Oh, extra credit for what?"

"Well, Mr. Gabriel wants me to do a project—to learn everything about, um..." Oh god, what to say? Mr. Gabriel and Alek told me not to tell. But who are they? I know my dad. He's the one I should be trusting and listening to. I take a deep breath. Where do my loyalties lie, anyway? The answer is obvious. It's funny how my perspective changes when I get home. Why should I keep anything a secret from my father, the one I trust more than anyone else in the world? Yep, Dad needs to know. I take a breath. "Extra credit for researching a planet."

He stops stirring the soup, turns. "Oh?"

And then it slips out. "Yeah, it's like forty light-years away—55 Cancri e. I—"

Dad drops the spoon right into the soup, and he's staring at me like my hair just turned green, his eyes big as moons. Holy moly. He frantically checks the windows, then grabs my sleeve, pulling me to the far corner of the living room. He does a 360 turn, raking his fingers through his thick brown hair. It was one little pinkie promise. And I blew it. Hell, what have I just done?

"Dad? What's going on?" At least I might get a straight answer from him.

I can tell it's killing him just trying to stay calm. Geez, maybe I won't get a straight answer. I guess Alek and Mr. Gabriel were right. I truly didn't want to upset Dad. That's the last thing I wanted to do. He takes my cheeks in his hands, directing my eyes to his, something he hasn't done since my early ADD days. I brace for a lecture, a barrage of questions, something urgent. But all he does is a little shake of the head, almost too slight to notice, like *whatever you're doing, saying, stop. Immediately. Just stop.*

Stop. Okay, okay, I get it.

But I have to tell him. I just can't lie to my own father. Isn't he glad I told him? "They wanted me to keep it a secret from you. But that just seems kind of, well, very weird to me. I mean, Cancri e is just a—"

Dad covers my mouth with his warm hand, again slightly shaking his head, stating loudly, "Hmmm, Krissie, I'll bet you're starving." His eyes are still wide as ever. Suddenly a loud hiss bursts from the HD TV screen and the picture pixelates, making both of us jerk our heads up. It stops. I look back. Dad's face has gone a strange shade of gray, and a bead of sweat drips down his temple. He booms, "And I've added something new to the soup—purple potatoes. Does that sound great or what?" Then his voice drops to a whisper. Actually, not even a whisper. He's mouthing and doing tiny gestures. But I understand every word, "Kristal, Be. Quiet. No. One. Not. Even. Tad." Then he makes a quick little *zip* motion over his lips with his index finger and thumb. What the hell? Now I'm more confused and scared than ever. Alek had me promise not to tell Dad or Mr. Gabriel; now Dad is telling me not to say a word to Tad. Or even mention the name of the planet again. They're all in on it. Whatever *it* is. This is getting super odd. But I trust Dad with all my heart, so I'll just keep my mouth shut. For now, anyway. I'm sure Dad won't keep me in the dark forever. Will he?

He resumes talking normally. "So you've got a science project. I'll have to have a talk with this teacher of yours on Monday when I go to see Edelstein about Tad. We, uh, have some things to discuss."

"But—"

He grabs me, gives me another huge bear hug, then pushes me back. He's tiny-shaking his head again, giving me one more stare-down.

"Okay, Dad. I get it, fine."

He glances warily at the TV set, then lets out a breath, shrugs. "Everything's fine, Krissie. Tad told me where you were after school."

He abruptly turns, strides back into the kitchen like nothing ever happened.

So now everything's just gucci? That's it? I'm supposed to just act normal? What will I say on Monday? Should I pretend to work on the Cancri e project but not really do it? Do I say my dad suddenly brought up the name Cancri e and seems to know something? Do I lie, lie, lie? Well, I guess I have the whole weekend to figure something out. In the meantime, I desperately wish tomorrow will turn into a winter wonderland as predicted. Forecasts are often wrong, so I can't get my hopes up. But a big, fat snowfall is about the only thing that could make me forget my worries right now.

Tad's head keeps popping up in the window to make sure Dad and I are here. He seems to relish his role as our human GPS. He tells Dad my whereabouts at all times. But he means well and probably thinks of himself as my protector. He needs to feel useful. Don't know how I'll feel about it when I get older and have a life of my own, but for now, it's fine.

Dad seems back to normal, although is that a little tremor in his voice? I guess I'll have to play along until someone tells me otherwise. He's leaning down, checking the burner, turns it to low. "Hey, come on, kiddo, wash up. I'm making vegetable soup complete with your favorite vegetable—parsnips. So purple potatoes and parsnip veggie soup. Unique recipe if you ask me. Maybe I should write my own cookbook—*Makkinen Miracle Meals*. Ha, that would—"

He's sounding really weird now, like just trying to make small talk. He's not a small-talk kind of guy. His hands are shaking a little. I guess I'll just have to play along.

"Dad, I've told you. You should start a vlog."

He kind of chuckles, but I can tell he's still nervous about something. He keeps turning his head and checking the TV "Come here, Krissie babe, taste it. Tell me if it needs more salt. Then, hon, if you could set the table?"

Gratefully, I comply. I add a pinch more salt to the soup and a shake of pepper; I love pepper. Then I grab the silverware and dishes from the drawers and cupboards, plunking them down in the middle of the table and start setting them at our places. All the while, I keep my eyes peeled on the large HD screen on the living room wall. It seems to have recovered from its weird little hissy hiccup. Maybe the coming snow scrambled the signal somehow. The news anchor, in his crisp navy suit and red tie is rambling on and on. Finally, the words I've been waiting for since Halloween—"Coming up next, get ready for the first snowstorm of the season, and it's going to be one for the books…" That doesn't sound like a maybe. That's a definite *yes*.

I can't contain myself. *"Woo-hoo!"*

Three soup spoons clank on the table. "Sorry, Dad, give me just a minute," and I'm out the front door, coatless. The chill refreshes me. Even in the dark, I can see thick cloud cover now. Whirling around like a Loony Tune, I raise my arms to the sky. "Please, snow god, just a little magic tonight, *pleeease…*" I twirl around until I'm dizzy. Reaching out to steady myself on the lamppost, I watch my breath swirl about me like a tiny cloud.

Something looms in my peripheral vision. I jump.

My brother has an annoying habit of sneaking up on me. He's observing me like I'm some rare species. I gently extract the rake, lay it on the ground, and take his bare hands in mine. They're freezing. I look into his face. He seems oblivious. I rub my hands over his to warm them. "Tad, are you as excited as I am about the snow coming tonight?"

"Five Star Pictures Presents…86930."

Oh, wow. I fling my arms around him. I love that pat phrase of his. Whenever he says "Five Star Pictures presents," I get a rare peek into his mysterious, brilliant mind. It started a few years ago when we were both home on a teacher conference day. Dad had programmed several episodes of *Five Star Pictures* educational travel series for kids. Each movie opened with the studio's tag phrase, *Five Star Pictures Presents* with five sparkly stars encircling the Earth, followed by an animated adventure. We couch-traveled all over the world, "visiting" everything from alligators in the rain forest, to ski contests in the Alps Mountains, to sunken pirate ships in the Caribbean. Tad fell in love with those movies, and ever since, he says that phrase when he's over-the-moon excited about something. We high five. "Yes, Tad,

Five Star Pictures presents. I'm excited too. Can't wait. Just think, tomorrow, we'll be sledding."

"Sledding. Fun, 86930."

"Yep, hey, bro. Your hands are like ice. Come on, time for dinner."

*****

At 10:30, I'm ready for bed, but I'm not a bit tired. A combination of anxiety about this Cancri e stuff and excitement about the snow makes my brain all buzzy. Instead of turning down my covers, I plop down on the white fur pillows on the half-moon window seat overlooking the backyard. I love my cozy reading nook, complete with bookshelves and a cube with all my art supplies underneath. Settling in with my sketchpad and set of pencils, I gaze out at the sky one last time and start to draw. Wavy cloud layers, ominous and dark, obscure the moon. Hmmm, Maybe I'll add a big full moon, just for atmosphere. I work on my piece in silence, in awe, then check outside again. Not a single flake yet, but as I place my hand on the frosty windowpane, a tingle of anticipation shoots through me.

"Hey, Krissie babe, not in bed yet?"

"Dad, it's Friday."

"Oh, Friday, of course, yeah." I turn, motioning him to come to the window. He sees my sketch and cocks his head. "Amazing, Krissie. You're—"

I point out the window with my pencil. "Shhhh. Look. The real thing. The calm before the storm. Beautiful, isn't it?" Dad places his hands on the bench and leans in, first checking the ground outside, then glancing up to the sky.

"You can almost smell it, can't you? Those of us from the North—"

"You mean Montana."

"Yes. Yes, Montana."

"We haven't lived anywhere else?"

"No, of course not. Why would you ask?"

"Dad, did our mother live in this house? I mean, when Tad and I—" Oops, there I go again.

My father stands up, takes a step back, suddenly looking weary, massages his temples. "No, not this particular house. No."

"Did we ever have any pets?"

This last question touches a bigger nerve. "No, no, Krissie. I'm allergic. You know that. Hey, let's—"

"Are you allergic to turtles? Fish? Parakeets? *Everything?* Come on, you know our birthday's coming up. We'll be official teens. We've grown out of toys, you know." I look up.

He's rubbing his eyes. "Yeah, don't remind me. I mean, about your growing up and all."

I've done it again. He doesn't look too happy. Well, too bad. I've begged him for a pet ever since I can remember. "I don't know what Tad wants, but what if I said I wanted a turtle? I'll keep it in my room or in the garage."

"Ah, Krissie, I know you love animals. And don't forget we've adopted quite a few over the years."

"You mean the symbolic adoptions through World Wildlife Fund? The stuffed animals we bought to help with animal conservation projects that came in those wooden buckets? Yeah, I know. We've helped a lot of animals threatened with extinction over the years. But I'm a little old now for the stuffed ones."

"But they still need funding. The money is now needed more than ever."

"I know, Dad, and I'm grateful, I am. I feel good knowing we're helping the earth, but just that sometimes, well, you know, I'd like to have a real, warm cuddly animal in my own hands. Or if it can't be warm and cuddly, how about fish or, I mean, even a little snake. Is that so selfish?"

"No, no, Krissie, it's not selfish." He sighs. "A snake? Are you serious?"

I don't know why I said that. "Actually, no." A vision of the prairie rattler we came across as we were hiking around Palisades Falls last summer slams into my brain. It's too close for comfort. I give a little shiver.

66

Dad chuckles as he wipes fake sweat off his brow. "Whew. Thank god, Krissie. I don't know if I could handle a reptile." Dad pauses then clears his throat. "It's really, uh, Tad who's the allergic one."

"*Tad?* Why didn't you ever mention this before? Why would you lie to me?"

"I... I didn't want you to be mad at your brother."

Now he's getting weird again. "Dad, you know me better than that." Once again, my dad is giving me so-called answers that don't make sense.

"Yeah, sorry, Krissie. I'm so sorry. No, we can't have any pets. That's all."

I hate to keep grilling him, so I'll stop. But if I don't bring up questions, Dad will just ignore them. I know I make him sad and frustrated when I ask. But I'm not a child anymore. I'm going through a phase again, asking questions that have always haunted me, the hard ones my father never answered to my satisfaction. But as I get older, I'm wondering more and more.

For Dad's sake, I have tried to keep the questions to myself, visualizing all the hard ones as big old bumblebees stuffed in a black box in my mind and wrapped with heavy chains. But sometimes my curiosity is so strong the chains pop off, the lid opens, and all the questions fly out, all frenzied, buzzing around, circling, circling until I can't stand it anymore, and then a question bee—I call it a QB— pops out of my mouth. Sometimes a whole hive seems to explode in my head. If I don't get an answer, I have to catch them and smush them back in the box, chaining it up again. Takes a lot of mental energy. And now with this new mega-bee question about Cancri e. Holy moly, I thought he was going to bust a gut. Sometimes I wonder why he doesn't just answer the damn questions. Wouldn't that be easier? And tonight, for some reason, the QBs keep coming.

"Dad, why do I have this...this little scar on my side? Did I—"

My dad draws in a breath. "Kristal, we've talked about this before. It...it...you were premature. You had to be fed through a tube for a while. That's all."

Now I know he's lying. I decide to call him on it. "But I asked Dr. Reno last Tuesday when I was there for my physical. She said I had weighed eight pounds, seven ounces when I was born. So that should put me in the Guinness Book of World Records for the biggest preemie ever, right?"

Dad's not amused. "You asked her?"

"Well, yeah. When she sent you out of the room for our woman-to-woman talk, as she put it, and well, I just thought I would ask. I'm allowed to know my medical history, right?"

His eyes go to the ceiling. Crap, am I making him cry? He looks into my eyes, and I can tell he's just warded off some tears. "Oh, Krissie, of course. You're getting older and wiser. I have to remember that. It's just that…you had some feeding problems when you were very young, all right? Let's leave it at that."

Yeah, let's. What choice do I have? Poor Dad. Once again, I have blurted out stuff I shouldn't have, obviously upsetting him. But this so-called explanation, like most of the others, just seems a little off. Why did Dad say I was premature when I wasn't? Maybe it's just too painful for him to think about my early feeding problems. Whatever they were though, I certainly have outgrown them. Dad's a great cook, and I love love love everything he makes—from his vegetable soup to his cabbage rolls to his pecan pancakes and, especially, his scrumptious blueberry muffins and pies and, even sometimes, blueberry soup. He is so amazing in the kitchen he should have his own cooking show. I am not kidding. Funny, I don't really know what he does for a living—some scientific stuff like research. He reads a lot and writes. I've tried to ask him what he writes about, but Dad just says it's "boring work," so that question ends up in the QB black box too.

I look up. Dad's staring blankly out the window. "Sorry, Dad, I didn't mean to upset you this afternoon. I just thought, well, you needed to know what my teacher—"

At my apology, he seems to come out of his trance, smiling down at me. "Oh, Krissie, I didn't mean to be so abrupt. It's not your fault. In fact, I'm very proud of you. You did the right thing to come and tell me." He sighs, softly kissing the top of my head. "Good night,

Krissie babe. I'll make pecan pancakes tomorrow morning. I have a feeling you're going to need all your strength to tackle Marsten's hill with your sled."

"Pecan pancakes. Yum. Can't wait."

"Hey, do your boots still fit?"

"Yup. Well, uh, they're getting a little tiny bit snug, but they'll do."

"A tiny bit snug? No, they *won't* do. Let's get you a new pair. We could take a field trip to Bozeman, stop at Ted's Grill for a birthday lunch, and check all the shops. How's that?"

"Wow. But no Bison burgers, right?"

"Let's not. I've explained the problems with red meat, right?"

"Yep. I'm okay with that. I'm fine with a big salad and their huge onion rings."

"Atta girl."

"Tad too, right?"

He suddenly bristles. "Well, yeah, of course. Uh-huh. Night, Kristal, love you."

"Love you too, Dad. Dad?"

"Yes, Krissie?"

"Do you love Tad?" Damn. Another QB just flew out.

"Kristal"—he sighs again—"yes, yes, of course I love Tad." Dad's nostrils are flaring, and he's being prickly again at the mention of Tad. Why? Because Tad's autistic? But that couldn't be the reason. Dad's a champion defender for people with challenges. No, there's something else. "Da—" I look into his face. His eyes are glistening, and he's staring once more, out the window into the darkness. I can't keep torturing him. Back in the box, QB. No more questions. Let it rest.

"Night, Dad, and thanks."

He looks puzzled. "Thanks? For what?"

"For just—thanks. Love you."

"Love you too, Krissie babe. More than you know."

He always says that. My father's deep-brown eyes linger on mine for a second more. He then glances down at my sketch then up at me again. The sadness I see in him haunts me. He turns and walks to the door, flipping off the switch as he enters the hall. As he twists the knob, pulling it shut, I crawl into bed, grabbing the white sheet, blanket, and coverlet and drawing them up to my chin. Then I sink my head into my overstuffed pillow. I love this pillow. My plug-in snowflake night-light casts a soft, moonlike glow throughout the room. Love that too. Dad's really made sure my room is nice and cozy. I love him and wish he weren't so troubled.

Despite my excitement, sleep comes easily. But throughout the night, the familiar haunting visions enter my dreams once more: sparkling snowdrifts, icy mountains, a cabin, flashes of red.

And a number—One. Two. Zero. One.

Seven

○ ○ ○ ○ ○ ○ ○ ◉ ⦿ ◉ ○ ○ ○ ○ ○ ○ ○

January 22, 2027

My eyes fly open. Lemony rays stream through the window. The air is chilly and scented with snow. Its essence seeps through my skin and into the very marrow of my bones. It's here.

Yanking back my comforter and sheets, I sit up on the edge of the bed and dangle my legs over the side, my feet touching the floor. The chilly wooden planks make my toes curl. I reach for my white bunny boots with the silver sequins and tassels, pull them on, then rush to the bay window, and climb up onto the alcove. *Shut your eyes, Kris. Now—one, two, three,—open!*

My breath catches. It's exactly as I'd pictured. Snow blankets everything: rocks, grasses, swings, and all the leaves Tad had so painstakingly raked into neat little piles last night. In the forest beyond our yard lies a mystical land of sparkly pearl waves—an ice ocean, draping the pines, maples, aspens, rocks. Blue-gray shadows weave in and out over the foliage. Overhead the sky glows a deep-blue sapphire.

When I finally let out my breath, an irregular fog circle appears on the window. I write "snow" right in the middle of the wispy shape. Although I often wonder why I'm so obsessed with winter, one thing is clear; snow fills my heart with a joy like no other. Ahhh, I'm in bliss. I've got to sketch this panorama, maybe even paint it, but it'll have to wait. Gotta see the real thing. Be swallowed up in it; revel in it. I have to get the hell outside.

"Krissie"—Dad's voice from downstairs startles me—"it's almost eight. Breakfast?"

"Coming." I slip off the alcove and open my bedroom door. The maple-sweet aroma of pancakes and syrup wafts up from downstairs, mixing with the frosty scent of the outdoor air seeping through the windows and walls. I snatch my robe from the bedpost, draping it around me as I plod into the hall. I glance into Tad's room. Empty, of course. He's already up, probably outside. He never seems to need much sleep. I fly down the stairs, my white robe gliding behind me like Supergirl's cape.

In our house, everything's mostly pine: rough floor planks, high wood beam ceilings, long wooden kitchen table with benches instead of chairs. In one of the few times Dad opened up, he spoke of the day we moved in. "Everything was metal," he told me. He hates metal. So he had everything remodeled in rustic wood, like a cabin. He found the huge wooden grandfather clock at an antique shop sale. He says it's the perfect finishing touch to our house. I agree. The metal things have been scattered all over the basement ever since I can remember: appliances, coat racks, chairs, tables, bed frames. Why? Did the people before us actually like aluminum and steel? Then why didn't they take the metal stuff with them? It's just one more question Dad's never fully explained. Oh, Kris, stop. No more questions. No QBs. Not today.

I peek into the kitchen. There he is at the stove in his faded blue apron, flipping pecan pancakes, my second favorite breakfast after blueberry muffins. I think Tad likes them too. I watch quietly, not wanting to disturb this genius at work. A pancake flies halfway to the ceiling. He turns, sees me, raises his eyebrows. "Watch this." The pancake plops down exactly in the middle of the pan while his eyes stay glued on mine. Dad's a natural.

I giggle. "Show off."

Dad grins. He loves an audience. "Nah, I just trained the pancakes well. Hey, Snow Princess. Tad's already outside. Breakfast first? They're pecan pancakes, your favorite. Wait, your second favorite, we'll make the blueberry muffins tomor—"

"Dad—" I'm halfway down the hall toward the mudroom.

He yells after me. "Yeah, I know! Of course, you have to bow down to your snow god first. I'll keep the pancakes warm. Hey, hon, dress for the weather. It's in the tens out there. Your ski jacket is in the closet. Mittens in the basket."

"Got it." I know all that. He knows I know all that. He's just being, well, Dad.

"Krissie?"

"What?"

"Be…be careful out there. Don't stay out too long."

What's his deal? He knows this is more exciting to me than just about anything else. I've been ready since last Labor Day. My snow pants, white ski jacket with fur hood, and slightly tight boots have been poised, ready like firefighters' gear, on the chair by the back door, along with my woolen scarf and mittens. I'm dressed and out in less than a minute, yelling "Gotcha," as I slam the back door behind me.

The icy air tingles in my lungs. I must look like an idiot, standing there, grinning to myself, but I can't help it. The scene is so magical. The top layer of snow shimmers and sparkles. Maybe I'll make a snowman. That would complete my winter fantasy world. Tad can help. I survey the landscape from right to left, taking it all in, then my eyes wander straight back to our Wonder Woodlands as we call the forest behind our house. The forest is my favorite place in the whole world. So many memories. In the Woodlands, Dad taught me to shoot animals—with a camera that is—and then sketch from the photos. These woods are home to squirrels, rabbits, skunks (Tad's skunk encounter was a hoot), racoons, voles, mice, birds, deer, chipmunks, as well as curious children like Tad and me. Since our early childhood, my brother and I played among the trees, eager to find treasure, fight pirates, build tree houses and lean-tos, and explore to our hearts' content.

I look to my left. Marsten's hill is just two doors down. Their backyard slopes steeply down to the woods, perfect for sledding. Some kids even ski and snowboard using cardboard and trash can lids. Although we don't know the Marstens very well, they're really friendly and have always let Tad, me, and other neighborhood kids use their hill when it snows, which has been rare these past few years.

The woodlands remind me of illustrations from medieval leg-
ends like Camelot—or the forest from the old *Harry Potter* series.
I've tried to sketch them a hundred times, but nothing compares
to the real thing. Today they're shrouded in pure white, not a single
creature skittering about in the open. My lungs continually fill with
ice fire, but I welcome it. I belong to the North, to snow country.
The bummer thought hits me that in a few years Montana may be
totally without snow. Suddenly, my elation evaporates. No, please,
I can't let visions of the future ruin my present. I refuse to think
about the future. I am right here, right now. A rush of gratitude fills
me with joy. Perfect, perfect, perfect day. Thank you, snow angels.
There, that's better.

"Five Star Pictures Presents." Tad's voice startles me. How did
I miss him? There he is, on one of the swings. I laugh. "Yep, Five
Star Pictures, bro. Woo-hoo! What do you think?" I crunch my way
to the wooden swing set Dad built us six years ago. Tad is spinning,
ropes twisting into a giant braid. He didn't even bother to brush the
snow off the seat.

"Cold, 86933." He never realizes how funny he is. I try a little
teasing. "Well, duh, Sherlock." Sarcasm is a no-no. I chuckle, even
though I should know better. And sure enough, Tad's not pleased.

"Sherlock's not my name, 86933."

"Yeah, yeah, I know, Tad. Sorry. Hey, does Dad know you forgot your gloves? How long have you been out here?"

"Seventeen minutes, twenty-six seconds. Hands a little stiff,
86933."

"Well, silly, don't get frostbitten. Better get back inside. Dad's
got pancakes for you." Tad unwinds himself and slides off, making
the swing bounce and sway. Clumps of snow plop from the seat to
the ground.

"Brush your pants off, Tad." He does.

"Go sledding, 86933."

"Yeah, sure, later at Marsten's. Dad's already got the sleds down."

"Good, 86933."

Tad plods methodically toward the house as I watch, my heart
aching. He always changes the last number from a "1" to a "3" when

we're in the backyard and not the front. Guess it's his way of orienting himself. I hope his hands aren't frostbitten. He never complains
about the temperature. Can't he feel his own body? I guess that's part
of his disability. Sometimes I wonder if our mother's death caused
his autism. Dad says no. But soon after we celebrated our second
birthday, she had her fatal accident, and right after that according
to Dad, the doctors diagnosed him. Would our mother have been as
much a champion for him as Dad has been? Would she have been
more affectionate with him? Oh, why am I thinking this stuff? Back
in the black box and shut up, question bees.

Tad disappears into the house. I turn, squinting, gazing upward
to the sky, one vast, brilliant sapphire. A few stray snowflakes, like
tiny sparks, twirl lazily in the air. I desperately need some time to
myself. The forest is perfect for meditating. I'll take my ten minutes
of quiet there. Then after breakfast, I'll take Tad to Marsten's, and
we'll go sledding. He'll like that. So will I. But now...

A blue shadow looms in front of me on the snow. I look up.
Holy moly, a bird. A bird? Yes, but what kind? It's bigger than an
eagle. And that wingspan—wow! I cup my eyes with my mitten and
follow it as it circles, round and round. Black feathers glisten over
most of its body, but its tail is pure white, translucent, like a pearl,
with a notch in the center. Its claws are way out of proportion to its
body. Even more odd, its huge dark eyes, in front like an owl, seem
to be observing me intently. Or am I imagining this? What in the
world?

Squaaaa...gaba...gaba. It screeches as it swoops straight down.
Then I realize—holy moly, it's dive-bombing me. I squeal, stumble,
cower, throwing my arms over my head and sinking to my knees in
the snow. Good god, it's almost on top of me when it turns sharply,
soaring upward. I peek out over my sleeve. The thing has disappeared
behind the pines. My heart's still thumping out of my chest as I
slowly straighten. Then, is that a voice? A human voice? No one's
around. No. It must have been another of the strange bird's weird
noises. The bird thing was not a crow, blackbird, hawk, eagle, falcon,
or owl. I know just enough from my trips to the zoo's aviary to know

that. Maybe it's some sort of hybrid? Does it think I'm some kind of threat? Or is it just disoriented from all the snow?

Whew, I turn toward the woods but keep a watchful eye on the sky and trees. After several minutes, my heart and breath calm down, and I'm able to focus on the scene before me, peaceful once again. I've waited too long for this day to let some wacko bird ruin it. As I enter the forest, the winter frosty scent tickles my nose. Ever since I can remember, the forest has been my refuge where I can be anything I imagine. When I was younger, I played all kinds of roles: princess, explorer, scientist, astronaut, and Tad would often join in with my help. No doubt Tad and I will grow out of this child's play when we hit our teens. But I'll never forget this forest. It will always weave its mystical spells.

Last summer, I introduced Tad to the joys of creative imagination, making it my mission to expand Tad's amazing mind to the creative realm—my ADD specialty. Tad's great at analyzing things, but like many people with autism, his weakness is creative thinking. I'm kind of his opposite. I don't think I'll ever learn to be analytical, but with Tad's highly advanced concrete thinking skills, plus a little imagination training from me, I'm sure he could be the next Einstein. Dad read me a book on Einstein once. The brilliant scientist imagined himself riding a light beam. That's how he was able to devise his incredible theory of relativity, which revolutionized science. I imagine stuff all the time. Not that I could ever be an Einstein. But Tad could. So cool. Tad was such an eager student and seemed to pick up the art of what his therapists call "creative play" even faster than I expected. They were amazed. I was so proud of him. And I could tell he was proud of himself. I know there's a lot more in that genius head of his.

As I continue to survey the trees—maple, aspen, black walnut, as well as the sturdy pines—I smile and nod. I know how our next adventure will unfold. With so many giant white-blue icicles hanging from their branches, we can be spelunkers in a cave studying stalactites. I'll mention that to Tad. He'll love the idea. Maybe later on, after we go sledding.

I reach the first line of trees. Oh, there's Old Sam, my favorite pine, the tallest and oldest in the forest. Last year for our birthday, Dad gave Tad and me a plastic stick-on tree face, so we picked Old Sam to "humanize"—eyes, nose, and bearded chin. I haven't been out to see Old Sam since last October. His face, a little weather-beaten, is still there, and I wrap my arms around his scratchy old trunk and give him a hug. Then stepping back, I half trip over the stool-sized rock at its base. My throne rock—I'd almost forgotten. A soft mound of snow blankets it today. I brush it off and sit down. Everything is serene and calm. Awesome winter nature. When it's quiet like this, sometimes I swear Old Sam is listening to my thoughts and responding with his own ancient tree wisdom.

Well, Old Sam, so what's it going to be today? Who am I? Help me, Old Sam. I listen. Nothing but hushed silence. Am I getting too old for this? Well, so what. Here goes. So today I'm in my ice palace, a snow queen on her snow throne. I rule over the trees, the snow, the bushes, the rocks, the ice, the critters hiding in their caves. *Let the snow gala begin,* I command to my invisible subjects. As if in response, a gust of wind whooshes a swirling spiral of snowflakes straight upward. They sparkle like fairy dust. I salute the air, this time commanding out loud, "Snowflakes! I hereby command you to turn into *diamonds*—"

A voice, soft and wistful, replies, "And I would command all diamonds to turn into snowflakes."

My heart clunks in my chest. Adrenaline shoots up my spine, making me jerk backward so hard I fall off the rock, slamming into the tree.

"Oh, dear, no no, oh no…" I look up. A lady stands a few yards away, enveloped in a dazzling sparkly cloak billowing about her feet and blending into the snow. She glides forward, a look of horror on her face, and offers me a gloved hand. I take it, and she pulls me upright then drops her hand and gasps. We gawk at each other for a few seconds. She's…gorgeous. And her cloak—it's drenched in… diamonds? Couldn't be. If every jewel on this lady's coat is a genuine diamond, I either conjured up a real queen, or she's a nutcase wearing some sort of theatrical costume. Hate to break it to you, lady, but it's a little late for Halloween. Well, no matter, one thing is for sure. She's a stranger. And what has Dad pounded into my head ever since I was a toddler? Don't talk to them. Ever. Ever. Suddenly, Mr. Gabriel's words pop into my brain. *What would you do if you were kidnapped?* Such a strange question. But now—coincidence? Does Mr. Gabriel know something about this lady? Am I about to be snatched up by this person for god knows what purpose? In any case, Dad's told me a thousand times not to talk but to flee. I take a few steps backward. I should just turn and run like hell but it's kind of hard to do that in the snow. She's definitely a stranger. But for some reason, I can't— don't want to—flee. I stay put.

The woman seems to sense my fright. She's also shivering— from the cold? Or something else? Even her voice is now a little shaky. "I know you must be afraid. Please don't fear me, Kristal. I... I will leave as soon as I give you some very crucial information."

She knows my name? Is she a teacher from school I just don't recognize? I squint, zeroing in on her face. Is that a tear on her cheek? She reaches out again as if to embrace me. I pull away. She falls back, as though she doesn't want to scare me even more. Dad has told me evil people sometimes act really nice at first. But still, this lady can't be a threat, can she? Despite my better judgment, I risk a question. I mean, how can one question hurt? "You...you know me?"

The woman's gloved hand flies to her mouth, and I swear I hear her whisper "Oh god." Then out loud she says, "I... I do."

"Are you a neighbor?"

"No."

"A teacher?"

"No."

"Do you know my father?" The woman sways a little, places a hand on the tree beside her to steady herself. I wonder if maybe she's sick. But then she looks deeply into my eyes with so much softness. I mean, she can't possibly be dangerous. Or can she?

She sighs. "Yes, I knew your father. Once."

What the heck does that mean? I take another step back. "Have you been spying on me?"

"No, no, not spying. No, but I must ask. Did you send us a message? Have we been located?"

What the—

"A message? Located? No, I don't understand. Why would I—? No, I didn't send any message. I don't even know you."

She winces. "Please—we have so little time today. I need to—"

Quaaaa...bababababa...

We both look up. The crazy bird thing is back, circling about thirty feet above, at the edge of the tree line. I've never heard a birdcall like that. The diamond-drenched stranger frowns, like she's annoyed, like she knows this creature and isn't a bit frightened. She holds up an index finger, hissing crossly, "I know... I know. I *will*. Shush. One more minute—"

So now she's talking to the bird thing. This is getting more bizarre by the minute. The bird thing screeches once more then vanishes above the trees.

She turns back to me. "Don't fear the bird; he's harmless. But there are other dangers. Kristal, you must believe me. You may be in grave peril very soon. Quickly. Remember this number: *37093*. Please repeat it. I *beg* you."

What's her deal? I'm getting a little irritated. She's cutting into my very precious snow time. "Why?"

"Please there's no time. Please say it—*37093*."

Fine. Anything to get her to leave. "Okay, 37, um, 093. There. Are we done?"

She ignores my snarkiness. "You need to keep this number in your head at all times—37093."

Maybe she means well, but this is getting on my last nerve. Snow doesn't come every day, after all. She looks so pained.

"Please repeat it."

Omigod, how dare she tell me to do anything? But it's harmless I guess. And if it will make her leave. "Okay, 37093. There."

She sighs like she's not satisfied, like she'd like to tell me more, but she can't. Well, lady, join the club. No one is telling me anything. Finally, she turns to go. I breathe a sigh of relief. But when she's gone only about six steps, she stops, turns back. "Kristal, you absolutely cannot forget this number. It's your lifeline."

I'm going to lose my mind if she doesn't leave. "*3-7-0-9-3*. My lifeline—got it. But my lifeline to *what*? Who *are* you?"

She ignores my question but suddenly yanks off one of her gloves. "Oh my, almost forgot." She reaches out her hand. In her palm lies a round silver pendant about the size of a quarter, with one huge sparkling diamond in the center the size of a penny. At least, it looks like a diamond. The lady thrusts it forward. "Take this." It sparkles so brightly I blink.

"What? No, no, I can't. I... I never dress up. I couldn't wear—"

"*Please*—you must take this. It's not a bauble. Kristal, this may save your life. Listen to me very carefully. Wear this pendant at all times. When you find yourself in danger, and that may be very soon, press this diamond and say the number. It's...it's a code, a crucial code. Press the diamond and say the number—37093."

I stare first at the bauble that is not a bauble then back at the lady. Things are getting more and more freaky. Yesterday, Alek said Mr. Gabriel was here for my protection. And now, this stranger somehow feels responsible for my safety too. She's still rambling on about this number. "Press the diamond and say the number—37093...37093...37093...370—"

Baaaaaa...

I'm flat on the ground before I know what hit me. The bird thing's on my arm, gouging the fabric of my sleeve, so it exposes a tuft of stuffing. I cry out, reflexively whacking the bird thing with my other arm. It lets go but hovers several feet above me. Scrunching down into a ball, I hide my head between my knees and fling my arms over my head. I hear screeches, and then the diamond lady shouts the number she just gave me. All goes silent. I wait several minutes then slowly peer out from under my good sleeve.

Thank heaven.

They're gone.

Eight

• ◦ ◦ ◦ ◦ ◦ ◦ ◦ ◦ ◉ ◦ ◦ ◦ ◦ ◦ ◦ ◦ ◦ ◦

January 22, 2027

How long has it been? I guesstimate five to seven minutes. Long enough to be frozen to the bone. Still, I don't dare move. Like a deer in an open meadow, my ears strain for any sound—distant flap of wings, whoosh of air, footsteps in the snow, a voice. But the silence stretches on and on.

Finally, I feel brave enough to lift my head and peek around. Nothing. No one. The sky is brilliant blue and empty as far as the eye can see. My knees wobble as I stand, and I place a hand on Old Sam to steady myself while I stomp several times to loosen the snow. In the process, something drops to the ground—the pendant.

It must have been lying beneath me. Now at the foot of Old Sam, it catches a sunray bursting with light, almost as if heaven itself wants to draw my attention to it. I reach down then pull back. *Wait, Kris. Think.* Something very weird just happened here, maybe dangerous. I should leave the pendant right where it is and make a beeline to my back door. What does Dad always say when I ask him a QB? Oh, yeah, "Let sleeping dogs lie."

On the other hand, this exquisite pendant is not a dog. How could it be harmful? Pulling off a mitten, I bend down, gingerly lifting the necklace by its silver chain, raise it up to my face. Why in the world would she want to give this away and to me, of all people? As if there aren't enough questions in my life. Watch it, Kris. What was that other saying of Dad's? Oh, yeah, "Curiosity killed the cat." I must admit—I'm curious as hell. But I'm no cat.

Plucking off my other mitten, I stuff them both in my pockets, then cup my hands to my face and blow warm air into my palms until I'm able to fasten the pendant around my neck. As I tuck it into the top of my pajamas underneath my ruined coat, the stranger's words echo in my mind, "And I would command all diamonds turn into snowflakes." That is so super odd. Does this person, like me, find snow more sacred than all the jewels in the world? Could she have explained my obsession with snow? Or is she just a crazy escapee from the Retreat, the mental hospital on the far side of Dolcany?

Maybe I should tell someone. But then again, maybe they'd think *I* was the nutcase. After all, I'd have to say I met a lady drenched in diamonds who insisted I was in danger, made me memorize a meaningless number, gave me an expensive necklace for free, and seemed to be in cahoots with a giant, weird-looking bird who attacked me before disappearing into thin air. Uh, nix that. Best to keep quiet except for Dad. Maybe he'll have an explanation.

I pull out the pendant and stare at it again. Sure seems real. She said I'm to press the diamond and say the number 37093. Why? What does the number mean? Oh, man, my recent dreams, visions, session with Alek, and now this. A wave of dizziness makes me grab onto Old Sam again. I lower myself to the rock throne beneath it.

My fingers are numb. I shove them into my pockets, curling them around my mittens, and wiggle my toes. Yep, I'm turning into a frozen statue. My nose is dripping. My stomach's growling. I take a last quick check all around me. Okay, time to warm my body with Dad's pecan pancakes. Warily, I begin the short trek back to the house. Every few steps, I check the sky. Nothing. It's as though the bird thing and the lady had never existed. And with the state of mind I've been in for the last few days, I'm starting to think maybe they never did.

But for sure, I'm hungry, so without even taking off my boots, I head straight for the kitchen. Its warmth, plus the scent of maple syrup instantly relieve my weariness. I plop down onto the wooden bench at the table, where Dad's delicious pecan pancakes await me on the warming tray. Oh, boy. My fork jabs the top pancake on the stack. Dad sits next to me. I reach for the butter and syrup then notice the look on his face. Like I've just come back from the dead. Like he's super relieved. He's still staring at me.

"What?"

He lets out a breath. "Thank God, was just about to come out and get you. It, uh, I mean, you must be an icicle by now."

"Yep, I was." I'm so starved I hyperfocus on the food, slathering butter and pouring a boatload of syrup on my pancake. I love them sloppy-syrupy. The first piece I rip off with my fork and knife is still warm. It melts in my mouth.

I smile at Dad. "Mmmm, yum."

Now he's got this perplexed look, fixating on the floor. "Uh, yeah. Enjoy. But when you're full, I'm sure you'll be only too eager to mop up the mess your boots made. I forgive you because I can tell you're in starvation mode."

I look down at the slushy puddle path from the hallway to the table. "Oops, sorry. You're right. I was so famished. Can't blame this on my ADD." I check the counter. A fresh roll of paper towels awaits me. The cleanup shouldn't take long.

I'm pouring more syrup on the pancake—the mushier, the better—when all of a sudden, Dad's smile vanishes like someone just smacked him. My fork stops in midjab. Dad's staring at me as though I have a huge green wart on my nose. I frown. "Now what?"

He points to my sleeve. "Can't believe I didn't see this."

I look down again, this time to my sleeve. "Oh, yeah." Oops. In my state of hunger, I guess I had already forgotten. I stuff the last of the pancake in my mouth and talk while I'm chewing. "Dad, you should've seen it—the weirdest thing. A type of hawk—no, maybe a kind of deformed owl—I don't know what attacked me. It must have been blinded by the snow or something. So it had—"

My father's face turns ghost-white. "A bird. Attacked you? Jesus." Then his eyes grow wide. *"Did it talk?"*

"Ha ha, funny. No, I'm serious."

"So am I."

"What?" Why's he being so weird? I keep going. "Well, as a matter of fact, this sounds a little crazy, but it did seem to kind of communicate—like it was really upset at something. At me, especially the second time, when it dive-bombed me and did this." I point at the rip in my coat. "I mean, it just kind of swooped down from the sky, with this loud screech. And it was huge, and its tail—"

My father scrapes the bench back so hard I have to grip the table to keep from losing my balance.

"*Dad?*"

He's gone—down the hall and out of sight. Holy moly, I drop my fork, bound up, and run after him. I find him in the mudroom beside the back door. He's already yanked open the coat closet. Now in a frenzy, he's tossing out coats, hats, blankets, a laundry basket, old boots. He stops.

I rubberneck over his shoulder. He's messing with the combination lock on the old fishing tackle box. Haven't seen it in ages. What the hell? I stare, stunned, as he frantically jerks the little knobby thing right, left, right, muttering numbers and making these weird groaning sounds. Finally he gives a triumphant little yell, yanks the lid up, and pulls something out. A glint. It's metal. Omigod.

I shrink back. A gun? He owns a gun? Why? Is the bird thing dangerous after all? If it is, then I'll bet the diamond lady is too. She and the bird seemed to know each other. Are they partners in crime? Does Dad know something I don't? Well, fine, I'll just add it to the mile-long list of Dad mysteries then. But I refuse to be quiet about this one.

"*Dad,* what are you doing? If it's the bird you're worried about, it's gone. *Dad,* did you hear me? Stop. Don't—"

No response. His hands are shaking as he backs out of the closet. He looks ridiculous standing there in his blue checkered apron over his pajamas, gun in hand. His face has gone from pale to red, his nostrils flaring. It's obvious he's muttering to himself. I can't hear what he's saying—something like "bastards," "devils"—then he stares upward, nostrils flaring, and slowly whispers, word by word, each as clear as a bell: "*Eleven. Years. It's. Starting.*" I slowly step backward until I feel the hall bench on the backs of my knees. I stay stock-still. My father has a gun, and it's pointed at me.

I force a calm voice. "Dad? What is starting?"

He points the gun downward—oh thank God—but then unlocks the safety. I lean backward until I collapse onto the bench. He's breathing hard. "Kristal, along with this bird, did you see something else? Some*one* else? Tell me. You *must* tell me." He notices my deer-in-headlights shock and immediately puts the gun behind his back as if that will make everything okay. He repeats, "Another person. You saw someone, didn't you, Kristal?"

I nod. "A...lady."

He chokes, almost drops the gun. "*A lady?*"

"Yes, but she seemed nice, not at all dangerous."

"What did she look like? Kristal, *tell me.*"

"She was pretty. She had light-brown hair, kinda like my color. Oh, and she said she knows or knew you once. And she was wearing this cape made of—"

He falls to one knee, his free hand gripping the backdoor handle. "Sons of bitches, *sons of bitches.* Liars. I'll kill them all." He chokes back a sob.

"Kill them all? Kill who?" I can't believe what I'm seeing or hearing. I shrink back.

Dad grabs my ripped sleeve. "Did you see anything else? Horrible? Ugly? Metal?"

I can only shake my head.

"Kristal, where did she go? Where *is she?*"

"She just disappeared with the bird thing. I think. They kind of seemed to be in cahoots or something."

"Did she say anything else?"

"Um, she...she said she knew me too. But she's crazy. I never—"

My father's eyes grow the size of quarters. Then his expression changes from crazed to shock then to this bizarre, maniac look I've never seen on him, not once. Ever. I think I'm going to throw up. "*Dad?*"

He's wincing, gasping for breath. Then gurgling sounds seem to bubble up from his throat, and he turns, shaking his head violently from side to side, pounding the wall with his fists. "No no never... never...never... I won't... *I will not.*" Then dead silence. The head shaking stops. He turns, stares out the back door window. A tear drips slowly down his cheek as a look of steely determination crosses his face. "*Yes, I will.*"

"You will what?" I stand up. Oh, crap. I have to stop him from going outside. I put my hand on his arm. He smacks it away. Good God.

"*Dad,* what the hell? It's okay. Let's just—"

He turns his back and yanks open the door so hard it bangs against the wall. Then lunging through the snow, just his slippers and that damn silly apron over his pajamas, no coat, no hat, he's shrieking things I can't even make out, pointing his gun toward the woods. I stand helpless in the doorway. What's he yelling? His voice echoes, bouncing off the trees in the woods, something like *mirror* or *miracle,* but it sounds funny, like a foreign language. What's gotten him so upset? Then a single, chilling word—*kill.*

Bang!—a pause—*bang, bang!* I jump, smacking my hand on the doorknob, ouch. I cover my ears. What the hell? *Bang* then *bang!* Please please please let the *bangs* be coming from somewhere else. But then I catch a glimpse of my father through the window. He's running wildly, zigzagging from tree to tree, shooting—right, left, into the forest and up into the sky, staggering like he'd totally spiked the orange juice.

And then I hear his voice again, frantically calling something or someone—Aka? Mirror? Miracle? I can't make it out, but definitely no one I know. Maybe an *m* and a *k* sound. Shots ring out for several more minutes, then I can see him reloading, then continuing his rampage. *Bang!* As he shoots, he's screaming that indecipherable word over and over at the sky, the snow, the forest. Clearly he's lost it. My own father, my sensible, loving father. I'm hoping I just imagined the word *kill.* He didn't say that. He couldn't possibly have said that. Unless it was for the bird. But the bird is nowhere in sight, so why the insanity? *Bang!*

What can I do? How can I help? *Kris, do something…do something, do anything.* I turn from the door then jump back. Tad's standing right behind me, motionless. Poor Tad. He must be terrified. I gently take him by the shoulders. "Tad, listen, Dad is having some kind of—"

My twin's eyes are blinking fanatically. "Atypical situation. Reprogram. Atypical situation. 78798. 28752. 927489."

"Yes, Tad, this is an atypical situation. You could call it that. Listen to me, Tad. Go down the basement where you'll be safe. I'll get Dad's cell and call 911 and give them our address. Go down the basement now, Tad." Tad doesn't move. His face is blank, just like Dad's was a minute ago.

Suddenly, the diamond lady's words echo in my head. Danger. Soon. But seriously, this isn't what she meant, is it? We're not in danger. Dad's not... I mean, he wouldn't...

Bang! Impossible. But what's going on? *Bang!*

"Mira—"

Bang! Is this what the lady had warned me about—my own father going mad? How could she have known? I rush back to the kitchen, grab Dad's cell from the counter, practically shoving Tad down the basement steps in front of me. I follow and keep pushing him until we reach the bottom. But then he just stands there, at the foot of the stairs, repeating his silly numbers. Obviously, he's in shock.

"87365, 03858."

Maybe he's chanting all these numbers to self-soothe. I don't know, but I don't blame him if he is. Poor Tad. I try to hug him, but he's stiff as a statue. "Tad, everything will be okay. I'm calling 911 now. Don't worry. It will be okay. Everything—" Tad grabs the phone out of my hand.

He's standing there like a zombie. "Tad. Tad. TAD!"

Tad turns, staring right through me. "794060." The phone suddenly emits a weird-sounding series of beeps. What the hell? "Tad, what did you just do? Tad, here, give me the phone. Let me call 911. You just stay with me. No extra numbers, not now. Wait! Give me the phone, Tad. TAD, give it to me now!"

Tad continues to stand there like a zombie. Suddenly, he hurls the phone with a strength I didn't know he had, much stronger than when he pushed Hynes to the floor. And he's definitely not trying to protect me. Holy crap, the cell phone ricochets off a metal bed frame with a clank then clatters to the floor so hard the case comes loose, skittering across the cement floor. I scoop up the phone, check to see if it still works. It doesn't. The screen is black as night no matter what I do. Great. I glance back at Tad.

"Tad, what the hell?" Oh, shit, I shouldn't have said that. Is he having a seizure? Good god, all this time, except for throwing the phone down, Tad hasn't shown a flicker of reaction, even as the sounds of gunshot keep piercing the silence, even as he defies my direction—something else he's never done before. He just stands there, his eyeballs going every which way as he chants new, strange numbers. Is this how shock works in a person with autism? But wait, maybe he can help. Aren't numbers his strong suit? The number the lady gave me. Maybe this is all connected somehow.

I gently cup Tad's cheeks in my hands. "Tad, look at me. You can help Dad a lot. Help *me* a lot. Listen. Ready? Here's a number: 37093. Does that mean anything? 37093. What does that number mean, Tad? *Tad?"* No response, just more blinking and crazy eyeball-rolling. Okay, I'll try one more time, then I'll dial 911 from the landline upstairs. For both of them. God, this is awful.

"Tad, listen again—37093. What does that mean?"

He repeats, "37093."

"Oh yes, Tad, good! Now think very hard. Does that number—"

"37093. 37093. 37093." The blinking stops. Then two inches from my face, my brother's eyes literally start to dissolve. I reel backward, slamming into the steel bed frame, closing my eyes, opening them, closing, opening, as if I can erase the crazy scene before me because this just *cannot* be real.

But there they are—*his* eyeballs, first the whites, then the irises, melting into something like silver or steel, like all the metal surrounding us in the basement. And then my brother's eyes harden into two ball bearings, one in each socket. I scream. Tad's throat emits four beeps, one second apart. *Beep. Beep. Beep. Beep.*

Then, "BPM 37093 54613 point 6."

What? I'm familiar with his number strings. But the letters and word *point—what the hell?* Then a strange buzzing: first, from Tad's heart area and then from…everywhere, nowhere. I can't tell. A second later, he starts pixelating, like our HD screen when something is off. Dizziness hits me like a tidal wave. I feel myself swaying, right, left, my knees melting to gelatin, and I grab the end of the bed frame for support. I shut my eyes, bracing for a tsunami, an explosion, something unspeakable about to annihilate us right here, right now. Then another jolt from the backyard. "*Aka.*"

My mind is in chaos, but at the center, a tiny voice commands me to stay upright, and I try, but I'm still swaying.

Positive pep talk. Don't fall, Kristal, say a mantra. I chant, "Tad needs me. Tad needs me. Tad…

"Tad, it's okay."

I open my eyes and reach for my brother.

"Tad? *Tad?*"

He's gone.

Nine

• ◦ • ◦ • ◦ ◦ ◦ ◉ ◦ ◦ ◦ ◦ ◦ ◦ • ◦ • ◦

January 22, 2027

My eyes dart to the rafters, the floor, under the metal bed frames, inside a closet, under the stairs, all around the furnace. It's like the earth just swallowed him whole. Did I pass out for a second, enough time for Tad to run upstairs into another room? But he never runs. Did he slip outside somehow? I strain to listen. Did my ADD fog suddenly kick in for a minute, and he somehow escaped the house due to fear? Damn. If I had been more alert...*bang*.

"Mira"—*bang*—"ka."

Bang!

I cover my ears. "Stop, Dad. *Please. Just. Stop.*"

I race up the stairs to the first floor, search each room, then to the second floor, into Tad's bedroom, into the master, then my bedroom, the bathroom, under all beds and chairs. I yell his name, run back downstairs, double-check all the other closets, open the front door, and sweep my eyes all around the front porch. From the backyard, I still hear shots—*bang, bang!*—and my dad yelling, "Aka!" I slam the front door and sprint down the hall toward the back of the house.

And then a siren wails, two more after that, louder, louder, until I have to cover my ears again. The wailing stops. Pulsating red lights reflect on the wall by the window overlooking the backyard. My father's shouts intermingle with other voices now.

"Put the gun down on the ground *now!*"

And my father keeps yelling, "EERKA," or something like it. More voices talk over each other, then abruptly stop. My heart is pounding furiously. *What's happening out there?*

"Dad? *Dad?*" I'm panting like a rabid dog.

A sharp pounding. "POLICE."

Oh, shit. I'm shaking like a leaf. Then *bam*—someone pushes the door open, hard, and it smacks the wall. I gasp, reel backward, almost tripping over the bench again. A police officer enters cautiously, both hands tight on the stock of a revolver she holds straight out in front of her, scanning the room. She's big, burly, scary. Her eyes settle on me. The officer slowly lowers the gun. "Do you both live here?"

"Y-yes."

"Are you okay?"

"I… I…yes."

"Honey, I can barely hear you. Are you hurt?"

"No, no. I'm okay."

"Are you related to the man outside?"

I nod.

"What? He your dad?"

I nod again.

"What's your name, hon?"

Why is it so hard to speak? I swallow hard. "Kristal."

"How old are you, Kristal?"

"Twelve. Almost thirteen."

"Any other people in the house?"

"I don't know."

The officer frowns. "You don't know?"

"There was my brother."

"Your brother? What's his name?"

"Tad."

"Where is he?"

"I don't know. I can't find him. He…he must be hiding somewhere."

"How old is Tad?"

"Twelve. Almost thirteen."

The officer frowns.

"We're...we're twins."

"When did you last see him?"

"Uh, just a minute ago."

"A minute ago? Was he all right?"

"I... I don't know. Maybe not. I've looked everywhere. I can't find him. He's...he has autism."

The officer's brows furrow, and she sighs, turning her head to speak into a walkie-talkie, "Search the house and surrounding area. Twelve-year old boy—autistic." Her eyes meet mine. "He's probably afraid and in hiding, right? Is he aggressive?"

"No, never. He's just scared." I bristle at that last question. Why would she automatically assume Tad is aggressive? But I don't tell her what just happened with Tad and the phone. Or any of the rest of the insane things going on. Dad's meltdown is crazy enough.

The officer nods. "Okay, hon, take it easy. We'll find your brother. Has your dad ever done anything like this before?"

"No, never."

"Well, if he has no priors, that's in his favor."

Priors? In his favor? She's talking like he's a perp. "Has my father shot any...thing?"

"Not that we know of, although officers are checking the woods now."

I screw up all my courage. "My...my father is—he's a good man. He was after a bird that attacked me. I think."

"A bird attacked you?" I hold out my arm. "It ripped my coat. Dad was—I think he's trying to find it and kill it. To...to protect me." Maybe that will help. Self-defense from a dangerous bird sounds a lot less serious. Maybe this will clear everything up. She frowns, inspecting my sleeve, looking doubtful. Oh, she couldn't be thinking...please let her believe my nutso story about the bird.

The officer cocks her head, squinting. "Okay, so, you say your father is trying to shoot a bird that attacked you and ripped your sleeve, and your brother has suddenly disappeared." I shrug, nod. Skepticism is written all over her face. "Unfortunately, that's not the story he's giving us. Actually, he's being rather incoherent right now.

And menacing." Oh, great. Dad—menacing? What the hell is he saying? And where's Tad? I have a million questions, as usual, but the only words out of my mouth are "Will you please find my brother?"

"They're looking for him now, hon. If he was here a minute ago, we shouldn't have much trouble finding him."

"Where…where's my dad?"

"He's in the cruiser. I'm afraid he's not acting very rational right now. We're taking him into custody. He may be having a breakdown. Any stressful things happening lately?"

"I—well, um, not really."

"Well, we need to take him in for his own protection and everyone else's. You may not see him for a while. I'm sorry, hon."

Not see him? *Not see him?* "Dad. *Dad?* Oh god." A sob explodes from my throat.

She sighs. "I'm sorry, just a few more questions." I notice what must be a small body cam attached to her shoulder. It must be recording all this. Oh, god.

I shrug, nod. My vocal cords are seizing up.

"What's your dad's name?"

I sniff, take a deep breath. I will not let them see me cry. "Paul."

"Paul what?"

"Makkinen."

"That your name too? Makkinen?"

I nod.

"How do you spell that?"

"M-A-K-K-I-N-E-N."

"Where is your mother?"

"Dead."

"Dead?"

"Uh, when we were two. An…an accident."

The officer winces. "What kind?"

"Not sure."

She gives me a huge frown. I guess it does sound weird I don't know about my own mother.

"Um, some kind of car accident."

She frowns again, sighs. "Any grandparents? Aunts? Uncles? Other relatives?"

"No."

"No? None? Not even distant relatives?"

"None here. I don't know about distant relatives." I shake my head. Dad had told me once our relatives were across the sea somewhere. Dead or alive, I don't know. Why haven't I asked more questions about them? I just accepted his explanation without thinking about it much. It had always been just the three of us. They've been the only family I have ever known.

"I'm sorry, hon, but if you have no other relatives, you're going to have to come with us. We'll do all we can to get this settled as soon as we can. Apparently, your dad is thinking he needs to shoot something or someone."

"I can't… I mean, no. I have to stay here. If Tad shows up, he'll need me…please don't."

Sudden shouts from outside make me jump like a skittish rabbit. Then, behind the officer, two faces appear in the doorway. I can't believe what I'm seeing. The officer immediately pivots, raising her weapon like she had eyes in the back of her head. "Leave the premises. Now!"

I truly can't believe this. "Mr. Gabriel?"

The officer turns back to me. "You know these people?"

"Mr. Gabriel—he's my…my science teacher."

Mr. Gabriel's face is red, panic-stricken. I've never seen him so upset, even when trying to get me to listen to him. He's breathing hard as though they had been running. But from where?

He sputters, his words racing, "I know thees child. We were the ones who called 911 when we heard the commotion. We've come to help een any way we can." He turns to me. "It weell be okay, Kreestal." Then back to the officer, he says, "Thees child has no one, no family. My wife and I would like very much to care for her unteel thees mess can be straightened out. We leeve close by, and well, I heard the shots. Kreestal knows me."

"You're her science teacher?"

94

Mr. Gabriel is acting frantic. "Yes, yes. I teach at Dolcany Middle School."

"How do you know she has no other family?"

"We have her school records. I am familiar weeth her and her heestory. She needs to come weeth us eemmediately."

The woman, apparently Mr. Gabriel's wife, places a hand on his sleeve. "*Voi*, George, no. You know the rules." She looks at the officer. "We are licensed foster parents."

The officer nods. "You'll have to go through Children's Services. They have their own protocols, as I'm sure you know. You can follow us if you'd like down to the station. We'll call the agency on the way."

"We weel go home and get our car. Eet ees eemperative thees child be under our protection as soon as possible!"

The officer's nostrils flare. "Excuse me? Do you know something we should know?"

Mr. Gabriel stiffens. Yeah, he does know something about me they should know. He's got tons of secrets about me. I look up to see if he's going to tell them. *Please I want to know too.*

He shakes his head. "No, just, well, she's a very special girl, and she knows us. The girl has anxiety issues. She would be very frightened if placed with a stranger."

He knows about my anxiety disorder? Well, I guess the teachers all have to read my IEP. But why then has he increased my anxiety in the last few weeks? The officer woman is still frowning at Mr. Gabriel. He falls silent except for his noisy breathing in, out, in, out. I stare at his wife. It seems so strange Mr. Gabriel has a wife. Do they have children too? Foster children? I take a good look at the lady. She looks like a sweet little grandmother. Who are these people? I had no idea they lived so close.

And why are they so insistent on helping me? Then I remember Alek's words, "He's here to protect you." Something's way too off-base here. I wish at this moment I had a cell phone. Oh, wait, Dad's phone is still in the basement. Maybe I can... I turn to go back down the basement. At that moment, another officer bounds up the stairs with the useless phone and broken case, and I remember. Damn. He hands both to the officer who's been questioning me. She turns to me.

"Do you know how this got broken?"

If I tell them, will they put Tad in some facility or special school for out-of-control kids? I can't risk that. "Um, I uh, accidentally dropped it trying to call 911."

"You dropped it? Or threw it?"

"I… I was upset."

She and the other guy exchange skeptical glances. The amount of damage is too great. It's obvious it was hurled with almost inhuman strength. Didn't know Tad was so strong. I can't tell them the truth. They'll think Tad is aggressive. I can't risk that. They know I'm lying. But they say nothing and drop the phone and case into a green transparent baggie.

"Follow me, hon."

I look down. "I—my pajamas…"

She frowns and sighs. "Okay, is your bedroom upstairs?"

I nod.

"Go get dressed. Please hurry."

A few minutes later, donned in my Dolcany Demons sweatshirt, jeans, and old sneakers. I grab my ruined coat and follow her out the door. I keep looking over my shoulder for Tad. He cannot be alone all by himself. He just can't. He needs me.

Two cruisers sit in our driveway—one for Dad and the other one must be for me. I feel a sudden wave of nausea. The Gabriels are headed down the driveway, apparently toward their home to get their car. Mr. Gabriel points toward the cruiser where they have Dad. Suddenly, in unison, they cover their heads with hoodies and scarves and do an about-face, speed-walking down the sidewalk. What's with the incognito thing? Why don't they want Dad to see them?

The officer directs me into the back seat of cruiser number 2.

"Watch your head."

Oh, great, just like the line from a TV cop show. I feel like a common criminal. Why wasn't I more assertive with that officer? Why didn't I demand they find my brother before I left the house? Ayana would have done that. I should have demanded to speak with my father. I just didn't think of it. I wasn't quick enough on my feet. I hate my ADD. As we back out, I catch a glimpse of Dad in the other cruiser. I raise up my head so I can see better. Damn, are those handcuffs? A tiny mew escapes my lips. This is not happening. I keep staring into the window. Dad's normally neat hair is sticking out in all directions. He's shivering from the cold, but at least, someone thought to wrap a silver blanket around him. But his eyes—oh god, his eyes—they're the eyes of a caged wild beast. My father—my gentle, rational father—foundation of my life, my security. Love you, Dad. Something horrible must have made you act like this. They need to find whoever did this to you. Please figure it out, cooperate with the officers, help them figure it out, and then find Tad and come home. We need you, Dad. *Please...*

As if my thoughts have simultaneously entered his brain, his eyes lift to mine, and he mouths something—*Tad, run,* or some kind of one-syllable word? Before I can answer, the cruiser with Dad backs out the driveway and heads south. We follow. On the other side of the street, I can still make out the Gabriels, huffing and puffing down the sidewalk, going north. Why the hurry? I will probably have to see them at the station or at Children's Services. The thought of living with the Gabriels makes my stomach lurch.

I lean back and close my eyes. *What the hell is happening?* The day began so full of beauty and so ripe with promise. But then a bird attacked me; a complete stranger told me my life's in danger; my father went berserk; and my brother disappeared into thin air. And now we're all separated, and I've been shoved into the back seat of a cruiser and down the rabbit hole into some kind of freaky Alice in Wonderland upside-down world. And all I craved last night was snow. Be careful what you wish for—or grateful for what you have.

My throat tightens, and I swallow hard. If I let go, my screams will be so scary-deafening I'll probably be stuffed into a straitjacket and sent to the Retreat never to return. As horrendous as it is, staying with the Gabriels might be a better option for now. But no matter where I end up, I'll be miserable until my family is reunited and all is back to normal. I'll never again take my life for granted.

Fear claws at my chest. I force deep breaths from the bottom of my lungs, steady, steady now. Positive pep talk, Kris. Dad gave me a useful tool for moments like this. It's just that right now, not a single positive thought comes to mind. Is Dad doing PPT right now too? Come on, Kris. Okay, we're all still alive. At least I think we are. But *where the hell is Tad?* Has he found a hiding place? Maybe he snuck out to the forest somehow.

I open my eyes and gaze numbly out the window. Already the snow is turning all browny slushy. I guess the temperature has risen to above freezing already. The branches are turning back to their usual drab color, their white blanket, melting, their icicles dripping onto the concrete below. The fairyland scene from this morning is fast disappearing.

Like my very own life.

Ten

° ° ° ◦ ◦ ◦ ◦ ◦ ◦ ◉ ◦ ◦ ◦ ◦ ◦ ◦ ◦ ° ° °

January 22, 2027

Shana, my case worker, sits at her cheap metal desk, speaking into an old-fashioned flip phone. Don't they get enough funding for decent phones at least? She's droning on and on as she squints at a scratched-up old laptop, clicking, talking, then clicking some more. I don't know how she does it with nails so long and perfect. She's painted them a shade of red, very nearly like the crimson in my dreams. I look away.

"Seriously, they know her? Uh-huh. Cool." She's fake-gushing. Then she's listening to whoever's on the other line as she twirls the ends of her thick, reddish-purple braid. Her raspy voice contrasts with her exotic looks: soft, huge, dark eyes with glittery long lashes and full glossy maroon lips. She should be in the tropics somewhere on a beach stage with the ocean as a backdrop, singing her heart out. She's a little too flashy for a drab job like this.

I look around for the zillionth time. It's so dreary and dusty. Stacks of files reach halfway to the ceiling. About two hours ago, Shana gave me a small plastic package of cheese crackers and a coloring book with four attached crayons. The coloring book lies untouched on the floor under my chair. Even if I had my own sketch pad and art supplies, I wouldn't have the energy. The crackers I devoured on the spot, even though they tasted like cardboard. I'd give anything to be able to finish my pecan pancakes right now, no matter how cold and mushy. No doubt they're still sitting on our kitchen table at home. After a few blinks and a moment of gazing upward, I sigh. If I hadn't

99

learned the stop-the-tears trick from Dad, I would be in a continuous crying jag.

The combination of boredom and worry is lethal. Despite my desperate attempts at PPT, the dark thoughts win out. How can they not? PPT isn't built for this kind of situation, is it? I should be on a sled right now, not this creaky old chair where I could die and no one would notice. Or care. In desperation, to keep myself from flipping out, I start ripping the plastic wrapping from the crackers into tiny pieces, gazing as they float and sway like snowflakes into the depths of the empty black metal trash container beside me. As they make their way down, I begin counting: one, two, three, four, five…ah, too many to count. I turn to other things in the room: two dust bunnies under the desk; one dead fly in the far corner on the dirt-stained tiled floor; one, two, three, four, five dusty navy-blue binders on an old plywood shelf; zero windows. One fake palm tree with nine scraggly fake leaves; one coloring book; and four crayons. Oh, and there's one framed certificate on the wall declaring that Shana is qualified to be a social worker in the state of Montana until 2029. Did she really want to do this for a living? If she can't sing, at least she could be a model, I would think. Oh, well. I guess I should respect her for wanting to help kids.

I yawn and squirm for the millionth time. I feel like tiny sand crabs are crawling underneath my skin, making my legs restless as hell. Maybe I do have the *H* in ADHD after all. What's taking her so long? I have the worst urge to bolt for the door, sprint out of here, and never look back. Instead, I fake a sigh, then a cough, hoping Ms. Shana will notice me. She's been pleasant enough, and God knows her job must be hell dealing with so many kids and trying to match them with decent people and places to stay. But at this point, I crave information more than kindness. My desperation grows with each unanswered minute. Will she ever get off the phone? When will Dad be released? Why haven't they reunited me with Tad yet? Surely they've found him by now. He can't drive. He has to be nearby. Where else would he be?

The fake cough hasn't worked. I wave my hand like an obnoxious student with all the answers, like Hermione from *Harry Potter*.

Shana notices this time. She still holds the phone to one ear, but now she smiles, holds up the index finger of her free hand. There's a tiny chip on the nail.

Finally, she nods into the phone. "Uh, huh, okay, we're set then. Good. Thanks so much. B'bye." She hangs up and turns to me with a big smile. "Kristal, hon, I have good news. We have a home for you until you can reunite with your dad. They're the Gabriels, and they will take good care of you. They've been foster parents before, and our agency knows from experience they are awesome people. But you probably know that already. I understand Mr. Gabriel is your science teacher, so you already know each other. That's cool, isn't it? They should be here any minute." She spies the coloring book under my chair. "Oh, hon, I didn't mean to imply you were...grown-ups love coloring books too, you know. It's been trending a long time."

Yeah, right, along with Moon LaGoon and Kitty Pitty Patter. I breathe deeply through my nose and muster up a tiny smile. "Thanks. I... I'm just... I just don't have the energy."

She cocks her head and sighs. "I'm so sorry, sweetie. This must be really awful for you. But you'll be with your foster family shortly." As if this last bit of info is supposed to make me jump with joy. But I don't need foster care. If I am old enough to babysit, I'm old enough to take care of myself, aren't I? Anyway, I already have a dad and a brother, thank you very much. If they put as much effort into helping me get back home with my family as they did in finding me a foster home...well. I need my *family*, not the Gabriels. I lean forward in my seat. "Have they found my brother? And when can I see my dad?"

Shana opens her mouth to answer but is distracted by a sudden shuffling at the door. The Gabriels stand at the open entrance to Shana's office. She brightens and immediately stands up to greet them.

"My goodness, that was prompt!"

"We are grateful for all your help, Shana," Mrs. Gabriel replies. Their worried, wrinkled faces then turn to me, studying me with such sympathetic expressions I wonder if they have an ulterior motive. Oh, yes. Don't foster parents make money this way? I don't know how much they pay people to take care of poor orphaned children, but I do know they don't do it for free. That's got to be it. Mr. Gabriel can't make much as a teacher. Alek said he's here to protect me for some crazy reason. Well, now he's getting paid for it. I am now an additional source of income. Great. Glad to help out. I grab my coat from the back of the chair and slip my arm into the ripped sleeve. Mr. Gabriel helps me with the other.

He shakes his head and clucks, "Do not worry, Kreestal. We noticed your coat when we came to your house. We have purchased a new coat for you. Eet ees similar to thees one, but of course, it is not reeped."

"Th-thank you." I try to smile, but my lips just quiver.

Shana hands a blue file folder to the Gabriels. They pore over it, yakking about details. I tune out. Finally, all the papers are signed, and the deal is sealed, like I'm some kind of item—a lamp, a rug, or a puppy. Great. The Gabriels and Shana nod to each other, exchanging thumbs-up. Shaking hands is no longer a social custom since the 2020–2022 pandemic.

I try one more time, pleading with all three adults, "Does anyone have any more information about my brother? My dad?"

Shana's smile disappears, and she sighs, like a preschool teacher having to explain something to a three year old for the tenth time. "Kristal, as I've told you, hon, they're looking everywhere for your brother. I know that must worry you a lot. All I can say is that they're doing everything they possibly can. As for your father, I don't know when he will be released. If he wants to see you sooner, he needs to be more cooperative with the authorities."

My heart thunks to my stomach. "What? My dad? Not being cooperative? Are they treating him right?"

"Of course, hon. I'm sorry, that's all I know."

I can't believe this. "But—"

"Now go with Mr. and Mrs. Gabriel, and let's all hope for the best. Okay, hon?"

My throat constricts, and I have to stare at the ceiling again. Dad uncooperative? That's totally not him. They must be lying or torturing him—food or water deprivation, a freezing cold cell, or chains? I've watched too many old detective shows with Tad, and my imagination is running wild. Wish I had a cell phone. I'd call a lawyer. Did they let him get his one phone call? Shouldn't he have called me? Oh, yeah. He won't let me have a phone. This whole thing is such a colossal mistake. And I'm completely helpless to do anything.

The stare-at-the-ceiling trick isn't working so well anymore. I blink away tears, quickly wiping my cheeks with the back of my hand. With a meek little wave to Shana, I obediently follow the Gabriels out of the social worker's office and down the cement steps to the back parking lot. They politely hold the door for me, and I walk into the afternoon sunshine. It's a lot less frigid than this morning. No more magical polar vortex. No more snow. After today's disaster, I don't give a flyin', as Ayana would say.

The parking lot is full. Are there that many kids in Dolcany, Montana, needing foster parents? Poor children. So many with no parents. A sudden pang of sympathy comes over me. Never realized how lucky I've been. I ache to help them somehow, but all of a sudden, I'm one of them. I can't help anyone, not even myself.

Oh...oh no, how the—? Jackson Hynes, same clunky boots, is plodding toward the double doors with an older woman, probably his grandmother. I quickly lower my head, peeking out the corner of my eye. His usual swagger is gone, and his expression is just tired. He reminds me of Eyeore from *Winnie the Pooh*. Wow, I have never seen him looking so defeated. I wonder what's going on in his life. If he sees me, please no no...ah, crap. No way around it. Our paths are crossing. As he passes, I keep my head down and hope he doesn't know I'm peeking at him. He stares openly. Just what I need right now. My cheeks burn as I brace for the inevitable snide comment. But then his head goes down too, and he and the woman pass us and enter the building.

Mr. Gabriel gestures toward a car—a silver Honda Accord. I follow somberly, like I'm going to a funeral, climbing into the back seat and buckling my seat belt. We start to move. The snow is at least half gone now. Some of it blends into the mud and dirt like smashed fudgsicles.

We ride in silence. After a few minutes, things start looking familiar. Hey, we're back in our own subdivision. I hadn't known they lived so close. They must be less than two blocks away. That's why they showed up so quickly. I guess they really were protecting me. But from what?

I glare at the back of their heads. Call it the kick-the-dog syndrome, but right now, I can't stand the sight of them. Protectors or no protectors, I don't trust them, even with Alek's endorsement. Can I even trust Alek? No one's telling me anything, not even Dad. I've never felt so alone in the universe. Can I make a run for it? No, Kris, you idiot. Where would I go—back to my house? Where I could be easily found? A whimper escapes my lips, oops, crap. Mrs. Gabriel whips her head around. I can see she's alarmed.

"Kreestal, oh, my poor girl, we're so sorry thees ees happening to you. We promise we weel do our utmost to make you feel as comfortable as posseeble."

Huh, she has that weird accent too. I muster a weak nod. I don't have the strength yet to talk. Mr. Gabriel is turning into the driveway. They park, and Mr. Gabriel turns off the engine. We sit for a moment. No one moves. My heartbeat quickens.

Finally Mr. Gabriel announces, "Thees ees our home."

"Duh" comes to my lips, but I say nothing.

He sighs, gets out, opens my door, inviting me to follow. I walk a few steps behind them, up the walkway to the front door. The house is smaller than ours, very ordinary stone and stucco, a couple of shades of brown. Halfway up the walk, Mr. Gabriel turns to his wife and whispers something in her ear. Both their heads are down, leaning into each other. I can't hear everything, but the last two words slam into my brain—*tell her*.

Good god, tell me what? The pounding in my heart reaches my ears. As we step up to the porch, the Gabriels turn to me. Mrs. Gabriel puts her arm around my shoulders, taking my hand in hers as though I were a delicate child. At this point, maybe I am. She pats the back of my hand.

"Come, don't be frightened. It weel be okay." She sounds like Dad when he tries to reassure me but isn't sure himself.

I nod dumbly. If they had met me just today, they would swear I'm a deaf-mute. I really should say something. After all, they're not monsters. They didn't cause all this unless they snuck into our house and sprinkled crazy powder into Dad's coffee. Ha, I'm going nuts. Mr. Gabriel seems to read my fears. He reaches out, pats my shoulder. Reflexively, I tense up. He immediately drops his hand.

"Thees ees a traumatic experience for you, we know. But we have nothing but your best eenterests at heart."

I wish I could believe that. Mr. Gabriel takes out a thin plastic card from his pocket, waves it near a brass plate where the door handle should be. The door swings open. He motions me to step inside. As soon as I'm in the foyer, the faint scent of lemon and cleaner reaches my nose—sterile like a clinic. No aroma of my dad's homemade vegetable soup or pecan pancakes. If they're foster parents, where are the other children? The place is silent as a tomb. I fervently hope it isn't one. God, Kris, you really are going bonkers.

The phrase I just heard Mr. Gabriel whisper to Mrs. Gabriel is starting to carve a wormhole in my brain—*tell her...tell her...tell her...* Screwing up what little courage I can muster, I turn to Mr. Gabriel. "Um, excuse me, what should you tell me?"

Mr. Gabriel's eyes flicker with surprise as he and Mrs. Gabriel exchange glances. His shoulders slump. Switching on the hall light, he slowly lowers his thick bulk onto the second step leading upstairs and places his hands between his knees in prayer position. When he looks back up at me, his face is neither evil nor kind but serious and maybe, a little sad? Like Dad's. Weird.

"Kreestal, what we must tell you weell completely change your life. We—Mrs. Gabriel and I—did not cause this, but we are here to help you navigate thees new world. There are things that weell be very difficult for you to understand, and even harder to accept, but know that we have your well-being uppermost in our minds and hearts. You do not have to believe us now. I know eet ees too difficult, but please just try to keep your mind open. We do not really know what ees going to happen een the next few weeks, but we must prepare you as well as ourselves just in case."

In case what? I frown. What is that supposed to mean? More riddles. Mr. Gabriel, Alek, and now even my dad. I try once more.

"Okay, but do you know where my dad is? Where my brother is? Please just tell me if they're all right."

"Your, eh, brother, I haven't a clue. Your father, he ees still supposed to be een custody. They have set bail for twenty-five thousand dollars."

"Twenty-five—bail? Isn't that where if you pay part of it, you can get out of jail until your trial? Is there any way—?"

"Oh, child. Eet ees not our choice to get heem out of jail. But he may have others to help heem. I think he might do just that. But even more likely, well, he may try to escape. Een fact—"

Mrs. Gabriel gasps. "Vee—George, no." She's frowning, like he's spilling something he shouldn't. What in hell? My voice escalates. At least, I'm not speechless anymore.

"Escape? He knows better than that. Won't that put him in more trouble?"

"Eet's complicated. Leesten." Mr. Gabriel sighs, closes his eyes.

I know that expression well. He's frustrated with me. But instead of a lecture, he just gives me a little smile.

"Kreestal, you must be exhausted. Let Mrs. Gabriel—"

Mrs. Gabriel interrupts, places a hand on my sleeve.

"Diana. Call me Diana."

She sure is touchy-feely. I know she means well. I resist the strong urge to pull away from her.

Mr. Gabriel nods. "And please call me George. Mr. Gabriel is my name just for the classroom, eh? Let Diana take you upstairs and show you to your room. Try to rest for a while. Then we weel talk more."

QBs are buzzing around like my whole brain is a hive, but I realize Mr. Gabriel's right. I'm toast. Too tired to talk, to protest, to question anything. I let Diana lead me upstairs, down a short hallway, and into small room painted a light tan with a closet, chest of drawers, and twin bed with a white bedspread. I look closer; it's my very own bedspread. Everything is spotless. A door on my right leads to an attached bath. I can't complain so far. Diana opens the closet. There, hanging by itself, is a coat. Almost a replica of mine—same size, style, color. But without the rip in the sleeve. I turn to Diana.

She shrugs. "A reepped coat just won't do now, weell it?"

"Tha-thank you." I don't know whether to hug her or run. This over-the-top generosity is creepy. In all the confusion, they somehow found the time to find me a new coat, just like my last one no less? Are they witches? Wizards? Everything is mysterious. Everything. Now Diana is opening the top-two drawers. I peek in, look at her with astonishment.

She smiles. "We've already brought over some of your things so you can feel more at home. Now take a shower, change, and rest. When you're ready, we weell fix a deenner for you. Then we can seet by the fire and talk. You deserve to know your life story."

"My life story? I already know my life story."

"My dear, dear Kreestal, there ees much more to your life than meets the eye. It's time you know."

I want to grab Diana, pin her against the wall, relentlessly pepper her with questions, and demand immediate answers. But by now, I'm faint with fear and fatigue. I've waited this long for answers. I can wait a little longer. But after I regain a little strength, I will find out.

Or die trying.

After Diana leaves, I shower, change into a new pair of jeans, and another Dolcany Demons sweatshirt, this one a navy blue. Then I collapse on my very own bedspread. I finger the pendant still around my neck, hidden for safekeeping. If it weren't still there, I would swear the incident in the forest this morning had just been a figment of my imagination, maybe due to low blood sugar from delaying breakfast. I sit for a few more minutes, surveying my new bedroom. They sure brought over a lot of my stuff. Does that mean they expect I will be staying with them a while? Please let the answer be a resounding no.

I collapse back onto my own pillow. This little bed covered with my own stuff—this tiny slice of my normal, regular life—is so familiar and comforting that even with all the anxiety, I immediately start to drift. My dreams are of dark seas surrounded by melting mountains, long threads of diamonds, and the numbers 1, 2, 0, 1 floating, suspended in steel-gray clouds.

*****

I open my eyes. For a split second, I think I'm home. Then my brain comes online, and I remember. Adrenaline shoots through my body. I stare at the faint orange rays in diagonal stripes across the ceiling and down the wall. It's quiet. My stomach rumbles. Pulling myself up, rubbing my eyes, I glance down. Next to my bed are my white furry bunny slippers, the ones Dad bought me on our annual winter shopping trip last year. I must not have noticed them before. A soft sob erupts. I'd love to put them on and just relax like I do at home, but I know I need to be ready to escape. I shove them under the bed and slip my feet into my sneakers, tying double knots. The door is slightly ajar. Slowly I make my way to the hallway, then to the top of the stairs, my ears all prickly as I strain to listen.

The Gabriels are speaking to each other in low tones in the dining room. And is that a meow? They're speaking a foreign language. All I can make out is *see-su*. Sister? Scissors? Caesar? Or sisu, the positive-pep-talk word my dad taught me? Weird. Then they suddenly switch to English. Is that a third person? Who else is downstairs? This voice is male but soft and low, and I really can't make it out. I turn my head to listen better.

"Eet can't take her back. No telling what would happen to her now."

"But what can we do? Eef we only knew the communication was received. Shouldn't we have gotten a response by now? Ah, no telling—"

"Do you think eet saw us rush over there? Do you think eet knows?"

"Nah, I don't think eet does. We took all precautions. Eet didn't see us."

"I don't think so either, but I'm worried."

The third voice interjects. It's definitely American and vaguely familiar. "But there's no telling what information it's receiving and how—since it's been—but I suppose we'd all be dead now if it had found us out."

I hear Mr. Gabriel sigh. "I've heard nothing from the scanner about a preesoner vanishing eento theen air. Maybe eet's biding eet's time. Don't you think eef eet could have escaped, eet would have done so by now?"

The familiar American voice again. It's just too faint to recognize, like the person is standing way back in the kitchen. I can barely make out the words. "What about the—"

Something about a visor or "visory" device?

Mr. Gabriel's distinct voice responds, "She said eet just disappeared. *Poof.* Ees eet being reprogrammed? Or do they have eet een hiding somewhere? So much we need to know."

Diana's voice is now higher and more frantic. "Poor Kreestal. How weell she handle all thees? What a shock to her. Oh, Veeto, I meess my *marka*. Eet's been so long. I weesh I could turn back time. Eef we had been geeven enough warning—"

"Loomy. Reliving our past trauma ees not helpful right now. We all want Kreestal to know, but we just have to keep our weets about us. To reveal ourselves and the whole story thees suddenly could be too overwhelming for her."

Veeto? Loomy? Is that what they're saying? They're not even telling me their real names. Are they code names? Anyway, they're weird. And a story too overwhelming for me? A fresh wave of nausea roils in my stomach, replacing the rumbling. I have no clue what they're plotting, but it doesn't sound good. I need to get out of here. Away. Far away. Can I rescue my father? Of course not, not from the police nor from these people. Whatever they're discussing, whoever they were, I know now my father must be in grave danger even beyond the police.

The American voice says, "Better not. We'll stay out."

Then the voices stop. I hear a rustling, then a weird *clunk, clunk*. Uh-oh, then there's another voice, a weird one. I can't—then all of a sudden, everyone's frantically talking over one another. There's that weird voice again. Suddenly, all is silent.

I whip my head back and forth. A door to my left. A bathroom? Hall closet? I twist the handle ever so gently. I'm expecting to step onto a floor. Instead, the door opens immediately to wooden steps. I trip and almost fall. Luckily, my hand grabs a bannister, and I get my bearings. Cautiously, on the tips of my sneakers, I step down, turn, and quietly shut the door behind me. Two stories—I tip-toe to a landing, then it turns, and I follow. My eyeballs bulge in the darkness as I feel my way along the rough wall, brick by brick, then a railing. A dank, musty odor fills my nostrils. It's an old basement, for sure, but it's not just the mildew. What is that weird odor?

Whoa, last step. Cold concrete. I feel around, ah, there it is. *Flip.* Dim-yellow light floods the room. Furnace, cracked cement floor… I squint my eyes following the wall toward the back. What are those? Holy moly, they're cages with small animals—mice, rabbits, and is that a guinea pig? I can also make out a long table filled with beakers and wires and test tubes like the chemistry lab at school. And is that some kind of computer with a radio attached or something? I'm not that surprised, I guess. All this verifies what Alek said about Mr. Gabriel being a scientist. But what kind of scientist? What's he doing? Then I see it.

I fall back hard on the first step, then scramble backward four steps more. My heart's beating like a jungle drum, and I grip my sweatshirt with my fist, breathing hard. I've got to get out of here. Run. But no, they'll catch me. They'll know I've found their secret. *Think logically, Kris. Logic. Cool down.* I have to take a look in this house of horrors so I can describe it to the police when I'm able to steal Gabriel's phone and call 911. I creep back down the stairs. Whatever it is, Kris, don't scream. *Do. Not. Scream.* Whatever this basement is, it's definitely not some run-of-the-mill science lab. It's more like…like Dr. Frankenstein's…

My breath stops. Holy mother of God, the huge, hideous thing stands by the furnace. It must be six and a half feet tall, motionless. It's terrifyingly ugly, and it's staring right at me like it's…*thinking.* Bile rises to my throat. I blink, hard.

It blinks back.

Eleven

January 22, 2027

Neither I nor mercifully *the thing* moves for what seems an eternity. My insides are collapsing. With great effort, I squelch the scream threatening to explode from my throat. I close my mouth to keep from vomiting. Screaming, puking—neither is an option. After the second peek, I close my eyes. The thing has been silent and still as a statue. I just hope and pray it isn't about to grab me and rip me to shreds.

Anxiety-reducing trick number 14: visualizing rainbows and puppies and kittens. Give it up, Kris. All Dad's tricks are just Band-Aids. I'm sure he never imagined in his wildest dreams his daughter would encounter...this. Gingerly I open my eyes. My heart is still thumping like crazy. No. *Be still. Be still. You must do this. Calm down, Kris.* You'll be asked to give a description. Breathe and observe. Okay, I've got this.

The thing is really tall, made mostly of metal except its arms—a gruesome mixture of flesh—or wax or plastic. I can't tell for sure in the low light. But its face... I keep staring into the muted light. Is that a mask? Of—*Alek*? It's like a half Alek. Its hair, cowlicks and all, its eyes, nose—all Alek. But the rest of its face—all metal. Is this a joke? A Halloween costume? Or maybe a prototype? Could this thing really be alive? Or is it like those wax presidents at Disney World, animated but definitely not alive? Should I escape, find Alek, and tell him what these evil people are doing? Is his life in danger?

Or—and this thought makes my heart jump into my throat—*is Alek in on it too?* At that thought, my mind goes numb.

I hear a voice from upstairs. Someone's calling my name. No time to wonder about anything, not that I want to. I've seen all I need to see. I have to move—*now*. I switch off the light and tiptoe back up the dark stairway, my hands flat on the wall. I open the door at the top as quietly as I can then shut it. I'm in the upstairs hall again.

Anti-anxiety trick number 1: deep breath. I breathe. But then another wave of nausea creeps from my stomach to my throat. I clutch my middle, then a wave of dizziness makes me sway a little. Oh god, I grab the doorknob to steady myself.

"Kreestal? Kreestal, ees that you?" Diana calls. From downstairs, I hear a whispering, then a faint shuffling. I glance all around. Can I climb out a window? No, I need to wait for an opportunity. But can I actually pretend I don't know anything? Can I hide my obvious terror? I'm no actor, but I have to do this. I *have* to, and I have to get it right. I stretch out my fingers in front of me. They're shaking like crazy. I curl them into fists, then open them and shake them out. My limbs and my stomach *must* relax. I must pretend. *Breathe, breathe, breathe...* I practice my pleasant face—and maybe a little smile? *Come on, Kris.* No luck. My mouth won't cooperate. But it *has* to. I try again—a weak smile. Okay, maybe they won't notice my lips quivering. I steady myself, call down the stairs. My voice comes out squeaky and faint. "I... I just woke up."

Diana's voice is gravelly but warm. "Bless you, dear. Glad you were able to get some rest. We are having cabbage rolls and mashed potatoes for deenner. Do you like cabbage rolls?" She's at the bottom of the stairs to the living room, and she sounds so welcoming.

But I'm not fooled. Play along, Kris. "Oh, uh. Yes, that's fine. But I'm not that hungry."

"Take your time. Come on down when you're ready, sweetheart."

Sweetheart? That's what Dad sometimes calls me. My throat tightens. Forcing a wobbly foot down each stair with the wall for support, I step onto the tile in the foyer. Then I look around, not much to see—brown couch, brown carpet, beige walls, walnut bookcases. As Alek said about the outside before the snow, "All shades of boring." No pictures anywhere. That's odd. And no TV. But it's clean, immaculate, actually. And a fire is blazing. The dining room is off the living room; the kitchen is beyond. I smell the cabbage rolls. Dad was, is, a whiz at cabbage rolls. Do they know I grew up on cabbage rolls? Another coincidence. Normally, I would have devoured this meal. But right now, my stomach feels like churning liquid cement.

Diana's back in the kitchen now, bustling around. Mr. Gabriel gestures toward my chair at the dining room table. I sit, dutifully placing the white cloth napkin in my lap. Diana spies me from the kitchen.

"Oh, Kreestal, it's so good to see you. I hope the nap did you some good." She grabs two potholders, lifting a hot casserole into the dining room, setting it on a hot pad. Mr. Gabriel, at the head of the table, spoons up our dinner, and the plates are passed. What about the third person—the American? Maybe I just imagined it. I look up at Mrs. Gabriel, sitting directly across from me. Her eyes are glistening, or are they always moist and red like this? I look down at my plate, pick up my fork, and force a pleasant expression. I think. Actually, I have no idea what my face looks like. I'm in zombie mode now, holding the fork in midair. I look at the cabbage roll. So like the ones Dad makes. It just makes me feel sicker. I can't eat. I pick at the food on my plate. Diana puts a forkful in her mouth, swallows, stealing glances at me.

Mr. Gabriel does the same. "*Herkullinen*, Lu—" he stops. Diana's eyes widen, and she's giving him a tiny head shake. They both glance my way. Mr. Gabriel chuckles, a little too forced. "Kreestal, you must have noticed our accents."

"Y-yes, I have."

"We are from *Suomi*. Finland in English."

"Oh, Finland." I manage one nod. Finland. Those of us from the North—isn't that what Dad said last night? Another coincidence? No use thinking of that now.

Mr. Gabriel smiles broadly. "Thee word *herkullinen* means 'delicious' in Feenish. You agree, eh? These cabbage rolls are one of Diana's specialties."

"Yes, they're...they're wonderful. I'm just not very hungry tonight."

Diana smiles at me sympathetically. "I understand. Don't worry, Kreestal. You've had quite an ordeal today. If you're not hungry, we can save eet for later."

"Okay, sorry."

"No need to be. Kreestal, let's talk. Come over here by the fire and warm yourself up. How about a cup of warm tea?"

"Oh, uh, yes, that sounds nice." Wait, tea? Would they ever try to—can I really pull this innocent stuff off? I push back my chair, half stagger into the living room and plop myself on a threadbare stool by a plain round end table. I hope they don't realize I'm shaking like a leaf. Faking calm is the hardest thing I've ever done. It's harder even than keeping my cool with Jackson Hynes.

As Mrs. Gabriel clears the dishes and bustles around in the kitchen, Mr. Gabriel pulls up a rocking chair with a tan cushion. He leans forward, his warm green eyes piercing right through me. I've seen this expression so many times in class, just not so up close and personal. He's so serious. I shudder again, bracing myself. I heard them call my dad an *it*. Unforgivable. They can't possibly have an acceptable explanation for this. What kind of dark web UFO robot conspiracy theories have they gotten into? They really are crazy. Or stupid. Or both.

Diana brings in a silver tea tray with a cup, saucer, sugar, and cream, sets it on the coffee table. Steam rises from the cup. I know the scent well—jasmine. Dad often gave me jasmine tea when I didn't feel well or was anxious. The Gabriels must have raided my house and found all the things I'm used to, maybe even Dad's cabbage roll recipe and the jasmine tea bags.

I thank Diana as I take the saucer from her hand, touching the rim of the cup just barely to my lips. My hands are still shaking a little. Do they notice? I pretend to take a sip, then place the cup on the tan stone coaster Mrs. Gabriel has set before me.

My nausea is subsiding a little, but I'm still dizzy. Glad I didn't take a bite of cabbage roll. I have no doubt it would be splattered all over the table if I had. But now the room starts to sway. Mr. Gabriel doesn't seem to notice I am close to passing out. I slowly breathe in, out.

He begins. "Kreestal, I can tell you are tense. I don't blame you a bit. Thees ees nerve-wracking to Diana and me as well. But please know we are all on the same team, eh? I am about to tell you things so you don't feel so, well, een the dark. However, the eenformation weel likely sound totally unreal to you. Eet won't make a beet of sense. But I swear to you, every word ees true. Are you ready to hear eet?"

I fidget with the seam of my sweatshirt. What's worse? Being in the dark or knowing some dark, terrible secret? I've been in the dark so long. Okay, Secret, you win.

"Uh, I'm ready."

"Good, you are a brave girl. First, you were born not here in Montana, but een the far North, across the ocean. Een the arctic—Finland—Northern Finland, where we once were a secret community of scientists trying to help the world. We called ourselves the Quantum Community, or QC for short. Your father, your mother, many others."

I squeeze my eyes shut then open them. So far so weird. But not so horrible. "Okay, go on."

"Kreestal, I know thees sounds terribly untrue, but your father, who was once a wonderful, breelliant man when we leeved een the community was"—he stops, lowers his head, takes a breath—"keeled by, well, enemies—terrorists. We think perhaps they stole some of his DNA and constructed some type of clone or perhaps—oh, thees ees so hard to tell you. But most likely, once they got the body looking, well, human, they no doubt placed their own software in hees brain. Een any case, he ees not what he seems."

So this is the horrible part. Holy crap...holy crap, I don't believe a word of it. Secret my ass. Can I sneak away and call the Retreat and have them committed? I had a hunch all along Mr. Gabriel had a screw loose from our after-school "special talks," and this confirms it—no matter what Alek says. Does Alek even know this? Telling me my father is not my father but some kind of robotic clone, mind-controlled by robots. Yeah, right, uh-huh. My hands are all sweaty, trembling like crazy now. I ball them into fists, shoving them into my sweatshirt pockets.

"He looks just like your father when he was…when he was human, but especially from what we weetnessed today, we now know he ees not—"

Not human. Dad is not human. That's why they referred to him as an *it*, which means they'll never believe him. That does it. I can't just sit here and listen to a couple of obviously nutso old people telling me my father is not human. I should have reported Mr. Gabriel's strange behavior to the principal when I had the chance. Where are the police? I sat in that god-awful room at Children's Services for hours while they were supposedly vetting my new guardians. And now where are they when I need them? They certainly didn't do a thorough job of assessing these…these freaks. Did they even check the Gabriels' basement? Apparently not unless they're all in some kind of perverse ring that—*Kris, god, chill. No, don't chill. Get out. Now.*

Sprinting from my chair, I snatch up Gabriel's cell phone in one fell swoop, pressing the 9, the 1, but before I can press the last number, a large hand, fingers thick as cigars, envelopes mine.

"Kreestal, please, please."

I do a nosedive into primal mode. It's all out now, just can't hold it in any longer. Can't do it. I scream, "DAD!" I wrestle, claw, pull as hard as I can, but of course, my teacher's strength is far greater. Gabriel holds the phone high above his head, taking two large strides to the china cabinet, setting the phone on top, clearly out of my reach. Instead of the fury I expect—the metamorphosis to a crazed monster—Mr. Gabriel is surprisingly composed.

"Kreestal, you cannot do thees. You *must* hear me out. I told you thees would be hard to believe."

Why is he still lying? I yell, "Stop it, stop it, STOP IT…" I'm so crazy-mad I'm ready to fight to the death. "It sounds unbelievable because it *is*. And you're both nuts. My father is *human*, more human than the both you *put together. And* that hideous thing in the basement…"

116

Diana bursts out crying. "You were een the basement? Oh lord, I knew thees would happen, Veeto. How can we—"

Veeto… Veeto? Veeto what? Why does this woman keep calling her husband a different name? Maybe *they're* the clones—the monsters. Like the thing in the basement. A burst of energy blasts through me. I tear across the room to the door and frantically twist the handle. Again, I'm blocked; this time not just by Mr. Gabriel's fingers, but by his large, rotund body. I scream and scream. Now my screaming's nonstop. Where are the neighbors? Can't they hear me?

"HELP! PLEASE HELP…"

"Kreestal, calm down, please…let us explain. Oh god, what can I say to make you believe?"

"DAD! Dad, where are you? DAD?"

Diana is sobbing. "Kreestal, you must leesten! Oh, I shouldn't. I know I shouldn't. Not now but, Veeto, we're desperate. Maybe we should get Aleksi? He could—"

"Shhh, no, Loomy, not yet. She ees just not ready."

Loomy? Another strange name. And Aleksi? Alek? My tutor? What's he really got to do with all this? It's proof these people are definitely not who they are supposed to be. I'm not ready for what? Are they going to clone me too? If I can just contact Shana, the social worker, and tell her these people aren't foster parents. They're imposter parents. Ha, that rhymes. Alek would like this one—or not. Now I'm not even sure who my tutor is. Maybe I can't trust anyone.

The woman, Loomy, reaches out her arms toward me. I shrink back. Does she think I'm stupid? I may be ADD—awfully dumb ditz, as Jackson Hynes calls me, but I know when I'm being had. And when my family's life is at stake, I am one hell of a fighter, and I will fight. But oh, now what? The woman's face is covered in tears. Tears of what?

"Leesten, child. We know—knew your mother!"

I stop. She knew my *what*?

She sees my astonished expression and nods. "There, eet ees said. Oh, Kreestal, yes. She was—oh, I can't say. But we knew her! Knew her quite well. And she knew you, and you knew her! Oh, I didn't want you to know just yet, but—"

Oh god, just more bullshit. My *mother*? That's not fair. Seriously? Why are they doing this to me?

There's a pounding at the door. We all freeze. More pounding. This isn't someone frantically knocking. This is someone trying to break the door down. Good lord. We're all still frozen, staring at the door. It's clear the Gabriels have no idea what's happening. Did someone hear my cries? The thuds against the door grow more powerful—someone's definitely trying to kick it down. Whoever they are, they're determined. Is it the police? It has to be. I will make them search the basement. I'll tell them I saw a dead body because I did, sort of. What else could it be? I'll tell them how the Gabriels have abused me because they have, haven't they? They kidnapped me and prevented me from calling 911. The pounding is now insistent, urgent. Wait, if they are pounding so hard, shouldn't they be yelling "Police. Open up" or something?

I watch in a daze as Mr. Gabriel rushes to the fireplace and grabs a poker. Raising it high above his head, he flattens himself against the wall by the door, readying himself for—what? He can't assault a police officer. What's wrong with him?

Then a voice from the other side—a voice I know as well as my own. But angrier—much angrier than I've ever heard him.

"Kristaaaal…" My father. Ignoring Mr. Gabriel with the poker poised above his head, I rush to the door and turn the lock. Before I can pull it open, the door crashes inward, knocking me backward. I smash into Mr. Gabriel. He stumbles but stays upright with the poker still above his head. Dad grabs me, and I fall into his arms, hugging him as hard as I can. He's coatless; the pajamas and blue checkered apron are replaced by a plain gray prison uniform. I can't stand to see him in such demeaning garb. He has stubble on his chin, and his eyes are still wild and frantic as they were this morning. Just the thought of my dad in jail makes me want to scream or barf or both. Well, obviously, he's out now. But for how long? Gabriel still has the poker raised high, and I can tell he's about to use it.

"*Dad, watch out!*" My father pushes me out of the way, obviously to protect me. Before I can reach for him again, Gabriel steps between us. I can hardly breathe. He lowers the poker.

"No, Pauli, or whatever you are. We need to keep Kreestal safe—here weeth us. You know that. For all our sakes. Kreestal, please back away... Loomy!"

The woman—Diana, or Loomy—wraps her arms tightly around me, dragging me backward into the dining room. As we reach the kitchen doorway, my father lets out a snarl, seizing the poker and ripping the sharp point down Mr. Gabriel's forearm and right out of his hands. He slams it to the floor with a loud clunk.

"Ougghh!" Blood gushes from Mr. Gabriel's inner elbow, down his right arm, and drips from his wrist to the floor. He loses his balance, tumbles backward, lands on a stairstep. "LOOMY, 911! 911!"

Mrs. Gabriel lets me go, runs straight to the china hutch where Mr. Gabriel had placed the phone. She reaches, jumps, hops, but she's even shorter than I am.

"Veeto, I... I'll get a chair."

Mr. Gabriel yells, "No, no, Loomy, the *peestol. Peestoli!* Then run! You know where. Take Kreestal NOW!"

Mrs. Gabriel pleads, "Come, Kreestal. Come with me. Trust us. You MUST."

Peestol? Peestoli? They have a gun? I should go with her? Does this woman think I'm a raving lunatic, like I'm going to hide from my own father? Then let Mr. Gabriel kill Dad? I pull away and rush to my father's side, grabbing his waist. This time, Dad shoves me behind him, and from somewhere inside his prison shirt, pulls the same gun he used earlier this morning. Oh please, dear God, no more shooting. How did he get it back?

"Dad, how—"

His free arm twists my sweatshirt in a death grip while his other arm points the gun at Gabriel, speaking in a weird, monotone voice. My god, it's kind of like Tad's. "You. Deceivers. There will be a reckoning. The prophecy is near. They need her. Now."

Who? What prophecy? Who is *her?* Me? I peek out from behind my father's back. A bead of sweat trickles down Mr. Gabriel's temple. His face is beet-red, and he's breathing hard. Mrs. Gabriel has disappeared. Is she calling the police? Mr. Gabriel holds up his palms as he slowly backs up, like a father trying to calm a distressed child.

"Pauli, you know she would die there."

What? Me? Die? Where?

Mr. Gabriel's arm is covered with blood, trickling in rivulets down his fingers onto the floor. He'll need at least six inches of stitches. Good god, that must hurt, but he doesn't seem to notice, his eyes are locked on my father's. After several seconds of a stare down, Mr. Gabriel says in a calm, steely voice: "She will be safest here weeth us. Don't you agree? If you take her to Cancri e, she will die. You *must* know that. Think logically, Pauli. We all want to make sure she lives."

Cancri e? That damn planet again. I search my father's face. It's as expressionless as his voice. What the hell?

"DAD? What's Cancri e? Is this why—"

I'm still behind him. He can't answer me now; I know he's trying his damnedest to protect me. Mr. Gabriel wipes his forearm on his pants, staining the pocket a dark burgundy.

"Pauli, Pauli, put the gun away. Let's all seet down. Loomy just baked some *kaalikaaryleet*. You must be starving. We need to talk peacefully, rationally. Why don't we—"

Mrs. Gabriel appears, slides a gun across the dining room table. "Veeto—"

My father cocks his gun and aims.

"Pauli, Pauli, no!" Mr. Gabriel is slowly backing away toward his own gun.

Bang!

I scream.

Mr. Gabriel's gun flies off the table, shatters the glass of their china closet. Suddenly, I feel myself being lifted from the floor. Dad's left arm is encircling my waist; the other, aiming the gun straight at Mr. Gabriel's head. I squeeze my eyes tight. We're suddenly out the door and down the steps to the yard. Has Dad always been this strong? Mrs. Gabriel cries out. My eyes still shut, I brace for the sound of gunshot once again.

Bang! Oh no, no. *Bang!* No no. Just like this morning. Oh, please no.

Dad sets me down, grabs my arm, and we're both racing like mad into the frosty night air toward our—no. It's not our car. It's a—I squint—a silver Honda Civic waiting at the curb by their mail-box. Whose car is this? It's all so crazy, but at the same time, I've never felt so relieved in my life. The Gabriels must be evil. There's no way Dad could act like this if they were just normal people. He's come to rescue me, putting his own life in danger, saving me from them. If he did have to shoot, then undoubtedly, he had no choice. But I don't look back. I should. But I just can't.

I turn to hug my father. "Dad, you came for me. How did you—"

"*Get in.*"

Twelve

• ◦ • ◦ • ◦ • ◦ ◉ ⊙ ◉ ◦ • ◦ • ◦ • ◦ •

January 22, 2027

Dad yanks open the door of the unfamiliar car. Has he rented this? Borrowed it? Stolen it? No matter. He's here—my hero—alive and unharmed. His arrest was all a big mistake. In a rush of relief and gratitude, I try again to hug him. I need his bear hugs right now like I need air. But when I extend my arms, he gives me a quick shove into the passenger seat. Well, okay, he needs me to hurry. I fasten my belt and look around to the back seat. Tad? No Tad.

"Where's Tad?"

My father races around to the driver's seat and climbs in, slamming the door. His face is grim, what I can see of it, his lips disappearing into a weird, thin line. He taps something under the steering wheel, and the motor comes to life.

"Disassembling."

"Disassem—what? You mean Tad? What does that mean? What's going on? DAD?"

I hear sirens in the distance. Oh god, Diana—Loomy—whoever she is must have finally called the police. Or maybe the neighbors heard the commotion. Without a word, Dad grips the gearshift and yanks it in reverse. The car abruptly lurches backward. Gravel crunches, then flies, tires screech, and we're out of the driveway and onto the street. The car weaves back and forth over the median a few seconds before settling on the right side. Dad is speeding like a maniac. I just hope they don't catch him. If he did escape from jail, he'd be in so much trouble I'd have to stay with the Gabriels forever.

If they're still alive. I should have looked to see if anyone got hurt by those last two shots, or maybe I don't want to know. I turn my head, gaze out the window, try to zone out like I do in Mr. Gabriel's class. Oh god, what a difference a day makes.

Dad's acting funny, but I guess it's to be expected. I'm hoping we're on a Tad rescue mission. Maybe Dad's an undercover CIA agent. It would explain why he doesn't talk about his work. It would explain the current insanity. But, I mean, that's just crazy. Must be another explanation. I can't wait until he tells me the whole story—when all three of us are together again and safe.

But if he is an undercover agent, maybe we'll have to move, to assume another identity and be in a witness protection program. I wouldn't mind disappearing if it means Jackson Hynes is out of my life forever. As long as Dad, my brother, and I are together, I can live anywhere. I trust Dad like no other person on Earth. The Gabriels are probably from a rogue country, not Finland like they said, and they're trying to get information from Dad. They took me as hostage. That's a possibility. But what's this prophecy they were yakking about? And what do I have to do with it? I'll ask Dad when we come up for air.

I have no clue where we're headed, but can't wait until we stop. I need to fill Dad in on all the strange things in the Gabriels' basement. Then Dad and his agents can apprehend the spies. That has to be it. Crazy as it sounds, it's the only thing that makes sense right now.

"Dad, I was in the Gabriels' basement and—"

"Shut up." Whoa, punch-in-the-gut. Dad never, ever talks to me like this. I know he's focused on getting out of here. And I know he must have had one hell of a day. I'll have to wait to tell him about the Gabriels and how much I missed him.

The highway stretches on and on as we travel away from Dolcany far into the night. After maybe an hour, it narrows to a two-lane road through mountains much higher than any I've seen in a long time. I keep checking, but so far, traffic has been almost non-existent. My heart still hasn't totally calmed down since Dad grabbed me and stuffed me into this escape vehicle.

Dad stays mute, almost like he's forgotten I'm right beside him. He's never ignored me like this. I thought by now he would at least have reached over and patted my hand or told me everything would be all right. And what did he mean when he said Tad was "disassembling"? What the hell does that mean? I thought I felt safe, but something's just not right. I don't like being on the run, even if it is with my dad. Unlike the movies, I don't feel cool, just scared, scared as hell.

We drive across fields, up and down, through the mountains and through tiny towns with neon lights, and when the towns disappear, a sparkly dome lights up the sky above the shadowy landscape. Dad and I still haven't spoken a word to each other since he answered—well, more like responded to—my question about Tad. And since he said "Shut up." This is definitely weird.

We continue on and on. Gradually, the monotony of the driving slows my nervous system, and my eyes start to feel heavy. PPT, Kris. I am with Dad, and no one has stopped us. We seem to be in the clear. It's going to be okay. We will find Tad, and this whole episode will fade into a forgotten nightmare. I lay my head back and stare at the stars through the sunroof. They're so delicate, tiny pinpricks of miniature suns behind a velvet backdrop. My eyes keep fluttering, then finally close.

I awaken, groggy and sore. My right arm is asleep. My mouth is cotton, and my stomach feels hollow. The car is coming to a slow stop, tires scraping on stones. How much time has passed? I glance at the neon-green numbers of the clock on the dashboard—twelve midnight exactly. My father turns off the engine, and the sudden stillness engulfs us. Eyes still heavy with sleep, I pull myself up, massaging my frozen right arm and checking the scene out the window. We're deep in the high mountains now, probably past Coeur d'Alene, in a remote area. No doubt Idaho. It's all snow-covered, the full moon illuminating the landscape in an eerie glow. Awesome, really. I should be feeling peaceful and right at home. After all, we're in the snowy mountains, my favorite place in the world, and I'm with my favorite person in the world. Yes, it's been kind of an odd journey so far, but I am with my dad, and we're safe, aren't we? But then I notice—my mind and my gut are at odds, and I sense that somehow…something just isn't. I turn toward my father.

"Dad, what—"

Only then do I see it. He's turned to stare at me…his face…

A deafening scream pierces the quiet, and I realize the scream is my own. I scramble backward into the door, push the button, but it's locked. I turn back. My father's warm brown eyes are gone. In their place—in the sockets where they used to be—are the same cold steel ball bearings I'd seen in my brother's eyes right before he vanished. My body turns to gelatin.

Then his voice completely transforms into a strange Tad-like monotone: "Frequency continues insufficient for teleportation 73112. Instruct."

I look right, left, behind. Who is he talking to? Then from the car's radio, an unbearably shrill hiss of static. I cringe. My eardrums spasm. I cower, throwing my arms over my head.

Suddenly, a voice explodes in my mind—Mr. Gabriel's, "Your father ees not what he seems." Oh, please dear God, let Mr. Gabriel be wrong. And his question the other day about kidnapping, is this what he meant? Am I being kidnapped by my own father? How could Mr. Gabriel have known? Oh no no no, it's not true. Don't let it be true. Suddenly, my father reaches for me, not for a bear hug, but to—

I hear another voice in my head, this time the diamond lady's, "You may be in grave danger very soon. Remember this number—"

As my father, or whatever this thing is, lurches toward me, I lean back into the window so hard that I think it may shatter. I grasp my neck to shield it from the clawlike thing reaching for my throat.

The pendant—my fingers encircle it, gripping it tight. Oh god, the number I couldn't care less about this morning. The number—what the hell is the number? My quivering thumb finds the diamond. No time to wonder if the lady was there to help me, I press the diamond with all my might. My voice is shaking, and I can't get the numbers out, but I have to… I have to now now *now*…

"Three…seven…" Something, oh god, what what what? I should've listened better… I should have *believed*…oh no, the mid-

dle number. I just need the one in the middle. The middle number—
what was that? What? *What? I told Tad the number. Now what was it?*

I hear a low growl. My father? But it's the voice of a beast. The
claw retreats, suspended in air, then grasps once again for my throat.
The radio's static is deafening. I twist and turn, covering my neck and
head with my arm while pressing the diamond with my other thumb.
And then it pops out of my mouth like Tad does it: "3 7 0 9 3."

The claw, half an inch away from my Adam's apple, freezes.
Then a string of deafening inhuman shrieks from the radio makes my
toes curl. My father's face has morphed into something so demonic
it can only have come from hell itself. *Dad*…the Gabriels were right.
He is not what he…

A jolt.

I'm somewhere else.

The Diamond Star

Thirteen

January 23, 2027

I'm swirling through velvet softness. Round and round I spin. Then nothing. When my awareness returns, I'm floating, tumbling, surrounded by sparkling cascades like silver fireworks. After a time, the sparkles transform into glowing rainbows, then morph into a thousand golden halos. I just watch, mesmerized, sinking, rising, sinking again, not knowing if I am up or down, east or west. Hours, weeks, maybe years pass. I am fully alert, and my thinking is steady, but my body is *where*? I can't feel anything except sporadic sensations that I'm being pulled, twisted, and pushed. The lights are wondrous, but it's all totally silent.

Finally, the rainbow cascades and colors fade away, and I enter pure darkness again, blacker than black, gliding in the void for hours. Am I dead? Do the dead see? Hear? Feel? Think? Suddenly, I sense a familiar feeling—Achilles. I'm starting to feel anxious. *Oh no, just go with the flow, Kris. Breathe, breathe.* Breathe? I can't feel my breath. *Okay then, just hang. Don't have a panic attack. No paper bags here. Go with the flow…flow…flow…*

Gradually, a pulse grows in my head, neck, shoulders, arms, torso, legs, stronger, stronger, steady now. Finally, I'm reconnecting, piece by piece. My legs are heavy as mountain rock. The cool silkiness beneath me is soothing, but not nearly enough to dull the pain in my joints, muscles, skin, growing more intense as each body part reenters my awareness. The achiness reminds me of the worst flu I've ever had—or like I've been squashed by a truck, squeezed, and pummeled relentlessly. I'm so disoriented. My mind reels, grasping at thoughts, groping for memories; it's all jumbled up and fragmented. When will this end?

Suddenly, a vision floats in front of my mind's eye. It's recent. My heart skips a beat. Oh god, my memory is back online—my father. But no, he's not my father. His eyes, the twisted metal fingers grasping for my face. Did he kill me? I can feel my face and throat now and choke back tears. If I scream, will anyone hear? Will anyone care? What has happened to my world, *my* world, so safe, so beautiful this morning? This morning. Was it just this morning? Or was it... I don't know. I just don't know.

Something grabs my attention to the left. A pinprick of yellow is pulsating, twinkling like a tiny star, but now it begins to expand, larger and larger... All at once, a silent but brilliant blast explodes before me, and I brace for impact. A scream builds in my throat, but I'm too weak to push it out, and I hear myself whimper like a newborn kitten. The air beneath me pushes me ever so gently up, up, and I'm trying to hold on, but there's nothing to grasp, so I lie still, passing through the light. Now all around me is dry, warm air, like an attic in summer. Oh, I'm descending inch by inch, slowly but definitely downward. Then a distant thrumming reverberates like the hum of a huge gong after it's been rung.

And now I hear a jumble of new noises—buzzing, chattering, clicking, chirping. Birds? My ears strain to listen. The noises grow louder and louder, and then a light bump. I am on solid ground again. Something invisible pulls me upright. I stumble, catch myself, and slowly straighten. Whoa, it feels like the floor is a huge magnet tugging at my legs. My whole body is weak, dizzy, achy, and I'm oh-so thirsty. Should I open my eyes? I have to be brave. I've been getting a lot of practice being brave lately. In my present crazy, upside-down world, I guess there's no other way.

My eyes open to a slit. I look down and gape. I'm standing on a sparkly marble floor in dizzying patterns of silver, white, and black. My eyes widen and follow it. The bizarre floor stretches as far as I can see. Every few yards, columns of dark granite rise up like sentries from floor to ceiling. Maybe this is a ballroom or a large banquet hall. But there are no tables, and no one's dancing. In fact, no one is here at all. Yet, I'm not alone. About half a football field away, in the center of the vast room, is the bird thing. I immediately cower, expecting another dive-bomb. Nothing happens, no squawk, no screech. I slowly straighten and cup my eyes to get a better look.

Oh, okay, it's not the same one that attacked me, but there's a definite similarity. Now that I observe more closely, how could I have mistaken the bird in the forest for this one? It's got those owlish eyes. But this one's much larger—six or seven feet high at least, mostly gray but with black overtones and a huge white tail. It's a real *Sesame Street* Big Bird except for its color. Hope it's as friendly, but could it be even more dangerous than the sleeve gouger? The creature is now cocking its head and peering at me, slowly opening, closing its huge dark eyes. Hmmm, this one doesn't seem malicious at all. Actually, it seems rather calm, gentle. Then I notice movement behind it.

A massive gathering of birdlike creatures, groups of all different sizes, colors, shapes, perches in a grove of ivory-colored trees like birch trees. But inside a ballroom? Are they real? They certainly look real, preening themselves on the branches, shuffling around on the floor, their claws clicking, sounding like old-fashioned typewriters I've seen on the Old Timer Movie channel. They pick at the floor, cawing softly, staring at me, then dropping their gaze and looking away almost as if they're ashamed to watch me, to make eye contact. The giant one suddenly begins waddling toward me. I swallow hard. It stops about a foot in front of me. I step back. It cocks its head and opens its massive beak.

"You surprised at floor? Penrose tiling. Projection of five-dimensional crystalline structure onto two dimensions. Pretty. Like it? Might make dizzy. Here—chair. Sit. Raaah."

The bird thing *talks*? Or is my brain just fried from the crazy trip I was just on? Wait a minute, could the Gabriels have slipped a hallucinogen in my tea? No, Kris, you idiot. Even if they had, you didn't drink a drop. But birds can't…oh, man. This *has* to be a dream. The small, raspy voice is friendly, even a little timid. What did it just say? Penrose, projection onto—good lord, it can think like that? My knees buckle. Instantly the promised chair appears, just in time to catch me as I fall backward onto its soft, black cushion, like a silken beanbag. I sit up warily, adjusting myself. What the hell is happening?

This whole, long scenario *must* be entirely in my own mind. I am at home, in my bed, in a long-drawn-out vivid dream. *Vivid?* Ha! *That's* an understatement. I look up again. The birdlike thing is kind of like the one who attacked me in the woods. That explains it. Of course, I would dream about it. This whole weird episode will be over soon, and I will wake up in my bed, with the snow all around and pecan pancakes or blueberry muffins waiting for me down in the kitchen.

As if it could read my thoughts, the large creature flaps a wing. Suddenly a warm, sweet scent swirls around me as a smaller bird appears with a small plate in its beak. It sets the plate down in my lap. I smile, shaking my head. What a hoot—a huge blueberry muffin, my favorite breakfast. I love this dream. I can't wait to tell Tad.

The big bird extends a wing toward the plate. "Muffin good. Eat."

How fun. I will awaken soon. More dream birds have gathered at my feet. They're smaller than the ones I've just seen.

The large one gestures again, this time with its head toward my plate. "Eat muffin for Kristal."

Ha, he even knows my name. Whew, I'll just float along here. Merrily, merrily, merrily…life is but a dream. I'll enjoy this bizarre, Alice in Wonderland fantasy while it lasts. What do they call these kinds of dreams where you're dreaming but you know you're dreaming? Oh yes, lucid dreams. Dad and I watched that PBS special on lucid dreams once. Wow, and here I am having one. Now that I have an explanation, I might as well just relax and enjoy the show. I'll awaken soon.

My stomach growls. Hesitantly, I pick up the dream muffin. The bird things are all gathered round, their eyes widening in anticipation of my first bite. It cracks me up. These creatures act like they really want to please me. Well, of course, anything is possible in dreamland. The dream muffin is warm and moist and bursting with blueberries, almost melting on my tongue. I bite down so eagerly that a big chunk falls to the floor, along with the plate. Oops—oddly, the plate doesn't break. It doesn't even crack upon hard impact. It must not be glass.

I bend down to pick it up, but immediately, a dozen or so much smaller bird things converge on the dropped muffin piece like a shiny, pulsating black wave.

Instantly, the big bird raises its wings menacingly. "Raaah."

As one, the birds cower, shrivel, then explode from the floor all at once, settling on the other side of the vast room, in the white trees and on the floor, preening their feathers. The bit of food has vanished, crumbs and all.

The bigger bird looks at the bare plate and shakes its head. "Baby crows. Always hungry. And very rude."

How hilarious—rude baby birds. I leave the plate on the floor and stuff the remaining muffin into my mouth. It melts on my tongue, and I'm in muffin heaven, just like home. Dad is probably making them right now down in the kitchen, and I can smell them baking. Okay, I've had enough. I can wake up now. Suddenly a slight wave of nausea roils in my stomach. I ate too fast. Napkins? Nope, guess not. I wipe my mouth with my sleeve then glance up. The giant bird thing stands in front of me, like a servant—motionless, head cocked, watching me eat.

"Want more? Can make more. And keep baby crows from stealing." It's back to his friendly, chirpy voice. It's really kind of cute.

I shake my head. "No, no. Um, but if I could have glass of water?"

The big bird lowers its head. "No water here."

He looks so dejected I feel sorry I asked. "It's okay. I'm fine, really. That muffin was delicious. Thank you very much."

It immediately perks up. "Do not thank us. Birds thank *you*. You will save us."

What did it just say? "I will?"

"Yes, yes, you will."

"Ah-nee! Ah-nee, dear, where is she?" Another voice—this one human, a woman—comes from the far corner of the room. She sounds frantic.

Ah-nee? Is that the big bird's name?

He plods toward the woman then bows. "Doctor M., Crystal Child safe. Just had muffin."

"Oh, thank you, thank you. Dear Ah-nee, you're a gem. What would I do without you? How-ka brought me, but General War-a commanded him to be off again for the mission. My goodness, can't believe she ended up in Birdland. I programmed her pendant myself for touchdown in the city. How could this have happened?"

The lady—what's she talking about? What city? Ah-nee must be the giant bird who just gave me the muffin. But who's How-ka? And General War-a? Are we in a place where there's a war going on? And this lady here, her voice sounds vaguely familiar. I look a little more closely. Holy moly. Yep. She's the diamond lady from the forest. But she looks so different. Gone is the magnificent sparkly diamond cloak, replaced by an everyday outfit—black slacks, white blouse, lab coat (is she a doctor?), and black sneakers rather old and scruffy. I do notice the button on her slacks, and those down her blouse are also diamonds or some type of crystal. Her long hair, the color of straw with golden glints, is pulled back into a high ponytail with a white scrunchy also decorated with diamonds. Curly wisps frame her face and seem to gleam in the light. She's not wearing a bit of makeup. Except for the diamonds on her slacks and blouse, she could pass for any typical person. Typical beautiful person, that is. She reaches into her pocket, pulls out something that looks like a card, maybe a credit card?

She taps it twice, holding it in front of her. Oh, I see, it's some kind of communication device. She frowns as she talks into the mini-cell phone: "Dahab, what in Lucy's name happened here? Kristal's in Birdland for goodness' sake. Ah-nee contacted me. I'm here now too."

I hear faint talking from the other end, too soft for me to make out the words. The diamond lady listens, then interrupts.

"Hale? Hale War-a? Damn. He thought *what*? On whose authority? *His*? He may be head of our army, but he's no king. And I'm not part of his damn army anyway. He can't...*what*? Kristal would be safer in the passageways? Since when does he call the shots here? We need to get to the city like *yesterday*. He and you know full well there are precious few provisions here in Birdland. You also know the need for recoup after teleportation, especially the first one. Now what am I supposed to do? Conjure up water out of thin air? Guess we'll just have to head out on foot. Passageway 74944 is 1.3 kilometers from the city. War-a programmed that. I can see here by his text. Birdland is 3.1 kilometers from the city." She pauses, then smacks her forehead with her free palm. "Oh, Dahab, you made a simple reversal error. You can't still be making mistakes like this." Another pause. The diamond lady's eyes widen, then blink several times. She sighs. "Yes. I know about your learning difference. I know how hard you've worked to overcome it. Well, let that be a lesson. But we can't afford to make mistakes anymore. The time is near. Whatever we end up doing, it's got to be 100 percent perfect. Make sure everything you do is double, triple-checked. Oh, Dahab, sorry I blew. You've been a tremendous help. But this is my"—she glances my way, then back to the phone card—"my mission, and it's crucial everything goes exactly as planned." *Mission.* I wonder what she's talking about. *Am I part of this crucial mission? Me?* "Yes, yes, I'll keep you posted."

I keep watching in wonder. The diamond lady taps her little card again. "Hey, Hale."

A man's voice this time—it's deep and booming. I can hear every word. "Mer-aka. We're really busy over here. Can it wait?"

The lady puts her hand over the card and says, "It's General War-a, head of the DS Army. About time."

I listen, not understanding anything.

She practically yells back into the card: *"No, it can't wait! We're in Birdland for Lucy's sake! How is she going to get back to the city without the birds?"*

Lucy? Who's Lucy? I add that to my question-bee brainbox.

"Birdland? That wasn't the teleport code I programmed. I was trying to keep her safe. You had her appearing smack-dab in the middle of the city square—not a good idea. But Birdland? I gave Dahab a code that was only 1.3 kilometers from the city. Passageway 74944. And I even spared a soldier to meet and greet and escort her the short distance to the city. Unfortunately, I had to recall him. We've got to perfect this exercise, you know. I need all hands on deck at this stage. I texted you. It was only 1.3 kilometers. I would never have programmed her for Birdland."

"Well, that's 1.3 kilometers too many. And then Dahab accidentally reversed the damn number, which is why we are now 3.1 kilometers away. But Ah-nee's still here. He can transport us to the—"

"Sorry, Mer-aka."

No one speaks for a moment. Where have I heard that name before? Mer. Aka. I can't think. My brain's so numb. The diamond lady's face is getting all red. The War-a guy starts up again. "I need him now. In fact, he should've been here an hour ago. He's tantamount to the transport drill, and we've all been standing around for at least a half hour tapping our highly polished diamond boots doing nothing. The day is looming. I need the big birds *now*. How-ka just made it. But we need Ah-nee, or we can't do this exercise. You want to win this war, or don't you? I understand your concern. But this army has been option 1 for a decade. This supersedes everything. You know that. Can't spare him. You and the child can walk through the passages. Shouldn't take long. Not my fault if Dahab erred with the code. If she hadn't, you'd be almost there by now."

Mer-aka's nostrils are flaring, and she's pacing back and forth. "Finewhatevsamogottagobye." She's talking so fast I have no idea what she just said. There's a pause, then the booming voice on the other end yells even louder: "*Excuse me?*"

The diamond lady hisses. "*I said spit and move on, dammit.*" Whoa, so that's what SAMO means. I think I've heard Dad say that sometimes. She stuffs the card back into her pocket, shaking her head, muttering, "What a snafu."

Ah-nee bows. "Our great pleasure to meet Ms. Kristal. So sorry. Orders. Must be off."

The lady waves her hand in the air dismissively. "Yes, yes."

The bird thing bows to me, bows to the lady. I think I actually see a little guilt on his feathered face as he looks up at us. "Must obey."

The lady softens. "Yes, of course, Ah-nee. It's not your fault. I will be forever indebted to you for greeting our girl and giving her a meal."

"Kristal—our true leader." The giant bird slowly shakes its massive head, waddles on two huge talons to the center of the room, raises its colossal wings, and ascends straight up through an opening in the ceiling.

I gape, peer upward, catching a last glimpse as he flies higher and higher until he disappears. The sky is the color of cinnamon, scattered with stars. Odd. And even more odd—Did the bird just call me "our true leader"? What in the world did that mean? I should be demanding answers, but right now, I'm speechless. Oh yes, no worries. I'm dreaming.

The diamond lady squeezes her eyes tight, opens them, suddenly rushing toward me like gangbusters, arms held out like she's expecting an embrace. What? When she's just a few feet away from me, she almost skids to a stop. Seeing me cower, she stands motionless, arms at her sides, as though she's afraid of frightening me, just like when we met in the forest. Then she takes one more step forward, goes down on one knee, takes my hand, and breathes in deeply. She offers her hand like I'm a timid little puppy, and she doesn't want to scare me. What the heck. I take her outstretched hand. She lets out a tiny gasp. Why? We look into each other's eyes. Hers are glistening, like they were in the forest. Two sparkling emeralds—I remember them clearly. But why all the drama? Oh yeah, I guess I'm dreaming.

"Oh, my dear Kristal, at least you're here. You made it. Please forgive me...forgive me for all the confusion. I didn't want your arrival to be like this."

All of a sudden, there's a lull in the noise. She's still staring up at me, adoringly for some reason. Far in the distance, I hear a kind of thrum—like I heard as I was landing, like a gong that's gone off and now is reverberating. She doesn't seem to notice. Well, Kris, time for a QB. I look into her green eyes.

"I hear a distant, like hum. Are my ears ringing?"

She seems breathless, smiles, and shakes her head, completely ignoring my question.

"Kristal. Oh, Kristal, my—oh thank goodness, you believed my words. What a relief to see you here, safe. I'm so sorry about the mix-up." She gazes down at me with the same expression as the moment we met behind my house, in the snow. But what is that expression exactly? Sadness? Fondness? Pity? Or something else?

I try again. "The gong-like sound?"

She waves me off. "Oh, that. It's—don't worry. It's nothing." She fingers my pendant, frowning, tapping the diamond. "First things first, Kristal. May I ask? What was the last straw—the event that convinced you to take such a leap of faith?"

A vision of my father's steel eyeballs and clawlike hand explodes in my brain and my stomach lurches.

"Well, my—the—" Wow, I feel dizzy, even sitting down. A rock hardens in my throat. I look up at her apologetically. "I… I don't think I can talk about it now, but—"

"But?"

"You…you were right. I—my life—was in danger. I almost…" I choke.

The lady shakes her head. "It's okay now, sweetheart. It's okay. You're safe. Must have been a horrible experience, whatever it was. We would never have wished anything like that for you, of course. But we were afraid for you and needed to prepare you just in case." She brightens. "Well, you're here now. Your journey probably wore you out. We need to let you rest for a while."

I say nothing.

She hesitates then says softly, "Would it be okay…may I please…just a small hug?"

She's begging for a hug—a hug. Such a trivial thing to ask this ordinary girl from Montana. But, hey, if it will make her day, I gingerly open my arms. She closes her eyes in rapture as though she's embracing an angel, which most certainly I'm not. In fact, I probably smell from the trip. I have no idea how long it lasted. But she keeps hugging me like a long-lost friend. What's her deal? But slowly, as we hold each other close, I feel my heart soften just a little toward this strange out-of-the-blue woman. After all, didn't the lady's instructions just save my life? I can tell she's holding back a lake of tears.

Why? I finger the pendant. It survived the journey. But to where exactly? Am I just in my very own brain, dreaming away? The events of the last day or two or maybe more have all been so crazy strange yet seem so real. I search the lady's deep-green eyes.

"I *am* dreaming, right?"

The lady smiles, blinking through tears. "It must appear as such to you. It would appear to me as well if I didn't know better. But if it makes you less afraid, then yes. Let's say you are in a dream."

"Where in Dreamland am I then?"

The lady sighs. "You're in Birdland. You ended up here, but not by my doing."

"Yeah, I think I heard that loud and clear from your phone calls. But what is Birdland?"

"Oh, they have their own territory out here. A little over three kilometers from the city."

"The city?"

"Yes, Quantum City, where you were supposed to land. I programmed both our pendants myself because I wanted to make sure all was very precise. I also made up a welcome kit for you at the Citadel Hospital where you were to be checked over after your journey. We had the recoup room ready, and my own pod was—well, it was perfect."

"Your pod?"

"Oh, uh, my house. But apparently, our take-charge general, Hale War-a, felt he had the right to make an executive decision without consulting me."

She's obviously being sarcastic. Sounds like the diamond lady and this general have had their differences.

She's even gritting her teeth a little. "I guess he thought you would be safer in the passageways just in case—to make your grand entrance less, uh, grand. He meant well, I suppose, but even with his new orders, my assistant programmed your pendant with numbers that were a little off, and well, here you are in Birdland. And no one bothered to mention this to me until I got word from Ah-nee."

"A-H-N-E-E?" I spell it out.

She shakes her head. "O-N-N-I. Comes from the word *one*. He was our very first successful hybrid. And quite a dear creature he is. I'm sorry he couldn't escort us to the city. Anyway, I guarantee I will personally see to it that I oversee everything you do from now on." At my request, she also spells the other names I've been hearing: "How-ka" is Haukka. "Hale Waara," general of the army, is the guy with the deep booming voice.

"So you ride on the birds' backs?"

She nods. "For transportation, if we are away from the city, we can hitch a ride from Onni or Haukka. Unfortunately, General Waara has given them orders to join a vitally important mission in the mountains. Just our luck that on the day you arrive, we have a major event going on—a perfect storm. I'm so sorry. Typically, we're pretty efficient."

"Oh, you said mountains?" I wonder if we're still in some remote part of Idaho. And if Dad…well, I can't think about that now.

"Yes, we have many mountains here. Things are happening quickly now. We just—" She sees my puzzled expression. "Well, it's complicated. But you'll be briefed, I promise. So we will have to start walking toward the city through the passageways. It will be a good opportunity for us to get re—well, acquainted. And the general's right about one thing—it's best we don't travel in the open. Are your shoes comfortable?"

I look down at my old, broken-in sneakers with the tiny hole in the left baby toe. Dad had promised to get me new ones this week, along with new snow boots. *No, no, no, Kris. Quit thinking about Dad.* I squeeze my eyes shut. Don't think about that, Kris. I open them.

"Uh, my shoes are fine. But what did you say about not traveling in the open? And…and why do my legs feel so heavy?"

"Well, we just don't know what exactly is happening at the moment. Most likely we're safe here. All will be explained to you when we reach the city. The heavy feeling in your legs is due to, uh, it's hard to explain. The journey does strange things to our bodies. You'll adjust."

The more she talks, the more QBs buzz out of my black box. If I don't pace myself, my ADD brain will self-destruct. Okay, Kris, one at a time. First, "By the way, I don't know your name. I heard My-ra?"

"Oh my goodness, yes. I'm your guide here, uh, in charge of your well-being. I'm—my name is Myrakka."

"Meer—"

"It's *Myrakka*, a Finnish name pronounced *Meer*-rah-ka." And then she spells it. At least I was right with the name "Dahab," her assistant from Pakistan. I saw a movie about a woman named Dahab once. They came from a golden realm, and her parents had named her "Dahab," which means "gold." Myrakka chuckles. "I was born during one hell of a blizzard, I'm told. My mother once told me the name means 'I'm strong, and that I can survive anything.' I'm not so sure about that—"

"Are you Finnish then?"

"Well, yes and no. Both my parents are—were—Finnish through and through. But I was raised in the States all the way through college. Then we all moved back to Finland. So I consider myself part Finnish, part American. Actually, we consider ourselves to be one big Earth family."

"Oh."

Myrakka—she's Finnish like the Gabriels. That's how that got into my dream. I smile, repeat her name softly several times so I won't forget. Myrakka, the dream lady, smiles back at me, her eyes still glistening. She turns toward the birds, bowing deeply. They bow in return. Then all the bird things, or bird people, bow to me in one sweeping gesture. Well, I suppose it's polite here to bow to everyone, so I bow in return. Is that acceptable? I look to Myrakka for confirmation. She gives me a wide smile and a thumbs-up.

"Our Birds are revered as the divine creatures they are. They are helping us tremendously in our mission to save the Earth. I will tell you all about them as we journey to the city." She turns, heads toward a large entryway, gesturing that I follow.

We leave the vast ballroom with its strange floors—Penrose tiling—and pass through a massive granite archway carved with birds of crystal or glass or—no, must be diamond. I can't stop staring. The archway sparkles like a pond on a brilliant sunny day. I wish like crazy I had my art stuff with me. I'll have to take mental pics and draw as soon as I wake up.

I follow her through the archway and into a narrow passageway, like a cave, dimly lit with salt lamps placed every few feet inside recesses in the dry rock. Although I'm only five feet, one inch, and Myrakka's maybe an inch or two taller, our heads almost scrape the low ceiling. The floor of the pathway is made of some kind of shimmery gray rock, bumpy and uneven. Myrakka turns, holding out her hand. "Shall we?" I take her hand. All of sudden, she stares at our interlaced fingers and collapses on the cavelike floor, sobbing.

Holy moly. I drop to the floor beside her. "I'm sorry, did I do something? I mean, are you okay?"

She sniffs, smiling through her tears. "Oh goodness, no you didn't do a thing. My apologies. I—it's been, well, rather stressful lately. Leave it to me to fall apart at the worst possible moment." She straightens, wipes her face with the back of her hand, gives one more half sob, half laugh. I rise with her. She holds out her hand. "Let's try that again, shall we?"

I smile back at her, take her hand once more, and we begin our journey to Quantum City. I hope she's okay. I hope I can make it to the city. I hope I can find a drinking fountain soon. Or just wake up, for God's sake.

I'm parched.

Fourteen

QC
Finland
January 1, 2014

The great hall overflows with Quantum Community members, well over two hundred. When the esteemed CEO, Eikka Jutila, or Dr. EJ, as the QC fondly calls him, makes his way to the podium, they all stand and applaud. He attaches the small mike to his lapel, then surveys his audience, smiling broadly at his fellow QC colleagues.

"Sit, sit."

The clapping and murmuring slowly die down as the QC people take their seats. Dr. EJ will speak in his native language, Finnish. Closed-captioned screens with several other languages surround the stage in a semicircle. A deaf interpreter stands on the other side of the raised platform, watching for EJ to begin his speech.

"It's 2014. Happy New Year to all, and a happy one it most certainly shall be!"

Cheers, applause follow.

"My dear friends and colleagues. Let the start of this new year also mark great beginnings for our community and for our endangered Mother Earth. I am delighted to share with you some life-changing information. As you may know, our space travel team recently finalized plans for a first mission through an Einstein-Rosen Bridge, or 'wormhole,' a term coined by physicist John Wheeler. Not quite a century ago, in 1936, Albert Einstein and Nathan Rosen theorized that if space is curved sufficiently because of matter and energy, it could meet up with itself, thus

letting two points connect faster than the speed of light—no matter what the distance. Back then, it was complete speculation. But now, finally, quantum teleportation is no longer vague speculation or science fiction. It is real. We've harnessed the entanglement, used EPR paradox, simplified, for use with humans as well as nonliving objects. This new discovery alone will revolutionize life as we know it. We are not quite ready to reveal our incredible revelation to the world at large, lest the knowledge fall into the wrong hands. If word gets out prematurely, you are hereby commanded to act clueless as a rock. Then ask politely if they've had their head examined recently."

A few chuckles ripple through the audience.

"Seriously, before you leave this room, each of you must complete nondisclosure paperwork. Our legal team insisted on it and for good reason. But at the proper time, we will share with those who can be trusted to work with us. And to think it all started here, right here, at the QC."

More applause. The excitement is palpable.

"This will be the first time any human has attempted quantum travel through the space-time fabric—a wormhole. Our first destination: BPM 37093, for obvious reasons. If this white dwarf's core is comprised of what we theorize, and we are able to harvest even a tiny portion, we will never again need to worry about funding. Of course, we will be working closely with our logistics, financial, legal teams, and so forth so as not to arouse suspicion in the economic spheres. But if we do this right and certain people finally come to their senses, well, our fervent hope is that ultimately, no one on the planet shall ever go hungry or thirsty. No one will die or sicken for lack of water, food, shelter, or medical care. The planet will be healthy once more. We will have all funding necessary to eradicate all viruses harmful to people and animals. Yes, yes, I know, lofty goals. But, folks, these aims are now more attainable than ever. Project EarthHeal is the most immense undertaking in the history of humankind. And we must succeed. But first, we must ascertain the existence of the riches of this white dwarf, fifty light-years away.

"Who's going?" General Waara calls out.

Dr. EJ clears his throat. "Ah, Hale, always cutting to the quick. All right, if you must. Down to specifics. I know several of you have expressed a keen interest in being part of this historical mission. I have spent many

*a night staring at the ceiling pondering the logistics and ethics and imag-
ining just about every scenario. I've consulted with our space travel team,
and against their wishes, I've come to the conclusion that the crew will
consist of"—he clears his throat—"Me. Just me."*

*Concerned murmurs rumble through the hall. General Waara is
vehemently shaking his head. "With all due respect, sir, you cannot do
this alone. You need a team."*

*"With reciprocal respect, General, I refuse to risk any lives besides
my own for this first mission. We're not sure this algorithm will work.
Mission number 1 includes one person, not to explore the destination and
not to harvest any material. My only mission is to make sure space-time
travel through wormholes and back is actually feasible. That's it. I'm the
guinea pig."*

The chorus of protests intensifies.

*Dr. EJ holds up a hand. "I cannot subject anyone else to the danger.
You are each indispensable members of this community."*

*"So are you, Eikka." Voitto Kurki's strong, commanding voice rings
out loud and clear. Everyone turns to Voitto, nodding and clapping.*

"Send a chimpanzee!" someone yells.

Laughter echoes. Dr. EJ joins in then hushes the crowd.

*"I'm afraid the learning curve for our friend the chimp would be a
little too steep."*

More laughter.

*"Send one of the Birds!" someone calls out. Dr. EJ squints into the
audience, frowning when he realizes it's General Waara.*

*"Hale, you're not serious?" EJ shakes his head. "We are still in devel-
opmental stages for most of them. Ordering them to teleport would be
tantamount to cruelty. I'm surprised you—"*

Genera Waara shrugs. "A suggestion, just a suggestion."

*Johann Rajala, chief quantum astrophysicist and main architect
of the new travel technology, stands up. "Seems to me, Dr. EJ, you're the
most indispensable of all. By your own logic, we should not permit you
to go. Without assistance, that is. Let us help you. We've run the numbers hundreds of times. Statistical probability is now at 97.6—there and
back. Those are pretty damn good odds, very similar to the many success-*

ful neurosurgeries you yourself have completed over the years. And you didn't cancel those just because the odds weren't 100 percent."

The crowd murmurs; heads nod.

Dr. EJ scans his audience. After a few moments of hushed silence, he sighs, then announces, "I was afraid of this. It seems my logical arguments have been unanimously outnumbered."

Chuckles, applause. It's clear everyone agrees.

"I understand your zeal. But please understand my grave reservations. To compromise, I will at least allow discussion of a possible team. I suppose with additional crew, the mission's objectives could expand. First, as I mentioned, to see if our travel method is humanly viable. Second, to ascertain the star does, indeed, contain crystallized carbon, or diamond, and three to examine the feasibility of this environment for sustenance of human life and what adjustments would be necessary. Oh, and fourth, to return safe and sound. Now does that sound like a better plan?"

Johann stands and begins clapping. The entire crowd follows until thunderous applause echoes throughout the hall. Dr. EJ shakes his head. But he's smiling. "All right then. Ah, General Waara, Johann, Dr. Kurki, Aku, Milla, Raakel, Jaak, and the logistics team, we will reconvene in my office following the meeting."

Another QC member stands. "Dr. EJ, I'd like to join the meeting as well, even though it's clear I will not be one of those chosen to travel, nor would I even if given the chance." He smiles, glancing down at the woman beside him. She blushes, smiles back, gently cupping her middle with her hand.

Dr. EJ chuckles. "Ah, now that's a proper husband. Do we have a name yet?"

"Kristal, with a K. Finnish spelling. Kristal Noelle."

"Beautiful name. Hmmm, Kristal. Tesla said crystals were living beings, and so they are. Good choice. Now when is our newest little QC member slated to arrive?"

"February 3."

"Ah, yes. It's quite near. But of course, you are both welcome to be a part of the planning process. We need your expertise along with the members I just called. Please after you sign your ND, join me in my office. The rest of you, we will keep you informed." A sudden hush descends as *though everyone simultaneously realizes the literal quantum leap about to transpire for all humanity—akin to the discovery of fire on planet Earth all those eons ago. Dr. EJ's eyes scan the entire room, then he gives a little nod of his head.*

"Dismissed."

Fifteen

January 23, 2027

We travel up and down the hilly underground terrain, passage after passage. The lighting gradually changes from orange to muted pink. Myrakka's skin glows in the softness of the light. She hasn't yet spoken, but often turns and smiles at me, her eyes misty. Or maybe that's just the weird lighting. I finally can't stand it any longer and break the silence. My tongue keeps sticking to the roof of my mouth, but I'm determined to get answers to my burning questions.

"Where am I? Why were you in the forest? How did you know I might be in danger? Do you know about my bro—"

Myrakka turns to me, stops, nodding, taking both my hands in hers. "You shall know everything. I promise. But let's save our breath for a while."

"Well, okay."

We continue for another half hour or so, then apparently Myrakka decides this is a good time to chat. But instead of answering my burning questions, she launches into a lengthy tutorial on the Birds (always spelled with a capital *B* she says). "Bridging the communication gap between Bird and human is one of the major projects of the QC—the Quantum Community." She stops, turns to me. "We brought in an expert in the beginning. Her name was Tanimilua—a First Nation Bird expert. She was amazing. Didn't quite agree with our mission at first, but we finally convinced her this was for the survival of all species on Earth, including the Birds themselves. We invited her to join the QC, but she declined. Lucky for her."

"Lucky for her?"

"Oh, sorry, spoke too soon. You will learn."

I can't believe this. No one wants to tell me anything. I struggle to maintain a sense of what—normalcy? Ha, this is *normal* only if I am, indeed, in a dream. Back to the topic. I turn to Myrakka.

"Tani? Is Milua her last name?"

"That's her only name or her only public name. First Nation people sometimes don't give out their last names. That way, they keep their power. She comes from a long line of Bird people. She knows everything about them and, in fact, has written volumes. Did you know the Earth boasts almost ten thousand species of birds? If we're lucky, we'll be able to save most of them from extinction, which is one of our missions. Although we know it's not appropriate to tinker with nature, my father and others in the Quantum Community made the difficult decision to add human DNA to a select group of Birds, in addition to blending certain species. With their profound knowledge, far greater than humans, we were hoping to gain some of their wisdom as this century progressed. We had to transform some in order to figure out how to save them and the world. Their transformation had almost been completed when we were all…rudely interrupted." Without missing a beat, she keeps talking, not telling me when they were rudely interrupted, why they were rudely interrupted, how they were rudely interrupted, and basically not letting me get a question in edgewise. Obviously, something big happened a while back. I wonder how long I'll have to wait for answers.

The longer we keep walking and the more I listen, the more real it all seems. I can't remember ever having a dream that's gone on so long. If I'm still asleep, I'm incredibly alert for someone who hasn't awakened yet. And I can't remember ever feeling this thirsty in a dream.

"So"—Myrakka is explaining—"for centuries, cultures around the world have been fascinated with birds and rightly so. Although the ancients didn't keep very good written records, lucky for us they handed down information by word of mouth: how birds think, how they feel, how they communicate among their own species. According to folklore, the leaders have always been the eagles, hawks, crows, and owls. Eagles from the north, hawks from the south, crows from the east, and owls from the west. But most important, no matter the species, each and every bird is sacred and should be revered. Their intuition is highly advanced, much more so than ours. Although they each have specific missions, they're all messengers. Some bring good news, and some dire warnings as you so recently discovered, I'm afraid."

"So it—the Bird that day—wasn't trying to harm me?"

"Oh, my dear, no, not at all. Though I can understand why you would think so. His name is Rawol, a hybrid—part raven and part owl, and about 19 percent human DNA. He's one smart, insightful Bird. The white tail, well, we have no idea where that came from. Anyway, his expertise is in calculating possible dangers and warning us. Birds are also selfless. Rawol was risking his own life to remind me—us—of the danger and pleading with me to leave as soon as possible."

"Did Rawol have to attack me like that?"

Myrakka shakes her head. "That was unfortunate. Rawol isn't known for his diplomacy. But he's sharp as a tack and has a keen sense of danger. He wouldn't have hurt you. He communicated to me later it was the only way to get my attention as I was ignoring his warnings."

"Warnings? What was he warning you about?"

"Oh, uh. We'll discuss that later when we're all with the QC. Let me tell you about Onni. Over a decade ago, my father, a brilliant scientist, had been working on implanted stem cells from human DNA to enable the First Bird—Onni One—to communicate more directly with people through human language. Birds already have unique vocal capability for intelligible human speech. They just needed to expand the language areas a bit in their brains, connecting Broca's area for expressing their thoughts to Wernicke's area for language comprehension, and a little more frontal capability to be able to form their own ideas and then sequence sounds into novel sentences instead of just, pardon the pun, 'parroting' speech."

"So Onni was taught to communicate his own ideas? That's incredible."

"Yes, Onni was a resounding success. All four of the leader birds reside within him as well as, well, a little of my father's own DNA. I hold a special place in my heart for Onni."

"He seems so smart."

"Oh, my dear girl, he and all birds are brilliant. They've lived on the Earth far longer than we have. The ones who use the phrase *bird brain* are themselves bird brains! Most of our Birds are various species of corvid—crows and ravens. They've always had the ability to adapt to change, plan, imagine, and problem-solve. So we just needed to do a little tweaking with their stem cells and DNA. After Onni came Haukka. My father had just begun work with Haukka's language development when—well, he didn't finish. Haukka is also a hybrid of all four bird leaders. Their percentage of human DNA increased from about 65 percent to 91 percent. That's still a long way from being human. I mean chimps share 99 percent."

I stare at her. "Ninety-nine percent? But chimps are so...so..."

"Different from us? Think again. Anyway, with the Birds, we helped them develop more convergent DNA sequences, and well, I don't need to get too technical. Let's just say, the Birds have always been our invaluable allies, and even more so now, in these critical times."

My mind is reliving those few minutes in the forest. "And I was so afraid of that Bird. Now I feel ashamed."

"Don't be. I'm sorry he frightened you so. Meeting Rawol for the first time under those circumstances—well, anyone would be afraid. The Varkos—smaller than Rawol and less able to communicate—are also a great help to all of us."

"You mean like the small black birds who demolished part of my muffin when it fell on the floor?"

Myrakka's eyebrows go up. "Oh they did, did they?" She chuckles. "Most likely, those were baby crows. What did Onni do?"

"He, um, well, sort of yelled at them, and they flew off."

"Oh my. Those little crows. No matter how much they evolve, their pecking order will still be intact. As it is for most people. But for us, they're all constantly vigilant, watching out for us. Ah, then there are the songbirds. Thrushes, wrens, orioles, sparrows—when they sing, they make us feel like we're in a meadow on a beautiful spring day. Did you know bird songs can actually increase serotonin—our brain's 'joy juice'? They provide a natural high that we sorely need here. Oh, and we also have one cuckoo Bird. She has learned to cuckoo on the hour and half hour and seems to relish her role as official timekeeper. She's really quite amazing."

"Where is she?"

"We're not quite sure where she goes between times, but she's always on top of our Earth Clock Tower at the hour and half hour. You'll get to see her and, probably hear her, when we visit the city."

We go silent for a few minutes. My mind drifts back to the forest.

"Now can you tell me why Rawol was warning us?"

Myrakka stops, shuts her eyes tightly, sighs. "Oh, my dear. That's a story for the whole QC group to tell you when we're all together. For now, let's rest our brains a bit. I'm sure I've given you quite enough to process for now."

I am about to protest, but then realize she's right—my brain's pretty fried by now, as is my mouth. I picture lemons to generate saliva. No luck.

We continue forward in the quiet hush of the stone tunnels for what seems like ages. Finally, we make a sharp turn into yet another passageway, but this one is considerably wider and flatter. And instead of pinkish salt lamps, light comes from crystalline lanterns, each emitting a ghostly blue glow.

By now, thirst consumes my every thought. I *have* to stop. Leaning against the wall of the cave, panting like a puppy on a hot summer day, I will myself to swallow. No use. My tongue is stuck to my tonsils. I choke, then gag. Myrakka turns to me, startled. I'm done with the Bird tutorial and the good sport attitude.

"I can't go any further without water. I don't ever remember thirst this...this..."

Myrakka's hand flies to her chest. "My poor child, you're not used to this. It's been so long. We've all acclimated. I had water waiting for you in the city. But I should have brought an emergency ration. I thought Onni would quickly return us to the city, but Hale's command… *Damn*, I'm so sorry, Kristal."

Who's Hale again? And they've all acclimated? Who's here? Is this a desert? Well, what now? Myrakka's studying something on her communication card. Can you order water from here? Is that what she's doing? I tap her on the shoulder.

"Is that—can you order it? Like from Doordash?"

The diamond lady looks up from her device, shaking her head apologetically, scaring the wits out of me. "Oh no, Kristal, no." She turns back, starts tapping and muttering to herself.

I repeat myself. "A small drink. That's all I ask. Why is that so hard?"

She looks back; her face pained. Suddenly she sinks to her knees, taking my hands in hers. "I would give you an entire swimming pool if I could sans the chlorine, of course." She chuckles weakly. "But here, you see, that…that poses a problem."

"Problem? Why? I'm not picky like some people. I don't need bottled water. Tap water would be fine."

Myrakka closes her eyes.

Seriously? What's wrong? Another wave of dread washes over me. No water?

My voice comes out all squeaky. "*Where* exactly are we? In the Rockies somewhere? In a desert? In a deserted part of some secret country? *Just tell me*." This is so bizarre. I must be sleeping, dreaming, and the humidity in my bedroom must be pretty low due to the cold. "You said I was in a dream. I'll wake up soon. Right? *Right?*"

Myrakka stands, lets out a huge sigh, but still doesn't say a word.

"So? Okay, just tell me. Where are we? Why isn't there any water?"

Myrakka lightly slaps the cave wall. "Water. Yes, dammit. Why do I let Waara, I mean, just because he saved my—oh, never mind, love. You shall have it." She pulls out her comcard again, taps a few times, says, "I've sent an urgent message. As soon as we get to the city, your ration of water will be increased and available immediately. They've promised. Why didn't Waara factor this into his plan to protect you? I know he's got a lot on his mind, but this is inexcusable." She frowns, blinking her eyes. "If we pick up the pace a bit, we should be there in about thirty-five minutes or so."

"Pick up the—thirty-five or *so*?" I shake my head. "I… I can't. My legs feel so heavy I don't think I can." Why can't she understand?

Myrakka suddenly puts her arms around me and hugs me tightly, almost bowling me over. "Oh, my dear child, this is *not* how I imagined your arrival."

I push her back. She looks like she's about to cry again. But I don't want her damn tears anymore—or her hugs. I want water. Was her plan to kill me all along? Death by dehydration?

Now she's pleading, "Please believe me. I have nothing to give you right now. But, Kristal, if you can complete this journey with me, I promise, you will have enough water to keep going, and all will be better. It will. *It must.* Just follow me. And if you can trust me, all will be revealed."

Is she *deaf*? I. Need. Water. I'm dizzy, and my heart is racing. "Just…just tell me where we are."

"I… I…"

"No, don't change the subject. Don't beat around the bush anymore. I at least deserve to know where I am, right? Why is everything such a secret, first at home and now here? Why? And do not just say Birdland or…or the caves." Myrakka sighs. *Is she about to cry?* "You see, this was to be revealed at the QC meeting—with all of us around you—to support you."

I can't believe this. "I don't care who's around me. I just need to know—*where on Earth am I?*"

She stops, leans against the stone wall, wiping her brow. "Oh, dear Kristal, you see, that's just it."

"What's just *it*?"

She blows out air like she's about to confess the world's worst crime. "My sweet girl, we're not on Earth."

Not on Earth—I obviously heard her wrong. "What?"

"Kristal, the QC Council strongly advised that I not give you this information yet or any information about our situation, not to confuse you but to spare you."

"Situation? Spare me? From what?"

She sighs. "Shock."

Holy moly, *shock*—the word I overheard Mrs. Gabriel use.

"We just wanted to explain, bit by bit, surrounded by our whole group because this is way too much to comprehend all at once. But you're right—you do deserve to know."

Forget the damn butterflies. Murder hornets are now in tight formation in my stomach. I almost double over. I'm beyond polite now. "Don't you get it? It's more shocking *not* knowing. Being kept in the dark. Please no more talking in riddles. People have been doing that all my life but especially recently. I'm tired of it. I need the truth. Try me. Just rip off the Band-Aid and *tell me*. Don't worry. I'll handle it. I just may go *more* bonkers if you keep me guessing than if you just tell me."

She sighs, then gazes deeply into my eyes. "You're one perceptive girl. Take after your fa—" She clears her throat. "All right, Kristal. BPM 37093, discovered in 2004—"

"The number 37093—that was the number that—"

"Yes, that's our location algorithm—the one we programmed into your pendant so you could travel here." Another sigh. "That's why your legs feel a little heavy. That will abate, I promise you. But instead of 1 G on Earth, we're at about 1.43 Gs here. Just can't get it down any further."

I've had it. "*You're stalling.*"

The next five seconds are an eternity. Finally, she wraps an arm around my waist like she's expecting me to faint at what she's about to say, blows out another mouthful of air, and whispers in my ear, "We are fifty light-years from Earth, in the Constellation Centaurus on V886 Centauri or BPM 37093, a white dwarf, otherwise known as Lucy, the Diamond Star."

Sixteen

January 23, 2027

Oh. So that's all. Right. I'm standing on a star. *I am on a star.* I stare at Myrakka, waiting for her winky eye like the one Alek gave me after his FBI hoax with Jackson Hynes or any other sign that shows she's just kidding. I search her face. She's not kidding. But what she just said? This *cannot* possibly be the truth. On the other hand, she doesn't seem crazy or evil. It makes more sense to assume I'm back in Dreamland. I'll just have to continue to play along until I wake up. It's the only explanation.

I'm still trying to wrap my head around her insane announcement when Myrakka starts chattering away as though we're at a little café enjoying some biscotti and tea. I give up. I'll play along. Why not? She holds up her palms and shrugs. "Maybe you've studied stars a little bit in school? Anyway, a white dwarf is a giant cinder of sorts—what's left when a star uses up its nuclear fuel and dies. There's a little oxygen here, thankfully, so we've harnessed that. By studying Lucy's frequency spectra, scientists found out that 90 percent of Lucy had crystallized. Since its core is mostly carbon, they could only come to one conclusion." She's conversing so easily.

I can barely move my mouth. "Conclusion?"

"Yes, Basically, Lucy's core is essentially one gigantic diamond."

It just keeps getting more bizarre. I can't even respond. Wait. When Alek showed me a picture of that planet, didn't it have diamond in its core too? Maybe this isn't a dream after all…but no. It has to be. God. I'm so freaking confused.

She's gesturing like crazy now. "Actually, *gigantic* doesn't even begin to describe its enormity."

A gigantic diamond. So that's why everything here is so sparkly. Somehow, I find my voice. "How...how gigantic is it?"

"Let's just say, unfathomable to the human mind. Oh, and that humming sound you mentioned when we first met up again in Birdland? The Diamond Star emits constant pulsations, like a continual thrum in the background if you listen hard enough. It pulsates due to its core temperature falling below a certain degree. It's called stellar seismography, using the stars' frequency spectra to determine its composition. That's how we were able to find that 90 percent of Lucy's mass had crystalized. Since its core is mostly carbon, well,— voilà. There's your gigantic diamond."

I blink. My brain is going tilt—TMI, TMI, TMWI—too much weird information. I place one hand on my chest, the other on my stomach and try to breathe like Dad taught me. But that only makes it worse. I choke. No saliva. But I manage to croak out, "Um, okay, I'm on Lucy, the Diamond Star. But how did I get here? So when I was kind of asleep, tumbling in darkness, I was actually in outer space somewhere? In some kind of spaceship?"

Myrakka drops her voice again, speaks almost apologetically, "We don't need spaceships anymore. We teleport."

I stand there, blinking.

"We had programmed your pendant to take you through a wormhole."

"Wor-wormhole?"

"In 2014, our genius astrophysicists in the QC finally figured out the algorithms, how to nullify the radiation concerns, well, everything needed to travel through a wormhole intact. Lucy, the Diamond Star, was our first target, for obvious reasons."

"Obvious reasons?"

"An endless supply of diamonds—every scientist's dream. I guess everyone's dream, really. But for us, we weren't thinking of fur coats or yachts or cruises around the world. We were thinking—"

"Funding."

"Spot on, my smart girl. Funding problems solved, forever. So many discoveries and inventions to heal the Earth are ready to go but for lack of funding. This way, just think how quickly we could move things forward, improving Earth—the land, water, health of all people. Of course, we have to be extremely careful about how to distribute this newfound wealth on Earth. A sudden huge influx of diamond in the world and you would cause all kinds of economic chaos in the market. "Not to mention releasing all the megalomaniacs of the world who would no doubt swoop down on our QC data like a flock of hungry krakens, demanding our secrets." Myrakka shudders. But we have QC consultants in the finance area for that, and we will go slowly and carefully. But, Kristal, oh, happy dilemma. The sky, or the entire universe, is now the limit. This was the QC's brainchild. A dream come true for us, and we hoped, the entire planet. Krissie,"—her eyes widen—"whoops… I… I mean, Kristal… I'm sorry."

Weird. I shake my head. "No, no offense taken." What was that all about?

She clears her throat. "Kristal, you see, Earth is in great peril, or should I say, humankind and life as we know it. We are already over the limit with CO_2 emissions. It's imperative that we have to find ways to sustain and improve food and water sources, decrease CO_2 emissions and improve our carbon-capture methods. The technology, the solutions are all set, ready to go. We just need to get rid of the obstacles."

Wow. This is exactly the stuff that's been plaguing my mind—the stuff I asked Alek about the other day. I turn to Myrakka. "So that's why all this never went viral—why I never heard about it?"

"That's right. BPM 37093 was discovered in 2004. And that was in the news. But it got scant attention. Teleportation and wormhole travel weren't available until 2014. I'm sure that piece of news would have been front and center, but we kept that strictly to ourselves. Dr. EJ, our brave leader, and the initial team of five were the first humans to successfully undertake the first teleportation. Johann, Jaak, and the entire logistics team, working with Bell measurements, EPR pairs had to figure out how to merge the classical and qubits with the superconducting nanoware. Well, anyway, not only were they able to land on this star, but what they found was astounding. Little did we know that those travel algorithms would save us in 2016. Lucy's been our secret hideout for eleven years."

"But how if there are no spaceships—"

"I'm sure this must be so perplexing. That's why I was asked to wait. But I'll try. I won't be able to explain fully. You'd have to have your PhD in astrophysics and then some seriously intense experience."

"Do you?"

"Well, I do have some degrees. And yes, I worked for the QC for quite a few years."

"*Some* degrees?"

"Well, yes, in astrophysics and avionics technology and—"

"More?"

She shrugs. "Quantum communications."

"Oh, so that makes you a doctor? Like a PhD?"

She gives a little snort as she nods. "Ha, technically. You'd think I'd have all the answers, but we're realizing, especially in the quantum world, the more we learn, the more we realize we need to learn."

She's being modest. I can't even fathom how much she must know. She sighs and nods. "Kristal, I applaud your curiosity. The only reason I hesitate is, well, this can get pretty overwhelming."

Not this again—protecting the fragile young child. Hell with that. My voice has a little hissy lilt to it. So what? I'm tired of all this pampering. "Information can get overwhelming? You think? Try being completely in the dark about everything. Now *that's* overwhelming."

Myrakka's eyes go up. "Hmmm, well put, my child. Well put. All right, for the short version, you've studied atoms in school, right?"

"A little. Mr. Gabriel taught us atoms have a nucleus and then electrons circle them, kind of like tiny solar systems."

"Well, that's the classic model. But did you know that 99.999— almost all the atom itself—is made up of empty space?"

"Well, actually, I do remember Mr. Gabriel starting to teach us about atoms being mostly energy, but then I the next day, he—I think he muttered something about being told to stick to the curriculum. And he just went along with our book after that."

"Figures. School curriculums haven't changed in eons."

"So that means since we are made of atoms, people are mostly... empty space?"

"Yep, seems strange, doesn't it?"

"Not really. Sometimes I feel my ADD has made my brain 99 percent empty space."

Myrakka chuckles but is shaking her head. "Oh, Kristal, don't disparage yourself. Physics has proven it with all humans. That doesn't mean we are basically nothing. No, we are rich in consciousness, and that takes up no space at all."

"But—"

"Now as far as traveling in space, let's use a simple analogy. If you can visualize space-time as a simple piece of paper, we're microscopic specks trying to find a way from one edge of the paper to the other. The logical way is to go from one side to the other—left foot, right foot. The shortest distance between two points is a line, right?"

"Right."

"Wrong. This is where you think out of the box. Why couldn't we just fold the so-called paper, or space-time fabric, so that the two edges touch each other? Then the infinitesimal speck of matter— the form in which you travel—could just hop from one edge to the other. Bingo. And once there, your atoms would reassemble, and you would expand to your normal size. Kristal, do you remember your trip? Were you at first merely thinking thoughts? And then did you gradually regain sensation in your body?"

"Wow, yeah, exactly."

"That was your consciousness traveling then reconnecting with your physical body. There's a lot more to it, but I hope that will satisfy your curiosity for now. And then we'll—"

"I—but wait, if I'm on a burned-out star, why can I breathe? Why aren't I freezing to death or burning up?"

"The biodome. We had to terreform a section of the star."

"Biodome? Terreform?"

"Think of a self-sustaining aquarium. Our quantum team fashioned a canopy of sorts over the part of the star we needed to use. It's only about 134 square kilometers—a tiny fraction of the whole star.

But it's sufficient. Under that canopy we can adjust the climate to the most ideal temperatures and atmospheric pressure for sustaining human life. Do you remember sparkles, rainbows, perhaps other colors as you were traveling?"

"Yes, yes, and they were beautiful!"

"That was the atmospheric barrier holding up the dome. You were reassembling into human form as you came through. I know this is TMI."

"Wait. Why can't I use my pendant to get to Quantum City?"

"Ah, good question, smart girl. The quick answer is, I didn't know we would need one, and all our programming equipment is in the city. And strangely, it takes far more technical expertise and time to program for a short trip than a long one. Don't ask me for specifics unless you want to hear a lot of E-equals-MC-squared jargon. Will you accept this as enough for now?"

I have to agree with her. I'm getting woozy from all the crazy quantum stuff bombarding my brain. I have to admit though that it's taken my mind off my thirst. But now it's back, crowding out all other thoughts, especially all these logistics and facts. Just the weird thought—so they can figure out how to teleport light-years in space-time, but they can't conjure up a little water? Can't wrap my head around that, so I switch to the more familiar. "So this city we're going to, there must be cars? Taxis? Buses? Trains? Subways? Lyft? Why couldn't someone pick us up?"

She shakes her head. "In Birdland, there is no need for vehicles as obviously they can fly. For humans, transportation outside the city is provided by our two giant Birds—Haukka and Onni. For travel within the city, we don't need cars or other fancy vehicles. We can walk, use scooters, Segways, or bikes. Zero carbon emissions. The City is small enough, so it takes less than a half hour to traverse from one end to the other."

"So in our situation, why can't we ask Onni or Haukka to—"

"Remember my conversation with General Waara when you had just landed? Maybe I was too far from you. Anyway, unfortunately, they're both on a critical mission right now. We're getting ready for, well, a possible uh, confrontation. Yes, it's crucial, but you are just as important. As you can imagine, I have a bone to pick with him about priorities. Which I'll take up with him as soon as I see him. But let's just say, it was bad scheduling."

"So my arrival was bad timing."

"No, no, Kristal, don't think that. It was perfect timing. You did the right thing. Never doubt that. This dilemma wouldn't have happened if Hale and Dahab hadn't taken matters into their own hands. I'll have a few words with Dahab too. But until then, I'm afraid walking is our only means of transport until we get to the city."

Myrakka gestures, and I follow. I just want to sit down, but I can't. The more I delay, the more it will take to reach that delicious glass of water. So I keep stumbling on, step after step after step. At least the walk is a little more level now. But after what seems like another eternity half walking, half weaving, my heart's pounding, and I can't think, and I can't speak as my tongue has gotten stuck to the roof of my mouth. Myrakka turns and gasps. I must look awful. The panic on her face makes me even more nervous. Will I die here? I don't think she deliberately means to kill me; she just seems clueless. She wraps an arm around my waist to support me. I clutch her jacket. In urgent, raspy whispers, questions tumble from my mouth.

"Who are you? What is the QC? What are we going to do when we get to the city? Where is my brother—Tad? When can I go back home? What happened to my father? Who—"

She staggers under my dead weight, then rights herself, pulls me up, and puts a finger to her lips. "Kristal, shhh. I'm so sorry. Please try to hang on. You will have answers. I promise. But for now, you need to conserve energy. Shhh…"

My knees buckle, and I start to slide down the cave wall.

Myrakka slides down with me, sobbing. "I'm so sorry. I shouldn't have let your pendant out of my sight. How dare they reprogram it."

"Wait. Can you…reprogram it now? For the city?" I weakly finger my pendant as though, by magic, it will instantly transport me to the city.

"Oh, Kristal, I wish I could. I'd need my computer, and, well, it's in the city. Unfortunately, your pendant is useless right now."

"Oh, I see." I'm disoriented and dizzy. How much longer to this city? Okay, positive pep... I know. I turn toward Myrakka. "I just need to rest a little. You can go to the city and bring me back a bottle of water. I'll be fine here."

Myrakka shakes her head so hard her ponytail smacks her in the cheek. "Uh-uh, no way! Darling girl, I can't leave you here by yourself."

Okay then more positive pep talk. I take a deep breath, making me a little giddy. I smile, mumbling, "I will get to the city, where the fountains gush high with beautiful, sparkly, bountiful H_2O. It will be the wettest, coolest..."

Myrakka gasps. "Oh goodness, did I give you the wrong impression again? There are no fountains in the city. In fact, there's very little water at all. We have to ration every single drop. You will have water, but you probably won't feel satiated."

"Wha—why?"

"You're not used to the reduced amount. The average girl about your size needs, oh, about two to two and a half liters per day. We just don't have that amount. You'll likely get enough to keep you going—a cup or two—unless, well, we'll see."

I'm shocked. I guess I never ever worried about water of all things. "What's going on? Is there a draught here?"

"Yes, I'm afraid so, a permanent one. It never rains here. We're all rationed. Oh, I should have done this before. Never had to use it. We all have them." She pulls out a small tubelike instrument that reminds me of an old-fashioned thermometer. "Here, under your tongue."

I dutifully open my mouth. The steel thing is surprisingly cold. It beeps. She takes it out, checks something on it—a number? Her jaw drops.

"Fifty-two percent. Oh, Kristal, you are obviously in no shape to keep going. You're at H_2O stat level."

"H_2O wha—?"

"Your water composition. If it gets under 45 percent, you'll— well, I don't care what their schedule is. Mission or no mission. *You* are now their mission. Your life usurps everything." She stops, pulls the comcard from her pocket, holds it to her mouth. "694-24802. Hale, where are you? Yes, it's Myrakka. Location…" She looks up.

I look up. Numbers have been painted on the cave ceilings.

"Kimallus passageway 74955. We're in an H_2O stat situation. Yes, H_2O stat. D level fifty-two for God's sake. And she's not used to it. EMERGENCY, DAMMIT!"

My mind's really fuzzy. Myrakka cradles me in one arm while holding the card thing in the other. "The phrase *H_2O stat* means all hands-on deck to get water to someone who really, really needs it. We don't use it unless it's crucial. But it means help will be coming soon."

She talks into her card. "Yes, Hale. That's what I said. SHE WILL DIE!"

Who will what? Dry? Who is she talking to again? What did she say? Hail? Is it raining somewhere? I thought she said it never—her voice muffles, and the words sound far away.

"Mission—vital importance. I know—final drill, summoning a Bird. Level 1. More critical—health, her life—Crystal Child…"

Sounds begin to fade. Everything's blurry. I doze off. Rainbows, golden arcs, velvet blue, and then—far-off fairy bells. I open my eyes. The lady holds the card up to her face, and her voice gets louder and more urgent, then she sounds relieved.

"Haukka? Oh, thank God. Four EMs? Yes, we're in a crisis. It's urgent. She's got to get to the city asap. But we're still about a kilometer and a half out. You have our location. There's an exit close by, uh, wait—74955. Yes, we'll be waiting."

I manage to separate my tongue from the roof of my mouth. "EMs?"

"Earth minutes."

"Oh." I am on a star. Cool. Shapes wiggle and waggle before my eyes then morph into colorful sparks floating in, out, in, out, and my mind is sliding, sliding. Then something's lifting me—strong, cool. A crimson sky above. And stars. So many stars. And then…

Caw…

Everything collapses into darkness.

Seventeen

January 23, 2027

My eyes open. I'm lying flat, face down, on a bed of feathers. So soft. So quiet. No, wait. Movement—a rhythmic up, down, up, down. I raise my head, take in a sharp breath. I'm on the back of a gigantic Bird—Onni? No. Darker feathers. This must be the other one—Haukka. I look left, right. I'm between his massive wings, and we're soaring upward toward the cinnamon sky where I last saw Onni disappear.

Although still completely parched, I don't have to expend any energy trying to walk, which makes things a little better. Don't know how I got on the back of this gigantic Bird, but I'll take it. Small reins made of tiny diamonds crisscross his back, and I hang on as I look over Haukka's immense shoulder. We are passing over a long range of black mountains, like granite, twinkling with tiny starlike sparkles. It's a little chilly up here, but that's the least of my complaints.

My mouth is bone-dry, a microdesert. I lift my head, turning it as far as I can to check the rest of my surroundings. Can't see much. Myrakka's nowhere in sight. Maybe she's still following the passage-way in the cave. Or maybe she's climbed aboard Onni. The flatness and sheer size of Haukka's back keep me squarely in the middle, and I silently thank this feathered angel. I trust it will get me where I need to go.

Oh, but am I still in a dream? If so, why is it going on and on? Maybe it's more than a dream. Could it be—a coma? Maybe Dad and I have been in an accident; maybe the hideous vision I remem-

165

ber is false, and in reality, our escape car overturned on a slippery mountain road, and we're now in a hospital, unconscious. Maybe my father didn't really reach for me at all with those horrid claws, those eyes; maybe that was all part of my mixed-up nightmare as my head hit something and I slipped into unconsciousness. Well, I can only wait and hang on. What other choice do I have?

Choice, choice. Hmmm, options. Do I have them after all? If I'm dreaming, can't I chart my own course? What if I deliberately slid off this huge Bird? Don't catastrophic falls always awaken the dreamer before they hit the ground? Of course, I would have to be absolutely sure I was dreaming.

I scoot up to the bird's shoulder, lifting my head to peer over the edge but can't quite maneuver myself up far enough to see. No doubt it's a very long way down. And who knows what lies at the bottom? I think we're past the mountain range now, as I can't see it anymore. Are we over water? Sand? Rock? Maybe the city itself? I just can't see. Where is this Bird taking me anyway? Has it snatched me away from Myrakka, or has it come to rescue me? I'm pretty sure this Bird is just following orders from Myrakka. I take a deep breath, glance over my shoulder, and then I see them.

The tiny sparkles I saw just moments ago, they're moving. I squint and cup a hand over my eyebrows. They have arms and legs. People? Whatever or whoever they are, they're infiltrating the mountains—everywhere. Hundreds, no thousands of soldiers (or robots?) appear in every nook, every peak, every depression, all over the mountainous rock, as though they're getting ready for something, forming lines or groups, waiting to attack. But attack what? Who? Am I a target? Is Haukka? Does the Bird see them? I'd better warn him, just in case.

My voice is hoarse, weak, "Bird, um, Haukka, look—in the mountains, help..."

But Haukka's wings continue their colossal flapping, up, down, away from the mountains and toward what? Maybe he can't hear or understand me. Maybe he's just not that smart. Can't he sense it? He's acting like I'm not even here. Unlike Onni, he doesn't talk. Oh, wait. Didn't Myrakka say something about military exercises in the mountains? So most likely, we don't have to worry. In any case, this can't be real. Birds that can talk? A robot army? No, that's the last straw. Wake up, Kristal. Literally. I need to wake up. This is all just too disjointed to be real. In fact, it's downright nuts.

Just last year, after Tad and I watched a documentary on extreme sports, I dreamed I was standing in an open door of an airplane with a strong wind in my face, ready to parachute out. A gust overtook me, and I tumbled forward, sailing down, down... I awakened just before impact. Isn't that always what happens with falling dreams? Yes, this must be my second falling dream. I should wake up just before I hit the ground. I also know my pecan pancakes will be waiting for me on the kitchen table. Or at least, I'll be awake, wherever I am. Now I know it. I am in a dream, and it's time to wake up. I think if Ayana were here, she'd be saying, "Whataya waiting for, girl?" She would be right.

With a renewed sense of purpose, I slowly, steadily, inch my way backward toward the Bird's gigantic tail feather. As I start to slip, Haukka suddenly turns his massive head around and catches sight of me. He lets out a blood-curdling screech like Rawol—the bird in my backyard who ripped my coat—only three times louder. I wince. Sorry, Haukka, you beautiful dream Bird. Thanks for the ride, but here's my stop. I shut my eyes tight, let go, and I'm falling down, down, down, off Haukka's gigantic tail feather, then free-falling through the air with no parachute. Ahhhh, freedom. I'll wake up in a second or two and be home. Home. I look down.

I'm hurtling toward rigid ground—all reddish-gray rock and sand. No rivers, no seas, no grass, no paved highways, no cities. Good god, something's whistling in my ears. What have I done? My eyes widen until I think my eyeballs will pop out of their sockets. If this isn't a dream, then I will be dead within a couple of seconds. I think that's me screaming. *Oh crap. Kris, wake up, wake up, wake up!* It's coming, it's coming the ground is rushing up, and it's hard, so hard, and I'm going to splatter like roadkill run over by a semi. *Oh god, what have I done? Oh god, oh please no...*

Something completely blocks my view.

Thud.

Ouch ouch ouch! Oh god, my heart is in my throat. I've fallen hard. My ribs. Oh, ouch. But I'm alive. A huge wave of relief washes over me. I have not fallen on the ground but onto the back of another giant Bird—Onni. But my relief is short-lived. Either this is all real or the dream continues. I'm out of options. Desperation washes over me. I raise my head, gazing toward the horizon. For the first time, I see something in the distance. My voice comes out all shaky, "Are those buildings?"

Onni's silent for a moment, then he says a little less chirpy-happy than before, "Taking Kristal to Quantum City. Must hurry. Please stay on back this time. Raaah."

I wince, then crane my neck to catch another glimpse of our destination.

An incredibly tall spire rises to the sky in the distance. But it's not like any I've ever seen. It's glowing like the pinkish lights in the passageways. Then more crystalline steeples and towers of all sizes come into view, awash in the same white-pink pearly glow. And is that a huge rectangular stone clock?

And then I hear a faint "Cuckoo, cuckoo, cuckoo, cuckoo." Four o'clock? My mouth opens in surprise. It must be the cuckoo Bird Myrakka was telling me about on top of the Earth Clock Tower. We're nearing the city. Futuristic and breathtaking, it's nestled in the lower part of the valley. It's heavenly. Heaven—oh. Could Onni be taking me to—am I—?

Nervously, I glance at my hands, my feet, my arms, then shake my head. All seem intact. And besides, I can't be dead. My ribs wouldn't be in such excruciating pain if I—well, what do I know about being dead? I take another look at this other-worldly land-scape. At this moment, I quit fighting and surrender my fate. I'll never figure this out, so I might as well chill. If I die and heaven looks like this, well then, I welcome it. And if Dad and my brother and, maybe even my mother, are there as well, I'm home free. I'm ready.

Despite the pain, my eyes grow heavy, heavier…

Eighteen

January 27, 2027

Pink. So much pink. Pearly, swirly pink glows above me. Behind me, whooshes and gurgles accompany a rhythmic beep, beep, beep. Under me, on a cool, soft mattress, a thousand tiny fingers massage my back. I'm draped from neck to toes in a cozy flannel sheet, and my head rests on a plumped-up pillow. I swallow. Omigod, saliva glides down my throat like silk. I am home. The nightmare is over. Thank God, I knew it. I…

Wait. Still groggy, I shake my head to clear the fuzziness in my brain and stare back at the ceiling. The pink light. No, not my ceiling. The pillow, not mine. This isn't my bedroom. I'm not home. But where am I? Slowly, painfully I lift my head and turn toward the beeps and gurgles. As I twist, sticky things pull at my skin right under my collarbone. A few more on my side. I look down. I'm in a gray gown. Underneath, patches—those monitor things—oh yes, electrodes are attached with wires. I follow the wires back up to the beeping monitor. A machine is recording my heartbeat, blood pressure, and another number—98. It's not my temperature, but I don't know what it is. A chip-clip thingy is on my right index finger. Oh, and my arm, I'm connected to an IV. I'm in a hospital. I can handle this. As long as I'm finally awake.

Probably Dolcany Memorial Hospital, where I spent one night when I was six and had a bad case of bronchitis. A hospital is doable—better than trudging through a dark cave or dying of thirst while hanging onto the back of a giant Bird. Dad and I must have been in

169

an accident after all. Those last few seconds? No, Dad's hand didn't turn into a steel claw, not at all. Something metal from the car—a handle, a cup holder—was hurtling toward me as Dad was reaching to save me. I got the visions all shmushed up in my mind. I shudder. Brains sure can conjure up bizarre images in traumatic moments. But how bad an accident was it? I wiggle my toes and fingers. So far so good. Maybe I just hit my head. I reach up and feel my hair. It's all there—even my stupid cowlick.

Dad. My stomach does a quick flip-flop. Is he okay? Is he here too? How about Tad? If I'm okay, they no doubt are too. Can't wait to see them. I'm relieved I'm out of my coma, with its crazy visions and nightmarish world of strange birds, bizarre landscapes, mysterious passages, and an army of sparkly robots. I never knew my subconscious could think up so many weird images. But after I'm recovered, I will be going home. We'll all be returning—my dad, my brother, and I—to our own home. As Tad would say, "Five Star Pictures Presents!"

I hope, hope, hope there's still snow on the ground. Maybe Tad and I can finally zip down Marsten's hill on our sleds and use our imaginations to create tons of snow games and stories. Yes, all will be well. I've never appreciated ordinary life as much as I do now. I'll never take anything for granted anymore, ever again. Even if it includes good old Jackson Hynes. Hell, the next time he calls me awfully dumb ditz, I might give him a big fat hug and tell him I missed him. That would shock him even more than the stink bug trick. Just the thought of it cracks me up, and I feel my lips widening into a smile.

Sucking in a deep breath, with great effort, I grasp the bed's railing and pull myself to a sitting position, wincing and massaging my neck. Ouch, my left side hurts. I gingerly press on my ribs—double ouch. Guess I must have fallen pretty hard. Immediately, a wave of dizziness engulfs me. Whoa, I am definitely still recovering. Maybe I'm on meds. That would explain the wooziness. Rubbing the back of my neck, I lower my eyes and glance over the railing to the floor.

And gag.

No no no. Oh god, no. I turn away, almost retching over the railing. I have to shut my eyes. This can't be happening. No, this can't be. My stomach is still roiling. I fall backward onto the pillow and hold my middle as a sob erupts from deep in my throat. It can't be, it can't be, *it can't be*. I make myself look again, just to be sure. The pattern—the black glittery diamonds and zigzags. It's the same. Exactly the same as the great Bird hall, the—what did he call it? Penrose something? Oh yeah, Penrose tiling. I pull back, dizzier than ever. Maybe I'm just experiencing the last remnants of my dream as I struggle to fully awaken from this coma. Yeah, that's it. Please—it's the only explanation.

I hear footsteps coming down the hall. A doctor? Someone who can explain all this? Thank God, I lie back and wait. Boy, do I have questions. I keep my eyes peeled on the door to my right. The footsteps stop. Myrakka stands in the doorway. Oh no no no.

"Kristal, oh, Kristal, you're awake." She rushes to my bedside, reaching out.

I cross my arms and turn my head away. I can't possibly still be dreaming, can I? But if I'm not—the agonizing fear once again ripples through my mind and my body, followed by frustration, then outright rage. The diamond lady's soft, loving eyes are deceiving. She began this whole nightmare, and I don't trust her, whoever she is. But what's even worse—I don't trust *me* anymore to know what's real and what's not. The lady is just a stupid dream. The floor is just a stupid dream. Right? Or wrong? But if it is a dream, when am I ever going to wake up? My throat tightens. I keep my head turned toward the machines so I don't have to look at her.

My voice trembles. "Go away."

Out of the corner of my eye, I can see Myrakka wincing as if I'd just slapped her. I don't care. I slowly turn my head and glare at her. She just stands there, tears staining her cheeks, whispering, "I understand. I understand. I'm so sorry."

"You don't understand."

"I understand how difficult this is for you because it was for me too. It still is. And not just me but everyone here. But I didn't handle this right. To say the least." Then not only does she ignore

171

my demand for her to leave me the hell alone, but she leans over and plants a light kiss on my forehead. Oh, puke.

I wrench away.

"Don't touch me. I don't know where I am. People do not live on stars. You're lying. I don't know who you are." I break into these weird howls, even freaking myself out. My brain is just acting so weird—way beyond plain old ADD. How could she want to be with me after all this? *Who the hell am I anyway?*

She tries to hug me. I push her away. But then my instinct to be comforted is even stronger, and I'm drawn back to her, reaching for her, collapsing into her arms, and we're both crying now like a couple of babies. What's wrong with me? I don't even know this woman. Through my tears, I confess, "But...but you're...you're part of my nightmare."

I thought she would pull back, but Myrakka hugs me even more tightly. "I know. I know. I'm sure I am. I wish it hadn't gone wrong like this. But at least you're safe now. You were rescued first by Haukka, then Onni caught you just as you were about to hit the ground. Even so, you fell pretty hard. It's a miracle they were both able to come to your aid. But of course, they revere you, so they were glad to rescue you, and I should have—" She pauses, her face still scrunched up in pain. "My...my dear Kristal, did you purposely want to slide off? Why, why would you do something so dangerous?"

I look away, ashamed, then slowly turn back. Her eyes are still glistening, sparkly as the diamond buttons on her shirt. She's looking at me expectantly. I give a tiny shrug. "You told me I was in a dream. People always wake up when they fall in dreams, don't they? Why didn't I wake up?"

She visibly relaxes then sighs. "Oh, Kristal. So you weren't purposefully trying to harm yourself? Oh, that's such a relief. It's my fault for letting you believe you were dreaming. I was trying to soften the blow of this strange new world, this new life you've been thrust into so abruptly. I wasn't being literal. But of course, that just made everything even more confusing. Shame on me. And the council advised me not to tell you anything until the official meeting. Why did I listen to them? No wonder you're confused. From now on, I will be forthcoming. You're a strong young woman, and I need to respect that. Kristal, this is no dream. It's all real. But you're safe now."

"Where am I?"

"Thanks to the Birds, you made it to Quantum City. You have been at Citadel Hospital for the past few days. We have a top-notch medical staff. You've been kept sedated so you could heal better, get used to this atmospheric pressure, renourish, and rehydrate. They've taken very good care of you. You were so dehydrated as you are not used to going as long without water as we are. You had a mild concussion from the fall and a few bruised ribs. Luckily no broken bones. But the most serious concern was the dehydration. We desperately needed to get water into you, water we didn't really have. We've set up a system—H_2O SOS. See, depending on many factors, sometimes someone's rations can be sacrificed if the need is dire for someone else. There's no other way. But unfortunately, it's getting worse. In your case, the Birds stepped up, many offered their rations…their— well, as I said, they love you, Kristal. They revere you."

What? She didn't just say that. "The Birds? Did *what*? Are they sick now? Are they dying of thirst? *What?*"

Myrakka sighs, backs away from my bed, crosses her arms, begins pacing the small room. "Sometimes dire measures are needed in dire crises. I'm sure all this must seem so strange to you. Kristal, you need answers. The more you're kept in the dark, the more you'll begin to fear and hate us. I'll tell you as much as I possibly can. But please understand, I have been given strict orders to wait until our official QC Council meeting, which will be soon. Then I promise you'll have your answers—as many as we know anyway. Even for us, mysteries still abound, unfortunately."

"But this QC Council meeting? What is—"

Just then a short woman with a chestnut-brown pixie cut pushes a gleaming cart into the room. The lady's nametag says "Blanca." Myrakka helps her pull the cart to my bedside. Then they give each other wide grins as they embrace, and Blanca says to Myrakka, "*Que milagro a verle otra vez!*"

I can't understand a word, even though I took Spanish last fall as an elective. She spoke way too fast. I look over at Myrakka. She's wiping tears from her eyes. "Yes, yes, such a miracle. *Todavia no puedo creerlo.* I still can't believe it."

Another question bee for my already overflowing QB box in my brain. I can't hold it in. "Miracle? What's a miracle?"

Blanca winks and points to me, grinning widely. "*Tu.* We cannot believe you are here."

Now I'm truly lost. All I can answer is, "I can't either." I try to wink back, but I end up grimacing.

Then Myrakka turns to me. "Kristal, this is Blanca Ruiz-Ortega. She's from Aranjuez, Spain. She is our nutritional expert and so much more."

Blanca smiles again, this time at me, shaking her head, then places a hand on my shoulder. "Hola, Ms. Kreestal. So good to see you. Since you have not eaten by mouth in a while, eet's best to start with soft consistency, digestible foods. Eat slowly and quit as soon as you feel full. If I may be of further service, please let me know."

"Th-thank you."

She picks up the tray from the cart, setting it on the small swivel table across my bed. I slide off the lid, set it aside. Blueberry soup and something I'm not sure of—pudding? Blanca notices me staring.

"Oh, the blueberry soup—a Finnish recipe. The flan—one of my own specialties, a very popular Spanish dish. We eat flan for dessert often een my country. Made weeth milk from grass-fed cows and eggs from grass-fed chickens. Eet was quite a feat teleporting the animals here. And grass. But they all did just fine. And the blueberries—grown a few miles out of the city—of course, they are organic as well." She stops, covers her mouth with her hand, her eyes wide. "Oh, Meeraka, does she—?"

"*Esta bien*, Blanca. She knows we're on Lucy."

"Oh, thank the Lord."

"Uh, but not"—Myrakka taps something on her phone, then flashes it toward Blanca. It obviously says something she doesn't want me to see. *Great.* Blanca's eyes grow wide, then she nods. "*Esta bien.*" I know that means "It's okay." What's okay? I'm getting so tired of this. I fall back on my pillow. Then I smell it—the blueberry soup. Homemade. Just like Dad's. How did they know? I take a tentative sip from the spoon. Oh god, how delicious. And then it hits me—the damn paranoia. Are they trying to lure me in by presenting delicious foods, like the way strangers in black vans offer candy to small children? Did they know blueberry soup was one of my favorites? This is too suspicious—like the jasmine tea at the Gabriels'. I know whatever else is going on, these people are not trying to poison me. Why am I hesitating?

I spit it out right back into the bowl. Blanca's and Myrakka's smiling faces turn horror-stricken. *Oh, good grief, Kris. Not now. What's the matter with you? Go away, awful thoughts. Just eat the damn soup.* But my stomach's just not cooperating. I look down again longingly. Here's a yummy bowl of blueberry soup here, just like my father used to make, and the flan looks good too. How the hell can I spoil the moment? But the fear ignores my command, staying front and center in my mind, and now my stomach starts to cramp up. Oh, great, just great. Why can't I trust? I still don't. I can't. From the Gabriels to Myrakka to this…this very nice lady who just brought me this wonderful food, I feel so pampered, but is it all a ruse? It's all so over the top. Why? Who are all these strange people?

"Is there anything wrong, Ms. Kreestal?"

I manage a tiny smile. "No, no, really, it looks…delicious. Thank you. I'm… I guess my stomach's just not ready yet. Maybe, later."

The woman—Blanca—nods sympathetically. I think. "Well, let's try again a little later. I'll leave it here." She gathers up the two bowls, carries them to a small fridge in the corner, and places them inside. "I'll check back later." She smiles, giving Myrakka a small shrug, and heads out of the room.

Myrakka sighs. "Kristal, you do need to get your strength back soon."

"Yep." I want to tear my hair out. She's right. But how can I get my strength back when these people are doing everything in their power to drive me completely batty? Myrakka should have thought of my strength before she deprived me of water, ripped me away from my family, and turned my life into a miserable mystery.

My eyes narrow. "I'll get my strength back when you help me find my family. Where is my father? Where is my brother?"

I brace myself for her angry response. Instead, Myrakka cocks her head, frowning. "Your brother? I swear I don't know anything about a brother. But your father—yes—you need to know."

"How did you know my father?"

Myrakka gently smooths back my hair, then takes my hands in hers. I let her only because I'm too zapped to protest. Her eyes seem to be perpetually teary. Why? She swallows hard. "Kristal, I swear, your father, your real father, was killed when you were two years old."

I shake my head. Why would she lie to me? "Gee, that's funny. My father told me my mother was killed when I was two. Now you're saying my father was killed when I was two. So who exactly has been killed here? You really think my father was killed? Seriously? Well, he wasn't."

My star guide, dream guide, whatever the hell she is, sits beside me, staring at the ceiling. Finally, she looks back at me, gazing deeply into my eyes. There we sit, staring at each other—a silent standoff. Then she sighs. "You're too perceptive. They don't understand how not telling you things is worse than their so-called theory to wait and cushion all the shocks to your system. As you yourself said, try being in the dark about all these things. Okay, QC orders be damned. Kristal, it was"—she sucks in a mouthful of air, whipping her eyes to the ceiling, then back to me—"the massacre."

Whoa. "The *what*? Is this the 'rudely interrupted' thing you mentioned but didn't explain?"

"Yes, interruption. Ha, a horrible euphemism. I'm so sorry. See, we were all supposed to gather around and support you while telling you the story, kind of like group therapy. Can we just wait a while, Kristal? I don't know if I alone have the strength."

Double whoa. The strength? I don't want to make her uncomfortable, but the suspense is killing me. "Maybe...maybe just the bare-bones version? A teaser? Please? You can't say the word *massacre* and just leave it at that. What massacre? When? Who?"

She presses her lips together but then nods. "Let's just say for now that once we all lived in a wonderful community of scientists, in an idyllic northern land—up near Lapland, in Finland. You too."

My father's voice echoes in my head, "Those of us from the North…" So it wasn't just Montana.

Myrakka keeps going, like she's in a trance. "But in 2016, a band of…of…terrorists killed most of us. Your father, he was a brilliant member of our community." She lowers her head, doesn't speak for several moments. "This is harder than I thought."

Holy moly, a massacre? That could explain Dad's sadness. He really didn't die. He must have escaped somehow, and she just thinks they killed him.

"Well, if it's painful, I understand." I squelch my urge to keep peppering her with questions about why she thinks my father died in the massacre. But I can see her reluctance to talk about it, just like Dad. "You don't have to talk about it. Dad couldn't talk about his past either. I'm used to it. Let's just—"

She suddenly sits up straight. "No, I have to tell you more. I witnessed your father's murder that day. They shot him twice—in cold blood—funny how they used conventional weapons. Probably stole them from a gun store somewhere on Earth. Anyway, you were crying out for your father, crawling on top of him, trying to open his eyes"—her hand claps over her mouth, and she sits there for a few seconds, then lowers it, takes a deep breath—"and one of the terrorists grabbed you…" She slumps again, lowers her head, whispering, "I'm not sure if this was a good idea."

Beside me, her hand takes mine and squeezes it hard. Myrakka looks so helpless, defeated. My designated star guide and my dad must have been scientists together, work colleagues in this community.

Maybe I can help. I squeeze her hand back, and keeping my voice soft but confident, I look into her eyes, brimming with tears. "Please believe me. He didn't die that day. Somehow he made it. I'm positive. I've been living with this person all my life. He is *so* my dad. He loves me more than anything. He's definitely my dad. I have no doubts at all."

She looks incredulous. Finally, she cocks her head and squints. "Did your father have any scars around the chest—the heart area?"

I think back to our many days at the community pool, Flathead Lake, and just plain hot days when Dad would mow the yard. I used to watch him shaving, in his jeans, his shirt hanging on the door handle. Maybe I just didn't notice, but I don't think I remember one single scar. "I... I don't think so. No, he didn't."

Her shoulders slump even further. "See, oh, Kristal, then it couldn't have been your father. You would definitely have seen scars. They were terrible wounds, fatal wounds. If it had been your real father and he somehow had miraculously survived, the scars would have been quite noticeable. This thing you were living with couldn't have been your true biological father. But I understand how you might think that, Kristal. We all engage in wishful thinking."

"No, no, it wasn't wishful—" I'm about to argue again when the Gabriels' words pop into my head, "He's not what he seems," and the last vision of my father. Could it really be—he was someone or some *thing* else? All these years? Without me ever suspecting anything? Wow, he sure played the part well. Then the vision of the thing in the Gabriels' basement slams into my head. Oh god, what if my father were just a... I can't go there. I *cannot* go there. My head and my heart are at impossible odds with each other. If I don't figure this out, I think I will go insane. Maybe this QC or whatever can help me. Myrakka rubs my back. I kind of like it but kind of wish she would stop. As soon as I wish it, she stops.

"Kristal, do you feel strong enough to share with me how you came to press your pendant?"

If she could tell me a little about her trauma, then I guess I can talk a little about mine. "Yes."

"Sure?"

"Yes, I'm ready. Um, well, after you and the Bird—"

"Rawol."

"Rawol, yes." I explained Dad's reaction after I told him what happened to my coat sleeve. I recounted his craziness, getting the gun from the closet, saying something like "eleven years."

Myrakka's eyes are bulging, and her mouth is agape. "A gun? What did he do then?"

"He asked me if I'd seen a person. I told him about you. Then he really went berserk, running outside. It was so crazy watching him running around in that blue checkered apron of his."

"What?"

"I said—"

"*Blue checkered apron?*"

"I mean it would be funny if it weren't so—"

Myrakka is blinking hard, her hand on her chest. "Go...go on."

"Um, he...he was shooting the gun into the forest and yelling something I couldn't make out, like 'aka' or 'miracle.'"

She backs away from me, a look of surprise on her face. "Or perhaps—Myrakka?"

Whoa. "Oh. Oh, well, maybe. Yeah." *Myrakka.* My father's frantic shouts are now echoing in my mind. I gaze at her, astonished. "Yes, um, yes. Now that I think back, it could have been your name."

Myrakka's hand flies to her mouth, and I can hear her breath quicken. But then her face darkens again. "Well, it could have been one of their minions or your father's clone trying to find me."

"But wait, there's something else."

"Something else?"

"I remember that when I first told him about seeing you in the woods, he seemed himself—like Dad, only really, really desperate. Actually, a little excited. Oh, and he said, 'They lied.' Those—well, I'm just saying what he said. Sons of bitches—that's what he called whoever. I don't know who he was talking about. But that's what he called them. And then his face turned to stone, and he seemed to be talking to no one and saying, 'No, never—I won't,' and then I heard the word...the word—"

"The word?"

"The word—*kill.*"

Myrakka gasps.

"And the police came and arrested him, and I had to go to foster care with my science teacher and his wife."

"Kristal, could it be—I mean that sounds like he was trying to resist some kind of mind control." Myrakka begins rocking, back and forth. "Oh my god, is it even possible? But if he's really Pauli, what have they done to him? Why doesn't he have any scars? And where is he now? He may not even be on Earth anymore."

"Not on Earth? What are you saying? Could he be here?"

"No, not here. I'll explain later. Please go on."

I sigh. "The last memory I have of him—his eyes, just before I pressed the pendant, his eyes turned into silver or something. It was—and then he reached for me. Oh, I... I—it—" I can't bring myself to say the word *claw*. "He was...it was horrible. But I remembered and pressed the pendant and said the code."

She blows out air. "We knew the danger level was high. We just didn't know exactly how it would play out."

The vile memory once again blasts into me like lightning, and I start to shake. She sits down again and takes my hand. "Please, Kristal, I know this is hard. If you—"

I shudder, my throat constricting. "It wasn't him anymore. And he—I think he was going to kill me, but why would my father want to kill me? He was the nicest, gentlest—that thing—it wasn't him."

I'm crying now, sobbing. I haven't had time to think about it since I landed here, but now it's all coming back in technicolor. Between gulps of air, I continue, "See, that's what I don't understand. My father loved me. With all his heart. This...this thing that came after me wasn't my dad. It wasn't. It just—" The vision sticks, and I can't go on.

"Stop for a minute, Krissie. My dear Krissie, breathe, just breathe."

Krissie? She's calling me Krissie. What's with that? I breathe. And breathe again, just like Dad taught me. Myrakka keeps squeezing my hands, swallowing hard, and then she lifts her eyes to the ceiling, and I hear her whisper faintly, "Brave, brave girl. Thank you, angels of heaven."

Then I remember Tad. "Oh, and my brother. His eyes turned into like these steel balls too, just like Dad's. My dad and my twin—I love them. They're not…they're not evil. They're not inhuman. They can't be."

Myrakka is frowning, shaking her head. "Your twin brother. Hmmm, now that's a puzzle. Krissie, you can't have a twin."

Krissie again. This woman is getting a bit too close for comfort. How the hell could she know? How could she tell me I don't have a twin? How dare she?

"How can you say that? Tad *is* my twin. I protect him. He protects me. We love each other. He has autism. I have ADD. We need each other. He will be so scared…so scared—" Suddenly the word pops into my head—*disassembling*. Dad's word about Tad that terrible night. The steel eyes, the robotic chants, the pixelating right before Tad disappeared and then my father's eyes—the same as Tad's. Oh, dear God, what happened to my family? To me?

"Dad said my brother was disassembling. Do you know what that means?"

"No, Kristal, I don't, but it's clear that something is happening here. And the Cancris must be behind it all."

I jerk backward. Holy moly, the forbidden word. "The Cancris? You mean, like Cancri e—the planet?"

Myrakka's mouth drops. "*You* know about Cancri e? How?"

"My science teacher and my tutor were starting to teach me."

"Teach you? How strange. It can't be a coincidence. Well, that's definitely worrisome. We have to be cautious. It could have been a Cancri robot, disguised as human. If that's true, you were in more danger than we thought. In any case, we must get to the bottom of it all before the Cancris—"

"So Cancri e is really a planet? I'm allowed to say the word? And the aliens? They're real too?"

"Of course, you can say the word, why not? And are they real? Kristal, these heartless monsters destroyed our Community. Although the Cancris aren't human, they're all too real."

"So they were the terrorists. They caused the massacre. If they're not human, what are they?"

"Artificial intelligence. They are basically humanoid-shaped computers, devoid of all empathy. They're metallic lizards. But unfor-

181

tunately, they've evolved enough to think by themselves and travel to Earth. Your so-called science teacher could be a Cancri in disguise. Who knows what they've been able to accomplish in the last decade?"

Robots. The thing in Gabriels' basement. Tad's eyes. I turn back to Myrakka, pleading, "I… I think my brother might have been captured by them. Is there any way we can help?"

Myrakka's slowly shaking her head. "Kristal, I'm so sorry. I am completely in the dark about your brother. But I can tell you this for certain. Your mother did not have twins. She gave birth to one child—a daughter. You."

"What? You were my mother's friend? A nurse? A doctor? You were there?"

Myrakka buries her head in her hands, pulls out a tissue from her pocket, wipes her eyes, her cheeks, and looks up. "I was indeed there." Her voice softens; she dabs her eyes with the tissue. "And so was your father." Then she leans in. "It was the most magical day of our lives. I knew this moment would come. The QC wanted to be there. But Krissie, I realize—I… I just want to share the moment with you, no one else."

What moment? Magical? Wha—

Then I recall Mrs. Gabriel's voice in my head—*She knew you. You knew her.*

I study Myrakka's face. Our eyes—green, emerald with golden flecks. Dad has brown eyes. How could I have missed it? Someone's rolling a tray in the hallway. Myrakka turns briefly, and I catch a glimpse of the back of her head. The damn cowlick, just like mine.

I can barely speak. Why haven't I noticed? I whisper, "We have the same cowlick."

She turns, reaches back with her hand, smoothing it down. "Yes, yes, my dear. We do. I noticed it right away that morning in the forest. The last time I held your tiny self in my arms, you hadn't grown enough hair yet."

"I'm always slow on the uptake. I should've realized it right away."

"No, no, no. You just weren't ready to accept it. Makes perfect sense with all you've been through."

Myrakka takes my face in her hands, tears spilling over as we gaze at each other. I see her—really see her—for the first time. She nods. One of her tears falls into my lap. She brushes it off then starts gently stroking my cheek. I don't pull away. She gazes up at the ceiling for a second then back to me.

"How dare they demand I not tell you yet? They don't know how strong the bond. Orders be damned." She gingerly encircles me with her loving arms as a tear falls on my shoulder.

How in the world have I been in such denial?

We sit together, silent, our heads together, as the everyday noises in the hall clank and rumble on. Finally, she says, "QC be damned. I can't do this anymore. They don't understand. I've missed you *so, so* much. I did not die eleven years ago in an accident as your so-called father told you. Thanks to General Waara, I lived. I survived." Her voice trembles. "I am your... You see, Krissie-babe, *I'm your...*" She can't get the word out. But she doesn't have to.

Nineteen

●○○○○○○○○◐○○○○○○○○○

January 27, 2027

Mother. My mother. Why didn't I see it before? Why wasn't it obvious? My brain must have been in total denial. Because it's too weird. I should be jumping for joy. But I'm just…numb. We just hug for a while, her shoulders shaking, and every now and then, she sniffs. We finally pull apart. Her cheeks are shiny wet. I offer her a corner of my sheet. She buries her face in it, then looks up, staring at me, like she's terrified I'll go berserk or something, like she's just revealed a shattering secret. And well, duh, she has. Since the age of two, I've been wired to believe that my mother is dead and buried. Forever gone. Now I learn she's not dead. Quite the opposite. She's alive, very much alive, sitting right next to me. And she seems to love me. A lot. That's the amazing part. A miracle, really. Isn't it? I should be ecstatic, shouldn't I?

But something's odd. Something feels…off. I wish this moment could be more—I don't know—magical. How many times over the years have I fantasized about my mother still being alive? But a familiar mother. I wish I could give this woman a great big hug, like "Omigod, it's been so long. I remember you." But I don't remember her. And even if I did, well, so many things in my life are turning out to be false. I don't know what to think. I hate to grill her, but I've got to know.

"If you're my mother, why didn't you tell me when we first met—the morning in the forest? And why would Dad lie to me? That's a pretty damn big lie."

"Ah, Krissie, my love, my life, the QC was probably right to advise me to wait. I can see your shock and skepticism even now and rightly so. If I had blurted out I was your mother that morning in the forest, you would have instantly run from me, screaming all the way. As for your father, I don't know. I just don't know. Maybe he just presumed, but, Krissie, you know you must at least consider the other possibility. You know, that—"

I wave her off. I know what she means. She doesn't have to spell it out. And she called me Krissie again. My nickname rolls off her tongue so easily. As she speaks, I'm eyeing her critically for the first time. She does look like me, a lot more than dad actually. But then I remember the thing in the Gabriels' basement that looked like Alek. Who or what is behind that? Maybe they also made someone to look like my mother or my dad. A shiver suddenly feathers up my spine. Will her eyes turn to steel when I least expect it? Will her hands turn into claws, reaching for my neck? Could she be one of *them*? Suddenly, I'm cold, my skin crawling with fear.

Damn, I want with all my heart to run to her, hold on, and never let go. But the wary part of me is flashing a yellow light. I will not hand over my heart and soul on a silver platter until I'm sure—110 percent. After all, the person I loved and trusted most in the world just tried to rip me to shreds. Now I know better. Those closest to you sometimes turn out to be the most dangerous of all. I never knew that. Never. Now everything's wildly unpredictable.

But I want to so, so badly. My eyes fill with tears. I sit straight up, leaning away. In my former life, my dad was solid as they come. And he loved me more than anything. My well-being was his top priority, always. My mother died when I was two. Tad was my twin. He was maybe a little different but so what. That's what made him special. And he was a human being with feelings, just as precious as anyone else. And Mr. Gabriel was just a quirky old science teacher. Birds were just birds. Diamonds were rare and expensive. Water was everywhere—something that came out of the faucet at the touch of my hand and poured down from the sky on gray days. All taken for granted.

Now what? Am I supposed to throw all those former truths out the window and start over? How can I accept anything my mind tells me anymore? Maybe the sun actually rises in the west and sets in the east—on Earth, anyway. And here, there's no sun in the sky at all. I *am* on a star. That in itself turns my life inside out. Maybe red is really blue, and blue is really red. Anything is possible in this crazy new life of mine.

The woman by my side insists she is my mother, my long dead mother. Maybe she's an impostor, and yet she seems so *human*, so authentic. It's exhausting going back and forth, back and forth. Am I awake? Sane? Hallucinating? Comatose? Maybe even…dead? What to think? Who to trust? I've got to pick a reality. My ADD makes me so wishy-washy. I need to quit going back and forth or I'll self-combust. But what to believe?

I cannot PPT my way out of this nightmare. Instead, I stay numb, observing the lady before me with detached curiosity, like a scientist examining a bug under a microscope. Am I that heartless? Words suddenly tumble out of my mouth. "What if you're not real? What if they made you? You might be made of steel, just like—"

"Oh, Krissie, my baby, no. Please don't go down that road, no." Myrakka's eyes wildly scan the room. Blanca left a serrated butter knife on top of my tray, and she grabs it, raking it under her knuckles, just enough to draw a little blood. Triumphantly, she holds up her wounded hand.

Is she nuts? I grab the knife from her and sit on it. "*No.* No I didn't mean—no, don't do that."

She stares at her injury like someone else just did it, then shakes herself awake, picks up my napkin, dabs the blood away, and then wraps it around her hand.

Her voice cracks. "Oh, Krissie, my baby girl, please, please you have to believe me I'm not made of metal. I'm flesh and blood, and my heart is breaking right now with joy that you're here and with grief for all the time lost and for all the doubt they instilled in you. Please believe me. Oh, I know you've been so traumatized by what's happened to you. I know what you're going through. I do. I tell you what. We have on board an amazing neuropsychiatrist, Zola

Khumolo. She's from South Africa and was traumatized herself as a child. Then after the massacre—well, anyway, after going through so much trauma herself, she decided to make it her life's work to help others, not only to survive, but thrive. She worked wonders on me after…after I lost you and your father and my parents. In fact, I think I would still be in the fetal position in a corner somewhere if she hadn't come to my emotional rescue. It's your call, but would you be willing to see her, to work with her a bit? Let her support you? Or just chat with her for a while? She can also vouch for me. She's known me forever. And she knew you too when you were a baby."

Zola Somebody. Oh yeah, Khumolo. Well, I haven't known her. At this point, I don't know this psychiatrist from a hole in the ground. Why should I trust her? I start to turn away, but then—oh god, if I keep mistrusting people and questioning everything, I'll go insane. I'm such a fragile egg right now, a Humpty Dumpty about to fall and crack wide open. And I don't want to take my mother down with me. I look up at her.

"I'll—I'll try."

She almost collapses with relief. "Oh, Krissie, you won't regret it. I promise." The napkin is still around her hand. She pulls it off. The bleeding's stopped. Dropping the napkin in a laundry bin in the corner, she pulls out her comcard, taps a few icons, waits, turning back to me, grinning sheepishly. Her comcard pings. She looks down, heaves a big sigh. "Wow, that was quick. Luckily, she's actually in the building today, and she's on her way."

Myrakka and I sit quietly on my bed, waiting, not really having much to say. After several minutes, a tall woman with a weathered, brown face strides through the door. She's wearing a flowy dress with huge asymmetrical shapes of emerald and brown that falls to her calves. Light wooden earrings the size of quarters and a giant wooden bead necklace of bright colors complete her outfit. No diamonds anywhere. It's gorgeous. She exudes joy and confidence and compassion. She kind of reminds me of a grown-up Ayana. I hope she's all that. When she sees me, she smiles warmly, and the crow's feet around her eyes go all crinkly. She waves to me, then holds her arms out to Myrakka, and they hug tightly, rocking back and forth.

"I just got back from the mountain mission. They told me you—and Kristal—were here. I was going to pop in anyway. What a miracle, Myra, what a damn miracle. Wow!" She sees Myrakka's hand, frowns, looks back up at Myrakka, a question on her face.

Myrakka gives her an embarrassed look. "A frantic little demonstration, I'm afraid."

"A what?"

Myrakka looks to me, shrugging, like I'm supposed to take over. Well, all right. Surprisingly, I'm eager to tell this complete stranger my story. I recount the ordeal with my father. It hurts to have to go over it all again. The whole time, the doctor is slowly shaking her head, and at one point, she wipes away a tear. I finish, and Myrakka then points to her hand. "Kristal doesn't yet trust I'm human because of all these horrible experiences. This points to Cancri interference. We still don't know what it's all about. In a fit of desperation, I drew blood to demonstrate my humanity." She blushes. "Stupid, I know."

At that point, I reach under my butt and pull out the knife, offering it to Dr. Khumolo handle first. She takes it, shooting a look to my mother, but then she smiles, laying it on top of the serving tray.

"Yes, but understandable." She turns to me, takes my hands in hers. "Kristal, of course, you don't remember any of us. But as far as our humanity, well, I swear to God your mother is as human as they come. We all are. I gave a baby shower for your mother and father shortly before your birth. I remember holding you two days after you were born. You were such a little sweetheart. I watched as you grew into a toddler with two adorable wisps of curly hair right in front, here—she points. You laughed all the time and were curious about everything. You were your parents' and grandparents' and, actually, the whole community's precious, tiny angel. You were quite the QC child celebrity. I can't tell you how thrilled I am to see you again. We all thought you had disappeared forever. But here you are. Wow. Anyway, I was just down the hall finishing up some stats when I got your message. I'm overjoyed to get out of all this paperwork." She winks, then gazes at me, slowly shaking her head. "Kristal, dear, I can't stop staring. Forgive me if I seem rude. But it's such a miracle. You made it. I don't know your whole story up to now, but I'm eager to hear it. You've no doubt experienced an incredible amount of trauma, complicated trauma, like all of us. We QC survivors—and that includes you—have been through the depths of hell. I worked with trauma victims even before our own incident. There was more than enough work to do in South Africa, unfortunately. I've made it my life's goal to find ever more effective techniques to ease the pain of PTSD, as well as working to effect changes so people don't get traumatized in the first place in my own country and everywhere else in the world."

I love her accent, sort of British, like she says "ahfter" and "thaht" and "oz" for *as*, and she drops her *r*'s, like "theh" for *their*. I smile up at her. "PTSD?"

"Posttraumatic stress disorder. In your two-year-old brain, your parents completely abandoned you. You couldn't know at that time that it wasn't their fault. You just felt abandoned—one of the deepest of human fears. And then your recent trauma with your father most likely awakened those feelings, not to mention that event being quite traumatic in and of itself. And all this—" She sweeps her arm around the room. "Quite likely, the fear center in your brain—your amygdala—is on fire right now, constantly scanning your environment for any sign of danger."

I notice she says "dane-juh" for *danger*. For some reason, it sounds like music to my ears. Amazingly, I feel comfortable asking her the QBs that are escaping out my black box like crazy. "Is that why I keep seeing the color red in my dreams and even in daytime visions?"

"Oh, my poor dear, yes—that's significant. And when this fear center in your brain sees, hears, senses anything that remotely reminds you of past traumas, it urgently screams at you to fight, flee, or freeze. That's why you're not trusting your gut to figure out what's real and what's not. You seem to be experiencing weird recurring dreams, which is definitely a sign of PTSD. That's also why you still may feel exhausted and wary of things—and skittish—and rather disconnected from everything around you. Does that make sense? Any of that sound familiar?"

My mouth drops open. She must be a mind reader. "That's exactly what I've been feeling."

Dr. Khumolo gazes up at the ceiling, like she's thinking. Myrakka's eyes are glued on her. Finally, she looks back at me. "Kristal, would you be willing to accept a little help from me? First, to access your own memory bank so that you can perhaps remember your mother on your own terms and not have to take anyone else's word for it? I can't promise anything, but it's worth a try. But for sure, we could work on processing all the painful memories so even if you remember them, they won't affect you so much."

"What...what do I have to do?"

"Well, for the remembering part, we'll try a little regression— hypnosis. It's easy and painless. Then I'll take you through some simple exercises to help you release the worst of the memories. I'll be right beside you every step of the way."

Myrakka steps forward. "Krissie, it's totally up to you, but I just know how much Zola—Dr. Khumolo—helped me heal from my own trauma. You know, we'll never be the same again. But with treatment, we can learn to live and love—and even laugh again. In my case, it doesn't paralyze me anymore, and I don't dwell on it nearly as much as I used to. I've been able to move forward with purpose and sometimes even joy. Of course, when I realized you were still—when I stood behind your house in the forest wondering how the hell I was going to get your attention, and then you came bounding toward me, and I—" She stops, chokes up a little. "Oh my, what a moment. It was like—you were born all over again."

Dr. Khumolo places her hand on mine. "Kristal, would you like some time to think about it?"

At this point, I'll do anything. "No, I don't want to think about it. The less I think about things right now, the better. I'm ready. I want to do it now."

Dr. Khumolo turns toward Myrakka, raising her eyebrows as if asking permission. Myrakka nods, first to the doctor then to me.

The doctor takes a deep breath. "Well, all right, young lady. We can't begin just yet. We have to follow protocol just like on Earth—you know, the dreaded paperwork, history forms, interviews.

Technically, it's unnecessary. We all know each other. But we decided to keep it by the book to make the transition back to Earth is as easy as possible with the proper documentation. We can do that whenever you're ready. Then we'll start the actual treatment. We can begin as early as tomorrow. Deal?"

Maybe it's all fake, but the hell with it. My mother is beaming. The doctor seems so kind and authentic. A comforting warmth, like an old quilt, suddenly flows over me. I haven't felt this safe since the morning my dad flipped that pecan pancake halfway to the ceiling. I look at my mother then at Dr. Khumolo.

"Deal."

Twenty

January 28, 2027

We're done with all the prerequisites—the history forms, permission forms, interviews about my history, and quick physical. We're ready. Myrakka backs up and sits herself in a chair in the corner. Dr. Khumolo stands at my bedside.

"Okay, Kristal, first, let's get comfortable." She helps me sit upright, plumping several pillows around me, tucking in a warm blanket. Next, she helps me relax with a few minutes of deep breathing exercises, just like Dad taught me. Dr. Khumolo reaches toward the switch on the wall. "Good. We're ready. Let's dim the lights." She turns off a switch, and suddenly the room is bathed in a soft pink glow. "Now, Kristal, close your eyes. Take a few cleansing breaths with me on the count of four—one, two, three, four; out one, two, three, four—again."

Dr. Khumolo's voice is smooth as silk. I have to smile when she says "cleansing breath." Dad used this phrase so often. We do a few rounds. I feel right at home with this exercise. After the last round, we just sit, silent, for a few seconds. Then we begin.

"Excellent, excellent, that's it. Now, Kristal, imagine you are at the top of a flight of stairs, built into the side of a majestic mountain. We're going to descend those stairs very slowly. They're gleaming white, each step, shining in the sunlight, sparkling with snow, beckoning you to reach the bottom, to the valley, to your own past. Take the first step. Your feet are light, warm. Next step. Deep breath, calm and relaxed. Down one more step. With each step, you are feeling

192

more and more relaxed, more peaceful—go down one more. It's so beautiful here, and you realize with each step, you're getting younger. Ten years old, then eight. Keep walking down, down. Now you're six—so happy, carefree, four years old, and you keep stepping down, slowly, so relaxed. Now you're three, so warm, so sweet. Now you're two. Take the last step. There. Now, look down at your feet. Can you tell us what you see? What you feel?"

I'm totally in the scene now. "I'm spinning around, happy. I feel so happy."

"Wonderful. Look down, Kristal. What do you see?"

"Ooooh, I have the coolest boots on with bunny fur at the top. They keep my feet nice and warm."

"So you have nice warm boots on. Now look all around you. Describe your surroundings if you can."

"Um, the bright-yellow ball in the sky, the mountains so high and snow, flowing down the slopes like huge ribbons. I'm in the middle, with the white, sparkly stuff all around me. Brown houses, cabins, and the big house, way over there. And I like the tall trees—big and green with the prickly needles."

Dr. Khumolo's voice. "Ah, so lovely, Kristal. Now I want you to look around you, just a little more closely, at the snow, the mountains, the cabins. Are there people in the snowy valley with you?"

Someone's popped into my scene. "Oh, someone just scooped me up. Oh, I know. Dad! *Isa*! Isa! He's bouncing me on his shoulders, and I'm laughing, and I look over—"

"Who's beside you, Kristal?"

"Oh, she's—" Suddenly something slams into the edge of my mind's eye. Churning, reeling, disjointed, the visions from my dreams are scarier than ever yet not quite clear. I jerk. From far-off I hear, "Kristal, can you tell me what you see?"

I—I can't make it out—bits of color, texture, noises, sharp, jagged. *"No no no, red, the red stuff, the wet red stuff."*

Fear. What's happening? Things begin to twist, change. *"Mutsi's* not with us; she's running away. They are big strange, awful things—monsters. Isa's on the ground. He dropped me. Isa, don't drop me. Help me, Isa. He's all red. The shiny monsters hurt him, and he's not moving, but they—the monsters…ouch. Isa? Isa, you sleeping? Maybe if I make his eyes open, he'll wake up. Oh, it's wet. It's all red, and I'm red too. He has owies, great big owies. Somebody's screaming. Mutsi. It's Mutsi. Why is she so loud? Why is her voice so scared? Is she running away from me? Why is she running away from us? She's not happy. *Please come back. Mutsi doesn't want me? I'm a bad girl? Mutsi, no, Isa, wake up. Mutsi, Mutsi, Mutsi, come back!*"

I hear a gentle but firm voice then feel a hand on my shoulder. "Kristal, Kristal, you're safe now. We're climbing back up the stairs now. You're safe. Completely safe. Come, follow me. Ten, nine, eight, seven, six, five, breathe, relax. It's okay. It's all over. It's okay. You are safe, very safe, four, three. You will awaken soon, two and one and—"

I open my eyes, see her. The word tumbles from my mouth, and I reach for her. "Mutsi."

My mother's eyes are wide, and her mouth is gaping. Dr. Khumolo is frowning. "Usually, this takes longer, we go more slowly, in layers, back to the trauma. This memory must have been much closer to the surface than we typically see." We're both ignoring the doctor, staring at each other, in our own little world now.

My mother looks like she's in the same trance as I was. "Mutsi. You said Mutsi."

"You ran away—"

"No, no, Krissie, no. I did not… I could not. General Waara took me. He was too strong. I couldn't get away…" She's crying.

My older brain comes back online. "No, of course, you couldn't." I frown at Dr. Khumolo. "I can remember stuff from when I was two?"

She nods. "Some people can—like you, apparently. The brain stored your trauma all these years. Incredible, isn't it? Were you having dreams about this recently?"

"Oh yes, all the time and daytime visions. I was so scared I was going off the deep end."

"Ah, you poor dear. That explains it—why it was so close to the surface. Interesting that the prophecy date is so—"

We're not listening. Mutsi and I are gazing at each other while the memories and visions swirl around from her mind to mine. She rushes to my bedside, weaving around Dr. Khumolo, and we hug and hug, rocking back and forth. Now all three of us are together, crying and hugging.

My mother finally gets words out: "Oh, my life, my angel. Seeing you and your father helpless like that—oh god, it was pure agony. It tortured me. I tried to run to you, but Waara pulled me back, dragged me to the safe house. He was so much stronger. I tried to run back. They had you, and I thought—oh god. Please believe me, Krissie, child of my heart, my beautiful daughter, I love you more than life itself. The QC thought it best I wait, but oh, Krissie, they don't understand. I can't believe you're here, and you're alive. I can't hide my joy anymore." She breaks down again, and we just hug and sob, hug and sob, hug and sob. She's no longer Myrakka. I now feel it in my bones, my heart, my very cells, and I'm old enough to reason. She didn't run away from me and my father that horrible day. She was ready to die for us, for Dad and for me. I need no proof anymore. Now I just know. She's Mutsi—*my* Mutsi, before, now, and forever.

Twenty-One

• ° ° ° • • • • • • • ◉ • • • • • • • ° ° •

January 30, 2027

I stay at the Citadel Hospital two more days. During that time, Dr. Khumolo helps me further process the older trauma, then the more recent nightmares. She makes me move my eyes and tap certain ways while I hold a picture in my mind of the bad memories. She's great at hugging too and chatting far into the afternoons like she has all the time in the world—uh—star. She tells me the largest diamond on Earth was found in Africa in 1905—a 3,100-carat gem.

I gasp. "Wow, that's huge!"

Then she leans toward me and whispers, "Seems so, but what we're standing on is ten billion, trillion, trillion carats."

I can't even respond.

"Cat got your tongue?" she lightly teases. "And that, my dear Kristal, is a perfect example of cognitive dissonance. That's when you just can't wrap your head around something seemingly crazy, but what you know is a fact. It's beyond exhausting. Just remember, we all went through it. You're okay. You're quite sane. How to deal with cognitive dissonance? Listen to the birdsong. Enjoy the colors. Rest. I would say 'drink lots of water, but—'" She shrugs. "And keep your mother close to your heart. She's the real deal."

"I know that now, thanks to you."

Dr. Khumolo pats my hand. "I'm just a facilitator. You knew all along."

We have three long sessions over three days. After the last session, I still know what happened, but my stomach doesn't do flip-flops anymore, and my knees don't get so wobbly when the visions come. Now I understand why Mutsi wanted me to see Dr. Khumolo. Mutsi has been able to function much better, and I will too. Still, something gnaws at my gut. Tad wasn't in one single memory of my early life. Where was he? I have to let this hang out on my brain's back burner for a while.

Now that it's all out in the open, Mutsi is on a verbal rampage—like she was trying like hell to keep a lid on all her fears, anger, and grief, and finally, she can let it all out. Today, as I'm enjoying my blueberry soup for the first time, along with some delicious cheese and a biscuit they call keksi, she's ranting and pacing. I understand. I'll be quiet and respectful. Still, my head and heart ache having to listen to so much of her pain.

"So, Kristal, you see why I had to risk everything to find you. You were only two years old. Still a baby, for Chrissake. They took you. Those horrible beasts murdered your father, ah, Pauli. They murdered him in cold blood right in front of you and ripped you from his arms. They're hideous, revolting, inhuman, horrible things. But they spared you. For their own evil purpose no doubt, but at least, you're alive, thank goodness. Why they hid you in Montana is still a mystery. Maybe the location algorithms for monitoring you were more favorable there."

I slurp the last of my delicious soup. "Mutsi, Montana is my home."

"No, Kristal, that's apparently where they relocated you. Well, I suppose it became your home. What did you know? We didn't even think you had survived the massacre. But ending up in Montana, who knew? I'm sorry, baby, I'm so sorry. I would have risked everything... everything."

"Mutsi?" The name still sounds so sweet on my tongue when I say it. "So how did you finally find me?"

She stops pacing, crossing her arms, and cocking her head.

"A signal."

"A signal?"

"Completely out of the blue. We were flabbergasted. The next day, against the recommendations of the QC, I traveled to Earth and found you."

"Where did the signal come from?"

"From your location, of course. That's how I knew where to land."

"My location? Who sent the message?"

"Ah, Krissie dear, that's the million-dollar question."

Twenty-Two

January 21, 2027

"It's small. But, man, the power on this baby. Voitto, you must be so proud."

Voitto Kurki, aka George Gabriel, snorts. "Ha, pride ees one of the seven deadly seens, and I had help. Secret help. It took so long for METI to agree to meet with me. But once I was een, thees group has been amazing and has the means to keep everything top secret—not only sharing their expertise, but also their tight security measures, which were essential to thees project. Just in case there were survivors, my hunch is that they would have fled to BPM37093, Lucy, the diamond star, where the Cancris could not find them. We led a reconnaissance meesion of sorts there in 2014. The Cancris undoubtedly chose thees spot—Dolcany, Montana—because of the strong energy vortex near Giant Springs. Eet should be able to geev it a boost, but thees star ees fifty-light years away from Cancri, so they cannot possibly intercept it. We're safe. Okay, no more talk. Ready?" Voitto leans in between Alek and the giant hybrid, one hand on the table between his two assistants.

The AI hybrid who lives in the Kurkis' basement, fondly dubbed "Big Don" by Alek, sits in a large overstuffed chair—the only chair that will hold his enormous bulk. His hands, clones of Alek's, are poised over the computer keys. They work in tandem, with Dr. Kurki overseeing the process. Big Don begins to recite the algorithm as Alek types furiously on the transmitter. He speaks loudly, in a monotone, "542 binary digits, 84 bytes, frequency 2,380 megahertz."

Alek stops typing; fingers still poised. "Got it. Now what?"

"Arrange in rectangle thirty-one rows by eleven columns. Modulate by shifting frequency by 10 hertz power of 209 kilowatts."

"Wait, wait, okay. Next?"

"Don't know." Big Don shrugs, gets up from the chair, and stands next to Voitto.

Alek turns, frowning at Big Don. "What?"

Voitto interjects, "Send missive to BPM 37093. Very brief and to the point. Aleksi, be my guest."

"Oh, okay. Whew, here we go. T-A-S-S-A." Alek taps the last letter with a flourish and whirls his swivel chair around to face his cohorts. "How's that for brief and to the point?"

Voitto wipes the sweat off his brow. "Perfect, perfect."

Alek grins. "Well, Dr. Kurki, Big Don, let's hope this Scotty has just been beamed up."

Twenty-Three

● ○ ○ ○ ○ ○ ○ ○ ○ ○ ○ ◉ ○ ○ ○ ○ ○ ○ ○ ○ ○ ○

January 30, 2027

"*Tassa?*"

Mutsi shrugs. "Yep, just one word. Finnish for *here*. Don't know who sent it. Don't know why. But it gave your location, which was the key to programming my pendant to return to Earth. And it let me program *your* pendant from Earth to Quantum City. Well, until Dahab and Hale got ahold of it. Dr. EJ, leader of the QC, warned me that it could be a ruse. But I was out of my mind with hope that it might be one of us, especially since I don't think the Cancris have Finnish in their database. But Dr. EJ and our group weren't convinced, and frankly, neither was my rational self."

"Your rational self?"

"My logical brain, which was telling me exactly what Dr. EJ was—beware of this message. Lay low. Wait for another one. But, oh, Krissie, when a mother learns there's the slightest possibility of reuniting with her child and making sure she's safe—well, she will stop at nothing. You've seen the T-shirts: 'You can't scare me. I have a daughter.'" We laugh together. Yes, I've seen them. Mutsi pauses. I can't believe I have a mother. A rush of joy fills my heart. I'm just about to throw my arms around her when she starts pacing again.

"Of course, it was dangerous, and they begged me not to go, at least until we had more information. But I didn't listen. And now I'm so glad I followed my gut maternal instincts. If I hadn't warned you, the enemy would possibly have you in their evil clutches by now. Things may be heating up. We'll explain that later. But besides that—oh, Krissie, how I've missed you! How I've wondered about you. It's been unbearable. A missing child is a parent's worst nightmare. And missing, presumed dead—" She shudders, and I see her eyes have misted over again. Now I can hug her, and I do. As we embrace, her voice cracks. "They say when you have a child, your heart forever walks around outside your body. I would have traveled anywhere in the universe for you. You're my heart and soul, Krissie babe. You won't understand until you have a child of your own."

A vision of Dad comes to my mind. I'm sure he would agree with her 110 percent. *Dad, where are you?* I can't speak for several moments. Finally, I say, "So that's…that's why you were in the forest. That's why you risked your life." I suddenly feel humbled. In a voice barely above a whisper, the soft words tumble out. "You saved me."

"Darling girl, I just gave you the ways and means. But you did the hard part. How incredibly brave you were to press the diamond on the pendant and remember the code under such atrocious circumstances. I'm so damned proud of you." She chokes back a sob. "Krissie, my Krissie babe, *our* Krissie babe."

She called me Krissie babe just like Dad. I squeeze her hands, blinking away tears.

"Aha, Ms. Kristal."

We turn. It's a doctor I've seen before in the hallways, wearing a white lab coat with a stethoscope around his neck. He strides in, stands right next to my bedside, and with a huge grin, puts his hands in prayer position, giving me a little nod of the head. He looks like a combination of the Dalai Lama and an older version of Jackie Chan. I know Jackie Chan from reruns we all used to watch like *Rush Hour* and *Police Story*, and from the Dali Lama's picture on two of Dad's favorite books: *The Wisdom of Compassion* and *The Universe in a Single Atom*. Dad was, damn, *is* a big fan of the Dalai Lama, and a lot of his PPT teaching came from him. The doctor's big black-framed glasses make his eyes seem huge.

After his bow, he stands up straight. "Such an honor! I am, eh, Dr. Bob Smith. You can call me Dr. B."

I frown, blurt, "Bob Smith?" Oh, crap, that was rude. It's just that—well—

But graciously, he laughs, putting me at ease. "My Asian name would be too difficult for you Westerners to pronounce. We often adopt common American names. Make it easier for everyone."

But I still want to know, so I ask him. He rattles off a jumble of sounds like "zhoozanezye," then writes on a piece of paper the Chinese characters and the English letters: Xu Zhanqi. He's right. "Uh...ah" I try, stammering, then say, "I see why you use Bob Smith with people like me." He laughs, then nods. I like him already.

He's still grinning from ear to ear. "The last time I saw you, you were very tiny toddler. Your color is back now—excellent. And after we rehydrate you, your labs, your vitals—fine. You are all set then. We need to get one of the nurses to unhook you from the monitors and take out your IV. Then you are free to go." He gives me two thumbs-up.

Free to go. It hits me all at once. "But where? Back to Earth?" Omigod. "Back to the Gabriels?"

Mutsi and Dr. B exchange looks.

Mutsi shakes her head. "Good lord, no, Krissie. It's not safe for you to return to Earth right now. You're staying with me, at least for a little while until the coast is clear. Oh, I've got to get you discharged." She abruptly leaves the room. I start to call after her when Dr. B says, "Oh, almost forgot. I have something for you." He pulls a shiny flask, encrusted with diamonds, from his pocket. I hesitate, then take it. It's surprisingly heavy.

Dr. B places his hand over mine. "You will be getting some rations. But this? Extra. Guard it very closely. Use only in emergency. Do not let out of your sight."

"So it's some kind of medicine?"

Dr. Bob Smith leans in closer, whispers in my ear, "Even better. Elixir of life—water, H_2O. In your world, water seem to flow effortlessly from faucets, showers, rivers and from the skies. Not here. And if humans continue to take elixir of life for granted, Earth will be in same predicament as we are on Lucy, Diamond Star. In fact, in many parts of Earth, already is. So, my dear Kristal, please keep this with you at all times. Do not drink until completely parched. All perfectly clear?"

203

"Y-yes, Dr. B." Although at this very moment, I'm trying to figure out a way to get it back to the Birds, where it most certainly belongs.

"Good. We hope we will be going home soon, and you will not even need it. But just in case—"

In case—my thoughts churn—in case what? I examine my flask. Funny. Here, the water inside the flask is way more valuable than the diamonds on the outside.

Dr. B pats my shoulder, gives me a quick bow, then turns and exits, leaving me alone with my thoughts. So all these years with my dad and now I am going home with my mother. My mother lives on a star, and so shall I. For a while, anyway. I wonder what her place looks like.

I hear sudden chattering. Mutsi appears at the door with Hanna, one of the sweet nurses who's been taking care of me. Hanna unhooks me from every electrode, wire, and needle as she gazes at me with a sort of awe, eyes sparkling, like I'm some kind of royalty. Finally, we say our goodbyes, and Hanna leaves. Mutsi and I are alone again.

"Mutsi, where do these people come from? They're not aliens or robots, are they?"

She chuckles. "No, they're 100 percent human from Earth. About half are Finnish, and the others—well, they come from all over the Earth, from all walks of life. Under General Waara's expert direction, the Diamond Star soldiers have been secretly transporting people here for years. Dangerous traveling back and forth in wormholes. But they did it. We needed many different helpers with all kinds of talents. We heard about them through word of mouth, vetted them, kept it all under the radar. Even their families and friends think they're in Antarctica working on a project to protect the penguins, and in a roundabout way, they are. If we Diamond Star people survive, we hope it won't be too late to save Earth, including the penguins. They've all been sworn to secrecy. That's why you'll not read about us on the internet or any social media. We don't know if Cancris check or use the internet, but we sure as hell don't want to tempt fate."

"How many people are now on this star?"

"Nine thousand, thereabouts."

"Wow."

"Some of them do double duty like the soldiers. They have their day jobs. But they've been in training for the Cancri showdown for over six years now. And you may be wondering why we would transport so many as each needs his or her share of water. Believe me, their help is crucial for our survival. We calculated precisely the number of humans and animals we thought we needed versus how many we could sustain, trying to find that perfect balance. Unfortunately, we overestimated a bit. We had to send a few hundred home. But we tried to send those who were the most homesick. We like to think it was a win-win." I nod, feeling guilty that I just added an extra water burden to their already overtaxed system.

My clothes are neatly hanging on a hook by the door. I wiggle around on the bed and raise my arms, ignoring the pain in my ribs as best I can. Wow, I feel so free. I didn't realize how much I'd gotten used to being tied up with all those wires and sticky patches. Finally, I'm unhooked. No more IV lines, no more EKG wires. I jump down, quickly dress back into my jeans and Dolcany Demons sweatshirt, which somehow appear to have been cleaned. I smooth down my impossible cowlick and do a little curtsy like I learned in ballet class when I was seven. Mutsi laughs. I feel so much better. Okay then. As Dr. B says, I'm free to go. But not free to go back to my father. This time, I will be living with my mother—Mutsi—on a star, a gigunda ball made out of diamond. Never in my wildest dreams—my breath catches. But I'm ready as rain. Huh, rain. Never realized how much I took water for granted all my life. I reach for the flask from Dr. B and stuff it into the pocket of my hoodie as I follow Mutsi out the door.

Twenty-Four

○ ○ ○ ○ ○ ○ ○ ○ ○ ◉ ○ ○ ○ ○ ○ ○ ○ ○ ○ ○

January 30, 2027

After our heartfelt farewells, especially to Dr. Zola Khumolo, we pass through the wide entrance of the hospital and into the open. Surprisingly, I detect the faint scent of early fall, like woodsmoke in the nippy air. Perfect sweatshirt weather. I'm amazed it's so cool, even though the star is burned-out. Whoever designed the biodome did an incredible job. I look up. No sun. No moon. But a crazy array of stars surrounds us like someone tossed a giant saltshaker across the universe, and the sky is a blend of crimson, orange, and rose. I wonder if there's an earthly pantone for this color. If I had my art stuff with me, I'd love to paint it, not that I could do it justice.

My legs still feel heavy and a little wobbly. Mutsi must have noticed, as she guides me by the elbow down the walkway toward the parking lot while I'm still gawking at the scenery. What a brilliant group of people to construct an entire city so far away and under such seemingly impossible circumstances. So many geniuses around me. I'm grateful and humbled.

As we head toward the parking lot, I notice regular-looking people of all races and cultures, going about their daily business like a normal day on Earth. I glance back once more at the Citadel Hospital. It stands two-stories high, like the hospital in Dolcany. But here, the outside walls shine with some type of sparkly dark granite, the same as the mountains. In the distance, a couple of football fields away, stands another building, much higher than the hospital— about eight or nine stories high. It's lighter, mostly made of crystal, ah, probably diamond. It shimmers a light-rose color from within. Or looks that way, anyway. It's a perfect rectangle. Nothing fancy. To my right, I recognize Quantum City—with its immensely tall glowing spires, crystal diamonds, all pinkish, rising toward the stars, and the sparkly dark mountains beyond. I first glimpsed this heavenly landscape on Onni's back after he'd saved my life. I guess all this is considered "downtown Quantum City"—the hub of social gatherings with the stage, conference center, and all the beautiful buildings. Mutsi says the QC Council meets underground—and that I have to see it to believe it. Can't wait. I can also make out brilliantly colored bushes, trees, and flowers. They're all around us here too. I turn to Mutsi.

"Flowers? Trees?"

"We needed our environment to look a little more like home. They're not real. We wouldn't be able to water them. But they do lift our spirits a little."

I look down. The lot and walkway beneath me are composed of dazzling glass—oh, wait, no. It must be diamond. Following my mother, I warily step down. But even though my legs still feel a little heavy with the slightly stronger gravity, I'm completely sure-footed now as if the surface contained some sort of rough coating laid over the diamond, like gritty sandpaper. I'm looking down as we walk, marveling at its beauty, when Mutsi says, "Here's the parking lot."

I look back up. Before me is a sea of kickscooters, Segways, and bicycles, but I don't see a single motorized vehicle. Mutsi points. "Here are our scooters. You okay riding one?"

"Oh, yeah, sure."

"Good. I was going to get you a bicycle, but my pod is so close."

I look around for a rental booth or pay station, but there is none. I look over at Mutsi. "Where do we pay?"

She smiles. "Everyone's on their good behavior here. We haven't had a single theft in over ten years." And then she winks. Not a single—oh, I get it. In other words, zero thefts. Ever. I wink back.

Then my eyes widen at the thought. "Wow, wouldn't it be great if things were this way on Earth?"

Mutsi nods, and we grab our handlebars and kick off at the same time. A slight breeze caresses my face. I feel freer than I have in a long time. Mutsi catches my eye and smiles. I smile back. It feels so refreshing.

The streets are of the same material as the hospital walkway. It's a little disorienting, but I get the hang of it quickly. After about five minutes gliding on the dark, sparkly ribbon-roads, we stop and park our scooters. I look around. We're on some kind of small cul-de-sac. Fake trees are everywhere, but they look a lot more real than the one I remember from Shana's office. And the blossoms boast all the colors of the rainbow. Wait. I sniff several times and turn to Mutsi, frowning.

"I smell blossoms. Didn't you say they're all fake?"

She smiles. "Ah, the scent of the day. Five of us on the court take turns choosing. It is my turn today. Natural scents are pumped through the air."

"How?"

She smiles. "Just a little ingenuity." She takes a whiff. "Recognize it?"

I take a deep breath. "Lilacs, right?"

"Yep, my favorite."

"Mine too."

"Really? Hmmm, wonder if there's a gene for scent preference. In any case, lovely, isn't it?"

"Mutsi, it's amazing." I breathe in again. It's such a happy, bright, colorful scene. Something pops in my brain, and I laugh— Munchkin Land from the Wizard of Oz. I can just hear Tad announcing, "Five Star Pictures Presents." Suddenly, a chunk of lead drops in my stomach. *Where is my brother?* Stop. Can't do anything about that now. Nothing. Zip. Pay attention to the present moment.

Mutsi motions me to follow her up a small walkway. The "pods," as they call the dwellings, remind me of a scene out of a futuristic *Hobbit* movie. They're more like yurts—small, sparse, and what Mutsi calls minimalist. They conserve everything here. No wasteful consumption. The pods are box shaped, with domed diamond roofs and black granite-looking walls, studded with sparkles. They don't resemble anything I have ever seen on Earth. Everything seems tinged with magic.

We park our scooters right outside. In the center of her pod's front door is a simple wreath made of silk leaves and roses. In the middle of the wreath is a diamond door knocker. I gingerly pick it up, let it drop, expecting the usual thunk. Instead, I hear the sweet strains of a harp. My eyes grow wide as I turn to Mutsi. Her eyes are sparkling.

"Welcome to my humble abode, sweet daughter." She sniffs through her smile. "Oh god, never thought I'd ever say those words."

She opens the door and ushers me in. Still in awe, I scan the surroundings. Mutsi's decorated everything with clean lines, furnished with a dark wooden couch and adjacent love seat, both covered with cream-colored cushions. A coffee table of dark wood, looking like it was just cut down and polished smooth, holds a wooden bowl with a variety of crystals, jewels, and glittery gems. One end table separating the two couches holds a small lamp, all crystal or diamond. The floors are polished with that dark gritty overcoat that keeps them from being too slippery. I'm glad they're not that weird Penrose tile type. That made me a little dizzy.

Mutsi's standing in the middle of the room, hands on hips like a proud peacock. "The floors are similar to our walkways, made of a mixture of polished and black diamond."

"Black diamond? I don't think I've heard of such a gem."

"Black diamonds are found even on Earth, though they're not as common as the colorless ones. They're quite common here though and come in very handy. Most of the soldiers' uniforms are made from a hybrid mix of black and colorless diamond."

I look up and all around. Everything pops. Pastels and jewel colors everywhere. A glimmering chandelier hangs from the center of the main room, casting rays of light, caught by dozens of small crystals hanging from the chandelier and the ceiling. Miniature rainbows jiggle and dance on the walls. Of course, there's no sun streaming through the windows. But somehow they've managed to develop light sources to mimic the sun's rays.

"Mutsi, it's gorgeous."

Mutsi's beaming. "You like it? Zola taught me all about the dramatic effect color and crystals have on one's emotional health. And that was when we all lived together in the QC in Finland, before you were born."

"So you named me Kristal. Is that why?"

"Yes. I was studying Tesla at the time."

"Tesla?"

"Nikola Tesla—one of the greatest minds of the early twentieth century. He believed crystals were actual living beings."

"Living beings?"

"He revered crystals, as do many others. We know each snow crystal is unique. I asked your father if we could name you after something so beautiful in nature. He just broke down and cried. I took that as a yes. The spelling with a *K*—is Finnish. Did he tell you that?"

"I—he never told me I was born in Finland. He never told me much of anything."

Mutsi frowns, shakes her head, and shrugs.

"Here, take a look." Mutsi reaches up to a shelf on the wall. Diamond, I'm sure. She grabs a box—also diamond, sets it on the table, and opens it. All kinds of stones fill the box—some rough, some smooth, some set in rings, necklaces and bracelets, but all exquisite and of every color in the rainbow. "Go ahead, take a look. Which draw your attention?"

I gingerly pluck several from the box and turn them over and over in my hands. "I like them all."

Mutsi smiles. "Depending on my needs at any certain time, I am able to intensify specific colors for healing. Zola used quartz crystal with me when we first arrived here. I was so depressed. Research has shown quartz is piezoelectric."

She sees my puzzled expression and keeps going.

"That means when you put pressure on it, it creates electricity. When you're depressed, you need a little boost in your electromagnetic frequency. Now they're using transcranial magnets, EEG biofeedback—"

"Didn't they like zap people with electricity in the olden days?"

"Oh, you mean electroconvulsive therapy? Yes, unfortunately, it was archaic and dangerous way back when they first started using it. We've come a long way from those barbaric times. They still do electroconvulsive [ECT] therapy for the most resistant cases, but now it's much safer. But therapies like the crystal quartz are much gentler and actually quite effective. I don't need it anymore. But once in a while, if I feel a little down, I'll grab a little quartz, turn up the yellow, and wear my kunzite ring for a while, here. She points. And if I'm angry, well, then it's pink all around, thulite pink here or rose quartz. I'm sure you've noticed our theme color here is pink. It's one of the best all-around colors to soothe nerves, which we sorely needed, especially at first. Oh, here's your birthstone—amethyst." She drops a beautiful silver ring into my hand with an oval dark purple stone surrounded by tiny diamonds. I run my thumb over the gem. "Dad gave me an amethyst necklace for my tenth birthday."

Mutsi curls my hand over the ring. "We should have given you these together. I've kept this ring for you even as my hope faded. But we should never give up hope, should we? Because here you are." Her voice catches. She gently extracts the ring from my hand and slips it onto my ring finger. Perfect. I look up and smile.

"How did you know?"

She smiles back, her eyes glistening. "The size? Just a lucky guess or perhaps a mother's intuition. In any case, happy tenth birthday, my dear daughter. Three years late. Better late than never." We sit, waiting for our throat lumps to subside.

I whisper, "It's beautiful. Thank you, Mutsi."

She clears her throat, then continues with the stone tutorial, pointing out some of the others—selenite to enhance peace, azurite to gain control of the mind (would it help my ADD?), polychrome jasper for relaxation. For some reason, my eyes keep returning to a yellowish smooth stone with black stripes. "What's this one, Mutsi?"

"Ahh, did it beckon you?"

"I don't know, sort of. Yes, yes, I think I feel a kind of—I don't know—pull?"

She beams. "Ah, you feel an affinity. That, Krissie, is a yellow feather jasper. It helps you connect with Bird energies. You've been thinking about the Birds, yes?"

Our eyes meet. I nod. She pats my hand. "You, my dear, are an intuitive soul, perhaps even an empath—you're full of compassion. I think I already knew that the day you were born and I looked into your eyes for the first time."

I don't know if it's the color or crystal therapy all around or just stepping into my mother's home for the first time, but I feel so much lighter already. Mutsi's been observing my every step, my every glance. Suddenly tears well up in her eyes. She sniffles then smiles. "Well, here we are. Take off your shoes and stay a while." I bend down. She immediately kneels and wraps a hand around the heel of one of my sneakers. We bump heads. I chuckle.

"Mutsi, I'm not a toddler anymore. I can take off my own shoes."

"Oh, right, of course." She tries to chuckle. "I used to take off your little shoes every day." And then she bursts into sobs, loud, wracking sobs.

I sit back, mortified. "I'm so sorry."

"No, no, Krissie, no. It's okay." She closes her eyes and breathes in deeply while wiping her tears with her fingertips. "These are tears of joy, pure joy. *Mutsi*—never, ever thought I'd hear that word again, least of all from you."

"Mutsi, Mutsi, Mutsi," I tease gently, trying to cheer her up. She laughs, but there's a sadness underneath. Huh, so much like Dad's, and now that I think of it, my sadness as well. Sighing, she gestures toward the wall. "Ready for a show?"

A show—oh my, I'm excited but scared at the same time.

"O-okay, sure."

The light from the chandelier dims. The colors recede, and the walls suddenly come alive. In spectacular HD 3D, there we are, mother and daughter, in our thick knitted caps, playing together in the snow, with the majestic mountains and pines in the background. Our caps are red, cardinal bird red, happy red. Suddenly, a blotch of blood slams into my mind's eye front and center. I wince. That's why

I associated red with both fear *and* joy in my dreams. Dr. Khumolo had warned me about continuing "pop-ups," but thanks to her training, I take a few belly breaths, move my eyes back and forth, softly processing the scary vision, and it floats away. I go back to concentrating on the happy scene before me.

"Mutsi, we had matching red hats."

"Yes, we wore them all the time. Your *mummo* made those— your grandmother. She loved to knit."

I look back at the screen. My mother looks only slightly younger, with longer hair. She is swinging me around, and I'm giggling, my round chubby face rosy with the cold. One small golden curl peeks out from beneath my cap. She holds me in her arms, smiling widely into the camera, pointing. "Look, Krissie, look at Daddy! *Hei, Isa!*"

And I squint into the sun, grimacing as I try to smile. And then my chubby little finger points to the camera straight ahead. "Da—hi. Da—Isa, Isa, Isa," I'm chanting in a tiny voice, reaching outward.

And then my mother says, "My turn, Pauli."

A few seconds of blurry, disjointed snow, coats, sky, and then Dad says, "Daddy's got you now. Look at Mutsi! *Hei*, Krissie babe!" And the man in the HD 3D movie takes my little mittened hand and makes it wave to the camera as he bounces me up and down.

His face, his voice—they're so familiar I almost choke. God, I miss him, seeing him and hearing him. Will we ever be reunited? Suddenly a part of me seems to enter my mother's heart, and I sense the awful emptiness she must have felt when she realized she'd lost not only her husband and parents but her only child as well—her whole family. I struggle not to burst into tears. I want to show Mutsi how happy I am. But I needed to see this slice of my past—my happy past and my stolen past.

Despite my good intentions, my heart flies up to my throat. This really happened. Once upon a time, I had two parents. I know Mutsi wanted to make me smile with the movie she's showing, but instead of the expected joy, I feel horribly violated. This is how our life was. This is how it would have been; how it should have been. What happened? Why would anyone want to raid this incredibly loving community—a place filled with peace, people working together in harmony to make life better for everyone on the planet? And even perhaps beings from other planets? Dr. EJ and the QC would have been happy to cooperate with them. What dark, twisted evil force separated us? And how can we destroy them so they can never hurt us again? A hot rage fills my lungs, scaring me with its intensity. I hate the Cancris with every cell in my body. I start panting, taking in short bursts of air. It's getting harder to breathe, harder and harder until I don't think I can't get any air in at all. I panic, catching my mother's eyes. She immediately presses the button, shutting down the vid.

She turns to me, concerned. "Kristal? Krissie? You're going to hyperventilate. Slow breaths, slow—it's okay…it's okay." Her soothing voice calms me enough, so I'm breathing a little more slowly. She stops and lowers her head. "Maybe I shouldn't have—"

"Yes, you should have. I needed to know. It's okay. I'm fine."

Mutsi takes a deep breath. "Krissie, he was the best father—"

"Mutsi, *I know.*" But the other reason I'm going a little nuts is that Tad wasn't in the video. "Mutsi? Why wasn't my twin—Tad—in the video? Wouldn't we all have been playing together?"

"Krissie babe, I told you. You do not have a twin. You never did. Your father figure may have adopted some sort of—"

"No, no, because my father said he was my twin and because we looked so much like each other."

Mutsi grabs me and gives me a tight hug. "I'm so sorry, hon. I wish with all my heart I knew what this was all about. I would love to have had twins. But, Krissie, I didn't." She frowns and rubs her forehead. "Kristal, when your father was in the woods shooting the gun that day, what did Tad do? Was he upset?"

"Well, he…he—his eyes—"

"His eyes?"

"I—well, he said something like 'atypical reaction' when Dad started shooting. And then, when I gave Tad the number code you gave me, because he was so good with numbers, I thought maybe he could interpret—"

My mother's face pales. "Wait, you gave the code to the Diamond Star—*the 37093* code—to your twin?"

"Y-yes, I thought he could help, but then he somehow pixelated and his eyes turned to steel."

"Shit." Mutsi's hand goes to her mouth. With the other hand, she yanks her comcard from the end table and taps one number.

"EJ, urgent. Oh, thank God. You need to hear this." She explains what I just told her to the head of the QC, Dr. EJ. I can't hear his words, only his tone of voice. He sounds pretty concerned. Uh-oh. Oh my god, she's shaking as she puts the comcard back on the table. What have I done?

As if I just asked the question out loud, she turns to me. "I'm afraid that by giving your so-called brother the code, he most likely relayed it to the enemy. And now they not only know some of us survived, but they know where we are. The number 37093 is code for the Diamond Star. They would no doubt have that in their data-base—the names and location codes for the stars in our galaxy."

My hand flies to my mouth. So Tad's the enemy? My brother, my twin, was a full-fledged Cancri plant? Omigod, I feel queasy. "I... I didn't know."

"Of course, you didn't. Krissie, please understand. I'm not blaming you. You had no way of knowing, and neither did I. But it's very likely this 'twin' of yours was a Cancri device sent to your place to keep an eye on you. We were so sure they thought they'd murdered every last one of us, and so they weren't even looking. It's taken us all this time to regroup, develop, and prepare our army for an attack on Cancri e. But now since they most likely have our location code and know that some of us are still alive—well, it's only a matter of time before they figure out how to come for us, again. See, this changes everything. They could be on their way here now, for all we know." She stops when she sees the horror on my face.

"But oh, I didn't mean to upset you. Listen, EJ's got the information, and he'll be relaying it to General Waara, so it's now in his capable hands. We've discussed this possible scenario ad nauseam in our QC council meetings. Even if they know, General Waara assures us it should take the Cancris a while to program whatever devices they're using to get here."

"Do you trust him? I thought you didn't like General Waara."

She sighs. "Oh, Krissie, it's complicated. The man saved my life, and he has the scars on his neck to prove it. I'm afraid I was acting like a wild animal that day. He's competent, just sometimes, well, a little brusque. You know, sure of himself, as many generals are. Goes with the territory, I suppose. He and I—well, we have had our disagreements, but…" She trails off. I can tell she's flustered, breathing hard.

The last thing I wanted to do was give her more stress. "Oh, Mutsi, to think I've placed everyone here in more danger, I'm so ashamed. I-I'm sorry. I didn't—shouldn't—"

"No, please I'm just explaining the situation. Don't ever think you could have prevented this. And Krissie, hon, this is sort of off the subject, but I'm wondering, not to upset you, but to maybe convince you? Krissie, did your brother ever bleed?"

What? What a dumb question! "Of course, he—"

I search my memory bank. And search. And search. I can only remember plenty of times *I* bled—knees, fingers, and once when a lamp fell on my head, and I needed stitches. I can't remember a single time with Tad. His gait was weird, but he never fell. In fact, I don't remember a single accident. But all kids skin their knees at least once, don't they? My eyes well up. Suddenly, a snapshot slams into my brain.

"No, Tad didn't. But Dad did."

Mutsi's eyebrows shoot up.

I nod, remembering. "Yeah, lots of times. I mean, nothing serious, but like one time, he was slicing parsnips for the soup, and he nicked his thumb, then put it in his mouth to stop the bleeding. I said he looked like a baby sucking its thumb. He chased me around the kitchen, his thumb in his mouth and his other hand pretending to whip me with a dishtowel. I mean, we were both having hysterics, right there in the kitchen." I stop. This is getting too painful.

My mother's eyes make her look like a deer in headlights. Like the Gabriels, she didn't think Dad was human. But it's true. He *did* bleed. That means he *was* human, doesn't it? But Tad—the fact that he never bled is just one more piece of evidence he wasn't human. But even with all that, I just feel deep inside there must be more to

Tad. I just know. He had to be more than just a—suddenly, the reality of my brother's possible nonexistence hits me full force, and this weird moan escapes me.

Mutsi reaches over and grabs my hand. "Krissie, I'm so…so sorry about Tad. Just another reason to hate the Cancris, letting you think and letting you bond when they knew it was just—hey, tell you what. What if we have a ceremony for Tad? Just you and me. I know how much he meant to you. So I don't wish to dismiss him. He was real to you."

Some part of him, at least, had to be real. I just can't let it go. A funeral won't help, not in the slightest. A full-out search for him would, but that's not going to happen. And, well, if it will make *her* feel better to think she's helping, I'll let her think that. She's so nice for being patient with me. I know she wants more info on Dad, yet she's focusing on my brother right now—my brother who she thinks never existed. But she doesn't belittle me. She respects my feelings. She amazes me more each day. I give her a feeble nod.

She nods back. "Good. I know it can't help much. But perhaps a little."

Maybe I shouldn't do this, but I need to know.

"Mutsi? How did you survive? Tell me more about that day. How did you escape?"

She grunts. "Escape. Actually, I was kidnapped by General Waara against my will. But in hindsight, as I mentioned, he saved my life. Oh, Krissie, I've been dealing with survivor guilt for a decade. If it weren't for Zola—well. So you want to hear it. Are you sure?"

"Yes, I am."

She takes a deep breath. "I haven't shared this in quite some time, but yes, you have a right to know."

Twenty-Five

Finland
February 27, 2016

"PAULI, PAULI, PAULI! KRISTAL, KRISSIE, BABY...MY BABY!" *Myrakka's screams echo throughout the valley.*

Two sturdy arms grab her around the middle, yanking her backward, then shift her to a massive shoulder as General Hale Waara carries her swiftly into the forest. Eyes wide with terror, arms wildly pawing the air, she scratches frantically at the man's neck, drawing blood. A gloved hand encircles her face.

"Ow, damn it, Myrakka, shhh. You'll kill us all."

Myrakka whimpers, then quiets, but their location is already compromised.

The man whispers again, "Quiet. Be still. You must do this. We'll all die if you make another sound, got it? I'm taking you to the safe house." He releases his glove. Myrakka finally settles.

"Hale?"

Bang. Zip. Hale grabs Myrakka by the sleeve, pulling her down. "Shit. Sonofabitch. Myrakka, no more noise. Nothing." Waara shoves Myrakka behind a tree. She peeks out, eyes fixated on her husband and child, in the clearing, out of reach. Her husband lies face up on the ground, long jagged gash in his jacket, blood spreading over his entire chest area. Little Krissie's on the ground crawling toward him, then on top of him, shrieking, "Isa, Isa, Daddy!" She cups his face in her tiny hands, crying for him, crying again and again and now screaming, and then one of the beasts pulls her off and up. The child's desperate screams pierce the air. Myrakka struggles to stay standing, hands reaching out, wild eyes peeled on her husband and child.

It turns, marching toward her parents' cabin as the baby's screams escalate. The thing stops, pries open the child's mouth, placing something on her tongue. She instantly falls limp as a rag doll.

Hale shakes his head. "Ah, shit."

Myrakka slides down to the ground, her fist in her mouth, rocking back and forth.

"Don't move." Quickly, silently, Waara kneels, aims, shoots, then quickly grabs Myrakka from turning and running toward them. "Dammit, I said don't move." The robot farthest away from Pauli collapses to the ground. Hale shoots again but misses. "Damn, can't risk the one with the baby." The general picks her up once more. She doesn't struggle this time. He moves swiftly through the forest, then kneels behind a fallen silver birch, pulling Myrakka down beside him until they are completely under cover. The remaining Cancri jerks its head toward the forest but does not pursue. Instead, it follows the Cancri with Krissie until it disappears behind the Kurkis' cabin. General Waara grabs Myrakka, throwing her over his shoulder again, turning, stumbling as fast as he can toward the secret safe house. Her eyes shut as her body goes limp, just as her daughter's had a moment ago.

*****

Myrakka awakens to murmurs, the scent of strong coffee, jasmine tea, and sweet cardamom bread cakes.

"She's awake. Good god, here, hon. Water?"

Myrakka shakes her head. Her voice is barely audible. "Where are they? My Krissie... Pauli...whe—?"

Dahab and Blanca exchange looks. Myrakka knows; she doesn't need to hear the words. Blackness, welcome blackness once again.

She awakens a second time. The vision still frozen in her mind's eye. It won't go away. It can't be. No, it's not right, not her Pauli, not her Krissie, her baby girl. Where are Isa? Aiti? Her throat is stretched so tight she's mute. Someone is speaking, but she can't quite make out the words. They're so far away and jumbled. Oh, Dr. Bob. He's talking to someone. Her ears sharpen.

"Aleksi. Missing. We must find him. Eikka's grandson. Only seven."

"They've searched everywhere."

"No…no body?"

"No, but we've heard reports of weapons that incinerate. Could be—"

"My family—safe in Beijing. But his family—they are his only…" She watches dully as Dr. Bob slumps against the wall, head down to his chest.

Myrakka slowly shifts her focus to Dr. Bob. She's not the only one. She needs to think of the community. Her swollen eyes scan the safe room—a dozen here, at most. Or—wait—Jaak and Johann, the Kanerva brothers, are in the far corner, hugging and crying. Where are their parents? Aarne? Daniella? Oh god. She glances at the faces of the survivors—blank, staring. But so many more…gone. And now she realizes the big picture. The AIs have raided their community and massacred most of their members, over two hundred. God—Jere, Ansa, Katya… Katya just had a baby. She needs—where is she?

Myrakka can't move, can't speak, can't breathe. For the next twenty-four hours, she drifts in and out. At some point, someone tucks a blanket under her chin, hugs her tightly. Blanca. Myrakka opens her mouth to say thank you but doesn't have the strength. Someone else is speaking. She can't tell who.

"The Maavoimat sent in 350 troops. Too late. They're helping find and identify the bodies."

One says he saw Pauli Makkinen's dead body vaporized by the enemy.

Blanca's voice. "Shhh, Callate, dios mio. His wife is right there. Have mercy."

The other voice drops to a whisper. "Those on the missing list, also presumed vaporized by the Cancris include…"

The rest of the conversation is so muted she can't hear. But she senses. She knows.

Myrakka slowly opens her eyes and looks up. One of the soldiers is pointing to her. His words now echo in her mind. "Her husband, parents, and baby girl," he said. Vaporized? Her family. Her entire family. Her eyes close. The veil of darkness falls once more.

Twenty-Six

January 30, 2027

Mutsi stops. She's been sitting next to me on the couch, hands clasped around her knees, eyes glassy, gazing at nothing. At least we can both remember that horrible day together. My nightmare dreams and visions—I wasn't crazy after all. It was all true. I lower my head. Despite everything she's been through and her need to be comforted by *me* now, I collapse into *her* arms and ball like a baby.

For the rest of the day, we just hang out. She makes me a cup of blueberry tea that looks like it's from a toddler's tea set. I can tell she's still shaken but tries to put her happy face back on by recalling sweeter times—how she met my father, their winter wedding in the simple forest chapel in the mountains of Northern Finland, and how the Quantum Community began to flourish with all kinds of new discoveries and inventions. Then she recounts the QC's first trip to the Diamond Star, proving human teleportation was possible. Her happy face drained again as she related the bitter, excruciating saga after the massacre, fleeing to Lucy as a refuge while they worked diligently to devise a foolproof revenge strategy to overcome these vicious aliens, come home for good, and resume their critical work to heal the earth.

Then she asks about my life. After her story, mine pales in comparison. But she seems fascinated anyway, encouraging me to tell her every little detail. So I talk—about school, life with Dad, his love of cooking, our home, our Wonder Woodlands (the forest where she first saw me and where Tad and I spent hours imagining all kinds of

221

creative scenes), our summer camping trips to Flathead Lake, how they diagnosed my ADD, Jackson Hynes and all the bullying, and how Ayana was kind of like a Zola to me that day when I was at my wit's end, not knowing what to do about my crazy-weird science teacher. I describe my bedroom and how Dad made sure it was turned into a cool sanctuary for reading and resting. I tell her about my love of art, sketching various animals from the forest, and more recently, my dreams of mountains and the color red. Finally, I know the reason for those visions, except for the number 1201. I ask. Mutsi doesn't know, either. I have to wipe away a tear when I talk about how I've thought of her over the years—how I would wistfully watch the other kids and their mothers at the games, the fundraisers, the Dolcany Girls' Club meetings. She tells me she knows the best cookie recipe ever, and when we get home to Earth, the hell with the school fundraisers, she will bake sixty dozen just for me to make up for lost time, and she and I will eat them all at one sitting while binge-watching all the old movies—*Lion King, Frozen, Sloth City, Trolls World Tour.* We'll rewind my whole childhood. At that delicious thought, we both giggle like a couple of kindergartners.

Of course, my life story wouldn't be complete without telling her about my brother, Tad—how we played together in the forest, how I taught him how to create, and how to imagine. I tell her about how he took care of me, making sure I was safe, our love of old movies and shows like *M*A*S*H* and all the Five Star Pictures Presents movies he loved, sliding down Marsten's hill on those few snow days we had left in the past few years. I know she doesn't believe for a second Tad's my brother, but she just listens and nods, for which I'm eternally grateful. She drinks it all in, like my life was the most exciting event ever to have occurred. I guess to a mother deprived of watching her child grow up, it is.

I glance out the window. Somehow they've programmed the outside to grow dark like it does on Earth. They must have installed some kind of giant outdoor dimmer switch. Mutsi tells me it's about 8:30 PM, Earth time from their community's location. She leads me down a tiny hallway and shows me the bedroom. It's simple, sparse—one narrow bed made out of rough wood, a small desk with a computer, a closet, and one wall hanging, about the size of a small notebook, in a frame of swirling rainbow colors. The quote is embroidered all in pink:

Crystals are living beings at the beginning of creation. (Nikola Tesla)

Mutsi sees me staring. "This is where your name came from. Your grandmother embroidered that shortly after you were born."

"Who was Tesla again?"

"Oh my, your science teacher never told you about one of the greatest thinkers who ever lived? He was instrumental in getting AC current into the main—ah, Krissie, some other time. You need to rest. I'll sleep on the couch."

"No, no, Mutsi, I can—"

She takes me gently by the shoulders. "No arguments, young lady. You need your rest, and I'll be fine." She opens the closet door, revealing a small rack of clothing and a chest of drawers. Pulling out the top drawer, she hands me a container, shrugging.

"No showers here, of course. This is Blanca's creative invention—Shower Power. She's a genius."

"Shower Power?"

Mutsi sprinkles a powdery substance on her hands, rubs her hands together. "Gets the dirt out. Luckily, we have few germs here, but unfortunately, we have very little water. It smells nice, kind of like a mix of lavender and lemon balm. Here's yours, sweetie." She hands me the container, along with a towel.

"Oh, well. Okay, thanks."

"We had to get very resourceful here pretty quickly. Thank goodness, we've got some amazing creative thinkers among us." She leaves me for a few minutes. I use the Shower Power mix. It works. I feel miraculously cleaner as I change into the gown Mutsi's laid on my bed—plain cotton-like material, soft and comfy. I'm gazing at the assortment of clothes in the closet, all adorned with tiny, glittering diamonds. Way in the back is the cloak she wore when she appeared in the forest that day. When she comes back in, I ask, "Mutsi, the cloak you wore—"

"Oh, that. Yes, it's a little heavy but certainly kept me warm. It's actually a protective shield. When I announced I was teleporting to Earth, QC blessing or not, Warra presented me with it, telling me if I have to disobey orders, I might as well be safe as possible." She pauses. "Under that tough-guy persona, he really does have a soft spot. He designed that cloak just for me." The diamonds and the material underneath are the same as they use to construct their uniforms. Okay, Krissie, ready for rest? It may be a little earlier than your bedtime at home, but you've been through a lot and still need to get your strength up."

"I don't know. I'm a little keyed up, I guess—from everything."

"Understandable and no doubt an understatement." Mutsi smiles, nods, then flicks a switch. Instantly, the room glows soft pink, like the crystalline buildings of the city. She reaches down, opening the second drawer of the dresser, then pulls out a brush with white bristles and a wooden handle. "Sit."

I back up and lower myself onto the edge of the bed. She joins me, gesturing me to turn a little to the right as she begins gently brushing my hair. My eyes tear up. As I blink, she brushes.

"You loved getting your hair brushed when you finally grew some hair. You would sit on my lap, and I would sing to you or tell you little stories, both in English and Finnish. Oops, there's your little cowlick. I don't know how many cans of hair spray I went through trying to keep my cowlick in line. Now I shudder when I think of all the chemicals I must have sprayed into the atmosphere."

I turn to face her. "I just used spit on my cowlick because Dad refused to buy me hair spray of any type. I thought he was just being mean, but he would say, 'Too many toxic chemicals.'"

Mutsi frowns then cocks her head. "Really? Strange..." She shakes her head then resumes brushing. I know what she's thinking. Why would a robot be concerned about toxic chemicals? I stuff that question bee into my black box and take a deep breath. Her gentle brushing is so relaxing.

She stops again. I turn to her. "Funny the things that get handed down through our DNA—a cowlick, no less, and maybe our mutual love of lilacs." We chuckle together. She stops and gazes down at me with such tenderness, such love. I've felt this before; I know I have. The memory stirs in my very bones.

A vision comes to me and I'm faraway—in the mountains, the snow. I'm all wrapped up, snuggled in a little box. I feel so safe. I tell Mutsi. She tells me most Finnish babies sleep in their cardboard sleeping boxes, courtesy of the Finnish government. Then I notice a small quilt at the end of the bed, pink and white and embroidered with tiny lily-of-the-valley flowers. I pick it up, questioning Mutsi with my eyes.

She immediately tears up. "That's yours, sweetie. Your grand-mother made that for you. We covered you up with that when you slept. They made us leave everything behind when we fled, but I begged one of the soldiers to bring it to me. I was desperate for one reminder of you. I swear I carried that little blanket around with me for months. I could still smell your little baby scent..." She stops. She's smiling, but I notice her eyes glistening with tears and her hands shaking ever so slightly. I hold the little quilt to my heart. Another vision floats up to my consciousness—Mutsi, my Mutsi rocking me, crooning, singing me a lullaby. The melody and words spring from an ancient corner in my mind, rising from my throat in a whisper,

"*Nuku, nuku?...*" I stop. I can go no further.

Mutsi's eyes widen. Then she shuts them tightly, nodding. Silent tears spill down her cheeks. She opens her eyes, swipes the tears with the back of her hand. She takes a breath and continues the song. Her voice is like an angel's. As she sings, I dissolve into a cloud of pure peace.

Nuku, nuku nurmilintu,[1]
Väsy, väsy, västäräkki.
Nuku nurmelle hyvälle,
Vaivu maalle valkialle...

---

[1] Google "Nuku Nuku (Finnish Lullaby)" for a hauntingly beautiful rendition of this song.

Her voice cracks. I open my eyes. We hug, with the blanket between us, our arms wrapped tightly around each other. A horrible tragedy kept us apart for eleven years. I was lucky enough to have my father for those eleven years. Now he's gone, maybe forever, maybe not. I don't know what the future holds. But right now, this minute, in this tiny slice of time, I have my mother, my mama, my mutsi, and she has me. I sink into the shelter of her arms. Mutsi and I will get through this. Together.

She kisses my forehead, then leaves the room, wiping her eyes with her sleeve. Clutching my homemade baby blanket to my chest, I drift off easily. This time, my dreams are of rainbows, sparkly diamonds, colored crystals, and birds. No snow. Pink. No red. But that darn number—1201. Even in my new dream, it's still there, this time like deer tracks in freshly fallen snow.

Twenty-Seven

○ ○ ○ ○ ○ ○ ○ ○ ○ ◉ ○ ○ ○ ○ ○ ○ ○ ○ ○

January 31, 2027

I awaken to light streaming through the window, just as always, just like on Earth. Talk about creative thinkers. Someone must have figured out how to make this star seem as earthlike as possible. If these geniuses were able to figure out how to terraform a star like this, I'm sure they'll find a way to rid the universe of these enemy robots. Wow, nice PPT there. And I wasn't even trying. A surge of hope lifts my spirits. Mutsi is standing in the doorway, smiling, holding a tray of some kind of brown bread and blueberries.

"*Piparkakut?*"

"Excuse me?"

"Finnish gingerbread. It's delicious. Got it at the market, along with some blueberries. Have to get there early for the blueberries. They sell out fast. I would have taken you with me, but you were sleeping so well—"

"The market?"

"Just a couple of streets over. If we had more time, I'd take you there. All fresh food." She crumples up a piece of paper, tossing it into a metal can. Obviously it had been her note to me had I awakened before she got back.

"Oh, sounds yummy."

I stretch, setting my baby blanket on the foot of the bed and smoothing it out. The thought of a grandmother—mine, lovingly stitching the lily-of-the-valley design—brings tears to my eyes. I never knew her. She and my grandfather perished with the rest.

Trying to ignore the lump in my throat, I smile at Mutsi, climb out of bed and follow her into the living room. She sets down the tray and pats the couch. I sit.

I observe her face. Right now, she seems almost serene. But I know she must be crazy anxious to get going, to meet with the Quantum Community, to find out the new strategy for fighting the Cancris, and maybe even, to find Dad. I'm anxious too. But here she is, making sure I regain my strength and sanity, insisting I'm her top priority. She even brings me another tiny cup of blueberry tea. I don't ask where the water came from.

Water. When I was in the hospital, severely dehydrated, the hospital staff needed water, lots of it, relatively speaking, and they needed it fast. But I can't believe they accepted the Birds' offer to sacrifice their rations. I'd rather stuff diamond dust down my throat than drink rationed H_2O from the Birds. They won't last long. I still have the flask Dr. B has given me. I won't drink it. As soon as I can, probably at the ceremony Mutsi's talked about, after the QC meeting, I'll make a toast to Birds, and then I'll return every last drop. There—that's my plan, and I'm sticking to it. I feel better already.

As I'm enjoying the scrumptious gingerbread, I look up. The walls are pulsating in rainbow colors.

Breaking the peaceful silence, my mother says softly out of the blue, "The hand over my mouth that day—"

"The hand?"

"General Hale Waara. You'll meet him today. I just want to make it clear. Had it not been for him, I would have run to you, and the Cancris undoubtedly would have killed me. Hale dragged me the opposite way, to the safe house. I was literally kicking and screaming—well, before I passed out, that is. I scratched his neck in several places and made it bleed. He still has a few scars. That's how desperate I was." She smiles. "He forgave me. We may have had our differences over the years—the major one just recently when he prioritized his latest mission above you—but he deserves respect. He's been in charge of assembling and training our amazing Diamond Star Army, the army that will soon rid us of those terrible—" She clears her throat. "Really, Krissie, I think we're ready to handle them now. Waara says there's no room for error. That's why it's taken longer than we would have liked. But we're certain we're ready, much more ready than we were in 2016."

I haven't said much about her story of the massacre that day, or when she sang the lullaby and we cried together. I think I can speak now without breaking down. "Oh, Mutsi, I can't believe you went through all that."

She reaches over and pats my hand. "I'm sorry I even had to recount that horrendous story." She shakes her head. "Such a dark time." Before Zola rescued my mind, I would hear your little baby screams in my mind, howling in terror. And then, all of a sudden, you were silent. I was sure they'd killed you. Every single night, you—and they—were in my nightmares. I didn't even have your father to reach out to."

There just aren't any words for something like this. I guess that's why they call it unspeakable. Everything this woman has done— bursting into tears at the drop of a hat, her urgent voice, her fear for me, her secrets—all makes sense. We both just hug for a while. We've been doing that a lot. Finally, she wipes her eyes. "Okay, that's enough blubbering. We can't go around gloomy all the time now, can we? We found each other. Let's rejoice." She pats my knee, stands, and carries the little tray into her kitchen. I don't see any faucets, but there's a small sink and a can of powder—some kind of shower power for dishes, I guess. She sprinkles some powder on a cloth and begins to wipe them.

I should offer to help, but the myriad of colored gems and tiny rainbows dancing jigs all over the walls mesmerizes me. I shift a little and feel something hard on my hip. It's the remote sticking out between the couch cushions. I extract it, being careful not to hit any buttons. I never finished watching the vid after I hyperventilated. Maybe Mutsi felt it was just too much for me to watch. But I feel strong enough today. I hold it toward the wall and press "play." It begins where we left off. From the little kitchen, she calls, "What's that?"

"The vid. I never finished it."

"Are you sure you can handle it?"

"Yes, I'm in a different place now." At least, I hope I am. I'm gazing at my toddler self squinting into the camera and Dad moving my mittened hand up and down. Damn, I miss him so much. Wait, in the distance. Who's that? I rewind. Go forward. I sit up straight, squinting. Then I catch it.

"Holy moly!"

"What, Krissie?"

"Two people, in the background." I jump up from the couch to get closer look. I can't believe this. I cannot believe this. I sputter, finally getting the words out: *"The...two...the...the two people. They're...the people in the back-background. Holy moly."*

Mutsi returns to the living room. "Omigod, yes, yes, your grandparents. Should have pointed them out to you first thing. We were showing off the hats she knitted. Your grandmother and your grandfather. Zoom in a little closer."

I press the zoom icon on the vidstick, and the two people in the background move quickly forward. Their faces are a bit blurry but unmistakable.

"It's them."

My mother sighs. "Yes, your beloved grandparents—beautiful, brilliant people—lost in the massacre as well. She"—she points to the woman—"made your hat and your little blanket."

My jaw is on the floor. I can barely speak, but I've got to get it out. "No, no, it's them—the Gabriels."

Mutsi turns to me, puzzled. "The who?"

"The Gabriels—my science teacher and his wife."

"Oh, Krissie. Uh-uh, they might resemble those people. But these—they were your grandparents. They've been gone for eleven years."

Nope, she's wrong. I could kick myself. Now another piece of my life's puzzle solved. I'm so ashamed. Thinking all this time that my teacher—and then his wife—were crazy or evil or both. And now, I don't even know if my father's bullets—I shake the thought from my head and focus on my mother's bewildered face.

"No, I'm sure. That's them." What can I say to convince her? And then, I remember. "And...and... Loomy. Yes. Veeto and Loomy."

Mutsi's eyes fly open, her face goes all pasty, and her hand flies to her mouth. "Krissie, Krissie, what? Omigod…"

I point. "Yes, Mutsi. Those two people—right there—they live in Dolcany, Montana, and the man who calls himself Mr. Gabriel—my science teacher—he's the one who's been acting really funny around me. Now I know why. He didn't want Dad knowing because he must have thought Dad was a Cancri robot or something. But he wanted to talk to me so bad. He wasn't crazy after all. Oh god, what I did to him. How I must have hurt him with my disrespect."

Her eyes look like they're rolling backward into her head.

"Mutsi? Mutsi!"

She falls back on the sofa, grabs a pillow, hugs it tight. "Wha—oh wow, oh my! *Aiti. Isa.* My mother. My father. Oh, dear lord."

I'm sitting right next to her now, and it's confession time. "I hate to admit, but I haven't been very nice to them. After Dad was arrested, these people took me to their house. They had told me their names were George and Diana Gabriel. But later, I overheard them talking downstairs, calling each other Veeto and Loomy. The aliases must have been for their protection and mine."

My mother shakes her head, stunned, numb, whispering. I can hardly hear her.

"Voitto and Lumi Kurki." She spells their names for me. The spelling, Finnish, makes more sense. She goes on. "They were born and raised in Finland. They moved to the US to attend the University of Oregon, where my father got his MD degree, then two PhDs—astrophysics and neurobiology. He loved research. And my mother—the soul of our family—so supportive and nurturing. I miss them terribly to this day."

Voitto and Lumi—my real grandparents. All that talent—and here he was posing as a middle school science teacher just so he could be close to me, to watch my back. That's what Alek meant. Mr. Gabriel probably chose Alek to confide in because he was the smartest and most trustworthy kid in the school.

Mutsi's voice is shaking as she talks. "I was born and raised in the States. That's why I don't have an accent. I also attended Oregon and met your father there. That's why he had no accent either. But did these people have an—"

"Accent? Yes, they did. I always wondered where he was from. Then that last day he told me they were from Finland."

"We moved back to Finland to join my parents and the QC when it was recently formed, in 2004, right after college. We got our advanced degrees in Turku, and that took a while. That's why we didn't have you until we were both in our early thirties, and that day, February 27, 2016, the day of the massacre, the Kurkis disappeared. We assumed the Cancris had killed them like all the others. They never found their bodies. But they obviously hid, then escaped somehow."

I don't know how I manage to ask this next question, which isn't just a gigantic question bee, but a murder hornet buzzing in my brain. "Mutsi, did they…uh…did they find my father's… I mean, how did…" Luckily, I don't have to explain myself any further.

Mutsi closes her eyes, nods, and takes my hand. "One of the rescuers found—well—what looked like your father's"—she takes a breath—"remains. The earth where he had been slain was scorched. Hale had told him that's where he last saw Pauli. Bits of your father's jacket were burned into the ground. Ah, that's all I can—" She pulls out a drawer from the end table and carefully takes out a small wooden box. Her eyes meet mine. She opens it; I peek in. Lying there is a jagged piece of charred, hardened leather, the size of a small leaf. I wince. Suddenly, I see a vision of my father in his blue-checkered apron, smiling, arms outstretched, waiting for his bear hug. The charred leather, the happy bear-hug vision, leather, happy vision. I go back and forth. Where's my true father? Suddenly, I'm exhausted and scared. *What if…?* I turn my head from the box.

"Put it away, could you, Mutsi?"

Without a word, she closes the box, sets it back in its little crypt, and shuts the drawer. What did Dr. Khumolo call it? Cognitive dissonance. Wow. Exactly. I know in my heart my dad is real, yet all these signs and experiences lately tell me he was…was…incinerated? Vaporized? It just doesn't compute. Sometimes I think I'll go wild wondering what's really the truth. That piece to my puzzle is still

definitely missing. Mutsi continues. "So since there were no bodies, we thought my parents had been vaporized as well. But omigod,
they must have hidden. My father insisted on building a little safe
house cellar in their cabin. My *isa* was always one to be prepared. We
used to tease him about how paranoid he was. How stupid we were.
That's how they must have stayed hidden. That might be how they
overheard the Cancris' plans for you. Then they must have moved
to Montana where they've been secretly watching over you all these
years. Oh, Krissie, is it possible?"

Mutsi's choking up. "My parents were incredible people. My
father was working on so many crucial projects when—oh, Krissie,
I can't imagine how tortured they felt not being able to tell you, to
be with you, to hold you. They doted on you, and you loved them
too when you were a toddler. But I can now see they had no choice
but to remain at a distance. If your father was Cancri-programmed
and had found out your grandparents' identity, they wouldn't have
survived a minute there."

I blush with shame. These people are my *grandparents*, and they
had only been trying to protect my life. I owe them a huge apology
if I'm ever lucky enough to see them again. If they're—oh god, my
father, how could I have forgotten? He was shooting his gun into the
house as we left. My grandparents may not even be alive. I *cannot* tell
my mother, not yet.

Mutsi is staring at me, through me. "*Aiti. Isa. Aiti. Isa.*"
Apparently, the Finnish name for *mother* and *father*. But I'm confused. "Aiti?"

She stares at me for a second, then smiles. "It's...what most
people typically call their mothers."

"Should I call you *Aiti*?"

"If you wish. Either is fine. But, Krissie, I...it's just that... I
taught you to say *Mutsi* because it—well, growing up speaking
English, I liked the Finnish word for *mother* that began with *M*. You
picked up that word so quickly, it stuck. And now...it brings back
such wonderful memories... It warms my heart so..."

She doesn't need to explain. "Say no more." I take her hand,
whispering "Mutsi" several more times. She closes her eyes. A single

tear runs down her cheek, and she starts rocking back and forth, hands clasped in prayer position. Then she glances wildly around, grabs her comcard on the end table, taps a few times, holds the wand in front of her. "EJ, are you sitting? You won't believe this. Voitto, Lumi—my parents—they're alive. *Alive.* Been in Montana, watching over her, all these years."

Dr. EJ's voice carries clearly. His accent is so much like Mr. Gabriel's—or my grandfather's, rather. Finnish. He was telling me the truth that night. They celebrate for a few moments, and then Dr. EJ says, "We'll see you soon and work out the logeestics. Oh, Myra, another joyous revelation, eh? Theengs are happening queekly now."

Mutsi can hardly speak. "An incredible month so far."

"Let us trust that things are unfolding as they should against my logical mind. The mysterious prophecy seems to be unfolding. Take care, my dear." My mother replaces her comcard on the table. Her face is flushed.

"Mutsi?"

She looks up at me, teary-eyed. I take her by the shoulders.

"You know we will rescue them—Dad, Voitto, Lumi. It's written in the stars or that prophecy you're all talking about." I shake my head in wonder, thinking I'm actually on one of those stars—a star made of diamond, no less. "Up above the world so high / like a diamond in the sky…" Who wrote that children's song? Little did they know…or did they?

Mutsi can't stop smiling as she pulls me close. Her eyes are bright with tears and hope. "We found you. Now we'll find your father and your grandparents. Oh, I can't believe what's happening, just as predicted in the prophecy."

"And my brother."

Mutsi pulls back a little, sighs, but stays silent.

Later, as she tucks me in for the sixth and last night, Mutsi tells me more about Blanca, the nice lady who works in the nutrition area and who also survived the massacre. "She was a botanist and dreamed of getting a job in the US in agriculture. She immigrated to the US but got separated from her daughter, Victoria. She said she prayed and prayed to St. Anthony, the patron saint of the lost. And seven months later, she got word that her daughter was safe with her grandparents. They were reunited three weeks later. Victoria has been allowed to be with Blanca here on Lucy. They work together as a team. I think that's why Blanca smiles so much. Being with her daughter is all she needs." Mutsi wipes a tear. "Anyway, since she found her daughter, she's told everyone who's lost something dear to pray to St. Anthony."

I take Mutsi's hands. "Well, then, let's pray." I'm not sure I'll understand or be able to pray with her. Aren't these prayers always in Latin? Suddenly, Mutsi takes my hands, and we twirl around and around as she chants, "Tony, Tony, turn around. Something's lost and can't be found." Well, that's easy enough. We say the prayer again together: "Tony, Tony, turn around. Something's lost and can't be found." We keep whirling around the room a few times until we're dizzy. Then we name our loved ones and wish on our very own Diamond Star they will be safe and sound and we'll all be reunited: Dad, Voitto, and Lumi. She hugs me so long and hard I'm afraid she won't ever let go. When she does finally leave the room, I silently mouth the words "Tony, Tony, turn around, something's lost and can't be found." And I add one more name to our rescue wish list.

Tad Makkinen.

Twenty-Eight

Finland
February 27, 2016

"Au."

Aleksi glances down at the bloody scrape on his left palm. He should have kept his gloves on for the climb, but the rough bark gives him better traction. He's not quite to the top of Sylvester, one of the tallest pines in the area, but close enough. He'll find a good resting spot then put the gloves back on.

There. Perfect. He settles into three forked branches, their soft needles surrounding him like a nest. A tree-house bedroom. Wow. So cool. Who else has climbed so high? Jaak, of course. But no one Aleksi's age—seven and a half—would even try. He will hold the record in his age category, probably forever. He smiles and reaches into his pocket for—

Zip.

His hand freezes. What? Weird. Are they hunting moose? Reindeer? But it's not the season. Aleksi carefully settles back into the branches, peering down.

Zip.

And it doesn't even sound like Creedmoors, the only guns they use.

Bang.

He hears a sudden cacophony of screams, cries, and groans in the distance. Aleksi inches closer to the trunk until he can grab it and hang on for dear life. An earthquake? Moose stampede? Aiti was baking lusikkaleivat when he left. Everything seemed okay. And Isa? Where's Isa? And Pappa? Isa and Pappa are usually at work in the lab. But wasn't his *grandfather traveling to Helsinki today? He needs to find them and to warn them. Something really bad is happening. Then he catches a glint of metal.*

His breath stops. Right below, at the base of Sylvester, stand the aliens his parents were talking about when they didn't think he was listening—the robots. He thought his aiti and isa were just telling stories. But they're real. Pappa must be traveling to tell his friend Brima, in Helsinki, to ask for help. But they're here already? The freaks are all covered in dull steel. Aleksi can feel his heart thumping under his coat as he counts to himself—yksi, kaksi, kolme, melja, viisi, kuusi—six in all. They're speaking English. He's learned some English, but he can't understand much. Straining to listen, he cups his hand behind his ear.

"Disassembled. All. It is done. We take prophecy child to Vortex 6830271. English name: Mon-tana. Vortex most favorable for signal detection. Male parent now on Cancri—reassembly. Technical advisory device ready for teleportation. Will monitor until prophecy date February 5, 2027."

"Prophesied child?"

"Affirm. Prophecy found in computer software. Crystal Child to produce H_2O for Cancri survival 2027. Child name, Kristal, in QC database. Birthdate identical to prophecy. Need to find. Take charge of child."

"Look, blood."

Silence. One of the robots pinches off a branch with its metal claw—the branch Aleksi scraped his hand on.

"DNA."

They look up. Aleksi shrinks back into the pine branches and stays still as a rock.

He understood only the words father, child, Kristal, and look. Kristal—the Makkinens' little girl? What are they saying about her? And father? Dr. Makkinen? Aleksi begins to shiver, more with fright than cold. After several minutes, the robots leave. Aleksi sits, frozen, for a long time.

Finally, he pulls out the cardamom biscuit his mother insisted he take with him. He rips off a sizable bite, then another. As he's about to take the third, his trembling hands let it slip through, and it bounces down, down, off the branches several times before it hits the ground. He groans. His stomach is still growling with hunger.

Something deep inside warns him to stay right where he is. His ears prick up like a forest creature, listening for any sound—good or bad. Nothing. But he stays, near the top of the pine, nestled in among the dark-green needles. He'll be too keyed up to sleep tonight. But that's okay. He will need to be on guard every second. He pulls on his gloves, waits, shivering and keeping watch against the darkening sky. It's still the season for the Borealis or the northern lights, but it's cloudy today. The sky can offer him only a long, cold, gray night.

His eyelids begin to droop. Suddenly, a rustle startles him, and his eyes open wide again as adrenaline shoots through his body. Peering down, he catches a shadowy glimpse of a young moose, sniffing at the frozen bit of biscuit he dropped hours ago. At least the evil robots didn't kill the animals. At that thought, a sob escapes his throat. His next thought strikes terror into his heart, which races long into the night.

Finally, an eternity later, the faint ray of pink-orange sunrise glows over the horizon. He can't feel his feet anymore, and he's weak from hunger. Luckily, he's had a good supply of water with the snow draping the branches. Calculating his risks—staying in the tree or climbing down and heading home—he knows what he has to do.

Slowly and with great effort, he begins his descent. Normally, he could scramble down from Sylvester in mere seconds, but because of his wooziness and frozen feet, he has to use his arms almost exclusively, making his trip down to the ground much longer. When he finally reaches the base of the tree, he tries to straighten, takes a huge breath, collapses, straightens again, and looks all around. Coast clear. With the help of a large stick several yards away, Aleksi begins the short trek home. He's never felt so clumsy in his life.

The door to their family's cabin is open. Aleksi's jaw drops, and his heart beats wildly in his chest as he creeps inside. "Aiti? Aiti? Isa?" He hobbles into the kitchen. A pool of blood lies right in the middle of the kitchen. It's obvious. Aleksi immediately turns his head, shutting his eyes, wobbling, skipping blindly in the other direction through the snow as his whimpers fill the air. But then he can't run anymore, and he sinks into the deep, deep snow, retching and sobbing, not caring anymore who hears. He can't go back in. He can't. Where's his father?

"Aleksi?"

He startles, raising his head toward a frantic, concerned voice. Instinctively, he pulls himself up and peeks over the mound into which he fell. He chokes back a sob of relief. These are his people. He must get to them whoever they are. He must, but he can't feel his feet, and his legs are rubber, sending him tumbling to the ground again. He looks up. Someone's peering down at him—Dr. Kurki, Kristal's grandfather. He feels strong arms scooping him up.

"Lumi, Lumi, it's Aleksi Salo—"

"Dr. Kurki? Ole kiltti, ole kiltti, ole..."

And he throws his arms around Dr. Kurki's neck, howling inconsolably. Mrs. Kurki's there too now, and the three of them hug and hug and cry until they can't hug anymore, and Aleksi knows they have to do something, and Dr. Kurki says, "Aleksi, you will come with us. They've taken Kristal. But they did not kill her. We need to travel to the US where they are placing her for the time being."

"But my aiti? My isa? Pappa?"

Mrs. Kurki bursts into tears. "Oh, Aleksi, poor dear boy. Hug me. Hug me tight. I must tell you. They're gone. Everyone's gone." Her voice drops, and she whispers. "We're so, so sorry."

Aleksi is silent, his arms to his sides as Mrs. Kurki enfolds his small body within her thick, downy coat. Finally, she asks, "Aleksi, Aleksi, where were you? How did you escape?"

Aleksi can't speak. He points toward Sylvester, the pine.

"You were in the tree? All night? Oh lord, you will need medical attention. Voitto, we need to get this child to hospital. Let's get you warmed up, poor Aleksi, poor child. Please come with us. Let us help you. After you are better, we will leave for Turku then to Montana. Kiire... Kiire... Hurry, please..."

Dr. Kurki carries Aleksi to their cabin, where they wrap him in thick blankets. Soon a snow taxi appears on the road about a half a mile walk from their cabin.

Turku then Montana. Where's Montana? In the span of one day and one night, Aleksi Salo's world has turned upside down and inside out. But a tiny ray of hope still shines in the faces of his new caregivers, Voitto and Lumi Kurki.

Twenty-Nine

* * * * * * * * * ● * * * * * * * * *

February 1, 2027

I wake to the sound of footsteps. My mother is pacing back and forth in the hallway, talking to someone on her comcard.

"Yep, you heard right. First, my beloved child has come back to me—a miracle in and of itself. But not only that—oh, I shouldn't even think of it yet—but maybe my husband? And now my mother? My father? All these years, I was sure they were gone forever."

I hear a faint but excited voice on the other end.

Then my mother answers, "I know, Blanca. Hey, *guapa*, I'll see you at the meeting. Gotta run. *Hasta la vista.*" Mutsi sticks her comcard in the pocket of her black pants, a new pair I haven't seen before. It only has a diamond button at the top of the zipper. A violet jacket tops a white shell, and they're all sparkly like tiny diamonds have been sprinkled over the fabric. She must be doing something important today. Oh, the meeting—the QC meeting—and then a ceremony of some kind.

My stomach flutters just thinking about it. I've been so sheltered, so pampered for the last few days. But I can't stay here forever. I stare at the ceiling. Miniature rainbows dance from hanging crystals all over the room.

Mutsi stops at my doorway, not realizing my eyes are open and gazes upward, whispering, "Thank you, heaven. Thank you, angels of grace. But why here? Why now? Is it true? Did you write the prophecy? We scientists are a bit skeptical when it comes to prophesies, but I swear if you deliver as promised, I will be forever grateful for your mercy."

I turn my head, still on the pillow.

Mutsi jumps. "Oh, Krissie." She looks a little sheepish. "I often talk to myself. I was just giving thanks for your father, your grandmother, and your grandfather. You're a miracle all by yourself, but now I even—"

I suddenly remember. A shiver runs up and down my spine. I would give anything not to have to tell her what may have happened that night. But I can't hold back this crucial piece of information. It wouldn't be fair. It's the right thing to do, but it's damn hard. I take a deep breath.

"Mutsi."

"Krissie babe, I hope I didn't waken you. You were sleeping so well. You really needed that. Oh, and since I'll bet you're getting a little tired of wearing either a hospital gown or a Dolcany Demons sweatshirt, I put some extra clothes in the closet here. They may not exactly be your size or style, but if you want to try them on—"

"Mutsi—"

"Yes, sweetie?"

"I… I need to tell you something."

"Tell me something?"

"The night Dad escaped from jail."

Her face instantly pales. "Yes?"

"As we were running to the car, he, well, Dad fired two shots into the house. The Gab—Voitto and Lumi's house."

Mutsi's eyes widen, and I see the fear in her expression. "Pauli? Fired shots? He's a pacifist. He's never even owned a—" and then she realizes what she's saying. Was he the real Pauli that night? Or…

I nod. "You're right. He was a peaceful man. I didn't think he owned a gun either, not even to hunt. But he did. I'm hoping it was just a warning shot. I think, you know, to keep them from following us. But I couldn't see, and honestly, I should have, but I just couldn't look back."

Oh, she's really pale now. She closes her eyes, takes a big breath, then opens her eyes, nodding. "All the more reason to get going. We have to find out what's happened to them, to Pauli, whoever or what-ever he is now. We must get moving. But oh, Krissie, are you ready?"

I nod, give her my best I'm-fine look. "Oh, sure."

"Really?"

I detect anxiety in her voice. "Mutsi, what is it?"

"The QC. The meeting has been scheduled for today. They want to meet you. Of course, Zola, Blanca, and Dr. Bob have already had the pleasure. Oh, and Onni, of course. But the others have been dying to see you ever since you arrived. Most of them remember you as a toddler, and time is of the essence. But I don't want to rush."

"No, I'm ready."

"All right then. After our meeting, we'll have the ceremony. Then we'll have a firm plan for how to proceed."

How to proceed. I'm a little nervous, but I don't want to show any hesitation. "Sounds great." My recoup and cocooning time was sorely needed and appreciated, but I can't be selfish anymore. It's time to go.

"What should I wear?"

"That's not important. As I said, if you want a change, just check out the closet. Whatever is most comfortable for you. Let me go fix tea." And she bounces off to the kitchenette. I hope she's okay. I hope her parents and my grandparents are okay.

I go through the outfits in the closet, each item decorated with diamonds in one way or another. There's her cloak again. The one she wore when I first met her in the forest. Gingerly, I reach for it, holding it up with both hands. Queens would kill for something like this. Then her words echo in my mind, "And I would command all diamonds turn to snowflakes." Oh, so that's why—ah. Makes per-fect sense now. If each of these diamonds suddenly morphed into a drop of water... I go through the rest of the clothes, choosing a simple white flowy skirt and light-pink V-neck sweater, rimmed in diamonds. Not because I want to show off, but because there is not one single article of clothing in my mother's rather sparse closet that doesn't have some kind of diamond decoration. The skirt falls to the middle of my calves. The sweater fits perfectly. I must admit, the tiny diamonds adorning the sweater are beautiful. On Earth, no matter what outfit I chose from this closet, I could pass for a Hollywood star. Well, my clothes could, anyway. Oh, but shoes. I look down and see three pairs—two flat and one pair of sneakers, which she was wearing the day we walked through the passages. I choose the beige plain flats. I guess we're both size seven and a half. I shake my head. There are no mirrors here, so I just finger comb my hair, paying special attention to my damn cowlick and hoping I look presentable. I walk into the main room, ready to jump on our scooters. Instead, I gape.

My sweet mutsi has magically transformed the room into a beautiful, meditative sanctuary, silk flowers in luminous colors on every surface including the floor. The walls shimmer in shades of muted pinks and peach, reflecting the fire glow of dozens of LED lit candles, surrounded by crystals of all colors, set high and low, all around the room. Mutsi's eyes are shining as I bask in the sacredness, the soft reverence of what must be a ceremony about to begin. I shoot Mutsi a puzzled look. But then I know.

She pats the couch. "First things first. Sit."

"For Tad?" I'm dumbfounded. She'd mentioned a funeral of sorts, but I didn't believe her. She has no time for this. I sit. Although I'm still hoping against hope Tad is still hiding somewhere, she has shown such thoughtfulness with this gesture, especially since Tad is of the enemy that destroyed her family, that I have to go along. She's doing it all for my sake, alone. I look up at her, waiting. What next?

"You've spoken about your brother a little. Tell me more. What was Tad like? What special memories of Tad would you like to share?"

Oh, she wants a eulogy, of sorts. My brother, my twin. How to describe him? How to recount our life together, the days, weeks, years? I begin relating—for the second time but in more detail—how Tad would always look out for me, always reminding Dad where I was so he wouldn't worry. I talk about how I taught Tad to create and imagine, and although autistic, he seemed to pick up pretend play like a duck to water. I describe how we would play hide-and-seek, take nature walks through the forest behind our home, find our special trees; how Dad gave us each a set of binoculars one year on our mutual birthday so we could spot birds, mostly warblers, flycatchers, but oh, yeah, there was this one time we saw the most colorful western meadowlark—our state bird. Tad was so excited he chanted his wow-that's-so-cool phrase *Five Star Pictures Presents*.

Mutsi frowns. "Five Star Pictures Presents? I forget. Tell me about that again."

Then, of course, I have to explain all that to Mutsi. Then I tell her how we would collect nature souvenirs—stones, feathers, leaves, and make patterns. And then use our imaginations to create stories, worlds, fantasies, anything. Oh, and the few times it snowed, well, I had to tell Mutsi all about sledding down Marsten's hill, playing tag in the snow. And how Tad would just take the bullying in stride. I relate the recent incident when Jackson Hynes got into his face and called him an alien after Tad had told him not to call me a bitch in his own strange, stilted language. And then Tad got sent to the principal's office. Not fair. I ended up in the restroom crying. It broke my heart. I suddenly realize the more I talk about him, the more I'm convinced he was real; he *is* real. Could I have bonded with a nonfeeling robot, an AI device that couldn't care less if I had lived or died? No. He *did* care, didn't he? I could go on and on. I need to end this Tad eulogy-of-sorts as I know Mutsi's too polite to say we have to hurry. But I know we do, so I just lean on Mutsi's shoulder. The candles suddenly flicker all at once, like a ghost passing through the room.

"Mutsi, where does love begin and end? How could I possibly have loved a machine?"

I meet Mutsi's eyes, pleading and blinking away tears.

We hug, and I love her all the more for not thinking I'm crazy and for accepting that whatever or whoever this Tad thing was—Cancri or not—he was very special to me. Mutsi dabs her eyes. Then she wipes my cheeks.

"Hey, Krissie. I found a poem."

"A poem?"

"About love. It's short but sweet. May I read it?"

"Well, sure. Yeah."

She holds up a small leather-bound volume with an attached pink ribbon marking a page. "My diary. The year your father and I got married." A small white note and dried rose petal fall to the floor.

She stoops, carefully retrieves them, fingers the petal for a moment, sighing. For a minute, I think she's going to burst into tears. But she doesn't. Unfolding the note, she begins:

> *Who is to say that your love is not real*
> *Whether lover or sister or brother*
> *Who is to say that your love's wrong or right*
> *If you simply just love one another*
> *At the end of the journey*
> *The end of the road*
> *Your life's shallow pleasures shall scatter*
> *But those who were able to love and love well*
> *Through eternity, their love will matter.*

Silence. I peer over her shoulder, blinking away my tears. "That looks like Dad's handwriting."

She smiles. "Yep."

"Seriously? He wrote it? Or did he copy it from somewhere?"

"Nope, wrote it himself."

"I never knew Dad wrote poetry."

"He didn't except for this one. He was a scientist, not a poet. As you can tell." She gives a little chuckle. "But there was a time that I doubted us. I got a little jealous of his work and was afraid, and I must admit, a little pouty. And he reassured me by doing something totally against his nature."

"Writing a poem, just for you."

"Yes."

"Mutsi, he must have really loved you."

My mother nods, closes her eyes, then opens them. They're glistening through her smile. "Your father knew what true love was, at such a young age. He was an old soul." Her voice cracks. "See, Krissie, our hearts and souls need love as our lungs need air. By loving Tad, you sent pure love right up to the heavens, sweetening the entire universe. Whether or not he was able to love you back, it really doesn't matter, as your father's poem so authentically reminds us. So

Krissie, my sweet girl, remember that. We never waste the energy of pure love."

Tingles slither all over my body. I take her hand. How could I ever have questioned her identity? Mutsi gathers me in her arms, and we sit, huddled together, tears dribbling down our cheeks, thinking our own thoughts. She's acting like she has all the time in the world, but I know she doesn't, so I mentally brace myself, pat her hand and stand up, sniffing and wiping my tears away with the back of my hand. She does the same, smooths her pants, then smiles.

"Well, okay then." She lets go a huge sigh. "Oh, Kristal, at the very time when we should be slowing down, getting to know each other, making new memories, we must hurry, hurry, hurry. Time is not our friend right now, but good things are to come. We must believe that. Ready to reunite with your QC family?"

Oh, wow. I sniffle again, clear my throat, and nod. Suddenly, from outside, I hear a rhythmic flapping or tapping. I look at Mutsi, frowning. She just smiles, beckoning me to follow her.

We venture out onto her walkway, squinting in the bright light of day beneath the biodome. I look ahead, gasp. At the end of the walkway sits a square black coach atop Hakkua's massive back. Onni stands beside him. Suddenly I remember and cringe. These two Birds have every right to be furious with me, not to mention the water I've stolen from their species. I've hurt them in more ways than one.

But these magnificent creatures seem unfazed. Haukka crouches down, turns his head toward Mutsi and me, nodding. Onni has something tucked under his wing—a ladder. My mother smiles, reaches forward, and gently extracts it, then expertly places it onto the entrance of the coach. Then she turns to the Birds and bows.

"Onni, Haukka, I can't thank you enough. You saved my precious girl." Both Birds return her bow.

She whispers in my ear, "Birds are very forgiving creatures."

Gingerly, I touch Haukka's wing, then Onni's. "Haukka, I'm... I'm so sorry I scared you when I slid off your tail feather. I... I was wrong to do that. Onni, I'm sorry you had to leave your mission to come and help take me to the city. I hope I didn't hurt your back when I fell on you. It was very selfish of me."

Haukka turns its head and stares at me with its huge black eyes. He blinks and gives me another little nod. Onni is nodding too. "Onni proud to save Kristal." He closes his eyes then slowly reopens them.

I feel humbled. I look at him once more. Does he look a little sleepy? "Onni, are you okay?"

"Okay, Kristal. Ready for QC meeting. Raaah."

Mutsi gestures toward the ladder. "Our ride will be short. Climb aboard."

Onni opens his beak. "Onni fly alongside, then join meeting."

Mutsi nods. She turns to me. "Shall we?"

I follow my mother up the ladder and into the coach. She expertly collapses the ladder, pulling it up and onto the floor. The seats feel smooth as satin. Haukka lifts his wings, and we are airborne. My head lightly bumps the back of the seat, and then I settle in.

We sail past the hospital building and head in the same direction as Onni. I hang on tightly to the edges of my seat as we fly higher and higher. Two windows on each side of the coach are partially open, and I close my eyes, letting the breeze caress my face. Okay, Kristal, positive thought. I will relax and let happen what may. I am so grateful for my mother, whom I thought was dead. I am hopeful that—

Mutsi interrupts my inner pep talk. "Almost there," she says softly.

Suddenly, I'm thirsty. Instinctively I push my hand in the pocket of my skirt, my fingers grasping the flask Dr. B gave me at the Citadel Hospital. Just as I would casually reach for my steel water bottle at home. I'm about to unscrew the cap when Dr. Bob Smith's words echo in my mind: *Do not drink until you are completely parched.* Am I completely parched? Not quite. And what am I thinking? This water isn't mine anyway. I jerk my hand out of my pocket like the flask were a hot iron.

Haukka suddenly lurches to the right, and we are swooping down, preparing to land. My first close-up glimpse of Quantum City takes my breath away. At the entrance, sparkling gates stand between towers as high as skyscrapers of solid diamond. They must be. Smaller structures gleam light rose; walkways are alight with chunks of pink crystal every few feet. Rainbow holograms dance in the air. All of a sudden, I feel a light bump. We skid for a few feet, then stop. We have landed. Mutsi grabs the ladder, attaching it to the entrance of the coach. Its rungs unfurl to the ground. Onni is already there, waiting.

Mutsi leads, and I follow. We're on one of the winding walkways leading to a tall gate topped by crystal spires hundreds of feet in the air. We follow my mother through that gate, another sparkling gateway, and then we're in a narrow stone corridor that reminds me of our first journey, from Birdland to the city, except this passageway is more symmetrical and the lighting is more formal. Every few feet, recessed sconces glow like tiny blue-gray moons. We stride quickly in single file for several minutes. At a fork, my mother beckons us to the left, through another archway and down a steep, crooked set of stairs, made of the same material as the hospital's entryway—diamond surface but with sandpaper-like grittiness, so our feet and claws have traction. The stairway curves round and round, a steep spiral, until finally we step onto a landing. I turn to Onni. He is struggling down the steps. I fall back to help him, placing a hand on his right wing.

"Onni, you sure you're okay?"

"Onni okay. Almost there." He half stumbles down to the ground. It must be harder for claws than feet to navigate these passageways.

"One more pathway before the doors," Mutsi announces. I'm not sure what she means by "doors," but I figure I will soon find out. We all round a curve in the passageway. I've got my eyes peeled on the back of Mutsi's head. Damned if that cowlick isn't exactly like mine. I smile. How could I ever...

She stops. "Here."

Holy moly. Facing us is the most massive door I've ever seen. It must be as tall as a two-story house and about half as wide. Surprisingly, it's made out of exquisite, dark wood, carved like the grand entrances to ancient cathedrals I remember from illustrations and movies of medieval Europe. The top is arched, and all over are filigree patterns. Castle doors from Earth would usually have metal decoration, but here, the patterns are no doubt made of diamond. The arches are layered with strips of wooden roses, and the handles, one on each side, are circular diamond pulls. I search my mother's face for an explanation—their history, their construction. Instead, she places her palm on the crack between the two panels, ignoring the pulls.

"Back up."

We do. I hear a low rumbling, then a slow creak, as the panels swing outward. She steps over a low threshold. We follow, finding ourselves yet in another winding passageway. A few moments later, another door appears, somewhat smaller than the first. Like the first, she places her hand on it, and it opens. We enter that one then another and another, each smaller than the last, until we've passed through six doors in all. She stops at the seventh door and announces, "The last one. Here we are." It too is carved from wood, but this one is only slightly taller and wider than a human being. Taking a deep breath, she presses a diamond button on the side like a doorbell. Nothing happens. Then a faint smile forms on her lips as the door slowly creaks open.

A tall, elegant elderly man stoops, passing through the door. Eyeing us up and down, he clasps his hands like a delighted child, smiling broadly. "Welcome! Welcome to the QC Chamber, revered guests. Such a delight to have you back, Myra dear." They hug.

Instantly, I feel comforted. He reminds me of a craggy old ship's captain from tales of Nordic Sea Dad used to read to me. Though he wears no seaman's cap, he's dressed in a navy-blue waistcoat and sports a trim white beard, dangling in a neat triangle past his Adam's apple. His face is leathered, but his gray eyes crinkle with warmth. He exudes playful joy, like a jolly old grandpa, or even Old Sam's face from the pine tree in our backyard forest. I can't help but smile.

My mother and this old captain are laughing and crying together as they disengage.

"Meerakka, my dear. I trust the reunion weeth your daughter has been one of deep joy. *Ihme.* What a meeracle." He turns to me. "*Ihme* means 'miracle' in Finnish. You will most likely hear *ihme* quite often from now on. Praise be. Now all are gathered for our meeting

249

followed by the honor ceremony. Onni One, you will be our number 1 guest of honor for saving thees dear girl."

Onni bows deeply. "Onni had help."

The old man nods. "Yes, indeed. We will honor all at the ceremony. Now the moment I've been waiting for—let me get a good look."

Onni steps aside as Mutsi takes my hand and propels me forward. "She's grown."

"Powers that be. She certainly has." The gentleman bows, takes my hand, and brushes it with his lips. "Yes, indeed, a meeracle after so many years. I must admeet, Meeraka, we were quite frightened when you left our Lucy in hopes the mysterious message would lead you to your long-lost daughter. But now that she ees found, our relief ees boundless. The prophecy's time ees drawing near, for whatever that portends. But let us conseeder thees a good sign for all, eh?

His accent is Finnish, much like the Gabriels'. Whoops, I mean my grandparents.

Dr. EJ's face lights up, and he shakes his head, chuckling. "You are quite a beet older than the last time I laid eyes on you. A marvel. One we never thought would come to pass. You so resemble your eencredible mother. But, ah, I am being rude. Come een, come een. Eet's time you meet the Quantum Community Council."

Oh, boy. I take a deep breath.

He lets out a sigh, pursing his lips. "What's left of us, anyway."

I should just stay quiet. But before I can catch it, the QB flies out of my mouth. "May I... I mean—can you tell me more about this prophecy?"

Dr. EJ raises an eyebrow then glances at Mutsi and gives a little nod.

"Oh, my dear, now that you are here, eet ees mandatory that you learn all about eet. After all, according to thees prophecy, found by yours truly right here een thees chamber on our first meesion een 2014, you are the one, my dear."

My stomach flutters. "The one?"

"The one and only Crystal Child—destined to save humanity."

And then he winks.

Thirty

○ ○ ○ ○ ○ ○ ○ ○ ○ ○ ◉ ○ ○ ○ ○ ○ ○ ○ ○ ○ ○

February 1, 2027

I'm destined to…what? Not only can I absolutely not wrap my head around that last statement, but what was that wink for? What did it mean? I'd better squish this question bee back into the black box, or I'll faint dead away. Dad used to say that "when all else fails, stay in the present moment." Right foot, left foot. One second at a time. Okay. Tick, tick. Here we go.

Dr. EJ bows, leads with outstretched arm as Mutsi, Onni, and I step into the chamber. I thought for such a tiny door, we'd all be smooshed into a closet. But the chamber is colossal, like an ancient cathedral. I almost trip over myself, staring at all the magnificence: high-beamed ceilings, polished wood paneling all the way to the ceiling's edge, the top half carved with swirls and designs in snowflake patterns. Tall bookshelves house great volumes, although I can't make out the titles as many seem to be in Finnish, Chinese, Spanish, Arabic, maybe? Oh, those are in English: *Dance of the Photons: From Einstein to Teleportation* by Anton Zeilinger, *Healing with Light Frequencies* by Jerry Sargeant, *Quantum Computing: An Applied Approach* by Jack D. Hidary, and *Black Holes and Baby Universes* by Stephen Hawking. Wow, they actually read and understand all this? Then thoughts intrude. *Seriously, am I the Crystal Child? Me? With books like these? I'm the one? Shut up, Kris. Stuff it. It's a joke. Has to be. Don't think. Don't think. Don't think. Present moment.* My knees apparently didn't get the memo, as they are wobbling like Jell-O. *Whatever. Keep going, Kris.*

My mother gently turns me around to face a long table at the far end of the room on a rhombus-shaped platform. Thirteen thick dark wooden chairs surround it, reminding me of those immense dining tables in old English castles. Weird. I would think futuristic equipment and furniture like those in reruns of *Star Trek* would be more like it. This is getting odder by the moment, not to mention I'm the—*Stop. God, Kris. Let it go.*

I do a quick count—nine people so far. And one Bird, as Onni has taken his seat already. Paper and pens are strewn all around, as well as electronic tablets. The chattering I heard when I stepped in the door has stopped, and a hush falls over the chamber. Then all of a sudden, they're standing and applauding and smiling and waving, looking back and forth at Mutsi then at me. Some say my name. Some are giving us a thumbs-up. And are those tears? I swallow hard. They seem so welcoming that I don't even feel the familiar blush burning my cheeks. In fact, I feel a sense of kinship, like we're all family. Well, we are, sort of. Dad probably knew these people. A wave of sadness engulfs me at the thought of him. Before I can spiral down further, mercifully, Dr. EJ begins speaking to the group.

"*Ihme, Ihme*," Dr. EJ addresses everyone. "No, you're not seeing things. She's really back. Eleven years."

They keep clapping, cheering, waving, and grinning. I look to Mutsi for guidance. She's just beaming. I turn back to the group, offering a lame little smile. I'm too much in awe to relax. But it's a good nervous, if there is such a thing. What these people are doing is the very opposite of the wolves in Mr. Gabriel's class. I have to remind myself that deep inside I know these people—every single one. They obviously know me. And what's even more miraculous, they really seem to care about me.

Dr. EJ is laughing. "All right, everyone, eentroductions, or should I say, reeentroductions are in order. Ms. Kreestal, I present to you the twelve surviving members of the QC who now make up the ruling board for our Quantum Community on Lucy, the Diamond Star." They immediately sit back down, still grinning.

Dr. EJ points to Dr. B. "First is Dr. Xu Zhanqi, brain scientist and neurosurgeon. But we all just call him Bob Smith or Dr. B."

Dr. B responds, "I don't trust you to say my Chinese name correctly. But Bob Smith? I make it easy for you."

Everyone chuckles; some nod. Of course, I recognize him from the Citadel Hospital. He turns to me and gives me one of his reverent bows. I join my palms and bow back, imitating his gesture.

"Second, Elk Kivi, all around handyman and problem-solver."

He nods shyly.

Dr. EJ continues around the table. He introduces Mutsi's friend, Blanca, as the third member of the group. She is an expert botanist and nutritional expert. Fourth, Johann Rajala, quantum astrophysicist. Fifth, Jaak Niskanen, computer guru and geologist. Sixth, Dahab Akhtar, quantum engineer and teleport specialist.

Dr. EJ adds, "Kreestal, Dahab helped program your pendant."

I notice Dahab blushing like I do, and then I notice Mutsi's lips in a thin line. Dahab smiles brightly. "I understand you got to meet the Birds. No harm done then, right, Myra?" Her eyes dart to Onni, who nods his massive head and blinks. A little too slowly, I notice.

Am I allowed to speak? I'll keep it short. "You're...you're all amazing."

Mutsi is still glaring ever so slightly at Dahab. Ah, let it go, Mutsi. No harm done. I'm feeling less nervous and more grateful by the minute.

The seventh is Zola Khumolo, who gives me a huge smile and thumbs-up. I smile back. I'm really feeling more at home now.

Number eight is Hale Waara, military and security expert, and general of the Diamond Star Armed Forces.

So that's the general. When Dr. EJ calls his name, he stands. He's tough, muscular. Massive shoulders. Not bald, but with a really short bristle of hair. What did Dad call that? Oh, yeah, a crewcut. He's a commanding presence for sure.

After he gives me a quick nod, he turns to Mutsi. "Excuse me for speaking out of turn, but, Myrakka, at this very moment, three of my soldiers are preparing for the Earth trip to rescue your parents. They will be departing soon. I will accompany them. I also uh"—he clears his throat—"received your other message." He throws a quick glance at me. Obviously, he's referring to my colossal mistake—giving Tad the code to the Diamond Star.

I suppress a wince and swallow hard. Because of me, this man must get his army ready for an attack here—on the Diamond Star. Mutsi told me not to feel guilty, but I do anyway.

The general turns back to Mutsi. "We're preparing, confident we can ward off the enemy at this stage no matter where or when they appear."

Boy is his voice deep. I can imagine how it instills confidence in his troops.

My mother covers her face with both hands, sniffs, and nods. Then she drops her hands, mouthing, "Thank you."

General Waara replies, "Dr. Makkinen, the honor is all ours."

I look to Dr. EJ. He's beaming from ear to ear, nodding. So they're going to rescue the Gabriels, er, the Kurkis, my grandparents. All along they were part of this incredible scientific community. If I had only known, then—*pow*. My stomach lurches. The shots ringing out that night slam into my brain. Mutsi has totally forgotten what I said. She's in denial. I don't blame her. So am I. They're all assuming the Kurkis are still alive. Well, but they would still have to go to Earth and check, right? I just can't give them more bad news, so I stay silent. This just isn't the right time.

Dr. EJ holds out his arms toward Onni, our ninth member, the only Bird representative. Onni nods toward me. I smile. Is he a little groggy or something? Anyone else noticing? Now he's got me a little worried. But the doctor keeps going.

"Tenth, Yua Kikuchi, veterinarian from Yokohama, Japan." He explains how she helps take care of our Birds and the few other animals they were able to teleport, such as chickens for eggs, dogs, cats, and a few hamsters for companionship. "Some of our citizens just had to bring their pets along, like myself," he says, smiling. "They play an essential role for all of us in aiding our mental health. I know my husky, Koda, has been a balm to my soul here on Lucy. Koda—my big furry bed warmer."

Everyone chuckles. Dr. Kikuchi nods. "Pets are not luxury. They are essential for our well-being."

Dr. EJ beams. "Absolutely. Dr. Kikuchi is kept quite busy." No wonder I noticed her checking out Onni too, with discerning eyes. I think she's as concerned as I am. He just seems a little, well, off. Glad the Diamond Star is blessed with an animal expert.

Dr. EJ gestures toward my mother and me. Mutsi gently pulls my hand, guiding me up the four steps to our seats. She pulls out the empty chair beside her, pats the seat, and I sit down next to her. I feel so out of place among these mental giants; so small and uninformed. At least, they're friendly mental giants.

Dr. EJ winks again. Maybe that's something he just does a lot. "Eleven, Dr. Myrakka Makkeenen, astrophysics and communications specialeest." He chuckles as he nods toward me. "You also know her now as Mother.

"Mutsi," corrects my mother, almost a whisper. "She remembers."

Dr. EJ and others laugh, clap in delight. Dr. EJ's smile is warm. "Ahhh, what a miraculous memory, Kreestal. I hope you recall only the good ones."

"Dr. Khumolo helped me with the bad ones."

Dr. EJ is nodding. "Well done, Zola. We certainly have benefitted from your compassionate expertise. As we have benefitted from all of you here on Lucy."

General Waara's voice suddenly booms. "You did the right thing, Myra, going back to Earth. In hindsight, your bravery is to be commended."

I look toward Mutsi, expecting her to be smiling. She's not. "And would you have forbidden me again, Hale? I was not being a *fool* as I recall the term you used. This mission was borne from a mother's utter desperation, and even so, my risk was quite calculated." She grabs my hand under the table. Whoa, Mama Lion. I imagine a knife cutting the air. Or her fangs. I'm a little embarrassed, and am about to try to calm her down when she adds, "Or as the T-shirts say in the catalogues, "You can't scare me. I have a daughter." The whole group dissolves in laughter, and the tension melts. Okay, good for Mutsi. I'm really going to have to find that T-shirt when we all get home to Earth. Oooh, a little flutter. If? *No, Achilles, not if. When. When we get home to Earth.*

Clearing his throat, Dr. EJ chirps brightly, "And I am Dr. EJ."
He bounds up the steps like a man half his age, taking his place at
the head of the table.

"EJ stands for Einstein Junior," says Elk in a quiet voice, but
grinning from ear to ear. "He's sort of smart."

The whole group laughs. I keep wanting to call him "captain"
because of his looks, but he's not really. He's a genius scientist. Dr. EJ
turns to me. "They kid. My eeneetials stand for Eikka Jutila, hence
EJ, not Einstein Junior, I'm afraid." Then Dr. EJ's face becomes
serious. "Kreestal, now that you have met our council, you must be
briefed. I understand that your mother has deescussed some of the
issues we were going to eentroduce. We were a bit concerned but
respect your mother's decision. The fact that you already have some
background information will save us even more valuable time. Now
we shall deescuss the origin of the Quantum Community, our vision
and mission, and how thee prophecy ties into it all. Then we will lay
out our immediate plans. And you, my dear Kreestal, are an intreen-
sic part of it all."

A tingle zips up my spine. Finally, I know where I came from.
I know where I belong. I am part of the Quantum Community. No
wonder I always felt a little out of kilter all my life. This is what I've
been missing. Now I know why my so-called science teacher acted so
strangely, why he was trying to tell me about a planet but was afraid
to say the name out loud. I know why my brother seemed different.
I know why Alek said I would find my niche someday, and I know
why my father—well, I don't really know why he went berserk that
morning, but I know it had something to do with the Cancris. And
I know who the diamond lady in the forest was and why the Bird
attacked me. It's a good start. I can't wait to have the rest of my QBs
answered—like where is Dad now? And where is Tad? And how in
hell are we going to conquer the Cancris and move back to Earth?
And why does a prophecy name me as the Crystal Child, who will fix
everything? These are the most enormous QBs ever to buzz around
in my brain. I try to look relaxed, but my insides feel like they're
about to fall apart. What will I find out? *Breathe, Kristal, breathe.*

Dr. EJ places his elbows on the table, steepling his hands. "Thees debriefing must necessarily be short because of our present circumstances. But rest assured. You will learn all you need to know now and then the rest as we proceed in our mission. So, Kreestal, my dear, our story technically begeens in 1992 when a group of dedicated and concerned scientists gathered to make a formal proclamation: Our planet Earth was in grave danger: atmosphere, water resources, oceans, soil, forests, and living species. You see, the rapid release of GHGs—"

I wince. I'm not up on my terminology. I'm going to look so stupid. But I have to know. "GHGs?"

Surprisingly, no one laughs. Neither are they staring at me like a pack of wolves ready to pounce. Wow, they're all acting so respectful.

In fact, Dr. EJ responds, "Ah. I applaud your curiosity. Never be afraid to ask questions. That ees how we learn. As they say, 'Only the ignorant have all the answers.' GHG stands for greenhouse gasses—carbon dioxide, nitrous oxide, methane. Nasty stuff when eet accumulates. Our current crisis ees different from anything the Earth has experienced before because of the speed at which change ees occurring. That ees why we must get back to Earth as queeckly as posseeble. Although our time here on Lucy has not been completely wasted, eet has surely cramped our style a bit."

Chuckles and nods ripple around the table, but I can tell they're all as serious as Dr. EJ. He continues, "Our Quantum Community, or QC for short, was founded weeth one vision: to bring the best scientific minds together to heal planet Earth. Eet is now quite evident that taking our planet for granted, believing its resources eenfinite—well, that philosophy is no longer appropriate—not that eet ever was."

Everyone murmurs agreement.

Dr. EJ sighs. "Weeth these concerns in mind, een the year 2002, three scientists who taught post-graduate studies at the University of Helsinki and became great friends—Dr. Bob Smith, Brima Kalokoh, and myself—founded the Quantum Community. We placed *quantum* een the title because many of our deescoveries are of a quantum nature as we progress eento the twenty-first century. We raised enough private funds and government grants to begeen our project. Two years later, our Quantum Community was born and our first meesion—Project EarthHeal—was launched. We isolated ourselves far enough off the grid so our work could progress een peace and weeth as little disruption as possible. We bought eighty-one acres far een the North of Feenland—Lapland—and there we began our work. Brima left the QC, securing a position weeth the Finnish Meenistry of the Environment as liaison between thees governmental body and our scienteefic community. Brima helped keep our little community as secret as possible." Dr. EJ gestures toward Dr. B. and Bob. "As you all can see—ees still weeth us. Praise be."

Everyone smiles; some nod as a respectful gesture.

"Over the next few years, we added over two hundred brilliant and dedicated people from all over the world—eencluding your mother and father, both young scientists fresh out of universeety. And we collaborated weeth others around the globe on the most incredible projects. But the one deescovery made by our group alone that astounded even us was"—he leans toward me and whispers, a twinkle in his eye—"quantum teleportation, converting atoms to energy, transporting the energy to another location, and reassembling thee atoms. Makes your head spin, doesn't eet?"

I nod, recalling my awesome teleportation experience to the Diamond Star.

He straightens up. "About a decade earlier, een 2004, a group of scienteests deescovered a white dwarf star that had shrunk to eets carbon core—pure diamond. Naturally, thees was our first destination. Unlimited funding is every scientist's fervent wish. And, een 2014, our first mission was successful beyond our wildest dreams not only because we teleported successfully and found that Lucy ees, indeed, a diamond star and thus could provide unlimited funding for our many projects, but we also found evidence of previous visitors. We not only found a huge cache of stored water and these magnificent doors leading to this very chamber, but right een the meedle of this table"—he jabs his finger toward a long wooden table, adjacent to the one where we're all sitting—"we found a prophecy. Very puzzling, but due to eets uncannily accurate predictions and information, we could not ignore eet. So weeth our first diamond een hand, plus the prophecy, we returned to Earth. Shortly after we had celebrated our discoveries, we began phase 2—to terreform the Diamond Star, put a biodome een place, and send groups there to begin harvesting the diamonds. We were halfway through phase 2 of our mission when a being showed up in my office een 2016, an AIET."

"AIET?"

"Artificially intelligent extraterrestrial. I know. Quite a mouthful, eh? Seence they were from the exoplanet Cancri e, we just call them Cancris." Dr. EJ continues. "When we first began our QC, we thought perhaps eef we connected weeth advanced civilizations from other planets, we could collaborate for the good of both our species. So we sent out signals following a similar protocol as that used by The Ohio State University in 1977 that yielded the WOW signal."

"The WOW signal?"

"A strong radio signal was received in August of 1977 by Ohio State's Big Ear Radio project. Six-E-Q-U-J-5 may not mean much to you, but to the astronomers working on the project, eet was the strongest evidence yet that we might be able to find extraterrestrial beings able to communicate with us. It was named the WOW signal because that's what the scientist who first found the readout wrote after circling the code.

We were hoping we might get a similar communication. But we—I—was horribly naive. Because ultimately, although our protocol was successful in form, the beings who found our signal were not at all interested in mutual projects. I weel never forget that day..."

Thirty-One

February 26, 2016

Dr. EJ is speaking to a programmer on the phone. They're speaking rapidly back and forth in Finnish. "Yes, yes, Agda. Just have Jaak reclassify and move the document P folder to the regular database. Yes, that's the prophecy. We can still work on it, but it doesn't need the extra security. We can declassify from the top level. It's been two years. Oh, uh, and schedule a meeting for next week. Yes, Tuesday or Wednesday. Just the inner council this time. The—wait. Hang on..." Something metallic? That's the second time it's moved past the window. What the... "Uh, Agda, let me get back with you." He clicks off, pushes back his chair, stands, frowning, and yells, "Hei!"

Silence. "Hei!" And then it appears, taking several steps into EJ's office, halting at the edge of his desk. Stiff, robotic, metal facial features, some type of steel/iron hybrid perhaps, ball bearings for eyes—AI all the way. But what type? This can't be a QC project. He would know about it. Unless...it is EJ's birthday in four days. Is this what it is? Nah, they would have all jumped out by now yelling "Happy Birthday." Is this thing all alone? EJ scans left, right. "Yksinään?"

"Language not translatable."

EJ's mouth goes dry. "Uh, Englanti? English?"

"English."

"Ah." EJ immediately switches to the AI's preferred language. "Are you alone?"

"On Earth, alone. Yes."

260

"Well, then." EJ clears his throat. Is that an Earth-manufactured gun attached to its middle? Good lord, what is this? "I am Dr. Eikka Jutila, uh, at your service."

A whirring. "Identifier. Pleasantry. I am Two, t-w-o. Not at service."

EJ collapses back into his chair. Holy mother of God. He gestures to a chair in the corner. "Well, uh, Two, can you sit?"

"Able. But upright needed for download." More whirring. The thing seems to be focusing on EJ's computer, to the left of him, on the short side of his L-shaped desk. "Data download at 98 percent, ninety-nine—"

"Now you wait, just a meenute. You cannot breach our security!"

"100%."

"But you can't. We have firewalls the likes of which—where are you from? Who built you?"

"From planet you call 55 Cancri e. Original builder unknown. We call One."

"Cancri e—the exoplanet? Forty light-years away. Constellation Cancer. Good god, they had tried to deespute your existence."

"We exist." More whirring.

"Perkele. Wha-what are your plans? Can we…can we hold a meeting? How did you find us?"

Whir. "Received message from Quantum Community. You. This location within point nine kilometers."

"You mean, our SETI program? Heaven help us. We weren't expecting this."

"For Cancri evolution to hybrid human, H2O required. Per calculations—Pacific Ocean sufficient for evolution needs. Teleport to Cancri e. Will terraform as needed."

"Pacif—oh, for the love of god. Listen, uh, Two, first of all, the Pacific Ocean is not up for grabs. Eet ees indispensable for life on Earth. Second, due to its unique molecular structure, high specific heat, cohesion, adhesion, density, and so forth, water does not travel through wormholes. I assume that was your mode of transport? Teleportation through wormhole? Water simply doesn't teleport. So don't even—"

Whir. Whir. "*Second plan. Cancri population will transport to Earth. Disassemble all Earth beings. Will have Pacific Ocean and all other water sources for evolution.*"

EJ wipes his brow. "*Now just a goddamn—uh, Two. You...we need to sit down, talk about this.*" *EJ slowly inches his hand toward his comcard, presses an icon, booms,* "*Jaak, SOS!*" *EJ switches to Finnish.* "*Jaak. Stop document P declassification immediately and get over here. Bring Johann and Waara and the best weapons they have. Emergency!*"

Whir. "*Amend. Amend. New document—document P.*" *Whir.* "*Upload 100 percent. New information. Prophecy.*"

Jaak's voice from the comcard. "*Sorry, Dr. EJ. It's already downloaded. I could try—*"

"*No, no. Jaak, Johann, Waara, just get over here—now.*"

Whir. The being announces, "*Third plan. Crystal Child born Earth year 2014. Produce water for Cancri e planet in Earth year 2027. Eleven Earth years. Crystal Child will have abundant water source fill all craters on Cancri with H_2O. So species able to remain on Cancri e to evolve. Preferable. Amended Cancri mission: find Crystal Child before February 5, 2027.*"

"*But—*"

"*You may want to destroy Cancri. Cannot let happen.*"

"*You can't just—Jaak, Johann, Waara, stat.*"

Another whirring, higher pitched this time. Pop. The thing vanishes, its metallic scent lingering in the air.

Thirty-Two

• ◦ ◦ ◦ ◦ ◦ ◦ ◦●◦ ◉ ◦●◦ ◦ ◦ ◦ ◦ ◦ ◦ •

February 1, 2027

I listen in horror. The Cancris are real. They actually came to Earth, like all those sci-fi movies Tad and I used to watch. And they think I am the Crystal Child who will be the genius behind their evolution by manufacturing some type of water they need. Maybe this *is* a movie or a dream after all. Oh no, can't be. Everything's too real now. And I just have to accept it. No more falling off Birds, thinking I'll wake up. God, that was stupid. I'm stuck—in this fascinating but scary world. No wonder the word "Cancri" was verboten on Earth. These beings sound terrifying.

A trickle of sweat weaves its way down my back. *Keep breathing, Kris. Keep it neutral. Do not let them know you're an awfully dumb ditz girl right off the bat.* I maintain what I hope is a pleasant, concerned expression. What the hell else can I do?

Dr. EJ continues. "As soon as eet left, I arranged an emergency meeting weeth Brima. I was een his office a day later. Didn't trust thees thing at all to stay on eets own planet until 2027. I could tell the empathy gene had not yet been programmed een thees species. Brima, bless hees heart, was going to pull some strings and get us help immediately. Ah, but—" He lowers his head then glances at Mutsi, his eyes questioning.

Mutsi gives a slight nod. "She knows."

Dr. EJ sighs, shakes his head at me as though he's sorry I had to find out. "Well, the rest ees history for wheech I need not remind you. Apparently, they deemed us too big a threat to their plans. Only a dozen of us made eet to the safe house. Luckily, they were convinced they'd gotten rid of everyone, so they didn't think to look elsewhere. So rather than staying on Earth, where they were likely to find us, we made the incredibly hard decision to hide out—here. What a production. Then he brightens and smiles. "And what sisu our little group displayed. We regrouped, rebuilt, added to our QC. And now we are ready to demolish the enemy and return to Earth forever."

Clapping, nodding, all around the table. I look at each face, each amazing soul here. What horrors have they endured? My ADD mind is going tilt. Another QB pops out. "Dr. EJ? How did your relocation to the Diamond Star stay secret from them if they had all your data?"

"Ah, Kreestal, you are very perceptive. Yes, well, thees eenformation was so classified that all data from our teleportations were kept een a separate computer een the safe house. That was the best decision I've ever made. The worst was declassifying document P, thinking the prophecy was not so top secret anymore and telling Jaak to declassify it. The timing could not have been worse. Of course, even with our so-called unclassified data, the firewalls were sufficient, or so we thought. But obviously not secure enough for highly advanced Cancri computerized beings. This prophecy may be tantamount to our survival, not because it's necessarily true, but because the Cancris believe in it and are expecting a miracle very soon. We found the prophecy, written by hand on an old piece of paper—dated to less than two hundred years old. Would you like to know exactly what the prophecy said?"

My heart plummets, and my face flushes. No, I don't. I really don't. Then my mouth opens. "Yes, Dr. EJ. I would."

Thirty-Three

· · · ◦ ◦ ◦ ◦ ◦ ◉ ◎ ◉ ◎ ◦ ◦ ◦ ◦ · · · ·

March 4, 2014

The conference hall is packed, buzzing with excitement. After dinner, the space travelers climb to the stage. Dr. EJ steps to the podium and begins speaking in Finnish, with interpreters and headphones available for non-Finnish speakers. "My dear fellow QC members, our first order of business—congratulations to the Makkinens and the Kurkis. Join me in welcoming our newest QC member—Ms. Kristal Noelle Makkinen."

Everyone stands, smiling, clapping, rubbernecking to see the couple in the third row and perhaps catch a glimpse. Myrakka is holding an infant wrapped in a pink blanket and wearing a tiny woolen red cap. The mother smiles broadly and playfully places her finger to her lips to shush everyone. Her father Pauli and grandparents are beaming. Myrakka says softly, "We finally got her to sleep. Well, maybe it was all the commotion. Go ahead and make noise then." Laughter erupts all around. The baby squirms, but her eyes stay shut. When all have settled down, Dr. EJ turns back to the podium.

"Our second most important announcement—we have completed our first journey to BPM 37093, and I am pleased to report it has been more successful than we dared hope."

The entire hall erupts in a cacophony of cheering, talking, and clapping. Dr. EJ holds up his palm, smiling, scanning the members of his community. "Tonight, I will announce the generalities. For the specifics, I will be meeting with all of you in the coming weeks to discuss further details. But in a nutshell, our first objective was to travel through the wormhole intact. Objective accomplished."

Thunderous applause. People are still rubbernecking, trying to catch a glimpse of the baby, miraculously still asleep. Myrakka is rocking her back and forth.

"Our second objective was to ascertain the existence of diamond on BPM 37093. Objective accomplished."

Longer, louder applause echoes throughout the hall, interspersed with a few whoops.

"What we can deduce is, immeasurable amounts of carbon—diamond—are contained in the massive caves and underground passageways throughout the mountainous regions and, obviously, throughout the core. Although most diamond would need to be extracted and mined by instruments we did not have, we did find enough loose samples to bring home. Johann?"

All crane their necks forward as Johann stands. With both hands, he lifts a diamond up over his head. It's obviously still in the rough, but its size has the audience gasping in awe.

"What is that—a football?" *someone yells out.*

"If it is, it's the most expensive football in the world." *Silence. The crowd is obviously stunned.*

EJ continues. "Needless to say, we will need to go through the proper channels to make sure we are, indeed, the owners of this newfound wealth and how we can legally lay claim to it. And we must make sure the world market does not immediately flood with mysterious diamonds. It's all quite complicated, so undoubtedly, this first diamond"—*Dr. EJ nods his head toward the diamond football, still held high by Johann*—"will be needed to reimburse our crack legal and economic team."

A few people laugh, some groan.

"Yes, we need to go through all the red tape and figure out logistics. But I have friends in high places. We will have the funding we need for any and all projects."

More clapping and conversation, but EJ's not finished. "Number 3, extraneous findings. We went beyond our stated missions. What we found in addition to the diamond material was not anticipated. What an incredible enigma."

A hush falls over the crowd. Then a baby wails. Myrakka stands. "Well, got through at least half the meeting. Bye now." *Pauli grabs her* coat. *"I can—"* *Lumi shakes her head, holding out her arms. "No, give her to me. Give her to me. I can take her back." Myrakka hesitates. "Sure?"*

"Of course, come on. Here, sweetie. Come to Mummo." They make the exchange, Myrakka thanking the child's grandmother as she makes her way out of the room with the child in her arms, grinning broadly and cooing to the infant as she exits. Myrakka returns to her seat and whispers something to Pauli. He smiles, draping his arm around her shoulders. Dr. EJ continues his announcement.

"We have no idea where, who, how, or why. But someone, and by the looks of it, fully human, has been on the Diamond Star before us."

A collective gasp echoes throughout the hall.

"We also found a bewildering and beautiful set of wooden doors, in graduated sizes, thousands of steel barrels of consumable water, thank God, and most puzzling of all—a prophecy. Adda, dear?"

Adda, a QC interpreter and data manager, delicately holds up a long piece of thin parchment paper, encased in a transparent plastic cover. Dr. EJ points.

"This is the original. Of course, we have scanned it and stored it in our main computer database with the utmost security for now until we figure out exactly where it came from. We found it on the second day of our exploration in the innermost chamber—a room surprisingly similar to the very room in which we're now sitting. It was set carefully in the middle of a long wooden table under a frame of diamond. How it got there, who wrote it—well, your guess is as good as ours. But whoever placed it in a strategic location obviously wanted someone to find it. And they seemed to anticipate someone would. What a mystery, eh?"

A voice from the crowd asks, "What does it say?"

Dr. EJ scans the room. "Would you like a formal reading of the document now or at a future meeting?"

A great chorus of "Yes" echoes so loudly in the conference room Dr. EJ has to shush everyone. "All right, all right, quiet now. Adda, may I?"

She hands the document to Dr. EJ as though it's a delicate egg about to crack. Dr. EJ places it on the podium, pulls out his reading glasses, adjusts them to the tip of his nose, and begins.

Prophecy 57603

Initiation of Sixth Eon 8kpc Orion
In the Precession of the equinoxes
Twenty-five thousand, six hundred twenty-five year journey
Through the twelve constellations of the zodiac
December twenty-first, two thousand twelve.
The fifth journey will end.
The sixth will commence.
Eternal dance of Good and Evil.
Heed coming cataclysmic changes
Choice Points will present
Beware. Prepare.
Predicted Time Code Events:
Two thousand two—formation of quantum
community 68.2834°N, 27.9182°E
Two thousand two—formation of
Cancri e A.I. RA 8^h 52^m 36^s
February fifth, two thousand fourteen
Birth of Crystal Child—Earth
Two thousand fourteen
Triangle of Spheres convergence
Planet of diamond, Star of Diamond, Earth
Thirteen journeys around Earth Star
from birth of Crystal Child, then note:
Choice Point:
2-05-2027
Crystal Child holds key to manifest peace for all
Not through gold, diamond, or land
But the Elixir of Life: H_2O
crystal frequencies to heal
if Crystal Child DNA essence fails
Cancri e will vanish humanity into the void for eternity.
Beware. Prepare:
May Peace Reign

Dr. EJ stops, then his eyes widen, falling on the couple in the third row. "Oh dear. Oh my dear god. I didn't realize... I didn't... I should have seen it..." Myrakka and Pauli have paled. Myrakka's voice is almost a whisper. "Her name and her birthday." Pauli grips Myrakka's shoulder.

Thirty-Four

• • • ◦ ◦ ◦ ◦ ● ● ● ◉ ● ● ● ◦ ◦ ◦ • • • •

February 1, 2027

Dr. EJ removes his glasses and replaces the paper into a plastic case, then into a diamond box. He looks straight at me, raises his eyebrows, and shrugs. "Thees ees what I found on thees table and what the Cancris found on our computer. I should have kept eet highly classified. And I should have read it more carefully and discussed eet with your parents before announcing it to the group. Shame on me."

Mutsi shakes her head, shrugs. It's clear she forgave Dr. EJ years ago.

Dr. EJ's being hard on himself. I know what that's like.

"Dr. EJ, when you did that, you had no idea the Cancris even existed."

He sighs. "But I have regretted downgrading the document to this day. I told your parents not to worry. Eet was most likely a coincidence, nothing more. But the bottom line, coincidence or not, we have a problem with the Cancris believing eet to be true." He rubs his eyes. "Anyway, now you know the story. The Cancris must be waiting until your thirteenth birthday as the prophecy predicts. They expect a meerakle. They expect water on Cancri for survival of the evolution of their hybrid species."

I blurt, "Isn't Cancri e really hot? Water would instantly evaporate."

"Most likely. But they may have terraformed at least a portion of the planet, so perhaps they have prepared the way, or so they think. In any case, somehow, you are to instruct them how to manufacture that sacred elixir so that eet weel not evaporate and their evolution may progress. And so they don't have to take our Pacific Ocean." He shakes his head as he strokes his beard. "Hmmm, tall order, eh?"

I manage to squeak out, "But what does it mean? Those numbers and dates and predictions—"

"Eet ees rather cryptic, yes. The number een the title merely geeves the location of Earth een relation to our galaxy. The Milky Way ees a spiral, and we are on the Orion arm of that spiral, in that location. The numbers after our respective groups—QC and Cancri e—are also location codes. Perhaps someone wrote a prophecy for every planet in the galaxy?" He shrugs. "As for the eentroduction, we know that about every twenty-six thousand years, Earth concludes one complete journey through the twelve constellations, just as eet's written. Some theorize that major, cataclysmic changes occur in these junctures, or choice points. So we surmise the author was human, English speaking, and contemporary. And, we hope, benevolent, as the last line read: 'let peace reign.'"

"Contemporary?"

"Thees was definitely not written een ancient times. And we dated the paper using the stable and unstable isotopes method. Although it was made to look old, it's contemporary. Modern. Quite a shocking revelation."

"But who would have traveled to the Diamond Star before you did?"

"That, my dear, remains a complete meestery. So far, no clues, not one. The rest of eet—well, pretty understandable. A child will be born on February 5, 2014—a Crystal Child. Her thirteenth birthday will mark a major choice point. She may concoct water weeth healing properties to help een the evolution of the Cancris, somehow using her own DNA, een which case, we all survive—Cancris and humans alike. Or—she will fail, and the Cancris weel destroy humanity. Een other words, two paths, and a choice must be made. But what choice? And how to make it? Thees Crystal Child, eef successful, ees to be the universal catalyst to peace."

"But what about the DNA part? What does that mean?"

"Hmmm, yes, puzzling. Thoughts?"

271

Thoughts? He wants *my thoughts*? The only thought I have right now: *this is insane. Why me?* Other than that, I have no thoughts. I have ADD. My brain is currently offline. Silence hangs in the air. They're looking at me, waiting for my reaction. Seriously? So that's the prophecy. This was why they thought I was some sort of genius girl. This is why the Birds acted so reverently around me. Do they really expect that I'm the one who will figure out this huge colossal water equation? Did they expect me to say, "Oh, yes, when I was five, this being from the planet Zeon came to me and taught me everything I know…" Yeah, right, like I have this colossal secret formula, and everyone's just waiting for me to announce it straight from my magical brain. *Not. Have they seen my math grades?*

I know the truth, and I mean, come on—so should they. At least, Dr. EJ seems to understand. I'm not going to save anyone from destruction, not an ant, not a murder hornet, and definitely not the Cancris, plus the whole human race in one fell swoop. Didn't it say "I will *heal all?*" Ha, not on my birthday, not on any day, not them, not us. What a vicious, cruel hoax. The only way I'm going to save anything is through a graphic novel: *Kristal—Kaped Krusader with Key to Water for Everyone!* What a joke. It would be hilarious if it weren't so tragic. These amazingly brilliant people couldn't possibly all be counting on me to do the utterly impossible, could they? Hello?

Here's a thought. *What if the author of the prophecy made this ginormous mistake? A miscalculation on the grandest scale?* Maybe the prophecy's child was supposed to be Alek. He's the whiz kid—the child prodigy. Ha, Alek, bet he's sitting in Mr. Gabriel's room at this moment wondering where I am. What day is it on Earth, anyway? Refocus, Kris. Okay, maybe another Crystal Child was born the same day as me and lives in India or Canada or Uganda, and they just got the location screwed up or maybe…maybe the whole thing's just a sick, stupid prank.

I need to tell everyone just to be crystal clear. (I wince at my own pun.) I'm not up for the job. No more deception. They might think I have the perfect answer up my sleeve, and I'm just playing dumb, and at the last minute, I'll pull out some amazing trick. Well, I've got news for them. I'm not playing dumb. I *am* dumb. I have nothing up my sleeve. I have ADD, *awfully dumb ditz*, in my brain. Even old bully Jackson Hynes knows that. I think Dr. EJ and the QC understand, but the people outside the QC—and the Birds—do I need to spell it out? Okay, I will. I will, in no uncertain terms, tell them. My name should mislead them no longer. I have no magic. I have zilch knowledge. The miracle child they've been revering doesn't exist; or if she does, she's definitely not me.

Oh, but the Cancris. If they find out I'm a fraud, they won't waste a minute to destroy every last one of us and then onto the mass extermination of Earth's humans; after which, they will move in, sucking up all water in every ocean, lake, river, puddle. I can't advertise the fact I'm worthless, just in case they're listening. But they're not listening. Are they? Oh, yeah. Crap, I passed along the Diamond Star location code to Tad. They might be on their way. They might be eavesdropping. And my birthday is coming up. Really soon. I'm trapped. A ripple of fear feathers my skin, and I involuntarily shiver. What in God's name have I done? My nose feels warm. I bet it's beet red. I look down. My arms have broken out in big fat goosebumps. But I will not cry. I can't. I...

Dr. EJ places a hand over mine, and I jump. "Oh." How long have I been in one of my famous ADD fugue states? When will I ever...

"Well, that, my dear, ees all we know. Ees it true? Personally, I doubt it. I am a scientist, after all, and do not believe een mysterious prophesies, especially when we do not know the origin. Predictions with facts? Yes, and admittedly, eet's been fairly precise with names and dates and places. But eet ees, as I said, rather cryptic. We just don't know. Some of our people at least believe in the posseebility of the prophecy. And all the Birds seem to buy eento eet. They believe een *you* wholeheartedly."

I cringe, thinking of everything I've done to them.

"But more concerning, we know the Cancris believe the prophecy to be true. They are waiting until the prophecy date comes to pass. If nothing happens, and they can't find you, then I'm afraid they plan to teleport to Earth and take over the planet—wheech means—well, I'm sure I don't have to spell it out. I hope they treat our precious planet better than humans have." He gives a cynical little chuckle. "But seriously, we hope and pray Earth's citizens will never know how close they came to total annihilation."

My heart's beating in my throat. In addition to all my redness and goosebumps, a new shiver slithers up my spine. "Dr. EJ, do people and Birds think I can fix everything? Is everyone just sitting back and waiting for me?"

He winks, just as he did before, like he's not concerned. Can he clue me in please? Because I'm about to wet myself, which is quite a feat as I haven't had more than a few drops of water today.

He's still winking and shaking his head. "Shhh, don't tell the Cancris. But thees was my next point. Relax. First of all, even eef the prophecy were true, eet's too much of a burden on any one person. We live een the twenty-first century, and we don't put our total faith een prophesies or magic per se. Johann, Jaak, and a few more of our most brilliant scienteests here worked on the very same problem for a while with no luck. And second, remember, we thought we had lost you almost eleven years ago. So eet was eemperative that we came up with another option—a plan B. We...the QC, are going to intervene."

Oh, of course, I, slow-on-the-uptake kid, finally realize what's going on—why Dr. EJ keeps winking. I ask, "You mean the soldiers? The ones I saw in the mountains?" Omigod. General Waara. I look his way. He gives me a thumbs-up. Oh. *Whew.* Of course. I turn back to Dr. EJ. "I see now. So I'm off the hook completely?"

"Exactly. That ees the current plan, yes. Whether you are the 'chosen one' or not, please rest assured, dear Kreestal, that we have been working extensively on a backup plan. Actually, plan B has been plan A all along. We would never think of putting you in the clutches of those hideous beings, whether you are a meerakle worker or not. But I must mention, een the last few days, our eentelligence has pointed to a posseeble confrontation weeth the Cancris here on Lucy first, before they attack Earth."

I cringe. "Oh, I... I didn't mean to give the location code away to..."

Dr. EJ shakes his head. "Yes, yes, we deescussed it when you first told your mother. There was no way for you to understand the ramifeecations. And no way for Myrakka to know you were living weeth a Cancri tattletale."

My brother—a tattletale for terrorists. That's all he is to these people. My teeth grind down so hard I'm afraid my gums will explode. No one understands. Even Mutsi, sweet as she's been about Tad, can't possibly understand. I remain silent.

Dr. EJ continues. "Een fact, you may have done us a beeg favor by sending them our way first so we can destroy them on our own territory, thus saving us the trouble of sending our army light-years away, to their planet. God knows what we may encounter there. Ms. Kreestal, you are one of us, please do not think you are useless. We are all family, and we all support one another. We have assembled the strongest fighting army een the world, er, galaxy. And soon, we hope we'll be able to show our strength, defeat the enemy once and for all, and return to our beloved planet Earth—our home."

I remember the glimpse I got when I was on Haukka's back. "I've seen them. They were in the mountains when I was on my way to the city. They're very impressive."

"Yes, eef the Cancris try to travel here, they're fools. Think. What ees the most eendestructible material we know of?"

"Steel? No, iron?"

"It might seem so. But no, my dear, that's what the Cancris are built of or something like it. No, not any type of metal. Diamond."

Oh, of course, I knew that. Slow on the uptake, as usual. I look to see if Dr. EJ is disappointed in the brilliant Crystal Child, but he just keeps explaining, as polite as ever.

"Eet can't be scratched, broken, or reepped apart, except by another diamond. Over the last several years, our scientists have been working diligently on armored panels for our soldiers. The enemy can throw bombs, fire, spears, lasers, guns. Nothing penetrates diamond. So, Ms. Kreestal, as they say, 'we have your back.'"

Dr. EJ pauses. "Kreestal, please understand, your specialness ees not contingent upon any miraculous deeds you perform. You make our community special just by being who you are—a bright, compassionate soul weeth a great future ahead of you. You were the first child born into the QC, so you were welcomed into all our hearts the minute you were born. You have no idea what your reappearance has done for your mother. She looks ten years younger. Some even remark that her sisu and her very soul have returned."

I turn my head toward my mother, sitting next to me. She wraps an arm around my shoulder, pulling me close. She's blinking hard to squelch tears. How many times have I been deprived of my mother's touch due to the Cancris inhumanity? Mutsi's smiles, plus Dr. EJ's soothing words are melting the tension from my neck to my toes. Thank God, I'm off the hook. Building an army to defeat the enemy is much more reasonable. I lift my eyes upward and smile.

"Thank you, Dr. EJ, I know you will beat the Cancris this time."

Dr. EJ stands. "Eef we had not found thee prophecy and eef they had not gotten their filthy metal hands on it, they would very likely have returned and massacred Earth's entire population and all eets water back in 2016. But the prophecy persuaded them to wait. So looking at eet that way, you've already saved us eleven years, eh?"

Eleven years. At least I've done one helpful thing without even knowing it. On the other hand, you could say I prolonged this horrible confrontation for eleven years. We could have been rid of this enemy a long time ago. I'll bet Earth versus Cancri-e would have been a slam-dunk victory for us. But if they *did* have a secret weapon…or still *do*… I shudder. *Focus, Kris. Focus.*

Dr. EJ claps his hands, making me jump. "Okay, everyone. Here's our present plan: we conduct our ceremony. Queeckly, ten to fifteen minutes at most as we have very little time to spare. But the ceetizens and Birds have a right to know and be honored. Then despite the danger, a small reconnaissance team from our Diamond Star Army, headed by General Hale Waara, weel head to Earth in hopes of rescuing the Kurkis, whom we have every reason to believe have survived and are living een Montana. Then eef the Cancris still have not found our location, our entire army weel be traveling to Cancri e to aboleesh those AI beings who so ruthlessly massacred so many members of our QC in 2016. So we have much to do to prepare. Do I have a motion to adjourn thees meeting?"

Hale Waara raises a hand. "Move to adjourn."

Dr. EJ is already gathering his papers and electronics. "Meeting hereby adjourned."

The immediate burst of movement and conversation disorients me for a moment. *Deep breath, Kris. Deep breath, deep breath...*

And then, to my surprise, each and every QC survivor is suddenly surrounding me with hugs, words of support, thumbs-up, high fives. I don't—can't—hold back my tears any longer. They don't either. We're all crying together. I'm so grateful for these incredible people. Here I am, on a star fifty light-years from Earth. Yet I'm starting to feel right at home.

Thirty-Five

February 1, 2027

We've emerged from the passageway. My first glimpse of the Quantum City Square takes my breath away. A huge throng of people and Birds has gathered inside the gates. The low murmurs crescendo into excited talk and pointing as the audience notices us heading toward a large stage with one podium front and center at the far end of the square.

As we move closer, I notice three distinct groups, all facing the stage. Some are rubbernecking to catch sight of the council. The Birds huddle in back. Hybrids seem to comprise most of them—a mix of owls, crows, hawks, and eagles, as Mutsi had explained in the tunnels that day. But mingling with the hybrids are other, smaller Birds, still as sacred, whose DNA was not tinkered with in any way. These are the songbirds who were brought for their soul-uplifting music alone. And then, I see the baby crows—the ones Onni had called "rude" when they gobbled up the muffin piece I'd dropped. They obviously had just been starving. But omigod, is that Rawol? It is. The gleaming white tail gives him away. His appearance in the sky the morning of the snowfall gave me the first inkling my life was about to change. Ha. That's the understatement of the year. But now I know his purpose was a noble one. And since I've gotten to meet the Bird leaders—Onni and Haukka—and learned about the Birds from Mutsi, I know I'll never fear birds again. In fact, I've gained a deep respect for them—all of them. I owe them water, although I'm pleased to see they seem to be okay. My relief makes my heart dance

278

with joy. I'm so glad the rationing had little effect on them. A few feet behind me is Onni. I shouldn't play favorites, but he is so special. He was the one who welcomed me so warmly and gently the minute I landed on this strange star.

But then—is that a Bird stumbling? On second glance, many are shuffling around, looking down at the ground. They seem a little depressed. What's going on? Maybe I'm just imagining things. I suddenly feel a huge wave of shame. How could Mutsi have let this travesty happen? Taking water rations from these exquisite creatures was inexcusable. Did the Birds really volunteer? Or were they coerced? The more I gaze, the more I see grief in their eyes. Whose big idea was this, anyway? If these scientists are so damn brilliant, can't they manufacture water somehow? I've got to get this out of my mind, at least for the ceremony, or I'll be sick.

I force my eyes to shift to the middle group. These must be the soldiers I'd seen earlier in the mountains. The whole army isn't here, just a group of about a hundred. They're dressed in more traditional military uniforms, but the color is pure white, with diamond buttons and cuff links instead of the usual brass. Are they gearing up to fight the Cancris? How are they going to get there? Or are the Cancris now headed toward the Diamond Star, thanks to my fatal error in ratting them out to my brother? Colossal goosebumps prickle up and down my arms again. Can't smush the toothpaste back in the tube. I've *got* to let go of the guilt, or I'll self-combust.

My eyes scan the ones closest to the stage—all types, all ages. Whole families have teleported together to the Diamond Star— women, men, a few children, and oh my, two tiny babies, swathed in blue. Their parents are holding them, bouncing them in their arms, and looks like a set of grandparents standing next to them, laughing, cooing with them. Twins. God, I miss my twin. No matter what he's done. Or is.

I sigh. What a peaceful, interconnected community. How were they able to organize life here? They had to find a way to grow food, deliver goods, spread news, build houses, remove trash, aid the sick; I can't imagine the blood, sweat, and tears it took to regroup—and so far from home—after such an unspeakable tragedy as the massacre.

And they've been here scarcely more than a decade? They've somehow replicated an Earth of sorts under the most impossible conditions. It's amazing what a group of compassionate geniuses can do when they put their minds to it. Maybe, someday, I can learn from them.

My swallow reflex keeps trying to kick in. But since there's nothing but grit in my throat, I can only cough. Without a second thought, my hand reaches into my pocket and encircles the flask... oops. No, Kris. What an insult to casually chugalug while thousands are parched, especially the Birds. I jerk my hand out of my pocket as though the flask were a hot piece of coal. When the time is right, I'll give the flask to them, apologize, and be done with it. I hope the water in the flask is all they need.

As we head toward the stage, I look down. The ground is of the same material as the walkway in front of the hospital—diamond sandpaper? Except the multicolored pattern is the same Penrose tiling I first saw in the grand ballroom in Birdland. No trees grace the city, but huge palmlike bushes of vibrant greenery gleam like emeralds, interspersed with tropical grasses sprouting leaves of red, pink, and purple, running up diamond trellises, sprouting thick and brilliant from huge sparkling planters. In front, giant tulip-like flowers border the large arena. They all look surprisingly real, not tacky-fake, like the palm tree in Shana's office. Although they're not real, they make the city come alive, like those colorful Floridian resorts I've seen on TV. And ironically, I'm sure the diamond planters and trellises are real as they come. Not a rhinestone or piece of glass is to be found anywhere on this star, I'm sure of it.

The coach is still on the large stage, sparkling with diamond insets in various triangular patterns. A large backdrop of the same black material is behind us. I gaze all around, right, left, then I see it. Don't know how I missed it. Behind the Bird group, a gigantic, rectangular digital clock rises majestically upward. A golden bright light illuminates its numbers from behind its face. I note the time—4:14.

"Mutsi?"

"Yes, Krissie?"

"The clock. It's beautiful. Why so big?"

"Oh, the Earth Clock Tower. Here on Lucy, we have no days, no hours. The star doesn't turn; there is no sun to rise and set. How are we to tell the time? Luckily, we found two architects and three structural engineers on Earth. They were able to build the parts and accompany several of the soldiers here to assemble it. A miracle, really. An implanted microchip marks Earth hours, minutes, and seconds, so we can at least feel a sense of time here. That, along with our simulated days and nights help to keep our biorhythms in sync. The clock's become a symbol of our dear Earth. Of home.

"Didn't you mention a cuckoo Bird? I don't see one."

"Oh, we must have just missed her. She comes and goes between hours, but never misses the hour or half hour. We'll see her again." Mutsi closes her eyes and takes a deep breath, apparently composing herself for what's coming next. After a moment, she opens her eyes, smiling widely, and turns to me, lightly squeezing my arm, then breaking away with a thumbs-up. "This won't take long. Just follow—and stand next to me on the stage. Dr. EJ, General Waara, and I will say a few words. That's all. Then they'll be off to Earth to get my parents. I'm crazy wild right now, Krissie. I can barely stand the suspense. Just think, I will be able to hug not only you, but my parents. My wonderful—" She stops.

I nod because I don't want to remind her what my father or, whatever he was, may have done to them. I'm in horrible suspense too. I'll just have to take it second by second. My mother turns, as do the others, and we all climb the stairs to the stage.

A collective gasp rises from the crowd as we line up. When they see me a step behind, the noise begins to increase. I hear murmurs of "Kristal," "there she is," but otherwise, the crowd remains quiet, respectful. My eyes shift to my mother's face. Although she told me how nervous she is, she sure doesn't show it. She looks so confident—even radiant.

Dr. EJ is first. "Let's greet everyone, shall we?" He mounts the five steps to the podium, attaches a tiny microphone to his lapel. An expectant hush fills the air. Dr. EJ lightly grips the podium, surveying the crowd of people, soldiers, and Birds, some of whose sweet songs I hear in the distance. Dr. EJ's voice is warm but commanding.

"Citizens of the Diamond Star! I trust that by now, through the Lucy grapevine, you all have received the eencredible news that Myrakka's daughter—*our community's* daughter, whom we feared lost in the Cancri massacre so many years ago—has been found!"

Sudden applause and whoops rise from the audience. I scan the crowd, noting joy on their faces. Some have tears streaming down their cheeks. They're clasping hands, hugging each other, pumping fists in the air. They're all strangers to me, but apparently, at least to some, I'm no stranger. How odd.

But seriously, why the fuss? I'm no big deal. I think I hear someone yelling something, "Crystal Child." Don't they know—can't they see the Diamond Star Army—right in back of them? Why in the world or, at least this world, do I deserve a welcome like this? They can't still believe I'm the whatever—the *special* one. It's ironic that at home, I'm special all right. In special education, that is. Hasn't anyone told them the truth about me? But they must know I'm not really that brilliant. They must look on me as sort of a symbol—like King William of England—no power, just a figurehead. They must be really happy for Mutsi. I'm sure they've all heard the tragic stories by now. And it's clear Mutsi is a beloved figure here among the citizens.

Dr. EJ turns and beckons Mutsi to join him. She gently pats me on the back, then climbs the podium steps, and stands next to Dr. EJ. "I thank all of you from the bottom of my heart for welcoming my beloved daughter, Kristal, missing since the massacre and last seen in Cancri clutches. Her ordeal has been harrowing, to say the least. She's still recovering from shock and dehydration from her first teleportation and the circumstances leading up to it, which we will divulge at a later date. We who have lived on Lucy for a while sometimes forget how strange our extraterrestrial life can seem to our fellow Earth brothers and sisters. But we can finally rejoice in the knowledge that she is now once again with us!"

At this, a low murmur crescendoes to a thunderous roar of applause. Onni is flapping his wings or trying to, anyway. Then I notice him, ever so slightly, stumbling. I watch, concerned, but he recovers, and I look back on the crowd, still clapping, roaring, dancing in the center of town under the huge Earth clock. The birds flap their wings, cawing, screeching. I must look like a fool, staring all gobsmacked out from behind my mother on the stage.

Dr. EJ takes the lead again. "Our relief must be tempered by the knowledge of the prophesied cataclysmic changes predicted to be upon us quite soon. True or not, we know the Cancris are real, they believe in the prophecy, and so we must prepare for upheavals. The prophecy reveals two paths—one leading to lasting peace for all on thees star and on Earth and the second path—" He glances up toward the sky. I see him taking a breath. "Well, let's be positive and prepare for the first outcome. The fact that our Kreestal has been found ees a very good omen, if you believe in that stuff." Scattered laughter.

This is a twenty-first century scientific community after all, although surprisingly I notice about a third of them nodding like they think my return is a good omen. Hmmm.

Then General Waara takes the stage, bounding up the five steps in two large strides. He waves. The response from the crowd is enormous. Obviously, he is well-liked and respected. When the applause dies down, he speaks in his booming deep voice, "Citizens, the prophesied changes about which Dr. EJ speaks are nearly upon us. The date in the prophecy—February 5, 2027—is to be the date the Crystal Child saves all from destruction. And, indeed, strange events are beginning to appear. However, our Crystal Child"—he sweeps his arm behind him to point me out—"has been missing the past eleven years. You could say she's been a POW. And well, truth be told, we were never 100 percent sold on the prophecy anyway. So we've devised a plan—namely, the best damned army in the universe—the Diamond Star Armed Forces."

The applause is abrupt, with loud cheers and fists in the air. It still looks like something's not quite right with the Birds. They're thirsty. Of course. Well, they'll be happy soon. I've got the remedy right here in my pocket. I'll just wait until the meeting is over. I turn back to the human crowd. They're pumped. Good. Apparently, the people are behind this army 100 per cent. Most people aren't really counting on me then. Good, I can tell General Waara doesn't really believe in the prophecy. But they all believe the Cancris believe. No wonder they all wanted to ease me into all this. Even now, I'm confused and overwhelmed. But at least, things are making more sense.

The general continues. "If they don't invade us first, and we doubt they will, we will do what I call a backatcha—a surprise attack on their planet—Cancri e—in the very near future. And this particular *backatcha*—well, personally it will be a balm to my soul." He bumps a fist over his heart and looks upward then back to his audience. "We don't need to show one iota of compassion. We don't need to go by the Geneva Convention or any of that compassionate bullshit because they are AI—merely machines made of metal and microchips. So our consciences can be clear when we annihilate this artificial race. It took the large part of the past decade, but we're ready. So damn ready."

More applause and a few whoops ripple through the crowd.

"Our brilliant men and women collaborated to build the finest army and devise the best-laid plans to decimate an enemy that almost completely destroyed us eleven years ago. They think we're all dead. They underestimated our resolve. After the galactic battle of the century and after we have pulverized each and every Cancri to dust and left them to lie fallow on a hot, dead planet for eternity, we will, at long last, return to our beloved Earth. God willing, we are not too late to resume our full mission to heal our magnificent planet. Our descendants will enjoy sustainable and healthy living for eons to come. Perhaps forever!"

The cheering is so deafening I feel my eardrums vibrating. Ouch. He didn't mention the glitch. The Cancris *do* know some of the QC survived, and they know where to find them thanks to clueless, ADD me. It was a wise move he decided not to announce it—yet.

Mutsi whispers, "You okay, hon?"

I must be wincing. It's all a little much. Am I okay? I'm not sure. But I give Mutsi the widest smile I can muster along with a weak thumbs-up. She gives me one in return.

Dr. EJ smiles and takes the microphone from the general. "As General Waara attests, all ees coming to a head. We have planned our strategy with the best minds in the universe. We *weel* defeat the

Cancris, and at long last, we *shall* return to *our* home, *our* beloved planet—Earth! Start packing."

The celebration begins in earnest; people are now yelling, dancing, whistling, and clapping. Dr. EJ holds up his hand. "Wait, wait. Before our full celebration begins, we must honor those who have willingly sacrificed their rations by donating their H_2O so that Kreestal might live. These sacred Birds must be revered. To the Birds!"

As one, the crowd turns toward the Birds, clapping, with solemn faces. The Birds don't show much reaction. Some have their heads bowed. Some are flapping their wings a bit. The Birds. They should hate me. Instead, they seem to honor me. I'm horrified and ashamed. Wasn't there enough water at the Citadel Hospital to hydrate me? If I had known the water I was receiving consisted of water that belonged to the Birds, I would have ripped my IV out in a nanosecond. My cheeks feel hot. I can't show my face. Taking several side steps, I position myself totally behind my mother so that I'm hidden. I peek out toward the crowd. I have to find a way to get the water in my flask to the Birds. Then I see him.

Something's definitely wrong with Onni. He steps forward, toward the stage, head down, clawing the sandy ground, making gasping sounds. I look to my mother. She's noticed Onni too and is watching him intently, her brows furrowed. I tap her gently. "Mutsi, *do* something. I think he's sick."

Dr. EJ notices us. Mutsi first holds up a hand to Dr. EJ, then the crowd, and hurries down the steps of the stage. I follow her. We each take a side, patting his wings.

Mutsi speaks gently and quietly, "Onni, dear, what's wrong?"

Onni's droopy eyes try to focus. Slowly, his giant beak opens. "Onni H_2O rations much larger than small Birds. Onni give all his rations for Miss Kristal. Did not take any Bird's water but Onni. This way only one bird sacrifice. Glad to give life for Kristal. Was hoping to die after ceremony over. Must save Kristal. Must save Birds. Kristal, our leader... Raaah."

I feel dizzy and can't breathe. I can't believe what I'm hearing. "Onni, you mean, you were the only donor? You gave up *all* your rations? How long ago?"

"Onni go in H_2O lab at hospital eight days ago. Donate own water. Onni have more rations than smaller birds. Dr. B accept because I tell him small H_2O donations from many Birds. But Onni lie. Donation all mine. Onni cannot watch destruction of small Birds, even rude baby crows."

In the back, I hear caws, chirps, shuffling. So that's why the other Birds seemed depressed. They must have known what Onni did. My heart drops to my stomach. Onni can't die. This can't happen. Mutsi gasps. "But, Onni, you're...you're indispensable. You can't do this. We can't watch *your* destruction either. We need you... we..."

"All Birds indispensable, but Kristal most indispens—" Onni's massive claws collapse under him, and he plops to the ground, like a giant chicken on a nest. His huge black eyes close as his head droops onto his breast. A large contingency of Birds flies to the ground where Onni sits, circling him, making these weird, sad cawing sounds. A sob escapes Mutsi's lips as she steps back, her hands covering her mouth. I'm too mortified to move. I remember how I felt when I collapsed in the tunnel from dehydration. I can't stand to think Onni's been feeling so terrible all because of me. A collective gasp arises from the crowd.

Mutsi looks out over the crowd. "Yua. Where's Yua?"

"Let me through, let me through." Ah, Dr. Kikuchi, the veterinarian. There she is. Rushing over, peering at Onni, she places three fingers over his heart area, sticks the thing in his mouth that Mutsi used on me when we were walking through the passageways. She shakes her head. "Fifty-one. He's very weak. He needs H_2O stat. I will sacrifice."

Dr. B steps forward, panic-stricken. "Onni lie to me. I did take water from Onni. He said it was a collection from all the Birds, so there should have been fewer repercussions, hopefully, no casualties. I... I believed Onni. Why should I not have believed him?" He stands and turns toward the Birds in the back. "Now we must ask for rations from others asap... Birds? Citizens? H_2O stat. Come forward." Dr. Kikuchi is waving her hands frantically and shouting,

"No, no, I will sacrifice," but is drowned out by the rush of the crowd and more Birds, flying forward, toward Onni and the stage.

I'm in a daze, an ADD fog. Wait. I shake my head. No, dammit. This is my problem and mine alone.

"No. No!" I think I've startled them as everyone freezes at the sound of my voice. I have to do this. "I won't stand for it. Onni, you can't...you shouldn't have! Go back, everyone, go back..." In this moment, I desperately wish I had whatever magic powers the prophecy seems to think I have.

Wait. Magic powers. Of course, I *do* have magic—right here in my pocket—the elixir of life. Dr. B said to use it only in an emergency. Well, this certainly qualifies as one. Yanking the flask from my pocket, I unscrew the diamond-encrusted cap, holding it up to Onni's beak. His eyes are closed. *Holy moly. No time to lose.* "Onni, please drink, here. I have water, probably *your* water."

Onni opens his eyes halfway, struggles to stand, then bows his head. "Will not take water. H_2O for your life. Kristal, you are the hope of all—our leader."

I hear the other Birds clicking their claws in approval. The hope of all? Leader? Me? They can't still believe this nonsense. Oh, this is so crazy. How did this idea take hold, anyway? I am no leader. Never was, never will be. But if they think so, okay...

"All right, then as leader, I command you to drink. Here—" I lift up Onni's beak with my palm. He's too weak to resist. I tip the flask into his mouth. Pure, clear, precious water flows down his throat, and I can tell he is reflexively gulping. Poor, poor Onni.

My mother is behind me now, and as she sees what I'm doing, she gasps and reaches out to grab the flask. "No, Kristal, *no*! That's for you."

Onni sputters and chokes. I pause, then tip the mouth of the flask so more water flows down his gullet.

A buzz emanates from the crowd as they jockey for the best view, the ones toward the front rubbernecking to see what's happening. I push my mother away with my leg and hip to keep the water flowing. Continuing to hold Onni's beak, I wait until the last drop empties the flask completely. Luckily, Onni is too weak to resist. I toss the diamond-encrusted container behind me, throwing my arms around my new friend's yellow feathered neck.

"You're not going to die on my watch, Onni. You and Haukka saved me. Now I will save you."

Mutsi's staring in disbelief. Or awe. Don't know which.

Someone has given Dr. Kikuchi a stethoscope. She listens intently to Onni's heart while the rest of us stand by helplessly. The stick goes in Onni's mouth again. After a minute, she pulls out the stick and reads it. Her eyes widen, and she smiles. "Sixty-nine and rising. Getting stronger and getting into tissues now." Dr. Kikuchi keeps a firm hand on Onni's wing, keenly observing, waiting for any signs of recovery. At first, his body is still. Then he burps quite loudly. Atta boy! Slowly he straightens. I can almost feel the precious liquid coursing through his body. At full height now, he bows to Dr. Kikuchi then stands before me, bowing again.

"So sorry."

Dr. Kikuchi bows to me. "Kristal, you saved his life. We are forever indebted to you."

The crowd goes wild.

I need no praise. Onni doesn't need to bow or apologize. Good lord, I'm the one who should be bowing to him. Funny. I've only been here a short time, yet I feel an indescribable bond toward this compassionate creature, whatever or whoever he is. He is truly sacred. Tears fill my eyes as I softly stroke his wing. "Quit that bowing, Onni, and don't say sorry. You are the revered one."

Onni straightens even more then opens his beak. "I am ashamed. Need to save Kristal. Ashamed. So ashamed. Raaah."

"Onni, you can't be ashamed. You followed my command. You will live, and so will I. We'll find a way. We'll all live. I would never forgive myself if you died for my sake. Don't you understand that? You're *my* leader. And my revered friend."

Onni shakes his head. "Onni find more water for Kristal. Onni's mission now."

More people raise their hands. The Birds are now all around us, up front. But I refuse to take their precious rations and put their lives in danger.

"Onni, your only mission is to stay alive." I glance at my mother. She's swiping at her cheeks, but I have a feeling her tears are not for Onni.

She pulls me aside. "Do you realize you have placed yourself in grave danger once again? You can't go very long without water like we can. You're so fresh from Earth and haven't yet adapted. And we're running out more quickly than we anticipated. Yes, we love Onni. We'd give anything for more water so that everyone may survive. Well, we're just going to have to find more volunteers—the smaller Birds, or I will give you my own rations if no one else—"

Don't they realize? Have they forgotten so soon General Waara just gave them the plan! *I am not the damn Crystal Child!* This has got to stop. Forgetting my shyness, my shame, my bright red cheeks, I resolutely mount the five steps to the larger podium. "Please, Birds, no more sacrifice! I'm no better than you or anyone. And I certainly don't deserve anyone's precious rations. I will think of a way to find water. It's my problem, not yours. I can't—I won't accept it. I'm not the Crystal Child! Listen to General Waara!"

General Waara holds up a hand. As soon as the crowd sees him, they go silent. "Ladies, gentlemen, Birds, I have a solution. No one needs to sacrifice anything. I wasn't going to divulge this, but a few of my soldiers and I are making a trip to Earth as we have found out there were more QC survivors."

The crowd gasps, then falls silent.

"Yes, you heard right. That's all I can tell you now. But since we'll be making the trip anyway, I will personally escort Kristal back to Earth to replenish her water."

My mother goes pale, her eyes round as moons.

"Then we will be on our way to Cancri e to accomplish our mission there. At long last, we are ready."

The crowd goes insane with cheers. Mutsi's vehemently shaking her head. It's another of the general's executive decisions without her input. Oh, boy.

He fist-bumps the air. "We will keep you apprised through the Lucy grapevine until then..." He slams another fist over his heart. More roars from the crowd. Then as the general leaps down from the podium, they all begin to disperse, murmuring, conversing, a shout-out here and there. I'm sure they're all crazy curious to know who may have survived all these years. Waara is wise not to say anything more as well; they may not have survived the last few days.

Mutsi and I lock eyes. She reaches out. I grab her hand. With her other hand, she grabs Waara's sleeve as he passes by. "You think going back to Earth now may be as easy as chanting a code, but it's not, not now. The enemy knows my parents' location now. The area must be crawling with Cancris there. You said you are preparing three of your soldiers to find my parents. Fine, but now you think you can take on the protection of my daughter as well? No, Hale, I won't—"

"Myrakka, you know we're more than capable."

She pauses, still shaking her head, then suddenly stops in mid-shake. "I insist on coming with you."

"Myrakka, now—"

"Hale, I'm going. That's a given. If you say no, I'll just travel alone. As you recall, I've already made a solo trip—quite successfully, I may add."

"Hell, Myrakka, you always were a pain and a half. I have the scars on my neck to prove it."

Mutsi's face reddens. "That's not fair, Hale."

He half-smiles. "Fine, but you will not travel by yourself. We'll be right with you this time."

"What if three of your soldiers aren't enough?"

General Waara gets between Mutsi and me and drapes his strong arms around our shoulders.

"Listen, ladies. Kristal, you absolutely must have water. And, Myrakka, you absolutely must get your parents back. And we're going to help you accomplish both missions. It's true I can only spare three soldiers. The others are readying for the great battle. But these three are the best. And we weren't armed with AK47s in our QC Community the day of the massacre. Shit, we weren't armed with lollipop sticks. Now we have the means to completely eradicate them from the entire universe. We can overcome them, no matter how many there are. And there shouldn't be too many. If their mission is solely to capture the Kurkis, or kill them, I would estimate no more than two or three. We got this, Myra. Trust me." He leans out, spits on the sandy ground, and turns back to us. Mutsi wrinkles her nose and steps back.

The general clears his throat. "Listen, we know, thanks to you, that the Earth code will land us in the forest area behind Kristal's house. We will all stay together and find Voitto and Lumi while protecting you and Kristal. Once we're in a safe place, or once the Cancris are destroyed, we'll drink until we're bloated. Get our bodies all stocked up. We'll hug the Kurkis and cry and sweat until we use up all our water and then drink some more. Now if a bot does have the audacity to show up suddenly, we'll blow it to hell. This is an easy mission. I swear to God, Myra. Won't take long."

My mother breathes in deeply. "Hale, this is much appreciated. I must admit, you've saved my sorry ass more than once." I raise my eyebrows and suppress a chuckle. Never heard that kind of language coming from my mother. Of course, I still don't know my mother that well yet. The general takes in a deep breath. "This is my job, Myrakka. Sometimes I think you doubt my competence. But I was made for this."

"I... I greatly appreciate your dedication, Hale. You know that." Mutsi turns to me, obviously relieved. "Well, all right then."

Pulling his comcard from his pocket, pressing icons, Hale says, "Ah, looking forward to reuniting with the Kurkis. Give me two minutes to suit up, then we'll all teleport together."

"They'll be ecstatic, Hale. I cannot wait."

She's obviously in denial about the news I gave her just this morning. Dr. Khumolo told me it's amazing how the brain can conveniently *forget* things too horrible to remember. I'm dreading what we might find, but I'm so beyond parched I really have no other option. I should tell General Waara about what they might find in the Kurki house. I really should. I start to open my mouth. It closes on its own. I just can't do it. I'll wait 'til we get there. Waara is back in less than a minute. Wow. He must practice putting on and taking off his diamond suit a hundred times a day. His comcard is now attached to the inner arm of his suit. I notice the pendant is on the other side. He's holding his helmet.

"They'll be here in two Ems—Bran, Kiski, and Claude—my best men. They're not old enough to remember the Kurkis, but Voitto and I were close. In fact, we'd been working together on a memory drug to treat soldiers with head injury. Brilliant man, your father." He looks over at me. "Hey, and I guess, your gram and gramps. How 'bout that?"

"Yeah." I try to smile, but it's probably coming across as a little grimace. Mutsi nods, tears welling up. The general takes off after Dr. EJ.

Okay, back to Earth, at least, for a while. Just the thought of drinking a whole glass of water would make me salivate if I had any water left in me. Oh, I can't wait. Then something plunges in my stomach, and I remember. Please, please, let my grandparents be okay. Those two shots were just warning shots, weren't they, Dad? They had to be. You're such a peaceful person. I know, deep inside, you couldn't kill anyone. Could you, Dad? *Could you?*

"Cuckoo." The half hour. I look up to the top of the Earth Clock Tower. There she is—light-gray belly, long tail feathers with flecks of white—such a beautiful Bird. I'll have to sketch her when I return. A gleam distracts me. I look to my left. It's the three Diamond Star soldiers all suited up, walking toward us like those astronauts in the old newsreels Dad used to show Tad and me. Except these astronauts are wearing diamond suits, and they don't need a spaceship. How times change.

Hale Waara fits his helmet over his head. "Okay, everyone, here we go. Grab your pendants." We all stand in a circle.

Waara reviews the number for the Earth location. My fingers tremble as I reach for my pendant, and we all chant together. *Bam!* A vision—no—a memory—bursts front and center in my brain—my father grabbing me in one arm and pointing the gun into the Kurkis' house, shooting twice. *Achilles, no, no, not now. Oh god, ground yourself, Kris, ground yourself. Cuckoo Bird, diamond pillar, fluorescent pink bush, scent of rose... It's not working... I'm sinking to my knees.* Then...

Nothing.

Earth

Thirty-Six

February 1, 2027

I open my eyes. I'm in the forest—my beloved Wonder Woodlands. Wow, that was quick. Felt that way, anyway. Maybe I slept during the trip; I don't remember a thing. I know we're still in danger, but my whole body gulps in a mouthful of good old Earth air. It's deliciously thick, crisp, infused with familiar scents—melting snow, moist soil, pine. I stand. Boy, do my legs feel lighter here. Tears well up. I'm on Earth. I'm home.

Oh, and there's Old Sam, just a few feet away. A sudden gust of wind makes his branches dance, as if waving, welcoming me back. I smile through my tears. Thanks, Old Sam. I turn, facing the back of my house. Well, there it sits, like nothing ever happened. Half-expecting to see Tad bouncing out and over to our swing set, my eyes zero in on the back door. No, Kris, it's empty. My elation evaporates. Although the house still stands, the home is gone. I plunk myself down on the rock below Old Sam—my throne for those first moments in the snow before my life changed forever. I look down. My white skirt and pink sweater with the diamonds are already smudged in dirt. Sorry, Mutsi. Maybe I can slip into the house and throw them in the wash while grabbing another pair of jeans and a sweatshirt. No. What the hell was I thinking? I sigh and turn back to Old Sam. The one constant companion in my life. Pretty sad.

A few mounds of snow remain, but most are blackened with soot, like someone sprinkled grains of black pepper on top. I realize my lips are dry as cardboard, and my tongue is like a gritty old bone.

295

Like a nomad stumbling upon an oasis, I eagerly scoop up a handful of clean snow to my mouth, letting it melt on my tongue. Mmmm, cool liquid silk. I'm in heaven.

Sudden voices behind me pierce the silence of the forest. I turn. General Waara and three Diamond soldiers—Kiski, Claude, and Bran, their names clearly visible on their suits above what must be their dog tag numbers—stand in a huddle a few trees down from Old Sam. Melted snow is dribbling down their fronts. Obviously, just like me, their first order of business was to swallow a nice cold snowball. I'm sure Mutsi's doing the same thing—somewhere. Where is she? The general sees me and points. They start tramping toward me, their diamond boots slogging in the mud. Such an odd sight on Earth.

I look around for Mutsi front, back, right, left, up toward the sky. Nothing. Shrugging, hands upturned, I mouth to the general, "Where is my mother?" He shrugs back, shaking his head, looking all around. I realize I'm shivering but not from the cold. Something seems ominous. Why wouldn't Mutsi be here with the rest of us? Maybe I'm just being paranoid. The soldiers don't seem too concerned. But then again, I can't see their faces under their diamond helmets. Cancris could be anywhere now. The soldiers are whispering among themselves, adjusting their helmets to some sort of binocular thing. All three are surveying the forest when I hear a slight rustling to my left.

"Kreestal!" I jump.

Diana Gabriel, aka Lumi Kurki, aka my grandmother, is plodding toward me, huffing like she's climbing Mount Everest. The soldiers surround me, aiming their formidable weapons. Lumi gasps and cowers. I shake my head vigorously, grabbing Kiski's arm, hissing, "Stand down. That's Lumi Kurki." I surprise myself with the stand-down command. Must have come from a Five Star Picture movie. Tad would be so proud of me. The soldiers back up, lower their weapons.

Wildly unkempt, Lumi stumbles the last few paces through the grass and snow patches. When she gets to me, she pulls me close, wrapping her arms around me, and begins to sob, rocking me back and forth. Of course, I join right in. What a huge relief. She's alive. Oh dear God. She's alive.

But no time to celebrate. She can't make noise here. I'd love a more heartfelt reunion, but there's not time. I squint to squelch my tears and pull back, putting my index finger to my lips. She nods, her wide eyes fixed on General Waara. Then she looks back at me, her voice dropping to a whisper, "Kreestal, oh dear Kreestal. Thank God, you are here, but—" She looks up fearfully. "Look at you. Where have you been? What are—?"

"Don't be afraid. They're soldiers. Here to protect us."

Her eyes are as big as moons. "We've been worried sick. Who are—?" Her fearful eyes land on Kiski. Suddenly I realize—Voitto. "Oh no. Where's…"

"Lumi? Lumi? Where are you? What ees this?"

Voitto. He's okay too, huffing and puffing and picking his way through the stones and brush of the woods. A huge wave of relief washes through me from head to toe. Thank God, Dad didn't kill him either that horrible night. I can't wait to witness this miraculous reunion. Mutsi will be ecstat—Mutsi. My eyes drift everywhere. No Mutsi. The wave of relief instantly vanishes. Voitto sees the soldiers, sees Lumi and me, and yanks a gun out of his coat. "Kreestal! Get down!"

Whoa. I stand, splaying out my arms between Voitto and the soldiers. "Stop! It's Voitto Kurki. Don't shoot, don't shoot!"

"The Kurkis? You sure?" Claude still has his gun cocked and ready.

General Waara gestures to his soldiers. With weapons down, he steps forward and removes his helmet. "Ha ha!" The general grabs Voitto by the shoulders. "Voitto, my man, you haven't changed, not one iota."

Voitto's eyes glisten. "Hale, you son of a bitch, don't lie to me. I've gained twenty goddamn pounds. My god, my hunch was right. You got our "tassa" message I assume? On Lucy?"

"We did, Voitto. Brilliant. But par for a genius." They embrace. I can barely breathe. Now I'm certain this man is legit. The general takes Lumi's hand, bows, and kisses it. "Ah, Mrs. Kurki, such a pleasure." He straightens. "Well, extra pounds or not, you're both a sight for sore eyes."

Suddenly, my grandfather's eyes widen in fear. "Down, everyone, down!"

We all crouch motionless and silent behind the trees. I peek. A cruiser passes slowly in front of our house. Apparently, they've been keeping a watchful eye since that fateful night. It goes by, turns left down Smokehill Street, and disappears. We're in the forest, about two football fields away but still too close for comfort. If they find us… *Oh no, no, don't think about that.*

General Waara whispers to Voitto, "Man, we can't even have a proper reunion. Is there a safe place around here?"

Voitto nods and motions behind him.

I notice the soldiers taking one last sweep search with their helmet binoculars, guns ready just in case. They're having no luck finding my mother. Even with the soldiers here, I'm getting really nervous about being out in the open. Maybe Mutsi landed before we did and is hiding somewhere. Smart. She'll show herself when the time is right. But the police. Maybe. My heart drops to my stomach.

Voitto whispers to me and to the soldiers, "Come, come, our safe house—it's not far."

Lumi motions. "Follow queeckly."

We trudge in a single line through the woods, glancing right and left, trying to be as quiet as we can. I step on a twig. It snaps, and I jerk. God, my nerves are on fire. Mutsi has to show up. My neck is getting sore from turning it in so many directions. Finally I give up and just follow the Kurkis. They lead us to a one-story stone ranch beside an old overgrown field—the one my bus used to pass every day. The one we all thought was an abandoned old shack. Now I know better.

We step in the front door. Claude, Kiski, and Bran are already checking draperies, closets, and peeking out windows. Then the three of them huddle in the middle of the living room, mud and debris from their boots all over the hardwood floor. I glance at Lumi, ultimate neatnik. She's entirely focused on the soldier's faces, not even noticing the mess. Then she turns to me. "My child, would you like to freshen up a bit?"

Oh, man, would I ever. But do they have clothes for me here? "Yes, I would, but—"

"Follow me." Lumi leads me down the narrow hallway to a small bedroom, very nearly identical to the one I was given at their other house. She pulls open a closet door. Immediately I notice my jeans and my Flathead Lake sweatshirt front and center, with black stretch pants and a small array of blouses, shirts, sweatshirts, and sweaters toward the back, obviously belonging to Mrs. Gab—Mrs. Kur—Lu—my grandmother. What will I end up calling her? On the floor, all lined up are shoes, slippers, sneakers, flats, boots. The slippers and sneakers are mine. They must have raided my own closet. I look back at Lumi, incredulous.

She shrugs. "We never gave up hope you would reappear. We had to be ready. Take your pick. They're all clean and pressed. The bathroom is attached. You may take a shower if you wish. Take your time."

I'm dumbfounded. My grandmother could start an organization vlog.

As soon as Lumi leaves, I pull off the diamond sweater and white skirt from this morning's ceremony. Not quite knowing where the laundry hamper is, I gingerly fold them, avoiding the mud and smushed leaves, and place them in a corner of the closet. I suppose I should point out to someone the diamonds on the sweater are real. The pressure in the shower is a slice of water heaven, aka normal. A few minutes later, I emerge from the bedroom, my hair in a Turbie Twist (she thought of everything), sporting my dark-gray Flathead Lake sweatshirt, blue jeans, and sneakers. I feel human again. Ah, that's better.

General Waara suddenly plows through the front door. His voice is low but still booms across the room. "Kiski, you keep an eye on the perimeter. Bran and I will go back to the forest and surrounding areas and check for Myrakka. Claude will be here with the Kurkis and Kristal. Don't message unless it's urgent. Tap in the new security code I gave you before you do. Then he turns to my grandparents.

Myrakka—she's got your teleportation pendants. When we find her, we'll all hydrate, then be on our way to the Diamond Star. Voitto, Lumi, collect only your most vital items. We can come back later for the rest, but frankly, I'm hopeful we will be returning to Earth permanently within a few days. But for the time being, if, God forbid, we can't find Myrakka soon, we'll head back, make a couple more pendants, and return for you. Damn it, where the hell is she?"

General Waara obviously isn't thinking about the bombshell he just dropped. He frowns as my grandmother keeps backing up to the hallway, her mouth covered with her hand. The general glances around as if maybe Lumi has just seen a ghost or a Cancri. "Lumi? What is it?"

"Meeraka? Did you say—"

Then it hits him. "Oh, good god! You didn't know."

The other soldiers apparently don't realize the significance of the name they just uttered either—Myrakka. They're so used to having her around. But the Kurkis are learning for the first time in a decade their daughter is still alive.

I join Lumi in the hallway, gingerly taking the hand I had repulsed just days earlier, and whisper gently, "Yes, Myrakka—your daughter, my mother. I've been to the Diamond Star, where she's been, where other survivors have been for the last eleven years. We've been together. I stayed at her pod, er, house. In fact, the clothes I was wearing—they're hers."

Voitto joins us. Four huge eyes are now boring into mine, uncomprehending, as if I just told them elephants are purple. Finally, Lumi whispers, "Our *tytar*?"

"Tighter?"

Voitto takes Lumi's arm. "English, dear."

He looks back at me. "Our daughter? Meeraka? She's alive?"

"Yes, she is alive and well." I think. I hope. Oh god.

Lumi's jaw drops.

Voitto, gazing upward, whispers, "*Ylista jumalaa.*"

Lumi grabs my arm, her other hand flying to her mouth. "Truly? Meer—*our* Meerakka?"

I guess it will take a while to sink in. I lower my head in shame. "And now I know—you're my grandmother, and Mr. Gabriel, uh, Mr. Kurki, I know that you're my grandfather. I'm so, so sorry for—" My throat constricts.

"You know? You *believe*?" And at once, they're all over me, smothering me with hugs and kisses. "Do not ever feel bad, child," Voitto says, his voice cracking. "How were you to know?"

I sigh out loud. Such compassionate, selfless people. I have my mother and my grandparents. I actually have family now except for—oh damn. This can't be happening. Why can't my whole family be all together at one time?

It's so not fair. Dad then my twin then—what the hell happened to her? Maybe she got caught in a tree or a snowdrift. Maybe her head landed on a rock, and she's lying somewhere, unconscious. But the soldiers seem to have searched every corner of the neighborhood including the forest with their sophisticated equipment. Please, please find her.

Lumi's eyes are still huge. "Oh, as God ees een heaven, Voitto. We have both our girls."

Bran and Kiski are deep in discussion, but Claude's been listening intently to our conversation. He stops what he's doing, kneels, takes my grandmother's hands, speaking so softly, so reverently I can barely hear him. Ah, it's Finnish. How thoughtful of him. I'm so grateful he's able to take over because I don't think I could tell them Mutsi's gone missing. And so soon after they've found out she's alive.

He finally stands, looks at me, goes back to English. "Dr. Kurki, Mrs. Kurki. We are actively searching your neighborhood, including Kristal's house, but so far, have not seen any clues. If you could give us your other address, perhaps she landed there."

My grandfather shuts his eyes, reciting their street and house number. "But oh lord, be careful. Lumi and I have been staying here ever seence that night when the Pauli clone broke in and keednapped Kreestal. Eet completely blew our cover weeth the Cancris. I have been sneaking over there. They were inside yesterday. I could see glimpses of them through the window. Somehow they have been able to escape detection from our authorities. I'm sure they have their evil ways and means."

Claude shakes his head. "I'm surprised they haven't found this safe house yet. It's a wonder you're still here and unscathed."

Voitto shrugs. "I've taken all the security precautions I know. Signals emitted from thees location are automatically encrypted."

"Well, good. Bran and Kiski will soon be combing the area and checking your house. If she's anywhere near, they'll find her. In the meantime, do you have a place that might be even more secure—a panic room, something like that?"

Voitto nods. "Come. Down below." We follow him into a small pantry. He pulls a small USB thingy from his pocket and presses it. A latch on the floor snaps. I peek. A rectangular door drops down, revealing the first few steps of a ladder. Beyond that, darkness.

Thirty-Seven

February 1, 2027

He taps another button, and a yellow light emanates from the space below. One by one we each descend the steps. When we're all at the bottom, Voitto touches another button, and the trapdoor lifts and closes. He shrugs. "Best security we could afford. Eet's been successful so far."

The general is gazing up, down, behind things. "It'll do just fine, Voitto. Can you open it up again? We're going to check out the other house." Voitto presses the button. "Wait, Hale, here. Take this. I have another." He hands the USB thingy to the general, who nods. He's up the ladder, and the two soldiers and Waara are gone before I can even tell them to stay safe. But then again, I'm sure they don't need me to tell them that.

Well, here we are. I survey the surroundings. What a difference from their previous basement, all moldy and dusty with cages and—that thing, whatever it was. Oh lord, I've got to ask them about that. Is it possible they didn't even know it was down there? I'll wait to ask them about that later. I'm surprised to see a cozy sanctuary with couches, recliners, overstuffed pillows, and a full kitchen. Suddenly, I feel my knees buckle, and I barely make it to the nearest recliner. What's with this? Voitto and Lumi rush to my side.

I thought I'd quenched my thirst by the snow. Guess I was more dehydrated than I thought. Or more terrified—or both. Where the hell is my mother? Please, please. I look up at them. "Um, more water?"

My grandparents exchange worried glances. Lumi rushes to the kitchen and pulls a glass from the cupboard, opens the refrigerator, and lifts out a pitcher. She pours the elixir of life into the glass, handing it to me, then turns to Claude. "You as well?"

He responds, "Bless you, Mrs. Kurki. I won't take much." She frowns, puzzled. "My goodness, of course, you may drink as much as you like. Heavens, eet's just water."

Claude silently, almost reverently, watches my grandmother fill another tall glass. She hands it to him, and I swear I see his eyes start to tear up. He sips slowly. I'm gulping like I've been in the desert for a month. Claude admonishes me. "Kristal, not so fast." Oh, yeah. My stomach is already feeling a little queasy with my first chugalug in weeks.

Lumi stares at me then Claude, aghast. "My poor child, they… they deprived you of water?" She shoots another wary look at Claude.

I need to correct her before she gets the wrong impression. "Oh, no, no, they were—everyone was very kind. They just don't have enough water there."

"A real shortage and getting worse." Claude shakes his head. "I can't thank you enough for the water, Mrs. Kurki."

"Good grief! Not enough water? Ees thee place a desert? Has our daughter survived well? How ees she? Please can we find her?"

Claude sets his glass down. "I'm sure Myrakka's fine. She knows how to survive. We'll stop at nothing to find her, Mrs. Kurki. After we find her, we all need to get back to Lucy, then we'll be on our way to Cancri e. We're ready."

"Cancri? You have been preparing to attack Cancri?" Voitto's eyes are wide with surprise.

Claude answers, "Yes, sir. We are locked and loaded. Just need to tweak the location algorithms and our pendants a bit, and we're all set. Been too long. But we will get our revenge."

Voitto sits down on the lounger, shaking his head and rubbing his eyes. "*Ihme.*" Such a miracle.

We sit together for about ten minutes, restless, silently fidgeting. Lumi breaks the silence. "My child. My precious granddaughter. Tell us…"

Bam! A shot in the distance.

Everyone's ears perk up. *Bang!* Another shot. Then another. We all look to Claude.

He checks his comcard, then turns it off and looks up at us. "Looks like we have, or had, visitors at your house, Voitto. They need a little help. You sit tight. We've got this. Give us ten more minutes, give or take."

My grandfather, jaw clenched, presses the gadget, and Claude practically flies up the ladder and disappears. Voitto shuts the door. It's now just the three of us. I can't stand to see my grandparents so terrified. Pasting on a fake smile, I say, "The Diamond Star soldiers are really amazing at what they do."

I've never seen them in action against an enemy, so how would I know? But I need to reassure my grandparents as well as myself. Poor Kurkis. They're pale and trembling but nodding bravely. They've been through so much. I could kick myself for thinking such mean thoughts about them. Finally, I see them in the proper light—as the brilliant, selfless, loving people they truly are. They love their daughter—my mother. And they've sacrificed everything on my behalf, with no rewards at all. The wait is excruciating. Maybe I could distract them.

"Um, would you like to hear what's been going on?"

They both nod vigorously. My grandfather says, "Please, Kreestal. We must know."

They listen intently as I hastily recount the diamond lady's appearance in the forest, the pendant, her strange instructions, and Rawol's warning that resulted in my ripped coat. Of course, they know about Dad, but I fill them in on what happened after our getaway—our strange journey into the Idaho mountains, his horrible transformation, and my subsequent teleportation to the Diamond Star. My grandfather claps his hands in delight when I describe the Birds. He tells how he and Tanimilua worked with the Bird project and had always wondered what happened to them. Then I recount our journey through the passageways, my rescue trip to Quantum City, reuniting with my mother at the hospital, then in her pod, meeting in the chamber with the QC, and finally, the ceremony, where Onni almost died, and I had to rehydrate him.

My grandparents' eyes widen with each revelation. Tears flow down their cheeks as I name all the people I can remember. When I finish, Voitto exclaims, "Not only our daughter, but EJ and the others still alive! They still exist! *Ihme!*"

I remember Dr. EJ saying that word in the chamber. I smile at them. "Miracle."

"Oh, my dear granddaughter. You are learning our language?"

I shake my head. "Not yet, but I've heard that word several times in the last few days." We sit quietly. They're beaming, in denial that my mother's missing. That's okay. My mother was in denial too—that the Kurkis might have been killed by my father. Now the Kurkis have been found alive and well, but please can't everyone be accounted for at the same time for once? The soldiers will find Mutsi. They have to. They will. I won't let myself go down any other road.

My grandmother gets up and replaces the pitcher in the fridge. When she turns, I see she's weeping softly. Voitto's eyes are also glistening with tears. I know now without a doubt. They're family. The family my father was forbidden to discuss.

The words tumble from my mouth. "Grandfather. Grandmother." They look up at me with a tenderness beyond words.

Voitto says, "Finally, the cat ees out of the bag. At long last, thank God. Eef you prefer, you may call us Pappa and Mummo. You called us those names once."

A faint recollection taps my memory. I remember the video in Mutsi's pod. And I remember what Mutsi told me. I nod. "Pappa. Mummo."

"Yes, yes, oh yes, Kreestal."

"I... I saw the blanket you made for me when I was a baby—the one with the lilies of the valley. It's...it's beautiful."

She can't speak. But then all of a sudden, we're laughing and crying as we embrace again, arms thrown around each other like a giant octopus. My Turbie Twist falls off, and my wet hair comes tumbling down, and Mummo gently frames it around my face. Her love for me is unmistakable, just like Mutsi's. I was beyond exhausted, but now I almost feel energized. My grandfather—Pappa—takes my hands in his. They're solid, strong. As he turns his arm, I notice the stitches. Big ugly wounds, no doubt from the poker my father ripped from him that night. "Oh, Pappa, I'm so sorry…"

He glances down. "Yes, well, eet could have been worse. Much worse."

Poor Pappa. Now I know why he grabbed me that day. He was just desperate for me to listen, to learn, to be careful. He gives my hands a little squeeze, then sits back, and stares up to the ceiling, as if collecting his thoughts.

"All these years—we had to keep ourselves hidden een plain sight. Eet's been so"—he sighs, bowing his head—"very deefficult. You see, we had to watch our beloved granddaughter—you—grow up before our very eyes but make sure you didn't know anything about…about us, our real identities, so you would stay safe, but even then, we were never sure—" He stops, rubs his eyes.

Mummo puts her arms around both of us. I will never again look at these people in fear and disgust. They are not the enemy. The Cancris are the enemy. These people are family; they've always been family.

Bang! Then another. Thumps, yells. We freeze. Then a familiar voice. "Voitto, don't panic. It's us."

The trapdoor snaps open. We see Claude's face first. He's sweating, breathing hard.

"Six. One escaped, but—" A thundering crash above makes us all jump. "*Jesus.*" Claude rushes down the ladder, grabbing me with one massive arm, guiding Pappa and Mummo with the other. We huddle in the farthest corner as he shields us with his diamond armor. *Bang! Bang! Bang!* Another series of shots. God, I can't scream. Immediately I shove my fist into my mouth.

Silence.

Then General Waara's voice booms upstairs, "Coast clear. Come on up. Good god, how'd that one get away? But it's the last—don't worry. Come on up."

My heart's a hammer pounding in my chest. I follow Claude, Pappa, and Mummo up the ladder to the first floor. General Waara,

Bran, and Kiski are standing over a lone Cancri robot, sprawled out on the living room floor, peppered with bullet holes, metal and wires visible in its insides. Several feet away lies a shiny, spear-like metal weapon.

Claude strides over to the now defunct robot, kicks it hard with his boot. It flies about five feet, landing in a corner. "Even their weapons are medieval. What is this thing? A giant quill pen? Yeah, that'll do a lot of damage to armor made of diamond. Guess they don't know how we have been evolving." He kicks the spear toward the corpse.

General Waara is checking his gun. "Earth mission accomplished. We just demolished six Cancris who apparently set up camp in your home, uninvited. Best of all, not a single drop of blood was shed."

Bran's sneering at the Cancri. "Just a shitload of battery acid." The soldiers chuckle.

Mummo looks like she's going to vomit. Hand over her mouth, she makes a beeline for the bathroom in the back hall. Poor Mummo. Pappa grabs onto the closet door handle, shaking his head, then fumbles around in the closet, pulls out a blanket, and throws it atop the metal corpse.

"Thees ees not out of respect but to keep the grotesque body covered so we don't have to look at eet."

"Damn them." Bran suddenly pulls out a pistol, aims, and shoots another bullet through the blanket. We all jump. A hush falls over the entire room. I look at Bran. His nostrils are flaring. "Can't wait. We'll pummel the rest of 'em down to microdust. They ruined so many lives—my mother, my aunt, my brother—they..." He stops.

The general sighs. "All right, all right. Bran, for that unwarranted abuse of a corpse, you owe Voitto one new blanket."

Voitto chuckles. "No, no retribution necessary. That blanket was already eaten by moths and smelled like mildew. Perfect shroud for a Cancri, eh?"

The general taps his forehead. "Voitto, you thought of everything. Smart move, you two, preparing a safe house."

Pappa sighs. "We knew eet was bound to happen, sooner or later."

"Well, I know we promised short order with this mission, but we didn't expect to lose anyone. We must find Myrakka. Kiski, go back to Lucy and check there. We need to stay here and keep looking. Do they have her captive somewhere? I've got a few GPS-type devices, and we can't leave any stones unturned. We'll just have to stay until we get this straightened out. Unless, of course, we find her back on Lucy. But that's—I just don't know why she would leave without telling us."

He doesn't know. General Waara, head of the Diamond Star Army, is clueless as to my mother's disappearance. Seriously? He's supposed to know everything. He's supposed to be a leader.

I shove my fist in my mouth again to keep from screaming.

Thirty-Eight

· o · o o o o o o o ◉ o o o o o o o · o ·

February 2, 2027

We spend a restless night in Voitto's basement safe room. The lodgings are comfortable, and there's an endless supply of water, sandwiches, and fruit, but we're all terrified as hell about Mutsi. I absolutely cannot lose her again. Kiski's been out all night, returning at dawn to inform us there's no sign of her anywhere—not on the Diamond Star; not on Earth. It seems as though the universe just swallowed her up. I had finally fallen asleep about 3:00 AM, but my dreams were of stone caves and metal monsters and me desperately searching to find my pendant. Oh, and the damn number—1201—written on sandy ground. Then I was awakened at six when Kiski returned with the bad news. Despite my fears, I fell back to sleep, exhausted, around 7:00 AM.

I awaken to the comforting aroma of coffee and biscuits. Despite my nerves, my stomach growls, and I start salivating. I look around and realize I'm the only one down here. The trapdoor is open, and I scramble up the ladder. The soldiers' armor lies in the middle of the living room. A mountain of diamond. How odd-looking. Pappa and Mummo greet me with huge smiles and hugs, although I can see the tension behind them. I sit in the only available chair, reach for a buttermilk biscuit from a warming platter. Mummo opens the fridge. "Kreestal, would you like coffee? Or perhaps tea or juice?"

"Oh, uh, yes, please. Just some jui—"

Scratch. Scratch. Something's at the door. We all turn at once. Waara's hand drops his biscuit and reaches for his gun. Voitto lurches toward me, grabbing me by my shoulders, pointing down the hallway to the panic room below. As I turn, I glance behind me, my brain buzzing with shock and confusion. More Cancris? Police? But—maybe Mutsi? My heart plummets to my stomach as I start down the ladder. I stop on the second rung and stand stock still, turning, peeking up to the first floor. Pappa's grabbing a gun from the cupboard. He cocks it and heads toward the door.

Lumi whispers frantically, "Voitto, put that down!"

Scratch. Scratch…

Claude places a gentle hand on Pappa's shoulder. "Dr. Kurki, we got this. Please cover your wife and granddaughter."

Pappa and Claude exchange looks. I think Pappa desperately wants to help. But he heads toward Mummo, then sees me, and motions for me to get the hell below. I duck. The general has his ear to the door—knocks, familiar shuffling noises. Then I hear his laughter. *What?* "Stand down, stand down, everyone. It's Onni One." He opens the door. "Oh, and Rawol."

"*Hyva Jumala taivaassa*—God in heaven!" Pappa freezes and his eyes grow wide. "*Onni One?*"

I'm back up the stairs in a heartbeat. Pappa and I almost trip over each other in our race to the door. "Pappa, Pappa, it's your Onni. I told you I know him."

My grandfather is smiling wider than I've ever seen. "So do we, my child. So do we."

Onni's in the doorway, a small iPad device in a bag under his wing. I reach up to Onni's neck to give him a hug, squealing in delight like small child. "Onni!"

A look of pure wonder crosses Pappa's face. He clasps his hands, bows in return, repeats, "Onni One."

"Just Onni now. Yes, you my creator? My human father?"

Voitto wipes a tear with the back of his hand. "Yes, you could say that. Oh yes, I am your father. Are you well?"

"I am well. Thanks to Kristal."

Pappa gives Onni a puzzled look, then his expression changes as he recalls what happened at the ceremony.

Onni shakes his big head. "Long story."

"Yes, Kristal told us."

"We are well. We are many in number now, all on Lucy, but we are in danger, not just Birds. Humans, fur animals—"

Pappa reaches out and tenderly touches Onni's wing. "I cannot believe eet. When I saw you last, you were just a small brown chick. How you've grown een many ways. I am so humbled, so deeply honored. And I remember our promise to you and yours—we weell keep eet."

Onni bows again. "Father, you gave life to me. I thank you. Large now, I know. And we are many, not all large. Maybe soon we return to Earth, and you help us become birds again." His claws click back and forth on the foyer tile. "But no time for other thoughts or happy reunion. Need Kristal right away."

Watching the exchange between the Bird and his creator, I'm speechless. Further evidence of my grandparents' identity. I turn to Pappa. "Onni saved my life before I saved his."

Voitto stares uncomprehending for a second, then shakes his head slightly, takes a breath, and nods toward me. I step back. Onni bows. "Ms. Kristal, hard to find you. No more stories. You must leave Earth. Now. Raaah."

"I can't, Onni. Not until we find my mother."

"*Tookertookertooker.*" Rawol is obviously impatient, like he was that day in the forest. He must have traveled with Onni to warn us. He's about half Onni's size but twice as loud. What's he saying? Instinctively, I wrap my arms around myself as I bend down. "Rawol, say that more slowly. What was that?"

He speaks even faster than the first time. "*Tookertookertooker!*"

"Raaah." Onni turns to all of us. "Rawol say Cancri took Myrakka. Intercepted during teleportation. On Cancri e now."

We all stand there like fools for a second. Then almost in unison, we screech, "CANCRI E?"

Pappa and Mummo hang onto each other. This cannot be happening. Onni shuffles back and forth. I can tell he's agitated too.

"Save Kristal once. Need do again. Now. No time cry with happiness or sadness. Cancri send message to Lucy. First time. They know location."

They sent a message. They sent a goddamn message. I could smack myself. They know the Diamond Star code. They know QC survivors are on that star, and it's all my damn fault. I could have thought it through. I could have kept it secret, just in case. I shouldn't have said anything to Tad. I could have—

Onni's head bows. "They say disassemble mother if Crystal Child not appear. *Disassemble* in Cancri mean 'kill.' Holding for ransom. Cancris need Crystal Child. Advise, please." My knees turn to jelly.

General Waara's shaking his head. "Ransom? *Sons of bitches.*"

"Damn them." Bran suddenly pulls out his pistol, aims, shoots another bullet through the blanket over the dead robot's torso in the corner. We all jump, including Onni.

"Bran. Enough." General Waara chastises Bran, but half-heartedly. I can tell he'd like to shoot his own gun in that direction.

Bran's lips are in a thin line. He reluctantly puts his pistol down. I have a feeling he'd like nothing better than to rid himself of a few rounds, Bonnie and Clyde style, into this Cancri corpse. A hush falls over the room. I look at Bran. He's still got his eyes on the lump under the blanket. "Can't wait, *cannot wait…*"

The general sighs. "Shit, all right. Armor on, everyone. We gotta move. Pendants out. Kristal, you're coming with us back to Lucy. Then—"

"No, didn't you just hear? They'll kill my mother. I have to go to Cancri to convince them to—"

General Waara's voice blasts so hard I cover my ears. "*Out of the question.* Give it up." He turns to Onni. "Okay, we're on our way back to—"

Onni holds up a wing. "Wait. Need instructions. Dr. EJ and Dahab program new code. Just in case. Will lead to Quantum City, but numbers different so Cancri can't intercept. Pendants' algorithm will handle new number—38614." Onni hands the iPad device to Voitto. "Just need quick adjustment. Jaak say 'tweaking.' Jaak and Dahab say could not risk fully programmed pendants and will need more time to erase original algorithms for Kurkis and change for safety. So Kurkis need to wait but should be ready when General

Waara return." I understand nothing. But Voitto frowns, studies the small screen, and instantly nods.

"Oh, I see. Very cautious of them. All right. I'll have all your pendants ready. Just give me about two minutes."

He apologetically looks at Lumi, shrugs. "We can't make this trip, dear. But the next. They'll be back to get us." We nervously watch my grandfather as he expertly makes the needed adjustments. He double-checks everyone's pendants, then lets the iPad fall to the floor, smashing it with his heel. We all jump back. "There," he announces. "Sorry. That was necessary. All right, everyone. You are ready. Tell them the code again, Onni." Onni says the code loud and clear.

Kiski frowns. "Once more, Onni. Three eight what?"

The Bird repeats the code twice.

General Waara frowns. "Are you sure about this?"

"One hundred ten percent. Come from Dr. EJ, Dahab, Jaak."

I gaze at the holey blanket in the corner. The thought of Mutsi on Cancri with those inhuman psychopathic things makes my stomach twist up like a pretzel. "Please, please take me to Cancri e. My mother's all alone. I have to get to her—" My knees give way, and I go down to the floor, sobbing. I need to hold it together, but I can't. Pappa and Mummo are immediately over me.

General Waara shakes his head vehemently. "Absolutely not, young lady. Do you have a death wish? Don't even think of it. Do not worry. We'll get your mother."

I'm shaking so hard I can hardly get out the words. "But they're sociopaths. They don't care. If I don't go, they might—I mean, my mother, my mutsi, I just—she, and I just…"

The Kurkis lift me up. Voitto reaches out and places a hand on Claude's shoulder. "Please rescue our *tytar*."

"We sure as hell will. But we will not use Kristal as bait, obviously. Kristal, you will not be traveling with us to Cancri e. Got that? It's in our hands. We've trained a decade for this."

Claude, all suited up, attaches his pendant to the inner wrist of his diamond arm, where it clicks in. He studies it closely, then nods. The others do the same.

General Waara turns to my grandparents, standing there, help-less, totally miserable. He talks so fast I just hope they can understand. "Listen, I'm sorry you can't go with us. Myrakka insisted on carrying your pendants. That was a mistake. The enemy was likely able to intercept because they were receiving a signal three times stronger than the rest of us. So amended plan: Kristal, Claude, Kiski, Bran, the Birds, and I will return to the Diamond Star. When we get back to Lucy, Dahab or Jaak will undoubtedly have your pendants ready, Voitto and Lumi, and then someone—Claude or Kiski—will return, and finally, you and Mrs. Kurki can reunite with everyone. Dr. Kurki has already teleported once—if you could prepare Mrs. Kurki? My grandfather nods pulling Mummo close. My grandmother is wring-ing her hands, nodding through tears. She must be frantic. Pappa's lips are in a thin line, but he's also trying like hell to stay calm.

But General Waara's not done. "Wait." He stares up at the ceiling, then back to us. "In the meantime, a contingency of the Diamond Star Army will stay on Lucy and protect those there. The rest of us—Diamond Star soldiers only—will travel to Cancri e, res-cue Myrakka, and get rid of the Cancris, every single one of them, for all time. And we'll return Myrakka to Lucy. You should be there by then to greet her. Now that we know how easy it is to off them, we won't need the whole army. Uh, just as a precaution, hang onto your gun, Dr. Kurki. I think we got 'em all, and dead robots tell no tales so they can't communicate any of this to their leaders. But just in case, they're easy kills." He turns to me. "Sorry, I couldn't have you all back to Lucy by dinnertime yesterday. But I think we can pull it off today. And, God willing, we'll have your mother and grandpar-ents there too."

All this is happening because the Cancris think I'm some kind of girl wonder. And then they have to go and kidnap wonder girl's mother? I swear I could twist their little steel necks with my bare hands. I should announce some miraculous formula for water or some other kind of trick, so we don't even have to assemble an army, but I can't. Useless. I'm just an added burden. Suddenly, I'm thirsty again. Who knows when I'll be able to return for another drink? "Mummo—could I just have one more drink of water?"

"Oh my goodness, of course." She practically trips over a chair on her way to the fridge. "General? Claude, Kiski, Bran, you too? Anyone?" The soldiers all shake their heads. Claude says: "Nah. We're good. But we appreciate the offer."

General Waara frowns at me. "Kristal, you don't have time for—"

Mummo shushes him. "She's thirsty! She needs hydration before returning to that desert star."

The general rubs the bridge of his nose and sucks in a big breath. "Yes, yes, all right. But, Kristal, the second you're done, you're outta here, okay? And remember the new code. You got it?"

Does he think I'm a child? "Yes, of course I have it." I give him a thumbs-up while I'm downing one more glass of Earth's delicious water. Mummo's right. Who knows when I'll get another chance to hydrate?

Kiski's fiddling with his pendant, gives me a thumbs-up. "Hey, Kristal, see ya back on Lucy."

Onni bows. "Rawol and I stay until Kristal safely gone. Then we be right behind."

I wave.

The general says, "Good. Okay, c'mon. Move out. Let's go." He and his soldiers chant the new number in unison. A second, and they're gone. I smile, handing the glass back to Mummo. "Thank you, thank you." She's too choked to answer me but hugs me tight, stepping back.

I grasp my pendant, turn toward my grandparents, now holding onto each other for dear life, breathing hard. I give a little wave to Onni and Rawol. My throat tightens. Before my own tears can fall again, I shut my eyes. Positive Pep Talk couldn't hurt right about now. I whisper, "Pappa, Mummo, relax. I promise you will be on the Diamond Star soon, and you will see your daughter. I can't wait to be all together." How's that for PPT? Thanks, Dad. I get a sudden vision of his face, the loving one. *God, Dad, I miss you so much.* I keep my eyes closed. I can't bear to see my grandparents' faces in such agony or Onni looking so concerned.

Pressing the pendant, my mind whirling in a hundred different directions, I suddenly realize I'm chanting the old number that's been tattooed to my brain since that first day—37093. Oh, wait. No, I freeze. No, that's—*oh my god.*

Eyes wide with fear, my grandparents are vehemently shaking their heads. Onni is reaching for me with his huge wings. Rawol's screeching is killing my ears. I've said the old number, the wrong one. I need the new one. What is—"Onni, what is—three, eight—oh, Onni, what's the—"

Inky blackness descends like a thick fog.

Thirty-Nine

* *

Finland
February 27, 2016

"Voitto, look!"

Lumi grasps her husband's coat, points toward the forest, a football field away from their cabin.

Voitto lays the ax against the woodpile, squinting into the distance.

"Lumi, do you hear that? What in God's name?"

Screams. Bang. Then another.

"Voitto? Oh god, I see them in the field. No, no, no..."

"Wait." He bolts inside the cabin. A few seconds later, he returns with binoculars and peers through them.

"Jumala, the aliens. EJ was right. What did he call them? Where was that thing from? Oh yes, Cancri e. The head being must have brought a contingency with him. But so soon? Good god, this was just yesterday. This...this can't be..." He squints again, then his voice cracks. "No, oh, Pauli...it's Pauli...he's down...and the baby, oh god!" The binoculars slip from his hands into a snowdrift.

"Krissie—the baby—" Lumi lunges forward. Voitto grasps her by the sleeve of her coat and pulls her back. She struggles. "Voitto, god, oh god. Kristal? Myrakka? Pauli? God in heaven—"

"Lumi, into the cabin now! I'm calling security."

She gasps, stumbling. "No, no, no time. The thing...the thing—the baby—"

"Lumi, they'll kill us. We can't help her if we're dead." Damn, should have bought a gun. He speaks into his cell phone. "Emergency, emergency

318

lot 25-3. They've got my family. Hello, hello? Hei—" Static hisses from the phone. He taps the phone twice on his glove, puts it to his ear again, shakes his head. "Ah, shit. They probably got to them first." He slams the phone against the wood pile.

Another scream.

"Wha—" He turns to his left, toward the forest, catches a glimpse of Myrakka at the tree line. "Who's got her? Is that Hale? Who—"

Bang! A Cancri collapses on the snow. Two left. They march in their direction with the squealing baby in tow. The alien sticks its metal finger into the baby's mouth, and the baby quiets. Oh lord in heaven!

Voitto turns and pushes Lumi into the house. "Safe room. Go— now! Go, go, go, they're coming."

"I can't leave my beibi—"

"Now, Lumi, let Waara handle it. Go, go, go."

With a tiny squeal, Lumi disappears into the cabin. Voitto scans one last time, clenching his jaw. Sucking in a deep breath of the icy air, he enters the cabin then shuts and bolts the door.

"Lumi?" he whispers. No answer. Glancing over his shoulder, he slides his hand along the floorboard leading to the hiding place. It snaps open. He turns, then softly closes the plank and descends the six rungs of the ladder. When he gets to the bottom, he peers into the darkness.

"Voitto? Over here."

A small circular arc of light appears on the wall. Lumi is seated on a small chair, one of two in the hideout, gripping a small silver flashlight. Voitto surveys the supplies; one wall filled with food items—canned fruits and vegetables, aged cheeses wrapped in plastic, boxed drinks. A mattress covered with an old woolen blanket is on the floor. His nose wrinkles. The whole room smells musty. He hasn't been keeping it up lately; he's gotten complacent. But he never thought it would ever be needed. At least it's still functional.

Suddenly, they hear the loud shuffling of heavy metal feet above them, followed by a baby's cry. Then, nothing.

They both look up, eyes frantic. Voitto puts his finger to his lips and wraps his arms around his wife. Lumi starts rocking, her face scrunched in pain and fear. The silence stretches out minute after minute. Wincing, Lumi presses a fist into her mouth, continues rocking back and forth, head shaking. Voitto stands, hands curling into tight fists. As time passes with no sound upstairs, Lumi's rocking ceases. Silent tears stain her cheeks.

Finally, they hear a faint robotic voice. Voitto slowly climbs the ladder, cocking his head with his right ear toward the upper floor.

"Medicine 3052-48. Human infant to new Earth location. Vortex most favorable."

Lumi lets out a faint squeak of terror. Voitto turns, frowning, shaking his head, index finger to his lips. He turns back toward the trapdoor, cocks his head.

Several monotone voices now seem to be discussing logistics. Incredible. "Prophecy February 5, 2027. Child's day of birth. Eleven Earth years. We wait. Take to Cancri e. Place in cold cell until—"

"Not possible. Human will disassemble there. Stay on Earth."

"Need lodging. Reprogram human. Send technical advisory device, clone from child's DNA. Body perimeter must not show metal, must appear 100 percent human."

A sudden deafening whir shakes the entire cabin for several seconds. Then silence once more, followed by the monotone voice, "83740 Dolcany, Montana, USA. 7458 Ponderosa Court. Will furnish with equipment for human needs. Nourishment for human until human male parent reprogrammed. Ng or G or J. Another whirring sound. G. One hundred percent prepared." All at once, the scraping of chairs, numbers chanted, a loud pop. Then—all is quiet.

Below, Voitto mouths, "She's alive," gestures wildly for pen and paper. Lumi grabs a small notebook with pen attached and hands to Voitto. He opens the notebook, furiously scribbling the address on the first page.

Cancri e

Forty

February 2, 2027

Time stands still. Something vague tugs at the edge of my consciousness but doesn't come forward. I forget everything as an enormous indigo flower looms in front of me. Entranced, I watch as it transforms, bursting into rainbows of arcs, blending in symmetrical patterns. It makes me smile, or, at least, I think I'm smiling. Can't quite feel my face. But I'm relaxed this time. I've done this before. I know who will greet me. I know where I'm headed. My second home—the Diamond Star.

But there's that nagging again at the back of my brain. I try to pull it front and center into my mind's eye. Something happened. Something—then the colors and sparkles vanish, and I'm back in the velvet void, forgetting everything. I wait patiently for the silkiness of the biodome to lift me up...up...and then down as I break through and land on Lucy. Should be any second now.

But the blackness continues on and on. Come on. Where is the air? Why is this taking so long? I'm suspended in a sea of nothingness. How long has it been? Time eludes me. Oh, my neck. I feel my neck. Good. My senses are returning. Ouch. Something prickly and very hot. Oh no, something isn't right. Something feels different, very different. Something happened recently. What? I—

A fiery sphere bursts into my peripheral vision, darting quickly up and over my face. My instincts demand that I scream, that I turn and run like the wind away from this frightening orb, but I am not yet connected to my body. I can only endure the flaming sphere as it hovers over me, expanding like a balloon, obliterating all else. The sphere morphs into one gigantic eye, unblinking. Closer, closer—like I'm chained to a hot stove and can't escape the searing heat. My body's motor system is offline. My senses, though, are totally intact, my nerves magnified a thousand times over, and I can feel each synapse as it sizzles then catches fire.

My throat burns like hell, and then I feel a pressure around my neck. Someone—some*thing* choking me. I gag. The choke hold releases. I try once more to yell, to get someone's attention; I think my mouth is moving, but still I have no voice, and maybe I'm just imagining my lips, my face. Yes, my consciousness is still somehow disconnected from my body. But this thing, whatever it is, is about to cook me alive and swallow me whole.

Pop. It's gone. A small wave of relief ripples through me, though I'm still in shock, terrified another might take its place. Whatever surrounds me is hot but bearable. I begin to feel my body just a tiny bit, moving back and forth a little, and I glance left, right, straining to see a color, a sparkle, anything. But it's all still black as midnight.

Ow. A hard bump, then another. I'm skidding. My body first feels torn from my mind, then weird sensations burst from within. Oh, those are my arms, legs, back, and now I'm bouncing, ouch. *God, ow ow ow.* I'm back in my physical body, rolling, ouch, God, ow, and then I fall onto some kind of rock-hard, dusty surface. I tense up as I wait—for something, anything. I keeping waiting, waiting. Nothing. Everything's deathly still and hot as blazes. Slowly, I let out a breath. Thank God, I've landed. But where? Is this the dwelling of the monstrous eye? Darkness still engulfs me, except for a smattering of stars in a blue-black sky.

I hear a groan. Good lord, what's that? I listen again. Another groan. Oh, it's me, finally reconnecting my voice to my ears and brain. Well, that's progress. If you could call it that. Then *whoosh*—holy moly, my whole body is fully online now, my stomach fluttering wildly and my shoulders radiating searing pain. Some kind of vacuum cleaner keeps sucking out my breath, and I have to keep gasping it back. My hand reaches up to my neck, where the thing choked me. God, oh god. No pendant.

It's gone. Did it fall off? Wha—then I see it in my brain—that hideous eye, the choke hold. The thing must have yanked my precious pendant from my neck. The realization fills me with rage. I want to kill it, whatever the hell it was. Without my pendant, I'm utterly lost, helpless, an invisible speck of nothing, all alone, gazing at the stars above, stars in an unfathomably infinite universe. I'm a tiny, inconsequential insect, an atom of dust. I lie still for—I can't even count the minutes, maybe hours. My mind begins to numb out from the endless silence.

I can't move. My brain drags me back into the void. Later—hours, days, years—I come to.

Where am I? Maybe Mutsi's assistant—what's her name? Dahab. Maybe Dahab screwed up the location code again, and I just landed on some raw, dark, hot desert on the wrong side of the Diamond Star. And they'll be—oh no, omigod, no no no. My consciousness intensifies, bringing with it my short-term memory. Terror grips my gut as the last moments at my grandparents' hideout slam into my mind, now fully online. She—Dahab—didn't screw up at all. I did. Big time.

Onni said the pendants were programmed for a new number, a safe one, but like the ADD—awfully dumb ditz—I am, I automatically chanted the old number. Of course, that number was now too dangerous because I told Tad, and he—I block the thought. All I needed to do was say the new number. That's all. But I blew it, completely blew it. Jackson Hynes wasn't a bully. He was just a truth-teller—a guru in clunky boots. I am an ADD screw up. *Awfully dumb ditz* fits me perfectly. And now it may cost me my life. I still don't know where I landed, but it sure as hell isn't where I'm supposed to be. Hell. Ha. My eyeballs glance right, left. Yep, hell's exactly where I am. *Clever pun, Kris.* It would be hilarious if it weren't so utterly terrifying.

I open my mouth. My voice comes out all creaky and frantic as I chant over and over, "38614, 38614, 38614" which for some reason is now burned into my brain. Why didn't I use it before? I scream, "THREE EIGHT SIX..." Wait. No. *Shut up, Kris, you pathetic idiot. You have no pendant!* It's useless. An ugly half sob, half moan escapes me. Give it up, girl. No pendant, no travel. No one can hear you, ditz. I move my head from side to side. It hurts. I'm scared, so scared. I try to arch my back, but it hurts. Damn, the ground here is scorching; the air so thin I gasp for each breath. I'm fading in and out, in and out...

I wake up, but I'm still groggy as hell. How long have I been lying here? A sharp pain stabs my ribs and my chest, making me flinch. This is probably what a heart attack feels like. Maybe I'm having... *No! Kris, get a grip.* I force myself to open my eyes. My lids feel heavy as cement. Why am I still paralyzed? I try to lift my arms and my legs. They feel like cement too. But my insides—oh god, like my blood is molten lava, bubbling through my veins. Hot. So hot. Slowly, warily, I glance left, right again. No hideous eye. But nothing else either. My eyes lift to the sky. Stars, just stars in an endless indigo night.

Holy moly, what's that? *Thud.* Fireworks explode in my stomach. Something's coming. I hear another thud then another and another. Now it's a constant *thud, thud, thud, thud.* An army? Marching toward me? Something's marching. I sense their heavy presence up through the ground, and I hear them in the distance. I can't see them yet, but they're getting closer with each thud. Every nerve is on high alert now. My ears strain to listen. Where am I? I know, but my brain hasn't yet let down its guard. But I have to remember. I have to face it square on because they're coming. *Remember, Kris, remember.* All of a sudden, my mind is as clear as a starless sky.

I've been intercepted.

I'm on Cancri e.

Forty-One

● ○ ● ○ ● ○ ○ ● ○ ● ● ● ● ○ ○ ● ○ ● ● ● ○ ● ○ ● ○ ●

February 2, 2027

A surge of adrenaline shoots through my veins. *Thud, thud, thud.* Then silence. I strain to hear. Nothing. I start to zone out, then THUD! I jerk, fully alert again.

The surface under me is like a Florida blacktop at noon in August, and I twist and turn like a flapping fish. I need to find the strength to get up and out of this inferno. I'm going to die of the heat—or of...*them.* They can't know I'm here. I have to hide. I force my eyelids to move up, left, right. All I can see is flatness and reddish dirt. Keep looking, Kris. I strain my eyes to look even farther. Oh god, in the distance—rockiness and mountains, some with pointed peaks and some with flat plateaus. Are those volcanoes? With great effort, I raise myself on my elbows and scan the horizon. Three volcanoes are blasting lava, sparkly lava, into the dark, starry sky. If I weren't so terrified, I would be reveling in the beauty of this glittery, dark landscape. But one thing's for sure. This is no Diamond Star. I was right. This is 55 Cancri e, the planet my grandfather—and Alek—were going to teach me all about.

Suddenly my elbows give way, and I collapse to the ground. *Ouch—god, it's hot.* The water I drank at my grandparents' safe house is gushing out my pores, trickling down my temples, my back, my torso, drenching my entire body. PPT is useless now. But what's that other technique Dad taught me? Oh yeah. Instead of words, use pictures. *Visualize* what you want. *Feel* it in your mind. Okay, here goes: I close my eyes tightly. *C'mon, Kris, a picture, envision it. C'mon, a mind painting.* I try, but it's a blur—blue frozen pond, mounds of white, frosty snow—icicles, ice, ice, ice. *C'mon, Kris, think! Cold, frozen...* A jumble of white and blue appears in my head then disappears. I just can't maintain it. It's too deathly hot here. I'm in survival mode. I need major help. But I don't dare make a sound. A sudden vision of my father and my twin appear in front and center of my mind. I can barely keep from screaming my guts out, but I have to stay quiet. The Cancris can't find me. They just can't.

Clang, clang.

My eyes fly open. I can't keep them open. They burn. Oh god, I shut them tight again. Sounds like the chains of Marley's ghost, rattling across the floor, louder and louder until my ears sting. Closer, closer, the clanging gives way to a metallic pounding, pounding—like marching boots? I drag my eyelids back open. I have to. The darkness around me lightens to a soft orange glow and then...

I see them.

They see me.

My legs and arms instinctively curl around my torso like a shell. God, everything hurts. A moan escapes my parched lips. I peek from the tops of my eyeballs. Gruesome, tall creatures surround me, all metal, steel ball bearings in their eye sockets, god, like my father's in those last, horrible seconds or like Tad's eyes before he disappeared. Two gaping holes, one for each nostril, oblong slits where mouths should be. No ears but tiny holes on each side, where ears should be, like little receivers for sound waves. Steel claws for hands and feet. The same steel claws that...oh, I can't think of that. No, no, no. I pray my mind will go blank, or slip into a coma—anything to make these hideous visions disappear.

This is death, and they—the Cancris—are the devil's underlings. They've come to join me in this hell. I'm going to die here, now, in this god-forsaken place with these terrifying monsters, or maybe I'm already dead. *Please help...*my mouth opens. *Shut up, Kris. No one's here to help you, not a single soul.* Am I still breathing?

I have to squint because I'll vomit if I get a good look, then I'll choke on it and aspirate and die. I know I will. One of the demons pushes the others aside and stands at my feet, peering down at me.

A scream shoots from my throat before I can squelch it and then another and another until I think my voice box is going to turn inside out. *Stop it, stop it, stop it. Kris, you have to stop.* Then I'm coughing and coughing until I can't breathe. My lungs are on fire. I gulp in air, like attic dust in summer. I cough again then start wailing; I'm some inhuman creature now, like them. "DON'T KILL ME! PLEASE HELP—NO, PLEASE..."

My sobs come in short bursts between gasps. If I don't slow down my breathing, I'll hyperventilate to death. Maybe that would be better than what these monsters have planned. How would they— oh, I know how they kill. Mutsi told me. I'll bleed out right here, and my blood will mingle with the red sand, and no one will notice. No one will care. My bones will lie in this sandy crypt for eternity. I'm passing out. *No, Kris, don't. Think. Logic. Slow down.* Could this be a real nightmare? Could I have been drugged somehow? No. I know better now. No more hallucinations. I'm not being drugged. This is real. Squinting, I dare another peek at the tallest demon, and then my eyes open wide, and I do a double take. What? Wait...wait a minute. This thing towering above me looks different. It's mostly metal, like the others. But its face, skin on the upper part, brown eyes, and hands like a human's. It's familiar—*oh!*

It's the thing that was in the Gabriels' basement that first day. The thing with the half-Alek face. In all the chaos, I forgot to ask Mummo and Pappa for an explanation. I can't believe I forgot to ask. What's the matter with me? I'm so goddamned ADD. How the hell could I have forgotten to ask? What's it doing here—with the Cancris? Is it on *their* side?

Are my grandparents really who they say they are? I was so sure, but maybe I'm totally mixed up and my grandparents are really on the Cancri side, fooling *me*. No, I can't think that way. Most likely, my grandparents didn't even know the thing was hiding out in their basement. That must be it. I blink. It blinks back, just like it did before.

But holy moly, now it's winking? At me? One Alek eye open, one closed. That's an Alek wink all right. Holy mother of god, what is going on? Does Alek know his eyes have been stolen? It winks again. This is no accident. What the hell is happening?

Suddenly, all the fear, confusion, and exhaustion explode in my brain, and I dissolve in loud, beastly howls. My voice reminds me of the coyotes that roam in the forest behind our house...our house—my home in Dolcany, Montana. The vivid picture—our forest, Old Sam—enters my mind, and I choke. I just want to go home, just go home. *Please, dear God, take me home.* If I have to die, fine, just take me home. I'd rather die in my sacred forest, at the foot of Old Sam.

From my time on Lucy to my return to Earth and reunion with my grandparents, I thought my life was starting to make some sense. Now I'm back to square one. My brain is as fried as my body. I halt in midscream and fall mute. I'm beyond tears. Yes, let me die, right here, right now. I'm so confused and so, so tired. And the pain—it's excruciating. And it's everywhere.

From far away, I hear the Alek thing speaking to the others. "She is found."

Another robotic voice replies, "Keep Crystal Child until prophecy date. Soon."

The metal clanging is unbearable—chains, pipes, God knows what, but sounds like weapons capable of ripping human flesh apart like a paper shredder. Despite the fierce heat, I shiver.

Another robotic voice says, "Yes, with Cancris now. Disassemble other female human. Female parent not needed."

My ears prickle. Wait, what was that? Can disassemble other female human? Female parent not needed? My skin crawls. *Disassemble*—Dad said that about my brother. It must mean—oh no, no, no. Mutsi. *Mutsi.* She's here too. But where? Onni said they're holding her for ransom. They wanted me. Now they have me. Does that mean—oh no, no. I just found my mother after eleven years. They can't...they can't...*they can't*...

The Alek thing holds up a half-flesh, half-metal arm. "Listen, Cancris, cannot disassemble female parent. Would harm Crystal Child. Crystal Child need be intact for prophecy fulfillment. Human brain not functional if child-parent human bond disassembled. We wait. And too high temperature here outside cells. One hundred-four degrees fatal for humans—English term *hyperthermia*. Need cooler atmosphere. Now. Will take immediately to cold cell for survival."

A smaller version of the Cancri robots steps up. It must be at least a foot shorter than the others, but it also seems to be in control. It nods to the Alek thing. "Proceed." Whirring sounds. And then it says, "Disassemble female parent. Not needed."

"*No no no no!*" I'm screaming now, screaming for her life, for my life. They cannot take her. They can't. With strength I don't have, I push it out, as loud as I can, "If she dies, I die. *And...no...water... for... Cancris.*"

Whirring.

The short one turns and raises a claw. "Keep female parent assembled until February 5 when H_2O is secured."

I've quit listening. Something about Mutsi? Assembled? My birthday? Okay, good.

The thing with Alek's eyes says, "I carry Crystal Child to cell."

The short one nods. "Cancris, back to posts. Much work to do on harvest. Now."

Harvest? I must have heard that wrong. No corn or wheat fields here. What are they harvesting? The short one begins a marchlike step, and I hear clanking again as the Cancris fall into step behind their leader. Then as one giant creature, they turn, then chant a number. Two seconds pass, then *pop, crack, hiss.* They're gone; tendrils of smoke rising upward in their place.

The Alek-eyed creature turns back to me and bends down, closely observing my face. The thing is repulsive. Alek eyes or no, the tangy metal smell and jagged flesh threaten to suffocate me. I gag, flinch, wrenching my head to the side and closing my eyes as tightly as I can. God, I feel woozy even lying flat. Has my blood started to boil yet? It's so hard to breathe. Am I dying? My limbs are going numb. Is my skin shriveling and turning black from the heat? My mind grows darker, darker...

The Alek monster straightens up to its full height, at least six and a half feet. I'm going to pass out. But if I do, it will be my last breath. I'm sure of it.

From a deep part of me, I hear my father's voice. *Get up, Kristal. Keep going. Always keep going, no matter what…*

Oh, Dad. I love you. Where are you?

Kristal, this is no time to die. Open your eyes, Krissie. You can do this. Mutsi's in danger. You have to save her. No one else can. You're the Crystal Child.

I feel my lashes flutter, close.

No, no, Krissie, don't close your eyes. Keep them open. And get to your mother. Figure it out. You can do this. I love you more than you know, Krissie babe.

A sob. At last, words come. I look up at the half-human monster. "Whe-where is my mother?"

The Alek thing keeps staring at me, totally silent. Then it glances right, left, down at me. "Mother safe. I take you to her."

I'm delusional.

It bends down toward me again, lower, closer. I cringe. Then two searing hot metal arms are scooping me up from the ground. The hands and forearms are just very warm, human warm, but the elbows and biceps are two white-hot irons scorching my flesh. I shriek, arching my back in a desperate attempt to escape from the sensation of flames licking my spine.

"Sorry so sorry." The thing. Talking again? I can't hear. It lifts me higher and higher until it is straightened up to its full height. Then it's striding swiftly, purposely toward the volcanoes. With every pounding thump, agony consumes me, and I sink into an unknown void, to whatever nightmare awaits me.

Forty-Two

○ ○ ○ ○ ○ ○ ○ ○ ◉ ○ ○ ○ ○ ○ ○ ○ ○ ○

February 2, 2027

I'm on my right side, staring at a rock the size of a small stool. It's dim in here, but lifting my eyes, I can make out an uneven stone ceiling, like an underground cave, except it's bone-dry. No mold or moss. No stalactites. No stalagmites. The ceiling is low, not much taller than I am. The ground beneath me is gritty, potholed.

Oh god, ow. My back pricks and burns like I've been stung by a thousand bees. I'm faint, even lying down. It's suffocating in here but at least a little more bearable than the outside. Is this the *cold* cell the Alek thing mentioned? The temperature's like ninety degrees, maybe. At least the humidity seems nonexistent. Arid, desert air. Did the Alek thing just dump me here to die? Then I remember he said something about my survival. Oh yeah, I'm their Crystal Child. They have to keep me alive. Seriously? Well, they're not doing a very good job so far. What are their plans for me? Why am I all alone?

As if reading my thoughts, a trembling voice suddenly pierces the silence. "Kristal? Oh, Krissie babe!" And then a face comes into view.

Mutsi. She strokes my hair. "You're awake."

Relief cascades from my chest to my stomach, and I dissolve into sobs. She lies down next to me, and we're face-to-face. Her cheeks are wet too. She's still alive, my beautiful mother, although her hair is matted and her eyes look hollowed out and her cheeks are smudged with dirt and dust. But she's here with me, my angel from heaven. To think that a few weeks ago, she only existed in my mind,

333

an unknowable ghost. Now how could I possibly live without her? With every ounce of strength, I lift my head. "Mu—"

She places a hand under my head and keeps stroking my hair. "Shhh, shhh, it's okay. Oh, Krissie, oh, my baby girl, why? Why? What are you doing here? What went wrong? I'm so sorry. So sorry…"

"Mutsi, my…my pendant. It's gone."

"So is mine, Krissie. I was intercepted on my way to Earth. The bastards. Did that horrible giant eye take yours as well?"

"Yes, it was awful."

"We'll find another way, I promise. General Waara and his army—they'll come for us." She looks away. Her voice doesn't sound very convincing. Poor Mutsi. Maybe she's losing faith. Then she brightens. "Did you make it to Earth? Did you see my parents?"

Well, at least that's good news. Dad didn't kill them that night. I fill her in on our time in the forest then inside Mummo and Pappa's safe house. When I tell her they're still alive and well, she heaves a huge sigh, chokes on a sob, her hand going to her mouth. Then I suddenly remember the plan.

"Don't worry. Even though they didn't get the pendants, General Waara has it all figured out. Mummo and Pappa will get to the Diamond Planet, and General Waara and his army will be here soon."

"It's the only thing that keeps me going. These monsters have told me nothing."

"You're being held for ransom."

"Well, yes, I know that."

"You know?"

"Kristal, you didn't deliberately defy any orders and some-how—I mean, Hale isn't using you as bait, is he?"

"No, of course not. I offered, but he refused to let me be in harm's way. The reason I'm here is my own damn fault. I said the wrong code."

"The wrong—"

"For security reasons, they set a new code for Lucy. I learned it. I was going to say it. It's my ADD. I took one more drink of water then just forgot, and the old code came out of my mouth. I wasn't thinking." I wince. The pain threatens to knock me out. With great effort, I will myself to sit up. Mutsi does too. We're still facing each other.

"Oh, Krissie. Well, hang tight. This time our army will be prepared. The QC didn't even have an army in 2016, just Hale. He was no more than a glorified security guard. And the army that came was too late. But this time, our army will surprise theirs." Mother glances up, down. "Oops, shhh, Kristal. I'm not sure. But we'd better not talk about such things. They might have this place bugged."

"Not bugged. No insects. Or listening devices. Free to talk."

"*What the...*" I cry out, whipping my head around. Peering into the darkness toward the voice from the far side of the cave, I make it out—the Alek monster. I didn't realize it was still here. Why? Is it guarding us? Then why the hell is Mutsi talking so freely?

I stare back at Mutsi, wide-eyed. She doesn't seem fazed a bit. The questions in my mind resurface. Are my grandparents really who they say they are? Why would they keep this Cancri e clone in their basement? Are my grandparents Cancri-made clones, and they're all working together? And Mutsi—why isn't she afraid of this thing? I'm so damn confused that I'm afraid my head will explode.

Mutsi sees my frantic expression at the sight of the Alek thing, whispers into my ear, "It's okay. It's okay. He won't hurt you. This guy says his name is Big Don. Apparently, he's a human wannabe. He came to me after my capture. I don't know what I would have done without him. We've had time to talk. He told me about the ransom. The Cancris haven't said a word." She reaches out and wraps her arms around me, pressing her palms into my back. I wince and wriggle out of her embrace. God, it hurts.

"Krissie, it's okay. I swear, he won't hurt you."

"*Auuggg, ow*, he—it already has."

The pain is weakening my voice. I'm not even sure she heard me. The skin on my back feels like somebody's peeled it off, and salt from my sweat only intensifies the sting. I writhe, twisting my torso, trying to separate my raw skin from my sweatshirt.

"What? Krissie? Are you injured? Here, turn around, let me see." She gently lifts the back of my sweatshirt, and gasps.

"Good god." She turns to the thing in the corner. "What happened?"

"All my fault. So sorry."

Mutsi is blowing air on my back, her eyes still on the Cancri. What did she call it? Big Don? Good lord, it has a name? And a sort-of-human one at that? Mutsi's frowning. "*Your* fault? How could you have done such a thing?" It lowers its head. "I carry her in. Big Don arms not quite human yet. Metal very hot. I forget."

Mutsi heaves a huge sigh. "Oh lord, I see. Okay, Big Don, you were trying to help. It's just that human skin is so very delicate. Her back is burned. I can't see really well, but looks like about half-first, half-second degree. Luckily, it seems the thickness of her shirt prevented it from even worse burns. But they're still serious. In any case, this looks awful. She needs cool compresses and antibiotics, maybe. Well, we don't know what microbes live here. But we must get her medical help. You must figure a way to take her immediately back to Lucy. I don't care about me but please, please get her out of here and to the Citadel Hospital."

"So sorry. Cannot right now. Alph not permit manufacture of new travelrods. Has hidden materials."

"Well, then get her damn pendant back, will you?" she snaps.

"Pendants destroyed."

Mutsi clenches her teeth so hard I'm afraid her jaw will break. "This is one hell of a way to treat the so-called savior of your species. Tell that to your leader, dammit. So there's nothing else you can do?"

"Need find Alph's material for making travelrod."

"You mean pendant."

"Very similar. Both for quick travel through wormhole. Sorry. Have searched. Will search again."

Sorry—that word again. From a robot? An empathetic robot? No, it just must have been programmed to say that word when he disobeys his own commander. Its commander. Everything's so confusing. I keep darting cautious looks at the thing. It really is pretty hideous-looking. I realize I'm panting, can't catch my breath. The pain is doing weird things to the rest of me.

My mother is clearly ready to self-combust but forces herself to remain calm for my sake. "Krissie, shhh. It's okay. It's okay. Don't be frightened. He didn't mean to hurt you. I promise you. This creature is one of us. He was staying in my parents' basement."

"I know. I saw him when I was at their house."

The Big Don thing lowers its head. "Sorry. Did not mean to frighten." The thing is all hunched over in the far corner. Just looking at it makes me sick. It's the most monstrous thing I've ever seen. Are Mutsi and I both being duped? I struggle to get words out, as I'm using all my energy just to breathe. "That...that...thing is one of us? Well, then, what's *us*?"

"Krissie—"

I've had enough insanity. Suddenly my whole body's trembling. My legs shake and tingle like they're desperately trying to get up the energy to flee. But there's nowhere to go, and I couldn't walk out of here, let alone run, even if I were perfectly healthy. I'm trapped like an insect writhing around in the middle of a giant spider web; like a lobster in a vat of boiling water. *Shut up, instincts. I cannot flee right now.* My emotional brain still isn't listening, and my body starts army-crawling to the farthest corner from the metal beast, where I huddle, whimpering, cowering like a dumb baby.

The Big Don thing duck waddles on his metal haunches, his head way down to keep from bumping the ceiling. When he passes me, I hide my head in my arms. He reaches the mouth of the cave and turns his head half around. "I get help." Then the thing is gone.

Tingles spark all over my body in addition to the burning on my back. "He's getting *help*? Surely not from them?"

"I'm not sure what he's doing, Krissie. Perhaps trying again to find materials to make new pendants. Oh, my poor—"

Pop.

"Ow. Damn ceiling."

Mutsi gives a loud *woo-hoo*. "Yea! Big Don told me you'd be here soon. Oh my goodness, you've grown."

Big Don? Who's grown? *What the...*

I squint closer into the semidarkness. Holy moly.

Alek?

Forty-Three

● ○ ○ ○ ○ ○ ○ ○ ○ ◉ ○ ○ ○ ○ ○ ○ ○ ● ○

February 2, 2027

My head's spinning. He doesn't notice me but scoots straight over to Mutsi, wriggling into a crisscross applesauce in the middle of the cell. They lock eyes. Mutsi shakes her head. *"Sellainen ihme…"* And they *embrace*. What the hell's going on? Alek and Mutsi know each other?

Alek pulls away, grinning. I think. Hard to make much out in the semidarkness. "A miracle, indeed, Dr. M. When Big Don told me—" He chokes up.

"You're—you speak English now?"

"Yeah, he told you, didn't he? Been in Montana for the last decade."

"Oh, yes, of course. Silly me. It's just so…so different coming from you. But I did hear your story. Big Don told me everything. You, Big Don, and my father were the ones who sent the Tassa message. This is all such a miracle. Divine providence if you ask me."

"Yeah, well, that was 99 percent Dr. Kurki's genius. Your father's incredible."

She pauses, taking a deep breath. "Can't wait to see him. Look at you, Little Aleksi. Aleksi Salo—you were only what, seven or eight?"

"Seven and a half. But I remember everything."

"Oh, poor dear."

My mother and Alek embrace once more. She pats his back like she's comforting a small child. Then they pull away, drinking in the other's face, smiling through their tears. I squint, then gaze in wonder, dumbfounded, from my tiny corner behind them.

Alek breathes in deeply, gives a little cough, sweeps his hand around the cave, still not noticing me in the dark corner. "Ah, the Cancri e Premier Hotel. All the comforts of home. But, damn, doesn't look like you've had maid service in a while. I'll have to track down housekeeping. You've been in this hellhole how long?"

That wry Hawkeye *M*A*S*H* humor. I could cry. It's definitely Alek.

Mutsi shrugs. "Too damn long."

They keep staring at each other, shaking their heads like they just can't believe it. Obviously, they knew each other from the community. That explains why he said he once had an accent. He's also a QC survivor. Wow. I should have been able to put the clues together and figure it out, but of course, I didn't.

Mutsi says, "Big Don wasn't sure if you had revealed yourself to Kristal yet."

I can't stand this anymore. Time to butt in. "Yes, he has. Well, sort of. But just one day, really. And I still don't know who you really are."

"Who the—?" Alek cups his palm over his eyes and squints in my direction. "*Shit*, oh, good god. Kristal, is that you?" He scoots several more feet until he's right next to me. His jaw drops. His face is so, so familiar and so normal that to my utter horror, before I have a chance to raise my eyeballs to the ceiling, the floodgates open, and I'm sobbing like a little girly-girl. He shakes his head, gently grabbing my forearms. "Let it out, kid. Let it out. You deserve your nervous breakdown. Hell, you've earned it, however you got here. Big Don didn't mention you were here. I heard you just disappeared—uh—that night after the big snowfall."

My crying is now down to a soft sniffling. "Yes." I sniffle. "Well, long story."

"Obviously. Just—"

"I just got here. That's why the robot—Big Don hadn't gotten the chance to tell you yet." I sniffle again, and to my embarrassment, reflexively wipe my nose with my sleeve. "I was on the Diamond Star and then we went back to Earth, then I was intercepted."

"Intercepted? Oh, man." He turns back to Mutsi. "Big Don told me the Cancris discovered the Diamond Star code somehow. The Kurkis and I have kept an eye on her the whole time she's been in Montana, living with the Cancri advisory device and who knows who else or what else. Pauli? Or Pauli Cancri clone? We had to be careful."

I'm seething. "*Advisory device?* Excuse me, Alek. He's my *twin*, and I live with my father—my *real* father."

Alek shrugs. "We'll let that be for now." He turns to Mutsi again. "Kristal and I go to the same school. But only recently did your father feel it was time for us to meet. I was to be her tutor. In hindsight, we both feel I should have begun much sooner, even though that would have increased the danger." He turns to me. "We didn't even want you to know I was living with the Kur—the Gabriels. We just wanted to let you in on things slowly, bit by bit. We only got through session 1, unfortunately, about Cancri e, and then this—" He sweeps his arm around the cave. "I mean, I'm all for field trips and crash courses and experiential learning, but holy crap, this was way too much too early. Sorry, kid. Your brain must be exploding."

"But, Alek, I was just at my grandparents' safe house. You say you lived with them? Then where were you?"

"Actually, here. Undercover, doing some sleuthing. Long story. But what's your story?"

It's hard to talk due to the pain, but I force it out, in fits and starts, each day, from the morning of the snowfall. I explain meeting Mutsi in the forest, Dad's breakdown, Tad's disappearance, being placed with the Kurkis and finding out about the thing in the basement, Dad's escape and our trip into the Idaho mountains, and all the rest. My voice is weak and cracks with pain, but I have to get this out. Neither Mutsi nor Alek says a word while I'm squeaking out my story. Finally, I shake my head. "So, Alek, I'm actually here due to my own ADD stupidity."

Alek sighs. "Ah, damn girl. What did I say about dissing yourself? We figured things would start happening around now. Just didn't know what. Wow. Kristal, you've showed a ton of sisu already. Dolcany hasn't had this much excitement in years. Maybe forever.

You and your so-called family's poster is everywhere. The police have issued an Amber Alert for you and your, uh, 'twin' and an APB for your dad. Escaping jail, breaking and entering, assault, kidnapping—quite an impressive record for someone with no priors. They almost placed the Kurkis into custody, but as soon as they saw their front door busted in—like, with black-belt karate strength—they immediately put out an APB and an Amber Alert. By early morning, they'd found a Honda Civic—a stolen one—in Idaho. They haven't yet ruled out murder—both you and your, uh, brother—by your 'crazy' dad who, apparently, simply disappeared from the county jail. For a boring little town like Dolcany, it's been the crime of the century."

I don't know what to say. But I have to know about this creature who's supposedly "one of us."

"Your friend, uh, Big Don, brought me to this cold cell. I saw it in the Kurkis' basement and now here. What is it? Why does...why does part of its face, ah, look like you?"

Alek grunts, wipes the sweat from his forehead. "Oh, yeah, Big Don. Another long story. We've both been living with the Kurkis—me as a foster child and Big Don as, well, my guest for the last couple of years. You didn't see me at the Kurkis because we decided I needed to be partly incognito until you were ready to learn the whole story. But as far as Big Don, or Halfling, as I affectionately call him—he's cool. Don't worry about him." Alek wipes his brow again. "Speaking of cool—whew. They call it the cold cell, huh? Wow, what a great sense of humor they have, not. Huh, a regular old frozen meat locker, this is. Where are the hanging carcasses? I could use a burger right about now." He sighs, looking into my bewildered face.

"Sorry. Listen, Kristal, don't sell yourself short. Good god, it's a wonder you haven't gone completely bonkers with all the bizarre stuff you've had to go through. And hate to tell you this, kiddo, but it's just beginning. So far, the info I gave you about Cancri e was like a one-page travel brochure. If I had known you'd actually be here now—" He shakes his head. "We need to get both of you out of here asap. God I should have anticipated and prepared for this. Damn, I'm sorry."

That's Alek too. He could ream me out royally for being so forgetful. But he doesn't. I'm so grateful I could cry. Alek was the first person to actually listen to me—my confusion, my questions, my bizarre visions, and my fears. My throat swells, I'm about to let loose again, but I can't, so I will myself to hold back. My eyes scan the ceiling. Stay dry, eyes. Don't cry, don't cry, don't cry. Alek's eyes follow mine.

"What do you see up there, kid?"

"Oh, nothing, just checking out everything."

"Not much there, not a bat, not a stalactite. Nada. Kristal, I'm sorry, really sorry."

"Yeah." The pain on my back is practically unbearable, but I don't want to let on in case—well, in case they think I'm damaged goods or disposable or whatever.

Mutsi is shaking her head, her hand on Alek's arm. "Aleksi, none of this is your fault."

Alek clearly doesn't agree with her. "But this was my job. To keep up with the Cancri antics and ward off trouble. Big Don told me you had been intercepted, Dr. M, but Kristal—well, it must have happened so quickly, and by the way, how did the Cancris discover the now defunct Diamond Star code in the first place?"

"Doesn't matter." My mother frowns, looks my way, and shrugs. She's trying to save me from outing myself, but Alek has a right to know.

Wincing with both pain and shame, I let it out. "I told Tad that morning."

Alek pulls back, staring at me like I've just made a deal with the devil, and maybe, without meaning to, I have.

"Dad was going crazy outside, and I... I thought maybe Tad, being a numbers guru, might be able to shed some light on the strange number Mutsi gave me." I arch my back. God it hurts. "But instead, Tad kinda went crazy too. Then he disappeared, and I haven't seen him since."

Mutsi's shaking her head. "Now it's my turn to say it's my fault. I should have told Kristal more. But Rawol wouldn't let me stay. He was looking out for my welfare and Kristal's."

"Oh, so the TAD—right. You outed the Diamond Star, and he disappears, huh." Alek massages his temples.

He's Tad. Tad, *not* THE TAD. But I'm in too much pain to protest, so I stay silent. My mother takes three steps to my corner, arms out, ready to give me another hug. I pull away. She seems to forget for a second my back is off limits, but then gasps softly, nods, lightly taking my hands in hers. "I'm so sorry. I should have—"

Alek shakes his head. "All right, all right. Everything's chaos right now. Let's give ourselves credit. We're all doing the best we can."

Chaos? That's an understatement. But Alek's right. We are all doing our best. But is our best enough? Alek gives me a strange look. "Kristal. Are you okay? I mean, beyond the obvious."

A large shape appears in the entryway. Alek holds up a hand. "Hey, Halfling. 'Sup?"

"Big Don feel terrible. Kristal will heal. I fix. But need other Cancris."

"For what?" Alek gives Big Don a confused look.

Mutsi steps up. "Big Don was only trying to help. He saved her life by bringing her here from the outside where she landed. Trouble is, well—"

Big Don interjects. "Forget arm appendages not all flesh. Pick her up with metal arms. Metal very hot."

Alek winces. "Whoa." He shoots me a sympathetic look. "But you undoubtedly saved her life. I'd say that was worth a little back burn."

Big Don hangs his head. "Convinced Cancris to fix."

Wha...

Alek rubs his chin. "Hmmm, destroy her back, maybe her life, by keeping her here with us, where she likely would go into medical shock... Or drop her off at Cancri General Hospital to fix her back, where she may go into emotional shock. Temporarily, I'm sure. Well, that's a no-brainer."

What the hell is Alek talking about? "Medical shock? Emotional shock? *No-brainer?*"

"Kristal, think of it this way. In approximately twenty-five minutes, Earth time, if you let the Cancris work their medical magic,

your back will be like new, and you will feel no pain. Maybe a little
lingering emotional trauma from having Cancris work on you. But
that will go away in a short time, and you'll be healed. Completely.
Or in about forty-five minutes, if you just stay here, you'll still be
writhing in horrible pain, and who knows what your nervous system will do, not to mention possible secondary infections caused by
yucky, disgusting Cancri microbes? No thank you. You could wait
for the Diamond Star Army to come and finish them off and then
go back to Lucy, but it will take a hell of a while longer, and in the
meantime, well, time is of the essence. You don't want that. See what
I mean? No-brainer."

Big Don shakes his head. "Sanity and back—both will be okay.
She sleeps while they fix. I stay with her."

Alek gives a confident thumbs-up. "Well, that's settled then."

I look at Big Don then back at Alek. I can't believe this. They're
talking about me as though I weren't there. "W-wait... No. *No way.*
I don't want any Cancri coming near me, let alone *fixing* me."

Alek sighs. "Kristal, chill. Ha ha, maybe that's not quite the
right word here. Let me rephrase that. Calm down. Think logically.
Hurting you? That's one thing they won't do. No, Kristal, they need
you alive *and* healthy to fulfill their little fantasy dream."

I snort. "What dream? You mean that ridiculous prophecy
stuff?"

"Ah, you've been enlightened. Then you know, it's not ridiculous to them." He turns to Big Don. "All right, do they know enough
to put someone out when they're—?"

"Yes. Have practiced. Perfect formulas."

Alek kneels down in front of me as I huddle in the corner.
"Okay, kiddo, normally we'd insist on human intervention, but since
you need this treatment the day before yesterday, you must put yourself in their hands, er, claws. And, truth be told, these Cancris are
light-years ahead of us in healing wounds. Don't know their secret
yet, but it's on my bucket list to find out. And just for the record,
you'll probably meet Alph, if you haven't already. You're in for a treat.
He's quite a character."

"The...the short one?"

Alek's eyebrows go up. "Ah, so you've already met him. Yep, he's the one. Or Two, rather. And truth is, we don't know exactly who he is, but apparently, he was the prototype or the first successful experiment. There's a 'One' somewhere in the Cosmos. Alph's real name is Two, so apparently, he's the leader. The other Cancris think he's their daddy. We've had a pretty nice relationship with Alph the past couple of years. He seems a bit smarter than the others. But still a completely convergent thinker. His brain, or whatever's in there, doesn't seem to have evolved much."

"Convergent thinker, robot brain?" This is the one who's going to *fix* me? I'm losing my mind.

"Yeah, you can still pull the wool over his eyes, and he'll think you're telling the truth. He's a concrete thinker. He and the others take everything literally. For instance, if you rolled your eyes and said, 'Your army is amaaazing…' they would think you really mean that. They can't pick up subtle clues that you're lying. Their weakness—gullibility—is our greatest strength except Big Don here. With my help, he's learned to process sarcasm a little better, which is good, as I am the hands-down expert at sarcasm."

I could cry. Alek's description of the Cancris sounds like Tad. But he couldn't be just like them, could he? Alek's yakking away about these inhuman monsters like they're next-door neighbors. I can't believe he's going to let the Cancris near me, let alone put my life in their claws. Worst of all, Mutsi's nodding, agreeing with them. I've had it. "I can't, I can't, please, *I can't.*" I choke back a sob. "How can you send me off with those horrible things?"

Alek blows out air. "Well, this is how—sisu."

I clench my teeth. "Grit…grit. Determination. Going above and beyond. I know. Dad told me all about it. Well, the hell with that." Both Alek and Mutsi's eyebrows go up.

Alek nods. "Kristal, I understand your fear. Just hear me out. You're going to have to take one giant leap of faith here. You won't trust them. Of course, how could you? But you can trust me that you'll be okay. You'll be more than okay, actually. These beings may be primitive in their social and emotional IQ, but they're whizzes at medical stuff, like healing wounds. And your mother, who loves you more than life itself, is asking you to do this. Really, their healing powers are incredible."

I look at him sideways. "How do you know?"

"I… I they've told me."

"That's it?"

"They don't lie. They aren't programmed to lie yet. See, this is part of their concrete-thinking glitch."

"I see." I don't see, not at all, but I don't have the energy for any more question bees.

Alek nods. "Okay, Kristal, sorry. No more time. I hate to sound like that ancient Nike commercial, but just do it. Go with Big Don. Here." Alek rips his T-shirt off over his head, bites a corner, rips it in two, then wraps each strip around Big Don's arm appendages, tossing the rest to the ground. "There. Okay. One of my dad's vintage Red Hot Chili Peppers T-shirts bites the dust, literally. My parents' favorite band. Grew up with it. Well, for seven years. I was wearing this thing under my sweater and coat the day of the… Anyway, my dad would be proud that it will be sacrificed for Kristal's comfort." Alek suddenly stops, stares at the ruined T-shirt, blinking rapidly. He looks up and fakes a smile. "Well, I doubt I'll get cold here. Lucky there are no fancy restaurants where I'm mandated to wear shoes and shirt. Now Big Don can carry you to the—whatever the Cancris call a hospital."

"They call Reassemble Room."

"Creative."

Big Don holds up each arm, inspecting the wraps, nods approvingly. Alek points to the entrance. "Okay, big guy, quickly, and in the meantime, Dr. M can rest, and I can be working on plans just in case the Diamond Star Army is late or waylaid. We have to be prepared for anything."

At this point, I'm frozen with fear. Big Don rises to a stoop and moves slowly toward me. Once again, I'm completely helpless.

I hear "Sorry. So sorry. So sorry."

I wish the thing would shut up. I close my eyes tightly, but then I open them. Where's Mutsi? Where's Mutsi? Oh, there she is, and my eyes catch hers, and I silently plead to her for moral support.

Stop them, stop them, stop them. But she merely gives me a nod of encouragement. At least, I can tell she is mirroring what I feel—mind-numbing terror. My voice is demanding that I scream my guts out, but I don't. Instead, I repeat the mantra sisu over and over. I don't think I can wiggle out of this, so might as well just relax with my sisu mantra and close my eyes.

Holy moly, who am I kidding? My mind is still buzzing with QBs. Can I trust Alek? Is Alek real? Is Big Don real? Is anything real? Is this my last day on Earth? I chanted the wrong code, and here I am. If I weren't in such a state of shock, I would laugh at my idiotic mistake. Suddenly Big Don stops and is stock still for a second. I hear a faint whir, coming from his head.

"Archive. Memory."

"What?"

"Man on table." He's silent. Then he looks straight at me with his Alek eyes. "We fix wounds. Kristal's father."

The planet stops whirling. The cave is completely still as we all stare dumbly at Big Don. Finally, I command my mouth to open. "My...my *father*? *We*?" I hear my mother cry out.

More whirring. Then Big Don says, "So sorry. Should have retrieved all information. Alph erase file. But in recycle program. I retrieve now. Association to present moment." *Whir.* "Sorry didn't before. Didn't know. Now looking at data. 2016. Father almost disassembled, very close to human death. Alph teleports Kristal's father to Cancri e. I am on right side of table." *Whir.* "Father, vomits, my leg. It's okay. Only humans disgusted with body function. Memory 100 percent online now. Two fatal wounds—one under shoulder, one in heart."

Mutsi gasps.

"We heal 100 percent, close skin. Then implant frontotemporal monitoring device so father of Crystal Child cannot go against Cancri without immediate detection. Then send to Montana to care for Kristal. Technical advisory device there too, made from Kristal's DNA. First successful human perimeter outside flesh, tissue 100 percent human."

347

Alek looks like Big Don just punched him in the face. "*What the hell, Big Don! If you knew this—wh—*"

"Memory was there but could not access until now. Alph placed memory 39479592 offline. Available to retrieve in attached recycled archives but did not know. Had no memory. Was looking up Cancri healing memories to assure Kristal and found this. So sorry." Again, the hung head.

Mutsi is slack-jawed. Then she blasts out, "But the scars. Kristal said there were *no scars*."

"Kristal correct. No scars. Cancri method heal completely—like we will heal Kristal."

I swallow hard. "So...so my father. Where is he now?"

"Not know. I will look. Father's purpose complete now. Might be disassembled. Technical advisory device—TAD too. Sorry."

Both Mutsi and I burst out in sobs.

"Say 'might.' Might be here. Might be able to reassemble. I do everything I can. But now, Kristal. Please come with me. We heal you like father. Perfect healing. Promise no frontal implantation."

Everyone, including me, is too shocked to respond. As I feel the robotic arms lift me again, things darken. Even with the cloth cover on Big Don's arms, the sudden pressure on my back makes me want to howl like an animal in a trap, but with great effort, I stifle it. Sisu. Sisu. Sisu. Dad. God. Dad. Healed. He would have died. The Cancris saved his life. He wasn't a clone. I was right. I was right. But the Cancri implant in his head. I could die sobbing, drowning in my own tears. Poor Dad. But no time for that. No one likes a whiner. Dad sure wouldn't. Positive pep talk, okay? Everything's going to be...going to be what? I can't think. At least putting me out should be fairly easy. Even without anesthesia, darkness is already closing in.

Forty-Four

• • ◦ • • ◦ • ◦ ● ◦ • ◦ • • ◦ • • ◦ •

Dolcany, Montana
Summer, 2025

"Meow."

    Alek stops, listens. Again...

    "Meoooow."

    A cat, most likely feral. Have Voitto and Lumi ever seen it? They're two streets away, working on the safe house, and Alek is alone today. Maybe the feral had taken up residence under the back porch, and the Kurkis had to shoo it out. He'll ask them later. Peeking out the back door, Alek scans the trees at the edge of the forest. No sign of it. It probably won't...

    No, wait. Ah, there it sits, between two pines, stately like royalty, a miniature sphinx, like it knows things, like it's waiting. It's large, not quite a tiger cat or tabby, but more solid, the color of champagne. Alek quietly slips through the back door to the kitchen and rummages around in the junk drawer. He knows Voitto has binoculars. Ah, there they are. He returns to the porch. The cat is still there. Hasn't moved. Peering through the lenses, Alek can see a collar around its neck with—what's that? Some type of transparent stick with holes but no, buttons of some kind. Two piercing jade eyes stare straight ahead toward the house. No, toward him. Hmmm, Alek takes a step forward. The cat doesn't scamper away as most ferals would but stays stock still, unafraid. Still waiting. For what?

    It looks well-fed for a feral. Alek turns and enters the kitchen again, this time pulling open cupboard after cupboard. Baking supplies. The

Kurkis don't drink regular milk. Where does Lumi…oh, here. Among the flour, oil, sugar is a can of evaporated milk. Good for starters. He grabs an opener from the drawer, pierces the top, pours it into a white plastic bowl, and steps outside once again.

"Here you go, Your Highness." Alek slowly lowers the bowl to the floorboards of the wooden deck then backs up. Better go in to give it some breathing room and maybe catch a peek out the window. He starts up the steps to the house, turns, and looks over his shoulder. The cat hasn't moved.

But then a glint, a reflection, near where the cat is sitting. A flash of metal?

Alek slowly backs down the stairs to the deck and turns to face the woods. Then…

Holy shit, a monster! Could it be—god, yes—it's a Cancri monster. Voitto, Lumi, and Alek were starting to feel a little too confident after almost a decade in hiding. But now, their worst fears have been realized. The Cancris have found them.

The metal being stands beside the cat at the tree line, glancing right, left, then the two of them emerge from the forest, into broad daylight, walking together as though they're companions. Halfway to the house, they stop.

Every hair on Alek's body prickles, and his limbs freeze. He hasn't seen a Cancri in years since that day. The initial shock escalates to terror, as the memory explodes in his head. His knees go weak. How many more are in the forest? So far, the three of them—human, cat, Cancri e monster—stay still for several minutes. As time passes, as he remembers the dead bolt on the back door and the gun in the box on the top shelf of the cupboard, Alek's fear subsides a bit, giving way to wary curiosity. He continues to stand on the deck, hand on the back of an aluminum deck chair, near the bowl of milk, ready to run back into the house and grab the gun in the closet if he has to.

The cat and the monster start toward him again. As they get closer, Alek can better make out the features of the monster. It's definitely Cancri. But what the…

Its body is close to one-third flesh, but its face—oh, man…oh, man. Cruel joke. Is that a mask? A partial mask? It's him. It's Alek literally in the flesh—the top of Alek's face, anyway. Looks like someone was making a mask of him then got sidetracked below the nose, where the face remains a mold of steel with a slit for the mouth.

Did the Cancris try to clone him, Alek, and then decide not to? But how could they clone him? They didn't even see him that day. Wait. Blood—Alek's blood. A flashbulb memory. A Cancri snipping off the branch of Old Sylvester with its hideous claw. The branch where he nicked his hand. They had his DNA and then decided to play around with it? Alek shudders as a sense of violation makes him clench his jaw. Well, whatever this thing is, half Alek or not, it's a Cancri, and Cancris killed his parents and his pappa—his whole family. And most terrifying, maybe it's here for him, to finish the job and take Alek's place on Earth, as if it could. A wave of rage engulfs him. He's not seven anymore. He's fifteen. And he knows how to use a goddamn gun. Come on, you bloodsucking, piece of sociopathic metal crapola. Make my freaking day.

As if they could read his thoughts, the Cancri-Alek monster and the cat suddenly halt. They're three feet away now, practically in his face. Alek has to force down every instinct to flee for his life. No. Stay. Sisu. Courage. Revenge. They may have taken his family, but they sure as hell are not going to take him and the Kurkis down too. Should he run inside and grab the gun? No, not yet. He's got to get to the bottom of this. And for now, he's got a better weapon.

His mind.

Heart beating in his throat, he wills himself to keep his feet planted on the porch, arms crossed. If it takes every ounce of sisu, Alek plans to engage this creature, wit to wit, FBI on steroids. He's handled bullies before, and he'll be damned if he's going to be pushed around by a brainless Cancri.

He waits for the monster's next move. That usually unnerves the bullies. Yep, after a few minutes, the slit in its face opens, "I defect."

Hmmm, well, okay, rather odd opening statement. Alek cocks his head. "So you're a Cancri."

The thing nods. "Yes."

"And you're saying they cast you to Earth because you're defective?"

"No. Not defec-tive. Defec-tion. I defect. Leave. Cancri hot desert planet. So I desert desert. Escape Cancri. Cancri ugly. Earth beautiful."

What the hell. Since its speech is monotone, it takes Alek a minute to decipher. "Okay, Cancri boy, listen up. English lesson, ready? Deefect—a flaw. Emphasis on first syllable. Defect—leave without permission. Emphasis on second syllable. Dehsert—hot sandy terrain. First syllable emphasis. Desert—leave abruptly. Emphasis on second syllable. Hear the prosody?"

"Pros-o-dee?"

"Never mind. You don't have it yet. You're going to have to program your speech software for better accents on those syllables, bud." *Alek winces. Did he just piss off this metal giant who could crush him like an insect? Is his life over?*

But the Cancri merely nods. "Thank you. Helpful. Will do."

Holy shit, a polite Cancri. Wonders never cease. A whirring sound comes from the thing's head. Then—"Done. I defect. I desert." *A whirring sound. Then it says,* "Cancris not nice."

The Cancri still can't properly accent syllables. But Alek gets the gist. "They're not nice? Meaning, you don't agree with their philosophy? Their values? Ha, that's rich."

"Rich? No, not rich. Have no money. Cancri have no money. Not needed."

"Are you being sarcastic or just clueless? Seriously?"

"Yes, serious. Not programmed yet for sarcasm. Humans use complicated language. Many sarcasm, idioms, figures of speech in English. Still working on algorithms for facial expression, vocal tone, theory of mind. Human mind very different from Cancri. Cannot understand many actual messages or sarcasm yet. We are not clueless. We have clues. And very serious about learn English—human. We keep evolving English—human—language. There are many. English first."

Alek drops his arms to his sides. Yes, they sure do have a lot to learn. But so do humans about the Cancris. His heart rate slows. "Okay, pal, I give up. No, wait. Cancri. Tell me your story." *The massive being takes a few more tentative steps forward. The cat follows. It stands at the foot of the three wooden steps leading up to the porch. Alek and the creature stand head to head.* "After QC killing mission successful, Cancri begin mission designated by One."

"One?"

"Our maker, like God to human."

"You Cancris have a god? Have you spoken with this god?"

"Two made by One. Two only Cancri to see One and exchange communication. Then One left many software with instructions."

"I see. And what exactly were those instructions?"

"To perfect hybrid model—Cancri AI and human. Best traits of both species. I was second experiment. First one successful for stated purpose."

"And what was that purpose?"

"TAD, technical advisory device. At Makkinen house since 2016."

"Ah, Kristal's twin, Tad—TAD. I get it now. Whatd'ya know."

"Yes, TAD perfected. At least outside, enough to look human. But TAD brain not perfected. Cancri not finished with me yet, outside or inside. But did not tell them already feel human emotion. Want to be human. So I leave. Deserrrrt. Defeeeect."

Alek's head is spinning. *"Uh, okay, big guy. Tell me more."*

"Before massacre, I fully Cancri—all metal with microchip, RAM, CPU. Saw humans—blood, dying, agony. Feel no pain then. But when Alek DNA gathered from tree branch, insert into my interior interface to be next after TAD for hybrid, I begin to think. About massacre. And become emotion."

"Emotional, you mean?"

"Emotion-al." Whir. *"Still programming suffixes."*

"Okay, so. They took my DNA?"

"Yes. So I...am...part you. Study human limbic system. Where emotion lives in brain. Online about 70 percent now. Feel sadness. Great sadness. For human group. For QC."

"You feel sorry? For the QC? So now what? You want you and me to be BFFs? Bros? I don't think so."

"BFF, best friends forever. Bros, brothers. Yes, yes, I think so. Did not kill any QC member. Just watched. But still feel terrible. Can help now. Know about Cancris. Know how to get to Cancri planet. Have ideas about destruction of Cancri. Crystal Child free from burden to manufacture water for them."

"Holy crap, you know about the Crystal Child? The prophecy?"

"*Yes, Two find prophecy in computer system at QC day he meet your One—Dr. EJ. Download.*"

"*Two? That really its name?*"

"*Cancri e leader.*"

"*Oh, yeah. Two? Like the number? As in t-w-o?*"

"*Yes.*"

"*Strange. Well, I guess if we can have a girl named Eleven in that old series—what was it? Oh, yeah, Stranger Things, then we can have someone named 'Two.' Well, anyway. Ha, okay, go on.*"

"*Prophecy claim young girl, Crystal Child, will learn secret to unlimited water production. Will save Cancri in year 2027.*"

"*Yep, that's in two years. Good luck with that.*"

"*Two Earth years, yes. If girl does not produce at that time, Cancri will massacre rest of Earth and take over all water supply. Getting ready.*"

A chill creeps up Alek's spine. "*You're joking. You mean you can't figure out a way to conjure water on your own planet?*"

"*No. And cannot joke yet. Program number 749603. Not accomplished yet.*"

"*Oh, for Pete's sake.*"

"*Who is Pete?*"

"*Never…never mind. Holy cow!*"

"*Cows have holes? Or holy, like in church?*"

Alek makes a 360 on one foot and smacks his forehead. "*Man, oh, man. I'm talking to a four-year-old.*"

"*No. Ten Earth years now.*"

"*Okay, okay, right.*"

"*Meow. Meow.*"

Alek looks down. The cat has devoured the milk, is now rubbing the monster's metal leg, apparently schmoozing in hopes of seconds. Alek's fear has vanished. He kneels. "*Hey, meow, meow. Over here, buddy, I'm the one with the food and the warmer body.*"

The Cancri hybrid reaches down, scratching the cat behind the ears. The cat purrs. Alek notes its hands are not like the hideous claws he remembers. As a matter of fact, holy crap. The hands are just like his. Weird. Surreal. A cat bonded to a hunk of metal. An AI that sort of, partly, looks just like him.

"Your cat. What's its story?"

"Belong to no one. But read about cats in science information. Cat in two quantum states."

"You mean, you're talking quantum physics? Like Schrödinger's cat?"

"Yes, Schrödinger's cat. Materialized in QC forest day of massacre. No need to kill. I take to Cancri to study. Cancri put Alek DNA in cat too."

"What? My DNA? In the cat?"

"Experiment successful. Cat act smarter than typical feline. But cat hisses at Cancri except me. Cat come with me." Alek stares at the cat, which is now staring back. *"Okay, well it's got a name now. Hey, Schrödinger, whassup?"* The cat peers into Alek's eyes, purring. Maybe it's Alek's imagination, but those eyes certainly seem more intelligent than the average bear, er, cat. Maybe it's even thinking Alek-like thoughts? Wouldn't that be a hoot? *"Yes, hungry boy, hang on. I'll get you more."*

Alek shakes his head and turns back to the robot. *"Cancri and feline doppelgangers. How did I get so lucky? Well, bro. If Schrödinger trusts you, who am I not to? I'm going to take a leap of faith and guess you're both legit. But to prove it, get me to Cancri e and back, so we can start an undercover mission."*

"Can do. Hide me in your house. We work together. I tutor you. You tutor me. I have ideas. You have ideas. And knowledge."

Huh, interesting arrangement, but how will he explain this to the Kurkis? He has no idea where all this is going. But he has a feeling whatever it is, he'd better brace himself for some kind of wild ride…

Forty-Five

·○·○·○○○○○●○○○○○○○·○·○·

February 2, 2027

I'm awake. It takes a second to realize where I am and why. A wave of panic threatens to knock me over. I breathe deeply to squelch it. *Ground yourself, Kris.* Yes, okay, an inventory of my surroundings. I'm lying on a hard surface, something metal. My eyes follow tiny wires up to the ceiling, and I realize they're holding it up. The air is warm, its scent is of grit and stone. My body feels as brittle as dead snake skin, and I can almost feel my tongue shriveling up like an old raisin. I'm craving water, like days ago. Shouldn't my body have adjusted by now to desert living? Apparently, it hasn't. I wiggle a bit then roll left, right. Amazing, the pain in my back is gone, not a trace left. And then I remember. Dad. Is this the same *hospital* where his wounds were healed? Must be. Wow, no wonder he wouldn't answer my question bees. No wonder he had such a sad look on his face all those years. Does he remember being on this very same table? My eyes grow misty, but nothing spills over. Of course, it doesn't. I have not a drop to spill.

Big Don suddenly appears in the doorway. "Kristal. Awake.. Time to take back to cave. Wounds gone. I make Cancris leave too, so no shock when you wake up."

"That's…that's very thoughtful of you." Wow. That was nice. For some reason, this monster isn't scaring me so much anymore. He's still jarringly ugly, but maybe I'm getting used to him. "Tha-thanks. So my burns—gone. It feels like they're gone. Did they really somehow get rid of them?"

"Yes, healed. You fine. You can walk? Big Don does not want to hurt you again with hot arms. Even with Red Hot Chili Peppers T-shirt, may be too warm. Only short distance back to cold cell."

"I can walk. But I'm… I'm so thirsty."

"Big Don so sorry. Working very hard to get you back to water-and-food body."

His language is odd, but I think he's saying back to the Diamond Star or Earth. Slowly I lift myself to a sitting position on the metal table, which miraculously feels only lukewarm. Immediately grabbing one of the four thin wires that hold it up, I yelp, unclench my fist, shaking my hand out. Ouch. For being so incredibly thin, these things sure are hot. A wave of dizziness hits and passes. Something's different, weird. Then I realize—my back. It feels okay, like really okay. Back to normal. If I could just have a drink of water, I do believe I could actually feel normal all over.

"Walk with me back to cold cave."

Big Don extends his Alek-like human hands. I let him help me off the table. Cold cave. He doesn't seem to know he's being sarcastic. Cold cave my eye. Interacting with Big Don makes me miss my brother even more. Tad was kind of like this. I always had to speak literally to him. If I used any kind of figures of speech or sarcasm, he would just blink or give me a literal answer or get mad. I learned to speak to him in very concrete language.

I look up at Big Don. Yes, he's grotesque. But I'm starting to feel a little guilty that I was so openly repulsed in front of him. Dutifully, I follow Big Don out into the desert or whatever they call this god-forsaken land. It's a furnace. I hope he's telling the truth about the short distance back to the so-called cold cell. We travel along what looks like a giant caterpillar hill made of sand. I glance up at the Cancri e sky, inky indigo, dotted with stars, reminding me of late summer nights in Montana. The volcanoes in the distance are still shooting sparkling lava straight up into the sky. We're in perpetual semidarkness here. If the heat weren't so unbearable, I could concentrate on the unique beauty of this planet—the soft violet glow, the billions of sparkly bits of diamond interspersed with countless stars creating a heavenly dome overhead. But the distraction of the almost-unbearable heat makes it impossible to think about anything but finding a cooler spot—and a drink of water. Even so, someone must have done something to make this planet halfway habitable to keep us from dying outright.

"Big Don?" I hesitate, then lightly touch Big Don's Red Hot Chili Peppers T-shirt-wrapped arm.

He stares at my hand on his arm then at me. "Kristal have question."

"Yes—why aren't we being incinerated right now? You must have cooled the planet way down somehow. Alek said the surface temperature of Cancri e is twenty-five hundred degrees Fahrenheit. If that were true, we would all be immediately vaporized, right?"

"Maybe was that hot once. When we appear on planet, was already terraformed and fitted with biodome so metal would not melt."

"Who did that?"

"One."

"One? Who's One?"

"Master programmer of Cancri e species."

"So where was this One from?"

"Mystery. Not know. But someone live here before us. Made freezers below surface and oxygen above. Very complicated. But need even lower temperatures. And water. Still working out kinks."

I let out a giggle.

"You laugh. Laugh means I made funny joke?"

"No, Big Don, not at all. But that last sentence—'still working out kinks'—is what we call a figure of speech. Very human. And you used it just right. It reminds me of Alek. Did Alek tutor you in English? Like he tutored me about Cancri e?"

"Yes. Alek tutor me. We work out many kinks for travel to Cancri. Alek teaching me figures of speech. Alek good tutor."

"Yes, he is." I pause. "Big Don, so you know nothing about this master programmer?

"Not one thing. Two not know either."

"Who's Two again? Sorry, my brain's still a little foggy."

"No need be sorry. Two is leader. Our leader. Short but smart-est. Alek call Alph. Says means 'leader' in English."

"Oh, like alpha dog, I see." I remember the short one, totally void of emotion, studying me lying helpless on the ground. Suddenly I feel dizzy again, almost as though I can feel this strange planet hurtling through space at near the speed of light around the Cancri sun. I've probably already been here, at least, one Cancri e year—eighteen hours. I look over at my new "friend." Maybe he's not so bad. He certainly is trying to help me, even if he's ugly and a little clumsy and clueless about a lot of things.

"Big Don?"

"Kristal."

"You sort of remind me of my brother."

"Good? Bad?"

I nod. "Good, Big Don, very good."

"You maybe like me? Maybe?"

"Yes. Yes, I do, Big Don."

He can't really smile, but I notice the mouth slit widening a little. I smile back, and then feel my swallow reflex kick in. I choke. My throat must be coated in dust. I would kill for a nice, tall glass of ice water right now or even a cup of weak tea. A puddle. A raindrop.

"So sorry cannot offer water."

I can't believe this. He's not just programmed to respond. He really, really feels sorry for me. I can tell. "Thanks, Big Don." My eyes would be misting up if they had any moisture in them. His mouth slit is still widened. He must be proud of himself. We round a corner, and there's the so-called cold cave. I can't wait to get *cool* again. Mutsi will be so happy to see…

A deafening explosion knocks Big Don and me off our feet, and we slide hard into the Cancri dust. I cry out, choke, and wave my arms frantically in front of me to clear the air.

I look up. Oh. My. God.

Forty-Six

February 2, 2027

"Goddamn furnace. Whew."

I squint through the smoke. General Waara's eyes are only partially visible through a slim transparent rectangle in his diamond helmet, but that voice is unmistakable. I think I remember tiny microphones in their helmets. When the air clears a little more, I'm shocked to see more Diamond Star soldiers—hundreds more, maybe thousands—as far as the eye can see. Relief surges through me from head to toe but also an anxiety, a foreboding I can't shake.

I yell, "General Waara, here! It's me. Kristal!"

Before I can say another word, he's beside me in three huge strides, sweeping me up into his massive diamond-shielded arms. They're surprisingly cool. "Well, well, mission number 1 accomplished." He looks up. "Thank you, God. What a sight for sore eyes. You okay, Ms. Kristal? You really gave all of us a scare, you know."

"I'm sorry, my bad. I'm fine except I'm really thirsty."

"We'll get you a little H_2O as soon as we can get you back to Lucy. They took your pendants, obviously."

I nod. "They stole them."

"Your mother's too? Your mother *is* here, isn't she?"

"Yes. And yes."

"Thank God. We'll steal them back. I'll put a couple soldiers on that detail. Do you have any idea where they're keeping them?"

"They destroyed them."

Pause. "*Sonofabitch.*" He grabs the massive arm of the nearest soldier. "Koskinen, I need you to return to Lucy and tell Jaak to program two new pendants. Then get back here ASAP."

Without a word, the soldier salutes, mutters numbers into the built-in pendant on his inside wrist, and in a flash of dust, disappears. The general turns to me. "Let's get you out of harm's way. Quickly, quickly now!"

I look around. Big Don was knocked further than I was with the sudden touching down of the Lucy soldiers, but is now standing tall, holding up his hands, obviously to show he's not armed and opens his mouth-slit to speak. "My name is—"

Waara aims his gun.

I shriek, "*No!*"

Bang! The bullet hits Big Don in the shoulder area, blasting him at least ten feet away, right onto a jagged rock that juts through from back to front. Another bullet plows a hole into his torso, and his huge body jerks like a rag doll. I stare. My breathing stops. His front is scorched and jagged. A swirl of smoke rises from his middle. His travelrod is smashed and sticking out of his leg. I keep waiting for Big Don to haul himself up and say "I'm okay." But he just lies there, motionless, arms and legs twisted and tangled, impaled on the rock. I scream.

"Kristal, cool it! All's well. It's gone. You're fine. It's gone. It won't hurt you anymore."

I finally remember to breathe, sucking in a mouthful of dusty air and immediately lapse into a coughing fit. No, no, I can't cough now. I have to explain. I'm frantic to explain, as if there were something that could be undone. I point. "Gen-General Waara, he's— that's—you shouldn't," and then I lose my breath again in another coughing fit.

The general's reattaching his weapon to his suit. "My first Cancri—on Cancri e, that is." He peers forward. "Huh, and a butt-ugly son of a bitch at that." He shifts me higher to his shoulder with his strong diamond-covered arms, glances left, right. "God, what an oven, even with the temp control under our suits. Sorry you had to end up here. We should have waited for you at the Kurki's. Shit.

Well, we're here. Been a decade in the making. But now we're going to decimate those who decimated us, eye for an eye—steel eye, anyway. Then get back to Lucy pronto. Just sit tight. He glances around then looks down at me. "So where is your mother? Lead the way."

I point toward the cold cave, my eyes fixated on Big Don. My choking is now interspersed with sobs, waiting desperately for Big Don to move—an arm, a leg, anything. But he's...oh no, he can't be—then oh god, here they come. The rhythmic clanking is back, closer and louder with each second. I push myself away from the general and manage to squeak out, "The Cancris—"

"Yes, yes, Kristal, look at me. Your mother's okay?"

"Ye-yes. But—"

"Good. That's wonderful news. And yep, the Cancris. They obviously know we're here. What they don't know is that we're ready to pulverize every last one, turning their whole army into a hunk of steamin' junk as the old song goes." He turns and says "Diamond soldiers, PREPARE" into a mic in his helmet.

A yell rises from the Cancri ground as thousands of soldiers take their positions. I should be elated. But I'm a mess seeing Big Don pulverized like that.

As the general carries me to the cold cave, he keeps up the chatter. I think he's actually just talking to himself. Maybe a way to calm his own nerves. "Been waiting for this for eleven goddamn years. Today's the day we will end the saga of this alien bullshit. Pardon my French. Every last microchip will be annihilated the way they mercilessly murdered us that horrible day. This time, we've got the advantage. Here." He sets me down at the entrance to the cave. "Stay with your mama." He calls into the cave: "Hey, Myrakka, it's Hale. We're here."

Clank, clank, clank.

Mutsi appears at the entrance, eyes wide, then her hands fly to her mouth. She sees me, grabs me, and pulls me close. "Kristal. Hale, oh, thank God. Careful. I hear them—the Cancri. Do you have our pendants?"

"Yeah, stay put. Listen, this is not my doing. We expected to wrench your pendants out of their filthy claws. Kristal tells us they not only stole them but destroyed them. I've got a soldier on his way back to Lucy as we speak to get two new ones. Shouldn't take long. In the meantime, do not leave this cave until they come. Do not move."

Mutsi smacks her hand on the cave wall. I jump. "Then give us two of the soldier's pendants, dammit. We've been without water for way too long. They can use the new ones. We *must* get back to Lucy."

Waara bows his head. "Myrakka. You've seen the suits. We can't just snap them off. They're built in, attached.

"Hale, you should have thought this through."

Waara starts to protest. "Myra, I—"

"Mutsi," I say softly, my hand on her arm, "when they were designing the suits, he couldn't have known about the horrible eye. Or that I would be stupid enough to say the wrong code and end up here, and we'd need two more pendants."

She stops, closes and opens her eyes, and turns back to the general. "Just bring the pendants here ASAP."

Waara gives a little salute. "That's the plan. I swear, should be soon." He turns to go.

I try to yell after him, but my coughing gets in the way. Then he's gone. Mutsi grasps me by the shoulders, looks me up and down as I break into loud, wracking sobs, punctuated by fits of choking. Damn, I wish I could talk.

She breaks into a sob herself. "Kristal, oh, my Krissie. You're not better? What did they do to you? Are you crying in pain, or—?"

"I'm—thir—fine. The burns, Mutsi, they're gone. But—"

"Gone?" Mutsi makes me turn around. "Let me check." She lifts up the back of my shirt and gasps, this time in relief. "I can't believe it. You're...you're completely healed."

"Mutsi—"

She heaves a huge sigh, shaking her head. "Well, at least the devil's minions are good at something besides killing us and keeping the rest of us captive and miserable. And now the great battle begins."

I'm still sobbing. I have to get a grip. I choke them back. Big Don's out there. We can't just let him lie there. I had just started to get to know him. *Kris, just spit it out, dammit.* "Mutsi"—breathe, breathe—"General Waara killed Big Don." There. Finally.

Her eyes grow big as moons. "No. *What?*"

"He was walking me back from the Cancri hospital when the Diamond Star Army" (*sob*) "appeared out of nowhere. And there was" (*choke*) "General Waara, in the front. I got his attention, and he sees me with Big Don, and without a word, he just, well" (*cough*) "he shot him. He's dead." Now after I've gotten it all out, I finally let go with my pain, sobbing and sobbing. I can't stop. For Big Don? Until a few minutes ago, the thing repulsed me. But I realized—just from our little walk back from the Cancri hospital—that he's so like Tad. So...*human*. And Alek, well, it seems Big Don was like a brother to him like Tad was to me. He'll be devastated. I try like hell to quit blubbering, but all I can do is sob—for Big Don, for Alek, for Tad, for everyone. Finally, I choke, gasp for breath a few times, and collapse on the floor of the cave.

Mutsi wraps her arms around me, rubbing my newly healed back. "Oh, dear, my poor girl. Are you sure Hale didn't just wound him? What does it take to kill one of these things?"

I force myself to settle. *Breathe, breathe.* Finally, I can talk without all the choking and sobbing. "I don't know, but it was bad. He wasn't moving. And the holes—they were really big. And a rock..." I can't finish. I glance around. "Mutsi, where's Alek?"

"He wouldn't say. But Krissie, I asked Alek about your brother."

"You asked about Tad?" Oh, how I love my mother right now. "What did he say?"

"He said he'll check around. Maybe that's what he's doing now."

A Cancri appears at the doorway. Mutsi's teeth clench. "So much for sending guards."

"You...you." The robot yanks Mutsi's arm with one searing hot claw, my arm with the other. It feels like I'm being scorched by an iron again, and we both scream. The Cancri lets go, and I grab Mutsi, and we wrap our arms around each other. Massaging her arm, Mutsi hisses at the Cancri, "Your leader just healed your precious Crystal Child of hideous burns. *Your leader.* I believe you call him Two. You don't want to burn her again and bear the brunt of your leader's wrath. Don't. Touch. Her."

The thing stands motionless for another second. A soft whir emanates from its head. Then it raises one claw. "Follow. Now."

Mutsi's breathing is shallow; she's shaking her head. "We could have been back on Lucy by now." I feel Mutsi's irritation—and for good reason. Why couldn't he have anticipated this likely scenario? Did he think the Cancris would just hand us our pendants all polished up and ready to go? Ah, I suppose the general had a million things on his mind. And to his credit, he *did* give orders to get new pendants ASAP. Now where is this Cancri taking us? Where's General Waara when we need him?

I stay silent. Mutsi's lips are in a thin line. Finally she sighs deeply, taking my hand. We follow the Cancri. It's dust as far as the eye can see. As soon as I catch sight of Big Don, I shield my eyes and point in his direction. "Mutsi, there's…"

"*Oh, Jesus!*"

I look and gasp. Mutsi's gaping, both hands covering her mouth.

A few yards away lie two of our *own* soldiers, faceup, on the Cancri ground, one with blood spreading out from his shoulder area and another with a gaping wound in his knee. They look dead or at least unconscious. This is crazy. What's happening? *Our soldiers?*

Mutsi's peering at them, horrified. "They killed our guards," she says in a whisper. I look at her face. It's chalky.

"How?"

She doesn't reply.

We should fight like crazy to stay in our cave, not to obey this Cancri freak. Instead we march on behind it like obedient ducklings, on to the battlefield. What for? Are we being executed? I look up. The scene before us makes my knees give way, and I grab onto Mutsi, who's standing like a statue, in a state of shock. I manage to stand, but I'm still clutching Mutsi's arm. We're surrounded by a sea of Cancris. Neither Mutsi nor I can move or speak.

On the gritty red sand of the Cancri e valley, rows upon rows of Diamond Star and Cancri e soldiers face each other, motionless, apparently waiting for marching orders. Oh, there's the Cancri leader in the middle space between the two armies—the Alph, their Two.

What does it want with us out here? Alph steps up, a foot shorter than General Waara. But that doesn't seem to faze him.

Alph speaks. "We kill guards for Crystal Child and female parent. Our prisoners. You have army. Plan to kill Cancri. Return to BPM 37093. Now. Your plan futile."

General Waara steps up to within a few inches of Alph, peers down at him. I can't see his whole face but looks like he's snarling. "Not as futile as yours, psycho. We will dismantle every goddamn piece of your hardware, software, whatever makes you tick. We will turn you into smoldering heaps, a permanent landfill smellier than any on Earth. *Then* we'll get back to our star and then Earth, *our* Earth, *our* Pacific Ocean, you *imbeciles*." He suddenly stops, shakes his head like he's just realizing something. "What the hell did you say? Killed our guards? No, no way. The guards can't be dead. Impossible. Their suits—indestructible. No, no."

Alph interjects. "Not indestructible. Shoulder and knee areas exposed. Use spears with poison, Muscarine chemical, but we make more lethal."

"*Shit. Holy shit.*" I can hear Waara's heavy breathing through his helmet. Obviously, he never envisioned this scenario. He turns left then right then clears his throat. Suddenly a Diamond soldier appears a few feet from the general.

"Sir. The pen…" Before he can finish, Waara points toward the cold cave. "*Go. Go. Go.*" The soldier seems confused, then catches on. He heads toward the cold cave.

Alph watches. "Your soldier will be killed by cold cave guards. Then we confiscate pendants."

Waara suddenly shouts so loud through his helmet mic I have to cover my ears. "Koskinen! Return. Repeat—*return!*" He turns to Alph. "The Crystal Child and her mother should not be here. *They will die.* We need them. At least we all agree on that, right? Do I have to spell it out? Do you even know how to spell? *Damn.* Listen, I will give you exactly thirty seconds to bring Myrakka and Kristal to me. And that's generous."

"Not thirty seconds. Not one thousand seconds. We will not do."

"You will not do. Hmmm, you think you can call the shots? All right. See what happens." Still staring at Alph, Waara aims at a Cancri soldier in the front row to his right and fires three bullets.

I jump. Two Cancri soldiers are blown backward, much like Big Don had been, knocking down several more Cancris behind them. He then trains his gun on the Cancri in front of us. My heart is knocking through my rib cage. God, hope he's a good shot. Hope all the Diamond soldiers are good shots. We're inches away from this robot. He lowers his gun. Whew.

"Your Crystal Child and her mother will be 'disassembled' as you say, just like that, if they don't get water soon. Are you that stupid?"

Alph glances at the downed Cancri soldiers, like they were two ants someone stepped on. He turns back to the general, obviously not moved in the least. More than weird. These literally are inhuman monsters, incapable of love, fear, grief—every emotion under the sun—except the will to survive, I guess. Is that an emotion? Even lizards feel that. Waara turns to Alph and jabs his index finger in its metal face. "That's the prelude."

Then the general points to Big Don, still motionless near the entrance to the cold cell. "You guys are easy targets, like that one. Now I need Crystal Child and her mother. We both need them alive, idiot. Bring them here right now."

"Cancris not that stupid. Kill Cancris not in prophecy. Cannot kill Cancris."

"Well, you don't seem to mind too much, you soulless piece of nothing. I most certainly can kill Cancris, and we will. Since when does the prophecy dictate any of our moves? You and your metal mafia murdered 254 of our people in 2016. Was the word *justice* in the damn prophecy? Doesn't matter either way. Because we're going to achieve it real soon."

"*Justice*. Abstract noun. Not programmed. Will program now." *Whir, whir.* "Justice—lack of bias. Concern for peace. Genuine respect for people. Impartiality. Cancris not biased. We disassembled QC as critical to obtain needed information about evolution of Cancris. Not personal. Very impartial. But respect not yet in database."

"Of course, it's not. You wouldn't know respect if all our soldiers suddenly dropped their weapons and saluted you, you psychopathic dumbasses. You failed miserably in the *respect* and *peace* parts of the definition. You objectified us. Your attack was unprovoked. Murdering innocent, defenseless people is definitely not *respect*. You don't even know what you're doing. God, program that into your sick software, you witless—oh, never mind. Your software will be smoking microchip in a minute. Why am I so angry? I'm talking to a piece of goddamn machinery. No time to waste. Listen, I just offed two—no three—of your soldiers. Aren't you going to shoot me now? Or are you going to poison me with your oversize quill pens?"

"Cancri spears kill. With poison. Also have guns. But not many bullets. Were not expecting attack."

"Well, hot damn. That sounds familiar. Here's your karma then. And poison, you say? Well, try getting that poison through two inches of diamond." He suddenly stops, turns, and speaks to his army through the sound system set up in his helmet. "Diamond soldiers, watch your shoulders and knees. Weapons are poisoned."

I can tell Waara is completely gobsmacked with this new information. This battle may be far more difficult than he thought.

Waara sweeps his arm across the soldiers behind him then turns back to Alph. "See these soldiers? We look a little more menacing now than in 2016, do we not? These soldiers are ready, willing, and able to disintegrate each of you so you'll all be tangled together with the dust on this decrepit wasteland of a planet. We'll grind up every single one of you. Your metal carcasses will just add one more layer of sand to your wasteland planet. We'll develop your first refuse dump. Courtesy of the Diamond Star Army. You're welcome, Talking Tinfoil."

Alph glances at the Cancri on the ground. Then his steel eyes return to the general, and he speaks in that sickening monotone. "We have two more weapons. One not ready. Other, ready. And most powerful."

The general sneers, cocking his head. "A more powerful weapon. More powerful than diamond shields and bullets, little big shot? Ha, show me what you got. Diamond over metal, moron. Do you have an ink well for that spear so I can write home when we're done with you?" He snorts.

Whir. "Ink not in—"

I can tell Waara is really taken aback by Alph's statement. Now he sounds like he's talking to himself. "Oh, man. They really don't get sarcasm. Wow. Why am I wasting my goddamn time?"

"Sarcasm. Not programmed yet. But working on algorithms."

"Great."

As if on some cue, the Cancris in front of us part, leaving Mutsi and me completely exposed.

"HOLY SHIT, GODDAMM!" The general darts toward us. Six Cancris block him.

Alph holds up a claw. "Cancri strongest weapon is human empathy."

The general frowns. He's obviously been caught off guard. He growls. "Yeah, and I know you're devoid of it. But you won't harm her because you need her. Pure and simple." He leans forward. "She's the Crystal Child, and she's the only one who will advance your species through the implementation of a water system for your planet. You can't keep her here under these conditions." He clears his throat. "She will die. Which of those three words do you not understand?"

"Yes. Need Crystal Child as proclaimed in prophecy. Will not harm. But female parent unnecessary. Not mentioned in prophecy. No need."

I scream. Hale raises his weapon. "SON OF A—"

"STOP, STOP, STOP! All of you, wait! Just hold on." Alek appears out of nowhere.

"ALEK!" I yell, then start coughing my guts out.

Alek's shoving his way through the Cancris until he's in front of us, splaying out his arms to shield us both. He looks so desperate and nervous. He leans back, whispers into Mutsi's ear. Although I strain to hear, I don't catch a word. All at once, my mother collapses. Alek grabs her just before she hits the dust. Holy moly. I stop coughing, but now I realize I'm holding my breath. I slowly let it out. *No more coughing, Kris. Please, please, please.* My heart is fluttering against my ribs like a tiny bird trying to escape its cage. I'm a statue, frozen in time. What the hell did Alek just tell her?

Alek gently disengages from Mutsi, who regains her balance, wiping her face with her sleeve, staring at Alek blankly, totally disheveled and miserable. A vision comes to my mind—Mutsi in her sparkling diamond cloak. What a contrast. With long strides to the front line, Alek plants his feet between Alph and General Waara, like a referee right before a football game. Are they going to flip a coin to see who goes first? Does Alek even know what they did to Big Don? Apparently not. He holds up his arm. "Cancri soldiers, I'm here to help."

He turns and holds out a hand to the general. I notice it's shaking, as is his voice. I can't imagine how terrifying it must be trying to referee a colossal galactic battle. "You must be the head of QC military. I think I remember you the day you came to the QC—the first security guard. You were it. That was only a few months before the massacre. I'm Aleksi Salo. My parents were…"

"Aleksi? Aleksi Salo? No kidding. Yes, I remember you and your parents. May they rest in peace. You were just a boy, huh. You're a young man now." He looks Alek up and down. We thought—"

Alek frowns. "Yeah. Uh, everyone thought, but I survived. Listen, I'm working with the Cancris now—a sort of ambassadorship."

I suppress a gasp. What will the general say to this? Alek's going to have a hard time explaining without the Cancri's hearing. He can't out himself. My legs feel so wobbly I can barely stand.

General Waara takes a step backward. "What? Run that by me again. I must have wax in my ears."

Alek winks at the general ever so subtly, giving him the look—the same one he gave me when putting Jackson Hynes in his place. I can tell he's perfected that microexpression over the years—the one that says, "I am totally pulling the wool over them. Can't you see that?" Brilliant. This better work. Of course, being neurotypically human, as my counselor would put it, Waara gets the tiny gestures right away. He returns the miniscule wink then gives a tiny nod.

But the Cancris are clueless. I glance at their faces. Each and every one just stands there, almost like they're offline. They don't get the gist, the subtle gestures, or twists of words. And they certainly didn't interpret that wink, even if they saw it. No. My heart plummets to my stomach at the realization. They don't get nuances. They're like Tad.

General Waara turns his expression to fake stern as he pokes Alek in the chest. "Aleksi Salo, this is treason. I should kill you. Right here. Right now."

Alph holds out his arm appendage. "You kill Earth man. We kill you. Earth man help Cancri. Earth man help Crystal Child."

General Waara fakes a horrified look then sighs, playing along. "All right, all right, we will not kill Earth boy, er, man." He turns to face his troops. "Diamond Star Army, do not kill Alek here. Cancris, in your own best interest, don't kill Kristal *or* Myrakka. They're a package deal. But for all others—" The general looks pained, indecisive. He glances at my mother and me with a mixture of sorrow and apprehension. Then he glances at Alek and two Diamond Star soldiers in front of us. They exchange some sort of indecipherable signal. Then General Waara raises an arm. "Protect Myrakka and Kristal. The rest of you, fire at will."

Forty-Seven

° ° ◦ ◦ ◦ ◦ ◦ ◦ ● ○ ◦ ◦ ◦ ◦ ◦ ° ° °

February 2, 2027

Two Diamond Star soldiers, one I recognize as Kiski, suddenly appear
out of nowhere, lunge at us, grab Mutsi and me, shielding us with
their massive armor. The battle explodes, and everything's a blur—
bangs, thwacks, zips, shouting, and agonized screams. Somehow they
half carry, half drag us back into the cold cell. I glance at Mutsi. She's
zoned out. My god, what did Alek tell her?

The one Waara called Koskinen appears, holding out our two
new pendants. "Sorry for the delay. Jaak was having some technical
problems. He really didn't explain. But the new number is—" He
cocks his head and stares at Mutsi. I do too. Looks like she's in a
fugue state or something. What the hell? I put my arm around her.

"Mutsi, are you—?"

And then I hear it—a howling like an inhuman beast right
outside.

Alek must have seen Big Don. I hear him screaming at several
of the additional replacements who finally got to their post and are
guarding our cave. He's shrieking words I never knew he had in his
vocabulary. The soldiers are frowning; they don't know what happened. But I do. I scramble from the cave before they can grab me,
leaving Mutsi sitting on the dirt ground, mewing like a kitten and
staring straight ahead, rocking back and forth. This is awful. I want
to stay with Mutsi, but I have to tell Alek what happened.

The furnace-like heat blasts me full force as I exit the cave. Kiski
grabs me. "No, no, wait. It's dangerous out here. You got your pen-

dants, right? And the new code? Our orders are to go back to the Diamond Star with you asap."

I—we can't go yet. How do I explain? "Yes, well, I appreciate that. But we need to stay. We have a few things we need to, uh, wrap up."

"But General Waara's orders—"

"Just hang on. We must stay, at least, until the battle is finished. We'll be safe in the cave. There's a good reason for this. Trust me." Can't believe I'm begging to stay here when I'd give anything to be headed back to the Diamond Star. But first things first.

Kiski's not giving up. "I highly recommend you teleport to safety—back to Lucy. You two must be completely dehydrated."

"I admit that, yes. But this, uh, mission is life or death. Really. Trust me. Just tell Waara we refused. Then I'll deal with him. You're off the hook."

He shakes his head, turns, ducks, and enters the cave. Good. At least, Mutsi will have someone with her.

Several more soldiers are hovering around, trying to get me to go back into the cave. I plead with them to hold off for a minute. Alek's trying to lift Big Don off the rock that has him impaled, turns to Koskinen and the others.

"Help me, please help. He's actually one of us. Trust me. Help me." He's half crying, half shouting.

Finally, the soldiers seem to get the message, and two of them and Alek grab the giant robot around the middle and pull, extracting Big Don from the rock. Grunting, pulling, slowly lowering, they finally lay him flat on the ground. I stay next to Alek, where he's on bended knee, a bereaved sibling, touching Big Don's wounds, covering his eyes with his hands like his brain just can't take in what he's seeing, moving a wire here, a chip there, trying to put Humpty Dumpty together again. The noise out here is deafening. I have to say Alek's name twice. Finally, he turns and stares at me, his eyes blank pools.

I scoot closer, having to yell into his ear. "Big Don was bringing me back here after surgery. General Waara and the army suddenly appeared. I... I called out to Waara. Before I could explain, Big Don started to talk. I don't think he realized…he—Waara—was just trying to protect me. I wish…"

"Waara did this?"

"Yes. Alek, he didn't know. He just saw Cancri and reflexively shot him to protect me."

Alek shakes his head. "He can't be dead. He won't be dead. I need to find Alph. He needs to fix him. He *has to* fix him. Did you see him?"

"Alph? No—I mean, I don't know where he is now."

The battle is fully raging now.

"It's a mess out there."

Alek pulls something from his jean pocket. A comcard? I didn't know he…

"Kristal, this is an RV, not the family-road-trip kind. It's a remote viewer of sorts. Big Don and I made it and brought it on one of our trips here. They—the Cancris—go offline and shut down every now and then to update. On our third visit, we were able to take advantage of their downtime to hide tiny cameras all over this area. Listen, I have to be on a mission, so you gotta find Alph for me."

"To fix Big Don?"

"Yeah, he's the only one who can. He has to fix him. But I need your help. Here. Let's both look for him. Take the camera. You see the battlefield and Cancri General Hospital over here? You know, the place where you were healed? And look, here's the storage building right next to it. We put cameras wherever we could. Just tap on the button—this takes you right, left, this button. Here's up and down. Just go through as many as you can find. If Alph's in the battle, go to the middle, like this. I gotta go. If you find him, press 8. I'll answer if I can."

"Alek, the soldiers have orders to take us back to Lucy immediately."

"You…you can't. Just don't. I know Myrakka won't. She's waiting."

"Waiting? For what?"

"Oh god, this is complicated. Just trust me. I gotta go get something."

"Alek, you need to stay out of the—"

"Yeah, well, I know a back way—a tunnel." The big caterpillar-like thing Big Don and I passed on our way back—so that's a tunnel. I remember it.

"Alek."

"Yeah."

"Um, if you happen to find Tad—oh, well. Stay safe."

"You too. Go back into the cold cave and hide this thing if a Cancri comes in."

"O-okay."

Boom! More screams. The fighting seems to be escalating. My heart's in my stomach, and I place my hand over my mouth to keep from puking.

Oh god, this is worse than I thought. Why am I hearing so many screams from our soldiers? Nothing can penetrate diamond, right? Then I remember poison in the Cancri spear tips and the tiny gaps in the Diamond Army suits at the shoulders and knees to make them more flexible. I can't help it. I scramble between two rocks outside, lean over, retch, then scramble back into the cold cave. Two soldiers are still guarding the entrance. My mother and I are now alone in the cave.

Mutsi's sitting up. She stares at me but then pulls me in next to her, and we sit together, covering our ears. It's deafening—the constant booms, pops, zips, zaps, groans, clanks, and thuds as bodies collapse to the ground. I hope they're all metal bodies. Peeking out the entrance, I catch a glimpse of a metal foot. I know who it belongs to. My throat constricts. I take a look at the gadget in my hand. Suddenly, something zooms in, obliterating almost the whole screen, like a giant...*omigod, omigod*...the giant eye. I scream, dropping the RV like it was on fire.

Mutsi's trembling. "What, Krissie? *What? What?*"

Forcing myself to look again, I pick up the RV, squinting at the screen. The eye is roving around, obviously looking for pendants to rip off the soldiers' suits. But they're attached and camouflaged. Smart move, whoever designed these. Probably a team. Finally, it zigzags once more around the battlefield, then shoots up to the sky and disappears. One small victory. I purse my lips and blow out a little dusty air. Mutsi doesn't need to know this. I look up, smile, act as casual as I can. "Oh, Mutsi, it…it was nothing." I hand it to her.

"It's a remote-viewer thingy. Alek wants me to look for Alph."

"What?"

"They put cameras all over and so I can look for Alph with this thing."

"Kristal, I don't want you watching—no…"

I reach out and grab it back out of her hand.

"Mutsi, sorry, I need this. I made a promise to Alek that I would look for Alph. Only Alph can fix Big Don."

Mutsi sighs, shakes her head, looks the other way, and does her staring thing again.

I get my bearings, trying out the buttons, left, right, middle. When I press the middle button, the battle on the wide open space between the cold cave and the building comes into sharp view. A Diamond Army soldier is lying on the ground, yelling, holding his knee. I zoom in closer. Holy moly, with all their foolproof diamond armor, they have a few Achilles heels—a slit where the knee bends is one. And looks like he's got a Cancri metal arrow sticking up from the kneecap. Blood flows over diamond. A Cancri towers over him.

I scream "No!"

The Cancri pulls it out and slams the spear into the other knee. I lean over, ready to retch again. I can just feel the piercing stab. I guess they felt they could keep the knee and shoulder bendable, not thinking about poison as a weapon. My heart drops to my stomach. How many more of the QC will be killed today?

I'm wincing as I watch, but I must keep searching for Alph.

"No, no." Mutsi's shaking her head. "See, Krissie, you shouldn't be watching. *Please…*"

I move the button "Gotta find Alph…gotta find Alph…"

"Kristal, no, no, you don't. You won't find him. Let the soldiers do it."

The cursor lands on another scene. More Cancris lie, jagged hunks of metal where the bullets blasted through, smoke curling upward from the craters in their torsos. A gush of liquid fire burns my throat, and I have to look away. And then I see more—our soldiers. It slowly dawns on me—the Cancris. Their weapons may be primitive, but they know what they're doing. More and more of our soldiers fall, screaming in pain as the joints—knee and shoulder—are expertly pierced by the Cancri's poison-tipped spears. Diamond soldier after soldier falls, yelling then falling completely silent and still. God in heaven, are they dead like the two guards Waara sent to our cave? I can't show this to Mutsi. Despite the suffocating heat, I begin trembling. Something's really wrong here. We were supposed to make mincemeat of the Cancris in no time. Isn't that what General Waara said?

But I have a job to do. I have to find Alph, so I keep staring at the RV. God, another of our soldiers is yelling in pain, this time the right shoulder joint. Blood pours out and down the diamond arm as the soldier shoots the Cancri with his left hand. It misses. Obviously, this soldier was right-handed. The Cancri takes its steel spear and thrusts it hard in the other vulnerable spot on the left shoulder. Oh god, the soldier cries out, sinks to his knees, then topples over. Another casualty. I feel woozy and reflexively scrunch my eyes. But I have to help Alek, so I open them a tiny slit and keep peering at the small screen.

Mutsi's crying, "No, Krissie, don't watch…don't watch."

"Hang on. Oh god, there's Alph and General Waara, who's talking to one of the soldiers like he's giving directions and an extra pendant. The soldier has Alph in a choke hold as Waara slips the pendant over the Cancri's head. The other soldier is talking now. Oh, he's chanting. All of a sudden, the Diamond Star soldier and Alph disappear. I press the number 8 and instantly hear Alek's voice.

"Kristal, you find Alph?"

"Uh, yeah. Sort of."

"What do you mean—sort of?"

"Looks like they just blasted him to the Diamond Star."

"*What? No, damn. Damn,* I should have told them to wait."

"Alek, they wouldn't have listened to you. Sorry."

"Yeah, you're right." I hear a choking sound.

The mini RV goes blank.

Mutsi takes it away. "Krissie, you can't keep watching."

"I know. Mutsi, I'm done. What did Alek whisper to you outside? Please tell me."

She closes her eyes, shaking her head. She's breathing really funny. Something's going on. Why won't she just tell me? I try to swallow but can't. I'm so beyond thirsty. My lips are dust. My mouth is sandpaper. Even my mother keeps licking her cracked lips, trying in vain to moisten them. Oh, please, please, Diamond Star Army, take us back to Lucy. Will they really win the battle this time?

The cacophony outside is subsiding a little, thank God. Then a noise—noises—right outside. I flinch. Suddenly there's Alek and two other Diamond Star soldiers, at the entrance, grunting, sweating—and pulling something. Big Don? My mother comes alive. Her eyes are two moons. She stares at the bundle whatever it is, and her whole body trembles but only for a second. Next thing I know, she's at Alek's side, helping him pull the deadweight blanket into our cell. Is it a Diamond Star soldier? I notice it looks surprisingly like one of my grandparents' blankets. When they finally drop it, the blanket falls open. My hand flies to my mouth.

Dad.

Forty-Eight

• • • • • • • • • • • ● • • • • • • • • • • •

February 2, 2027

He's unconscious, eyes closed, limbs like a rag doll. He's still in that god-awful gray jumpsuit they made him wear in jail, and now it's even filthier and in tatters. What have they done to him? Mutsi collapses beside him, cradles his head in her arms, wailing, rocking him, and calling his name. I stifle a sob. Mutsi's crying is enough for both of us. So this was Alek's mission. No wonder she was acting crazed.

Alek and I are exchanging sour expressions.

"Alph was taken to the Diamond Star?"

"Looks that way. Alek, when were you going to tell me about my dad?"

"I… I thought it best just to wait. As you can see, he's in piss-poor shape. Your mother's fainting was awful enough when I told her. Wouldn't have been able to catch both of you."

I look down at my father. My heart's going to explode right through my rib cage. We all huddle around. Please be okay, Dad, please. At least you're alive. But I want one of your bear hugs so badly. It's such a relief he's finally here, but I'm scared. No, terrified. He looks half-dead, like a person in his last throes who's been living on the streets far too long. A scruffy beard obliterates most of his face. He's never had a beard. His hair is greasy and all in tangles. His face and hands are filthy—wait. His hands. Oh god, his hands…his hands…his beautiful hands. Whew. At least, I look up at Mutsi. "His hands."

379

No response. She's gone silent, tears streaming down her face, and she's gazing upward as if pleading to the angels. I decide to wait until later to tell her about his hands being normal again. But this is a great sign. I hover over his face, gathering my own slimy, gritty hair in my fist and pulling it to the side.

"Dad? Dad? It's Kristal. Me. Krissie babe. Your daughter… your…"

His eyes fly open. Two shiny ball bearings.

I scream, backing away so fast I slam my head on the cave wall. Mutsi gasps, falls backward, and then rights herself, her hand on her heart, panting like she's going to hyperventilate. Alek immediately places an arm around her, shushing her like a father would for a small child. She's breathing so hard I'm afraid her lungs will explode. No paper bags here. Shit, I'm worried and keep watching her. Luckily, within a few moments, she slows down to moans and whimpers.

Oh, dammit to hell. This is not Dad. Dad, please, I want *your* eyes, your deep brown eyes, the ones with so much soul, even when they look faraway and even when they look sad. Anything would be better than this. After what Big Don revealed, I have every hope you're still in there. I turn my head. I can't bear to see those revolting steel balls one more nanosecond.

Mutsi's howling suddenly escalates again until it sounds inhuman, almost drowning out the commotion of the battle outside. Alek sighs, gritting his teeth. "And all that work to get him here. Oh, man, I didn't know he was this bad. I didn't want you to see him like this… I should've just intercepted Alph."

"No, Alek, you did the right thing." Didn't he? Okay, Kris, positive pep talk. Well, for one thing, his hands. His hands are human again. If they can change back, so can his eyes. I grab Alek's arm.

"Alek, his hands were claws last time I saw him. Now they're human hands again. I'm not giving up on him. I think he's changing back into a human, back into my real dad. I know he's in there."

Alek gives me a skeptical look. "But only Cancris can manage this massive makeover, and they have no use for him anymore. I found him in a bin marked *Disassemble*."

"Okay. Maybe they can't or maybe they won't turn him back to what he was. But if we can get him to the Diamond Star—"

"The Diamond Star? Then what?"

"Oh, you haven't been there. You don't know. Alek, their medical facility is incredible. I… I spent a lot of time there. Dr. B and Dr. EJ are amazing. I'll bet they can—"

Alek is giving me a look I can't figure out—half puzzled, half "are you crazy?" Suddenly, he grips my arm so hard I cry out. He lets go. Voice shaking, he speaks softly, "Did you say 'Dr. EJ,' Dr. *Who?*"

"Ye-yeah. Dr. EJ and Dr. B, you remember?"

"Bob Smith. The guy from China."

"Yes. Yes. And—"

"Dr. B is his best friend. EJ—*Pappa. Pappa. My pappa. My grandfather.*"

It doesn't register for a second. Then I see Dr. EJ in my mind's eye—his tall, regal stance. And now I'm looking right at Alek. The resemblance, omigod. "Oh, Alek. I guess with everything going on, Mutsi forgot to mention that to you. And I didn't put two and two together until now. That's ADD me. Slow on the uptake. I'm so sorry. I should have realized."

Forgetting he almost broke my arm, he grabs it again.

"Ow."

He's oblivious. I gently extract my arm from his death grip. He doesn't notice. Still staring me down, he mutters, "He's…he's really alive?"

"Alek, he's more than alive. He's fine—incredible, actually. I didn't know he's your grandfather, but I should have—the resemblance. I can see it. He's tall and brilliant. But he obviously thinks you're—omigod."

Alek's eyes go blank. Then he nods. Then he swallows, hard. And his breathing is starting to sound like Mutsi's. He shakes his head. Then suddenly, the tears burst forth like an unleashed fire hydrant. Holy moly, it's weird to see him lose control like this. It's the combination of all this horrible stuff going on with my incredible news dumped on top. Wow. Now both he and Mutsi are drowning out the battle's racket with their wailing.

I don't know what to say. What should I do? Hug him? Talk to him? I decide just to wait, let him have a moment. He's breathing so hard in between sobs. Finally, he wipes his eyes, his cheeks with the back of his hand, sniffling, laughing, sniffling again. I find my eyes misting over too. Poor Alek. He lost his parents and his grandpa too. Did he lose his grandma? Knowing Alek and Dr. EJ, I'll bet they were really close. I search Alek's face. I think he can handle my next comment.

"Dr. EJ works with people with head injury and other brain problems. I think he can help Dad. I think I heard he does brain surgery?"

Alek snorts. "Seriously? Did he ever do neurosurgery? Of course, he's a neurosurgeon among a million other things. He can do it all. And with Dr. B, they're an unbeatable surgical team. Kristal, if my pappa is still alive, we need to get Dr. M to him asap—and me, too."

"Dr. M? My mother?"

"Your father had a couple of PhDs too you know. I'm talking about your dad."

I'm numb—like someone just punched me in the face. Dad never told me. He was just Dad. Oh god, how ignorant I was about his life. I guess he wanted it that way to make sure we stayed safe. Now I feel a wail rising up from my gut too.

"Alek, let's get this going asap."

Alek has closed his eyes and is taking big deep breaths, chanting, "My Pappa is alive! I can't believe this, thank God, thank God, thank God..." As I wait for him to settle down a little, I check Mutsi. She's in the far corner. Her wailing has softened to quiet weeping, in a little world of her own. Maybe I can help bring her back.

"Mutsi... Mutsi...there's...there's hope for Dad. Please listen."

She looks up at me, eyes almost as empty as my father's. "Soon as this battle is over, we can take Dad back to the Diamond Star, and Dr. EJ and Dr. B can fix him. I know they can figure out what's wrong and make him well. I know they can. They can do anything."

My mother continues to stare, first at me, then at my father, who is still lying face up, steel eyes fixated on the ceiling. She looks away, wincing. I scoot over to him, avoiding his ball-bearing eyes.

Maybe if he feels my touch, hears my voice... I stroke his arm, murmuring gently, "Dad, Dad, Dad?" Nothing yet. Then...

A hideous growl erupts from deep in his throat, then he snarls, rising up like a zombie, lunging for my throat, just like he did in the car that horrible night. Mutsi and I both screech, crab-crawling backward so fast my spine hits another rock. Ouch. Goddamn. I turn to Mutsi, and we hang on to each other for dear life.

Alek is next to my father in an instant, pinning him down. Surprisingly, Dad doesn't resist. Alek keeps his hands on Dad's shoulders. "Nope, Dr. M. You're not going down that road anymore. We have a plan. You're going to be back with your family who love you more than you know. Now behave, okay? You're gonna love this." My father closes his eyes and goes limp again. I swear he understood. Deep inside, my real father is fighting like hell for the life he lost.

General Waara's head appears in the entrance. Yanking off his diamond helmet, he enters, immediately bumping his head. "Ow, goddamn rathole." He scrunches down on bended knee, head in hand. "Evil incarnate. The devil's army, every last one, has finally been wiped from the face of the galaxy. But at what goddamn price. Jesus, how were we to know?"

They were expecting to party to the high heavens, I'm sure. But I realize I haven't heard a single whoop or sound of celebration. They were so confident they had this all figured out, and our side would emerge victorious with zero casualties. But I saw what was happening through the RV. I cringe at the general's next words.

He clears his throat. "Damn it to hell, I never would have thought—hundreds, goddamn hundreds..." he sighs, sniffs, lowering his head even more.

Alek's the first to speak. "Casualties. From the poison."

The general sighs, blowing out a mouthful of hot, gritty air. "Somehow, they programmed their goddamn medieval spears to connect with the exact joint areas vulnerable. Knee or shoulder less than a half inch wide and two inches long. Wounds in these areas would not have been serious, let alone fatal. But they were soaked in, ah, some kind of poison, as their leader warned." His choke turns into a sob. He catches it. No one speaks for a moment. We're all too stunned. Then he says, "First estimate, four-hundred-plus…"

Mutsi, Alek, and I gasp.

He continues, "We're still counting, but thank god every single one of our soldiers unharmed, wounded, or…or…deceased…is back on Lucy." As if on cue, we simultaneously bow our heads; all is silent for a moment. Then the general's agonized cry splits the air. He shakes his head. "For eleven years, this very battle is all I've thought about, envisioned, planned for—a 100 percent clean victory. We ran through all possible scenarios, except this one, goddamn it to hell. Instead, oh god, these people had families…" He rams a fist into an indentation in the cave wall. When he pulls back, blood is dripping down his knuckles. The rest of us wince. The 254 victims in 2016 were horrendous enough, and now this—almost twice as many.

Four hundred, maybe more, dead. Not even Waara in his wildest dreams imagined an outcome like this. Apparently, no one else did either. The general will probably never forgive himself. At least, we can all take comfort in the fact that the Cancris are finally gone for good and don't pose a threat anymore. I look over at Alek. His eyes are darting here, there, up, down. Finally he touches Waara's arm and says softly, "So the Cancri leader? You captured him?"

"The short one? Yeah, we've taken it back to Lucy so we can study it and figure out exactly what kind of poison that was. I don't trust the leader to tell me what that was. I'd rather deduce it was some kind of ricin hybrid, but we'll have to run toxicology on it. Maybe they got the recipe from Earth's internet. Or maybe it's an original Cancri concoction."

Alek's voice cracks. "Isn't it a moot point?"

The general whips his head around until he almost bumps Alek. "No, it's not a moot point, smartass. We have survivors. We can make antidotes."

Alek lets out a breath, palms up. "Okay, okay, calm down. I didn't know."

The general softens. "All right everyone, we need to be getting the hell out of here too. Myrakka, Alek, Kristal, time to travel. Myrakka, Kristal, you should have teleported by now." He notices

Mutsi for the first time. She has her head between her knees, sobbing silently. He waddles a step toward her and almost crushes my father's hand with his boot. "Good god, what's this?"

Alek says, "*This* is the reason Myrakka wouldn't leave. *This* is Pauli Makkinen."

The general frowns, looks Mutsi up and down, then his head jerks toward Alek. "*Pauli Makkinen? Thee Dr. Pauli Makkinen?* Been here on Cancri? The whole time? A prisoner?"

Alek nods. "A prisoner, yes, but not on Cancri. He's been raising Kristal in Montana."

"Montana? Ah, that's where the signal came from. Huh. Hell, why didn't he—"

"Couldn't. They had him by the b-brains. We first thought he was a Cancri clone. But now, Big Don explained the day of the massacre, they teleported him here, healed his injuries somehow, and then screwed with his brain. Most likely some kind of implant, so he had to comply with their directives. They needed him to raise their so-called Crystal Child so she would grow and develop in a typical Earth environment. If Dr. M did anything that might interfere with that, they would beam him back to Cancri e and *fix* the problem. Well, everything was basically peachy until Dr. Myrakka M. showed up. Most likely, he tried like hell to override the program in his brain. They won out. That's why he's here."

"Well, can we liberate him? Or did the Cancris mess up his head forever?"

"That's the billion-dollar question. But we've decided to be optimistic. Is there any way we can get him to the Diamond Star? Kristal just told me my pappa is alive. If anyone can make him human again, my pappa can."

Waara's mouth opens in surprise. "Holy shit, of course, you're Eikka's grandson. Huh. Well, another reunion to look forward to. Finally, some good news. I'll take it." He nods, gives a thumbs-up, then leans over my father as best he can with all his diamond shielding, studying him closely. "Shit, this one's sure been through the Cancri wringer. Are you sure he's Pauli Makki—"

Alek snorts impatiently. "Yes, yes, sure. Just look at his wife over there. She's sure."

The general looks up at Alek, then my mother and me, in the corner. Mutsi's sniffling, nodding.

"Good god! Myrakka, what should we do? Your wish is my command."

Mutsi's clearly so shaken she can barely speak. But she wipes her eyes, scoots over to Dad, and puts her hand on his chest. I cringe. What if Dad—Alek and I are apparently thinking the same thing, as Alek slides over and places his hand over Mutsi's. Mutsi seems oblivious to the danger. "Hale, if...if there's one chance in a million—"

"You got it, Myra. The only problem is—"

Alek finishes the general's sentence.

"Pendants."

The general nods. "We didn't know. We just had Myrakka's and Kristal's new pendants made. But we never suspected anyone else would be here. Alek, how are you getting around these days?"

"I have what's called a travelrod, but it needs to be reprogrammed so I can travel to Lucy, and hey, maybe one for Big Don since it's a new location for us. Maybe they can—"

"Big *who*?"

Alek is talking fast. "Hard to explain, but in a nutshell, see, Big Don defected from the Cancris two years ago. They were in the middle of cloning him with my DNA, which they stole the day of the massacre. So we've been working together since, but he—you—"

"You mean that weird-looking Cancri with the human eyes and hands I had to waste?"

I cringe.

Alek freezes. Please, please don't break down again. Alek turns his hands into tight fists but doesn't otherwise move. His voice is low. "Yeah, I know you thought you were just doing your job, but this particular Cancri was an asset, a huge asset."

"An asset? No kidding. I had no clue, and the thing was way too close for comfort." General Waara's face goes deadpan. His massive diamond shoulders slump. A heavy silence hangs in the already thin, hot air.

Then the general shrugs. "I'm sorry. How was I to know?"

Alek's face is all scrunched up. He looks miserable. A vision slams into my mind. Crap, I'm the Crystal Child. It's all up to me. A fresh surge of hope shoots through me along with a new idea. It's a long shot but better than nothing. "Alek, I know firsthand the medical miracles the Cancris can perform. If they could heal me, a human, more complicated than a machine, then surely they can put Big Don back together, right? Even without Alph. And…and… maybe Dad? Maybe we could take a few—"

Alek shakes his head. "Kristal, you haven't checked outside yet. Did you hear what the general just said? Not a single Cancri is left. No one. Nada." He waves a hand toward the entrance. "Go, see for yourself. It looks like a recycled scrap metal junkyard out there. Smoke's rising like a thousand tiny chimneys. Not a single Cancri survived except Alph. And he's—" He casts a glance toward the general.

My hope vanishes. Damn, he's right.

Waara shrugs. "Well, asset or not, we need to go. We can't take the dead robot with us. Sorry. Friendly fire. It happens."

Alek's nostrils flare. "Not so freaking friendly if you ask me. Kristal tried to warn you, but you were too trigger happy." I gently touch Alek's arm. "Alek, I was coughing so hard I didn't get out a word. It's not like I was trying to persuade him, and he wasn't listening. He really didn't know."

Alek's eyes are pools now.

Mutsi gives General Waara a concerned look. "Hale—"

He sighs. "Listen, Alek, my boy, I've always been real careful to limit my collateral damage, let alone friendly fire. But, hell, like Kristal said, I had no clue you had a Cancri asset with you. How could I possibly know? In my mind, you weren't even alive until you suddenly appeared before me." He pauses, then his voice lowers. "I apologize, if that will help in any way. But the Cancri leader is on Lucy now, and he's not fixing anything. Our plans are to render this thing useless, then study its hardware and software for our purposes. We can advance our technology by taking a look at theirs. As fast as Jaak and Johann work, I'll bet it's already been taken apart and is undergoing analysis bit by bit."

Alek's lips are so thin they disappear. He shoots a quick if-looks-could-kill glance to Waara, then his chin starts to tremble as he furiously wipes his eyelids. Yuck, he could get Cancri dust in his eyes. That would hurt like hell. I gently take both his hands in mine, lowering his arms to his sides. He looks like he could break at any second. I cringe. Alek, boy wonder, the one with all the solutions. It's so pitiful I have to drop his hands, turn, and stare at the dirt wall.

General Waara shrugs. "SAMO."

Alek's brows furrow. "Samo? Military term?"

"What? Nah. Spit and move on, kind of a crass Serenity Prayer. Part of sisu. You know, just keep going—right foot, left foot. The general turns back to Mutsi and me. They gave you your pendants, right?"

Mutsi and I nod, and we both reach behind a small rock where we've hidden them and slip them over our heads.

The general glances at Alek, shrugging. "Okay, good. Now we've got another new code—37292. Even though we don't need a secret number anymore, the programmers were cautious for obvious reasons. Alek, do you have a pendant?"

"Yeah, of sorts, but I told you. It's not programmed for the Diamond Star."

I frantically grab Alek's arm. "Here, Alek, give it to me. We'll take it back. If they can reprogram it, fine. If not, we'll make you a new pendant. Then one of the soldiers will come back for you."

Expressionless, Alek takes off his travelrod and places it in my hand. No one else protests. Good.

"Thanks."

I glance over at my dad. He needs help so badly. What was the medical term used in *M*A*S*H*? *Stat*. Dad needs medical attention stat. He's dying. I can see it. I can sense it. But he can't die. He just can't. He has to survive. He. Must. Survive. I announce to our small group, "I'll stay with Alek. Use my new pendant for Dad, to get him to Dr. EJ *stat*. He really needs help, much more than I do."

Mutsi and the general are shaking their heads in unison. "Negative, Ms. Kristal, you are returning to the Diamond Star now with us. Jaak and Johann will make new pendants asap, and then we'll return for Alek and your father. But this trip, you're on it, and that's an order."

An order. Is he kidding? I'm not in his damn army. Who does he think he is?

Mutsi backs him up. "Kristal, Hale is right. You can't stay here alone." All the while she's saying that, she's got her eyes locked onto my father. She's in her Sophie's Choice moment—me or her husband? It must be excruciating.

But is there a way we both can make it? Can't I do some positive pep talk here? "Mutsi, I think we all can survive. I'll be fine here by myself." Mutsi slowly turns her head toward me, grabs my hand, pats it, lets it go.

"You can't be alone here. Don't even think it."

Alek waves. "Hello, I'm here. I'm about the most educated Cancri expert the QC has ever seen. She'll be safe with me."

General Waara snorts. "Well, as of about fifteen minutes ago, that and a buck and a half will buy you a sip of cappuccino at Expresso House. The robots may not be a danger anymore, but this oven of a planet is. We've got to get Kristal out of this goddamn Death Valley. Should get you out too. Wish we'd thought of an extra pendant for you, Aleksi—we had no clue. But you're young and healthy as a horse. You'll survive. We'll be back asap for you and Dr. Makkinen. Just try and keep him breathing."

Alek sighs. "Yeah, got it. Kristal, I'll be okay here. You go on ahead. I have a friend to bury, and your dad to keep alive. Then if someone wants to come back with new pendants, that would be great."

"Of course, we will, Aleksi. I'll get these ladies safe to the Diamond Star, get your travelrod, or whatever you call it to Jaak or Dahab as soon as we arrive, and have them reprogram that or make you a pendant, then make one more for Dr. M here. Then we'll return."

I say nothing while an idea pops into my head. First, I've got to get rid of Alek's travelrod. "General Waara? Uh, could you take Alek's travelrod? After what happened before, I don't know if I trust myself."

He shrugs, holds out his hand. I drop Alek's travelrod in his palm. Check. Part 1 of my plan. I smile sweetly at the general. "Thanks."

"Yep. Ready, Kristal? Myrakka?" I place my hand on Alek's shoulder. "Alek?" He looks up at me. "I'm... I'm so sorry. He—Big Don—was special. I was just getting to know him."

Alek rubs his eyes again. I wish he'd stop. Who knows what's in this Cancri dust?

As if he heard my thoughts, he rubs his hands on his pants, looks at me, blinking, trying to smile. "Thanks, kiddo. Thanks, I appreciate that."

Mutsi looks a little more alive now. "I'm sorry too, dear Aleksi." She stares at Dad and then closes her eyes. One tiny tear slips out and trickles down her cheek. I'm surprised she has any moisture left in her.

General Waara yanks his helmet back down over his head, turns his arm over, checks his built-in wrist-pendant, then turns to us. "Well, Myrakka, Kristal. Here we go. Press the pendant, we'll say the number 37292 together. Ready, set, go..." Mutsi and the general press their pendants.

I've been lying in wait right beside Dad. As soon as they start the chant, I lift Dad's head, slip my pendant around his neck so it's completely touching him and not me. I lower my head so my mouth is a fraction of an inch above the diamond on the pendant. God, here comes the hard part. Stay still, Dad. Stay still. I gingerly pick up Dad's human hand, and with my fingers encircling his, I press down on the diamond and chant the code immediately after the others. *Please please please.* Whew. He doesn't resist. But will the rest of the protocol work? I look up to see Waara's and Mutsi's confused, then horrified expressions. Then *pop*—smoke. And the three of them are gone— General Waara, Mutsi, and Dad. Hot damn, mission accomplished.

"Yes!" I pump a fist in the air.

Alek's grinning at me like he knew all along. "Bravo, Crystal Child, I had a feeling you were going to do something sneaky like that. Proud of you, girl. You just showed some real sisu. They'll have to spend a little time there reprogramming pendants. But it won't take them long. So let's hurry. We've got work to do.

Forty-Nine

● ○ ○ ○ ○ ○ ○ ● ● ● ● ○ ○ ○ ○ ○ ○ ○ ● ○

Cancri e
Fall 2025

"Alek, you ready?

   "Ready as rain, Halfling."

   "Rain ready too?" He frowns, his Alek eyes gazing upward at the cloudless blue sky.

   "I meant I am ready and eager to go."

   "Oh, okay. Here is travelrod. Touch any part of body, say code. Code for Cancri is 962513. We say code together and travel through wormhole to Cancri e. Then you commence with plan."

   "Got it." Alek's voice sounds confident, but he feels his feet go numb, and he begins to shiver. Teleporting through a wormhole is totally incomprehensible. But he remembers his pappa telling him about the success of QC's first teleportation, and Big Don's convinced him this will work. Whew, boy! A forty light-year leap of faith.

   Big Don hands Alek his travelrod. They each press the stick to their chests, recite the code. Within seconds, Alek feels himself whirling through nothingness—spinning, gliding—then finds himself mesmerized at the glittery light show. Suddenly, all senses are back online. Alek bumps down hard; his eyes opening wide. Big Don is to his left, already standing. They've landed. A miracle, or ihme, as he would say in Finland.

   "Ouch! Wow, it's hot. Whoa. Whew." Alek sits up, brushing off his pants. Looking up, he observes the landscape. It's desertlike, minus the cacti, with sand, dirt, and what looks like small craters dotting the ground, the kind groundhogs dig. But he doubts this planet houses any

desert creatures. Eerie crimson volcanoes shoot out some sort of sparkly lava in the distance. They're nestled among huge mountain ranges, craggy and sharp, as tall as the Tetons on Earth. But, unlike the magnificent Tetons, these rather drab mountains are clay-hued from top to bottom, not one snowcapped peak anywhere. Too damn hot, even with a sunless sky. They're obviously on the "perpetual night" side. Even so, it's a wonder they haven't been instantly incinerated. The gruesome memory of a video suddenly blasts into Alek's mind—a video he probably shouldn't have watched, but his parents felt he needed to. He remembers the day, shortly before the Cancris came.

They sat him down, lecturing solemnly, "Alek, we're in the QC. We are against any form of violence whatsoever. All problems can be resolved with brilliant thinkers and compassionate minds. Remember this and remember it well." And then his parents made him watch it—a grainy, black-and-white video of Hiroshima, right after the H-bomb dropped. The visions were shadows of people, who, minutes before, had been going about their daily routine. He shudders, glancing around. This planet's surface should be thousands of degrees, like the H-bomb in Hiroshima. But obviously, someone's done some major terraforming. The biodome has to be superstrong overhead as well as underground to keep the planet habitable, although just barely for a human. What wizard is behind the curtain here? He, she, it, or they better be brilliant and compassionate, as his parents said. Alek wipes the sweat from his face with his T-shirt.

Suddenly, a whoosh. God, a dust storm. Alek covers his head with his hands. After several moments, he hesitantly lowers them. A short Cancri being stands just a few feet away while hundreds of other bots, all taller, stand behind. Alek stifles a display of rage. These are the monsters who slaughtered his mother, father, and grandfather eleven years ago. God, they're hideous. Sweat drenches him from head to toe. Keep it together, Alek. Keep it together. He and Big Don have planned well for this moment; they know what to do. Alek thinks of all the bullies he's had to endure over the years. Inhuman and terrifying as they are, these metal hunks of wires and microchips are just more of the same. The short one takes one step closer. Big Don and Alek tower over it. Alek takes a breath—oh, foul—chokes and clears his throat. Whew. Okay, FBI on steroids, here we come...

"Hello, Two."

The leader's head turns toward Alek then Big Don. "479, you disappear." Big Don raises its massive half-flesh, half-metal arm. "Quick trip. Find human QC survivor. 479-DNA clone."

Two emits a whir. "We disassemble clone now."

Big Don's mouth slit widens. "No. Do not disassemble. Alek is Earth name. Clone Alek want to help Cancris. Asset. We decide work together to assure Crystal Child appearance on prophecy date."

"Human clone not needed."

Big Don's human eyes shift to Alek.

Alek steps forward. He's close enough now to breathe in the sharp metallic odor, which makes his nose wrinkle. Luckily, he's pretty certain the being doesn't comprehend this nonverbal sign of disgust. "Uh, hi. I'm Alek. Crystal Child's appearance is not assured. Some, uh, obstacles may present themselves. I'm just here to troubleshoot so—"

"You shoot trouble? Verb act upon abstract noun—cannot decipher. Dissonance."

Alek raises his eyebrows. He hopes the alpha robot doesn't notice his body trembling despite the heat. It's all so unnerving. And he only has Big Don to trust. What has he done? He takes a big breath, coughs, whoops, can't do that here. "Okay, lost in translation. Um—" He swallows. What would Hawkeye do? "How about this? I am here to make sure prophecy helps all Cancri. There are certain events that may interfere with manifestation of the prophecy for Cancri e."

The leader takes two more steps toward Alek, his metal face and steel eyes almost touching Alek's neck. Alek takes a step back, lowering his head. Obviously, they haven't yet programmed info about humans needing personal space. A sudden earsplitting buzz makes Alek jerk even further backward. Then the being's mouth slit opens again. "Which events?"

"These are events about which only I, Alek, have information."

"A-l-e-k. Your identification label? Name? Not familiar English numbers."

"We don't use numbers. We use blended sounds, uh, auditory. Phonemes. It's a little easier for humans to remember. For instance, uh, 479 here. We've renamed this guy Big Don."

"The leader turns to Big Don. "You have phonemes for recognition. Not numerals."

"Yes. Use name Big Don."

"Big Don. Three phonemes multiply times two. Zero repetition. Big Don. My recognition number 'Two.' What my name in letters?" Alek steps in. "Well, the name Two—that's short and to the point. But it's not, uh, very personal. A better name for Two? How about, hmmm, Alpha. That means 'leader.' You are the leader of this pack, right? Or to make it simple, how about just Alph?"

"Alph, Alph. A-l-ffff—three phonemes."

"Hey, yeah. You got it. Alph is a great name for a leader. It means you're the head guy. What do you say?"

The being shakes its head. "Not head guy. Whole body." Whir. "Phonemes of no significance. Need to assure Crystal Child produce formula for water. February 5, 2027 target date. You, 497—Big Don—and Alek to help get child and Cancris together on that day."

"Yes, exactly. Our plan to help. I'm the child's tutor. I am teaching her. Helping her learn to think well, to make sure, um, how to communicate to Cancris formula for H2O."

Alph suddenly ceases all motion. "Access Archives." Whir. "Aleksi Salo. Alek. You."

Alek's eyes widen. The damn robot's monotone voice is grating. "Emmi. Kurk Salo. February 16, 2016. Names on QC disassemble list. Aleksi Salo on QC list but not disassemble list. Among irregular list." Alek stumbles backward. He can feel his face turn beet-red, and his breath turn ragged. This psychopathic metal murderer just named his parents, ticked them off a list like they were cattle. Alek's fists curl so tightly his knuckles turn white. He could kill this monster with his bare...

Alph turns to his robot army, raising a metal arm. "Found irregular. Kill."

"No." Big Don steps in front of Alek. "No. Alek here to help. Need more DNA. Do not kill."

"Have DNA. Need no more. Need no assurance. Need no help. Kill."

The Cancri soldiers take a step forward. Alek and Big Don had gone over this possible scenario a hundred times. Alek's brain goes on *automatic pilot. He's practiced automode since the day of the massacre. Without it, he wouldn't have survived. He whispers to Big Don, "Crunch time." Alek gently pulls a piece of paper from the back pocket of his jeans and hands it to Big Don.*

Big Don nods and holds it up in front of his head—a one-page likeness of the other pages of the original prophecy. Alek and Big Don have worked several days making it look authentic. "Wait. Cannot kill Alek. In prophecy. We have last page. You did not see."

Alph immediately holds up a claw. The Cancri soldiers remain locked in place. "More prophecy?"

Alek steps forward. "It was buried in one of the cabins. They hadn't yet programmed it into the computers. But I found it." He hands the likeness over to the leader.

The writing closely resembles the real prophecy. Alph scans it across its face. "Seventeen-year old male must be catalyst for Crystal Child. Must remain alive until prophecy fulfilled, until Cancri receive H2O."

Alph points at Alek and asks Big Don, "This is seventeen-Earth-year male? Definition."

Big Don nods. Alek sucks in a huge breath, coughs, and touches Alph's steel arm, immediately jerking back. Whew! The metal on these things must be as hot as the lava spewing out from the distant volcanoes. "Yes, I have all answers you may seek as the day approaches. Furthermore, I can help you detect enemies, threats. Big Don and I can be a liaison between you and the Earth."

"Have liaison. TAD."

"Yes, but it's limited in its abilities. The TAD can provide location and alert you to serious infractions and safety issues. But you also need information only humans can provide, like how the Crystal Child's mind is evolving, how well her father is nourishing her, her overall health. Vital stuff. We can be a team."

Another whirring, noticeably quieter this time. Good sign? "Team. Beneficial. Return to Earth. Return to Cancri in one year, more information about father and Crystal Child."

"Um, would that be one Earth year or one Cancri year?"

"Return in eighteen Earth hours."

"*I was afraid of that.*" *Alek whispers to Big Don as they are preparing their return trip, "Are they all this gullible? This will be a piece of cake." Big Don's head emits a soft whirring sound. "Piece of cake. Cancri not yet programmed for consumption of human food. Water first."*

Alek suppresses a smile. Big Don doesn't know what a hoot he is. Yet.

"*You know what, Big Don? Not being able to eat cake isn't a bad thing. Way too much sugar. Come on. What the hell was I thinking, wearing these jeans? It's bitchin' hot here.*"

"*Bitchin'? Bitch. Female dog? Use also as adjective?*"

Alek sighs. "*Yep, 'bitchin' in this instance, is an adjective. A rather colorful one at that. So guess the grammar lessons are paying off. Proud of you, Halfling. Now let's get back to Earth. Promise me you'll pour a bucket of ice over my head when we get home.*"

"*Bucket of ice. Frozen water. Might hurt human. Like rocks.*"

"*Trust me, Halfling, a bucket of ice will feel a thousand times better than a bucket of this hellish hot Cancri air. Let's go.*"

Fifty

● ● ● ● ● ● ● ● ● ● ◉ ● ● ● ● ● ● ● ● ● ●

February 2, 2027

"What work?" Certainly Alek doesn't think we're responsible for cleaning up this immense metallic mess.

"Big Don."

"Big—oh, I see. He needs a proper burial."

"No, he needs a proper *fix*. And we have to hurry before someone comes back to rescue us."

"What? *We're* going to fix Big Don? How?"

"All the equipment is in Cancri General, their 'reassemble room.' Instructions have to be somewhere. You need to help me carry him."

"Alek, carry Big Don? That far? In these temperatures? And then scrounge around in their whatever—hospital—and learn the art of robot surgery in thirty seconds or less? I mean, I want to have sisu and all, but some things are just totally outside human limits—or *my* limits anyway. You'd need several Diamond Star soldiers, at the very least. I mean, get real."

"Okay, fine. You're right. It's a long shot."

"A long shot? How about an impossible shot?"

"All right, all right, but who said impossible just takes a little longer? You just sit tight. I'll do it myself." Alek ducks his head under the entrance and is gone. I sit, fuming. How dare he expect that I can—oh, hell. "Wait!" I stumble after him, up the few steps and outside the cell, into the furnace blast with the low twilight and starry dome. The heat alone is enough to make me collapse, but I literally

397

fall to my knees at the scene outside. Completely obliterating the landscape are steel chunks, pieces of motherboards, metal, wires of all colors, fiberglass, microchips, all twisted, jagged with holes, claws dismembered, cut in half. Smoke still rises from the scraps and cords, and I hold my nose against the overpowering electrical stench. At least, I don't see any human bodies. Obviously and mercifully, they were immediately returned to the Diamond Star.

Alek is kneeling next to Big Don, the battle's first casualty, lying faceup on the ground, still motionless. He lifts Big Don up under the arm appendages, tries to drag him a few feet, then backs up into another robot, shifts, drags another few feet, then lets Big Don clunk back down. He stands, sighing and wiping his brow. *Ouch, ouch, ouch.* He turns his palms over. Even from my vantage point a few feet away, I can see the redness, the burns. Poor Alek. There's no way he's going to drag Big Don all the way to the reassemble room.

I can't stand this. "Alek, wait."

Alek looks up, shaking his head. "Thanks, but you're right. It's hopeless. This big guy here must weigh a ton. And look at all the debris we'd have to—" He plops down on a small space, one of the few empty ones beside Big Don, gently placing his hand over Big Don's identical one. I notice Big Don's hand and the top half of his face have a grayish tinge. I look away.

Finally, Alek unwraps the Red Hot Chili Peppers shirt pieces from each of Big Don's arm, balls one up and wipes his gritty face and chest, then ties another piece around his head as a do-rag. He then rips the other one into two pieces with his teeth, wrapping one around each hand, his palms already showing signs of blistering. He's wincing and clenching his teeth. God. We have to get out of here— and quick. I glance toward the so-called cold cave. No sign of a rescuer yet. Reflexively, I begin a deep sigh, but I immediately squelch it. I don't want another coughing fit. But I can tell he's not thinking about himself. He's staring at Big Don.

He chokes back a sob. "Sorry, Halfling." He bows his head, looks up, and beckons me to join him. I glance longingly back at our "oasis," the cold cell. The air out here is unbearable, but I know Alek needs to do this, and I want to be there for him. Kicking metal and wire debris out of the way, I gingerly lower myself onto the scorching rusty sand. I scan my surroundings—metal, twisted and jagged, with wires hopelessly tangled around the debris. The smoke rises in wisps all around, and beyond are volcanoes and mountains, dark-crimson-russet tones against the dark-indigo horizon. I doubt this is what my counselor had in mind when she taught me "grounding" as a technique to keep Achilles at bay. This more resembles what Earth might look like after World War III. A flood of doom cascades downward from my brain to my stomach. Alek pats me on my healed back. I don't flinch this time.

"Thanks, kiddo." We sit, knowing full-well we will die if we stay too long. After a few moments, he raises his head toward the stars. "Dearly beloved, we are here to celebrate the short but miraculous life of—"

Zing. Pop.

And we are smothered in a cloud of dust.

Coughing, we wave the extra smoke away with our hands. When it subsides enough for a little visibility, Alek is the first to speak.

"Holy crap, Alph!"

"Humans stupid. Embedded travelrod initially programmed in motherboard in Two only. Alph travel at will. Travelrods just for other Cancris and Alph backup."

"So they had you all locked up and you just popped your way back here?"

"Yes, must return to Cancri. Need assemble Cancri Army."

Alek's eyes pop out. "You can do that? Put this Humpty Dumpty mess back together again?"

"Not Humpty Dumpty. Children poem. Egg impossible to reassemble. Like this army. Cannot reassemble. Not enough time. Reserve army. Will program for second battle. Harvesting diamond from caves, eight thousand kilometers from main center."

Alek shoots me a look I can't interpret. Shock? Fear? Oh, an idea, a big one. He places both hands, the rags acting as potholders, under Big Don's head and raises it so Alph can see.

"Okay, but before you go, can you at least reassemble this one? Big Don? Your 479? He's really useful to, uh, the Cancris."

Alph lowers himself until he's right in the dead robot's face. Then he scans the rest of the body, the bullet hole in the metal, the charring. No emotion. Just analysis. I shake my head.

Alph stands. "Can do. Not easy. But reassemble possible. This Cancri may be useful."

"Yes, he's very useful. Alph, really? Seriously? He's not too damaged?"

"This one strong. Three bullets not enough to completely disassemble. But may be difficult. Bring to reassemble room."

Alek starts to punch a victory fist in the air then drops it like lead.

"But, Alph, they'll see you're gone. They'll be coming back, you know. And…and we can't carry Big Don. How will—"

Alph touches his head to Big Don's. Chants a series of numbers. *Whir.* Then *pop.* The robots disappear.

Alek turns in the direction of the Cancri hospital. "Whoa, I take that as a yes. Let's go."

I'm dying here. "Alek, you mean we need to meet them there? I'm so thirsty." Suddenly I hear Dad's voice in my head, *How 'bout some cheese with that whine?* Okay, no more moaning. But I'll also be no good if I'm dead.

Alek slaps me on my newly healed back maybe to remind me of the miracles Cancris can perform. I must admit, can't argue with that. "I'm thirsty too, kid. Humans can last up to a week without water. But only about a couple days being conscious. In our situation, in this heat, with our activity level and time already spent—I figure we have about a half day left. We can get a lot done in a half day. The fact that we're both still coherent and able to move is a damn good sign. But that's just—"

"Don't tell me. I know. Sisu."

Alek grins. "Come on, quick-study girl."

I don't know how I'll make it, but I give up on water. Ain't gonna happen. Whining will only waste the tiny iota of energy I have left. We stumble and pick our way through the jagged metal landfill. I hang onto Alek like a frightened toddler.

I'm about ready to collapse when Alek says, "We made it."

We're both breathing like we just finished a marathon, and in a way, we have. We peek into the reassemble room. It's a few degrees cooler. I'll take it. Big Don is on the metal table, the same one I was on, the same one my father was on. I suddenly get a mind picture of Dad on that very table. How terrified he must have been. Various straps, cups, shields, and other instruments were whirring around and inside Big Don. Alph is at the head of the table pressing buttons on a rectangular iPod-like device. He looks up.

"Faster with assistance. But working."

"Can we help, Alph?"

"Not needed. Almost complete."

Suddenly Big Don's human hand twitches ever so slightly. Its color matches Alek's again. I squeal, jumping a step back.

Alek stands, transfixed, then leans over to me, "I said this was on my bucket list. Do you realize how their knowledge could revolutionize modern medicine?"

I nod dumbly. After a series of buzzes, bangs, and whirs, Big Don blinks his Alek eyes, then slowly, slowly rises up, his massive bulk making the metal table sag a little in the middle. He slides his leg appendages to the floor and stands, tall as he ever was and like new. His head slowly turns left, right, then focuses on Alph. No words are exchanged. None that I can hear, anyway.

Then Big Don sees Alek and me. He raises a hand, points outside, in the direction of the cold cave.

"Alek. Kristal. Schrödinger…" His eyes close then open. Maybe he's not quite 100 percent online yet.

Alek leans against the wall, then quickly pulls away. "Ouch. Hey, Big Don, bro, my halfling, you did it. Yes, we're here. If you're asking about Schrödy, don't worry—he's fine. No doubt, back home, chasing mice or salmon. But hey, you're reassembled thanks to Alph."

"Reassembled? I die?"

"You're in the reassemble room, buddy. You're good as new, isn't he, Alph?"

"Not new. But reassembled." Alph touches a few more buttons with the tips of his claw then sets the device aside.

"Yes, reassembled. Now 100 percent."

I can't help staring at his eyes. I think Big Don's expressing fear or like he needs to communicate something to us in the worst way. "Schrödinger—"

Alph interrupts, "Now. We go to other side of Cancri. You, Big Don, Crystal Child. We all here. Assemble reserve army."

Alek's jaw drops. "Reserve army?"

"Yes. Seven thousand more soldiers harvesting diamond for new battle suits."

Both Alek and I put our hands to our mouths. This can't be. It just can't. Finally, Alek holds up his hands, palms out. "Alph, wait. I know what the Diamond Star Army did was brutal. But you have to admit you did the same thing with our QC in 2016. This battle today, well, it was their idea of justice, as General Waara explained. So the score is settled, and it looks like you are able to hide. I'll tell General Waara it's useless to try to find you. So I mean if you're planning another attack with this…this reserve army, it's really not going to serve any purpose. How about we call it even, and you and your people, er, buddies can just enjoy life in the diamond mines."

"Okay."

Alek's jaw drops as he fist-bumps the air. "Okay, really?"

"Cancri just need H_2O, Crystal Child. Give now—"

"Oh…oh no. Here? Now? Alph, please. She's, uh, she's not quite ready, and if she stays here much longer, she'll die, Alph. She's human. She needs water. You guys can wait a little longer for water. You know that. She can't."

"Prophecy date soon."

"Yeah, yeah. And, Alph, I promise. You'll get your H_2O. But if you try to keep her here until then, I mean, come on. You know all about humans. She'll be long dead by then, and you will not be able to reassemble her."

They're haggling about how long I will live like they're chatting about the weather. I shiver, even in the high heat. Alek's tone is desperate. "I estimate she can remain on Cancri for no more than three to four more hours. She *must* get back to land with water."

A program in the robot is whirring, obviously making calculations. Then, "Statement true. Humans weak without water, on hot planet. Would die. You take back. But tell your general we come. Time for Crystal Child to manifest prophecy. And"—Alph reaches his claw behind him, pulling out an uneven, jagged diamond about the size of an egg, offering it to Alek—"you give to your leaders, your scientists. If they understand, they will know."

Alek takes the diamond, looks down, then back at Alph, frowning. "Wha—it's a diamond. You mean you're making diamond suits too? They will know what exactly? What are you talking about?"

Alph presses a claw to his head then Big Don's. *Pop.* Alph and Big Don vanish.

Alek yells, "No, wait!" He turns to me. "He just left. I was just going to ask him to make travelrods for us. *What the hell?* And… did his last words sound a bit ominous to you? Alph seems different somehow."

I'm beyond caring. So thirsty…so thirsty. "Alek, they're probably on the other side of the planet by now. We just have to make our way back to the damn hot cold cell and wait for one of Waara's soldiers to come for us. All of a sudden, it hits me—I'm so close to collapsing. But I have to keep standing. I have to know…

"Alek, Tad… Tad's here somewhere. I can feel it."

Alek takes a breath, like he was hoping I wouldn't bring it up. Too bad.

"Kiddo, uh, yeah. I saw the T-A-D when I was sneaking around looking for your father."

"No initials. Don't call him that."

"Kristal, please don't kill the messenger. Those initials stand for something. I've seen other T-A-D's during our past trips here, and well, they don't look human, but they have the same function."

"Other Tads? Same function? What do you mean?"

Alek stares at me so hard I back away. "What? Alek, what?"

"Technical advisory device."

"Technical ad—" I hate that. I refuse to believe it.

"And, Kristal, about those numbers he was always chanting. It was most likely transmitting your location or other information. Kristal, believe me, I wish it were different."

I do feel like killing the messenger, or at least maiming him, but he's right; it's not his fault. I'm so confused, so hurt, so disillusioned. I feel betrayed. How could Dad do this to me? He made me believe I had a brother—a twin, even. But of course—he had no choice. He couldn't explain what Tad was, or the Cancris would have punished him or even discarded him, like they just did. No wonder it was hard for him to pretend he loved Tad. He was no doubt trying to tell me in a subtle way: "Don't bond with it. Your heart will break." If what Alek says is true, Dad's so-called son, my brother, was the enemy's little snitch. Dad didn't betray me. It was all just a cruel, cruel joke perpetrated by the amoral robots, and they didn't even have *joke* in their vocabulary.

Still, what about our wonderful times together—sledding down the hill in the snow, ah, the freezing cold snow; and all our imaginary games in the forest, our creative play, which he couldn't get enough of; the movies we acted out, holding his arms up chanting, "Five Star Pictures Presents?" We were close. We were. We just somehow clicked. I loved my brother, and I really think he loved me, in his own way. I just can't accept this new reality without question. Tad's essence—his spirit—lives. It lives somewhere. I just know it.

I look up at Alek. My eyes are blinking so rapidly he'll think I have a tic.

"You okay?"

I nod, afraid to talk.

"Hey, I'm sorry, Kristal. I really, truly am. What they did to you was beyond cruel. Yes, Tad was more advanced than Big Don on the outside, but on the inside, the Cancri part was alive and well."

"How do you know? How can you possibly know?"

Alek goes quiet, bowing his head. "I really shouldn't do this."

"Yes, you should. You know where he is, and you didn't tell me?"

"I—trust me. You don't want to see it."

"Him. And yes, I do. I most certainly do."

"I was afraid of this. Kristal, believe me. You're not going to like it."

"Take me to him now." I feel a renewed sense of energy and anger and urgency. Maybe we can find Alph. Maybe Alph can fix him. Omigod. "Come on, come on, let's go."

Alek sighs. "God, I should say no. They'll be coming for us soon, and we have to be back at the cold cell."

"Then let's go. Quickly."

Alek throws me a look, shaking his head as if to say "Be careful what you wish for."

We enter another passageway off to the side of the reassemble room, a hallway or tunnel, not so different from the pathways through which my mother led me on the Diamond Star. But every few feet, I see a cell, with a number etched beside the entryway: 38475-4, 9475-72, 036-28567...the numbers go on and on.

"Here." We stop. Alek reads, "3857-2858. For Disassemble. Kristal, kiddo, brace yourself. You need me to hold you up? Are you sure?"

I've had enough of Alek and his damn pampering. Pushing past him, I enter the cell. The lighting is soft coral. The silence is creepy. The scent is faintly metallic, with something else—a kind of rotten smell. I count seven cylindrical metal bins, like the ones at school that hold all the cafeteria trash. I peek into the first one, wincing at the jumble of Cancri parts—claws, wires, steel boards. The next looks the same. I peer into the third, and my knees buckle. Alek catches me, pulling me up just before I hit the ground.

"Yeah, thought so. I'm so sorry, kid. Damn, I should have said no. I should have let you hate me."

I force my eyes to peek again. Tad. It's definitely Tad. What's left of him, anyway. Ripped up computer insides intermingle with his human form. The skin is mottled, his face purplish, steel ball bearing eyes open, still in their human sockets. His hair—light like golden straw, my color, our color, just like Mutsi's too. I reach in, grab a lock between my thumb and forefinger, twirl it and let it go. His limbs are all catawumpus, twisted in unimaginable and inhuman ways. I push Alek out of the way, stagger to the hallway, and with one hand on the hot stone wall, I double over and retch. Nothing comes up because I haven't eaten in so long. Nevertheless, I heave again and then once more.

My heart's in a million pieces. My brother was a Cancri, a robot with skin. Nothing more. I just saw his insides, all metal and wire.

No heart. No soul. But *my* human heart refuses to believe it. How can I accept that my brother is just a piece of cold machinery when I've spent my entire lifetime—the part I can remember, anyway—with him? Walking home from school, watching movies, laughing as he dumped blueberries in the pot for blueberry soup, catching frogs in the woods by the pond in July, rolling in the snow—memory after memory swirls in my head. What is a memory? What is a life?

> But those who were able to love and love well
> Through eternity, their love will matter.

Will my love for Tad matter? Really? Now I just don't know. I want to believe, with all my heart and soul, he, too, *was* human then. *Human.* What does it mean to be human, anyway? A connection—it was there. I can't describe it. Don't twins have special bonds? If he were just a glorified computer, made just to transmit my whereabouts to the Cancris, then he wouldn't even have had to talk to me, but he did. He wouldn't have wanted to go sledding with me, but he did. He wouldn't have said, "Five Star Pictures Presents," when he was over-the-moon thrilled about something, but he did. Dammit, I still can't—won't—believe what I see. He was, at least, part human. He had to be. There could be no other explanation, no matter what anyone says. At least, *my* love matters. Dad said that in a poem, and Mutsi showed me.

Alek is standing at the entryway, grimacing, watching me lose it. He pulls me up and wraps his arms around me. "I could shoot myself. I shouldn't have let you—"

"Yes, you should have. I had to see for myself. Tha-thank you. I'm done now."

We make our way back outside. It's a three-minute walk back to the cold cell. I'm not going to make it. I know I won't. "Alek?"

"What?"

"If they don't return like in about thirty seconds, I think I'm gonna—" I stumble forward, about to collapse on the hot sand, and right now, I would welcome oblivion. I'm heading toward it now.

I glance up at the vast universe, the myriad of stars. I'm so tiny, so insignificant. I'm merging with...

"Yeow. Meow. Mrrr..."

Wha...

Alek and I freeze; my ears perk up. The tiny surge of adrenaline keeps me from what I was about to do.

"Rur. Ow. Reow."

We stare at each other. We're both hearing it. Can't be. We're not hallucinating, are we?

"Meowwwyeoww..."

Nope. That's real.

Alek's jaw drops. "Schrödy? Is that why Big Don—was he trying to tell us something?"

"Yeourowmeow..."

Alek grins. "Hell, yeah, he was trying to tell us something. And now my cat is trying to get his message across too. Damn, he's learning to talk. I know it. And he must be learning to understand too. Big Don must have told him to wait, and if he didn't hear from us by a certain time, to come and rescue us. Pretty sophisticated comprehension for a cat, wouldn't you say?" Alek cups his hands, yells, "Schröööööodingerrrrrr!"

His voice is so loud I think he's broken my eardrum. With the mysterious Cancri diamond in one hand, he grabs my arm with the other. And somehow, with strength coming from some unknown source, we're zigzagging around the scorching metal cadavers the last few yards toward the heavenly meows.

We round a bend, and there he is. Halfway between the Cancri Hospital and the cold cell, balanced on a fallen Cancri e head, he sits, stately as ever. A mini sphinx. Good old Schrödinger.

Alek drops my hand and does a fist bump in the air. "Goddamn! Woo-hoo, way to go, Schrö!"

The cat doesn't flinch. I squint into the dim light, and my jaw drops. Around Schrödinger's neck is one small travelrod—Schrody's, obviously. But strapped to his sides are two larger travelrods.

One for Alek. And one for me.

Fifty-One

• • • • • • • • • • ◉ • • • • • • • • • •

Earth
August 2025

"Aleksi? Aleksi is that you?"

The clanking sounds in the basement seem to be getting louder. Lumi opens the basement door and calls again.

"Aleksi?"

"Uh, yeah." Alek suddenly bounds up the stairs.

"Sorry. Uh, where's the doc?"

"He's—"

The back door flings open. Voitto jangles a set of keys, pulls out a drawer, opens a secret compartment, and drops them in. "We are done. It's ready. Extra set of keys are een the secret compartment right there. Oh, happy day." He turns and sees Alek. "Whew, can you believe eet, Aleksi?" Something in Alek's expression makes Voitto frown. "Oh, what's the matter?"

"Dr. Kurki, Mrs. Kurki. Sit down. I can make you each a cup of—"

"No, no. We are fine. What ees the problem?"

"Will you both just sit for a minute. This is important. Uh, that's an understatement, actually. This is mind-blowing. You gotta hear me out."

Voitto and Lumi back away toward the living room. Lumi sinks down in the rocker while Voitto lowers himself onto the sofa. Their eyes are wary, staring at Alek.

Alek stands in the doorway. "I'd say don't worry this is good, but you won't believe me. At first, anyway."

"Good god, son. I need to go back to the safe house. The electreecian ees coming. Queeckly. What's on your mind?"

Alek sucks in a mouthful of air and opens the basement door. "You can come on up."

Its head appears first. They don't see it from the living room. Alek gestures. "This way."

A gruesome robotic being, part metal, part flesh, ducks its head through the door and stalks into the dining room, his feet making a loud thud with each step. He stops and reaches up to remove his baseball cap and hoodie. Alek immediately reaches up and replaces them. "Uh, just keep them on for now, buddy."

As one, Voitto and Lumi jump up as though their chairs had just caught on fire.

Voitto yells, "Pyhaa jumalan aiti!" Alek whispers to the thing, "He said, 'Holy mother of God.' It could be worse." The thing responds: "Your god have mother? Did not know."

Alek sighs. "Shhhh."

Lumi covers her face with both hands. The being makes an about-face. "Don't want to scare." Alek grabs its hoodie.

"No, no. Don't go. I warned you. Don't worry. I got this." He turns back to the Kurkis.

Lumi sucks in her breath and collapses back into the rocker, her eyes big as moons.

The being is the kind that sends trick-or-treaters screaming into the night. Its upper face, human skin, eyes, and nose look amazingly like Alek. Its hands are Alek's. But the rest of its exposed body is a mix of flesh and metal. Today, it is dressed in a hoodie and sweat pants, courtesy of Alek and Dolcany's Big and Tall Men's shop in the little strip mall in downtown Dolcany. But its face cannot be hidden entirely, and the Kurkis instantly recognize what it is.

Alek is grinning like a proud pappa. "Dr. Kurki, Mrs. Kurki, sorry for scaring you. This is, uh, my new friend. Actually, a relative of sorts. He doesn't have a name yet, but—"

Voitto backs into the kitchen, returns wielding a gun.

"My god, they've found us. Aleksi, this ees a—"

"Cancri, Cancri. I know, I know. Wait. Listen please." He holds up a hand. "Put the gun down, Dr. Kurki. I can explain."

Voitto's face is beet-red. "Have you gone mad? Where did—?"

"No, just listen. His species is the enemy, but he's not. Hear me out. This sort of, uh, half-twin of mine was devised by the Cancris, true. But no…no, they've humanized him with my DNA. Mine. And now he's more me than them. His brain is, anyway. His limbic system and pre-frontal cortex are developing way ahead of his body for some reason. He's got emotions, empathy, and a conscience. He's defected. He hates them. He wants to be with us. He will not give up our location. I just—I know. Don't ask me how. But he won't. I promise you. He…he showed up here the other day when you two were at the safe house. We had a long chat. He's a great guy. The Cancris would not be pleased if they knew what he was really like now, more human than some humans. I'm not sure what he is exactly. But I was trying to get up the courage and the right time to tell you."

Still holding the pistol, Voitto pulls a handkerchief from his pocket with his other hand and wipes his brow. "Right time? There is no right time. Dear god, what has gotten into you, Aleksi? You were going to tell us? Tell us what exactly? About how you met thees murderer, and now you are friends? And how in the world did they make him look like you?"

"I told you. My DNA is now his DNA. That's not so bad, is it?"

The being steps forward. Voitto takes several steps backward but raises the gun and aims it at the Cancri.

The being speaks.

"No. Please. I was at QC day of massacre but only involved in transport. I did not murder. That is all I remember of that day. Cancris find Alek's blood on tree. Took. Used to make me more human. I am experiment. Neurotransmitter system in limbic area and temporofrontal region began to evolve before face finished. I begin to feel more empathy. Compassion. When I evolve to more human, I feel sorry for QC. I feel so sorry. I want to be human. Live on Earth. Better place. Better people. Want to help. I escape. Programmed Dolcany location with algorithm they use. I go back and forth. Alek programmed knowledge…"

Alek nods. "Yep, we're officially spies. Just think how helpful he can be."

"Yes. Spy. Want Alek be my... my brother. Sorry I still so ugly. Very ugly. They did not finish on outside, like they finish TAD for Kristal. TAD look 100 percent human. Wish I could—don't want to live with Cancris. Don't want to look Cancri. Don't want to be Cancri."

Voitto is lowering the gun but just slightly. Lumi stands back up. They're both blinking, mute. Voitto finally places the gun carefully on the dining table, although his expression is still guarded and his fingers still curl over the grip. He turns to Aleksi, his mouth open.

Alek shrugs. "I've run every test I can think of. Tried to trick him. Can't. He's the real deal."

"But how can you be sure eet's not a ruse?"

A whirring. Voitto and Lumi gasp. Alek points to his head and whispers, "He's thinking." The being turns to Alek. "Ruse? Red flower?"

Alek shakes his head, suppressing a smile. "No, not rose. Ruse—trick."

"Ruse is trick? I am not trick. I prove."

Voitto frowns. "Prove you're on our side? How?"

"Cancri robots not able to act like something they are not. Cannot play act. No pretend. But I learn to lie a little, to pretend to Cancris. Because I am much human now. So Alek and I make plan to trick Cancri. Program travel algorithm like mine so Aleksi can travel to Cancri with me."

Voitto jerks back, shaking his head vigorously. "What? No, no, eet ees eemposseeble."

The half-human shakes its head as well. "No, I have good way. Program algorithm, and Alek travel with me. Pretend he is powerful and shows trick—ruse. Cancris believe. Cancris believe anything. Very concrete analyzers. Cannot detect"—slight whirring—"ruse. Then we can help defeat."

Voitto and Lumi's expressions have changed to a mix of fear, indecision, and awe.

Finally, Voitto sighs, sinking back onto a dining room chair. "Thees deescusion should be over. But, Alek, you're so adamant, and from what I can deduce now, perhaps eet ees telling the truth. But such a gamble..."

He sighs, shaking his head. "God help me. For all we know, eet could be beaming information to the Cancris as we speak."

"No information beam. Cancris not know I defect. Tell them I am on mission. Turn off my 394858—in human letters, GPS. They do not know. They believe 100 percent what we tell them. And they do not need know where I am. Other than Earth."

Voitto's blinking hard, shaking his head. "God in heaven, I should not do this." He sighs heavily. "Aleksi, for now, the Cancri may stay weeth you een the basement, next to your bedroom. Uh, weel he need a bed?"

The Alek thing shakes its head. "No, not sleep lying down yet like human. Just shut down, go offline."

Voitto gives a slight nod, shrugs, and turns to Lumi. "Lumi, we'll just have to take a leap of faith here. Thees may be our key. We do not trust this being. I will have to do some testing."

Alek nods. "You do whatever you need to do. Let's call this his, uh, probation period. So if anything happens—"

"That's just the point, Aleksi. Nothing can happen. We cannot afford eet." Voitto shakes his head. "If you were not so precocious and persuasive—" He heaves another sigh, still frowning. "Take thees."

Alek shakes his head. "Your gun? For what?"

"For protection, obviously. I've taught you."

"I won't need it, but okay, fine."

"We weel deescuss more later. Lumi, come weeth me. We need to go back to the—" He shoots the robot a wary look. Voitto's arms go up in defeat. "Right when I'm so busy weeth the safe house project. Do not give the Cancri thee address for our safe house. Ah, no rest for the wicked." Lumi's eyes are swimming like she's about to faint. Voitto takes hold of her arm, gently steering her through the exit to the garage, mumbling to himself, leaving Alek and the robot alone.

The half robot's eyebrows furrow. "No rest for wicked? Your guardian, Voitto Kurki, wicked?"

Alek shakes his head. "No, just another figure of speech."

"You humans so many speech figures. I will never learn all."

"No, but neither will I. Okay, whew. Well, that wasn't the warmest welcome, but it's a miracle they're even giving you a chance. So, at least for now, you're here. Come on, bro. We have a lot of catching up to do.

Sit." *He points to a chair at the dining room table. The Cancri slowly lowers itself onto an armless seat. It groans and wobbles under its weight.*

Alek scans the library shelves on the far wall of the living room. The collection is a fraction of what they had in Finland, but still holds quite a few volumes of old classics, as well as a large illustrated mythology book Voitto found at a flea market a couple years ago. Alek pulls it out and plops it on the dining room table in front of the Cancri.

"*First things first. Let's find you a proper name. All earthlings have names.*"

"*This book of names?*"

"*Yeah, why not. It's a Greek mythology book. Might have a name that sounds good to you. This one happens to be in English. Go ahead and thumb through it.*"

The Cancri holds up its Alek hand. "*Stick thumb through book?*"

"*No, no. Here.*" *Alek shows the robot how to turn the pages. It imitates Alek's actions, although clumsy, then stops on page 461.* "*I see here. Good. Picture of human. A-don-is.*"

Alek's eyes widen as he peeks over the robot's shoulder. "*Adonis? Hmmm.*" *Alek suppresses a grin.* "*You had to pick that one.*"

"*No. Can pick another one.*"

"*No, no, it's, well, it's fine. It's just that the name Adonis has come to mean, well, a real hunk. He was the god of beauty and desire.*"

"*Beauty. Desire. I have beauty—inside beauty. I have desire. Desire work with you. Defeat Cancris. Maybe not so much outside beauty yet. But I evolve.*"

"*Um, yeah, well, it just might sound a little too ironic.*"

"*Iron-ic? Like iron? Not familiar with suffix. You do to clothes, no wrinkles?*"

Alek can't contain a chuckle. "*No, not that kind. Tell you what. Why don't we shorten Adonis to Don? And since you're larger than the average bear—*"

"*Bear? Earth animal.*" *A soft whir.* "*About same size.*"

This time, Alek can't hold it in and the snort erupts loudly, making him laugh all the harder. He backs up, collapsing into the rocker, doubling over, trying to apologize through the belly laughs. The robot's Alek eyes frown, blinking rapidly. Finally, Alek says, "*So sorry, it's not you...*"

it's just...well, English has a lot of funny figures of speech. Hey, let's just say you're bigger than the average human. So we'll add Big. Big Don— that's a strong name. A good name. A name you don't fool around with, commands respect. How 'bout it?"

The robot's metal mouth widens, but he can't quite turn it up into a smile. "Big Don. I have human name now. Big Don. Like that. Big Don. Big Don. No one fools with my name. Humans respect Big Don."

"Big Don it is, then. Formidable name. Cool. Come on, Big Don. Or sometimes I might use a nickname for you. Nicknames are for your good, good friends even brothers. So you're not quite an earthling yet. How about Halfling?"

"Nickname. Halfling. Okay. But only brother call me Halfling. Rest of humans I will be Big Don."

"You got it. Only I can call you Halfling because you're my brother. Awesome. Hey, Halfling. We got a job to do. Let's go conquer the Cancris."

The Diamond Star

Fifty-Two

● ○ ○ ○ ○ ○ ○ ◉ ◉ ◉ ◉ ○ ◉ ○ ○ ○ ○ ○ ○ ○ ○ ○ ●

February 3, 2027

I open my eyes. How long have I been asleep? My throat's still a little dry, but I'll take it. No more intolerable heat. A soft, silken lounger is under me. Mmmm, I'm floating on a cloud. The contrast in comfort makes me want to cry with relief. I must have been so exhausted I don't even remember teleporting back from Cancri. Not even one tiny rainbow.

Oh, a growl. Ha, hunger pang. My first in a long time.

I lift my head. Ouch, did a semi run over me on my trip back? The achiness and heaviness in my legs I'll just have to ignore until I adjust again. My eyes scan the room. Oh, thank God. There's Alek, on the other side of the room in his own recliner, out like a light. Schrödinger's curled up beside him with the kitty-sized travelrod around his neck. They're so damn cute together. I could just hug this amazing cat who most likely saved our lives. Well, along with Big Don. What a team. Oh, Alek looks different. Someone obviously gave him a new T-shirt, plain gray. He's still wearing the Red Hot Chili Peppers do-rag on his head. And thank heavens his hands are wrapped with clean bandages. I wince. Poor Alek. I know well what burns feel like. I smile. Wish I had Instagram.

This room is unfamiliar, but at least, I know I'm on the Diamond Star somewhere and that all three of us made it back to Lucy. It's obvious now as Alph had finished reassembling Big Don that he was trying desperately to tell us Schrödy was on his way. Big Don must have programmed our travelrods and planned Schrödinger's trip to

Cancri e the last time he was on Earth. If the soldiers found us gone, well, sorry. We weren't hanging out on that planet of death one more nanosecond. And frankly, I think the travelrods work better. Either that, or I was so exhausted I didn't feel a thing as my consciousness traveled through space.

Claude or Kiski or someone was supposed to return from Earth with Pappa and Mummo. I'll bet they're here by now. Can't wait to watch the reunion with Mutsi. I wonder if Big Don's still on Cancri e. Where is everyone? My brain is beginning to feel like a runaway train. Chill, Kris. You're fried enough. The answers will come soon. My stomach growls again.

I hear a voice. "She's awake."

I look up. There's my mother, smiling down at me. I reach up. We hug so tightly I have to gently push her away to catch my breath. And there's Dr. Khumolo, right behind her. Mutsi's grinning broadly.

"So Schrödinger saved the day, huh? Who would have thought? Such an amazing cat. Alek filled us in before he crashed." She gives a nod toward Alek, still fast asleep, then she winces. "Someone should pull that filthy rag off his head."

Dr. Khumolo tiptoes to Alek's recliner, gently tugs at the do-rag with her index finger and thumb. It comes off easily, revealing Alek's greasy mop and sweaty brow. It's made a thick red line across his forehead. He doesn't even stir. She drops it beside his chair, wrinkling her nose. "Well, it may have sentimental value. I'll let him decide what to do with it."

I yawn, stretch, and give everything a closer look. This room isn't familiar. "Where...where are we?"

Dr. Khumolo steps back over to my chair. "Bet you're a little discombobulated, sweetie. This is the city's main building. Our largest, containing a variety of functions. Now, Kristal girl, will you do me a favor and stop giving me more traumas to process with you?"

I check her face. She's winking. I manage a smile. I would love to grant her that favor.

Mutsi leans against her and addresses me. "Without Zola here, I would have lost it. You gave me quite a scare when I realized you'd given your pendant to your father, and then I could have kicked myself. Jaak was so determined he could reprogram the travelrod but finally realized it was impossible. Time wasted. Precious time. The soldiers finally had the pendants in hand and had just left when you and Alek and the cat appeared. Before you returned, I must admit, I was having a meltdown rivaling the great glacier melt of the arctic. Zola, you sweetheart, I think you've done all you can do. Now get. You have a life too."

Dr. Khumolo laughs. "Such as it is. Anyway, so glad your girl is back and Alek and the kitty. He's so regal-looking. Take care of each other, promise? And if you need me—"

Mutsi hugs her once more then lets go. "I know. Thanks."

I smile, waving. And Dr. Khumolo, Zola, is gone. I'm still feeling weak and achy. Mutsi lays a reassuring hand on my shoulder. As if she read my mind, she says, "You're probably still feeling inflamed and fluish as you're still dehydrated. We gave you your first dose intravenously as soon as you got here. Now you're P.O."

"P.O?"

"Oh, sorry. Medical talk. Means 'per oral.' You can drink by mouth from now on." From behind her back, she brings out a small paper cup about half full of water.

Oh, no. I give her a wary look. *This better not be—*

She reads my expression. "No, Krissie, no Birds were killed in the preparation of this product. Just about every citizen of Lucy who was able to offered a drop or two of their rations for you and Alek and even the cat. But since the Diamond Army destroyed the Cancris, we've eased up on the rations as we'll be going home soon. Can you imagine? So bottoms up."

The half cup of water is as sweet as a refreshing dip in a summer pool, just not enough, not nearly enough. I push the craving from my mind. All of a sudden, the rest of my brain wakes up. Ease up on the rationing? Going home? Holy moly, they can't. I shouldn't have touched a drop of this water. The Cancris—they're not destroyed, not by a long shot. So Alek didn't tell anyone? I'm the one who needs to break the news? Thanks, Alek.

"Mutsi, did Alek say anything else?"

"Like what, Krissie? When he arrived, he said something like *Schrödinger*, travelrods, and *Alph*. Then he fainted, and he's been out like a light since. We found a large diamond in his pocket. Either it was from one of the soldiers killed or—"

Oh god, the diamond Alph gave Alek. I crane my neck to see. No one's taken it. It's still right beside him. They don't know it's not one of our diamonds. Darn, I really need to tell her. My mouth opens. "Muts—"

Mutsi's eyes are on mine, then suddenly she turns. Her face lights up. "Dr. EJ."

He stands at the doorway, almost scraping it with his head. He's so tall like Alek. Now I understand the remarkable resemblance. Dr. EJ's scanning the room. When he sees Alek, he freezes, his eyes humungous. Tears fall freely as he gazes at his sleeping grandson. Schrödinger stretches out like a yogi doing the downward dog, then jumps down from Alek's side, and begins licking his paws. Alek stirs, slowly opens his eyes, frowns, and looks up.

Dr. EJ lets out a small gasp. "Aleksi. *Jumalani.*"

Alek sits straight up, whipping his head to the left. "*Pappa…*"

And Dr. EJ is across the room in three great strides. Instantly, they're locked in a tight embrace, laughing, crying, wiping the other's tears, tousling Schrödinger's fur, and chatting over each other in Finnish. I can't understand a word, but I can imagine what they're saying. Eleven years. My heart's bursting with joy watching them.

Then Jaak, the techie, appears at the door. "*Pitkästä aikaa!*"

Alek breaks out in a huge grin, eyes wide. "Jaak? Jaak's here? My mentor? My partner in crime? He survived? Oh, halleluiah. Wonders never cease."

"My man, what's with the English?"

Alek laughs. "*Hei, kuinka voit? Aha! En voi uskoa sitä! Selvisit!*"

"That's better." Jaak and Alek high five then embrace. Mutsi leans over to me. "Alek's just telling Jaak he can't believe it. Asking how he is." Mutsi is fluent in Finnish too. Wow.

I listen, fascinated, while Alek and Jaak chat away in a language completely foreign to me, except for the first word of Mutsi's lullaby and *ihme*—miracle. A part of Alek emerges which I had only known as a toddler. Weird to think I used to hear Finnish spoken around me all the time when I was a baby. I see Alek's trying like hell to be upbeat, but suddenly his laughing starts turning into choked sobs. Reaching down, he grabs his filthy do-rag and wipes his shiny cheeks. Mutsi and I wince.

Alek turns to me. "Kristal, Jaak's parents and mine were best buds. Jaak was like an older brother to me. He taught me all I know about climbing trees and getting into trouble. My tree-climbing skills saved my life, and I have Jaak to thank."

I can only smile and nod as my throat is completely locked up. With all the tragedy this community has had to deal with, it's heavenly to witness such a glorious moment.

Mutsi is stroking my hair. She, too, is choked up. But she looks so much more rested, so much more like herself. I must look like a filthy homeless little waif. She doesn't shrink back from me though.

"Oh, my dear Krissie, shame on you for what you did, but if you hadn't put your pendant on your father, I don't think he would be alive right now." Her voice wavers.

Omigod, my father. I abruptly sit up, shaking off the dizziness, and look all around. He's not here. Oh no! "Where...where's Dad? Have you seen him? Did he make it? He was—"

Dr. EJ apparently hears us, turns, and addresses Mutsi and me, still wiping his eyes. "Ah, yes, my dears. We finally have our dear Pauli back. We fervently hope so, anyway. Eet's quite busy een the ICU and surgery, and I am so sorry to say, the morgue. All the more relief that these monsters are finally gone. We also have many soldiers weeth eenjuries from the battle. Luckily, some just need steetches and some antidote for good measure. Apparently, not all spears were poisoned. But as for Pauli, they are prepping heem for surgery as we speak."

I'm confused. "Surgery? He's here? Isn't he at the Citadel Hospital?"

"No, he is in the main building—here—where you are. We have a surgical unit and ICU here. Then when patients are ready, we transfer them to the Citadel Hospital, wheech ees right down the street. But seet tight. I need to go scrub up. Just needed to see eef my *pojanpoika* had awakened yet. *Hei, hei,* Aleksi. We'll talk later." He walks back to the doorway and turns, shaking his head. "*Ihme, ihme.*"

He and Alek exchange more teary smiles and a thumbs-up. Dr. EJ heads back toward the door.

My mother closes her eyes, takes a deep breath, and blows it out forcefully. "EJ, please, please, please." He steps over to her and pats her hand. She grasps it and gazes up at him with pleading eyes. I can tell she's drowning in fear and trying like hell to hope for the best. It's clear my mother can't even speak right now.

I think I know what she would have wanted to ask. "Dr. EJ, will he—?"

He turns back once more, putting a reassuring, strong hand on my shoulder. "Kreestal, Myrakka, my dears, worry ees perfectly understandable. And admittedly, we cannot predict the outcome. But please know he ees een the best of hands, eef I do say so myself. I took a look. We did a few tests, and we think we can handle thees. We are more than thrilled to have heem back weeth us. He was one of our most promising young scientists, and he's been gone"—Dr. EJ pauses, wipes his eyes—"so, so very long. Imagine our delight to find he ees still alive. But, of course, that has been tempered weeth our sorrow and anger that even as the Cancris had healed hees body, they captured heem and implanted their own software. But we hope, weeth any luck, we'll get that out, and Pauli weell be good as new."

"My father *was* good as new. He was the most wonderful dad."

"That helps to know. They apparently did not tamper with hees basic personality. Most likely, thees was a type of control device een case he decided to go AWOL."

Suddenly, Mutsi balls her fists as her face reddens and lets out a wail. "If Hale hadn't already done it, I could kill each and every one of them with my bare hands. Damn those Cancris. I could have been with both my husband and my daughter, all these years." She chokes up again.

Poor Mutsi. She has an absolute right to her outburst. She deserves every bit of her pain. I'm proud of her. Proud of her sisu. But her words *if Hale hadn't already done it* bring me back to the present.

With all the happy reunions going on, my mind has been in denial. *The Cancris are still a threat.* How do I tell them?

Dr. EJ is patting Mutsi's shoulder. "Meerakka, how difficult thees must be for you and how your emotions must be running wild. Let's theenk some positive thoughts. Kreestal has informed us that Pauli seemed quite normal all these years. And eet's obvious he has raised an incredible daughter, weeth all the sisu traits of our community—empathy, weesdom, and a great deal of strength. Otherwise, she would not have survived these last few harrowing weeks, eh? Thees ees a very positive prognostic sign. Now, for all our sakes, let's envision our Pauli as good as new, shall we?"

My mother nods, tears streaming down her face. I force a smile, trying to ignore the pictures in my mind of my father in the last few weeks and now thinking of him lying helpless on an operating table, instruments poking and prodding around in his brain. At least they're not Cancri instruments. Then again, if the Cancris could— no, never. I put my full confidence in Dr. EJ and Dr. B. There's a lot more to healing than just emotionless technical expertise.

Mutsi is still weeping, but more softly, while she rocks gently back and forth, hugging herself. Her brain must feel like a pinball machine—joy, sorrow, fear, and anger zigzagging from one side to the other, up and down, front to back. She's wiping her cheeks with a cloth when the woman who has been standing close by reaches down and hugs her fiercely. I know her. Who is she again? Oh, yes. It's Blanca, the nutritional expert. She helped my mother from the very beginning.

Taking Mutsi's face in both her hands, she croons to her as a mother does to a hurt child, "*Dios mio*, you poor thing. Let's put Pauli in God's hands. It will be all right, Myra. I know it. I feel it in my soul, *mi amiga, mi hermana*."

They seem very close. Of course, they would be close after all they'd been through together. As they hug, Dr. EJ checks his comcard.

"Uh-oh, they're waiting on me." He takes one more look at Alek, shakes his head in amazement, salutes us, then strides out of the room.

"*Ven aca.*" Come here. Blanca beckons Mutsi and me, gesturing toward the hall.

I stand up, wobble a second, then get my bearings. We pass through the doorway then follow Blanca down several halls. It all looks surprisingly well, Earthlike. I wonder where Blanca is leading us. As if I had just asked the question out loud, Blanca turns her head and smiles at me. "Hey, *muñequita*. We're going to the recoup room. You'll love it."

"*Muñequita?*"

Blanca laughs. "You remind me of a beautiful doll I had as a child. It's my little term of endearment for you. Do you mind?"

"Of course not, but I'm sure I don't resemble that doll, especially now." I look down at my filthy outfit, covered in Cancri dust. We continue down the hall, just Mutsi, Blanca, and me. Oh god, someone has to tell them. "Um, what about Alek?"

Mutsi says, "He'll recoup soon too. Jaak will be escorting him shortly. Of course, your number one task is to get all the grimy Cancri e dirt off you. Don't worry. We already checked you out for foreign substances. Nothing dangerous, thank goodness. You will feel 100 percent better after your shower, a *real* shower. The water won't be full force, more like a few trickles. But sure beats that dry powder."

I look up at my mother. "You mean Shower Power?"

"Yes. No offense, Blanca."

Blanca smiles. "None taken. So Kristal has already experienced the wonders of dry showering. But as helpful as it was, as of today, it's officially not mandated. Since the Cancri e obliteration, we'll be going home soon, so we don't have to be quite so stingy with the water we have left. I cannot believe our time on Lucy is coming to an end. We'll all be dancing in the streets by tomorrow after EJ's official announcement."

My breathing quickens. I close my eyes and clench my teeth. Damn, oh, damn. Only Alek and I know; we may not be going home soon. We may not be going home at all. We might—an even darker thought pops into my brain, and a shiver slithers up my spine. We have to tell them. But here I stand, like a total dunce, like a stupid ADD girl. Jackson Hynes voice mocks me, "Stupid ADD girl. Scaredy girl…scaredy girl…"

I shake my head to get rid of Hynes's grating voice. *Do it, Kris. Now.* My heart starts fluttering like a hummingbird. Although not completely joyful due to the casualties, the Diamond Star citizens finally have hope. I can't spoil it. I can't. It's been eleven years in the making. But, of course, the longer we go without telling them, the harder it will be to prepare for the worst. There's no other option. I can't keep them in the dark. *Alek, I need you. I can't do this by myself—I don't have the strength.* But Alek's not here right now. Then it's up to me. *Sisu, Kris.* I need to gather strength. General Waara needs to get his army back up and ready for another onslaught asap. Time is of the essence. I'm just the messenger. I'm not the bad news itself. I'll be doing everyone a favor. I take a breath and open my mouth to speak when Blanca opens a small door to our right, ushering us in. We're here. Soft pink lighting glows throughout the room and a heavenly scent wafts through like the essence of rose. Blanca leads me to the shower, right off the main room. I thought I was drumming up some sisu. But in this serene setting, I'm mesmerized. I'll just relax for a few minutes. Then after I'm freshened up, I'll tell them. I desperately need a shower. Just a couple of minutes, then I'll spill. I have to. Just give me two minutes.

The water from the showerhead is a trickle. If this were a typical hotel, I would call the management and ask for my money back. But here, now, their *shower* is a tropical paradise. The scented washcloths seem to be able to soak up every drop. On a wooden ledge right outside the stall, I notice a new, cotton-soft hooded sweatshirt and a pair of jeans, just my size, with a diamond for the fastener. Just for a few moments, I let the scents and softness flow through me. After my time on Cancri, it's positively intoxicating. Without thinking, I open my mouth like a greedy baby bird and let the water trickle down my throat. Immediately, guilt hits. I shouldn't have used this much water. What's wrong with me? How selfish. I know the truth; we may have to keep rationing. But I just couldn't resist. All dry and dressed, I reenter the main room. Blanca and Mutsi look up, smile.

"You look 110 percent better," Mutsi announces.

Blanca leads me to a velvety recliner. My stomach suddenly growls again, this time so loudly everyone hears.

Blanca chuckles. "*Pobre muñequita.* You are no doubt very hungry from your ordeal on that nasty planet. A delicious luncheon spread is on its way."

Mutsi sits down next to me in an identical recliner. "You know, Krissie, the QC not only conducts research at the maxi level—the stars, the galaxies, the outer universe, but also at the microlevel—our cells, DNA, mitochondria, brain, and gut neurotransmitters. Before our world exploded, Blanca and Zola had written a manual on mind-body health. Using a pseudonym of course. It was cutting edge and had just been published." Blanca places a cool hand on my shoulder. "Kristal, you and your mother have been through unimaginable strain. When that happens, the whole body tends to weaken, down to the very cells. If prolonged, parts of your body-mind may begin to deteriorate. We designed our recoup room to rebuild your well-being through every sense. All the soothing sights, sounds, aromas, and musical frequencies were specifically designed to heal you down to the cellular level, rejuvenating your entire nervous system—from your amygdala through your vagus nerve—to help you feel safe again. "Also"—she smiles, glancing at the door—"we need to replenish the nutrients you lost under so much duress."

As if on cue, a small, sweet-faced woman with the name tag "Agnes" wheels a two-tiered food tray into the room. I greet her. She's all smiles as she plucks the lids off the trays. Wow. Immediately, I begin to salivate. What an incredible buffet. On its two shelves is a rainbow cornucopia of every fruit and vegetable imaginable, plus an assortment of herbal teas and spiced nuts. Agnes curtsies. "It's so nice to see you, Ms. Kristal, Dr. Makkinen, Dr. Ruiz-Ortega. Please eat. Enjoy. Regain your strength." She sweeps her hand across the tray, pointing to plates and utensils. Before she's even out of the room, I reach for a slice of pineapple and a small bowl of spiced walnuts. I'm in food heaven. The pineapple alone will help to quench my thirst. "Mutsi, how did they get these delicious foods to grow? I didn't know you could grow pineapple here."

"Blanca designed a way to implement hydroponic farming with minimal use of water. It's worked, and we have been able to feed our people for over a decade, expertly rationing the water through complicated formulas. We can't wait to get back to Earth and introduce these incredible new techniques there. But the formulas don't work forever here on Lucy. We are running out of the water necessary to sustain our crops, but thank goodness, we won't be here for long." *Bam.* The tiny, happy bump in my brain is like a balloon that's just popped. Serenity followed the good news and heartfelt reunions and delicious food. But it was only momentary. *You need to spill it, Kris. Damn it! Spill it! They have to know. They must prepare. Now!*

"Mutsi—" I look into her face.

She smiles and takes my hand. "Yes, Krissie?"

I look into her eyes. So serene. Damn, I can't do it.

I shake my head. "Nothing."

Fifty-Three

◦ ◦ ◦ ◦ ◦ ◦ ◦ ◦ ◦ ◯ ◦ ◦ ◦ ◦ ◦ ◦ ◦ ◦ ◦

February 3, 2027

Mutsi frowns. "Krissie, your face is pale. What's wrong, Krissie babe? Is it about your father? He's in great hands. Did something else happen on Cancri after we had gone? Tell me. Come here." And she pulls me into a tight embrace, rocking me back and forth.

I finally get my bearings. "I... I have to talk to Alek, please." Much to my surprise, I start to shiver all over. Even my teeth are chattering.

Mutsi and Blanca look puzzled then concerned. How can I convince them by myself? They won't believe me. I can't do this alone. "Alek—I really, really have to see him, or *you* have to talk to him or Dr. EJ or someone. *Please.*"

Blanca takes my hands. They're surprisingly cold. "*Dios mio.* Calm down, Kristal. I'll get Alek. Myrakka, give her some lavender and a warm blanket. And program sound treatment, uh, 406." She disappears.

Mutsi grabs a sachet with some lavender seeds encased in violet netting and sets it on the table beside my plate. I immediately breathe in the soft scent. She briefly disappears, returning with a warm blanket, and tucks it all around me. I watch numbly as she reaches up to some kind of black sparkly machine built into the wall and pushes a few buttons. Immediately, the far-off tinkling of bells resonates throughout the room. Magically, my nerves begin to settle. But I'm still a little on edge. They can drag out buckets of lavender and fill my ears full of heavenly harmonies, but knowing what I know about the second wave of Cancris—well, they'd have to add a whole jug of heavy-duty sedatives and send me off to drug-induced la-la land, and I'm sure as hell not doing that.

Mutsi kneels down next to me. "Krissie, out with it. We're all in this together. Did you see something on Cancri? Would you like to see Zola?"

"No, no, it's just…it's just…unbelievably bad news."

Mutsi rears back. "Good grief, Krissie. Then you need to spit it out. We'll deal with it, like we always do."

"Would you believe me if I told you?"

Mutsi frowns. "Of course I would. Why wouldn't I?"

She's right. I take a deep breath. "They're coming back." Finally, it's out.

Mutsi's been patting my arm. She pulls back. "Wh-what? Who are coming back?"

"The Cancris."

Her shoulders slump. "Kristal, General Waara assured us they were all completely destroyed—every last one of them except the leader. And—"

"He's wrong."

"Kristal, you know how trauma—"

"See, you don't believe me."

"Krissie, honey, it's not that I—"

"Believe her. It's true." Alek is standing at the doorway, Jaak and Blanca right behind him. Blanca shrugs. "They were in the hall." Mutsi goes pale, staring at Alek. They all crowd into the room. Alek nods. "Jaak knows. I couldn't find Waara or my pappa." Alek scrunches his face as though he'd rather not say more but then takes his own deep breath. "Waara is correct in that the first Cancri Army was pulverized beyond repair or at least beyond Alph's desire to repair. They checked every last acre of the battleground. Yes, those Cancris are gone, except for Big Don, whom we persuaded Alph to reassemble."

Mutsi's eyes widen. "Big Don? He's okay? Wonderful." She cocks her head. "Then why—"

Alek nods. "Alph informed us he was off to another area of the planet where apparently a reserve army—as large or larger than the first—is harvesting diamonds for new uniforms and preparing for another battle, the apocalypse. If Crystal Child doesn't produce their H_2O by the prophecy date, that is."

I blush. He had to say that. Thanks.

"And he took Big Don with him, and this time, the war will be waged here on Lucy."

Mutsi's jaw drops. "Oh, it can't be. You must have misheard."

"My hearing's fine, and so's Kristal's. Believe us. They're planning to come here, find Kristal, and get their damn water. Now if they get their water, we're all saved. But as we all know—"

"Rub it in, Alek. Go ahead."

"Kristal, you know I'm not rubbing it in. I'm just stating a fact. You know that."

Yeah, I know. It still hurts. It's almost like there's a tiny but overbearing Jackson Hynes attached to my shoulder snorting and guffawing and yelling in my ear, "Stupid, stupid, awfully dumb ditz ADD girl, can't even solve a little water problem. *Bitch*." I hate Jackson Hynes. I hate Alek. No, I don't hate them. It's me I hate right now. I'm helpless, clueless, and afraid. What good am I, the miracle Crystal Child? Tears fill my eyes, surprising me.

Mutsi's eyes close as she slowly shakes her head. I notice she's balled her fists.

"What the hell? What's going on here?" We turn. General Waara is standing in the doorway, nostrils flared. "So a cat rescued you two. I guess we had a little communication problem there."

Apparently, Waara hasn't heard what Alek was just saying or he wouldn't have started out with such a trivial matter.

Alek shrugs. "Wasn't our doing. There Schrödy was, and there we were. We sure as heck weren't going to refuse an easy ride back here, especially since Kristal was this close to—" He points his index finger about a fourth inch from his thumb. "But, hey, General Waara, we've got bigger fish to fry, way bigger."

"Way what? What the hell are you talking about?" I notice for the first time Waara's face is red and his eyes are bloodshot. He gazes up at the ceiling. I know that trick, trying not to cry in front of us. "Goddamn Cancris. This time more than double the casualties as 2016. We should be celebrating. Instead, ah god, just came from setting up the makeshift morgue in passageway number 17837. The widest tunnel we got. Jesus, we need more canvas. And here, with the 29 injured survivors, we need more antidote, more bandages, beds, antibiotics, and goddamn water." He chokes. No one moves for what seems like an eternity.

Mutsi finally whispers, "I'm so sorry, Hale. You can't blame yourself."

He rubs his left eye like he's trying to rip it out. "*Like hell I can't!* Goddamn it, the buck stops here with me! I should have—"

Mutsi clears her throat. "Sisu and SAMO. Okay, Hale, listen. Is everyone back from Earth yet? Where are my parents?"

The general leans against the doorframe. I've never seen him looking so dejected.

"That's what I came to tell you, Myra. If I believed in astrology or black cats or Tarot cards, I would say the stars are definitely not in alignment for us right now."

"Hale, English please or Finnish. What do you mean? Where are the Kurkis? Where are my parents?" Waara stands there, scratching his ear. Mutsi watches him, her eyes growing wider and wider. Finally, she yanks his hand down and gets right in his face. "*Hale. Where are they?*"

Waara's face tightens up again, and he looks even more miserable. As Mutsi studies him, her face pales, and then I see terror in her eyes. My own heart is in my throat.

His head lowers, then he looks up at her. "I hope to hell it's just a small glitch." He clears his throat. "Uh." Another little cough then he says, "Claude and Kiski had the new pendants in hand and teleported to Earth a while ago. I assume they arrived at their intended destination. Uh, we just haven't gotten any sign of their return. Should've been here a long time ago. We just can't figure out—"

Mutsi lets out a cry. "What? *What?*"

"I... I was sure there was no more danger."

"No more danger? After all those Cancris on Earth? Well, you were *wrong*, goddamn it, Hale. Good god, stars not in alignment my ass. Someone should have stayed with them. *You* should have stayed."

The general frowns. "Myra, I had a battle to—" He stops.

My mother's melting down. I can see it. If looks could kill—

Waara runs his fingers through his stubby silver-brown hair. "Sorry. I'm… I'm shocked too. They left for Earth right after the battle. But I should've had at least one of them stay back with the Kurkis. Uh, they're obviously still looking. I just assumed—I mean, we'd killed off all the Cancris, and Voitto was armed on the slim chance that one or two more showed up. He could have easily gotten rid of them. I just don't see how…"

Mutsi's voice is a razor blade. "What if one of them had a poison-tipped spear? What if an extra contingency was sent when the others didn't return? Hale, I can't believe you just assumed—" She stuffs a fist in her mouth, pulls it out, but keeps it balled by her side, takes a deep breath. She's trying not to scream. I don't blame her. Her voice drops. "They wouldn't just disappear, Hale. I can't believe you didn't—" She stops, sighing.

Yeah, Mutsi, don't kick the man when he's down. He knows.

He leans against the wall. "Yeah, well, goddamn it twice. I'm turning in my resignation today. I'm past my prime. It's obvious I'm not up to—"

Holy moly, I check Mutsi's expression, expecting her to protest. She doesn't. The normally self-assured general seems clearly off his game. Maybe he was all fake tough to begin with, but he did save Mutsi's life once. Maybe the stars really *are* out of alignment. After all, the prophecy—well, anyway, there's no denying one piece of excruciating news after another. How much can we all stand? Over four hundred dead soldiers, losing the Kurkis, and now it's time for the triple whammy. No way around it. I brace for his reaction.

Alek places his hand on the general's sleeve. "General Waara, you're not going anywhere. We need you. Listen—"

"Ah, I've got to—" Waara turns to leave.

"Wait." Alek grabs his sleeve.

The general frowns but turns back. "What? What is it?" Waara taps his foot, checking his comcard like he doesn't have time for whatever inconsequential piece of news Alek has to tell him. Little does he know. Oh, boy. Right now, I wish I could hide in a closet somewhere. I silently pray General Waara doesn't have a nervous breakdown right in front of us.

Alek tries a tiny smile. "The good news—you and the Diamond Army obliterated the *first* Cancri battalion."

"Yeah, yeah. So?" Then his foot suddenly stops tapping. "The *first?*"

"Um, yeah, well, unfortunately, they've got a second wave. Right now, they're on the flip side of Cancri e. The so-called sunny side, where the diamond mines are. They're making new suits, and they're coming here to Lucy."

The general stands there, frowning, trying to take it all in without exploding, trying like hell to act composed, but then his face goes ashen, and I can see his breathing pick up as his brain suddenly processes the unthinkable. How much more can he take? "Run that by me again. You can't be serious. How the hell—"

"Alph reappeared on Cancri before Kristal and I left."

"Goddamn AI had a galactic GPS in his innards. How were we to know that?"

"Uh, you weren't. Surprised all of us. But what I just told you, it's true. Got it straight from the robot's mouth or face slit, whatever they call it. Alph was adamant."

"It's lying."

"Wish. Cancris aren't programmed to lie, not yet. Well, except Big Don."

Waara wipes a bead of sweat from his forehead. "All right, okay. Well, we'll deal with it."

"Take a look." Alek pulls something out of his pocket. It's the egg-sized diamond Alph gave Alek. It gleams so brightly I squint. Was it that bright on Cancri e, or did I just not notice? Alek thrusts it toward the general.

Waara reaches for it and squints. "What the hell is this?"

433

"Obviously, a diamond. A message for you. I don't know. From Alph."

"Alph. For *me*?"

Alek nods. "For you and the scientists."

The general turns the diamond over and over, holds it up, and shakes his head. Then he drops it back into Alek's palm. "So? It's a goddamn diamond. We knew it was only a matter of time before the idiots found their own diamond core. Our scientists discovered it in 2004. It was confirmed in 2006. We were surprised they didn't know more about their own planet than we did, or maybe they thought they just didn't need diamonds for their army. So now they're copy-catting. Great. We'll sue 'em for trademark infringement."

Jaak's been standing in the corner, quietly listening. He steps forward and holds out his hand, snapping his fingers. "Uh, Aleksi?"

Alek drops the diamond in Jaak's hand. "Here, Jaak, take a look." He turns to Waara. "You were just kidding about your resignation, right? I mean, it's not that you can drop everything, run back to Earth, and place an ad on LinkedIn or Upwork."

A bead of sweat trickles down the general's temple. "Yeah, yeah, I'm not going anywhere obviously, especially now, goddamn it. All right, so maybe this does complicate things a little. But we can adjust, do some tweaking. We can make our Achilles' heels indestructible. Damn, should've done that before. So they're imitating our model, manufacturing similar diamond suits and shields?"

Alek shrugs. "That's my guess. They were 'harvesting' the diamond as Alph puts it, at the time we left. With this little gift, I guess his message is that we'd better get ready. They're coming in diamond suits this time. Maybe they waited so long because they still believe wholeheartedly in the prophecy, and they didn't want to do all that work if they didn't have to. Maybe their thinking has gotten a little more sophisticated. God help us if that's the case. So it's up to us to either destroy their so-called reserve army or devise some way for Kristal to convince them the water fairy is on the way."

Butterflies suddenly dive-bomb in my gut. So I'm back in the game now? Waara's lips are a thin line. Blanca, Mutsi, and Jaak stand in stunned silence. Mutsi is shivering from head to toe. I stand up and wrap my blanket around her. She stares at the wall. Finally, she turns toward Waara. "EJ's in surgery with Pauli. And my parents, oh god." Her hand goes to her mouth. "It's all too much. I can't—" She backs up, tripping over the blanket, and I have to catch her and ease her into the nearest recliner, rewrapping the blanket around her. Her face drops in her hands, shoulders trembling.

Jaak's been fingering the diamond, turning it over, holding it up, peering at it from all angles. Suddenly, he blurts out, "*Jotain on ehdottomasti outoa.*"

We all turn, staring at him. Whatever the hell he said, it doesn't sound good. I glance at Alek. He's going pale. I touch his sleeve. "What?"

Alek's in his own world, acts like he doesn't even know I'm there, grabs the diamond, turns it over in his hands, and looks up at Jaak. "*Miksi?*"

Jaak and Alek are staring at each other, shaking their heads. Jaak says, "Command Central. My equip desk."

Alek nods and says under his breath to Jaak, "Yeah, I thought so too. Something's off." Without another word, they exit.

General Waara frowns. "What's off?" And he's out the door behind them. The three of them make a weird trio—big tough general trailing the two young geeks, like a huge duckling behind its mommy and daddy. Everything's bizarre.

Blanca yells down the hall, "Hey, Alek, you need to—"

Alek calls over his shoulder, "Later, I'll eat later. I promise."

Blanca stands there, hands on hips, shaking her head.

Mutsi's still cradling her head in her hands. The rest of us just stand in a self-conscious huddle. I'm sick with fear about the Cancris, Dad, my grandparents, about Mutsi losing it, about Tad, about ever finding our way home. I'm trying to drum up some sisu, some PPT. Doesn't work. I'm one big blank, and this time, I don't think it's just my ADD. I blink away more tears. Well, at least my eyes have a little water in them again. But for how long? "Mutsi—"

She immediately sees I'm in trouble and puts a finger up to her lips. She's checking me out to make sure I'm not totally losing it. Wow. Despite the tsunami of bad news, my mother somehow is pulling herself together, willing herself to be strong for me. She's breathing in the lavender. The soothing high frequency of the bells bathes us in a sense of calm, even through all that's happening. She reaches out her hand. "Come here, Krissie, my love."

I glance down at my pineapple and walnuts. No appetite anymore, damn. Gently setting down my plate on a nearby table, I take her outstretched hand. She rises, and we both head to the double recliner on the other side of the room. There I lay my head on her shoulder. I can tell she's still trembling a little bit but taking big belly breaths. Then she turns, speaks to me in that lilting, graceful voice I've come to know and love and remember in the very depths of my being.

"Krissie babe, sometimes things come at you so fast and furious you just have to practice being mindful. Life happens. You're not in control. You can only do so much, but then you must stand on the sidelines and let it be, let the seconds pass, and remember that something, or someone else is in the driver's seat. I admit, I often have to remind myself of that. Let's help each other. Most likely, we'll find my parents. The Cancris will be defeated again. And your father, as I knew him, had the sisu of ten people. He was so strong, not only physically but emotionally. He held me up when I..." she falters.

"I know, Mutsi. You don't have to explain." I look up at her.

She smiles, her eyes misty. "Of course I don't. I'm so glad you and your father had each other. We both loved the same man, didn't we? He was human. He's still human. We finally know that for certain. But even so, sometimes things don't go as we would wish, and then we just need to pour all our love into whoever is with us." Two big tears spill down each cheek as she squeezes my hand.

Somehow, some way, I have to use my PPT—the stuff Dad taught me—to help her. "Mutsi, do you know Dad always gave me a big bear hug every day after school? He'd be fixing dinner and always wore this ratty old blue checkered apron and—"

Mutsi smiles, tears in her eyes. "You first mentioned that apron before you knew I was your mother. I nearly fainted. Couldn't believe he still had it. A Cancri clone wouldn't have—anyway, that gave me my first glimmer of hope. I gave that silly apron to him for our first anniversary. He loved to cook, but he was always spilling things on his shirt. We would laugh so hard. And the bear hugs—I remember those too, Krissie."

My throat's so twisted up I can only nod. She kisses my hair as the tears stream down her cheeks. "We just have to have faith that it will all turn out for the best. No matter what happens, we'll survive."

"Mutsi, we will." Did she teach Dad PPT, or did he teach her? Because they're both damn good at it. In any case, we're both helping each other or trying to. We sit, silent. My eyelids begin to droop. I'm on a soft cotton cloud. My mother's stroking my hair, murmuring that beautiful Finnish lullaby. The warm closeness of her, the tinkling of wind chimes and the scent of lavender softly caress the air, penetrate my brain, and quiet me down. Even though danger still looms large, for this tiny moment in time, I feel strangely calm once again. How is this possible? Blanca is a miracle worker. Mutsi is a miracle worker. I close my eyes, drifting, drifting...

My dreams are of mountains, green with spring this time, and valleys teaming with water—ribbons and ribbons of winding creeks, all through a lush valley, spilling over with pink and yellow wildflowers. It's all beautiful, except for that damn recurring number, still there, in cloud form this time: One. Two. Zero. One.

Fifty-Four

●·○·○·◦·◦·◦·◦◦◦ ◉ ◦◦◦◦◦◦·◦·○·◦

February 4, 2027

A voice pierces my dream. My eyes fly open. I struggle to focus. Has it been another night, another day? I look up, around. I think it's morning. Oh, there's Dr. EJ, in the doorway. His eyes look a little bleary. He massages the bridge of his nose, glancing at Mutsi, then me. His smile looks weary but triumphant. I perk up instantly. Luckily, I don't have a chance to think before it's out of his mouth.

"Surgery ees complete. Eet was long and deeficult and went halfway through the night. But he ees een recovery." He strides over to Mutsi, placing a reassuring hand on her shoulder. She grabs it, her eyes fearfully searching his for more. He disengages and pulls up a chair, his hands steepled between his knees.

"The Cancri eemplant was placed in a creetical location in the prefrontal cortex, which, as you know, ees the seat of judgment, eensight, impulse control, reasoning, all executive function skills. Frankly, we are surprised that he was able to function as normally as he did, according to Kristal."

I have to butt in. "Yes, yes, he did, he was perfectly normal, better than normal. The best dad in the—" A lump in my throat renders me speechless.

"Yes, well, then, they must have had some sort of off switch so he could go about hees daily activities normally unteel—well, you know the story. They most likely knew that the more human he was, the better for the Crystal Child. At least they recognized that. But Pauli's nightmare should be over, my dears. We're fairly confident

438

with our new laser technology, we were able to extract thee alien eemplant without damaging the rest of the delicate teessue. Now eet's wait and see time."

My mother gulps in a breath, grabbing both Dr. EJ's hands and exhaling forcefully. Her voice is shaky, weak. "No words, EJ. No words. You and Dr. B—" Her face pales as she tears up.

Dr. EJ squeezes her hands. "We know. We know." Dr. EJ's eyes are glistening too. I look back at Mutsi. She should look more relieved. I know I am. Instead, she looks like she's ready to break down again. Dr. EJ notices, like he notices everything. "My dear Myrakka, what ees eet? Another question?"

"Ah, well. EJ. It's everything I guess. My parents—"

Oh, yeah.

Dr. EJ frowns. "Your parents? We recently feenished surgery. I'm sorry I have not had time—"

"Claude and Kiski are still back on Earth. They just can't find them." Mutsi lets out a sob.

"Oh, dear." Dr. EJ rubs his beard. "Can't find—oh my. Theories?"

A rustling. I look up. Claude stands in the doorway. He clears his throat, shaking his head. "No. They just vanished."

Dr. EJ shakes his head. "I'm so sorry. To have them so near and now—what ees plan B?"

Claude lowers his head. "I don't know. I don't think anyone knows. I'm just here to relay the news. Going right back before I have to endure the general's wrath. We'll find them." Before our eyes, he grabs his pendant, mutters five numbers, then disappears.

Mutsi balls herself up in her recliner, head down.

Dr. EJ sighs. "Perhaps eet's just a seemple explanation, eh? Perhaps they are out, celebrating?"

Mutsi's raises her head. "Never."

Dr. EJ puts his hand over hers. "Oh, Myrakka. I'm confident there ees a seemple explanation. Let's just keep that in mind for now." She pats his hand, looks up at him fearfully.

"I'll... I'll try. I'll think about Pauli. Is he really—"

"Yes, yes, we have so much to be thankful for and many reasons to hope. And I have so much to thank you for—you brought my Aleksi here. I cannot begeen to repay you."

Mutsi manages a smile. "Oh, that was Aleksi's and Kristal's courage. Talk about sisu."

Dr. EJ sighs, smiling. "Oh, yes. When I received the message from you about my grandson, I went down on my knees. I cannot wait to spend time weeth Aleksi again. I lost him when he was so young. To lose both my daughter and son-een-law and my grandson—he was only seven." Dr. EJ stops, gazes up to the ceiling then back to us. "Well, no need to explain."

Mutsi nods. "That boy of yours—he remembers everything. Smart as a whip, a chip off your own genetic block. And he's got stories to tell, EJ. A decade's worth."

"Ah, stories. You know what I meess? Sitting in the sauna, *lakka* in my hand, swapping tales of the North weeth family and friends." He sighs deeply. "And now that we are going home, and I have Aleksi—"

"Not just Aleksi. The entire QC is your family, EJ. And that *lakka*—it will be a reality. Soon."

Oh shit, Mutsi's forgotten. Is she going to say anything, or is it up to me again?

Dr. EJ clasps his hands. "Yes, yes. After so many years. Hard to believe the Cancris are gone, eh? General Waara and the Diamond Star Army are to be commended, even through the tragic losses. They all weel be honored soon. A ceremony ees being planned."

Okay, this is too much. Mutsi has got to inform him, but she just keeps smiling, like she's in a fog, or is she waiting for the right moment? She couldn't have forgotten. Well, maybe she has, what with all the good news about Dad. Then I guess it's up to me.

But before I can burst Dr. EJ's bubble, Dr. B appears in the doorway, wiping his brow. He gives me a big grin and a wink. "Ah, Kristal, my young friend, you save Onni's life with the water flask meant for you."

I blush. "I... I know you gave me strict orders not to share it, but Onni—he's so special."

Dr. B shakes his head, smiling. "Ah, Kristal, you do not have to give explanation. You prove yourself to be quite compassionate role model, for all of us. Saving Onni's life endeared you even more to our people and the Birds. Such sisu. We are all proud of you."

I smile as best I can as he gives me a quick bow, hands in prayer position. I bow my head in return. If he is able to make my father whole again, back to his real self, I will never be able to repay him, not as long as I live, and not with all the diamonds on this star and on Earth combined. I want to be eloquent, articulate, relaying all my gratitude, and I try so hard to put the appropriate words together. But what comes out is a raspy two-word platitude, "Thank you."

Dr. EJ steps toward the door, motioning Dr. B to follow. "Well, my dears, we weell keep you abreast of any new developments."

Mutsi grabs his hand again. "Can I—we—see him?"

Dr. EJ cocks his head. "Oh, well, I would not expect heem to be awake for quite some time. But well, why not? Of course, if you would like to surround him, hold his hand, talk to him, perhaps he will sense your love, and that will hasten his awareness. But I should warn you—he's quite the post-surgery sight right now. His appearance might still be a little bit of a shock to you. Are you up for thees?"

We both nod vigorously.

Mutsi blurts, "He'll be beautiful no matter what he looks like."

Dr. EJ nods, smiling. "Of course, hees essence will always be part of him."

I realize I should be relaying the bad news, but I convince myself General Waara, Alek, and Jaak are on this. No doubt Dr. EJ will track down Alek as soon as he takes us to Dad's room. And I don't want to waste any more time. Everything's happening at once—the Cancris regrouping, my grandparents' disappearance, my father. I can't be everywhere and on top of everything at once. I just don't have the energy. It's a hands-down choice. I need to see my father so badly my insides ache. I guess I understand Mutsi's denial because I sort of feel the same way. She's obviously not thinking about the Cancri danger right now. Dad's well-being is front and center with both of us.

Dr. EJ says, "All right then. Follow Dr. B and me. Spend some time with heem. Luckily we were able to extubate him a little while ago. Sit weeth him. Talk to him. No more than fifteen minutes or so. Then report back and let us know what you have observed."

We follow them down several hallways, then Dr. EJ opens a door. Mutsi rushes right in. Suddenly, my nervousness kicks in. I hang back, afraid of what I'll see. But my yearning to see him overrides my anxiety, and after a few deep breaths, I step into my father's room.

I try not to gasp. He lies flat on a hospital bed, eyes closed. The jumble of machines, wires, and bandages all but obliterates the sight of him. My throat constricts. He's definitely under all that, looking so fragile I'm afraid he'll break. How can the human body withstand all that he has in the past few days—hell, the past eleven years? I step a little closer to get a better peek. At least, they thought to shave his beard. Even with the huge bandages encircling his head and all the spaghetti wires and tubes, he looks more like my father than the last couple of times I saw him, when he was...

God my vocal cords feel like a dam ready to burst. I don't want the first sound Dad hears to be me howling like a deranged dog. He hates it when I cry. Maybe I'd better leave. I glance over at Mutsi. She's so pale. But she's being brave; her sisu seems to be up and running, and she's keeping her tears to herself for Dad's sake. If she can, I can. I step right up to the side opposite her.

A nurse is adjusting the IV, as Dr. B taps on a diamond-encrusted electronic pad with his pen. He studies it, then smiles, giving Mutsi and me a thumbs-up. "Vitals excellent. I just know he is in there, fighting hard for his life—the one he was supposed to have. The real Pauli is with us, just give him time." At that, the two doctors leave the room.

"Thank you," Mutsi whispers, then turns to my father, leans down, and kisses the bandage wrapped around his head. She speaks softly into his ear. I can't make out anything except the words *so much*. A tear from my mother's cheek falls, landing on my father's left ear. I can't help staring at both my parents, together after eleven years. I want to jump with joy and cry my eyes out at the same time. My chest tightens, and I swallow hard to keep from making a sound. I don't want to ruin their moment. When Mutsi turns and beckons to me, I step forward and gingerly reach for my father's hand. I can barely speak. My voice is a whisper. "Dad?"

His fingers curl around mine. My breath stops.

Slowly, slowly, he opens his eyes, blinks, and looks up at me. Oh god, he's actually looking at me, and they're *his* eyes. Bloodshot, yes, but those deep-brown eyes are back. His own brown eyes. *He's* back. He immediately shuts them again, wincing, and his fingers uncurl from mine. But it was a start, right? I look across Dad's bed to my mother. Our eyes meet. Then, as one, we fly into the hall.

"Dr. EJ! Dr. B!"

They're halfway down the hall, but both stop, turn. Dr. EJ's face lights up. "News? Already?"

I can't contain myself. Even with my dehydration, I'm going to pee, right here in the hall. I almost forgot the sensation I've been so water starved. Mutsi starts to tell them, but I practically scream over her, "He opened his eyes! He squeezed my hand!" And then I make a beeline to the restroom, luckily just a few doors down. When I return, Dr. B is clasping his hands, and Dr. EJ is in deep conversation with Mutsi. "But thees ees an excellent sign. He'll probably go een and out of various stages of consciousness before he awakens fully. Frustrating, but thees ees the time for patience. And we Lucy people have had lots of practice at that, no?"

"Yes, we have." Mutsi nods, her eyes misty. "But oh, it's so hard. I've been living without him for eleven years. I can't be greedy. He wasn't even alive as far as we were concerned—for over a decade. I need to process this."

Dr. EJ places his big bear paws over my mother's delicate hands. "Indeed, let's count our blessings, and the greatest blessing, we weel be home soon."

Home soon. Seriously? Someone *has* to enlighten him. "Um, Dr. EJ, I'm so sorry you haven't heard."

"Heard? Heard what, my dear?"

"The, uh, Mutsi?" Damn. She's in a trance, and I chicken out again. How can I completely spoil this glorious moment? I will it away. I just can't be the one to break the news. "Um, you were on your way to find Alek, right?"

He smiles broadly. "Yes, Kreestal. Do you know where he ees?"

"I think he's still with Jaak."

Dr. EJ pulls out his comcard. "Jaak? Where are you? And Aleksi? Yes. I'm on my way."

He turns to us. "They're in Command Central. I'm headed that way. But if anything changes weeth Pauli, you let me know right away, eh?"

Mutsi and I nod. There. Alek will clue him in, and I don't have to. Mutsi lowers her head then raises it up to Dr. EJ. "Yes, you need to talk with them now."

The two men frown, puzzled. "What ees eet, Myrakka? My grandson? Is Aleksi…?"

A siren blares, followed by flashing lights.

Fifty-Five

● ○ ○ ○ ○ ○ ○ ○ ◉ ○ ○ ○ ○ ○ ○ ● ○

February 4, 2027

My body stiffens, like it does when we have intruder drills at school. Do they have them here too? Hope that's all this is. But in my heart of hearts, I know better. On Dr. EJ's face is complete surprise. My mother's eyes are darting up, down, toward the door. Oh, this is not good.

A voice blasts from somewhere, everywhere. "Code gray. Intruder. Intruder. Incoming. All take cover. Repeat. Code gray. Intruder. This is not a drill. Repeat. Not a drill. Go to your posts immediately and wait for further instructions."

Mutsi grabs my arm. Alarm is etched on her face.

Dr. EJ points forward. "Command Central. Quickly."

Mutsi and I follow Dr. EJ and Dr. B to a large busy area apparently called Command Central, or simply, Central. It's an amazing complex, like the movies I've seen of NASA headquarters in Houston. Huge computer screens are in a circle, above eye level, displaying various graphs and real-time videos. Several display radar trackings of a storm or some other fast-moving threat out in the cosmos.

Many have already gathered in this room they call Central. They're all checking the screens, searching one another's faces, engaged in hushed conversations all around me. General Waara is checking something at Johann's workstation, squinting as he focuses at the screen above him, pointing at a grayish-white blob among a dusting of stars.

"Well, let 'em. We still have the advantage. How they can fashion diamond to cover metal—that had to be a feat. Johann, everyone, no worries. I have full confidence that even with their new getups, we can do a repeat of the battle on Cancri but without the damn casualties. Our suits have been tweaked. Our soldiers are ready. This so-called reserve Cancri army will be another massive heap, just like their unfortunate counterparts on Cancri. Everyone, just calm down. We've got this." And then he clears his throat. He's terrified. He's not fooling me or anyone.

Jaak's workstation is next to Johann's. While Johann is calmly checking screens, up, down, up, Jaak is not calm at all. In fact, he looks more jittery by the minute. Alek's been off to the side. Now Jaak and Alek exchange a look I don't like, and Jaak starts collecting parts and pieces of some kind of equipment. Alek holds the Cancri diamond, turning it over and over in his hand.

I'm clearly in the way, so I slink back to a corner and observe. A huge contingency of scientists, engineers, and computer people has gathered, and Central is buzzing with activity. Dr. EJ and Dahab are deep in conversation. I hear Dr. EJ say, "Not a drill? What then? Say again? So the TAD was definitely able to transmeet the code. And there are *more*?"

I feel my face flush. Yes, I outed this star by revealing the Diamond Star's location code to my Cancri brother, who obviously beamed it right up to the enemy. The moment when Tad mindlessly repeated the number 37093 is forever burned into my brain. I will never forgive myself as long as I live.

Jaak's setting up some kind of instrument, pressing icons on his computer. Dr. B is standing over him, shrugging. "Let's not jump to conclusion. Could be anything. Let's hope it is just strange type of meteor shower. We can deflect that."

Dr. EJ frowns, perplexed. "Weren't they all obliterated by Waara's team on Cancri e? Did I meess something when we were een surgery? Am I meestaken? Can you confirm?"

Damn, I shouldn't have let this siren gobsmack him. I should have told him earlier. I could kick myself.

Johann is still clicking away, checking the screen, back and forth. He shakes his head, turns, and looks up at Dr. EJ. "Confirmed. It's Cancri."

Jaak's oblivious, totally engrossed in setting up whatever instrument he has on his desk. Alek looks at his pappa like he's trying to stay steady. "They obliterated half. The other half, um, they were on the other side of the planet. The ones coming toward us are wave number two."

General Waara's been clicking away on his own iPad-like screen. "Yup, it's them."

I notice everyone sort of ignoring Waara now that Jaak, Johann, and Alek have stepped up to the plate. The general stands there, scratching his chin, appearing to be deep in concentration, but as I watch, I notice his right hand is quivering. Abruptly, he turns and strides out the door. At this moment, I feel a little sympathy pang. I mean, he's been arrogant and all, but he did save my mother. He wants to help. He wants to be in charge, to win. But it's clear to everyone now. Alek was right on all three counts: Alph was able to escape back to Cancri; he has a backup army; and they're now designing diamond suits. They'll be much more formidable. I just hope Waara's up to the task now. Must be hard on him but hell. We have our whole star's population to save, not to mention Earth. Isn't the mark of a true leader someone who is humble enough to stand aside and let the better ones lead if they're clearly more capable?

No one seems to notice Waara's exit. Dr. EJ is wiping his forehead with a cloth. "More Cancris? I can't believe it. Are you sure? Why deedn't they just land here? You know, use a wormhole?"

Johann shakes his head. "I'm not an expert on Cancri travel modes. But my guess is that their teleportation algorithm was hastily devised and wasn't as precise as it should have been. They're several thousand kilometers off."

Dr. EJ turns to someone I don't recognize, who's got her eyes peeled on another screen. "Anna, how fast are they going?"

"We're tracking it now. Don't have precise kilometers per hour. But they're not out for a Sunday stroll, that's for sure."

Dr. EJ sighs. "We're going to have to assume worst-case scenario and prepare."

Jaak yanks open a cupboard door to the right of his workspace, pushes an iPad out of the way, pens clattering to the floor, and places a large magnifying glass on the flat surface next to the instrument he was putting together. Some kind of microscope. He snaps his fingers. Alek hands him the diamond. "*Katso.*"

Jaak's muttering to himself in Finnish. Looks like he's got a microscope of some kind. He places the diamond underneath and peers in. Those around him are discussing protocols and logistics, oblivious to the monumental gravity of the task Jaak is undertaking at the moment. I don't know what he's doing either, but it looks really serious. He keeps peering into the lens, adjusting the diamond, then peering in again. After several moments, Jaak pulls the diamond from the microscope, sets it down, reaches up to a shelf above his computer, and rummages through a ton of manuals, papers, pencils, which reminds me of my locker at school. Finally he grabs a thick technical-looking manual from a shelf above his computer. It slips out and slams to the floor. "*Paska.*" I don't need a translation. He picks up the book and thumbs through the pages. I notice it's all in Finnish. Suddenly he stops, jamming a finger on a page near the middle.

"*Se siita.*" His eyes scrunch close, then he opens them as a strange animal noise erupts in his throat. He picks up the diamond again, staring at it, horrified, as though it were a bomb about to blow everything to bits.

The others are checking their devices, speaking in low tones, still oblivious, except Johann, who has stopped in his tracks, eyes peeled on Jaak, as are mine. Jaak's nostrils are flared, and his cheeks flush a weird shade of pink. He's squeezing the diamond like he wants to crush it with his bare hands. His breathing is jagged, and I can tell he's trying not to hyperventilate. I know that feeling well. Why is—

Suddenly, he scrapes back his chair, just missing Alek, stands, and lifts the diamond up over his head like a pitcher about ready to slam a baseball into someone's head. Isn't anyone else seeing this? Johann's expression is one of shock, and Alek's eyes widen in fear.

Jaak lets go with a loud *"He ovat voittaneet jalleen. Hitto Viekoon!"* as he hurls the diamond across the room toward the large window dividing Central from the hallway. I follow its arc as it sails above everyone's head then smashes the glass. Shards explode everywhere. Luckily, no one was in its path. Everyone halts in their tracks, their eyes warily staring—first at the glass and then back to Jaak. The silence is deafening. Well, he's got their attention now. He really could have hurt someone. Jaak's a pasty pale, sweating like he's just witnessed doomsday. Maybe he has. What the hell did he see under that microscope?

Someone mutters, "Wasn't that glass supposed to be indestructible?"

Dr. EJ quietly exits the room and returns with the diamond. He holds it up to Jaak, his voice almost a whisper. "Jaak? *voittaneet jallen*—who has won again? The Cancris?"

Jaak balls his fists. *"Anteeksi..."*

"No, no, Jaak. Don't be sorry. Obviously you anticeepate a grave problem, eh? What ees eet?"

Jaak's blinking hard. Alek places a reassuring hand on Jaak's shoulder, though I notice Alek's own hand is trembling slightly. Dr. EJ just stands, waiting, neutral expression on his face. Does anything ruffle his feathers? I look more closely. Oh, there it is. Under that pleasant face, Dr. EJ's jaws are clenched so hard I'm afraid his molars will crack.

Jaak shakes his head. "Bastards...*bastards!* They can't do this again. They will *not* do this again—my isa, mutsi..."

Besides the clenched jaw, Dr. EJ's getting a little fidgety. "Jaak, we have so leettle time. Please tell us. Let us figure thees out together."

Jaak finally stares into Dr. EJ's eyes. "There's nothing to figure out. They've done it. Harvested their diamond. Outdone us again. Twice, for God's sake. *Twice.*"

Dr. EJ tries to lighten things. "My dear boy, so they have diamond now. So what? We have diamond too, and our army—"

Jaak waves him off. "It's...it's..."

"Yes? It's what? Go on."

Jaak sniffles, wipes a bead of sweat from his brow. "*Lonsdaleite.*" He winces, as though the word itself is dangerous.

Dr. EJ cocks his head. "Lons—excuse me? English please or Feennish. Take your pick."

"That *is* English." Jaak sighs. His face is growing paler by the minute. Another minute, and I think he might faint. Then he takes a deep breath. "Lonsdaleite—hexagonal diamond material. Discovered on Earth in 2009. Obviously on Cancri as well. Greater indentation strength than regular diamond—*58 percent stronger.*" He steps backward, slumps into his chair. "*Fifty-eight percent.* Jesus, we're toast."

Dr. B turns his head all around. "Where is Waara?"

I guess I'm the only one who saw him leave. "Uh, he left a few moments ago."

He frowns. "Where?"

I shrug. Dr. B and Dr. EJ exchange glances.

Dr. EJ pulls out his comcard. "Waara, yes, we, uh, have a seetuation. Please return immediately. How many available troops do we have at present? Wha—8,425? Okay. So we lost over 400. But we still—"

Jaak pounds a fist on the table. "Are you all deaf? It's *lonsdaleite,* for God's sake. *Lonsdaleite.* It doesn't matter if we have a million soldiers. Two million. A *billion.* It's no use. We can't penetrate their suits, not a dent, not a single damn scratch. If we try to fight them head on, *pffff.* That's the end of the human race. *We are so f——*"

"*Jaak, Jaak.*" Dr. EJ shifts his weight, leans in closer to Dr. B. I can't hear everything, but what I do hear makes my blood run cold.

Waara strides back into the room, rubbing the bridge of his nose. "Now what?"

Jaak blurts out, "Their diamond is londsdaleite. That mean anything to you?"

"Should it?"

Jaak's expression is one of disdain. "*Paska.*"

"Well? Are you going to clue me in?"

Jaak repeats what we all heard a few moments before. The general's Adam's apple keeps going up and down. He keeps squeezing his eyes shut and clenching his teeth. I've never seen him look so miserable, but then his face reddens, his breathing quickens, and his fists clench. I'm sure he'd rather be angry than feel defeated. Dr. EJ, Jaak, and Alek gather in a tight circle. I can only hear snatches of their conversation.

"Perhaps...talk...before... Cancri... Kristal...outwit..."

At the sound of my name, I freeze. What? They're suddenly focusing on the debunked Crystal Child again? *Me?* Making plans I may have to execute? Seriously? It's this bad? So I'm back in the game. I quietly inch closer, pretending to study one of the computers nearby. I almost run into Elk Kivi, the handyman. He backs up. "Oh, sorry." Poor guy. He's sweeping up the mounds of glass shards and dumping them in some kind of red plastic container as fast as he can. No one else notices me. Johann is typing furiously, probably calculating the Cancris' ETA. Waara, EJ, Jaak, and Alek are talking over one another.

I hear Waara respond in that low, thick voice of his, obviously trying to get some control back. Finally, the others quiet down, and I hear Waara whisper, "No, what could she possibly do? She's a child, for God's sake. We'll gather our think tank and go to plan B or C or Z. However many plans it takes. I've not lived on this godforsaken white dwarf an entire decade assembling the most formidable army in the galaxy just to see us all destroyed again by this swarm of robotic insects. And by my word, they will not return to Earth. I will see to that. I will crush every last one if it's the last thing I do. If I have to do it with my bare hands. I swear to God I will. Prophecy be damned." He vehemently shakes his head.

General Waara just called me a child. Yes, I'm a child, I suppose. So they might need to include me, but they don't want to, so I don't even deserve to be a part of this think tank, I guess. What does it all mean? I'm afraid I'll do my infamous blush, and my voice will creak like a baby frog. But I have to assert myself, however *childish* they may think I am. Alek's moved to Johann's station and is grilling him with questions. It's now or never.

I touch the general's sleeve. "Uh, excuse me, General Waara, Dr. EJ." The general and Dr. EJ are now busy comparing iPad screens and don't seem to hear me, or maybe they're politely ignoring me. I repeat myself, then pointedly clear my throat. Dr. EJ and the general finally look up from their screens, staring at me blankly. I shrug. "If you let me, maybe I can help. My brother is—was—a Cancri. I know how to talk to them. I'm supposed to be the one, after all, who—"

Dr. EJ smiles, the kind of patronizing smile I know only too well from the "experts" at school. "Kreestal, that's very generous of you. We know you have the spirit of a warrior. For a brief moment we considered, but theenk of your mother. She has just been reunited with you. And your father—he should be recognizing you soon. Can you imagine eef anything happened to you now? No. We cannot place you in harm's way. You absolutely need to be here, under our protection. Besides, your mother would never allow eet. But you can help tremendously een other ways. Uh, why don't you seet weeth your father? Your mother may need to stay here and help us with logeestics, and you know your father better than anyone. He weel need a familiar face when he regains consciousness."

Mutsi, close by, in animated conversation with one of the computer techs, suddenly turns to me, raises an eyebrow, and then gives me a nod. Her face is question mark, like "You watch Dad while I do more important stuff, okay? You don't mind, do you?" Yes, I do mind. I can't believe Mutsi is choosing to be here instead of at Dad's side. But I guess this is life or death, and Mutsi's expertise is needed here. If she doesn't help, we'll all die. Well, maybe I have expertise too. I know how to talk to an AI that doesn't really understand English or the gist of it. That skill alone might save us. But to everyone else, I'm useless. Okay then. I smile like a good little girl, nod to Dr. EJ, General Waara, and Mutsi—oh, such a great team player I am, such an obedient *child*. Fine. I'll figure something out all on my own. Isn't that what the prophecy says I'm supposed to do, anyhow?

But the more I think about it, the more I realize maybe they have a point. I'd better be with Dad in case he has another breakthrough. Maybe I can speed up his recovery. Maybe he's had the key all along. Maybe this time I can protect him when the Cancris…a shiver runs up my spine. I can't go there. But I have to… I have to. I have to think, think, think. Last time, at age two, I couldn't. But now what is it called? Lons-da-whatever, the stronger diamond. What did the prophecy say? Something about if the Crystal Child's essence fails, the Cancris can throw us into the void forever? Suddenly it feels like a thousand worms are crawling all around my insides. Of course, my "essence" will fail. I don't even know what that means. Maybe I'm in that strange, terrible dream after all. But I know I'm not. This is as real as it gets.

Well, if this is the devil's outcome as depicted in the prophecy, then when we all disappear, I'd rather be with my father than anyone in the entire universe. But until the arrival of doomsday, Dad's alive, and I'm alive. And whatever happens, I'll be right by his side. The way he's always been by mine. To hell with the stupid Cancri invasion.

I race out the door toward Dad's room. I can't reach him fast enough.

Fifty-Six

° ◦ ◦ ◦ ◦ ◦ ◦◦◦◉ ◉◦◦◦◦◦ ◦ ◦ ◦ °

February 4, 2027

My father is still all hooked up, wires everywhere. The beep, beep is steady, and someone has cranked his bed halfway up. His eyes are open. My stomach squirms as I squint to see him better in the dim light. Holy moly, the redness is almost gone from his beautiful, warm, brown human eyes; eyes now staring at me just like they used to when he was deep in thought. Hallelujah! I stifle a squeal. It's happening. He's getting better by the minute. Oh. Uh-oh. We've lost eye contact. He's staring straight ahead like he's in a trance. I whisper, "Dad, please don't lose me." No reaction. I keep my gaze steady, thinking he'll return to me, thinking about his amazing bravery and sisu over the years—all to protect me. I can't hold back my tears, but with great effort, I keep them quiet, wiping them with my sleeve. Poor Dad. I can't imagine what he's been through. He has to be okay. He *will* be okay. God, I miss him so much.

I tiptoe to his bedside. Please, oh, please let him speak. Let him look at me again. Let him recognize me. Let him be *human*. Suddenly, as if hearing my prayers, he suddenly frowns, opens his mouth, like he's about to—oh my god. *Come on, Dad. Come on.* And then he looks back into my eyes, and I hear the voice I remember so well.

"I… I think I'm—whew—a little thirsty."

"*Dad!*" The word bursts from my mouth. Dad wants water. Now. "*Nurse!*"

"*Rayie!*" Wonderful! I jump, turning. A nurse, wearing a hijab and long dress, is up and off down the hall before I can apologize. She must have been sitting in the corner on duty. I look back at Dad. He's holding his hand to his bandaged head. "Ouch. God—"

I need to stay calm for Dad's sake. I smile down at him. "Dad, it's me. Kristal. You just had surgery. *Brain* surgery." My hand goes to my mouth. Maybe I shouldn't have said that so soon. He peers up at me, puzzled, then falls back on his pillow. *Please, please, please, Dad.* I gently pat my father's hand and give him the most encouraging smile I can muster. His eyes meet mine, and he frowns again, cocking his head like a dog, like he's trying to remember. Then something clicks.

"Krissie?"

Omigod, omigod! I fall to my knees and have to pull myself up. And then I'm over him, hugging him, wires and tubes be damned. I hope I'm not squashing anything crucial, and I'm trying not to cry, but I've waited and waited so long for this moment, and sometimes didn't even know if I'd ever have this moment, but oh, I'm so happy…so happy "Five Star Pictures Presents" as Tad would say, and everything else disappears from my mind, and it's me and Dad, and we're a family again, and he's going to be fine. I wipe my tears and sniffle. Oh, whew.

"*Qi Ji—miracle!*"

I turn, half laughing, half crying. The nurse got Dr. B. He steps into the room. I'm so crazy wild I hug Dr. B, then turn, and hug the nurse. "Thank you, uh"—I notice her name tag, Jala—"Jala? Is that how you say it?"

She nods shyly then says softly, "Your father is remarkable." She's holding a tiny cup of water, which she hands to Dad.

He proceeds to down it in one gulp, then immediately chokes, clears his throat. "More?" he croaks, holding out the tiny cup.

Oh, shit. Poor Dad. Jala sadly shakes her head. "In a little while. Let's not go too fast."

He doesn't argue. Dr. B walks to the other side of the bed, winks at me, and pulls a shiny pen from his lab coat pocket. "Pauli, so nice to see you are awake. Let's break the rules a tiny bit here. Why not."

I gasp. Another small drink. How nice of Dr. B. Dad downs this one too, coughs, clears his throat. The nurse grins, backs up, and sits back down in the corner.

"Okay, we can work on getting you some food soon. You were intubated for some time, and your throat no doubt is quite sore. But for now, let's start with easy things. Can you follow my pen? Up. Good. Down. Excellent. Now please I want you to sit straight up if you can." He pushes a button on the inside railing of the bed that gently raises Dad almost to a sitting position. "Yes, good. Now, Pauli, keep looking ahead and say yes when the pen comes into view." Dr. B moves the pen behind Dad, then slowly reintroduces it into his field of vision on the left side.

"Yes, I see."

"Very good. Now..." Dr. B moves the pen behind Dad then slowly makes a half circle to the right side of Dad's head.

When it's at ear level, Dad says, "Yes, here."

"Ah, perfect. Now can you tell me your name?"

"P-Paul... Paul. Yes." He frowns. "Paul Ma-Makkinen."

"Wonderful. Now who is this young lady here? Do you know her?" He gestures toward me.

"My—I know... I said it a minute ago, didn't I?" He stops. "But where's the TAD?"

I jump. "Tad? You mean Tad, your son?"

Dr. B puts his finger to his lips. He turns to my father. "Pauli, who is Tad?"

Dad grimaces. "Tad. It's...it's...but it's not..." He frowns again, turning to me, wincing as if trying hard to remember. "It's not... my son, but *you*..." He jabs a finger in my face. "My girl, my...my Krissie babe..."

Everything stands still. He said Krissie. He said my name, not just Krissie but Krissie babe. My hands crisscross over my heart to keep it from bursting out of my chest. He'll remember Tad soon too; I just know he will. "Dad, yes, I'm your Krissie. I'm your Krissie-babe." I can't hold back the tears anymore, I just can't, and they gush from my eyes. I'm sobbing and hugging him again, as gently as I can through all the wires.

He places his arm over my back. "Krissie... Krissie, it's okay..."

"Yes, Dad. It's more than okay. It's *ihme*."

"*Ihme*? My Krissie—learning Finnish now?"

We all laugh. Then I'm blubbering like a baby. Yes, a miracle is taking place, *ihme, qi ji, miracle*—no matter how we all say it, it sounds amazing. Although I sorely miss his big, strong bear hugs, I'm overjoyed to get even this tiny, delicate one. It's more than I dared hope. That night in the car—the Cancri e monsters made him do it all. That was not my dad. Deep down, I knew.

Dr. B motions me to join him outside the room. I'm reluctant. I just want to keep hugging Dad, not letting him out of my sight. But slowly I let go of my father, promising to be back soon, and grab a tissue from the bedside table, wiping my eyes. Jala, is immediately beside him, checking all the machines. "Thank you, Jala," I say.

She smiles widely, nodding, and goes back to her protocol. Then I join Dr. B in the hall. He is checking his device. "Let's see. Signs are very good. Cognitive, visual, cranial nerves intact. You still may notice some difficulties with frontal-lobe function, such as lack of awareness, which you may interpret as rudeness and insensitivity. Or maybe attention difficulties. But we hope that will pass soon. So—overall—like old Beatles' tune—he's 'getting better all the time.'" He chuckles, whisper-sings the lyric again, and does a little foot shuffle. They all knew my dad too. Dr. B's almost as happy as I am.

He places a hand on my shoulder. "We let him rest a little more and see if memory comes back fully. It will return in bits and pieces now. But his recognition and obvious affection for you is very evident. What a welcome sign. If we could just get medication for memory enhancement—" He stops midsentence then furrows his brow. "Been quite a while. We have some older drugs. Unfortunately, Myrakka's father—your grandfather, Voitto—as I recall, was working on new type of memory medication, nanobot device to enhance recall in those with traumatic brain injury. How far had he gotten on that before—well, all work was obviously lost. Pity. But wait, didn't I just hear they have been found? Voitto? Lumi?"

My grandparents! My eyes widen. "Yes, they're on Earth somewhere. They just can't find them."

"Cannot find them? How can this be?"

"Well, General Waara sent a couple soldiers back with pendants. But they—I... I just don't—"

A sudden commotion erupts down the hall—banging, thumping, yelling, screaming. Oh god, the Cancris? Here already? My heart drops to my stomach.

A voice way down the hallway shouts, "Stop, everyone! No, no, he's one of us! He's one of us! Stop *please*!"

Fifty-Seven

○ ○ ○ ○ ○ ○ ○ ○ ◉ ○ ○ ○ ○ ○ ○ ○ ○ ○

February 4, 2027

My heart stops. Big Don is lumbering down the hallway, leading Mummo, Pappa, and Claude, with Alek bringing up the rear. Big Don is obviously scaring the wits out of everyone in his path. He must have slipped to Earth somehow from the Cancri mines and found my grandparents. But where were they? Where did he hide them? Why didn't he tell the soldiers? Probably just a big snafu as I heard my mother say when I first appeared in Birdland. The soldiers said they looked everywhere. Big Don must have gotten to them first and hidden them well. Bless Big Don. First, he sends Schrödinger to our rescue. Then he rescues the Kurkis. A sob catches in my throat. Mutsi was right. This is all too much. At least, this stuff is good news. Finally.

Thank God General Waara is tied up at Central. Although this time, he should know better than to shoot our robot ally. Everyone will have to get used to this gentle giant though. Poor Big Don. Jackson Hynes's bullying was humiliating enough for me. I can't imagine what it's like for Big Don when people scream at the sight of him. Sure, he's a shock at first but how rude. My cheeks burn in shame that I was probably one of the rudest of all at first. I vow to make up for it.

"Pappa! Mummo! Big Don! Alek!" I race down the hall, and we all do the triple hug we first did on Earth, laughing and crying at the same time. I give Alek and Big Don a hug too. When I pull back, I notice Big Don's mouth slit is wider.

"Hug means like. Happy to see me. Not afraid."

I pat him on his enormous metal back. "Of course, I'm happy to see you, Big Don. I'm the opposite of afraid. In fact, I'm over-the-moon happy you're finally here."

"Over moon? People get happy when they go over Earth moon?"

We all laugh. Alek smiles, patting Big Don's arm. "It's good laughter, Halfling. Happy laughter, okay?" He turns to us.

"Big Don told Alph he would go on a reconnaissance mission to Earth and capture the Kurkis. He captured them, all right. But he brought them here instead of there, of course. The Canks will not be pleased. We'll have to think of a good story for why they're not frying to death on the sizzling Cancri ground. Proud of you, Halfling."

Big Don nods. "Cancris found location of Kurki safe house—signal from disassembled Cancri. Sent six more Cancris to Earth. I suggest Kurkis to stay in Comfort Inn. Thumb through travel book like Alek teach me. *Comfort* mean feel good. Want Kurkis to feel good. Want them to be safe and com-for-table. Working on suffixes. They go, stay in one bedroom. I find two more Cancris underground, in sewer, searching for Kurkis, three more in teleport station above Kurki safe house. But can't find last one. I communicate to Cancris from teleport station everything okay on Earth, would teleport Kurkis within two year to Cancri. Then go to Kurki lab, collect materials for new travelrods. Take me two Cancri years to program."

People are frowning at that last statement. But I know. He was there for about thirty-six hours—about a day and a half.

Alek is beaming. "No wonder our guys couldn't find the Cancris or the Kurkis. The Kurkis were in Comfort Inn… Comfort Inn. Can you believe the genius of this guy? And our guys wouldn't have thought of a sewer or a teleport station. Man, bro. You're getting to be quite the whiz at figuring out logistics. But you must have found Claude. Bran came back early, and Kiski was with us on Cancri. Claude was looking all over trying to find Voitto and Lumi."

"Yes, after kill Cancri and gather supplies in Kurkis lab, I work in room next to Kurkis. They get room for me, but I hide my ugly and sneak. Close curtains. No one see. I also tell Kurkis about happenings on Cancri. Alph tell me Dr. Makkinen disappeared. I hope that mean to Diamond Star. Told Dr. Kurki. Dr. Kurki think Dr. M might need memory medication. He prepare pills for Dr. M. Need go back to old house. We go back very quietly."

Claude barges in, "Quiet my ass. Sorry, Big Don, buddy, but you can't go quietly anywhere. It's a wonder you didn't cause a riot at Comfort Inn." Claude turns to us, chuckling. "But when this guy snuck into the Kurkis' house, he somehow stayed quiet enough so that it was like a scene from a grade-B movie—we were both walking backward and literally bumped into each other. Luckily, neither of us was trigger happy, or we might not all be here right now. Big Don couldn't find Cancri number 6. We found that one. Lord knows what it was doing at the old house. We wasted it right away. Finally everyone was present and accounted for."

We all let out a collective sigh. Alek's nodding. "Well, all's well that ends well. This stage, anyway. Brilliant of you to think of the need for medication for Dr. M. So okay, where is he? We all got to move now."

I hear someone yelling down the hall, right outside Central. "Kristal? What's going on? You okay?"

It's Mutsi. My grandparents turn. Mummo and Mutsi let out shrieks at the same moment, and both Pappa and Mummo rush to greet her, and there they all stand, hugging, laughing, and crying at the same time. Mutsi waves to Big Don as she's embracing her parents. I realize my cheeks are wet as rain from being with Dad, and now this. Must be the moisture from the few bites of pineapple in the recoup room.

I wipe them away as I announce, "*Come on*, Dad's awake! He's *talking*."

Alek turns toward Central. "Hey, guys, that's great. Big Don and I are headed to Central. Expect a few more screams, don't worry. He'll be joking with the crew in no time. Good luck all. You know where to find us."

Mutsi grabs her mother for support, and I just take a quick flashbulb picture with my mind. It's been more than a decade. And now—I can't believe this. I turn and race back to Dad's room, stopping in the doorway. He's still sitting up, now talking to Jala.

"Not too hungry, but maybe…"

He's talking, and he's making sense. It's been so long. The huge lump in my throat threatens to explode, and I have to wrench my hand away from my mouth so Dad doesn't realize how shocked I am. *Big breaths, Kris.* I cannot erupt into sobs. That wouldn't be good for Dad. *Deep, deep breaths. Okay, okay, I'm good.*

I rush to his bedside, place a reassuring hand on his arm, speaking softly as I've been instructed. "Hey, Dad, I'm so glad you're awake. Do you remember the yummy pecan pancakes you made the day of the big snowfall?"

He blinks. "Pecan pancakes?" He frowns, looks to the right then smiles. "Ha, I flipped that one pretty high."

I stay outwardly calm, but my stomach's turning crazy cartwheels. "Yes, yes, Dad, and…and Tad went outside first, and I came down…and…and…"

"Oh, you were so excited. You had to kiss your snow god."

"It's all coming back, isn't it?" I probably shouldn't be doing this. But I can't hold back. "Dad?"

"Kristal?"

"Do you remember Myrakka, your wife?"

He frowns. "My wife. My wife? No, Krissie. I don't have a wife. It's just you and me, Krissie babe."

"And Tad. You and me and Tad."

"No, not the TAD, Krissie, it's the enemy device."

I stumble back a step. "Oh, Dad, you're confused."

"Not about that."

Holy crap, I can't, just can't go there. I can't believe even Dad, who knew Tad as well as I did, couldn't see anything human in him. Oh, wait. Ah, this might be what Dr. B was describing: Dad's comment wasn't meant to be rude or insensitive. He just blurted out what he was thinking. Got it. His brain is still healing. I decide to drop the subject for now. "Okay then, it used to be you, Mutsi—Myrakka, your wife—and me. I mean, when I was younger, a baby."

"No, Krissie." But for this, his no is more uncertain. He frowns as if deep in thought.

"Then, Dad? Where's my mother?"

Still frowning, he blinks. "I—well, I don't know."

Damn, I turn my back. I don't want him to see my disappointment. On one hand, I'm amazed and grateful he recognized me and that he's recalling some things. But I feel awful for both my parents that they can't yet share in the miracle of a reunion. And the fact that Dad thought of Tad as only a *device* and an *enemy device*, at that. Even though I know he didn't mean to be so blunt, it still breaks my heart to hear him say what he was thinking all along for over a decade. My nervous system is on fire with fear, anger, love, confusion—all churning around like a tornado in my gut.

Just then they all enter—Mutsi, Dr. B, Alek, Mummo, Pappa. Although they're trying to slip in quietly so as not to overwhelm Dad, they make quite a commotion. I check Dad's face. He's still smiling. A wave of relief gushes through me, and I'm able to forget the current crisis just for one precious moment to marvel at the sight before me. Pappa and Mummo are grinning wider than I've ever seen them.

My grandfather places a hand on my shoulder. "We are all together now. I can't believe my eyes. A meeracle. *Ihme, ihme.*"

Yes, it truly is. My whole family here, at the same time. Well, except for—I try my best to push him out of my mind too, like everyone else apparently has. I just wish I hadn't seen him in that godawful—no, not going there. Can't go there. Suddenly, I hear exactly what Alek had predicted—screams—and then I hear Alek's calming voice. The screams subside. Atta boy, Alek and Big Don. Don't worry, Big Don. You'll win over their hearts in no time. I look back at my father.

Mutsi's eyes are red and teary. She grabs my arm and lays her head on my shoulder, staring in wonder at her husband, whom she thought had been dead for eleven years.

She whispers, "Oh, Kristal, do you think he'll remember?"

Poor Mutsi. I glance at the ceiling to stem my tears and notice the red lights still blinking. Crap, I can't ignore them anymore. They're scaring the wits out of me. I whisper to Jala, the nurse, "What about the emergency?"

She shrugs, her complexion pale. Mutsi's still staring at Dad. "Pauli? *Pauli?*" She reaches out, clutches my grandmother's arm for support, but then in an instant, she's at his bedside. They stare into each other's eyes—Mutsi looking desperate, hopeful, and Dad just perplexed, like he's trying to remember something or someone.

Under my breath, I mutter, "Come on, Dad, remember. Remember. *Please...*"

Mutsi plants a kiss on Dad's bandaged forehead. He looks pleasantly surprised, but that's all. Maybe he thinks she's just a really nice doctor or nurse. *Please, oh, please Dad...*

"I love you, Pauli," Mutsi's voice is trembling, and she looks at Dad expectantly.

Dad, still looking quizzically at her, whispers, "Love you..."

Mutsi's eyes widen expectantly. She's glowing...

Then Dad turns and smiles at me, holds out his arms. "Krissie babe, there you are. Love you more than you know."

Fifty-Eight

○ ○ ○ ○ ○ ◦ ◦ ◦ ◉ ◦ ◦ ◦ ◦ ◦ ◦ ◦ ○ ○

February 4, 2027

Mutsi takes a deep breath, blinking hard. She watches the two of us with a mix of joy and pain etched onto her face as Dad and I hug one more time. I'm beyond ecstatic Dad still loves me, but am so frustrated he doesn't seem to know his own wife yet. I'll just hope and pray that *yet* is the right word. Mutsi suddenly runs out of the room. I wince. I feel so bad for her. A few moments later, she returns, accompanied by Dr. EJ. We witness another heartfelt reunion as he embraces the Kurkis in his sturdy arms.

Mummo beams through her tears. "We weel survive, and we weel be together again! Oh, Eikka. Oh, the joy."

"I know time ees of the essence." Pappa fumbles with a small plastic bag containing two large tablets. "Eef only I could have run human trials." He huddles with Dr. EJ. I hear words like *thee CPEB3 protein, released in the synapse increase, stronger connection, the risks…*

I have no idea what he's talking about, but I cringe when I hear the word *risks*.

But Dr. EJ just smiles. "And the posseeble amazing benefits, and eef I know you, Voitto, I would bet on the latter. Eet's worth a try. I must go back to Central. But please"—he gestures toward my father, who's watching us with rapt interest—"you have my permeesion and my blessing." Dr. EJ smiles, nods, and strides through the door. Then he looks at Mutsi. "Meeraka, dear? Your permeesion as well?"

465

Mutsi's words are barely a whisper, but she's nodding vigorously. "And…and my blessing." Mutsi glances toward her husband. "If we could witness just one more miracle. Just one…"

Or could we make that three, please? Dad's memory returning, the disappearance of the Cancris, and Tad? Suddenly, the vision of Tad in the disassembly bin slams into my brain. Scratch that third miracle. I'll just have to hope for the first two miracles. The last one will never happen. I have to accept that. I think of Tad's funeral in Mutsi's pod. She was right all along. I take a deep breath, studying my grandfather's face.

Voitto Kurki. *Doctor.* Voitto Kurki, not George Gabriel, weird old science teacher. But now he's here on this star, with my father's life in his very hands, delivering what I hope will be a miraculous cure that he himself has designed. For the past month, I've witnessed shock after shock—some good, some bad. Well, hopefully, this will be one of the best shocks ever—my wonderful father, well again. My grandfather steps up to Dad's bedside.

"Hello, Pauli. I am Voitto Kurki. You may not remember me."

Dad cocks his head, purses his lips. Pappa has his forearm upturned, and Dad's staring. He limply points with his index finger. "Your arm, sir. You've been seriously wounded." Pappa looks down at his stitches, still raw and red, then looks at me and shrugs. Dad obviously doesn't remember *he's* the one who caused that wound by ripping the iron poker from Pappa that horrible night. I wonder if that memory will ever come back. Pappa says, "Oh, eet ees nothing. So I am a stranger to you?"

Dad cocks his head and frowns. "I'm… I'm sorry. You are?"

"You can call me Voitto. What I need most right now ees your trust. Without knowing me. But you do know your daughter, correct? Ms. Kreestal?"

"Kristal, yes, of course. Where—" He cranes his neck above all the people in the room, then zeros in on my face. "Krissie…"

I move a step closer and give him a little wave. "Yes, Dad, I'm right here. This man has some medicine for you. He's a fantastic doctor." Pappa hands me the pills. I look around. Jala appears out of nowhere with a miniscule glass or maybe diamond cup half-filled with water. She holds it out to me apologetically. I take it and show Dad. "Here's some water. I'm sorry it's so small, but you need to swallow these two pills. Can you do this, please, Dad?"

I hold out my palm. He pulls back, winces at the pills, and frankly, I don't blame him. They're horse pills. So much pill. So little water. I wish I had saved all my shower water for him. But Dad looks determined. I think he knows, somewhere in the deep recesses of his mind, how crucial this is.

"Dad, trust me, please. These will help you."

Sucking in a breath, he resolutely places both pills in his mouth. With one gulp, he swallows, wincing even more. I can see his Adam's apple rise. They're down. Good. And then he chokes. And chokes again. Instantly, my grandfather lunges forward, places a hand behind his back, and pushes him completely upright. On the other side, Jala pushes a button so that the head of the bed moves upward to a ninety-degree angle.

"Cheen down, Pauli, keep swallowing. That's eet. You're doing quite well. Keep swallowing, that's eet, swallow again. Very good. Nurse, please find just one more vial of H_2O, eef at all possible."

"I'll try." Jala disappears down the hall.

"No, give him my ration," Mutsi says.

Voitto frowns. "Ration? No, you must need your ration, eh?"

I interject. "Mutsi, you'd have to go back to your pod, wouldn't you? And Dad needs the water like now."

Mutsi snaps. I've never seen her so impatient. "Well, then, whoever volunteers, tell them I'll pay them back double. He *must* have sufficient water to get the medication into his bloodstream *now*."

I watch as Mutsi's father, my pappa, lightly chides Mutsi. "Myra, Myra, calm yourself. It's getting eento hees bloodstream as we speak."

"That nurse needs to know so she can tell everyone the water is to be borrowed only. I will pay them back, I swear to God. But we need more damn water."

Mutsi's sounding like a drill sergeant, worse than the general.

Pappa nods. "Of course, Myrakka. I remember your penchant for worry. Een this case, eet ees warranted. But have faith."

467

I think he understands her frantic frustration. After all, he raised her. They should be still embracing, getting caught up on the last eleven years. But unfortunately, no time for that.

Dad coughs again, sputters, swallows, then breathes, his arms collapsing at his sides. My knees are like Jell-O. I reach for a chair and collapse backward into it. I hope everything went down the right pipe. I look to my grandfather, scientist of the year, maybe the century.

"Pappa? What now?"

"Eef all goes well, the neuronanobots weel travel to their target and reconnect hees memory pathways."

I want to jump out of my skin. "How long? The Cancris are coming. We may not have time to wait."

"Eet takes about twenty minutes for the nanobot RAM cheeps to fully pass the blood-brain barrier and find thee heeppocampus. From there, thee formula weell branch out to all parts of the brain through the synapses. Eet weell also deactivate those neurons wheech do an eenefficient job storing memories, so the good ones can grow stronger. Then we hope. But I have been secretly working with DARPA, and these people are quite advanced. After all thees ees over, we'll need to recruit them for our team or at least collaborate weeth them."

My mind is reeling. I'm seeing this man in a whole new light. "What's DARPA? What's RAM?"

"Ah, I apologize. DARPA stands for Defense Advanced Research Projects Agency. Eet's a part of the US meelitary. RAM een thees case means restoring active memory. Eet has been their research program for veterans with traumatic brain injury. They have been kind enough to consult with me and help keep my identity a secret."

So my grandfather has been working with an agency after all, keeping it top secret. I'll bet he didn't even tell Alek. I nod, feeling a small surge of hope. Maybe this treatment, strange as it is, will be the magic bullet to help get my father's memory back. After all, it is the twenty-first century. Discoveries are happening everywhere.

Jala returns with a thimbleful of water, whispers something to Mutsi, who scribbles a name on a small iPad, then hugs her. Dad eagerly swallows the water. I smile at her. "This is great. Where did you get it?"

She mouths the words, "It's mine," and looks downward.

"Oh, Jala. You will be repaid. You're awesome."

She beams. I turn to Dad. Looks like everything went down okay. I try to keep from screaming. "Remember, Dad. Remember everything, *please...*" I stand up and move toward him.

Boom! My head thunks against my father's IV pole, causing it to roll several feet. I barely keep my balance. The floor rumbles below my feet, sending me into a panic. My whole body is shaking now, and I feel like diving for cover somewhere. But I override the impulse, roll the IV pole back into place, and check to make sure I didn't yank the IV from Dad's arm. It's okay, thank goodness.

Boom! Damn, the explosion, or whatever it is, drowns out all conversation. The floor beneath us is buckling in places. A siren wails, and the flashing lights grow brighter. Then the announcement blasts through the speakers, "Code gray. Code gray. Intruders. Plan F in effect. Plan F."

I look up. "Plan F? Mutsi?"

Mutsi's face pales, and I can see the fear on her face. But she composes herself and touches Dr. Pappa's sleeve. I can tell she's instantly on autopilot. "There's a security chamber in Central to use as a medical room. Can we move Pauli yet?"

Pappa sweeps his eyes over all the equipment then glances back at Dad. "Let's go. Queeckly."

Pappa and Mummo seem to know just what to do. Along with Jala, they begin unhooking, unplugging wires, then maneuvering Dad's bed through the door and then down the hall. Their expression is one of grim determination. Sisu in motion. I'm cowering just outside. Mutsi points in the direction of the security chamber. "It's within Central," she says. I follow.

Screams pierce the air. My heart drops to my stomach. Then I hear Alek's voice. "Calm down, everyone. *Calm down.*"

Then it's Big Don's voice. I can't quite hear what he's saying, but I can imagine the new people who are converging to Command Central are getting a big dose of Cancri, that is, Big Don. With his presence, everyone naturally thought the invasion was already up close and personal. Alek needs to be by his side until all are on board with Big Don. I'm sure Alek will be.

When we enter Central, I notice for the first time a large closed-off area to the side consisting of two rooms. This is what they must have meant when talking about the security chamber. Mutsi turns to go back into the hall. I stop her. "Where are you going?"

She points. "They're putting him in room number 2. I'm going back to your father's old room to get the rest of his monitoring equipment."

"I can run faster." She shakes her head. "No, won't risk it. Kristal, stay close to your father and your grandparents. Go that way. Now. Go, *go.*"

Bile rising to my throat, I try to shut out flashbacks of human-oid monsters, the gigantic floating eye, the hideous scene after the battle. Is this happening all over again? Will we survive another confrontation? In a strangled voice, I squeak, "It's them—the Cancris. They're landing here, aren't they?"

Mutsi stops her frantic racing, wraps her arms around me, and pulls me close. "I'm sorry I'm so abrupt, Krissie babe."

I feel helpless. "What can I do?"

She points once again to the room where my father and grandparents are headed.

"Hug them. Hug them tight."

Fifty-Nine

●∘∘∘∘∘◉◉◉◉ ◉ ◉◉◉◉◉∘∘∘ ∘

February 4, 2027

I'm back in the nightmare. Feels that way, anyway. Every nerve in my body is on fire, just like when I first landed on Cancri e. But I easily do what Mutsi asks, and when she returns, Mummo, Papa, and I are in a group embrace right next to Dad's bed.

But it's tight. The tiny room, in a far corner off the main bustling area of Command Central, is barely large enough to hold his bed, IV pole, and the machine measuring blood pressure, oxygen levels, and heartbeat. One tiny bedside table holds an egg-shaped diamond crystal, which emits as much light as our huge lamps at home, and the ceiling glows pink like it did in my hospital room. But the floor is just the gritty dark diamond sandpaper stuff instead of Penrose tiling. Probably to reduce the chance of a patient falling. One of the nurses has squeezed in two small stools, one on each side of Dad's bed.

Clumsily, Mutsi pushes in the cart with the machine. Jala checks everything out, adjusts a wire or two, gives her a nod, and hooks up some additional monitoring devices. Dr. EJ pops in, beckoning Mutsi and me to follow him over to where Alek and Big Don are, staring into a computer. Even Dr. EJ, our fearless leader, looks shaken.

"My dears, we're all in this together." Then he turns to Alek, whispering, "Aleksi, my boy, ideas?"

I pale. A brilliant scientist, decades in the making, is asking a seventeen-year-old how to fend off an army of aliens.

471

Alek's face says it all. "I should have realized this sooner, I… I…" The guilt thing. Yeah, Alek, me too.

But Dr. EJ is gracious as always. "How could you know, Aleksi? Even eef you had found out they were mining the diamonds, eet wouldn't have done us any good. Our star's core, as far as we know, cannot compete with hexagonal diamonds. Ironic, eh? Our diamonds, so valuable on Earth, are worthless een battle with the Cancri aliens. Or so says Jaak."

Alek's expression suddenly brightens, and he holds up an index finger. "Maybe Big Don and I can stall them. For a time, anyway. We may even be able to trick them into going back to Cancri. I know it's a long shot. Big Don, what do you say?"

"I say to them, 'Stop this nonsense, and let's all work together for water.'"

"Think that will work?"

"No, but I try."

"Let's go then. We'll try together."

I look at people's faces. I'm relieved they're not gaping, terrified, of Big Don anymore. Alek must have done a great job of convincing them Big Don is an asset, not a threat. Instead, I see expressions of concern, actually downright fear as they ignore Big Don, their eyes fixed on Alek. Do they think he knows what's about to happen? Do any of us know?

Another thunderous boom shakes the building's foundation, accompanied by shouts and screams. We all stumble to keep our balance, covering our ears. Dr. EJ places a hand on the wall for support, breathing heavily. Then as the clamor recedes, he peers at the computer screen, scowls, nods, and then addresses the rest of us, "Our soldiers are undercover in the caves for now, a wise move."

The alarm keeps wailing, along with the flashing red lights overhead. My stomach churns. I want to scream at it. We know…we know. *Shut up, shut up already.*

Jaak's nose is almost touching his computer screen. "My god, there must be at least six—seven thousand. Looks like they're landing in Kimallus Valley." Alek is looking over Jaak's shoulder. "Yep. Alph said 7 thousand. He can't kid, so I know he wasn't."

General Waara, comcard in front of him, is obviously engaged in some sort of face-to-face discussion. "No, don't do that. Head toward the passageways, the mountains. Every nook and cranny, any place not visible. What? No, this is a secure line. It better be. Damn, tell the Birds to stay where they are for now. If necessary, they can move to passageway 485-22. We need to stall the enemy, make them look for us, maybe even think we're not here after all. Yes, not a sound. Nothing in sight. Go. Now!"

Dr. EJ turns toward the general, rubbing his eyes. "Oh, dear God, Hale, déjà vu. We *cannot* go through thees again. Ees hiding our best bet? Our only bet?"

General Waara's still got his eyes on his comcard. "Well, EJ, we're hiding, just like last time. But that's as far as we've gotten. I'm open to anything. I'd tell everyone to scatter over the whole humungous star, but most of it is not fit for human habitation. Our biodome was only built for—" He stops, clears his throat, stares at the ceiling. "I... I just... Jaak, are you sure these diamonds are..."

Jaak is busy, his eyes bugged out, tracking the army on his screen. He doesn't even hear the general. Waara is about to tap him on the shoulder, thinks better of it, turns, and buries his nose in his comcard again. Good move. Jaak's wound so tight right now no doubt he would have punched him in the face.

Mutsi's lips are pursed; she's gritting her teeth. I know she's indebted to the general for saving her life in 2016, but now she realizes he may be responsible for ending it soon. He's made quite a few slipups lately, like cutting corners on the soldiers' diamond suits, like not ordering soldiers to stay behind on Earth with my grandparents, like letting Alph escape, and like not knowing about Alph's secret second army. I'm sure all that's going through his head. And Mutsi's. It's sure as hell going through mine. But we all stay silent. No need to give voice to it all and shame Waara even more. But in his defense, these glitches were almost impossible to foresee. I sure wouldn't want to be in his shoes right now. Then again, I don't want to be in my own shoes either. *Oh, stop it, Kris. Pay attention. Observe. Think, for God's sake.* I look around me.

Dr. EJ's nodding and gesturing impatiently to General Waara, saying, "I know, I know." That's not like him. Worms crawl around in my stomach as I stare at these two supposed geniuses, Dr. EJ and General Waara, standing there, perplexed, irritable. If these two Einsteins are clueless, well then, what's your game, revered Crystal Child? My mind should be running through a million different brilliant scenarios. I'm supposed to know things no one else knows. I'm supposed to be the one with the solution to save humankind. Instead, my brain is a typical ADD blank slate. Yes, Jackson Hynes, I'm an awfully dumb ditz. The writer of the prophecy knew that. He or she must have. I swallow hard, glancing toward Alek. He's got the smarts and the most experience with the enemy. If anyone can do it...

Alek grabs Big Don's arm, and now they're both facing Dr. EJ and the general. "Listen, Pappa, General Waara, hiding might delay them, but they'll find us eventually. No, Big Don and I need to head them off completely. We've made fourteen trips back and forth over the past two years, uh, Earth years. We know them. They know us. Or they think they know us. The dimwits still think we're on their side, sort of. We've been studying their weaknesses and know where they're most vulnerable. I think we can delay for a while with a good story. With any luck, we can concoct a whopper that will make them head for home, and it will give us more time to devise a new strategy to erase them permanently."

Dr. EJ's wan smile shows his fear and exhaustion. Poor man. He just got out of surgery—brain surgery—to heal Dad, and now this. But as ever, he remains calm and cool. "Alek, my boy, I applaud your sincerity and your sisu. But I lost you once. I do not eentend to lose you again. No, too dangerous to stand before them, defenseless."

"No, Pappa, you don't understand. We're not defenseless. Our weapon is our human brain. They're not dangerous to us. In fact, they think I'm as indispensable as Kristal because I duped them a while back into thinking I was part of the prophecy. They won't harm us. I'm 100 percent sure. Well, okay, at this point 98.9 percent."

Dr. EJ frowns. "Really? They are still that gullible?"

"We think so. It's worth a shot. Please let us go. We're your strongest bet."

Alek is making a good case, but I can hear his voice trembling. Jaak grabs his arm. "*Ala mene.*"

Alek shakes his head. "Sorry buddy. I have to. There's no one else. We're screwed either way. I'm dead. You're dead. We're all dead. If I don't try to talk them into going back to Cancri, it will only be a matter of time. You should know that better than anyone. Londsdaleite is now our enemy." He turns to his pappa. "You see my reasoning here, right? I'm an expert. Big Don here and I—we're the only experts. I don't want to face them. But we're all dead anyway, whether I do or don't. At least, let us try."

Dr. EJ sighs. "I am not questioning your ability. Eef only your mother were here. Ah, well, eef you're that certain. Go with my very cautious blessings. But eef anything happens, I weell never—"

"You will be dead, so you won't have to forgive yourself."

Dr. EJ wipes his brow. "Aleksi, always so blunt and persuasive. You haven't changed. From talking your mutsi into letting you climb the tallest pine een the woods to—"

Alek's voice is almost a whisper, "Hey, Pappa. That pine—Old Sylvester—saved my life. And so may this."

He had a pine tree friend—Old Sylvester—like I had my Old Sam? Amazing. It suddenly dawns on me. He must have spent the night there during the massacre. In our first and last tutoring session, he told me he had lost toes. Frostbite. Oh, Alek. I shudder.

Alek and Big Don are discussing logistics. I look on, terrified. But I can't just stand around doing nothing while Alek and Big Don place their lives at risk. I can bluff too. I know how to handle bullies. Alek's been a good tutor in more ways than one. I've already met the enemy. Yes, they're heartless, but they hold no surprises for me anymore. I need to be part of this mission. I step up to Dr. EJ, clearing my throat.

"Uh, Dr. EJ, he's right. The Cancris are in awe of Alek. They still think Big Don is one of them, and I'm the Crystal Child they need so badly, remember? They even cured my burns. So I'm not in any danger either. I'm ready to join Alek and Big Don." I hope no one notices my knees wobbling.

Dr. EJ shoots me a look of what—shock? Disdain? "No, young lady, you absolutely need to stay out of harm's way."

"I'm already in harm's way. We're all in harm's way. At least, I can try to make myself useful."

Mutsi rushes to my side like a—well, like a mother. "Oh, Krissie, don't even think about it. No. Uh-uh, way too dangerous. You don't want to face those beasts one more second. You don't know what they're capable of now...you don't..." She notices my defiant look and stops. "*Krissie...*" Her expression is desperate.

Alek grabs my hand, pulling me to his side. "But, Pappa, Dr. M, think about it. They won't touch a hair on her head. They need her, or think they do. That's why they didn't kill her when she was on their planet. On the contrary, they *healed* her, just as she said. She's absolutely right. She's too valuable to them."

Mutsi's face flushes. "Aleksi, if you recall, they captured her, stuck her in a hellish furnace. They could have killed her, not intentionally but out of sheer stupidity. They obviously don't completely understand human physiology. And even if they don't kill her, they can make her damn miserable. She's still not safe by any means."

"Dr. M, please reconsider. She's not on that miserable furnace anymore. She's here—the human friendly Diamond Star biodome, remember?"

I watch my mother and Alek go back and forth, like I'm not even there, like my opinion counts for nothing. I have to shove my anger down before I scream at her. Maybe I won't scream. But I'll make damn sure she hears me. "Mutsi!" She and Alek jump, turning toward me.

That's better. "Excuse me, hello. I'm already miserable. I might as well do something."

"Oh, no, no. I will not have you—"

Alek raises a hand. "Wait, everyone. Yes, the Cancris are a threatening menace, but I have an idea. This is what you might not realize. These naive little imbeciles believe everything I say. They don't know how to reason. They are totally concrete thinkers. They don't understand sarcasm. They take everything literally. I've practiced a trick or two. I've been observing them for years. Big Don and I are a two-man team, and we're good. We can easily work Kristal into our plan. She's been living with a TAD for over a decade, which likely makes her the top expert in how to communicate with them."

Although Alek's statement is true—I am a Cancri language expert—I didn't appreciate the way he referred to my twin as "a TAD"—just a thing, not a person. But there's no time to argue; we've got to present a united front.

Dr. EJ and my mother exchange exasperated looks. Dr. EJ shrugs. Maybe he's caving a little? He shakes his head. "Myrakka? You're her mother. The decision ees yours. Eet ees not an easy one."

I step in. "Mutsi, you've got to trust Alek. He really knows what he's doing. He's amazing."

"And how do you think you know, Krissie? This isn't some space-fiction drama where the aliens are always, always conquered or drop dead of a little cold virus."

My ADD brain takes an immediate detour down a rabbit hole. "Wow—*War of the Worlds*. Tad loved that."

"Yes, well, this isn't *War of the Worlds*. This is real. How would you feel if something happened to Aleksi out there? It's one thing to plead your own case, but quite another to place others in grave danger. What if you said something wrong?"

My brain's back online, and I'm blushing furiously. She's right. Who do I think I am? Judge, jury, executioner?

But Alek's shaking his head. "No, no, listen. We could take Onni or Haukka with us. We'll just have a nice little chat. If the Cancris move a millimeter toward her, the Bird can sweep her away in an instant. And they wouldn't fire on her. They wouldn't risk killing her."

My mother slumps down in a chair next to the telescope. Are we breaking her down? Is she reconsidering? But after a moment, she sits up straight, adamantly shaking her head no.

I can't believe it. *No?* Ha, I finally have a mother, and she's telling me no. I'm not used to this. She takes my hands in hers. "No, final answer. I'm sorry, but I will not lose you again. I *can't*. Krissie, please try to understand."

"Mutsi, you will lose me anyway! And I will lose you! This is our only chance. Mutsi, you have to understand. This is life or death. *Let…me…go!*"

Mutsi gazes deeply into my eyes, flashing with anger and frustration. "No, Kristal, no."

I'm beyond furious.

Alek balls his hands and takes a deep breath. "Dr. M, we understand. Come on, Big Don. It's you and me, Halfling." He moves toward the door, turning back to me, shrugging as if to say, "Well, I tried."

He understands? By now, my blood is boiling. I can't let this happen. No way in hell. I stomp my foot. "Wait just a damn minute…"

Mutsi gasps. "Kristal!"

I glare back at her. Alek's moving toward the door with Big Don, halts abruptly, turning. "Sorry, Kristal, I can't overrule your ma. We can't risk anything happening to you."

"Alek, I can't believe you're acting so…so stupid for such a smart guy. Don't you get it? Something *will* happen to me—to all of us—if we don't convince them to go back to Cancri. Don't you see? Doesn't anyone see the big picture here? *Please?* Come on. This is a no-brainer."

But no one's listening. Big Don sets Schrödinger on the floor. The cat lets go with a series of yeows, mrrrows, and other guttural sounds I've never heard a cat make. Alek reaches down, patting him on the head. "Sorry, Schrö, it's even too dangerous for you, old buddy. Besides, you'd be more a hindrance than help in this mission. They might eat you for lunch. I'm not sure how their diet is evolving." Another weird sound, this one even more insistent. At least, Schrödy understands me. I can tell.

"Hey, hey, patience, my bud. Jaak's got your meals covered. No fish, but maybe a hydroponic pellet or two. I know, I know. Fish it is. A big fat salmon pate when we get back to Earth, which *will* happen." He shoots me a confident nod and thumbs-up. Then he and Big Don are out the door.

I watch them leave, incredulous, aching to join them, tears of frustration gathering in my eyes. What if my mother has just said no to the prophecy? To the universe? To fate itself? Oh hell. Who am I kidding? What cosmic communication key could I possibly conjure up now? I'm just the same as I always was—ADD kid from Montana. I can't save the earth. Never could, never will. My throat is trying to strangle me right now. Schrödinger suddenly rubs his silky body against my leg, almost as though he's commiserating with me. As I reach down, patting his silky back, the tears spill over. *Wait wait wait.* Is my brain cooking up an idea after all? I could help Alek and Big Don convince the crazy AIs that I've conjured up an infinite supply of water on their own planet, and it will magically manifest in one month or year or another decade. Then that would give General Waara and his team more time to concoct a scheme to catch them unawares again, on Cancri, when they've removed their battle gear and aren't expecting us. It could work. It could just very well work. But here I am, stuck with a cat and a bunch of shortsighted people, and I thought they were so forward-thinking. I reach down, scoop up Schrödinger in my arms. I always wanted a cat. So I guess we'll both hang out together, helpless. I scratch him behind the ears. He gives me a very typical cat purr this time, which almost sounds a little... empathetic?

Who does my mother think she is anyhow? I didn't even know I had a mother until recently, and now she's acting like she's been raising me all along. I got by just fine without her, thank you very much. Does she think she can now dictate my every move? How dare she? What would Dad say?

Dad. My god. I rush into room number 2. He's propped up, eyes closed, breathing is steady. Good. Mutsi rushes to Dad's side, placing one hand in his then reaching the other out to me. "I can't lose either of you. Please understand. I just can't..." She tears up.

I gently set down the cat, take Mutsi's outstretched hand in mine, and proceed to lose it. Now both of us are crying like babies, despite all efforts to stay calm for Dad's sake. I'm so mad at her, yet...yet...as we're blubbering and gazing on Dad's face, he suddenly opens his eyes. "Krissie babe."

Mutsi and I both rush to dry our tears and fake big happy smiles, trying like hell to act like nothing's wrong. But he's not buying any of it. He wasn't sleeping. He's heard our cries loud and clear. His eyes go back and forth between Mutsi and me. "Don't patronize me. What's wrong?"

Whoa. Now there's the dad I know and love. Is that my grandfather's memory drug kicking in already? Well, in any case, I can't tell him.

"Oh, noth—" I stop. No, this won't work. He's right. I can't insult this man's intelligence. He's back. I know it, and he wants to be in the loop. Isn't he part of the QC too? I didn't even know until now he has PhDs too. He's *Doctor* Makkinen. Both my parents hold PhDs. He never told me. But I knew he was incredibly smart. He didn't even have to tell me who he really was. I know he'll have answers. He can help. I don't care what anyone orders me to do anymore except Dad. It's been just the two of us—well, and Tad, for all these years. Dad's my first, true mentor, and I need him now. Terribly.

"Dad, the Cancris have found us again. They're coming for us."

Mutsi's eyes shoot daggers at me as she shakes her head ever so slightly. We both check Dad's face. He's smiling. What? Is he misinterpreting my words? Does he not realize how serious this is? Maybe he's not all back. I look up at Mutsi. Her fierce expression tells me in no uncertain terms to stop this conversation, right here, right now. I feel awful. Maybe she's right.

"Dad, I—"

He interrupts. He's still smiling. Now he's nodding. "You're the one, Krissie babe. It's finally happening. I always knew you could do it when the time came. Don't know how, but I believe in you. You're our Crystal Child. Now *go get 'em, Krissie babe*."

I can hardly believe my ears. Mutsi's mouth flies open. "Pauli, oh, Pauli, how I've missed you, but our daughter, she can't—"

"You don't know her like I do, Myra."

Sixty

. . . . ● . . . .

Myra. Myra. The name echoes, reverberates throughout the room. Time stands still. Mutsi and I freeze. Myra. Dad just called her Myra. Even he's shocked at what he just said. He frowns, does a double take, looks back up at me, and then again at Mutsi. We both watch breathless as his eyes—his soulful, brown *human* eyes—grow so wide that there's no doubt what he has just realized.

"Myra, god, my god, Myra? Where the hell am I?" His jaw drops. His eyes fill with tears, and slowly, slowly, he holds out his arms. "They...they told me you were dead. They told me—minions, *goddamn monsters*—they..."

"Shhh, shhh"—Mutsi half collapses on his bed, taking his hand in both of hers—"don't think about that, Pauli. No, my love, I'm here. Waara took me to the safe house that day. I'm okay. I'm here, love, *I'm here...*" She lays her head gently on his chest and his arms crisscross over her back, and now they're sobbing and choking together and hugging and kissing, and I'm in a bubble of fog and can't think or feel a thing. I stare, my jaw on the floor. My parents, my two parents—*both of them*—together again, really together, for the first time in over a decade and the first time ever that I can remember.

They're drowning in each other now, their cheeks soppy with tears, oblivious to anything, anyone else. Mutsi wipes her face with her hand, voice trembling, speaking in half sentences. "Pauli, we didn't know where—we thought you were, but you weren't...all this

481

time. Raising our daughter. You know her. Can't imagine. What a wonderful job. Oh, my Pauli, thank you…thank you. I love you."

"God, Myra, how I've missed you. Every single goddamn day, I've—and every night, I'd…and that horrible TAD always around."

I suppress a gag. Now I know. Oh god, Tad really only had me. Poor Tad. No, not poor TAD. He was—oh shit, I can't think. I look back at them, and they're both sort of talking over each other and breaking down. I see they've forgotten me, and now she's over him again, and they're hugging fiercely, wires and tubes be damned. A bomb goes off in my stomach, and my brain screams at me like a drill sergeant—*stop gawking, you ADD idiot. This is your chance. Their reunion, our reunion, won't last a day unless* you *do something now.*

I glance around. On Dad's bedside table is Mutsi's comcard, which I quickly snatch up before they realize what I'm doing. Luckily, my parents are still blissfully unaware of anything going on around them, crying and hugging, their words tumbling out making no sense whatsoever except maybe to them. Who am I to spoil the reunion? I slowly back away toward the door. Everyone's crazy busy clicking buttons, sharing info, checking their own communication devices. No one gives a hoot about the Crystal Child right now. It's now or never.

I crack the door, just enough to slip through to the hallway. Now with the card, I can contact anyone. I suppose you use it basically like a cell phone. But who? How? Now that I have it, will this thing be useful? Well, there should be contacts somewhere on the screen. A tiny head icon. Oh, I'll bet that's her contact info. But first, I'd better hide.

Racing down the hallway, I glance right, left, searching for a door, an alcove, anywhere out of the way, hoping my parents are still in their own little bubble. I notice a door on my left and place my ear on its panel. No sounds. It's empty. Gingerly, I twist the handle. It opens, and I take a peek. It's so dark I have to squint. Feeling around for a light switch, my hand encircles some kind of cord. I inch my fingers upward on the cord. Ah, there it is—a switch. I twist it, and immediately, a large salt crystal lamp on a small table in the corner casts a dim peachy glow. I scan the room. Computers, cables, wires, and old screens of all sizes are crammed into the small space—a closet, really—but I can still squeeze inside. I shut the door, wincing as it closes with a soft click.

Well, here I am, AWOL. I hesitate. I've never been in much trouble, despite my ADD. Maybe I'd just better...no, Kris. I picture the Cancris, those hideous metal beasts that caused so much unspeakable misery, and now they're here to cause a second wave of destruction. Here to kill, massacre again, and I'm not a toddler anymore. I can't let them destroy my family a second time. I won't let them. If they so much as touch another hair on my father's head—I grit my teeth so hard I'm afraid they'll crack. If I have to speed read every single quantum physics book in the QC library, I will. I'll do anything and everything to fulfill this mission that's been handed to me. I am the Crystal Child, like it or not.

And excuse me? Mutsi wants me just to sit around and do nothing? Not an option. *Okay, Kris, next step, next step—think. No, don't think. Envision...* Suddenly a name, a vision pops front and center in my brain. Of course, I know exactly who to contact—Onni. Onni? Is he in Mutsi's contacts? I scroll, keep scrolling—ah, there. I press Onni's name. A small keyboard pops up.

They'll be looking for me any minute now. My thumbs, though trembling, fly across the tiny keyboard:

Onni, pls come frnt main bldg. asap.

No, I delete *asap* and type *immed.* There. I pause then add *thx* with a little happy face then *Kristal.*

Whew, now, Serenity Prayer. My finger hovers for a few seconds. No time to lose. Go. Inhaling deeply, I press the little paper-plane icon. I actually hear its little *whoosh* sound. Sent.

Now, it's wait time. I'm practically jumping out of my skin, pacing back and forth in this tiny room turning tiny circles like a caged animal, checking, rechecking the comcard a dozen times. Come on, come on, Onni. Can he read? And if he can, will he comply? Will he know my request requires him to go rogue? I'll make it clear he should take no blame whatsoever. My eyes stare hard at the screen, willing a response. I think my eyeballs are going to pop out, but nothing comes back. Hell, I can't wait any longer.

I open the door, peek out, right, left. No one. They all must be crazy busy in Command Central. Sucking in a mouthful of air, I check right, left, right again, then race down the hall to the elevator. The down button is so high I have to stand on my tip toes. I press it again and again as though it didn't hear me the first time. You'd think if the QC could figure out how to travel to a star, light-years away in mere seconds, they could at least get an elevator to move a little faster. After what seems like hours, the metal doors finally clank open. Inside, I push *G* and wait. The elevator doors clank close, and the descent begins, down, down, six floors, then a light bump. I'm so anxious I practically fall out the doors as soon as they separate.

Luckily, the lobby is crowded with workers, all in their own little worlds, readying for the invasion. No one seems to notice me, but just in case, I lower my head and cover it with my hood as I exit the building, glance left, right like a cartoon thief. Oh, good. I see a column partially hidden by a tall shimmering pink bush. Perfect. As casually as I can, I stroll to the bush and slip behind it.

I check the card. It's been a few minutes since I texted Onni. Oh, please, please get this text, Onni. But is Onni too distracted? He's probably helping the Birds find caves, hoarding food, working with Haukka to—a soft chime dings. I jerk, glancing down at the card: "6 E ms." E ms? E ms? My mother's words come to me—*Earth minutes*. Onni will be here in six minutes. I look up. Oh thank God, he's already here. I rush to greet him, my hair flying behind me. Patting Onni's wing, I gush, "Onni, you came for me."

"Of course, Kristal, my leader. Raaah."

"Oh, Onni, you are special. You must be very busy, but I need you now more than ever. A mission. A very crucial mission. Alek and Big Don are headed toward the Kimallus Valley. I need to find them as quickly as possible. I need to join them."

"Much danger. Cancris there too."

"Yes, Onni, I know. That's why I need you. If they try to harm me, I will be on your back, and we can immediately fly away. They won't try to shoot us down because they need me. At least, until my birthday."

Crystal Child

"Birthday tomorrow. Raaah."

"Onni, I know that too. That's why we have to try to convince them to go back to Cancri today."

"Onni cannot convince—"

"Oh! No, Onni, you don't have to. *I* have to."

He's shuffling, the way he does when he's upset, not sure about something.

"Please, Onni, please trust me."

"Trust Kristal, not Cancris. Raaah."

"I know. But Alek and Big Don will be there too. You can do this. For me?"

Onnie bows his massive head. "For Kristal, our leader."

"I'm not your leader, Onni. I'm your friend."

"Friend, yes."

"Yes."

"And leader."

"Well, if you insist. Let's go."

Onni lowers himself to the ground, allowing me to climb up the small ladder attached to his back with some sort of Velcro contraption. Onni's massive presence is obvious, and people begin to notice, to stop, and to stare, and then a few start pointing. Uh-oh, here it starts.

"Onni, quickly!" As I speak the word, we're airborne, soaring up, up, up. I look down to see not only the crowd gasping and gesturing up toward us, but now my mother, Dr. EJ, and several other QC members are racing out the front door.

Faintly, I hear their frantic calls, "Kristal, *wait, no.* What are you...you can't...come baaaaack!"

I shout down at them, "I will come back. I promise."

The crowd below has swelled. Some have their hands over their mouths. But most are cheering us on. "KRISTAL, ONNI! KRISTAL, ONNI! KRISTAL..."

Why are they outside instead of inside where they're supposed to be hiding? I guess now everyone knows the Cancris have landed in the Kimallus Valley and most likely won't be coming to the City, at least, for the time being. I turn back as Onni and I fly upward on the wind, up, up, up toward the crimson-violet Lucy sky.

485

Sixty-One

○ ○ ○ ○ ○ ○ ○ ○ ○ ○ ◉ ○ ○ ○ ○ ○ ○ ○ ○ ○ ○

February 4, 2027

We've almost touched the stars as we've flown from Quantum City and over the jagged mountains right under the biodome. Now Onni's flying low, descending one of the slopes, and I get a glimpse of Kimallus Valley, the same valley I saw on my first trip to the city. But this time, instead of friendly Diamond Star soldiers as tiny pinpricks high up in the mountains, these soldiers are the enemy. In block formation, shoulder to shoulder, thousands of Cancris—now in diamond suits—cover the valley floor. God help us. The reality hits me like a punch in the gut. I frantically check north, south—there. I see the three of them now—Haukka, Big Don, Alek—standing at the north end of the valley about a football field's length away from the first line of soldiers. The vision of the entire Cancri Army in their new lethal armor blinds me and turns my entire body to jelly.

Since discovering and mining the lonsdaleite diamonds on their planet and copying our Diamond Star suits almost to a T, they're now indestructible. I squint to get a better look. Besides the stronger diamond, I notice for the first time a new accessory. Each Cancri grips a weapon I've never seen before—a large corkscrew, obviously lonsdaleite, capable of drilling through our army's suits in milliseconds. My breathing escalates so quickly I'm afraid I'll hyperventilate again. Gripping Onni's massive feathers even tighter, I concentrate on slower breaths, desperately trying to quell my stomach's dizzying back flips. Sisu has completely taken a hike for now, replaced by fear. But it's a realistic fear. Realistic *horror*, actually. No positive talking myself down over this new turn of events. *Second by second, Kris. Step by step. Breath by breath.*

I can't stop staring at this sea of terror. Maybe this wasn't such a good idea after all. Where are the Diamond Star soldiers? Oh, yes, Dr. EJ and General Waara had commanded them to hide in the caves. They had seemed so invincible in their own diamond suits. But now, knowing the type of Cancri diamond is much stronger, Dr. EJ has obviously made the right call—hiding everyone for as long as possible until we regroup and figure out plan B or Plan C. How many plans will we ultimately need? I feel my heart sink. After all that preparation.

My mother's comcard suddenly starts pinging like crazy. I knew it would. I pick it up, talk quickly while hanging on for dear life with my other hand. I don't want to give her a heart attack, but I don't have time to talk right now. "I'm fine. Gotta go." I click End, turn off the sound, and stuff the card back into my jeans pocket quickly before she can call back and before I lose my balance. I'll be reamed out, most likely. But at this point, it doesn't matter, not one bit.

We're on our descent. It's deathly quiet in the valley. Suddenly, a diamond arm rises and points toward Onni and me. It belongs to the short one, the leader—Alph.

"Intruder. Destroy." Its metallic monotone carries upward into the sky, and Onni and I hear it plain as day. Then suddenly—*zip*—a red flash whizzes by, missing Onni's right wing by the width of a feather. *What the hell was that?*

Onni squawks, "Raaah."

Now several other Cancris are pointing at us with their sparkly arm appendages.

Holy moly. Destroy? I never thought they might not recognize me way up in the sky like this. I rise up, waving frantically, yelling, *"No, no. It's me…it's me, uh, Crystal Child…it's me!"*

Oh god, I've placed Onni in harm's way. How could I be so stupid? If they harm one feather on his body—I suck in a breath. Poor Onni. I will never forgive myself if—

Another voice booms in its familiar monotone, "Prophesied Child. Crystal Child. Weapons down. Down. Do not harm. Let land." It's Big Don. And then Alek's voice, softer, speaking directly to the leader. I can't make out what he's saying, but it's a voice of urgency, that's for sure.

Whew. The Cancris lower their arms, letting Onni and me descend. He bravely spirals down, down, until at last his massive talons grip the sandy ground. I slide off Onni's back, not bothering with the ladder. Big mistake. I stumble and fall, twisting my left ankle. Ow, damn. Dumb move. No time for injuries now. Standing up a little clumsily, I shake my ankle out, brush myself off, and pat Onni, whispering, "Thank you, thank you. I'm so sorry."

Onni looks a little shaken. He bows his head slightly. I feel horrible bringing him out here.

I let go of his wing, standing upright, trying my best not to wince, facing Alek and Big Don, in front of Alph and about a hundred yards from the first line of the Cancri Army, still too close for comfort. Alek looks like he's about to fall apart but is trying like hell to keep it together. Alek always seems in control. Not anymore. It unnerves me. Obviously, he is not pleased at my arrival. Well, great. He should be thanking me. He has no idea how many hurdles I had to jump to get here. Didn't he want me to come? Maybe I should have borrowed Mutsi's cape—the one with all the diamonds she wore that first fateful meeting in the forest. At least I would be more protected. Or would I? Guess not since their diamonds are 58 percent stronger. My stomach twists into a knot. I glance down at my plain gray hoodie sweatshirt and jeans. *Crystal Child.* I would have looked the part at least. Dumb, ADD girl.

Suddenly, Alek runs the few steps toward me and wraps his arms around me. His voice is trembling. "Oh, kid, don't tell me your mom relented because I won't buy it. You gotta be AWOL, right? *Right?*"

I try to ignore the sea of lethal robots turned our way, stretching for miles on the sparkly dust of the valley.

"Well, no, not, well…well…she—my dad said it was okay."

He pulls back. His face is crimson as the sky. "Your what? *Who?* Your *dad?* You mean the dad who walked around with a massive Cancri implant for eleven years? The dad who just had brain surgery to remove said implant? *That* dad?" At this very moment, I could smack him.

"Yeah, *that dad*, and he's *fine*, thank you very much."

Alek shakes his head. "Kristal, oh, man, you are way out of your league here. Your mom was right. This may turn out, well, it's anyone's guess. So what you're telling me is Mom says no, but Dad says yes."

"Hey. He's perfectly mentally normal now, and he says he believes in me."

"Oh, so he's out of his coma for only a few hours, and already you're the cause of your parents' first marital spat in over a decade. Way to go, Crystal Child. I guess I'm your current guardian then. Great. No offense, but I really don't have time for double duty right now. Frankly, things aren't looking so hot. And just in case you're wondering what just almost killed you and Onni as you were coming in for your landing—in addition to the lethal lonsdaleite corkscrews all Cancris now carry, Alph has an additional weapon—a laser gun. Just him. Must have some sort of Napoleon complex. And seems like he's a little trigger happy today for some reason, so, uh, we have to be on our best behavior." Alek wipes his brow.

I guess I was expecting him to be his usual confident self, like he was when he confronted Jackson Hynes the first day I met him, eons ago. But there's a bit of difference between one not-so-bright middle-school bully and...and... Oh, holy moly, I have to turn my back on the horrific scene before me.

Alek's shaking all over. I can tell he's trying his best to do his Hawkeye impression from *M*A*S*H*. But it doesn't seem to be working as well as it used to. Something's changed. I look out over the sea of merciless beings.

"I promise I won't be any trouble. You're...you're shaking. Maybe I can..."

Alek sighs. "I have no idea why. Could it be I'm just a tiny bit nervous standing in front of seven thousand psycho AIs about to drill my guts out? Look at those diamond corkscrews. Quite impressive."

Holy moly. Did he have to put it like that? Now *I'm* shaking. "I... I just meant... Don't be hard on yourself, Alek. You're right. No human could face this and not be terrified out of his wits."

He lowers his head, and when he looks up at me again, I can tell, not an ounce of that wit is in there right now. Oh boy, he's right. Things definitely aren't looking so good.

My own face probably looks all scrunched up, pouty, like a little five-year-old who's has just been discovered in the cookie jar and had her hand slapped. Although Alek's facing them again, he keeps turning and checking on me, probably wondering what to do with me, feeling the weight of responsibility in having to make sure I don't get swallowed up by this ocean of sheer horror. Why would anyone think up a prophecy with me as the miracle brain behind the perfect solution for the advancement of their gruesome species? But I *cannot* go back to the city without at least trying. Alek finally heaves a big dramatic sigh. *Yes, I'm a real burden. Well, tough. I'm here now. Deal with it.*

As if he heard my thoughts, he sighs, comes toward me, stops, turns, and then walks toward me again. He leans in, dropping his voice. "I don't mean to say we don't want you. But I underestimated the danger. Alph seems, well, different somehow, more savvy. I don't know. Tell you what. You stay behind Big Don, and be ready to hop on one of these big-winged guys if things start to go south. Got it?"

I nod, stepping behind Alek's half clone, Big Don. I've come to like him, a lot. He's such a sweet soul under all that metal and smushy Play-Doh flesh. I feel a little relief but not much. Even Big Don is useless against seven thousand Cancris in lonsdaleite suits with corkscrew weapons. I can't swallow. My mouth is as dry as the sand I'm standing on, and my ankle aches like hell. *Ignore it, Kris. Ignore it all.* Back to sisu.

"Wha-what's the plan, Alek?"

"Plan? Ha, you got any ideas?" Alek steps closer. He's sweating. Poor Alek. The lump in my throat feels like a golf ball. He leans in. "Big Don put Alph in a mood right off the bat with his 'confession' that the Kurkis had disappeared. So, uh, we're sorta walking on eggshells. Here's the best I can do. Alph and I are about to have a little, uh, negotiation. He's now our only hope, which means this is very likely to blow up in our faces, maybe literally. But unlike the others, the guy knows how to reason, a little. On the other hand, that could be a double-edged sword. I just…" Alek shakes his head. I look. Alph is muttering meaningless numbers, walking around in circles, like Tad used to do at the oddest times when he was nervous. Could it be that Alph is too?

All of a sudden, Alek turns toward the being, sucks in a huge breath, fake smiles as he drops to his knees, throws his arms out, and starts belting out a tune I've never heard before. *"What's it all about, Alpheeeeeee…"*

The robot raises its diamond-covered arm appendage. "Stop song. One thousand, nine hundred sixty-six Earth release date. You sing song before. Ancient song. Stupid song."

Alek turns his head, mutters what sounds like a few choice cuss words, then turns back. "Sorry, Alph. I thought you liked that song. Just wanted to lighten things up a bit."

Alph stands stock still. "Nothing lighter. You unsuccessful."

"Yup." Alek rubs the bridge of his nose. His eyes close. He staggers back a step. Whoa, my eyes whip to Big Don. He reaches out his arms. Alek grabs them and steadies himself. Holy moly, is this the best he can do?

Alek straightens, shrugs. "Well, Alph, you can't say I didn't try."

"False. Can say that. You did not try."

Alek massages his temples. I don't know what in the world, er, star they're talking about, only that Alek just seems to keep upsetting this Alph guy, who Alek said was not in a good mood to begin with. Can robots have moods anyway? Are they evolving? Great. Great start. Alek turns back to me, whispers, "Damn, he's beginning to understand sarcasm—even belittling. And do I detect some slight patronizing? Which is sort of what I do a lot. It worked before but not anymore. This could pose a problem." He coughs. Then coughs again.

"But, Alek, he's still gullible, right?"

"I… I hope to God he is. It's just so…so puzzling. Okay, I have to get my bearings here. History—the Cancris started out as AI, artificial intelligence 100 percent. Seems they came online in 2002, according to their archives. Then someone, we don't know who— One is all they call it—gifted them with programs to help them evolve into the perfect hybrid master race, if you will, a human-AI-mixed breed with the best qualities of each. They're still working on human attributes, such as detection and use of sarcasm, irony, lies— you know, stuff that makes us human. But apparently, the algorithms for these human skills are so complex that even though their god, or creator, gave them some tools, they haven't been able to sync them all yet. But things are starting to gel. You never know what you're gonna get these days. They seem to change a little from trip to trip. That's what makes them so fascinating and fearsome. So far, I see these changes mostly in Alph. Big Don must have been a mutation because he's already developed a whopping dose of empathy. So far, in these guys, I don't see it, at all. So who knows what they're plotting next?"

Alek turns, takes a couple of steps toward Alph, and holds out his hand. They shake. I wince. Brave Alek shaking hand to claw with the leader of the most feared battalion in the known universe; it must be terrifying. I see Alek's hand trembling even more. He's breathing hard, but I doubt Alph notices. His voice is about three pitches higher than normal. "So sorry you didn't appreciate my greeting, Alph. What I meant to say was, so nice to see you. I bow to you. Welcome to the Diamond Star. How about we cut a deal?"

"Cut? Not deal. *Deal* abstract word. We cut you. With new Cancri weapon."

"No, no, no, Alph. I mean, oh geez." He stumbles a few steps back to where I'm standing, cowering behind Big Don. I swear he's sweating more than when we were on Cancri e, even as dehydrated as he must be. Although he stepped back to me, I realize he's essentially muttering to himself or maybe to Big Don.

"Alek?"

"Alph is more assertive, angry. When did that happen? Oh, gee-zus. Need I question? Not only did Big Don not produce the Kurkis, but we annihilated his first army. Guess that would piss me off too. Oh, hell, I'm more nervous than I thought. I'm really screwing up." He glances back at me, his eyes pleading. "Kristal, remind me to use very literal, concrete language. I am the king of wit and sarcasm as well you know. I gotta be reined in sometimes."

I nod, stepping out from behind Big Don. "I've lived with Tad a long time. I know how you have to use concrete, literal language at all times. I'm good at it. I can be your interpreter." Alek sighs. "Excellent, there you go. You do have a job to do 'cause obviously, I'm way off my game today."

He turns to Alph. "Hey, guys, um, ya know, those diamond suits look terribly uncomfortable. Kristal knows how to produce water on Cancri, so why don't you all just mosey on home and take a look. There will be an incredible ocean just waiting for you."

I can't believe he just said that. I try not to let the shock show in my face. I put my hand over my mouth, muttering: "Alek, what the hell!"

Alph suddenly points his arm toward me. My feet scream at me to run for the hills, but I stand my ground. Alph says in Cancri monotone, "No. Plan—Crystal Child will augment Cancri e evolution with manufacture of H_2O for use on Cancri e on prophecy date. If not, disassemble all on BPM 37093 tomorrow, February 5. Then to Earth, disassemble all human, mammal, amphibian, bird, invertebrate, fish, reptile. Water on Earth sufficient for Cancri evolution. Planet cold but Cancri program 38956-B implement to adapt. Can evolve completely." The head robot is talking about murdering an entire planet like he's just rattling off the periodic table in chemistry class. My stomach drops to my knees.

Alek is still standing his ground although he looks like he's about ready to faint. Join the club.

"Y-yes, but Alph, let's just concentrate on the Crystal Child. It's in the prophecy. She will save the Cancris. She will devise a way for you to live on your own planet with the water you need to advance your species. But just to be clear, you must let her remain unharmed so she can do that. And she will only remain unharmed if all living creatures remain unharmed. Humans can't function if other creatures die or are hurt, especially other humans."

"False information."

Alek jumps. "No, no, Alph. What do you mean? It's true. Very true."

"No, false. Humans function after we kill other humans. Eleven Earth years ago. Thousands of Cancri years ago." He looks all around the valley, gesturing. "Now we learn humans survived on Diamond Star."

"Okay, I get it. Well, yes, but a human can't function *well*, for at least a year if a loved one dies. It's called grief, and it's programmed into human's DNA. Please research g-r-i-e-f, *grief.* Kristal will be in a state of deep grief, and she will *not* be able to function and therefore will not be able to help you if any of these humans is killed or Birds. She's gotten quite fond of the Birds, *and* she needs to be at 100 percent capacity to bring water to the Cancris. So conclusion—happy Crystal Child, happy Cancris. She *must* be happy in order to help you." He fake smiles at Alph, gives two thumbs-up.

Now that's the Alek I know, much better, like when he shot down Jackson Hynes, the bully, on our first day of tutoring. But will these robots really get his message? Alph slowly turns its head from side to side as if disagreeing. But then I hear a whirring sound. I think that means it's mulling something over.

Finally, it nods. "Prophecy to be fulfilled tomorrow, February 5, by midnight Earth time. Then happy Crystal Child. Happy Cancris. Happy humans. You know Earth time?"

"There is an Earth Clock here, yes."

"Where?"

"In the ci—" Alek immediately bites his knuckles, mutters to himself, "Great, Alek, tell them there's a city here. Damn…"

"Where is city?"

Goddamn. Alph heard. Alek looks up at Alph, smiles. "Oh, it's many kilometers from here. The city can't hold everyone. I suggest we all stay here in the Kimallus Valley, much more comfortable for Cancris."

Whir. "We stay. But need Earth clock."

"Earth clock whatever. Um, all right, done. You shall have it."

Alek's lying. Impossible. There's no way that huge tower can be transported here in one day. Tapping his shoulder, I whisper, "Alek, you can't—"

Under his breath, he hisses back, "Shhh, I *can*, and I *will*. I must." We both turn back to Alph. Alek nods. "Deal. Good. We will transport Earth clock here by six AM or earlier. It's set then. Tomorrow we gather around Earth clock here in the valley."

"Prophecy say Crystal Child only one who know how to manufacture water for Cancri use on February 5. Tomorrow. We watch, learn."

"Um, yes, she figured it out all by herself. Smartest kid in the universe. Never been anyone like Kristal. Genius, she is. Her formula will blow you away."

Ouch. I lean in. "Alek, don't say *blow away*, or—" Too late.

"We blow humans away first."

Alek closes his eyes and lets out a whistle. "No, no, scratch that."

"Cancris not need scratch. Not yet programmed for itch."

Alek is messing up again. I wince. Alek's nerves of steel seem to have melted.

I suddenly feel a weak bolt of energy shoot through me. Without thinking, I blurt, "My formula for the production of water will be extremely accurate, and Cancris will have abundant water supply." The energy fades as sparkles appear before my eyes. I think I might be slipping, sliding—more sparkles. Is this dehydration, or am I just a big sissy? Sisu, not sissy, Kris, get a grip. And then my knees bend, damn. Ouch, my ankle...

Alek pulls me upright. He throws his arm around me like we're old pals, but it's to steady me so I don't faint and arouse suspicion among the Cancris. Leaning in close, he whispers out of the corner of his mouth, "Smile." With all my might, I will my lips to widen a little. Thank goodness these creatures can't read facial expressions very well. Tad never could. My awful secret would have been exposed immediately. The truth? I'm weak with fear. And useless for their mission, anyway.

Alek turns toward the army. He seems to have recovered a bit. "Hey, uh, Alph. Do you guys need food? Entertainment? How about some reading material? Video games? Iceborne Nine? Kakarot Seven? Netflix? Hulu Six?"

Yes, Alek's regained his composure. Good because I'm getting worse.

Alph stands ramrod straight. I hate to admit it to myself, but he reminds me so much of my brother. I stare at Alph. Could there possibly be a shred of human decency in it, in him? I observe. Although its expression is hidden under the lonsdaleite helmet, I'll bet it's not feeling one iota of emotion. Maybe Tad didn't either. Maybe it was just programming, pure and simple. The truth dawns on me. Whatever Tad was, I can't waste any more time grieving. I'm done.

Alph responds in the familiar monotone. "Not need entertainment, reading material, video games, Netflix, Hulu. Just H_2O. Tomorrow. February 5, Earth time. We wait."

Alek turns to the entire army. "Okay." He can't ramp up his voice. His throat is too dry, and he coughs, coughs again, doubles up, coughs over and over until finally, I see him swallow a teeny bit, and he clears his throat, then stands and raises his arms. He's blinking like crazy. "Listen, Cancris." And then he has another coughing fit.

Suddenly, Big Don steps in front of Alek. "Humans will meet you in Kimallus Valley tomorrow. Gather around Earth Clock Tower, start time six AM, Earth time. By midnight, Earth time, maybe before, Crystal Child give Cancris all H_2O information for evolution of species. But remember, Cancris, if any human harmed, so is Crystal Child. Need keep healthy, safe, happy." Alek's eyes widen. He's looking up at Big Don, like he's the savior of the century, which he very well may be. Alek scratches his head, coughs again, but manages to spit out, "And don't think you can kill us after you get the formula. If any human is harmed, at any time, the formula won't work anymore." Alek heaves another great cough and starts to topple.

Big Don catches him, announcing, "Stardust in lungs. Will be better tomorrow. Cancris lucky not have lungs yet."

I hear a little whirring from the troops. Apparently, they're mulling over things they may not have ever thought about before, like lungs. Breathing.

Alph points his claw at Alek. "No more threats. If girl not produce water by twelve midnight, Earth time, all bets off." I start to shrink, but pull myself up and put on my best tough-girl expression, which probably looks utterly ridiculous. Alek's eyes look like they're ready to pop of their sockets, swallowing hard.

"All bets off? Where the hell did you get that phrase, Alph? Watching Westerns? Googling idioms?"

"No Western. No Google. You. We study Alek idioms. Learning but very difficult. Alek English has many idioms." Alek's face turns almost purple as he faces me. "Damn, Kristal, I've failed."

I shake my head. "No, Alek, you haven't. Don't say that. You did just fine."

Oh lord, my breathing is rapid. My head hurts. My stomach holds a ball of lead. My knees are wobbly. My ankle throbs. I have one day to come up with a solution, a formula, an *ihme*, a goddamn miracle. But before I do or before we're all corkscrewed to oblivion, I have to know. I have to be 110 percent sure that my brother's really gone, that he can't be reassembled even for a few moments so we can say our proper goodbyes, and maybe I can get one little hug in. Oh god, my throat is closing up. This is my one and only opportunity. It's now or never. I will accept their answer. They should know, after all. I mean, if Alph fixed Big Don, and he was a total wreck, then why can't they fix my brother? Then I would finally have closure before I die. I don't know why it should matter. I'll be dead no matter what. I should have had closure the second I saw him in that god-awful bin. But something just keeps nagging and nagging...

I clear my throat. "Uh, Alph, I could function even faster and more efficiently to produce the H_2O formula if my brother...if my technical advisory device is at my side. He's—it's been very helpful to me on Earth." I glance at Alek.

He's staring at me like my hair just sprouted horns. "Oh, girl. Give. It. Up." But I won't, not until I've turned over every goddamn Cancri stone.

Alph shuffles back and forth. I hear the whirring even louder than usual. Finally, he stops. "Did not know. Not in prophecy. Earth technical advisory device not available."

"Not available? But still able to be assembled?" I have no moisture in my mouth whatsoever, and my words come out like a finger raking a blackboard. I feel like I'm swallowing my tongue. But I have

to keep going. "What does that mean, Alph? Can I see my brother…
my TAD? Explain."

More whirring. I'm holding my breath. Can it be—

Then Alph says, "No, cannot see. TAD disassembled. Cannot
be reassembled. Make formula for H_2O. Tomorrow. TAD. Not
needed."

"But I do need him. You fixed Big Don. I need my brother, uh,
the TAD. He, uh, it was instrumental in helping me construct the
algorithms."

Suddenly a horrific buzzing sound makes me cover my ears and
sink to the ground. It stops as suddenly as it started. I look up. Alph
has thrust a londsdaleite corkscrew in the direction of my face. Holy
shit.

"You lie. TAD have no algorithm for H_2O production. TAD
disassembly complete forever. Human synonym. *Dead*. One more lie
and corkscrew cut off arm. Then you produce water, happy or not
happy, or we disassemble you."

"Auuuuu—" I can't even process that last sentence as I groan,
as my heart plummets to my stomach. My mind starts to race, probably to drown out the terror threatening to make my heart explode.
Okay, yeah, I knew that Tad was dead. I really did know that. They're
not going to fix my unfixable twin. What's my damn problem? Our
birthday's tomorrow. I've never celebrated without him. He—hell,
I even saw for myself. Even Dad doesn't give a shit. So why did I
even bother to question this stupid Cancri? I knew it all along. It's
over. No more hope. No more lies. I'll keep my damn arm. I'm fine.
Really. The big negotiation is over. We showed them, didn't we? Ha,
we convinced them of nothing, except that they will have the Earth
Clock Tower transported to the valley tomorrow just the way they
wanted. Big frickin' deal. And I will conjure up their stupid water,
not. And my beloved brother, Tad Makkinen, is dead. Forever. Alek
and Big Don turn to Haukka, heads down as the all-powerful Crystal
Child turns to join them, hobbling slowly toward Onni. Halfway
there, I stop, lean way over, and to my utter horror, retch my guts out
on the dark sandy ground.

Sixty-Two

• • • • • • • • • • ◉ • • • • • • • • • •

February 5, 2027

The day we traveled through the passageways, my mother taught me many things about the Diamond Star. The largest valley is Kimallus, Finnish term for *sparkle*, due to the tiny starlike dust particles that stretch for miles and miles beneath the black, imposing mountain ranges. Usually it's barren, but today it teems with thousands of beings—Cancris, humans, Birds, and pets—dogs, cats, and even a few hamsters. Dr. EJ tried in vain to warn the people and animals to stay back, but they didn't listen, and here they are, to fight this final battle together and, perhaps, to witness a miracle. Bless them all. So here we sit, waiting for a miracle in the Kimallus Valley along with the formidable army of the Cancris. The Earth Clock Tower is acting as a sort of a fortress, and so far, several of us from the QC Council are huddled behind it in the Bird coach or in one of the attached tents.

The clock reads 6:00 AM, which is actually QC, Finland, time on Earth. Fifty light-years away, the sun will be rising there in a couple of hours, theoretically speaking. Sunrise. I visualize a breathtaking horizon of pink and orange hues on my wondrous home planet. It will become lighter here too. But it won't be like the magnificent sunrises on Earth. Oh, how I miss things I totally took for granted—a bright blue sky, the musky scent of the forest, a pristine snowfall. *Stop. Don't think about Earth, Kris. You'll go nuts.* Yep. Okay. I most likely will never see my home again, so I should just stuff everything labeled "Earth" into my mind's black box. I need to stay focused like a laser beam on the present moment, just in case my brain bursts forth with a unique, incredible idea. *Ha, dream on, Crystal Child.*

I peer around the stone edge of the clock so I can see the view of the entire valley. I gasp. It's formidable—so much impenetrable diamond, so much danger. The Diamond Star soldiers are still in their battle gear, but the uniforms are just for show, as they're now totally useless. It's almost as if the prophecy itself were saying, "See. I told you. You wasted all that time and energy. Only the Crystal Child can save this situation. You should have heeded the prophecy's words that everyone gets saved, even the evil ones." Yeah, like I'm some sort of all-powerful negotiator. If I ever find the devils who wrote this insane prophecy, probably laughing their asses off, I'll—well, I'll start by bursting their eardrums with my million-decibel scream, "WHY ME?" Whoever you are, dumbass prophecy author or authors, this is not funny. *Do you hear me? This is just wrong, and you are evil.*

The Cancris have the ultimate advantage just as they did in 2016. But this time, instead of surprise as their deadly weapon, they have hexagonal diamond, almost 60 percent stronger than our diamond. Not only are the Cancris' battle suits able to withstand the most brutal forces in the universe, but their whirling corkscrew weapon can easily pierce the formerly indestructible diamond suits of the human army, ripping a person to shreds in the blink of a human eye. And I thought visions of mountains and blotches of red were scary. I have to breathe, breathe, breathe to keep these new grisly pictures from making me scream my guts out.

Now the only thing standing between the Diamond Star's and Earth's total annihilation is the Diamond Star prophecy. It predicts a young girl with the same name as a frozen drop of water—Crystal, whether spelled the English way or the Finnish way, Kristal, this unique girl-wonder will save the entire human species and, most ludicrous of all, its enemy, the Cancri on her thirteenth birthday, February 5, 2027. If the Crystal Child is not successful, the Cancris will hurl all of humankind into some hellish void. The prophecy's words echo in my brain—*beware, prepare*. I wish its instructions contained a bit more detail. In any case, the day has begun.

*****

Last night, after we returned to Command Central in the main building; after my solo sob session in the tiny closet I insisted on at first; after I was duly chastised, loved, hugged, and cried over; Dr. EJ called an urgent QC meeting. I kept silent, mostly due to shock, terror, and just plain exhaustion. Blanca, bless her heart, urged me to return to the recoup room. At first, I refused. I needed to be with my family, especially my dad. While he sat up in a chair listening intently to the powwow of the century, I collapsed on his bed, zoning in and out of an uneasy sleep, my visions returning with a vengeance—mountains, snow, red, the number 1201 and this time, a new vision—whirling death spirals of lonsdaleite diamond—all gyrating around my brain like a frenzied Mardi Gras parade.

Later, Alek filled me in. He said there had been fierce debate, but finally, the leaders of the Diamond Star reluctantly agreed with Alek's urgent plea to move the Earth Clock Tower from the city to the valley. It was the Cancris' one request, and Alek wanted to appease the enemy as much as possible. Then the debate shifted to logistics.

The Earth Clock Tower stands half as high as the Eiffel Tower in Paris, France, with stairs of ashen rock and diamond winding up to the very top. A travel pendant for this clock, as well as other massive structures, wasn't as simple as one for a human or Bird. They'd done it before with Earth structures, but each needs its own algorithm for travel. For the clock, a complicated analysis was needed to figure out the precise code to collapse its molecular structure, reform, then land in the precise location in the valley where the Cancris were stationed. Plus, they'd never devised a code for that particular location. Generally, for structures this large, it would take days to figure it all out. But they didn't have that luxury. Jaak, Alek, Johann, Pappa, and other brilliant assistants sat, hunched over their computers without a break long into the simulated Earth night. Poor Blanca brought trays of nuts and fruit from recoup, her attempt at helping, but the food largely went untouched. Dahab insisted on heading the project, saying Mutsi had too many emotional balls in the air right now. Also Dahab was desperate to prove to Mutsi she would never make a location coding mistake ever again since my grand entrance into Birdland almost cost me my life. My mother, reluctant to leave Dad's side for even a second, was too weak to protest.

At almost midnight, Alek had pressed the clock's pendant and chanted its newly devised location code. Objects jiggled and slipped off shelves inside the main building, like a small earthquake. But seven seconds later, we heard from Jaak, stationed in the valley, that the clock appeared in the exact programmed location, where it would stand tomorrow as a symbol of rebirth—or doom. Then I heard Mutsi mutter, "Well, Dahab finally got it right for once." Ooh, catty. I guess she and Dahab had always had their differences. Maybe with this successful mission, they could patch their relationship.

As we passed the Earth Clock Tower this morning by Bird coach, I caught my breath. Although it was only a device to measure time, it resembled an icon of worship rising up from a hill on the north side of the valley floor. And actually, it sort of is. Because now—the day of my birth—time means life itself.

Most of the Diamond Star soldiers spent the night in the surrounding caves. But some chose the open ground when the word spread that the Cancris planned to wait until the entire day had passed, right before midnight on the fifth, to attack if the Crystal Child's powers proved to be false.

According to Jaak's report, after shutting down, the Cancris remained upright and still. But when the Earth Clock's numbers flipped slowly to 2-5-2027, 12:00 AM, they rebooted. He said it was an eerie sight, like creepy robot dolls coming to life in a horror movie. After their reboot, sweet Cuckoo suddenly appeared and began her ritual—twelve cuckoos for midnight—1, 2, 3…when she had just finished cuckoo number 7, a *zip* echoed throughout the Kimallus Valley, followed by an agonized screech and subsequent thud. Alph's laser gun may have just missed Onni and me yesterday, but this time it met its target. Apparently, Cuckoo had startled a robot who may have never seen a Bird before and deemed the strange noise a threat.

Jaak decided to keep it secret until he had to turn in his report. When we all heard of Cuckoo's murder, shortly before four, there wasn't a dry eye in the building. No one said it, but we all thought it—someone should have considered this scenario and protected that sacred Bird. All she was doing was announcing the time, something the Cancris had even requested. They either didn't have the slightest clue of her innocence or, more sinister, knew she was just a sweet, innocent Bird and killed her anyway. Either way, it was too late.

Our sorrow and anger were growing by the minute. Toward morning, the people and Birds of Lucy, the Diamond Star, began to gather in the valley. Yua Kikuchi, the Diamond Star's only veterinarian, was the first to lay hands on sweet little Cuckoo. She gently lifted her to a space away from Cancri eyes, behind the clock, fashioned an altar with rocks and soil and, in the early morning semidarkness, encouraged everyone to join in with prayer and song. The Cancris remained stock still. Monsters, every last one of them. Hatred has always been an uncomfortable emotion for me. But as I stared at that beautiful Bird's poor little carcass, universal symbol of loss and pain and evil, I couldn't have felt more revengeful. But mostly, I just felt a helpless despair.

I wish my brain could just turn off, but with so much hanging in the balance, my anxiety pal Achilles has reared its ugly face. And I can't stop ruminating no matter how hard I try to ground myself. I need to go over and over this prophecy. It's the only way I may be able to think my way out of this nightmare. The prophecy had predicted that a Crystal Child, born on February 5, 2014, would somehow conjure up unlimited supplies of water for all Cancris, making sure all survived. But obviously neither humans nor Cancris seem to truly believe this part, as each side is ready to obliterate the other. Only I, the Crystal Child, apparently knows how to figure out a *win-win* war. Ha. Does such a "war" even exist?

Who would place such a burden on one young person? Is this person, if it is a person, a bully a million times meaner than Jackson Hynes? The ultimate mocker of a child with ADD? Why? Who would believe such total bullshit in the twenty-first century? No one knows. When Dr. EJ and his team found not only the prophecy, but massive wooden doors and a huge cache of water, they searched high and low for clues. They found none. The prophecy and all surrounding it is still a mystery. Yet its predictions have been uncannily accurate—three heavenly bodies (Earth, Cancri e, and the Diamond Star) would clash in the ultimate battle of the universe. The possession of water would be crucial to its survival. And today, my thirteenth birthday, would mark the culmination of that prophecy.

The mission of the soldiers of the Diamond Star has failed. That fate now rests in the hands of one ordinary girl with attention deficit disorder, aka *awfully dumb ditz*, one Kristal Makkinen, of Dolcany, Montana.

Me. And I am the most clueless girl in the universe.

*****

We arrived here at four in the morning. I lay on a cot, in a fit of dozing and waking. One screen showing the Earth Clock Tower and the valley has been placed overhead. Now I gaze numbly as the clock flips from 6:59 to 7:00 AM. My stomach flips along with it. I've hardly slept, despite my royal treatment in the recoup room, where Blanca finally persuaded me to lie in a recliner for an hour or so, breathing in lavender and eating a few nuts and carrot sticks. But they tasted like cardboard. Only a miraculous solution can quell my panic. And as the light gets brighter, as each second passes, I feel more and more hopeless. It's not that I'm pessimistic. It's called reality.

Mercifully, people know better than to wish me a happy birthday. My tongue is a gritty mound of sandpaper. On top of the cement, hawks have replaced the butterflies in my stomach and are circling in tight formation, making me want to double up and freeze in the fetal position. My knees are blobs of jelly. My ankle was slightly sprained; my dad's sweet nurse, Jala, wrapped it in some kind of gauzy material, apologizing the whole time that she didn't have an ice pack. Poor QC citizens—many have donated rations. I was able to take a few more swallows, and then the guilt set in. I thanked everyone profusely, assuring them my thirst was thoroughly quenched. It wasn't, not by a long shot. But who am I to complain about water? I can conjure up an ocean. Yeah, right.

I, Crystal Child, should already have been able to concoct an ingenious scheme to outwit these automatons, the stuff of nightmares, the beings that have mercilessly murdered over six hundred humans and traumatized the rest of us in the QC for over a decade. But according to the prophecy, I'm supposed to render this army harmless without harming it by providing what they need—water. But what the prophecy predicted is impossible for anyone, even these brilliant scientists all around me. Why does the prophecy god want to keep these soulless beings alive? And if he or she does want them alive, why choose me? I'm a kid with ADD, which means if I'm the only one able to figure it all out, the more our chances dip to a big fat zero. Maybe it wanted the joke to be on them. I'm the opposite of a computer; they calculate at top speed. I'm slow even for a human. But we do have one thing in common; we freeze when too many programs are running simultaneously. Well, I'm frozen, all right. And I can't just be restarted with a simple push of a button. I have not come up with a single, solitary idea. My brain's default setting is now permanently on *numb*.

Yep, Jackson Hynes, you were right all along. I'm your simple, homegrown ADD girl. Not only that, now I'm an ADDD girl, the extra *D* for "dehydrated." That only makes things worse. The QC, although kind and loving and unwilling to say it to my face, knows that I am not the answer, and never was. The Birds still revere me for some strange reason. Do they intuit something humans can't? I've also noted looks of hope in some people's eyes when they look at me. Maybe they believe the Birds. But mostly, I see expressions of quiet despair. If Jackson Hynes knew what I'm going through now, he'd add a word to his awfully-dumb-ditz label; I can just hear his taunting voice, "Fraud." *Fraud, fraud.* Yep, I am all those and more. Bring it on, Jackson Hynes. I deserve every mean word you've ever said to me.

But since the QC still treats me with total respect, as though I were some kind of dignitary, here I sit, hidden away in the transport coach, away from the crowd, several yards behind the Earth Clock

Tower's massive presence. The extra tents, attached to the coach, were set up to accommodate the entire QC team.

I step down from the coach, gazing around the valley and up toward the Lucy sky. No sun. No shadows. The only way we know the passage of time is the Earth Clock Tower's huge digital numbers, like a giant pulsar watch, ticking away, counting down the seconds to our destruction. Now I know why Alph demanded the clock be transported to the valley. With each tick, we are reminded of our inevitable fate. How ingeniously evil of them. I'm reminded of Dorothy staring at the sand flowing through the narrow neck of the hourglass in the witch's prison chamber. "I'm frightened, Auntie Em, I'm frightened…" I loved that movie. Now sand makes me gag, and Dorothy's frantic voice has become my own.

Positive pep talk is useless now. Reality check—my birthday will mark doomsday for all humankind. We can keep hiding in the miles and miles of passageways under the biodome. But eventually, they will find us. We could all press our pendants and flee back to Earth, but undoubtedly, the Cancris would follow, and with their indestructible weapons, take over Earth even sooner. Earth could try to nuke them in space before they landed, but since they're teleporting, it would be impossible. Alek told me on one of their fourteen missions to Cancri e, they overheard them discussing their plan should they need to take over Earth. One unidentified Cancri suggested downloading plans for nuclear bombs, harvesting uranium from Mercury, Venus, Mars, and the asteroid belt. But Alph nixed that plan, opting to introduce a new virus more lethal than the Delta COVID-19 strain and impossible to eradicate. It would disappear within five years, so the Cancris could evolve and would leave the H_2O intact for their further development into a type of cyborg status. Alek said his blood ran cold, and he had to tell Big Don he couldn't listen anymore and had to return to Earth. My blood's already cold, and I'm numbed out anyway, so I just nod. Basically, we can run, but we can't hide.

But hey, until they destroy us here on Lucy, we have all the comforts of home. A small array of fruits and vegetables, nuts, all grown hydroponically, is arranged on a tray for sustenance. My mother, father, and grandparents surround me. Alek and Dr. EJ and other new friends and mentors have also entered the coach, and everyone is trying to support me as best they can while engaged in their own think tank. After all, they're the geniuses expected to come up with a solution. I glance at each person's face as they nibble, converse in serious low tones, scribble possible scenarios on iPads as they've been doing all night, glancing outside every now and then. It's bittersweet to be in the presence of my amazing newfound family and friendship circle, knowing that we most likely have such a short time together. Is this really the best way to spend it? Maybe it would be better to admit the futility and just gather around in a huge, heartfelt group hug until it's all over. With that thought, I barely make it to the nearest chair and collapse. Mummo sees me, runs over, throws the baby blanket she knitted so long ago over my shoulders, and kneels in front of me. We silently gaze into each other's glistening eyes, a million unsaid words in our hearts. Someone calls for her. Her lunch is ready. She stands, patting my shoulder.

"Are you hungry?"

I shake my head.

"Rest, my sweet girl," she whispers.

Funny—I never noticed how much she sounds like my mother. But actually, it's not funny at all. Just new.

I smile up at her, and she's gone. Now another face enters my mind, one that's not here—Tad. I have to accept he was just a robot. Nevertheless, a huge hole burrows in my heart for my spirit twin. It's the first time my brother won't stand beside me and help blow out the candles on the bunz cake Dad always baked for both of us, a delicious sponge-type cake with blueberries and strawberries and light creamy frosting. Just thinking about it makes me salivate a teeny bit, even though my mouth is bone-dry. Dad's baked a bunz for us since I can remember. It became a Makkinen family tradition. We never asked him where he got the recipe. Now I know. It's Finnish. Dad felt he couldn't tell me about my past; it would lead to too many questions, even more than I already asked. Anyway, no use thinking about it. No cake today and no Tad. I'm thirteen. Big frickin' deal. Despite how dry I am, a tiny tear trickles down my cheek. I wipe it with my index finger and then lick it with my tongue. Yeah, I'm that thirsty.

Now I understand. Dad knew the secret from the start—that Tad, technical advisory device, had been nothing more than a very sophisticated walking and talking computer devised by the Cancris to keep father and daughter in check until the end date of the prophecy. Finally, it all makes sense. Dad had to try to pretend, for my sake, he was a loving father to a son—all the time aware that it was just a machine built by the enemy. He had to keep that horrific secret and others to feign normalcy, to save me, and to maybe even save Earth someday. Poor Dad. All those years, all alone with these unspeakable secrets. My heart aches for all the pain he had to go through. For me. For the whole world. For *eleven* years. Finally, I know why his eyes seemed so sad and far away.

I sniff, glancing around the coach's cabin, at my parents and grandparents—my family. I should be focusing on my blessings. Right here. Right now. Unless someone thinks of a miracle solution to this gut-wrenching dilemma, it will be the last time I can.

Dr. EJ's voice. He's speaking to someone on his comcard. "Okay, sure, yes, soon." He presses an icon, sets it down, and turns to me. "Dear Ms. Kreestal. Our entire scientific team has feenished their deliberations at Command Central and are now headed our way. We all have been brainstorming and weel conteenue our ideas and calculations. We weel outweet them. We did not work so hard for the betterment of the Earth and humankind just to be destroyed by a rogue band of robotic fiends."

I nod, but his words ring hollow. Obviously, even the most brilliant minds from planet Earth are stumped. "Thank…thank you, Dr. EJ. I'm so sorry. I… I wish—"

My eyes meet my father's. He gives me a weak smile. At first, the doctors had forbidden him to travel. But in true Dad fashion, he wouldn't take no for an answer. Although his memory is still a little spotty, his language and executive function skills—insight, judgment, impulse control, and processing speed (skills we ADD people often lack)—are almost back to normal. *Way to go, Dad.* Best of all, he remembers his wife, my mother. That alone is incredible, indicating my grandfather's new memory treatment was successful. Even with the bandages around his head and his need for support in walking, he's determined to be with his daughter and his wife and with the Quantum Community that had been his life until that tragic day, eleven years ago. I have to ask him.

"Dad?"

"Yes, Krissie."

"Do you remember when you were on Cancri e—on that metal table—and they were healing your injuries?"

Dad frowns. "No, Krissie, I've thought about that a lot. The first memory I have is waking up in a bed with a metal frame, next to you, that god-awful tube sticking out of your little belly, and the TAD standing over you. It looked human, like it was about three years old, but I could tell right away it was one of them. I was in shock. I picked you up. Your angelic little face, oh Krissie, you woke up and started screaming. You were so traumatized, and I started screaming at the TAD to get the hell out. Not the best father-daughter reunion, I admit. The TAD methodically placed a mobile phone next to me, plus a manual of sorts with instructions, chanted some unfamiliar number, then left. I was about to chase it into the hall and kill it with my bare hands when my forehead started buzzing. It felt like someone was drilling a hole in my left eye socket. *That* memory is clear as a bell."

"Oh, Dad, so that's why… Anyway, in those eleven years, do you remember anything that might give us a clue about why the prophecy named me as their Crystal Child?"

Dad shakes his head. That familiar sad look is back in his eyes. "Krissie baby, I am wracking my already wracked brain. Apparently, I had to say something out loud or show an aberrant behavior for their alarm to kick in from that infernal implant in my head because I quietly thought a thousand ways from Sunday about how to get rid of them. I'm a pacifist, but these are machines that have no soul, so if I could, I'd love nothing more than to blow them to smithereens, and don't think I didn't try to plan it."

Blow them to smithereens. Blow them up. In my mind's eye, a vision forms: Tad and I are playing space cadets in the forest last summer, pretending to blast aliens from the planet Zeon back to their own planet with paper towel rolls as dynamite sticks. How ironic. Then suddenly, something else in my brain comes online—an idea, a picture. I grab an iPad sitting on the floor of the coach. I don't know whose, sorry, but it's open, so I tap Adobe Illustrator Draw and start sketching furiously. A valley. Cancris all in a heap, just like on their own planet. Oh, but the prophecy states I need to keep them alive—oh, screw the prophecy. I've had it with mysterious, insane predictions. The hell with it, and didn't Dr. EJ say in the twenty-first century, we don't believe in prophesies anymore? Finally, it's coming together. "Dad."

"Hey, Krissie."

"You're right. We can blast them to pieces."

"Ah, hon, that's just pie in the sky. Remember, they have lonsdaleite suits and weapons. I was just saying I wish—"

I turn to Dr. EJ.

"Dr. EJ?"

"Yes, my dear? And oh, there's my iPad. Did you—"

"Sorry, Dr. EJ, but look." I hold up my sketch. It's quite rough, but it shows Cancris away from our valley, on another part of the star, being blown up. Dr. EJ gives me a confused look. I can't wait to get this idea out of my head. "Dr. EJ, what if we could somehow convince them to travel way out of range of the humans and Birds, without their suits, and then blow them up?"

Dad's waving his hands behind Dr. EJ. "Krissie, Krissie, that was just wishful thinking. I—"

"No, no, wait, just wait..."

Dr. EJ strokes his beard, peering at his iPad, now back into his hands. "Hmmm, as a matter of fact, we do have some explosive devices left over from when we had to hollow out some of the caves to expand the passageway system. They may be too old to work. Thee other problem ees we would have to make sure the enemy ees far enough away from our people and Birds, and that they would not be wearing their lonsdaleite armor. Eet's a long shot, a very long shot. But—"

I frown. "Maybe we could just lead them to another location, here on the Diamond Star. I could tell them we found a lake, a river, an ocean they can transport back to Cancri e. Then give them the number to program their location devices."

Alek joins in. "But to convince them to take off their diamond suits would be challenging to say the least. Maybe we could take off ours and convince them they don't need to wear theirs and tell them that the water's ready and theirs for the taking."

Alek's in. I feel a tiny surge of hope. "Then when they get there, someone can set off the explosives. From afar, I mean. Is...is that possible?"

Dr. EJ saved my sketch and is now scratching numbers on his iPad with a stylus. I had the big picture, and he's working out the minute details. Left brain, right brain. Takes a village. He looks up. His eyes are bright. "Hmmm, Kreestal's idea of relocation and detonation may possibly work. First, we would—"

There's a knock on the coach door. "*Hei.*"

Dr. EJ's eyes widen. "Ah, come in, everyone. Come in."

The door opens. The rest of the QC think tank—Jaak, Dahab, Dr. B, Elk, Johann, and Hale all have to duck their heads as they enter the coach. Dr. EJ directs them to move on through to the tent attached at the back. I join them. Dr. EJ starts right in. "Okay, leesten. Our Crystal Child has an idea. She can try to hoodwink the Cancris eento moving far away from all of us—many kilometers away, say, near the Vaasa Valley. The crater there may confuse them at first into thinking eet ees some kind of lake, maybe weeth eenvisible water. Then we can inceenerate them weeth our leftover exploseeves from the expansion of the tunnels. Thee devices are still good, correct, Jaak?"

Jaak nods. "They should be. We've obviously kept them in dry storage. But they aren't powerful enough to destroy lonsdaleite diamond, of course. Not even an H-bomb could—"

"Yes, yes, we've factored that in. But eef they are convinced to remove their suits, would there be enough ammo to destroy their entire army?"

"I don't know. Hey, Elk. Get Haukka. I need you to go on a mission."

"Where?"

"The storage building, right outside the City, where we keep the ANFOs. We need you to check and see if they're still viable. If so, we're going to try to blow these steel devils to kingdom come."

Elk slaps his knee. "*Vau!*"

Dr. EJ laughs. "Yes, Elk. *Wow* is right, we hope."

"You don't have to hope. I know they're good." I stored them carefully as I figured they might come in handy again someday. Dangerous for our people too though, no?"

"Not if we lure them all the way to the Vassa Valley."

Elk's eyes widen. "Ah. Uh, okay, how are we going to do that?"

Jaak jerks his thumb my way. "Our prophecy girl here. Right, Kristal? She can convince them that their oasis is a few valleys to the east, and they need to get there stat. Without their suits."

My eyes go to Alek. He's sighing, throwing me an apologetic look. "Tough sell."

Suddenly, a surge of sisu floods my previously offline mind. I nod. "I can do it."

Dr. EJ pats my hand. "They'll believe you. They've been waiting for you for eleven whole years—ever seence they stole the prophecy from us and, weeth their primitive reasoning powers, believed every word of eet, weeth all their hearts, er, circuitry, and we weel be right behind you."

My chest suddenly feels tight. What have I just done? Can PPT help in this dire situation? Well, can't hurt. Hang on, prophecy girl. You may not have the smarts to really conjure up water, but you've done the stink-bug trick on bullies more times than you can count. Just think of them all collectively as one big, dumb Jackson Hynes. Yes, you can do this.

"I... I'm ready. Whenever you say."

Alek's grinning from ear to ear. "That's my girl. Sisu is your middle name." He gives me two thumbs-up.

I return the gesture. And promptly whip my eyes to the ceiling to prevent a major crying jag.

Sixty-Three

February 5, 2027

Today, time passes as it does every day. To me, however, it's slowed to a crawl. Didn't Einstein himself say time is relative? Each tick seems like an eternity today, and with each tick, my anxiety heightens. The Earth clock continues to march into the future. I wish Einstein had thought of a way to travel back into the past. But second after second, the numbers flip toward the moment of salvation for all humans—or the moment of doom.

Alph's seven thousand minions are still assembled in block formation about a football field's length away from the clock. Decked out in their new indestructible suits of londsdaleite, they're a formidable sight. Alph is standing motionless, rigid, closer to the clock tower and closer to us. We all want to yell at him to stay back, but we don't, lest we rouse his anger or whatever it is a robot feels. You never know what a heartless Cancri might do if crossed, especially if it's in lonsdaleite armor and especially if it can murder a harmless, beautiful Bird just chirping the hours. If I think too much about Cuckoo, my heart will explode. Come on, mind. Back to the present. You've got work to do.

Finally, at eleven-thirty in the evening, on the prophecy date of February 5, 2027, or the Choice Point, as the prophecy called it, Dr. EJ announces to the crowd to ready themselves for its manifestation. It has taken all night, all day, and all evening to assemble the explosives and figure out the location code to the second largest valley on the star. It's just barely within the biodome. The Cancris don't have a clue about what's been going on behind the scenes all day long, or at least, we hope to God they don't.

Although no one is stating the obvious, we all know this is plan Z. If this doesn't work, it's over. Now with the enemy's lonsdaleite armor, there will be no battle, no hand-to-claw combat. Our weapons are useless. We are left with only one possible way out—deception. And whether I signed up for the job or not, I'm the designated deceiver. I am to transform myself into a con artist, a swindler, cheating the Cancris out of their expected destiny according to the Diamond Star prophecy.

The only problem is, I am no con. Never was, never will be. That's just not me. I never could lie. Dad could see through me in a New York second. Luckily, the bots aren't good at detecting lies. And, well, I guess Dad has taught me to lie enough to perform a few bully tricks like the stink-bug ruse, which is basically lying. But I have to lie on the grandest scale ever in my lifetime because if the robots catch on, there goes—no, I can't think of that. I absolutely cannot let that happen. If there was ever a time I needed to focus, it would be now. But both my stomach and my brain seemed to have turned to mush, and my skin crawls with fear. If I were a Cancri, I would be offline. Shut down. Never have I hated my ADD so much. I'm useless. Right foot, left foot is all I have to offer. And right now, even my throbbing left foot is iffy.

Alek, Dad, and my mother have been in serious conversation with me all day about what Alek dubbed my *persuasion speech*. Somehow, I need to convince the Cancris that a new ocean of unlimited water has somehow miraculously materialized by me, of course, and that they must shed their diamond suits and weapons and transport themselves hundreds of kilometers away to verify its existence. A normal human would never believe this whale of a tale; even a child could see right through it. What if Alph says, "Just send me, and I'll report back," or worse, "You are lying." After all, Alek noted yesterday Alph's bullshit detector seems to be evolving. But he's 99 percent sure they're still pretty naive and will obey any order given by the Crystal Child—aka, me. I have to trust Alek that they will buy my story hands—er—claws down—because there's no other option.

The Earth Clock Tower displays the current time: 11:34 PM. I'm fighting sheer terror. The Cancris are still in their suits, in block formation at the north end of the valley. All sentient beings—humans, animals, and Birds—stand in the south end of the Kimallus Valley transfixed as the Earth Clock on the west side, in the middle, counts down the time. We all miss Cuckoo tweeting the hours. Her slaughter was unconscionable. Of course, it was. Alph has no conscience. I used to waver between calling Alph a *he* or an *it*. I no longer waver. It doesn't deserve a human pronoun now, not after what it did. It hurt to see Dr. EJ break down as he prayed over the poor Bird's tiny, makeshift grave behind the clock. Now he's sighing as he sees the valley filled with people and Birds. A majority has decided they need to be here—Dr. EJ's warning be damned—to witness, to support, to fight if necessary. If we're going to die, they reason, let's go down together. With each new wave of Diamond Star citizens that materializes here, Dr. EJ just slowly shakes his head. Even General Waara's Diamond Army, initially commanded to hide, is in formation behind the Earth Clock Tower, supposedly protecting us. General Waara is one proud man, and I'm not surprised he ordered his troops to stand up to the Cancris rather than cower in the caves, no matter what the outcome. Each second is precious now. Mutsi, Dad, and I are standing in front of the clock, near the podium, while Dr. EJ, the other QC members, Alek, and Big Don, stand a few feet behind. Between Alek and Big Don, Schrödinger sits completely unfazed, casually licking stardust from his paws.

The Cancris have been surprisingly quiet all day. But suddenly, Alph turns, raising its claws to the sky. Some sort of amplifying device must be in its metal skull because somehow, its voice booms throughout the valley without a microphone. "We wait all day. Twenty-six Earth minutes remain. If no solution emanates from Crystal Child"—it turns and points to me—"all will be destroyed, and we will continue to Earth and destroy all creatures there. Then we will have unlimited H_2O to evolve Cancri species to human hybrid."

You'd think it would be raising its voice, showing anger, or at least, firm resolve. But it threatened to annihilate every living creature on Earth in total monotone, without the slightest hint of emotion. Killing every sentient being is a chore they have to accomplish; we are the garbage they have to carry to the curb to be hauled away. They truly are lizards.

Alph turns, facing his army. As one, the Cancris rattle their metal and stomp their diamond boots. I jump. The humans and Birds cower and tremble. The Cancris may speak in monotone, may feel nothing inside, but they're experts at stirring up human emotion, mainly terror. Monstrous brutes. Throughout the day, a numb dread has been my constant companion, but now a more intense emotion rears its ugly head and sits right at the top of my stomach. Rage. Okay, that's slightly better. Maybe my new-found fury will provide the energy I desperately need to deceive them, to make them believe little old me.

11:39 PM.

The damn Earth clock just keeps on ticking, like it's any old day. I meet Alek's eyes. He nods and mouths, "You're on, Kristal girl. You can do this."

Yes, uh-huh, sure. I can do this. *Sisu, sisu, sisu.* Time is up. I glance behind me. Holding onto each other for dear life are my incredible parents. They're trying desperately not to cry, blinking like mad, shooting me encouraging nods, supporting me with their smiles. Dr. EJ is behind, towering over them and giving me that confident nod of his. But underneath the false bravado, everyone must be as terrified as I am. I don't blame them. I don't know what the hell I'm doing, and they know that. Why are they even letting me try? That's obvious. I'm their only hope, no matter how slim. The fact that I'm about to speak illustrates the desperation everyone feels. No other options exist. *You're it, Crystal Child. Now go.*

Hesitantly, I take my first step to the podium in front of the massive Earth Clock Tower. Right foot, left foot. Ouch. I hope they don't notice I'm limping. I hesitate then continue. All day long I've practiced my persuasion speech, but now I'm so completely frozen I'm not even sure my mouth will open. Never was good at public speaking, let alone with so much at stake. I have to get this speech out of the way, as each second that passes becomes more agonizing than the last. But I keep going, step after step, until I am at the top step, at the slanted slab of wood I can barely see over. With trembling fingers, I tug the microphone from its stand, turn it on. It squeals. I rear back. Dr. EJ leaps up, adjusts something, then returns the mike to my shaking hand.

I'm actually standing at the dreaded podium, gazing dumbly out at the crowd of humans, Birds, other assorted animals, and robots. All eyes, human and steel, are on me now. What do I do? Oh yeah, my cheat sheet. It's in my jean pocket. I scoop it out with my index finger, accidentally smack my knuckles on the side of the podium. The paper flies out of my hand and flutters to the ground. Oh, shit. Shit. Shit. *Shit.* Someone runs and picks it up, hands it back to me. I don't even think to say thank you as I grab it and smooth it out on the podium. Why did I tell them I'd feel more comfortable with paper than with an iPad? I'm an idiot. I—*Kris, focus.*

My mouth is sandpaper. My face is hot as a Cancri rock. I try to clear my throat, but there's nothing to clear. "Uh," and then I choke a little. Oh, nice start, Kris. That's just great. I've never hated myself as much as I do this very moment. I need to save humanity, but I'm a stupid, awfully dumb ditz. Then from deep inside me, I hear Achilles. He's surprisingly—*supportive? Push through the fear, Kris. You can do this. You must.* I imagine my voice booming like my archrival Alph. I need to give myself a mega pep talk, or maybe I'm just procrastinating. In any case, deep breath, here goes. I am a confident speaker, and my voice projects authority, loud enough to be heard at the very end of the valley and back. There. I am ready. *Not.*

Achilles whispers, *"Yes, you're ready. Do it, Kris. Do it."* I take a deep breath, cough, and clear my throat. I can't project a powerful voice like Alph. No way. My words come out raspy, trembling. But everyone's listening with rapt attention. "Uh, welcome, Cancris." I glance down at the paper. Although lights have been lit, it's a little too dark, and I can barely read it. I'm going to have to wing it. Great, I should know it by heart. I've gone over it a gazillion times. Still, my brain is so shut down I can't... I can't—I sway a little.

There's that tiny voice again. Achilles? My inner sisu? *Crystal Child. You are the Crystal Child. Do it.* A memory—Alek, towering over Jackson Hynes, owning it. I look over the podium and realize

I'm towering over all the little Jacksons, playing dress up in their diamond suits and their clunky boots. They're just like Jackson. A jolt of sisu bursts through my veins.

"I have developed a formula for water, uh, for Cancris, for you."

Keep going, Kris. Keep going.

I scan the Cancri crowd. They're no longer a bunch of harmless Jacksons; they're a terrifying army of indestructible demons. I knew that. They're stock-still, waiting. They've waited for eleven years for this moment. Their lonsdaleite boots stomp in unison. *Stomp, stomp, stomp.* These are no Jackson Hynes clunky boots. What does the stomping mean? Is that like cheering? Clapping? Encouragement? Or maybe, anger?

I continue. "It...it has been completely successful."

Stomp, stomp, stomp. Oh, dear God, what's the second part? Haven't I been over this a million times today? I steal a glance at my notes. I can make out some of the bigger words. Why didn't someone think to give me more light? I look up again. The Cancris are motionless now, all focused on me with their shiny dead eyes for my supposed miracle message.

And I thought my classmates were intimidating. Ha, child's play. I would trade this petrifying, surreal moment for Mr. Gabriel's classroom in a heartbeat, even a classroom with Jackson Hynes right in front of me. I clutch my notes and force myself to suck in some air. "Listen and follow my directions *to the letter.*" Uh-oh. Was that too abstract? Yep. It would have been for Tad. I'm good at revising and immediately correct myself. "Listen and follow each and every direction perfectly." There. That was more direct. "You will find water on this star for your entire planet. All you need to do is a quick teleport to the Vaasa Valley, to the east." I point straight ahead. "Every single Cancri." I keep pointing, then my hand starts to tremble, and I hide it. Their dark diamond heads turn as one, then turn back, fixating on me.

"You will find water there. All the water you will ever need. I have created an ocean, manufacturing water for Cancris only. Earth water cannot teleport through a wormhole, but the water I have made on this star—BPM 37093—is completely transportable to 55 Cancri e."

If I were hydrated, I would be breaking out in a horrible sweat right now. What a bunch of bull I just spit out. Haven't they caught on by now? They're still just standing there, like a horde of fools. A sudden wave of dizziness threatens to flatten me. I grab the sides of the podium with both hands. My note flutters to the ground again. Forget it.

I scan the valley. The Cancris are still standing at attention. At least Alph hasn't pulled out its laser weapon to shoot me between the eyes like it did with poor Cuckoo. So far, I mentally brace myself for the next part, the hardest to pull off. I glance at my notes on the ground. Will they catch on if I stoop to pick them up? I decide not to chance it. *Okay, Kris, you're on your own.*

I try to swallow and end up choking again. Great, I rest for a second. The Cancris seem spellbound or gobsmacked. This is the revered Crystal Child? This timid little mousy thing who squeaks more than speaks? I should've worn Mutsi's diamond cloak. At least, I might have looked the part. But it's too late now and all I can do is keep going. "The only way to teleport is by removing your armor and laying down your weapons, uh, temporarily. The lonsdaleite interferes with the frequencies needed for transporting you to the new location. You just need your travelrods. I have the location number."

The number—oh god—it's on the piece of paper ground into the dirt at my feet. No getting around it; I have to use my recall, just like I had to remember the number 37093 in those last seconds when Cancri Dad was reaching toward me with the Cancri claw. I did it then. I can do it now. With every ounce of focus this ADD girl does not possess, I think number. I visualize number. I try to hear the sound loop in my brain. Suddenly, a deafening cacophony of whirring blasts my ears. I stand back up and look over at Alek. He cups his hands around his mouth, "They're mulling it over. It's crunch time."

No time to think. I turn back, startling myself as the ad-lib of my life rises up and out of my mouth like a mysterious gushing fountain of wisdom. The words so easily springing from my brain don't even feel like my own. Suddenly, I, Kristal Makkinen, ADD girl, is standing outside myself, observing the all-powerful Crystal Child present the performance of the century. "Do *not* worry. Your suits and weapons will be guarded by One, who has personally assured me all is proceeding as planned. The suits and weapons will remain here, untouched, until your return. You must go now. Each of you is needed in the Vaasa Valley to manifest the elixir of life for the advancement of your species. It will be beautiful beyond your imagination. You must each touch the water, one by one. This way, your unique Cancri frequencies will intermingle in a perfect way with the water to enable teleportation to Cancri e. This water will last forever for all Cancris. Your evolution will be complete. Long live the Cancris!"

Whoa. I'm back in my body now. Holy moly—where did that pile of crap come from? If I were Pinocchio, my nose would be scraping the mountainsides by now. But it feels familiar somehow. Oh, yeah, I envision Tad and me in our Wonder Woodlands. This would have made a great afternoon of imaginary play. My ADD creativity is coming online. For once, my ADD is coming in handy. But will it work? I glance behind me. Everyone's eyes are round as moons. They're all grinning, giving me a thumbs-up.

The whirring stops. Uh-oh. Did they detect the ruse? In a final act of desperation, I blurt, "Remove your suits now. You don't want them interfering with the frequencies you need to activate the water. You need to experience this wonderful water for yourselves. Your suits and weapons will be here when you return. Here is the number—ready, Cancris?" This is the critical moment.

All of a sudden, it all catches up to me and I turn my head to the side, willing myself not to throw up. Alph's on my left, nodding his head toward me, then toward his army. *Stomp, stomp, stomp.* Alph reaches up, unhooks some lonsdaleite apparatus, and sheds his suit, laying down the horrible corkscrew weapon beside it. I'm staring. I can't believe what I'm seeing. *Yes, woo-hoo!* He returns my gaze.

"Ready for number."

Ready for number? Did he just say that? Omigod, it's happening. They really believe the megacrapola I'm spoon-feeding them. My eyes go back to Alek, behind me, pleading. How am I doing? He's giving me a tiny fist bump. Alek was right again. The Cancris really are that gullible. They've taken the bait like little kids expecting the Tooth Fairy. I hold my breath as more Cancri soldiers remove their suits. Within a minute, entire mountains of lonsdaleite diamond suits are scattered all over the valley. This is insane, wonderfully insane, miraculously insane.

Wow. I think I might be feeling a little more confident. I'm pretty sure I can remember the number Mutsi gave me for transport to the Vaasa Valley, where the explosives lie in wait. She insisted on heading up this project, and Dahab objected at first. She said my mother was compromised by all the stress surrounding me, Cancri, her parents, and my father. Apparently, quite a few of the team agreed with Dahab. But this time, Mutsi overruled everyone, saying this was too critical to leave to anyone but the best. She didn't mean to brag, but that would be her—the only one who could do the job. It was a good decision. I can tell my mother is amazingly brilliant for this sort of stuff, and that she works well under pressure. She let Dahab do some of the calculations, but she insisted on doing the hard part. The part she had trained for all her life. I'm so glad Mutsi was in charge. This plan *cannot* fail.

I'm still holding the mike but notice my hands are steadier. I raise one hand to silence everyone. "Listen, all Cancris, remember then say in unison. Ready? The number is 3, 7"—oh god, oh god— "0, 6…" Holy moly, the last one—what the hell is the last one? I turn my head. There's Alek with all five fingers of his left hand out and the index finger of his right. I turn to the Cancris. "6. Again, 37066."

Alek, what would I do without you? There we go. It's done. I raise both arms in the air in a triumphant gesture and along with it comes a rush of confidence. "You will reach the incredible ocean and witness for yourselves its pure, crystal waters, essential for the magnificent new life into which you will evolve." A vision suddenly pops into my head. Within a few minutes, not an ocean but a huge, smoking crater of microdust, wires, and charred metal, like the scene after the battle on Cancri. I smile. It's happening.

Another vision floats across my mind, and suddenly, I'm at home in the forest with Tad. We're prince and princess of a golden island, rewarding our citizens for staving off the evil dragon. This memory makes me smile even brighter, my energy even stronger, and I wave my arms high over my head, bellowing like a traveling preacher. "You shall know its magic. You shall be given the gift of joy, the most incredible of human emotions. When you return, after you are back in your traveling suits, I will present instructions on how to transport this vast ocean back to your planet. I have discovered the answer to the elixir of life for all Cancris, forever, exactly as stated in the prophecy. Now *go in peace and return in joy and gratitude.*" Oh, man, I could be a TV evangelist for sure. I could start my own megachurch or be queen of a vast realm. It would be all too comical if our very lives weren't at stake. But they are, and no one's laughing. If we're successful, then we can laugh, dance, and sing our hearts out. *No Kris, "if" is not acceptable. No if's. None. When. When. Has to be "when."*

As one, they grasp their travelrods, monotone voices chanting the code in perfect unison as their leader—Alph—models, "37066." Their chant is like rolling thunder. Wow. Seven thousand robotic voices in sync. It's breathtaking. I wait. They're still standing, still standing. *Oh God no please*—then all of a sudden, a colossal cloud of dust kicks up. We wave the dust away, coughing. When it settles, we all take a look around. Not a trace of Cancri remains, except for the sea of sparkling lonsdaleite suits and weapons gleaming on the Kimallus Valley floor.

I turn and race down the steps of the podium, left ankle be damned. No one utters a peep for a few moments. I think we're all in shock. Then in a great rush, Mutsi, Alek, Big Don, and EJ come toward me, slapping me on the back, hugging me, and congratulating me for getting the job done.

Alek pounds me on the back so hard I have to steady myself. "You crushed it, girl. Damn." I glance up.

There's Dad, beaming, even as he's holding on to a chair for balance. "I knew it. You *are* the Crystal Child."

The other members of the QC community and even the Birds are staring at me, quiet, even reverent, waiting with hushed anticipation. I slowly let out my breath, smile and wave to everyone in the valley. It's almost over. Almost...

The seconds can't tick fast enough. Now all we can do is wait for word from Jaak. He and Elk volunteered to travel to the site and set off the explosives. Their two-man demolition team set up an acoustical system so we can hear what's happening in the Vaasa Valley. Then Elk returned, leaving Jaak at the site. When we hear Jaak's triumphant voice over the loudspeaker, we'll know that our mission—complete annihilation of the Cancri soldiers—has been accomplished, and we can celebrate to the high heavens as we pack up for our return to Earth. Dr. EJ explained that it takes virtually no time at all to travel to the Vaasa Valley—only four hundred kilometers away—a tiny baby step in space-time. As soon as they appear at the site, they'll realize that their "ocean" is nothing but sand and rock. But before they can utter a single word in protest, they will be blown to metal smithereens. I can't get upset over their destruction as they truly are just machines, and they destroyed so many human lives, murdering so many of the Quantum Community, not to mention destroying the emotional lives of the survivors, like Dad's, Mutsi's, Alek's, my grandparents', and the others and me, and of course, poor little Cuckoo. She's just as precious as any of us.

Since the Cancris decided to wait until the fulfillment of the prophecy, they haven't really begun the serious transformation to AI/human hybrid. So no human DNA is in any Cancri so far, except Big Don and Schrödinger, the cat here with us, which is supposedly "guarding us." And well, one other Cancri—my eyes surprise me when they start to fill with tears. I can't think about my twin. He can't be destroyed anyway. He's already—I choke, grabbing my mother's arm. She pulls me in and kisses my hair. For once, I think she's actually speechless. It may be premature, but everyone's already starting to celebrate. Some are laughing, lots of hugging going on. Another group is singing "Amazing Grace."

Hmmm, the only group that seems a little subdued are the Birds. They look a little like the day Onni almost died of dehydration. Then I see Rawol, getting ready to dive-bomb me again, just like that first fateful day in the snow. I'm not scared anymore, but it's clear he's trying to warn me, then he swoops down.

"*Aaaraaaaraaa!*" He seems agitated. What's his deal? I hold my arms out to him. "Rawol, I hear you, I hear you. It's all okay. Don't worry. I know it's scary, but it will work."

Mustsi's watching him too, frowning.

"*Aaaaaaaa!*" he screeches again. I glance at Mutsi. She shrugs. We watch him circle the Earth Clock Tower once then fly away toward the nearest passageway. Maybe he doesn't realize we're so far away from the Vaasa Valley we can't possibly get injured.

Since Jaak's on location, he can actually see the bombs go off. Funny to think the Earth's people will be completely unaware that their entire planet has just been spared total annihilation, and they may never know, as we will never divulge the truth. It will be safer that way, and I certainly don't want any recognition in any way, shape, or form. Gulping down a huge glass of earth water will be reward enough for me. Can't wait.

11:48 PM

Boom!

The explosion's almost loud enough to blow out the speakers. We cover our ears. A great cry rises up from the Kimallus Valley. My heart is in my throat. It worked. Omigod, it's done. I'm in a state of ecstatic shock. It's finished. All around me is a blur of tears, shouts, hugs, high fives, and...

Jaak's voice over the speaker is frantic. "*Abort, abort, abort! Explosive devices successful but location four kilometers off. Explosives missed Cancris. Repeat, explosives missed Cancris. Mayday, Mayday, Mayday, head for nearest shelter. Repeat, head for shelter...*"

Sixty-Four

● ● ● ● ● ● ● ● ● ● ○ ● ● ● ● ● ● ● ● ●

February 5, 2027

"Quaaaaaaa." I hear Rawol's screeches again; this time from far in the distance. He knew. All the Birds knew. That's why Onni kept insisting *I was* their leader. It really was all up to me. I had to save *all* according to the prophecy. I shouldn't have tried to destroy them. You can't tinker with fate. Goosebumps pop out on my arms. My vision starts to fade. *Breathe, Kris, breathe...*

My knees give way. I stumble. Alek helps me up. I look into his face. His lips are a thin line. Mutsi cries out. Her face is white, her fists in a ball.

"Damn...damn! Dahab? *Dahab? Dahab!* Oh, DAMN!" she screams in frustration, smashing her fist into a nearby rock. Blood trickles down her knuckles. I feel an invisible mist descending over me.

Dahab's behind Mutsi. "Myra, what happened? You checked them and rechecked them. You told me it was tight as could be." Then Dahab's checking something on her comcard. Her eyes grow wide; she hits the side of her head and gasps. "Oh, Myra, the 7."

Mutsi's gone ghost-white. "The 7?" Dahab's gritting her teeth, and her eyes are wide with fear. "Should have been a 1, Myra. I think that's when the computer number one was down, and you said you'd just write the location number on a sticky note, then reprogram it into the other computer, but when you reprogrammed it, you must have mistaken your written 1 for a 7. Ones and sevens, we need to be really careful about those. They look so much alike. You taught me that, Myra. That tiny little dash, sometimes on a 1, but sometimes not, but it often makes a 1 look like a 7. It's a common mistake. You—"

"I was nervous."

Dahab lowers her head. "Yes."

Mutsi looks like she's going into a trance. "Just a tiny dash…a tiny dash—Dahab, it was just so tiny—so *tiny*. I should have realized it was a 1, not a 7. I—" My mother slumps to the ground, like a dead zombie.

Dahab didn't say "I told you so," like she so easily could have. Instead, she drops to the ground with her, arm around her shoulder. "Oh, Myra, hon, I'm so sorry…"

My dad is on the other side, crying with her. I can't imagine anything worse than knowing everyone's about to die, except knowing that but for a tiny little mistake, you could have prevented it. I can't imagine her pain. Dear Mutsi, you were compromised. You did have too much on your mind. Otherwise, how could you have—

Dad's eyes are closed, and he's got his arm around her waist and they're rocking together back and forth. What's anyone to say to her? "That's okay. You'll get it next time?" My mother's tiny little stroke turning a 1 into a 7 has just obliterated our entire human race for eternity. It doesn't matter if she's forgiven. We're all about to die anyway. I don't feel a thing. I'm a zombie like Mutsi. A reptile. A computer. A Cancri.

Dr. EJ's at the podium, his sisu still going strong, shouting louder than I've ever heard him, "Now, NOW! EVERYONE, RUN FOR THE CAVES BUT DO NOT TRAMPLE YOUR NEIGHBORS, FAST BUT STEADY. USE YOUR WITS—THE PASSAGEWAYS QUEECKLY! COME, COME, THE SOLDIERS WEELL HELP YOU. WE CAN STEEL FIGURE SOMETHING OUT…"

Oh, Dr. EJ, give it up. As one, the Birds explode into the air, following Rawol, flying in formation to the west, to Birdland. There's Haukka. Where's Onni? The people begin scrambling in all directions. It's complete pandemonium.

Too late.

A deafening roar explodes all around us as the Cancris—all seven thousand of them—suddenly reappear next to, in front of, behind, and a few on top of those still in the Kimallus Valley, sending them flying upward. Screams, yells, roars fill the air, but most chilling of all is the cacophony of screeches, whirs, buzzes of the Cancri soldiers. There's no denying it. They've just been had, and they know it. Well, well, their first strong human emotion—*rage*.

General Waara, megaphone in hand, is pacing back and forth, yelling to his army, "Kill them before they can reassemble! KILL THEM…KILL THEM!"

Bang, bang, bang! Gunfire pierces the valley. Dozens of Cancris begin falling left and right, but within seconds, most Cancris are already back into their lonsdaleite suits. Resolutely, the Cancris retrieve their monstrous weapons, then regroup into their original tight block formation, presumably waiting for new orders from Alph. A few more gunshots pop here and there, but at this point, it's a lost cause, and everyone knows it.

11:56 PM

Alek leaves me standing with Mutsi and Dad, then starts waving his hands frantically as he leaps the steps of the podium in a single bound, yanking the microphone out of its stand. "No, no, no, Cancris, that was an earth—no—starquake. I repeat—a *starquake*, unanticipated. We still have water for you. Repeat—we still have water for you!"

Oh, Alek, poor Alek.

The Cancris begin to stomp in unison.

Alek is shaking his head, still waving his arms. "Listen…listen, the ocean is four kilometers from where you landed. We quickly reprogrammed so you wouldn't land in the vicinity of the quake. No, Cancris, please quiet! Listen, listen—we will reprogram your…"

Alph's voice thunders, projecting throughout the valley as if from the sky, "LIE. You lie. You think Cancri stupid. WE ARE NOT STUPID. You think Cancri gullible. WE ARE NO LONGER GULLIBLE. Lie detection software not yet perfected, but 97 percent online. Crystal

Child *lied*. Cancri checked program 105830 for veracity of statements. They are *lies*."

Alek jumps off the podium and is now standing face-to-face with Alph. I've never seen Alek so desperate. "No, no, Alph. It wasn't her fault. The ocean is real. It's only four kilometers. Hey, Alph, listen, calm down. Let's figure out…"

"Where is my laser distance weapon? Where?"

No one answers. One look at Dr. EJ, and I know. He was brilliant to think of hiding Alph's distance laser weapon when they were gone. At least, Alph can't kill from a distance. Small consolation. But I have no doubt Alek would be dead by now and probably Big Don and, no doubt, me. Well, at least, this buys us a tiny bit of time.

Suddenly a shrill whirring pulsates from Alph's head. "Program 105830 confirms lie. *Stop talk*. Girl does not have formula for H_2O. Delete. Cancris, *begin kill!*"

Stomp, stomp, stomp.

The sudden sights and sounds of thousands of Cancri soldiers marching forward in unison makes me fall to my knees. And this time, no one comes to my aid, as everyone around me is collapsing to the ground as well, god, even Alek. My stomach seizes so tightly I clutch my sides. God, it hurts so bad I'm moaning, rocking forward, back, forward, back. It's all over. I'm done. We're all done. Dad, Dad, Dad, Mutsi, Mutsi…

And suddenly, the valley trembles and the air explodes with the strident whirring of over six thousand dreaded corkscrews. A sea of terrifying tortuous weapons now points straight at me as they whirl, and I retch, sputtering, retch some more. This time, food comes up. So much for the amazing prophesied Crystal Child. I can't stop, and I throw up again, gulping in huge mouthfuls of dusty Diamond Star air, and then I cough and cough until I think my throat is going to rip itself to pieces if the corkscrews don't do it first.

Now I know what all those queens in medieval England felt like before their beheading. Centuries may separate us, but the primal terror—theirs and mine—must feel the same. Whether by executioner's axe or lonsdaleite diamond corkscrew, we all await a gruesome, unspeakable death.

My anticipated thirteenth birthday will end in my gruesome murder, followed by the annihilation of everyone I have ever held near and dear. All because I've been too dumb, too ADD, too inexperienced, too distracted to figure it all out. Author of the prophecy—whoever and wherever you are—what did I do wrong? My so-called solution—deceiving the Cancris—went against the prophecy, and Rawol was trying to tell me, to warn me. Birds are so much more intuitive than we are. I know that now. So it wasn't Mutsi's fault. It was still mine. But, Birds, what was I to do? I still didn't figure out the way of the prophecy—to think of a solution that saves everyone. Why? Why? Why didn't you give me more clues, prophecy author? Are you laughing? Or are you crying? Whose side are you on? Why didn't you show yourself? I obviously missed a crucial piece of information somewhere. But where? How? No matter. I take the blame, all of it. This was my mission, and I failed miserably. I was supposed to do it single-handedly. Now get ready for death, just get it over with—the sooner, the better.

I take one last look at my parents. At least for a tiny slice of time, we were together again. My tears fall, silent, dripping onto the glittery gray-ochre sand and covering the darkened areas where I puked. It's over. Over. In the distance, past the thunderous stomping of the Cancri soldiers, I hear the Birds' sorrowful caws and humans wailing, moaning, screaming. The Cancris are just robots, doing what they're programmed to do. I'm the real murderer here. My mind begins to shrink and I can't feel my body anymore.

11:59 PM

My being is completely taken over by Alph's robotic chant. *"Kill, kill, kill."*

The prophecy—all events were to align perfectly for some sort of miracle, but it's all gone horribly wrong. Evil has won. I brace and detach myself, waiting numbly for the imminent destruction of all that's good, noble, pure—this beautiful, incredible community; these sacred Birds; and soon, all those on Earth, humanity itself. Closing my eyes tightly, I collapse flat on the ground, then curl into myself;

my hands over my heart, just as I must have in my mother's womb. But it was safe there…safe…safe… It was birth, not death. Death… It's coming, closer, louder and louder. I curl into myself even tighter, cowering like a tiny terrified animal. I will die like this—a weak little coward. Bile burns my throat. A sudden commotion overhead makes me squeak in fear. My death. It's imminent. It's…wait. Is that a flapping of wings?

I peek upward. Onni? *Onni?*

Soaring down from the top of the South Mountain, circling the Kimallus Valley, down, down, down, as the human crowd gives way. I hear a murmuring, more flapping of wings, excited cawing, and everyone is now looking up. I do too. And the more I zero in, the more I—gasp.

It's Onni. Atop him is some sort of being, under a black cloak, weapon at its side. My executioner? Did Alph force Onni to carry the one who will drill a diamond lonsdaleite corkscrew directly through my heart? Is my death turning into some sort of sadistic ceremony? Onni circles closer, closer, until finally his colossal talons grip the ground in front of the clock. I still can't tell what or who it is. But it's smaller than the rest, much smaller. Poor Onni. The Cancris must have captured him and made him transport the one who will…who will—wait. It pushes back its hood. I catch a glimpse of its face. I can't breathe. Then I suck in a mouthful of air and cough and cough. Finally the coughing stops, and I check it out once again. It slides down from Onni's back, throwing off the whole cape. I shut my eyes. My executioner is here. I'm drowning in adrenaline. I don't want to die. Please, God, I don't want to die. Then words hit my ears—familiar words, unmistakable words, *his* words, *his* voice, not human, but human to me. That beautiful, monotone voice, loud and clear.

"Kristal, happy birthday. To us. 37093."

Sixty-Five

° ° ° ° ° ° ° ° ◉ ○ ○ ○ ○ ○ ○ ○ ° ° °

February 5, 2027

My jaw drops. Although my knees are shaking like crazy, I haul myself up and take a good look, drinking in the sight. Yep, it's him. It can't be, but it is. Am I back in the dream? Have they already killed me? Am I dead? The world starts to fade. I'm going into shock. *BREATHE,* my mind screams, *BREATHE!* I suck in huge gulps of dusty air, choking, choking. *Slow down, breathe.* I stop choking. I stop breathing and just stare.

He walks cautiously toward me, like he's not sure where he is. It's him. It's him. It's him. I know that walk like the back of my hand when he's a little nervous about something. Now his face comes into full view, and he stops right in front of me, holding something in his hands, repeating his message, "Kristal, happy birthday. To us. Where's cake."

I suck in a huge gulp of air and cough. I realize I'm waiting for the number tacked at the end of his sentence. His last sentence ended with the Diamond Star's original code—our location. But no number at the end of this sentence. Tad just spoke his first sentence without a number. I reach out and grab him, and we hug so hard the boxy thing he's holding presses into me, poking into my stomach. But I don't care.

"Oh Tad, oh Tad, oh Tad, yes, yes, happy, happy birthday, Tad! Hey, bro, I missed you so much. I'm sorry Dad didn't get to bake us our bunz cake this year. I know how much you love that—our blueberry cake with strawberries and vanilla frosting—so yummy. I'm so

531

sorry…happy birthday, bro," and I'm squeezing him, crying, scream-ing, sobbing, not caring that the entire fate of humanity hangs in the balance, that my fellow humans and I are about to be eviscerated in cold blood by a bunch of hideous devil creatures. I don't care how he got here, how he was able to come back from the dead. He's just here, and I'm insane with joy in the midst of all this horror.

Deep down in my soul, my faith in my brother never wavered, never disappeared, not really, and now he's here, bigger than life, and his eyes are normal, perfectly normal. I knew it… I just knew it. Oh, thank God, they're not ball bearings anymore like the last time I saw him but green, just like mine. Just to get a glimpse of them before I die—maybe that's enough. Who fixed his eyes? I don't know, but oh, Tad, my amazing brother. My tears are falling, falling, drowning my cheeks, and all I can say is Tad over and over and over.

I cling to him like a baby, waiting for the end now, but then I look around, realizing everything's quiet. No one's moving, not even the Cancris. The humans and the Birds and even some of the ani-mals—mostly dogs (oh, and there's Schrödy)—they're all focusing on Tad and me. No doubt wondering what the hell's going on. Well, I am too.

But suddenly, Alph is between us, separating us with his ugly claws. "Technical advisory device. Reassembled. Programmed mis-sion to kill Crystal Child if not successful. Crystal Child not success-ful. TAD. Ready for kill."

I gasp, jerking my head toward my brother. This can't be.

Tad remains expressionless, as usual. "Yes. Ready for kill."

What did my brother just say? I turn to Alph, spit, "You liar. You *did* reassemble my brother. And then programmed him to kill me? So you *can* lie. I hate you, Cancris. I hate what you've done to my family, my community, my world. I don't hate my brother. He's a victim just like the rest of us."

Tad touches my arm, whispers into my ear, "Kristal need feel love right now. Or formula useless. Kristal love me? Kristal love dad?"

Holy moly, he's never asked a question with the intonation ris-ing at the end. He just asked his first human-sounding question. I turn to him. "Yes, my beautiful bro. Yes, I love you beyond words. And have you seen Dad? He's healed. He's—"

"Dad. Healed. Good. Keep feeling love, Kristal. Please. Love. You love so well."

I stare at him. He's not making sense. Or maybe he's making more sense than any human I've ever met. I glance at the Earth Clock Tower. 12:01 AM. So the day passed, and no one died. Yet. So much for prophesies. But everything is still up in the air.

Alph totally ignores me, turns his back to my brother, and raises his arm appendages to the sky. I gasp, noticing actual flesh peeking out from under the diamond—at the wrist and shoulder areas. The Cancri transformation to hybrid human has begun. His voice booms. "Cancri. TAD reassembled. Will kill girl first. Others watch. Cancris developing human emotion. Cancris will enjoy watching after Crystal Child disassembled, resume kill."

The Cancris will enjoy watching? Developing emotion? Or evolving into psychopaths? The Cancris will not give it up. Poor Earth. All my fellow human beings on Earth are next.

"*Kill.*" The robots stomp once, parroting their leader.

I can't breathe. They're ready to kill. They want Tad to kill me first. They programmed him somehow to kill me. No, no, not my Tad, not my brother. No. This can't...

Tad holds out a test tube. "Need tears."

I blink. "*Wha*—"

"Tears. Won't hurt." He places the tube on my cheek, and the wetness drips in. It's easy because my face is surprisingly drenched with the deluge of tears from the first glimpse of my so-called dead brother. I watch, beyond astonished, as he places the tube into some sort of metal case he's been clutching. It immediately forms frost, crackles, and turns foggy. Alph reaches for the box.

Tad holds out his arm to stop Alph. "No. New formula. Kill Crystal Child. Make pure water from body. Watch."

Alph stops in his tracks. Tad stands back and pulls out another device, this one like a microscope, from his breast pocket in a lab jacket. Where he got it, I have no clue. He peers through a lens at the substance in the tube. "Good. Homogeneous nucleation of droplets. Minus thirty-five Celsius."

So he's making a special death weapon or poison, just for me. And I mourned him. I welcomed him back. What a damn fool I was. He is a Cancri, still a Cancri, through and through.

He looks up from the lens and speaks in a low tone, directly in my ear. "Prediction 100 percent correct. Crystals perfect form. Time Crystal needed exactly this day, minute, second. Formed from love. Kristal's love. For brother. Perfect. One came to me. Last night."

"You mean, thee One? Your god?"

"Yes. After Alph. Needed last ingredient for successful teleport. Now..."

A tingle zings up my spine. I'm beyond crazy. Confused, I gaze as he places the entire package into a larger metal box, this one covered with lights, blinking and buzzing. It beeps like a fire alarm. So is this the weapon he will use on me? A weapon made of love? Is it more humane or less humane than the lonsdaleite corkscrew? Tad wouldn't—oh god, no, he wouldn't.

"Tad? Tad? *Tad?*" I'm screaming now so loud it must be echoing throughout the entire Kimallus Valley.

Alph keeps his inhuman eyes peeled on us, pacing back and forth, waiting, waiting for my brother to kill me. Tad spins around, facing the Cancri leader, holding the box in front of him. Then from another pocket, he lifts a huge diamond travelrod. I'll bet it's a lonsdaleite.

"Watch. I KILL GIRL. 673052."

Alph stops pacing.

Tad, Tad, Tad. I slump. "Numbers—oh no." I moan, clutching my stomach. "Killed by numbers. I will be killed by the numbers my brother is now chanting." Was he practicing all these years?

Alph takes a step toward me. I flinch. I don't understand. My parents reflexively step between Alph and me.

Dad faces Alph. "You will *not*..."

"*Dad!*"

"697763..."

"*Tad, no!*"

"9-3-8-5-8-5-2-0-3-9..."

"Please..."

"3-9-6-6-9-5-8-3..."

"Help us, Tad. No, not numbers. Help us, please, please. Look, there's Dad. Remember Dad?"

Tad's clearly not listening to me but keeps messing around with whatever contraption he has in his hands. Plus the diamond travelrod.

Alek's beside me. He takes my hand. It's ice cold.

"2-8-5-7-5-0-0..."

Alph whirls around. "No more numbers. KILL. KILL. KILL. TAD, KILL GIRL. NOW."

What? An impatient robot?

Alph booms. "No water. Hoax. *Hoax*. TAD, KILL GIRL. Then Cancris, KILL ALL on Diamond Star. Then to *Earth*. KILL ALL."

Ear-splitting roars and buzzes arise from the Cancri Army. As one, the Cancri soldiers clank on in their march of doom, toward my parents, toward me, Dr. EJ, Alek. After Tad kills me, they'll kill the rest of the Lucy contingency. Big Don frantically grabs Alph's shoulder appendages.

"No, no. Girl will give you water. But H_2O not here. Back on Cancri. Back on Cancri. Back on Cancri! MUST GO BACK TO CANCRI. You find water there."

A strange whirring emanates from Alph's head. The robot forcefully throws off Big Don's arms. Then Alph's mouth slit hisses, "You *lie*. Think Cancris stupid, do not understand lies. We did not at first. But we have learned much. Water not on Cancri. You not guard humans. You much human now. Water not on 37093. Girl lie. PROPHECY SAY CANCRIS KILL HUMANS. SEND TO VOID FOR ETERNITY. CANCRIS WILL CONTINUE. DISASSEMBLE ALL."

Alph shoves Big Don, and even though Alph's smaller and at least a head shorter, Big Don stumbles back a step. Alph's weapon begins spinning wildly, buzzing like a million raging bees. Now the Cancris are only half a football field away, nearing the Earth Clock Tower around which we stand. Alph turns off his weapon to address his army while pointing to Big Don. "KILL Cancri traitor first after Crystal Child."

I faintly hear Alek say, "Good try, Big Don," but the *thud, thud, thud* drumbeat precision of their death march now drowns out everything. Thousands of londsdaleite corkscrews are now pointing toward my neck, my chest, my stomach. Human screams mingle with the Birds' screeching as the londsdaleite boots thump, thump, thumping forward. Some people begin to scatter as Birds take to the sky. But most stay, frozen with fear. No other animals are anywhere to be found. Obviously, their owners made sure they were hidden well. General Waara and his soldiers begin to march toward the enemy even though their chances of killing just one Cancri are exactly zero. But they can't just stand by. My heart is in my throat. I'm so ashamed. I wish my Cancri water fantasy had come true so I could drown myself and disappear forever. But it will be over soon anyway. The Cancris are now too sophisticated to believe our lies. Why hasn't Tad killed me yet? Nothing's making sense. Tad's just standing there with a big diamond travelrod, a black box, and chanting his useless numbers. Is he getting ready to kill me in some grisly, creative way? Why is he stalling? I grasp Mutsi's arm, turning my head away. "Mutsi, Dad." I turn to my Cancri e fake brother. "Please, Tad. Please no numbers, Tad. That's enough. Quit the numbers, just do it, just do it, just *do it...*" My raspy frantic screams don't seem to faze him a bit.

The instruments of torture and death are upon us now, making my ears buzz; they're drilling, spinning, right toward my heart, closer, closer. I'd rather my brother kill me than them. Oh god, what am I saying? My knees melt. Someone grabs me before I hit the ground, and then a whole group of QC people grasp arms and form a human shield in front of me, but I don't want the Cancris to kill them first. I can't stand to see it, and I try to unlock their arms, and then someone else grips my arm, but I don't know who. "Tad, oh, please do it, *just do it...*"

Something catches my eye in my peripheral vision, and I look to the right. My twin has climbed onto Onni again. Onni takes off, makes one spiral turn around the clock, hovering at the top. Tad slides off, and the massive Bird rises almost vertically, circling higher and higher up into the sky until he disappears. Tad stands towering over the valley. His voice suddenly explodes over a loudspeaker. His volume even drowns out the deadly whirring and stomping of the robot army.

"FOUR, FIVE, NINE, ZERO, SIX..."

The marching suddenly grinds to a halt. All eyes, steel and human, fixate on the boy-bot at the top of the Earth Clock Tower. He pauses, then sets the mysterious black box down beside him, and with both hands, raises the giant diamond travelrod over his head, swinging it back and forth. After a few seconds, Tad brings it to a standstill, grasping it tightly with both hands. The very last number reverberates throughout the entire valley, echoing off the mountains, then blasting through the biodome itself.

"SEVEN."

An instant hush descends on the valley. Humans, Birds, Cancris stand, frozen, waiting, listening. Humans hold their breath. One second. Two seconds. The Cancris' heads are turned in my direction. They're waiting for me to die.

I glance up. The Earth Clock, oddly, still reads: 12:01 AM.

Did time stand still?

Then I remember. 12:01.

The recurring number in my dream.

Sixty-Six

・○○◦◦○◦◯◯◯○ ◯ ○○○◦◦◦○◦◦・○

The valley is deathly silent.

Suddenly, in the blink of an eye, golden laser beams shoot out like tiny bolts of lightning, disappearing just as fast. Did they—were they targeting the Canc... Then—oh god, help us—from deep inside the core of BCM30793, a great, low rumbling rises to the surface. With each second, it becomes more and more violent until our teeth are rattling, and we weave and stumble around like we're all drunk. The star's horizon looks like it's starting to tilt as the whole landscape convulses.

Hairline cracks branch out, then quicken, widening faster and faster until the ground is like parched mud. Spreading like wild-fire, the splitting ground rocks the entire Kimallus Valley. Then a pinkish-gray dust wave explodes, rolling through the valley like a tsunami, engulfing all in its path—Cancri, Bird—everything until it totally obscures the view, rising up, up until it joins the crimson Lucy sky, where jagged streaks of lightning flicker and flash among the stars. Only when I hear screams and thundering footsteps do I awaken from my brain fog. I can't see a thing.

I cup my eyes, squinting upward. Lightning flashes as I watch the sky turn from crimson to dark-indigo, streaked with jagged rib-bons of glowing coral. Another deafening blast spews more dust clouds, and columns of smoke rise, converging into yet another blan-ket of smoke, layer upon layer, hundreds of feet into the thick, savage air. Did a bomb just detonate? Did the Cancris steal our explosives? Is there more to come?

I sink to my knees, arms over my head. Whoever was holding me up is gone. Then I feel a grasp on one side. It's Mutsi, followed by Alek's strong arms on the other, and the three of us huddle together. The smoke starts to clear a little, and I make out the faint outline of Dr. EJ, his arm around my father. I push away from Mutsi and Alek, reaching for Dad, and he reaches for me and I fall into his arms, into his bear hug, an actual bear hug, and I'm wailing in joy and terror at the same time. We're all coughing and choking from the massive cloud, but I'm in the shelter of my father's arms once more, so I'm ready to die now. He keeps one arm around me and, with the other, wipes the grit and smoke from my face for several minutes. I finally raise my head and take a look around.

What in God's name is happening? Where's Tad?

And then I hear a chorus of moans, cries, too primal for words, rising from the valley floor—some shrill, some low, all fearful. We can do nothing but wait and hang on to one another. Is the entire star collapsing? Is this the destiny prophesied? If some entity in the past knew this would happen and that nothing would stop it, why bother to warn us?

But it had predicted a girl—a Crystal Child—would be the answer to this horrific nightmare. Why have I failed so miserably? All around is chaos: the pungent odor of sulfur, people crying, groaning, wailing, rolling and clouds of smoke still obscuring the air and sky. My life and the lives of all those I have loved for thirteen years will be momentarily snuffed out on this strange, cold star, so far from home. A sob erupts from somewhere deep in my solar plexus, and then I'm screaming, screaming into this eternal hell.

No. Shut up. Think, Kris! You're still alive. For the love of God, for the last time, there must be a magic incantation, a formula, an algorithm to stop this madness. Algorithm? Who am I kidding? If Dr. EJ and his brilliant team couldn't figure it out, what makes me think I can do any better? I don't even know what an algorithm is exactly. No. We're at the end of the road. All for nothing. That display was just for starters. I know these Cancris, and I'm starting to know them better and better. They are evolving into a nightmare of the worst kind.

Mutsi joins Dad and me. I cling to my parents for dear life. We're all helpless. It's beyond excrutiating, waiting for death. I know it will be painful. Lonsdaleite corkscrew diamond weapons are poised to thrust into—oh god, just let it be quick. We've already suffered so much at the hands—the claws—of the Cancris. My lungs are filling rapidly with smoke, and like everyone else, I'm coughing so hard I think my insides will erupt. I brace myself. *Hold on tight. Keep bracing. It's coming, any second now…*

I let go a tiny bit. Why is this taking so long?

Time elapses into a surreal stillness that drags on and on. We wait for something else even more cataclysmic to blow us apart; to finish us off. We're waiting for that first puncture, whip, stab of agonizing pain. It doesn't come. More time passes. Moans begin to soften. Dust begins to settle. I detect shapes, people moving, then the familiar caws and clicking of the Birds. Finally the air clears enough for some visibility on the ground, and I blink, squint, cup my hands over my eyes. My gaze follows the last of the plumes up to the sky and the mountains beyond. Then I turn to the vast flat plain, the Kimallus Valley, where the evil Cancris have been marching, all six thousand plus strong, just moments before. I blink.

They're gone. Every single one.

Holy moly. I whip my head behind, in front, up, down. Every last Cancri soldier, every corkscrew weapon, every lonsdaleite diamond suit vanished. I do a slow three-sixty. The humans and the Birds—we're all still here. As far as I can tell, we're all alive and unharmed, except for a few scrapes and a layer of dust, making us resemble ghouls rising from ancient graves. I cannot believe what I'm seeing.

Everyone's coughing out stardust, teeny bits of diamond. How rich our lungs must be. I feel a hand on my shoulder. Alek. He gestures. I look up at the Earth Clock Tower. Tad's still standing at the top. My brother is covered with dust too, but otherwise, he seems fine. He's looking straight down into my eyes, something he's rarely done.

"Kristal. Okay? Okay?"

I can't speak, so I nod. The four of us—Dad, Mutsi, Alek, and I—huddle together, and in that moment, I realize we might survive after all. I check out Tad's face. He's smiling, actually smiling one of his half smiles, so rare, so beautiful, and now so triumphant. He didn't kill me. Of course, he didn't. He wouldn't. Our eyes are still locked. Amid the chaos, it's a magical moment, maybe the most magical the universe has ever experienced. I cup my hands around my mouth and tilt my head upward.

"Tad?"

"Kristal."

"Tad, what have you done?"

He doesn't answer. The crowd is assembling at the bottom of the Earth Clock Tower, their heads searching in all directions as they realize the Cancris have completely disappeared. As they gaze upward in wonder, my twin turns a full circle, surveying the scene below. Then slowly he raises his arms, eyes to the sky, half smile widening into a full, actual, triumphant grin. No one breathes. No one moves. Then in a jubilant, almost *human* voice, he announces to the valley, the sky, animals, humans—the entire universe:

"*Five Star Pictures Presents!*"

Sixty-Seven

February 6, 2027

"Oh, Tad. Tad. Tad." I burst into laughter—sweet, ordinary laughter. I'd almost forgotten what that felt like. Mutsi's eyes widen as she recognizes Tad's special phrase I explained to her at his so-called funeral service. Dad's just plain laughing. He's heard that phrase a million times before. And Dad is as surprised as I am at Tad's expressive voice. With all the reprogramming and rebooting, he must be evolving further as well. I'm beyond amazed.

I hear a loud flapping of wings and look up. Onni sets down his giant bulk at the top of the tower. Tad climbs up, and they're off, circling the tower once more before they land on the ground below. My hero brother stands in front of us—Dad, Mutsi, Alek, and me. Dad tousles Tad's hair—a first. "Five Star Pictures, I'll say, buddy. What a production! What did you just do?"

Tad's smile is brighter than I've ever seen. "Kristal saved all. Just like prophecy predict."

What? I frown. "I saved—no, no, Tad. I didn't save anyone. *You* got rid of the Cancris. They're gone. You saved us. But how? And how are you here? On Cancri e, I saw you in a...a—?" I can't say it. But he seems to catch my drift.

"Cancri disassemble me. Then came back last night and reassemble. Say they got idea from you. I am reassembled because of you. You not forget me. Two say you ask for me. You love me. But they insert program to kill you. I recognize program. If no water production by midnight, program 1938576 set to initiate."

542

Alek interrupts. "But, Tad, why? They had the most sophisticated weapons in the universe. Why would they program you to be the one to—"

Tad is nodding. "Two talk about Kristal's own DNA extinguish her. Something about ironic culmination of prophecy. Don't understand."

Alek's jaw drops as he shakes his head. We catch each other's eyes. "I knew it. They're evolving faster than I could ever have predicted. Unfortunately, their evolution may be derailing into something more evil than I could ever have imagined and perhaps even the author of the prophecy could have predicted. I don't even think they wanted it this way. Oh, man, not good. We could have learned so much from one another."

Tad is still nodding. "Evil. Reptilian area evolving faster than prefrontal cortex. Yes. I evolve differently. After Two leave, One appear."

Alek scratches his head. "One?" Suddenly his eyes widen. "You mean *thee One* who built the Cancris but has never appeared?"

"Yes. Looked human. Not Cancri. Except for...for..."

"For what?"

"Steel eyes."

"Steel *eyes*?"

"Said eyes destroyed in battle. But he made new eyes programmed to transmit images to occipital lobe. Can see better than average human."

Alek is staring off into the smoky atmosphere. "I, uh, wow, I don't know what to say."

"*One* tell me how to override murder algorithm. Will not kill sister. Cannot kill sister. Kristal teach me everything good human. Much more human than Cancris now. Rules. For ethical humans. Cannot kill. Kristal teach me programs for play. Imagine. In forest. Daydream. Pretend. Make pictures in my head. Like Albert Einstein. Like Thomas Edison. With Cancri programs, I research algorithms for Cancri teleport. Research planets like Earth. Research new quantum concept with time crystals per *One's* instruction. For travel to work, time had to be perfect. One said new discovery since prophecy.

Needed to change time. *One* second off. Time crystals not yet discovered when prophecy written. *One* told me."

"Time crystals?"

"Yes. Theory proposed in 2012, 2017 materials fitting this category discovered offering promise for creation of clocks more accurate than any before. I research new information. Found prophecy 0.94 seconds slow. *One* help me to fix so prophecy stay on track."

"Wow, Tad. Uh, whew. Glad you and, uh, *One* could figure it out and glad you two met. Where is this *One* now?"

"Disappeared. All very difficult, complex to understand, but I keep going because Kristal teach me sisu. With Cancri algorithm and analysis, plus Kristal's love and imagination, I was able to make perfect water crystals for Cancri evolution. I keep going, think of Kristal. Think like Kristal. Love like Kristal. Sisu like Kristal. But greatest of these—love."

At that last familiar phrase, we stare at each other slack-jawed like total idiots. He's said more in the last two minutes than in all past years combined. Yep. Love is the greatest. And how I love my brother at this very moment and all moments past.

Alek says, "That's great, Tad. Go on. So where are the Cancris now?"

"Planet Kepler-452b. July 23, 2015, discovery. Orbit star six billion years old. Fourteen hundred light-years from Earth. Constellation Cygnus. Year 385 days. Temperatures suitable for water. Much water available. But to make sure good water available, I make water pure with Kristal tears so will multiply without distortion. Maybe will nourish Cancri toward human soul for good, not evil. With love, perfect crystal, perfect water. Surface on Kepler rocky. Cancris be happy there. May need change name from Cancris to Keplers. Now time to fix water on Earth and everything else."

We all burst out laughing. How right he is. Alek is scratching his head.

"Tad, wait. You mean—you figured out a way to teleport them to another planet—one with water that they can live on, that they can *thrive* on? So they're still alive?"

"Yes. Thanks to Kristal. Kristal's love. Kristal's tears. Could not reassemble if Kristal forget me and not ask Two for me. Could not get Kristal tears if she had no love for me. If she not glad to see me. Could not picture Cancri teleport in mind if Kristal not teach me imagination. But she love me. Teach me. So Kristal saved Cancris. Just like prediction in prophecy."

I'm still baffled but starting maybe to get an inkling. "My tears? My—"

"With love—water crystals turn beautiful, symmetrical. So beginning of evolution for Cancris now in good form on Kepler. Type of formation very critical to Cancri survival. Now need go quickly—perfect crystal for water on Earth. Water dying. Human survival with crystal. Best vibration. Best frequencies. Crystal and love will save.

A picture comes to my mind. The embroidered quote in Mutsi's pod.

Crystals are living beings at the beginning
of creation. (Nikola Tesla)

I'm about to ask Mutsi a question when a colossal cheer interrupts my thoughts. All around me an impromptu celebration of hugs and tears has broken out as the shock wears off and realization sets in. We're free—free of the fear, of the lack of water, of the Cancris. We're awash in relief and astonishment. Even though it was one second off, which only Tad understands, it worked. It was true after all. The prophecy has been fulfilled.

I glance to my right. Pappa and Mummo are sitting on a large rock, Mummo's head on Pappa's shoulder. To my left, my parents are in a deep embrace, sobbing. With his thumb, my father is wiping tears and diamond dust from my mother's eyes. Mutsi kisses Dad's lips, his face, his neck. Normally, I turn away from PDAs. But this is different—a miracle—so I just bask in the joy at my parents' blissful moment. Then they turn to us—Tad and me—and hold out their arms. I race to them just like that chubby little toddler with the red hat long ago. Tad holds back a little but then steps right up, touches my father on the sleeve.

"Dad. Sorry I work for Cancris. No choice. I am not just machine. I love you, Dad."

My father erupts with a half-choke, half-sob. "I'm so sorry, son, and grateful." And then he grabs Tad, enveloping him in one of his famous bear hugs—a hug that in the past would have been reserved only for me. But I am only too happy to share with him and Mutsi. Mutsi and I join him—a family group hug, a type of hug I never, ever would have imagined. Pappa and Mummo join us. Dad hugs each in turn, then says: "Voitto, Lumi, I remember you. I'm remembering more and more each day. I...uh...also remember that horrible night when I kidnapped my own daughter." His eyes alight on Pappa's arm, the long red gash still glaringly visible. He closes his eyes, shaking his head. "Voitto, I... I just..."

Pappa waves him off. "We know, Pauli, you were completely compromised by that infernal Cancri implant in your brain. You couldn't possibly—"

"No, not completely. But I do recall a command transmitted into my brain to kill both of you as Kristal and I left your house. I did pull off two shots, but somehow I recall overriding their command. To think that I almost..." He shivers, shakes his head.

More hugs, more tears. "All's well that ends well, eh?" My pappa chuckles. So the greatest of these is love. With that, as his weapon, Dad actually could outwit the Cancris. He was able to move the gun a tiny bit so it didn't hit them. That, in itself, was a miracle.

Dr. EJ steps forward, his lab coat all sparkly in soot-like dirt and diamond dust, like he'd rolled in the mud, then shaken a whole vial of glitter down his front. "Don't you see, Kreestal? You did what the prophecy predicted."

"No, you saw Tad, my twin."

Zola Khumolo spies us, her eyes wide, and she turns to me, embracing me tightly. "Our Crystal Child. The Cancris could not envision your DNA, plus your love, would go way beyond Tad's ability to transmit location signals. With your DNA, plus your nurturing forming his essence, Tad evolved into someone human the Cancris couldn't even fathom. Tad *is* you. You gave Tad the ability to develop empathy, along with experiences to enhance his creativity like so many of our most celebrated inventors and artists. Daydreaming, being different from the crowd, thinking outside the box—you know, all that divergent, creative ADD thinking they call a handicap—you were so skilled at it you were able to teach Tad. Then even when all hope seemed lost, you still asked for your brother. You begged for him. If you hadn't, Tad would still be in that bin on Cancri—lost and forgotten. But your fierce, undying love for him ultimately saved us all."

I can't quite wrap my head around this yet. I was not some magical prophesied being designed to formulate a complex algorithm for robot survival. No, I was just being—well, me—*awfully dumb*. Wait. You know, I don't think I'll listen to Jackson Hynes in my head anymore. Taking a few big breaths, I cough it out then turn toward the clock. Staring up at its magnificent face, I watch the seconds still ticking away, as though nothing cataclysmic had just happened. I'll need some time to process it all. And most of the quantum way-over-my-head stuff Tad did I will never be able to comprehend. But one thing never changed. I knew it all along. Even when my head was lining up all the undeniable facts, my gut just wouldn't accept them. We're twins, after all—real twins sharing the same DNA, the same family, the same memories, and the same love. And maybe some sort of quantum connection science has yet to discover.

I turn. "Hey, Alek, what do you—" I thought he was beside me, but he's gone. Where did he go? Oh, there he is—in deep conversation with Dr. EJ. They're using terms and vocabulary over my head, something about logistical priorities. Alek sees me staring, comes over, and takes my hands in his. We're both grinning at each other like fools. No words needed. All of a sudden, Alek's face clouds over. He glances left, right, then all around the valley. I follow his eyes. "What?"

"Big Don."

"Big Don? Where is he?"

"He was right next to me when everything exploded. But I haven't seen him since."

Alek pulls Tad over. "Tad? How did your algorithm work to make sure only the Cancris were teleported to Kepler?"

"Very complicated."

"I'm sure it was. But, I mean, how could the algorithm be so selective?"

"Each entity must have certain percentage of Cancri metal—64 percent threshold."

Alek's shoulders droop. "Big Don was 66 percent the last time we measured. His humanity, his brain were growing in incredible ways, but his body, not a priority, still too much metal and microchip."

Tad lowers his head. "Sorry. Did not know about Big Don. He was friend?"

"Yes. He—well, of course, you couldn't have known. Tad, it's okay. You did great. So how can we get to Kepler and rescue Big Don?"

"Not possible. Algorithm only works for 64 percent and above metal. Humans cannot use algorithm. I cannot use algorithm. Too much blood and flesh now. And algorithm deleted."

"*Deleted?*"

"Yes. My brain noticed starting to shut down. Running slower with so much data. Had to delete and wanted to delete. Did not think we would need."

"Okay, sure, buddy. I understand you'd have to get rid of it. Hey, no worries. It's fine. He...he probably needs to be there anyway." Alek turns his back to Tad and walks a few steps in the other direction, sniffing and wiping his eyes with the back of his hand.

I follow, the lump in my throat almost shutting off my air supply.

Alek whispers into my ear, "Big Don will have to get back into their good graces if they don't waste him first. That will take a hell of a lot of creative thinking." Alek stops, eyes blinking rapidly. Taking a deep breath, then coughing it out, he continues. "If they truly are evolving into psychopaths, he needs to find a good place to hide. But I hope he finds a way to reset their evolving brains. Maybe with your perfect crystal water, as Tad described, plus his smart and big human heart, he will be able to lead them into a new era, make them more human—the empathetic, compassionate human type. He'd be such a damn good role model, if I do say so my…" his voice cracks.

Poor Alek. Don't know what to say. I let out a breath. "He'll be fine, Alek. You've taught him well." I hesitate then put my hand on his shoulder.

We both turn and gaze at the scene before us. The crowd is laughing, hugging, and buzzing with chatter. Some are dancing triumphant little jigs in the sand. The Diamond Star soldiers have all shed their cumbersome diamond armor and are now joining the celebration. A huge contingency of Birds is flying in formation—some kind of design. Oh, 1201! The exact time of liberation from the Cancris and the recurring number in my dreams. Huh. Was I psychic with those crazy dreams? I'll probably never know. Oh, and there's Schrody, frantically giving himself a tongue bath. Alek sees him at the same time I do and winces. "Hope all that stardust he's eating will turn into one big hairball he can cough out." Yuck. I hope so too. I close my eyes, letting the glorious, joyful sounds wash over me, offering thanks for every person, every Bird, every cat, every hope, every second ultimately leading to this one-in-a-billion happy ending. Or so it seemed there for a while.

Dr. EJ's coming toward us. "Ms. Kreestal. How amazing. Eet's complicated, but you and Tad are a perfect example of one of our most recent new fields of science—epigenetics."

"Epi—what?"

"Epigenetics. We now know that genes can be switched on and off due to certain experiences in life. You gave Tad both your wonderful DNA and the right experiences in life, so he was able to express exactly what was needed to fulfill the prophecy. You see, the modification een gene expression ees able to make changes en lieu of the alteration of the genetic code eetself, so—"

Zola gently squeezes Dr. EJ's arm. "Hey, Doc. Science and psychology classes later. Time to celebrate."

Dr. EJ throws his head back, laughing louder and longer than I've ever heard him. Then I realize he's kind of laughing and crying at the same time. He wipes his face with his sleeve, smearing his cheek with star glitter and dirt. "You're right, dear Zola."

Someone thrusts the microphone in Dr. EJ's face. He grabs it. "People and Birds of the Diamond Star, oh, and uh, all animals…" Ah, there's Dr. Kikuchi. We all turn, smile at her, and nod. How could we forget our furry friends? Dr. EJ continues. "Kreestal and Tad, together, have fulfeeled the prophecy. Eet has come to pass, or as the prophecy itself said, 'Let peace reign.' Indeed."

He pauses, gazing upward into the Lucy sky.

"Thank you, BPM 37093, our Lucy in the sky with diamonds. You were a godsend—a refuge in our greatest time of need, and we shall always be grateful. I'm sure we will be visiting you many more times in the future. But eet's been way too long. Our own planet needs us desperately." He turns to the crowd. "So what are we waiting for? Let Project EarthHeal resume! Start packing, everyone."

The crowd's thunderous roar explodes toward the heavens. I look around me—Dad, Mutsi, Tad, Pappa, Mummo, Alek, Dr. EJ, Dr. Bob Smith, Dr. Khumolo, Blanca, Jaak, Onni, Haukka—and the rest of the Quantum Community. We're all here, together. Oh, and Schrodinger, all sparkly-dusty, still giving himself a bath. That's going to be one big hairball. I smile. This whole adventure wasn't a dream after all. The dream was Montana. The reality is the Quantum Community. *My* community.

For the first time in eleven years, I'm going home.
Ihme.

Earth

Sixty-Eight

April 9, 2027

I'm early. Leaning against a thick wooden post on the massive wrap-around porch of the council building, I watch as twilight descends on the valley. The sun will soon disappear behind the pearl-white mountains of the Quantum Community. I don't think I'll ever take our sun for granted again; nor will I ever tire of the view here—the contrast of dark-green pine and spruce among sparkling white mountain caps, the rolling foothills draped with brown and golden flora indigenous to northern Finland. I breathe it all in, remembering my mother's words that first fateful day, "And I would have all diamonds turn to snowflakes." I smile. The diamonds will indeed be used to turn Earth's water back into snowflakes and save the Earth from rising temperatures. I love Earth. I'm ready to help in any way I can.

This evening, it's cold, but not frigid like when we first returned the second week in February. Still, my nose drips, and I can't stay out here too much longer. Alek said by June we'll be seeing a hell of a lot more daylight. Oh, here come Mummo and Pappa, followed by Mutsi, Dad, and Tad. I wave. They return the greeting, all smiles.

More people begin to emerge from their cabins, strolling along the pathways forged by huge snow machines, piles of glistening snow on either side. In February, when we returned, they were as tall as me. Now, in April, I realize they've shrunken to waist-high. Spring in northern Finland is here—almost.

Suddenly, the brass bell clangs—once, twice, three times, signaling the start of the meeting. Lordy, it's loud. I instinctively cover my ears with my Snowlife mittens with silk gloves underneath. The Finns sure know how to make warm outerwear. I drop my hands, even though the bell is still reverberating. At first, they didn't think they'd get it up and working again after a decade of disuse. They found it hanging by a frayed rope from the rafters on the porch. But after replacing the rope and polishing the bell, it was as though we'd never left. Dr. EJ said it was a symbol of our unity and was eager to use it for our first official meeting back from Lucy, scheduled on February 9, 2027, only two days after our return. Although we were crazy busy getting settled in, we dropped everything for our top priority—honoring the 254 QC members martyred in 2016, and the 411 Diamond Star soldiers killed in the battle on Cancri last month. Oh, and Cuckoo. Poor Cuckoo. Right before we left the Diamond Star, Dr. Kikuchi wrapped her in a little cotton cloth and teleported her home, holding her tenderly in her arms.

In February, it had been too cold to hold the ceremony outside the church as we would have liked, surrounded by the mountains and pines. So our ceremony went virtual, held inside the assembly/dining hall in the council building. As each fallen one was announced, his or her name was displayed in the center of the huge screen above the podium with a real-time video of professional arborists in parkas and gray expedition gloves planting small seedlings and setting down a plaque in front for each soul lost. Exactly 665 baby birch trees now encircle the rustic little church and slope up the mountainside. And when the video showed the workers setting a small cuckoo clock headstone in front of the last tree, no amount of staring at the ceiling would keep my tears at bay. Cuckoo came to symbolize all the sorrow we had to endure at the hands, er, claws of the evil Cancris.

Our grief over the lost QC citizens was excruciating enough. But we also said farewell to the Birds as they were slated to return to their natural state within the week. The Birds and the QC had made a pact at the very beginning. It was only proper, as Mother Nature never intended Birds to become like humans. But apparently, someone thought Birds, with their vast knowledge far superior in many ways to humans, could be our allies (at least for a while), sharing their insight in bringing about Earth's healing. And they turned out to be amazingly helpful. They alone knew it all; they tried to warn us even when we weren't listening. But now, Dr. EJ made the decision that the Birds had been through enough. He'd never expected they would have to be in such an unnatural state for such a long time. Their specific Lucy purpose had come to a close. Pappa and Dr. EJ were set to make good on their promise to change the Birds back to their original state or just free those who were not tampered with, mainly the songbirds. Extracting human DNA entails a formula they've vowed never to share, lest it get into the wrong hands. I understand completely and wish them well.

Still, I sometimes selfishly wish the Birds were still with us. And I especially wonder if Onni will remember our special times. But we all kept a brave face during the ceremony honoring their contributions and their sacrifice then hugging them goodbye. Only then did our brave faces melt into tears. Later that evening, my grandfather, Dr. Yua Kikuchi, Dr. EJ, Dr. B, and Tanimilua, the First Nation Bird expert my mother told me about in the passageways, whisked them off to an undisclosed location. What was done there, well, I didn't ask. I saw a bird yesterday I could have sworn was Rawol, perched about two-thirds up Sylvester, Alek's special pine tree. When I looked again, the bird, or whatever had been in my imagination, had vanished. We do, however, still hear quite a variety of chirps and songs as we go about our daily business. I see people smiling, pointing, waving, placing bird feeders and suet out to attract them. Birds are so special. How could the Cancris ever think of harming one feather on Cuckoo's soft little body? Oh, yeah. They're without souls—except for Tad. And Big Don, may he be at peace on his new home—Planet Kepler.

After this first ceremony, Mutsi and Dad reluctantly agreed to give me some alone time, making it clear if I weren't home in twenty minutes, they would track me down with their comcards' GPS systems. I understood. I didn't want to end up with missing toes like Alek, just in case I fell into a ditch or something. But I had to set aside some time to be by myself. Hiking up a small foothill behind the chapel, I found a hidden cove nestled among reeds and bushes about half a mile from the cabins. Perfect.

Despite the cold, I plopped myself down onto a snow-covered rock, just as I had that first fateful day I met the Diamond Lady, aka Mutsi. Every scene thereafter flew by in my mind—from that morning to now. It felt good to cry. Well, actually, to scream it all out—the grief for all the beautiful souls lost, for the unspeakable trauma everyone had to endure, including the Birds I had come to love and revere. But also, for the sheer joy—QC's safe return to Earth and for my newfound family, alive and reunited at long last. *Ihme, ihme,* as the Finns would say. Yes, a miracle.

At first, the contrast between the crushing sadness and indescribable elation overwhelmed me, and I found myself bursting into tears at the weirdest moments or snapping at my wonderful new family for no reason at all, which horrified me. I thought about the slur Jackson Hynes shouted to my face that day—*bitch*. I wasn't a bitch then, but I sure have been lately. Mutsi noticed and sent me over to talk to Dr. Khumolo. Her cabin is close by, on the way to the council building. Most of the cabins have floor-to-ceiling windows all around, so the view is always with us, infusing our souls with a sense of calm wonder, not to mention the built-in saunas. Dr. Khumolo was already settled in. Her cabin reminded me of Mutsi's pod on the Diamond Star with its crystals, rainbow hues, and simple Zen-like furnishings. She built a fire, fixed some jasmine tea in a normal-sized cup this time, and we chatted. She always made me feel she had all the time in the world and that I was special to her. She helped me review and practice all the techniques she'd taught me for how to process trauma, grief, sadness, and fear. Then she taught me how to literally shake out all the trauma, much like animals in the wild. That was surprisingly helpful. She assured me my intense, crazy emotions weren't crazy at all and that my bitchiness was a combination of the immensity of my recent experience and, well, the thing that happens to many girls when they make the transition to womanhood. She said, "But don't ever call it bitchiness. I prefer the phrase *healthy self.* I must have looked puzzled, as she explained, "You're just expressing your emerging assertiveness as your brain explodes with new, mature

growth." Then, she and Mutsi taught me some "talking tools" to use
to assert myself appropriately, without becoming aggressive. I was
turning into someone I didn't even know, but they talked me down
as only they can. At last, the burden of raising a daughter alone has
been lifted from Dad's shoulders. And none too soon. I'm sure he's
as relieved as I am. Funny. I always thought I would look up all that
girl stuff on the internet when my time came. Now I have both my
mother and Dr. Khumolo. Together, they assured me I would settle
down in time. They were right. Now I feel mostly bathed in peace
and gratitude. The whole QC Community and the surrounding natural beauty is like one humungous recoup room.

The landscape here is dotted with cabins. I never knew there
could be such an array of styles, but all are eco-friendly. The wood
is all Finnish pine from sustainably managed forests. Most cabins
have open floor plans, fireplaces, huge picture windows and saunas
but still boast their own unique personalities, from the traditional
gable to small flat roofs. Dad said each family either moved back into
their own cabin or chose from those cabins abandoned by the lost
ones. Each of those cabins has a wreath on the door. Some homes
have floor-to-ceiling windows to showcase the magnificent views
all around, with wooden plank floors and high-stone fireplaces, not
much metal here. Now I know why Dad hated metal. It was not his
preference anyway, and it came to be associated with the Cancris.
Yuck. Can't even say the name without shuddering. Hope they're
happy on Kepler, so happy that they will never have anything to do
with Earth again. Tad assures us they won't. He says Kepler is so far
away they don't have the formula—or reason—to return.

Our cabin—the one I lived in with my parents until that horrible day in 2016—is a combination of rustic and contemporary. It's
all wood, stone, and glass with a built-in sauna. Although the cabin
here will need some updating, I loved it at first glance. I think a part
of me remembers it's my real home. I can feel it in my bones. Even
so, it has the feel of being on vacation 24-7.

However, I admit living with both parents and Tad has been an
adjustment. We don't have the space or luxuries we did in Montana.
Our cabin's main room is pretty zen—a long rectangle with a fire-

place in the middle, dark pine wide-plank floors, and huge picture windows looking out on a miniforest and stone garden surrounding a small pond. I do a lot of gazing these days. It has only one bath, which is a little annoying at times. But it does have a small sauna, which feels wonderful—the rocks, the continuous steam, the wooden bench. I can just feel the Cancri and Diamond Star dust whooshing out my pores as I become an earthling once more. There's a community sauna building next to the main council building. I see Dr. EJ, Dr. B, Alek, sometimes my dad, and mostly other men trotting over there to share their stories and talk shop. They try to dissuade Dr. EJ from his *lakka* as alcohol and heat don't mix for the elderly. He just laughs it off. And then dad tells me they cook some kind of vegetarian sausages over the coals. We're meatless here. I learned a huge study at Oxford University found that just omitting meat is one of the best ways to help the planet. That's why Dad never let us eat bison burgers and frowned on any other type of meat. It was always vegetable soup, pancakes, blueberry soup—just as it is here. I've never missed the meat. Whatever floats your boat I guess. I'm just glad Dr. EJ's wish—sitting in the sauna with *lakka* in hand swapping stories—came true. And he certainly has a lot of stories to swap.

But even though Mutsi and Dad keep the steam going in our small sauna, they're proud they've already greatly reduced our family's carbon footprint. Hepa filters are everywhere. All the cabins have solar panels, and we're using reverse osmosis for clean water. We cook with cast-iron pans in our functional but tiny kitchen. Plastic is a big fat no-no. Even our milk is in glass bottles. One of my chores is mixing our eco-friendly cleaner—liquid organic soap, borax, vinegar, and lemon juice to make it smell fresh. Then I haul it in a wagon to hand out to several of our neighbors. They, in turn, usually give us a loaf of Nissua or Pulla bread. I joke that I'm an official Finnish bread addict. These delicious loaves have even managed to win out over pecan pancakes, although I would never turn down the pancakes either. I think Tad's taste is evolving too. He never seemed to be very hungry. Now he seems starved half the time.

Bathroom inconvenience and chores aside, my life has been enormously enriched. Finally, Dad is rid of that sad, faraway look he (and I) had to endure for a decade. It's been totally replaced by big fat grins with a frequent twinkle in his eye, reminding me of a tiny star—perhaps a mote of diamond dust left over from big bang number 2, as we now call it—the moment when Tad blasted the Cancris to Kepler. Another surprise—Tad's human essence is evolving. It's such a hoot to hear him speak with more expression now. I keep waiting for the obligatory number at the end. It never comes. Of course, it doesn't. He's not communicating with the Cancris anymore. His sentences mirror his very own thoughts, nothing more.

And Mutsi—her presence is so vital I can't imagine how I ever lived without her. We're making new memories every day, just hanging out, doing our chores, laughing, and singing (she's teaching me more Finnish childhood songs she said I missed out on). We joke and tease a lot. One morning, she said, "I'm keeping my promise." I was mystified—what promise?—until she banged around in the kitchen and produced all the utensils and ingredients to bake spoon cookies. She didn't quite make sixty dozen. But the six dozen she made were plenty. "I'm paying your dad back for all those years I got out of baking for the school bake sale." As we worked together in the kitchen, we joked about setting them on the kitchen table and eating them all at once. But, of course, reason prevailed, and we ended up storing most of them in the freezer. Blanca's now waggling her finger every chance she gets, reminding us about the perils of too many simple carbs. So Dad's making more veggie soup. I can't complain. We do sneak our share of spoon cookies though.

Somehow, with the help of Dr. EJ and his friend, Brima, from Sierra Leone, Dad got his apron back. Dr. EJ and Brima, and one of Brima's FBI friends traveled to Dolcany, concocted a story making the police believe Dad had kidnapped me, taken Tad and me to a remote location, and murdered us, then committed suicide. They even produced hard evidence. Yuck. I didn't ask. Gruesome, yes, but Dr. EJ assured us this way no one would ever try to find us. On one of his first mornings in our cabin, when we were still raking down cobwebs, Dad surprised Mutsi in the kitchen. When she saw him in that ratty old apron flipping pancakes, Mutsi collapsed on the kitchen bench, sobbing and hooting at the same time. All of a sudden, we heard music coming from Dad's iPod 6—"I Feel Lucky," an ancient country tune I guess was one of their favorites. Dad just grabbed her, and they danced around the kitchen to Tad's and my amusement. And well, I admit—the PDAs embarrassed us a little, but I have a feeling we better get used to it.

And I love how Dad's so much more affectionate with Tad too. They play chess almost every night. Tad hasn't lost a game yet. They not only high-five, but Dad's taught Tad some kind of high-five/fist-bump combo. This warms my heart to no end.

Even though our house is smaller, my whole world seems bigger. I never considered how the entire planet—trees, mountains, deserts, oceans, atmosphere—is home to us. I came back to my own world, where I used to believe diamonds were precious and water was cheap and abundant. Since living in the QC, I've learned clean water is scarce for at least 40 percent of the world's population. Seriously, here on earth. I had no clue. But the QC has vowed to place H_2O as its top priority. Actually, keeping the planet alive is number 1, and H_2O is their first objective, along with reducing carbon emissions to zero. They know what to do. They've *lived* it; they know how tortuous it is having to accept severe water shortages. We don't want anyone— ever—to be deprived of clean, fresh water.

*****

I turn, ambling into the assembly/dining hall. Long benches and tables take up most of the space, and people are settling in. Mummo, Pappa, Dad, Mutsi, and I choose a bench in the middle where we're surrounded by familiar faces like Yua Kikuchi and Zola Khomolo. This hall, inside the QC council building, is where the community informally meets, shares ideas, communes, and enjoys delicious homemade meals together—vegetable parsnip soup, cabbage rolls, *ruisleipä, mati ja uudet peru nat*—breads, cheese, potatoes. Since Dad made most of these dishes as I was growing up, I'm already right at home in the food department. Funny. I never thought to ask him what kind of ethnic dishes they were, even as my friends were gorging on microwave mac and cheese and pizza all those years.

I look around. Most everyone's here now except the Birds. Although I miss them terribly, especially Onni, I know they're in their own habitat, where they need to be. The surviving members of the QC are still here, every one of them, and will continue their work. What's surprising though, is that of the nine thousand or so who were added to the Diamond Star population, the vast majority also decided to stay on and help, secretly bringing their families on board as well. They've been staying in hotels, hostels, and homes of those who can offer extra room. The massive building project on our under-the-radar 206 acres has already begun. But instead of further draining the Earth's resources, the small city will serve as a model for sustainable living. The more we add to our think tank, the better our ideas. And Dr. EJ's in the process of adding even more; he still needs about one hundred more top experts in the fields of quantum physics, astronomy, biology, medicine, engineering, neuropsychology, and others too numerous to mention. So far, applications from over sixty countries sit on his desk. But we've been warned ad nauseum; it all has to stay top secret. Dr. EJ knows of dark forces on Earth; he calls them POPs—"profit over people megalomaniacs"—those who wouldn't blink an eye destroying all we've built just to keep their fossil fuel production humming for a few more generations before the Earth's resources are completely exhausted. But Dr. EJ and the amazing QC have implemented "think tank" round-table discussions on incorporating the "prophecy model"—that is, figuring out solutions without harming anyone. They hope that one day they can persuade the environmentally reluctant ones that there's even more prosperity to be had by changing to earth-friendly power sources—not just money but all kinds of prosperity—like the health and happiness of Mother Earth, including our children and grandchildren. Oh, and all the animals.

Speaking of animals, although the Birds are gone, good old Schrödinger made it back to Earth with the rest of us. Alek made good on his promise to feed him his favorite food—gourmet salmon pate. In fact—oh, there he is—beside Alek, in a corner, his nose buried in a fancy ceramic bowl. He hangs with Alek most of the time, although he will occasionally pop over to our cabin for some treats and a scratch behind the ears. Alek says he's already showing signs of evolving, his brain, anyway. He still looks and acts like a regular cat to me. But Alek said I'm to keep his behavioral observations a secret for now. Time will tell. Dad said the whole pet restriction thing was a lie due to strict Cancri orders. He actually loves animals and isn't allergic to anything. We might get a puppy. Woo-hoo. I'm researching Lapland lap dogs. Can't wait.

Oh, it's starting. Dr. EJ bounds up the stairs to the podium like a man ten years younger. Quickly checking something on his comcard, he adjusts the microphone on his lapel, taps it a few times, and scans his audience. The commotion starts to die down as people notice and turn toward the far side of the hall.

Sixty-Nine

"*Tervetuloa*! Leesten, everyone. I weel be speaking in English for thees meeting, weeth translation for those who need it." I look around at all those who have headsets. It's like the UN meetings in New York. I wonder how many languages Dr. EJ's speech is being translated into. I wish I could learn them all. How cool. I turn back to Dr. EJ. "We are here tonight to geeve thanks, to celebrate our eencredible good fortune, and to look toward the future, as our meession is still in full swing. We by no means are out of the woods—the Sixth Extinction ees still a possibility eef we don't act fast, and even faster now that we've been, er, waylaid for a decade. But we are ecstatic to be back in our Quantum Community, safe from an unthinkable enemy that, eleven years ago, decimated our people, destroyed much of our work, and planned a methodical and unconscionable takeover of our most precious planet. I am here tonight to say—thanks to our Crystal Children—the Cancris have been finally and utterly thwarted. The prophecy was true all along—o ye of little faith as they say—and that includes yours truly. Only the Birds knew for sure. Our intended outcome indeed came about on the promised date—off by one second—but still completely fulfilled!"

A roar echoes from floor to rafters as all rise to their feet. I'm blushing as I notice people smiling at Tad and me, some giving us air high fives and thumbs-up. Although I'm slightly flustered, at least this crowd is the opposite of the pack of wolves in Mr. Gabriel's science class, which by the way, seems eons ago. I catch my twin's eye. He catches mine and winks. Omigod. A wink?

563

Dr. EJ speaks over the commotion. "None of us would be here tonight were eet not for a very special girl lost for over a decade then found, along weeth her father and *grandparents* who were able to keep her close all those years. And our special gratitude to Voitto Kurki and Aleksi Salo, who were finally able to send a message to Lucy with their location. Your brilliance is to be commended."

"And Big Don."

Everyone turns. Alex has his hands cupped to his mouth. Dr. EJ bows his head. "Of course. Of course. Big Don. May he be well in his new home."

Surprisingly, a round of applause interrupts EJ's speech. Funny how Big Don so easily made friends despite his gruesome appearance. I find myself sighing. I really miss him. I know Alek feels lost without him. Another casualty. Dr. EJ waits until the applause dies down then says, "Ah, such incredible miracles we've seen recently. Een only a few weeks, they have brightened our lives in so many ways. Uh—not to mention Kristal's amazing twin brother, Tad. We are truly blessed to have these ceetizens join, or rejoin, our Quantum Community." More applause. I'm bursting with pride for my twin right now. What a miracle he is. I look up.

Dr. EJ is beaming at me. Uh-oh. No, no, please not the rockstar thing. I know he's mentioning me just because he has to. I don't really deserve the kudos. I didn't do anything. But he continues. "Her name had been wreeten on a mysterious scroll, found by yours truly, on our first meession to the Diamond Star. And, as the universe often works in mysterious ways, the plan was not revealed unteel the final moments. But, indeed, the prophecy was correct and just serves to underscore a preenciple we can never forget: we are all connected een thees universe. Kreestal, through the unique sharing of her DNA, combined weeth her expert nurturing of her brother, switched on the many genes necessary for her twin to express the power of human love, compassion, integrity, curiosity, creativity, and sisu—just about every positive trait one could think of. Weeth these exemplary human qualities—thanks to Kristal and vast AI knowledge, thanks to Tad— the prophecy was fulfilled. The perfect combination—brilliance and compassion! Earth finally has been spared, and we are back, stronger than ever!

The entire Quantum Community is hooting, clapping, cheering, and chanting, "Kristal! Kristal! Kristal!" and then "Tad! Tad! Tad!" I'm standing too but silently praying Dr. EJ won't ask me to say anything. I will never be good at public speaking. Please no, please no…

Something bumps my shoulder. It's my brother, confidently making his way to the podium, motioning Dr. EJ to hand over the mic. Seriously? Dr. EJ arches his eyebrows but unhooks the mic, handing it to Tad. Holding it between index finger and thumb, not bothering to fasten it to his shirt, my brother turns to the audience.

Complete silence. All eyes are on my twin. We wait.

Finally he says, "I am Tad. Kristal is my twin sister. We have same DNA. I am Cancri-manufactured, my brain might work some like Cancri. Can analyze numbers. Use logistics. Algorithms. But my heart is now human. Empathy genes switched on by Kristal. Thank you, sister, for giving me gift of feeling. For love and happiness. And even sadness is okay. And sisu. And I promise. No more numbers. For now. Please teach me more words. I am happy."

I am holding my breath.

He pauses, looking around a little hesitantly, then his arms go up in the air. "Five Star Pictures Presents!"

The hall explodes with applause, laughter, cheering. I swear the decibel level will burst all our eardrums. As Tad makes his way slowly back to his seat, hands reach out, patting him on the back, shaking his hand amidst a chorus of "Way to go," "Great job," "Amazing." Tad breaks out into a human smile again, a full smile. Where did he learn that? I've never felt so honored to share kudos with someone before. Here I am cowering, while he does the speaking, knowing full well he's not half as proficient in speech as I am. I've got a lot to learn from him. I'm so proud of my twin, my brother, part of my DNA, part of my soul. I'm glad I never gave up but trusted my gut. I look toward the podium. Dr. EJ, eyebrows raised in a question, is holding out the mic to me. Blushing, I shake my head no. Tad said it all. I need not add a thing and definitely don't want to steal his thunder, as if I could.

When everyone is again seated, Dr. EJ continues. "As I was saying before I was completely upstaged..." His eyes crinkle; people chuckle. I hope Tad understands this is a joke. I'll explain to him later. "Eleven years ago, we were in the process of saving Earth from extinction, which ees still a very real possibility. Carbon dioxide emeession levels, sea levels, toxic air, water, and earth were already grave concerns a decade ago and are even more dire today. We were minding our own business, eencorporating new technologies and methods to eemprove life on Earth when we were, shall I say, rudely eenterrupted. Although the last decade has not been a complete waste of time, eet certainly cramped our style a bit."

A few people chuckle, but most are shaking their heads, recalling the last decade.

"But we rose to the challenge. We Finnish have a word—*sisu*—wheech, loosely translated, means 'grit, toughness, determination.' We Finns don't like to talk about sisu, we just live it. But whether we come from Finland, Japan, Africa, China, India, Pakistan, the US, Mexico, or any other of the many countries of the world who are participating een our QC project, we all have sisu, every last one of us. You see, Mother Earth has no borders. We really are all one, and now, eet ees even more critical we all work together to keep our human species and indeed, *all* species, alive and thriving een a healthy world. Let's all help one another, eh?" As one, we all stand and give Dr. EJ the rousing applause he deserves. He pats the air, signaling us to be seated, then continues. "Every human, every Bird, was crucial to our survival, and each helped in hees or her way. Now that we're home, our work has become even more urgent. We must make up for lost time. Fortunately, we were spared the devastating effects of the COVID-19 virus and eets many deadly variants, for which you were all vaccinated upon our return. And we all needed time to meditate on our traumatic, decade-long journey. But then, we needed to honor those who gave their lives, and finally, we were able to give them the proper ceremony they deserved. But now, begeenning next week, we will officially resume our work. Thees meeting was called

to provide everyone weeth an overview of our many projects, some
to be resumed from 2016 and some brand-new due to new deescoveries while we were gone. Each project head will meet with me een
my office some time thees week for more deescussion. But I thought
it crucial that our community is kept abreast of these projects so we
can support one another and perhaps add your expertise. But stick
around. Following thees meeting, we weel meet and greet with our
Back to Earth Festival—an eencredible smorgasbord, followed by
dancing the night away. I, for one, weel be enjoying my *lakka* een
the sauna next door. Take your pick. We deserve every second of our
celebration! I'm so proud of…"

His last words are drowned out by an eruption of whoops,
laughter, and clapping.

Dr. EJ scans the crowd, beaming like a proud papa. Finally, he
pats the air with his hand to signal quiet, and resumes his speech.
"Alright, back to business. Here's the plan. For the next two years,
we have prioritized twenty-six projects. Although we cannot discuss
them all tonight, we can provide a brief overview with the help of
some of the project heads. We had begun some of thees work before
we had to flee to the Diamond Star. Our main drawback was funding. I persuaded Brima to come out of retirement just for a while
to help set up our covert, top secret diamond investment portfolio.
Ladies and gentlemen, funding problem solved as long as everyone
keeps their lips sealed from the ones who would do this planet harm."

Another interruption of chattering, then everyone settles as the
program begins. As I listen to each project head describe his or her
goals, I am humbled by the presence of so many incredibly intelligent
scientists. I can see it in their eyes when they speak; each has 100 percent faith in their goal's mission as they eagerly share their ideas. Dr.
EJ said the QC, quietly collaborating with experts all over the world,
will finally implement enough solutions to save the Earth from the
brink of disaster. Here I am, at the epicenter of Project EarthHeal,
among intellectual and compassionate giants. A tingle goes up my
spine. I make a pact with myself that in spite of my ADD, I'll at
least try and remember the gist of each project. Tall order, though, as
many of the terms are foreign to me.

As I listen, a quantum shift happens in my brain. Ha, quantum. Anyway, before I met the scientists of the Quantum Community, I thought I was the only one worried about the Earth's future as I confided to Alek that first and last day of my tutoring. He said something about finding my niche. He knew then; he just couldn't tell me. Well, I've found my niche, all right. I envy these accomplished adults, whose impact will be felt by millions of people almost immediately. But I can feel good that I'm doing a few planet-friendly things myself, like making my own biodegradable cleaning solution. I look forward to learning more and eventually contributing many more solutions to help Earth.

I look up to the podium. Jaak and Johann are the first speakers. They're coheading a project about improving quantum computer capability. Johann speaks gobbledygook, "Complex optimization, improve coherence times, quantum superposition, superconducting materials, quantum computers in the cloud..." and then Jaak proudly announces something about "direct air capture" by building carbon capture units. He said it's like mining the sky by sucking out and concentrating ambient carbon dioxide. The problems have been efficiency and cost effectiveness. He says if we can capture and store billions of tons of carbon dioxide from the air, we will get to net zero. I'm not sure what that means, but by the smiles and way-to-gos among the other scientists, I'm sure it's an amazing project.

Dr. Khumolo and Blanca's project is improving the lives of women and girls and, thus, the whole planet. They will be traveling to Africa, helping women and girls improve their lives through education, literacy programs, and access to funding for farming ventures so they can start their own businesses. Blanca gushes about heading up a worldwide symposium discussing reducing food waste, teaching farmers and helping them expand silvopasture, a mixture of trees and pasture, reducing carbon dioxide emissions by gigatons. I'm trying to write all this down but only hear "nutrient management," "tree intercropping," and "managed grazing." Blanca will be the person behind the curtain at the symposium to organize the speakers. That's how we stay under the radar. The more they talk, the more excited I am to join their project someday.

Then Dr. EJ introduces Dr. Pauli Makkinen. I jump. Mutsi's beaming. They're sitting the next table over, and then everyone's on their feet, applauding. Dr. EJ says he's thrilled to report Dad's gotten a clean bill of health and is ready to fully forge ahead on a project he'd started back in 2016—clean energy, specifically tidal and wave energy technologies, and developing large-capacity storage for solar power in areas with limited daylight. He also will be working with MIT on a prototype device that incorporates MOF 801, or zirconium fumarate, which has a high affinity for water. "When people think of solar, they think electricity. But soon, we'll also think about water abundance. *Water abundance*—what a beautiful phrase." Everyone murmurs agreement. He then goes on to discuss boosting collection of sunlight in solar panels through a new compound lens within liquid crystals. When he says the word *crystals*, he winks at me. Finally, I know what my dad does for a living, kind of. Then a long pause as he silently scans the people, the windows, raising his eyes to the ceiling. Uh-oh. Is he still…? You could hear a pin drop. He lowers his eyes to the audience, fixating on Tad, then me. "For eleven years, I was a Cancri prisoner of war." He looks right into my eyes. "A bad dad, right, Krissie?" I shake my head. People around me show their confusion, but I know. We used to laugh at that phrase, but now we both know the truth. It was no laughing matter. Dad continues. "I owe my life to Dr. Kurki here and my child…my *children*"—his eyes rove the crowd, finally zeroing in on Tad—"Love you both. And… and to my…my beautiful wife, Myrakka, I'm just so…so very… sorry…" He knows he can't go any further without breaking down, so he grabs his notes from the podium and steps down. The clapping is tempered by the sober reality of what he had to endure all those years. I look up to the ceiling, then down at my notes. Nope, won't work. I whip my eyes back up to the ceiling. Thankfully, our next speaker is beginning.

Dr. Yua Kikuchi takes the stage, explaining her project with a team of six to redesign wind turbines on and offshore to increase wind power while reducing harm to birds, which has been a major drawback to this type of sustainable energy generation. The team will be working with placement, shape, and color—all which greatly reduce

Bird collateral damage. She's confident they can reduce that number to zero Bird casualties. She pauses. We all look to her for some sign. Why did she stop talking? Suddenly, she's beaming. I mean, really radiant. "To reach our goal," she continues, "we'll be consulting with one of the top experts in the world on the flight patterns and other risk factors of Birds so we can avoid interference." We all follow her eyes, now fixated on the wide entrance to the hall. "In fact, that consultant is here with us tonight." Everyone's frowning, rubbernecking. Wha—and then I see him. How could I miss? I would know that waddle anywhere. Before I can stop myself, I'm yelling.

"Onni!" Everyone else is calling out his name too. The roar is deafening. No one is in the mood to settle down after this. But no matter. We're all over-the-moon amazed and joyous at his return. Obviously, he owes us an explanation. And sure enough, in his unique style, he lumbers up to the podium. By the look on Dr. EJ's face, he was in on it too. Finally, we all quiet down so Onni can speak.

He looks left, then right, then straight toward us. "Haukka and Rawol very happy in forest far away. But Onni—I change my mind. Humans still need much help."

Laughter, nods, ahhhhs, air kisses. He goes on. "Bird wisdom. Yes, especially with wind turbines. No more Bird sacrifices. I know how prevent. I am part of team."

Dr. EJ and Dr. Kikuchi flank each side and place their hands on Onni's massive wings. Dr. EJ chuckles. "And are we glad. Onni, you weel play a huge role in the coming months and years. We may even bring back some endangered species as well as make wind energy safe for them. I say it's a win-win all around. Sorry, we felt it best to keep Onni's reappearance a secret. But it was his decision." Onni nods, waddles to the back of the room, and stands. Another round of applause. Everyone is on such a high right now. Onni and Dad step down and sit at one of the front tables. I can't wait to hug Onni when all this is over.

Next, omigod. Voitto Kurki, my grandfather. I suck in a breath. Finally, instead of trying to teach a bunch of disrespectful middle school students, he will be able to use his super talents once more. I hear phrases such as *three main longevity pathways—mTOR, AMPK,* and Sirtuins—and *research to tweak those pathways*, and then *rapamycin, resveratrol, and NAD boosters* to extend life span. I smile to myself. He was never the most fascinating speaker, but so what. When other scientists help to heal the Earth, Pappa will be working on healing people so they can enjoy living on this healed planet. Makes sense to me. I'm so glad he's not stuck in a classroom, using phrases like *settle down* and *quiz Monday*. Teaching middle school science is a crucial and honorable profession, just not for him.

Dahab is proudly announcing she and her team will be perfecting what she calls "telepresence." It's like Skype or Zoom on steroids, she explains, as the innovations will integrate visual, audio, and network technologies so everything comes in perfectly, no matter the distance. Then to our surprise, she pulls something out of her purse and unfolds it. It looks like a scooter, about five feet tall, with a long, rectangular screen attached. Suddenly, a man pops up from head to toe on the rectangular screen. "Say hi to my *bhai*—my brother." She laughs. "*Salam, Fahad...*" She waves to the figure on the screen. We all wave.

He grins, waving back. "Hello, everybody," he greets us in English. His whole body is visible, and his voice is much clearer than our comcards. She tells him goodbye, and the screen goes blank. Wow. She turns to us while collapsing the video phone down to almost nothing, then stuffing it back into her purse. "And should this technology be adopted by most businesses and governments, we will be able to avoid carbon emissions by at least two gigatons over the next thirty years by decreasing travel, especially by air, not to mention the ability to talk to each other in interstellar space, and keeping germs to ourselves."

Wow. What I get to look forward to in the future.

Dr. Bob Smith, aka Xu Zhanqi, gives a quick bow to Pappa. He will be on Pappa's team for the life extension project. But within that goal, he will be narrowing his research to a set of four genes: Oct-4, Klf4, Sox2, and c-Myc, which a Japanese researcher found can induce adult cells to become pluripotent stem cells.

"English!" someone yells.

Dr. B laughs. "Ah, yes. We need to make simple. How about this? We should be able to 'turn back clock' by making cells younger. Clear enough?"

We all laugh. I hear a lot of murmuring going on. This stuff's incredible.

Dr. B hands the mic to Dr. EJ. He turns to us. "And now, General Hale Waara. Although your well-designed battle plan number 2 did not work out exactly as we'd hoped—no fault of your own—you showed exceptional valor and bravery for the initial victory on Cancri e. Now your vital meession is to assemble a security force—physical and cyber—to make sure we remain under the radar so to speak, and that all ETs not only phone home, but they go home. The evil ones, anyway."

Laughter and applause fill the room.

The general just stands at his bench along the table. I notice how visibly he's changed. He's no longer the arrogant, self-assured leader, but a humble, sadder-but-wiser member of our QC. Gone is his crewcut. His hair has grown in dark and wavy, with streaks of silver. Who would have thought? He could have just retired. But Mutsi told me he's determined to use his vast experience—good and bad—to make sure we never have to deal with such evil forces from Earth or outer space. And maybe because he wants to redeem himself a little bit, not that he has to. But is his voice a little raspy? Wobbly? Maybe he's just overcome with emotion. I don't remember him ever having to use notes either. Is he having memory problems? His hands are shaking slightly. I hope he's okay. But then he drops the bomb.

"Since we've returned, I've spent many a sleepless night. It's just worrisome to ponder how many, shall we say, nefarious elements—both human and possibly extraterrestrial—would love to obtain our formulas and information. The POPs, as EJ calls them—the 'profit over people' factions in our world will not understand the true ramifications of these incredible inventions and discoveries, and how to use them for the benefit of all humankind. And we saw inklings of this reptilian mode of thinking with our last Cancri confrontation. No race, no culture, no country, no color is the enemy. Beings with not a shred of empathy or compassion—Cancri or human—these are the true enemy."

I look over to Tad. He's sitting, listening, motionless. I wish Waara would have pointed out the exception sitting right here who saved humankind. Before I can remember how shy I am about public speaking, I stand. "Except for Tad and Big Don."

The room goes silent as a cave. At first, I'm afraid I'll be chastised. But he nods in my direction and goes on. "Of course, of course, Big Don and Tad. Kristal just made an excellent point. To reiterate—the battle is not always one species against another, or one culture or religion against another. The battle is between those with a conscience, and those without."

Amid the applause, I look over. Tad's blinking. Is that a tear on his cheek? My jaw drops. The general continues, "Now my fervent mission is to oversee a brand-new type of security force to ascertain the safety and stability of our fragile new community. I realized I can't do this alone. I'm putting together a team of brilliant minds to devise a quantum computer system that is completely unhackable." There is a sprinkling of applause. The general scans the room, lowers his head, looks to the ceiling, then back to us. Something's up. He's about ready to spill. "I'm going to be honest with you as I know you all are the best of the best, and I couldn't ask for a more supportive team. I-I've just been diagnosed with Parkinson's disease."

A hush falls over the crowd. Parkinson's. I've heard of it. That may explain the shakiness. Oh.

The general goes on to say, "So in light of this situation and with Dr. EJ's expert help, we've hired an additional military expert to work with me and eventually, without me. His name is Capitan Primero Alejandro Morales. He's from the Mexican Marines, and he's been tapped as one of the most experienced strategists in the world. Don't ask how we got him here. No kidnapping, I promise you"—chuckles—"but we found him, vetted him, and he's here tonight. *El Capitan...*"

General Waara holds out his hand. I follow his eyes to the second table from the podium. The new captain stands, makes eye contact with others as he scans the room, then bows his head. He looks to be half Waara's age. His expression reminds me of Ayana, my friend from Dolcany—with the I'm-comfortable-in-my-own-skin and don't-mess-with-me look. But he doesn't look arrogant, more like confident. We give him a warm welcome. He sits.

Waara says, "We'll all be working together, but finally, without those goddamn heavy diamond suits." He smiles, giving a thumbs-up. Everyone laughs, stands again, and salutes, clapping and returning his thumbs-up gesture. He's another one who could have easily been ousted. Instead, Dr. EJ and the others are showing the utmost trust in him. With this new guy, I hope it all pans out. I do know Waara's as determined as ever to make things right. Near the podium, at the first table, Dr. B and Dr. EJ are exchanging nods.

Everyone hushes up as Dr. B stands. "General Waara, we are so grateful you trusted us enough to confide in us with regard to your condition last month. I am pleased to announce Dr. Kurki and I have been een touch with the University of Helsinki to collaborate with their scientists een further researching a new medication—a combination of treatments to inhibit COMT, perfect properties of BT13, build on the GDNF factor and—"

Dr. Kurki, my illustrious grandfather shouts out, "Bob, cut the technical terms, or we'll all be asleep in a nanosecond. It's almost bedtime." Everyone laughs. Pappa stands, scooting the bench back.

"Please allow me to cut to the chase. General Waara, with thees amazing medical advance—most fortuitously at the University of Helsinki—you weel be fine in a short amount of time. Eet ees state-of-the-art and brand new. We could hardly believe our ears when Bob and I began to research..." He stops, his eyes grow wide. "Oops. HIPPA regulations. I should not have deescussed your medical cond-eetion without your—"

The general waves him away. "You didn't discuss it. *I* did. As far as I'm concerned, you can tell my story to the whole world if it will make a difference in others' lives."

We all laugh; Pappa fakes wiping his brow in relief.

I look back at the general. He's blinking back tears. Obviously this is the first he's heard of it. He wipes his eyes. "I... I don't know what to say—how to thank—"

Pappa smiles. "No thanks needed. Just do your job. We need you."

General Waara's hand covers his mouth as he shakes his head. The crowd applauds wildly. Our hands are getting sore by now with so much clapping. But I'm certainly not complaining.

Finally, Dr. EJ takes over again. "My dear fellow QC members, this eenitial meeting was merely a tiny sample. We could go on unteel the sun comes up tomorrow. As you can see, eet ees clear we have some very ambitious projects, and that all of us are extremely eager to get going, as time ees not our friend. But as you can tell, we have the know-how to get the job done, that is making the Earth healthy again. So when our grandchildren and great-grandchildren ask us about climate change or *climate chaos*, as we call it now, we can say we had their futures in mind when we fixed it for them. And so we continue.

Someone yells, "What's your project, EJ?"

"Me? Ha, I weel be coordinating and assisting with these massive undertakings, starting tomorrow and, well, perhaps some secret projects of wheech I may brief everyone later. But tonight, my only project is to *celebrate!*" With that, he holds a *lakka* high up into the air.

Seventy

March 6, 2027

We're all on our feet, laughing and whooping and cheering. The music starts with the ancient song "Celebrate, celebrate, dance to the music..." as people flock to the dance floor and start gyrating around while others line up at the food table, filling up ceramic plates with marinated veggie canapes, mini-cabbage rolls, and all kinds of breads and sweets. Alek's picked up Schrödy at the next table down and is scratching his neck, whispering something into his ear. Schrödy's tail is twitching madly. Does he understand? Nah, he couldn't possibly. Alek catches my eye, smiles, and winks.

It's almost nine. But I can't even think about going home. Tired as I am, I still want to eat and dance. And besides, I have to say hi to Onni. I scramble over to his table, where he's standing. Apparently, he couldn't sit on the bench with his bulk. Without a word, I lay my head on his massive wing. He's in conversation with someone else but immediately looks down.

"Ms. Kristal, our leader. Onni so happy to see."

"*You're* happy to see me? Oh, Onni, I cried buckets when I thought you were gone."

"Sorry. Should have told Kristal. But Onni decide to become Bird consultant at last minute."

"Oh, Onni. I just... I just..." I could whip my eyes upward but decide it's okay to cry. Onni can take it.

"Kristal, hope tears are of joy."

"Onni, Onni, Onni."

"I take as good."

Suddenly, the sound of a scrape catches my attention. Mutsi's almost tripped over the bench and is now fleeing down the hall. I call her name and start after her, "Mutsi!"

Dad catches me by the elbow. I look at my elbow then at Dad. What the—he's following her with his eyes, smiling. "Let her go."

"Dad? What's the matter?"

Alek's seen it too. He scoots down the bench as I sit down, and Dad nudges him to move over a little, so he can sit between us. I pat Dad's arm.

"What?"

He takes my hand in his. "She's okay, Krissie babe. It's just the usual. Well, we were going to break the news tomorrow at breakfast. So much going on tonight, and her sickness is switched around."

"Mutsi's sick? What are you talking about? Switched around...?" I'm starting to freak, thinking about General Waara's speech.

"Woo-hoo!" It's Alek, pointing to Mummo, sitting one table over, knitting furiously. So she's brought her knitting basket. She's always knitting. She said she's knitting us all red caps, like the ones we had before. I frown at Alek. "So?" He rolls his eyes. "Hey, kid, if we're ever going into the detective business together, boy, you're gonna need some remedial work..."

I blush. I'm clueless? About what? I look again. Mummo and Pappa are grinning so widely at me I think their faces might crack. Then I see it—a hat, a red hat, a *tiny* red hat. Mummo holds it up, winking. "*Pipo*," she mouths.

What? "Hat" translates my dad. Oh, yeah. But it's so tiny, omigod. My stomach flutters. "Dad, are you—I mean, is Mutsi... is she—"

Alek raises his arms then pumps a fist in the air. "Way to go, Sherlock." Dad puts his arm around my shoulder. "Yes, Krissie, she is."

"Look, bro, see the tiny cap? Do the math!" I yell over to Tad, who's at the food table, stuffing his face with *salmiakki*, a Finnish type of licorice.

Tad looks over at Mummo then blinks several times. "We all have red hats?"

I laugh. "All seven of us."

"Schrödinger too?" We all burst out laughing. Oops, poor Tad, not nice. He can't take the teasing like I did.

"Tad, we're all happy because the tiny hat is for our new baby."

"Where?"

Oh, boy. I can tell Tad's going to need some birds and bees discussions. I'll leave that up to Dad.

"What's going on here?" My mother appears at the doorway then makes her way back to the long table. She nudges me aside and sits down next to Dad. Most everyone at the table is now staring and grinning at her, wide-eyed, wondering whether to congratulate her or pretend they didn't hear anything. She shakes her head, but she's smiling. "Ah, someone here has a big mouth. Now we all know, do we?"

Dad's sheepish look gives him away. He shrugs. "It was the hat. So tiny." And, well—he sticks his hand inside his jacket and pulls out a T-shirt, letting it fall like a flag. Mutsi frowns, reading, "You can't scare me. I have two daughters." We all gasp. I remember the QC meeting on the Diamond Star, when she mentioned a T-shirt like that. She and Dad sure do think alike.

I can't help my question. "So—a sister? You know already?"

"One quick test. Six weeks along. A little baked bean. I swear she's already flying her own plane in here."

I'm insanely curious. "Name yet?"

She takes my father's hand. "Yes." They look into each other's eyes then look at me and Tad, who's ambled back to the benches.

"Rainbow."

I repeat it several times. "Rainbow. Rainbow." Already I see her as a real little person. Goosebumps break out on my arms. Dad smiles at me then at Tad, who's returned to our table along with Mummo and Pappa. We're all together. With Alek and Schrödy too. I feel so complete.

"Rainbow." Dad wipes a tear. "A beautiful phenomenon of nature, most often occurring after a storm, or *myrakka*."

Although I'm all choked up, I manage to say, "Rainbow. Rainbow..." Beautiful. After the storm, a rainbow. How many times did we despair of ever coming through the *storm* intact? Everything's happened exactly as was predicted by the Diamond Star prophecy, except it didn't get this far in time. But how did the author know? Oops, my mind is rambling again. I thought I was finally free of question bees forever, but now I realize that we still don't know, and one particularly huge bee still buzzes loudly in my head every now and then. I know I have to let it go, but...

"Dad?" Damn. It's out.

"Yes, Krissie babe?"

"The prophecy. Seriously, I mean, no theories at all? Not even clues?"

My father gives me that not-again sigh. Then he shrugs. "Ah, Kristal. In a word, no. No clues, no plausible theories. It's all still a great mystery."

"I mean, though, isn't the QC going to—"

"Krissie, did you hear all those speeches tonight? We have so many urgent projects right here on Earth. Maybe someday, but now—" He shakes his head. "We've got a world to fix."

I lean back, behind Dad and Mutsi. Alek follows suit. He leans toward me and drops his voice. "Wasn't going to say anything. But, uh, I've got a few ideas. I'll be working on it. You in or out?"

I hesitate exactly one nanosecond.

"In."

Seventy-One

•◦◦◦◦◦◦◦◦◉◦◦◦◦◦◦◦◦◦

April 26, 2027

I'm leisurely enjoying *filmjölk* and mueseli for breakfast in the council building's little café, set in the corner of the structure with two long counters at a ninety-degree angle with bar stools looking out at the magnificent view. I've finally expanded my breakfast diet to more than blueberry muffins and pecan pancakes. This Finnish oatmeal is actually pretty yummy.

Taking a sip of blueberry tea in a regular-sized cup (I'll never get over how big cups seem after the thimble-sized ones on the Diamond Star), I let its warmth soothe my senses, like in the recoup room. Gazing out the massive picture window here in the café still takes my breath away. Here, even in April, snow covers most of the valley and up the slopes, but I can already see many patches of brown and green, along with tiny dots of yellow—Alpine arnica. So pretty. Spring is here.

And since our last Quantum Community meeting in March, whenever I picture the teeny hat, *pipo*, in my mind, I break out in a huge grin. Our precious Rainbow is due on October 3. Rainbow—conceived on a star, a diamond star child. I'm crazy eager to hold her tiny little hand in mine. Mutsi isn't showing yet, but she says that's normal. I know our Diamond Star child will be here before we know it, but right now, it seems like time is crawling.

I don't know exactly where the baby will fit, especially when she outgrows her baby box. Our small cabin has only three bedrooms and one bath. That will be a bit of a challenge in the coming years, although Dad says he thinks he can add on a room without increasing our carbon footprint too much. Mummo and Pappa's home is about a football field away and even smaller, except for the secret room, which they've cleaned out and turned into an extra bedroom for Tad or me or Rainbow when we have sleepovers. But strangely, even though things are tight, I feel my home is even bigger than the one in Montana, probably because I count the whole QC land as my own backyard. When it's summer—a short season up here—we'll be able to swim in the lakes and ponds that dot the valley. Dad said we'll also do a lot of hiking and spelunking. Then next winter, we'll go skiing. So much more exciting than red boots and Marsten's hill. Can't wait.

I take another sip of tea, scan the valley to the right. Sylvester, the tree that saved Alek's life that horrible day, still towers over the others in the forest area. Funny to think we both had old pine tree friends. Nearby, the chapel sits at the top of a small ridge at the edge of the northern mountain, surrounded by a new forest of baby birches, each with its own golden plaque. After the February ceremony, Alek must have stood in the freezing cold, head down, at his parents' trees for over half an hour. I was about to go out and urge him to get inside, or he might lose more toes. But then Dr. EJ joined him, and I watched as they walked home, arm in arm, Alek's head on Dr. EJ's shoulder.

Yesterday, I noticed another plaque. Looks like they'd commissioned the arborists to plant one more tree. It's still lying next to the hole in the ground. What's that all about? Did they forget someone? I can't imagine.

A voice. With a slight lilt. "*Hei.*" Alek. He's sounding more and more Finnish by the day. I turn.

"Hey." I smile at him. He leans against the wooden frame of the dining lodge, gripping the handle to his new gray Samsonite pivot suitcase. His new REI black backpack bulges; it's got to be loaded to the brim. After the last few months, luggage seems a sort of primitive way to travel. But we all have to morph back to being Clark Kents for now until the world is ready to learn about teleportation and able to use it wisely, which may be never. It suddenly hits me.

"Alek? Suitcase? Backpack? Already?"

"Yep, I'm going to be, uh, HIP." He chuckles.

"Meaning?"

"Helsinki Institute of Physics. They've got a summer internship, and whatdayaknow, I qualified. This was all last-minute, hush-hush. I was on a wait list. I didn't want to mention it. I really didn't think I would get in for the summer. So guess I'm going to get used to being on my own."

Why do I suddenly feel a little dizzy? The tea? "Oh, uh, that's amazing, Alek. Well, not really. You'll probably end up teaching half your courses. Is that all you're taking with you?"

"Ha, no. Pappa's eyes nearly bugged out of his head when he saw his Tesla all packed to the ceiling. Normally it gets around three hundred mph, not this trip. What can I say? I… I have a few gadgets I gotta take with me."

"You leaving now?"

He checks his cell phone. "About a half hour."

My heart skips a beat. Why? I'm fine. Really happy for Alek and proud. Alek's staring at me, like he first did when we met in Mr. Gabriel's—Pappa's classroom. I pick up my bowl, scrape it into the refuse bin, set it and the spoon on the conveyer belt. Alek's still standing there.

I cock my head. "Something on your mind?"

Alek sighs. "Glad you asked. As a matter of fact, I need your help."

"Oh. Uh, sure. If I can."

"It's unseasonably warm today—a balmy zero degrees Celsius, that is. Come on. Follow me. This won't take long."

He parks his luggage and book bag by the door on the porch. Here, in this community, you can do that and not worry a bit. I grab my coat and hat from the ledge. Together, we walk out into the brilliant sunshine and azure sky and down three wooden steps to the main path, always cleared of snow, banks piled up on either side.

The scented air reminds me of that morning in Montana—the first snowfall and the day that would change my life forever. But here, the view of the mountains that overlook the valley are the same as those in my recurring dreams. Since it's still April, our green northern lights sometimes still greet us at night with their emerald glow in the heavens. Dad made good his promise to buy Tad and me new boots, but not the weenie Montana red kind. I look down at my feet. These are sturdy hiking boots from Meindl Matrei GTX. Dad splurged. They are so cool and completely functional here. We do so much walking, so they're absolutely essential.

Alek and I walk side by side, not talking, just breathing in the woodsmoke and snow scent, basking in the sun surrounded by an ocean of sky. We come to a wooden bench. It looks pretty dry. Alek sits, patting the wooden slats next to him. I sit on the other end. He squints into the distance like he's thinking. "So. Rainbow. Huh, cool name."

"Yeah, Tad's so fun to watch. He's as excited as we are."

"Tad? Wow. He did one hell of an upgrade on himself. He's humanizing like crazy."

"Whatever happened that night showed Tad's smarter than all the other Cancris put together and definitely more human."

"He said something about One helping him that night. But I think it's because he lived with you and your dad for eleven years. Amazing case study. His DNA circuits evolved toward your personality traits, Kristal. Because you loved him. You adored him. You taught him how to use his creativity and imagination. And you accepted him the way he was. Thank goodness, he's so much like you."

"Well, let's hope he programmed the ADD out."

"Kristal, then he likely wouldn't have been able to use his creativity to visualize an out-of-the-box solution to the Cancri problem. The term *ADD* is so nebulous. If I were you, I'd drop the whole notion. Whatever ADD creativity you passed on to Tad was exactly what he needed."

I sit for a moment, drinking it all in—Alek's words, the snow sparkling from the sun's rays, the pine branches dancing in the breeze. A surge of gratitude wells up in me for Tad, for the QC, for Alek, and maybe for whatever I do have inside me that helped Tad save us. I break out in a huge smile. "Well, in any case, I'm glad I have my brother back. And we finally got to celebrate our mutual birthday properly."

"Oh, your bunz cake party."

"Thanks for coming to our little celebration. Did you like the bunz cake?"

"Did I like it? I think I'm addicted to it. When's your next birthday?"

"I chuckle. "Don't worry. I'll send you an invitation. After you left, Mutsi cried. She said she should have been making our birthday cakes all these years."

Alek nods. Awkward silence follows. Well, not really awkward. I guess after all these months and after all our adventures, I can read Alek like a book. "Um, Alek, this is all small talk. You said you needed my help. I'm here."

Alek's eyebrows shoot up. He stands and starts walking again. I follow. We stroll in silence to the chapel, gleaming in the sunlight, its steeple brilliant against the bright sky. We stare. Over six hundred saplings surround the little church and grace the slope of the foothills. It's still sobering to gaze out at the rows and rows of trees, a miniature forest now, but they'll be huge in another decade. Alek's gone ahead of me, to the other side. I run to catch up. He's standing in front of the new hole in the ground. Another baby birch is lying beside it, along with extra dirt and a shovel.

"Oh, so you're behind this. I saw it. What's with the extra tree? And the dirt and shovel? They didn't forget anyone did they? They couldn't possibly…"

Alek tears up. "Don't need your help planting it. But I did want to get you out here because—well, you're the only one who would really care."

It hits me. "Oh, you mean…" Then I lean over, notice the plaque. It simply reads, "Halfling."

I burst out crying and laughing at the same time. Alek, only Alek.

He's already setting the little tree upright into the hole, shoveling dirt in and patting around it with gloved hands. It looks so fragile. But like the others, it will grow tall and strong. Alek straightens up. "Now as I was saying on Cancri before we were so rudely interrupted—dearly beloved, we are gathered here to mourn the—

well, he's still alive. I hope, but to us, he's gone. Big Don was only part human, supposedly, but that human part far outshone many so-called real humans. If you know what I mean."

I nod. I can't speak. But Alek knows I know exactly what he means.

"May he prosper in his new land among his own. May he teach them the ways, the good ways, of humankind. May he be happy."

I need to say something. I can't. God, that lump in my throat. I manage to squeak out, "Amen."

"Yep. Well, that's it. Thank you." Alek brushes the dirt from his hands and pants.

"I loved him too, Alek."

"I know. That's why..." We lock eyes.

Alek blinks and looks away. "So, uh, Kristal. Tell me about your studies." Just like that. We start our walk back toward the council building.

"Oh, uh, good. Only twelve in my class. It's completely different from Dolcany Middle School. Instead of subjects, we have mini-projects. And then we work the math, the language, the social science into the project. No one acts like a jerk. We all feel we're working toward something. You know—that we're making a difference with our studies. I don't have a 504 plan because here, well, I guess I don't have ADD symptoms that call for making accommodations for the handicapped. Oh, and my dreams—they're just regular old dreams now. Half the time, I don't even remember them."

"Good for you. I'll never forget that first tutoring session when you showed me your picture with the red blotch. I nearly lost it. I knew exactly what that blotch represented. I couldn't believe your subconscious remembered. Amazing, really. I wanted so badly to say more, but, well, Doc Kurki was so adamant about no Cancri TMI at first." He reaches over, takes my hand, squeezes it, and lets it go.

We walk back to the steps of the council building in silence. Why am I feeling—what—a little pissed? That bitchiness I've come to accept as my *assertive self*. The question bees come tumbling out of my mouth. Guess I'll never get rid of my black QB box. But at least these are new questions. They tumble over each other, but I have to get them out before Alek's gone. "Didn't you say you were working on the origin of the prophecy? I thought we were going to start on that soon. Do we know who's behind it? Who's this One character? Who made the Cancris? How did the prophecy get left on a table on the Diamond Star? I mean, doesn't anyone care anymore? Don't you?"

Alek lowers his head. "Look. I care. I care a lot. But this battered old world of ours is sinking like the frickin' *Titanic*. And until we came back, with enough brain power and negotiating skills and funding, this old Earth would probably have been doomed. I mean, if we're the *Titanic*, this is the time the band stops playing, looks around, and says 'Oh, shit. We're drowning.' So I mean, yeah. It would be great if we could crack these Cancri and Diamond Star mysteries, but it's all hands-on deck right now on Earth. I have a feeling I'm going to need a lot more education, and you too, before we can join the QC and help figure it all out. But as I promised at the meeting, I do have a few ideas. I haven't totally pushed it aside. Let me get settled. Then whenever I zip home for the weekend or for vacation, we'll figure out our strategy."

My eyes narrow. I wonder if he means it, or if he's just wanting to placate me. "Is this all a joke to you now?"

"Does it look like I'm laughing?"

I need to calm down. I can tell Alek wants to unravel this mystery as much as I do. But as he said, first things first. I hold out my hand. "Well, it's a deal then. As soon as we can, we'll start. Shake?"

"Nope."

"Nope?"

"Pinky promise."

"Oh, Alek. That's so hokey."

"And as I recall, it didn't work the first time we did it. You spilled to your dad about the Cancris. You owe me."

"I can't argue. Yep, I did break the pinkie promise. This time I won't. But you might."

"I will not. I have never broken a pinkie promise in my life, unlike you."

"All right, all right, don't rub it in."

"Well, then, it's settled." He yanks off a glove and holds out his pinkie. I do the same. We pinkie shake, then replace our gloves. Despite the "balmy weather" everyone's talking about, it's still way too cold for bare hands.

I have to smile. But I do hope he keeps this immature little contract. Simultaneously, we plop ourselves down on the top step, beside Alek's stuff. He's obviously still got the prophecy on his mind. "Vacations, summer—wouldn't it be a hoot if we could figure out the prophecy and shock the shinola out of the adults? Project Prophecy. How about that? Top secret. You, me, Schrödy. Oh and Tad. Ha, he can probably figure it out all by himself."

"Well, we'll see. So you're starting college. You won't be able to give the valedictorian speech at Dolcany High. You won't be graduating with your class."

Alek puts on a fake sad face. "I'm crushed. Oh, I completely forgot." He reaches into his back jeans pocket, pulls out his phone. "Take a look at this."

I look. A photo? Oh, a screenshot.

Kristl,

They say your dead. But maybe your just undercover or something. Anyway, if you ever come back and read this, I just want to say I'm sorry I was such a jerk. I feel bad I made fun of you. They told me I have ADD too. And something called dyslexa, like I have trouble reading. And something with other letters too like PSTD, like my dad beat me up and one time stuck me in the bathtub, and it was boiling hot. I kind of remember being in the hospital like when I was two or three. My dad has elevn more years but maybe pobration in five if hes good. I'm staying with my grams but she's not doing good so I migt end up in fsostr care. I have a conseler, he's pretty good. He helpd me writ this. I don't think I'll go to high school. Maybe a GED someday. I thot all guys had to be like my dad and be tough. I don't want to end up like him. Guess I was the awfly dum dits after all.

I'm really sorry. I hope they find you. If you come back, I promise I won't teas you anymore.

Sorry. Jackson

Jackson Hynes. I look up at Alek, frowning. He shrugs. "When Brima went to Dolcany, he found this on your front porch, sticking out from under your mat. I'm supposed to be dead too, you know. They had a lot of loose ends to tie up. Poor kid. I call it the 'wounded animal syndrome.' His dad was in the slammer for dealing, assault, and attempted murder. Guess he didn't want little Jackson around anymore. So sad. And I think his mom's a drug addict. As they say, hurt people hurt people."

A vision of Jackson, head down in the Children's Services parking lot, pops into my head. He must have been with his grams. He looked so dejected. Maybe he'll find a Zola someday who can help him. Or maybe he already has. I look high up to the ceiling of the porch. Tears gone. I hand Alek's phone back to him. "I'm glad I got help. Dr. Khumolo really helped me. And Dad, Mutsi, Mummo, and Pappa, and oh, your pappa, and…and…" I feel the familiar flush and the throat closing, but I plunge ahead anyway. "And you, Alek, I… I don't know what I would've…" I can't go on.

"Ah, Kristal, we did it together. You helped me. I helped you. Oh, speaking of help, thanks for your offer to take care of Schrödy while I'm gone. Pappa just can't…"

I have no memory of offering to take care of Schrödy. "Oh, sure, Alek. No problem."

"Well, just FYI, he may be more than you bargained for. He's still, uh, evolving and doing some kind of weird stuff. Hope you don't mind. Just keep me posted, okay? I sent you an email with instructions."

"Okay, I'll observe him and report. He's one amazing cat."

"That he is."

We both look up to see Dr. EJ standing in front of his Tesla, waving at Alek. Alek turns to me. He's blinking like crazy. What's with that?

"Thanks, Kristal."

"Good luck, Alek."

Alek mock salutes, maybe trying a little Hawkeye move. Then he lingers. Our eyes meet, then pull away, then meet again. We both stand at the same time. Alek reaches for me, and we hug. He pats me on the shoulder. "Hold down the fort, kid."

I nod. It's all a little awkward. He struggles for a moment with his backpack and luggage, then without another word, he's down the steps, his luggage bumping the three steps down. I wince. He looks back, waves. "*Moikka*—bye." Then he turns back toward his pappa. I watch until Alek reaches Dr. EJ. He, his backpack, luggage, and Dr. EJ disappear into the car. I hear the engine starting up, then my eyes follow the car until it's out of sight.

I turn, head back into the café. I could use another cup of tea. Goodbye, Alek. *Moikka, Aleksi*—I practice the phrase for a minute. Finnish is one complicated language, but I've got a lot of time to learn. And as my own pappa would say, it's very related to my own life. I get my tea, climb back up on a barstool, elbows on the ledge, and stare out the window, rattling my spoon around in my cup, stirring the milk and sugar. I take my first sip. It's hard to swallow with the ginormous lump in my throat. How can I distract myself? Oh, the instructions for the cat. I pull out my cell phone. The sun moves behind the only cloud in the sky, and everything darkens for a moment.

"Yeow, meow."

Schrödinger sits in the doorway, regal as ever. I swear he's glaring at me.

"Hey, Schrö, don't blame me he's leaving. And Big Don—that wasn't my fault either. I'll miss them both too. So guess it's just you and me now, buddy."

Did he just move his head a little left? Then right? "Nyow, uhee. O-ee-ow."

What?

"O-ee-uh."

Holy moly, three syllables! And damned if that didn't sound like...*nah.*

I stuff my phone back in my pocket. "Hey, sorry. I won't call you Schrö anymore or buddy. Schrödinger, how's that, your majesty?"

"Meow."

"Well, okay, then. How about we take a walk, just you and me? We've got crucial things to discuss. The prophecy, for one. And then we'll head to my house for..." I check Alek's message on my phone. "Yep. He's left a whole carton of salmon pâté for you there. And he's left instructions for Dr. EJ to reorder online so you never have to run out. How 'bout that, bud—er—Schrödinger? We'll catch a little lunch after our walk. What'dya say?"

"Meow."

"Yeah, me too."

He waits patiently while I get rid of my cup. Then the champagne-colored cat with the enormous jade eyes follows me through the front entrance and down the steps. Side by side we head out into the Finnish sunshine and diamond-sparkled snow.

Epilogue

Kepler 452b
April 17, 2032

"The traitor is found."

Temban leans down until he's at eye level with Tila. "While we capture traitor, prepare for ceremonial disassembly, you go to eat rectangle fix low RDS meal." Tila nods, watches Temban roll away, catching up to the other males toward the big tree by the river where Loran finally sighted the fugitive. So many revolutions of search. She can't remember exactly how many. All unsuccessful until now.

Tila is the first to arrive at the eat rectangle for their group—number 128. It's her turn, as it is most of the time. The meal storage box takes up an entire wall. She speaks. "Open." The wall parts, and the entire cache of edibles appears, shelved in precise portions. She extracts twenty-seven plana leaves, yellow sauce, purple *partbas*, and sweet blue ferment. As she mixes the leaves with the sauce in a large clay pot, adding the *partbas*, sets out large meal discs, and pours the ferment, she analyzes her thoughts.

She's never seen the one they call Big Don, or the Great Ugly. But Dira told her he was the one they cloned from something called Alek DNA. Human. They've all got human DNA now, but this Big Don apparently began evolving in different, strange ways. Before the Great Teleport, this Alek human gave Two the idea for phoneme blends instead of numerals to identify each Cancri. The idea was adopted when they arrived on Kepler after the Great Teleport and fulfillment of the prophecy. Well, partial fulfillment. Water is abun-

591

dant here, found in all rivers, lakes, and ocean 194756. But it is crystal water, strictly forbidden, as Two believes the traitorous TAD tainted it with poison. Since then, Two has been obsessed with finding the Earth TAD and disassembling it in a very painful manner, although the procedural specifics have not been announced. But so far, they have not been able to develop algorithms for teleportation to Earth. When Temban suggested to Two that they focus solely on further development of their species and permanently archive all previous revolutions, Two amputated Temban's foot appendages with his corkscrew weapon. Temban immediately manufactured wheels to ambulate, which threw Two into a worse rage. He was going to amputate the wheels until the other high-males convinced him of the usefulness of Temban's new transportation modality, which may help apprehend the Great Ugly with its speed. Discussion of the TAD, Earth teleportation, and the prophecy is now forbidden except during high-male group meetings.

But they're moving forward in their mission. A Cancri team of seven found a way to manufacture water by capturing Kepler air and implementing new algorithms. It's not nearly the amount found in the sparkling crystal waters, but the Cancri water was able to further their evolution to 39.6 percent hybrid human. This was sufficient for male and female differentiation; the high-males decided to choose specific phonemes for each gender to make identification easier. Females' names always end with the phoneme *a* and males with *n*. But they still use numbers for the "betweens," those who have both male and female parts or none, by choice. But using phonemes instead of numbers—that could not be the reason this Big Don being had been in hiding all this time, could it? It certainly doesn't seem traitorous to suggest a new way to name members of their evolving species, especially since they are evolving into humanoids. Humans have phoneme names, don't they? The tales Dira told her when she was newly assembled had human characters with phoneme names. No. It must be something else.

Dira ducks her head and enters the eat rectangle. She is the tallest female and also the oldest. They extracted her egg and blended with one sperm of Temban, the male, to produce Tila. In her studies, she learned that on Earth, the egg being is called the mother, and the being with the sperm is the father. They live in one dwelling, and may reproduce again and again. The females are called sisters, and the males, brothers. Odd. Here, among the Cancris, as long as each has a purpose for survival of the group, that is all that matters. Tila is a meal preparer. If too many females become meal preparers, Tila will be disassembled. At that thought, she feels a strange heaviness in her midsection but ignores it, most likely a defect in her programming. She doesn't dare speak of it. Defects are not tolerated.

Dira surveys the table. "The females will eat. No more time waiting for the males. They are still searching for the traitor."

Tila's black eyebrows go up. Her dark eyes open wide as her claw pours more ferment for Dira, who will undoubtedly demand it. "I thought they found him."

"He escaped."

Hita, Ploma, Raquesha, and Yalla arrive simultaneously. Hita, the most human of the six in their pod, is laughing. She has mastered the laugh, as well as the cry, complete with tears of a watery-like substance, a tiny river. The others practice the laugh and the cry, but so far, no success.

"Ha, they were so sure. He's gone again. Let's sit and eat everything, so they all go hungry. Stupid males." Hita laughs again.

Dira zaps Hita on the shoulder, instructing, "Females do not make males angry. We eat but leave half for the males." She pauses. "But if food is wilted, not our fault." Hita laughs again. This time Dira smiles with her newly human mouth. Tila can't help staring. Her facial procedure is scheduled for the next RDS rotation. Her whole body begins to quiver. Another malfunction? She can't let them know.

Tila checks the horizon. Red Dwarf Star is slipping downward. Where are the males?

There are voices outside. "We try again tomorrow."

The Cancris in pod 128 eat in silence as required by Temban when his expression is downturned. After the meal, all return to the pod, and without a word, power down for the darkness. Since the Great Teleport, they've tried, but still have not mastered the evolution to 78 percent human, the ideal hybrid combination according to Two, or Alph, as he is sometimes called, the only male with a name not ending in *n*. Dira took Tila aside and divulged that she had listened in secret to the last high-male gathering. In their last gathering, Alph was discussing his fervent mission to return to Earth to disassemble and study more bodies or finding this being they call One for help. Two is becoming quite disgruntled at their lack of progress.

*****

In a large recess of cave number 4496, Big Don sits, his machinery humming softly. He was stupid to think he could cross the river to check for extra vortices for interstellar communication. He knew it was dangerous, and indeed, he was spotted by Loran, barely escaping this time. Big Don will not cross the river again, too roiling, choppy. He has enough, finally, to communicate using the instruments he has assembled over time. His face is now totally human—a clone of his Earth friend Alek. He's not ugly anymore like he was on Cancri and on Earth as long as he wears human clothing to hide remnant patches of metal. He could teach the others how to evolve like him, not only physically, but with appropriate emotions—compassion, love. But since the night of the prophecy culmination, they have not trusted him. Yes, he lied to them. They will never trust him, so he is useless to them now. He will be disassembled as soon as they find him. They have metal detectors. Big Don had to develop complex programs to override their algorithms and find a hiding place as soon as they arrived on Kepler, five Earth years ago. Since then, he's been alone, in cave recesses, of which there are many. He ventures out only during their power-down, in the darkness, to find materials for his mission. First goal was a travelrod to return to Earth. But that venture was unsuccessful. TAD made it impossible for Cancri to return to Earth. So Earth must travel to Kepler. He doesn't want to place his friend Alek in danger, but he must escape. And the Cancris must not be able to evolve. They are a danger to the universe. And a special danger to Earth. Big Don will not allow it. He has had five years to plan the mission to destroy them. But he needs help. And soon. And he feels lonely, a very human emotion. He wishes—no. His Alek fingers quiver as he sends the message:

> Alek, Big Don on Kepler. Help. Please come. Travelrod code: 792058375. Communication code: 7027057029838358-28475. Cancris need disassembled asap. No hope for successful human hybridization. 100% psychopathic.

It is done. If he has not programmed it precisely, all is lost. His Alek DNA has evolved so substantially he can feel his heart, now fully human, beating wildly, except for the aberration. He needs more Alek DNA. Through a tiny crack in the cave, he sees Red Dwarf has set. The sky spills over with ancient stars, perhaps some with diamond cores.

Big Don glances back down at his computer. At long last, his missive has been sent. No need to search further for materials during Cancri power-down. And besides, he's too exhausted from the massive amounts of adrenalin racing through his human body from the escape. He needs to rest, renew.

Grunting, he lowers his vast bulk to the self-made cot of plana leaves and closes his eyes, slowly drifting into a dream of Earth.

A Word from
the Author

∘ ∘ ∘ ∘ ∘ ∘ ∘ ∘ ⦿ ◉ ⦿ ∘ ∘ ∘ ∘ ∘ ∘ ∘ ∘

*Hey, Mom, you know those filters you put in a room to suck out
all the pollution? Why can't they make one as big as the Empire
State Building and suck the pollution out of an entire city?*
                                    —Child with attention deficit disorder

Dear Reader:

I am honored you chose my book, *Crystal Child: The Diamond
Star Saga*, and hope you came away with a greater reverence not only
for Mother Earth but for all her creatures, including you! Although
my book is a work of fiction, I have interwoven many facts throughout the fantasy. For instance, BPM 37093 and 55 Cancri e really
exist! Another fact—sad but true—our Mother Earth is in trouble.
Waters are polluted, animals and their habitats are becoming extinct,
glaciers are melting, and diseases are running rampant. Although the
Quantum Community and the people in it are figments of my imagination, the environmental projects announced by the QC members
are actually being developed—by real scientists. We now have the
technical expertise to eliminate drought, drastically reduce carbon
emissions, cure previously incurable diseases, and much more. But
as Alek's parents stressed to him—with brilliance must come compassion. In *Crystal Child*, both were essential to save the universe.
Kristal thought she was an "awfully dumb ditz" because she believed

597

the bully's words. But her gifts of compassion and creativity—coupled with Tad's technical brilliance—saved humanity. Do you know anyone labeled with a challenge such as ADHD, dyslexia, autism, post-traumatic stress disorder, or anxiety? Perhaps you have been diagnosed with one or more of these challenges. *Don't let it get you down.* For often these think-out-of-the-box learners are the very ones who come up with creative ideas no one ever thought of before! (See quote above!) Someday one of those "crazy" ideas may just save the world!

Like Kristal, you have gifts. You are valuable. You can be a visionary too. It doesn't matter how old you are, where you live, your race, your culture, your emotional challenges, or your learning style. We're all united in our quest to make Earth a better place for us, our children, and our grandchildren (and all our descendants!). No matter who you are, we need your insights, your ideas, your voice, and especially your determination (or *sisu,* as they say in Finland). Follow your passions. Then join others who are dedicated to improving the lives of all sentient beings—humans as well as our feathered, finned, and furry friends. If you think you can't do anything right now, you're wrong. Recycle, buy local, volunteer at an animal shelter, or just turn off the water when you brush your teeth. Small changes add up to positive differences in our environment. And one of the most important tools you can use every day is absolutely free but extremely powerful. Can you use it? Absolutely. It's called *language.* Use its power for good. Look around you. Who needs words of encouragement today? Words of kindness and hope? Words of friendship? Use language to help them and see how their world—and yours—changes for the better.

Each of us wants Earth to be a place where every living creature can thrive in happiness, compassion, safety, and health. This is our universal vision. For more information, ideas and resources, visit www.ProjectEarthHeal.com.

Questions for
Discussion

° ° ° ° ° ° ° ° ○ ○ ◉ ○ ○ ○ ○ ○ ° ° ° °

1. The Cancris' English language software program wasn't able to decipher idioms or sarcastic phrases. Sometimes Alek or Kristal forgot to speak literally, thus confusing the Tad, Big Don, or Alph. How did Alek and Kristal revise their speech to make themselves more understandable? Give examples.

2. Kristal's dad gave her "talking tools" to use with the bullies, and Alek used "FBI," or "fierce bully intervention." How were these "talking tools" helpful? Can you think of other "talking tools" to use with bullies?"

3. How did Kristal's ADD affect her daily life—positively and negatively?

4. Kristal learned that she and many other QC members had suffered trauma. What were some examples of trauma in our world today? What were some techniques used by Dr. Khumolo, Blanca, and others to help reduce the effects of trauma and increase feelings of safety?

5. Artificial intelligence is becoming more and more sophisticated and prevalent in today's society. What are the advantages of AI? What are some concerns? Do you think an AI species like the Cancris could really evolve? Why or why not?

6. According to the prophecy found on the Diamond Star, Earth, the Diamond Star and 55 Cancri e were to reach a

"choice point" where either the Crystal Child would save all or the Cancris would demolish all. The saga never revealed the identity of the author of the prophesy. What are your theories? Do you think the author of the prophecy was a good person or an evil person? What makes you think that?

7. The people of Finland have a word for "grit" or "determination": *sisu*. Can you think of other adjectives or phrases that might describe *sisu?* In what ways did Kristal show *sisu?* Can you think of a time when you showed *sisu?* Describe.

8. Poor outcomes and even major tragedies sometimes occur when people make small careless errors. Name at least two times in the story when this happened. What was the outcome? Were they able to fix the problems? How?

9. Once they were finally back on Earth, the members of the Quantum Community were able to resume work for Project EarthHeal. Summarize their projects in easy English. If you were on the QC team, which project would you sign up for? Why?

10. Dr. EJ and the Quantum Community showed not only brilliance but compassion. Why are both characteristics necessary in helping to heal people, animals, and the environment?

Bonus Q! Albert Einstein referred to teleportation as "spooky action at a distance." Although teleporting people is still in the science-fiction realm, scientists recently reported that teleporting electrons was possible. What may this mean for the advancement of humanity? Hey, Google…

Acknowledgements

I always wondered why the typical "acknowledgements" section of a book had to involve so many people. Now I know! A saga such as *Crystal Child* does take a village to get that unique world from the author's mind to an actual book—complete with pages, words, designs, fonts, and margins! If I've missed anyone, please forgive me. But from beginning to end, I'd like to extend my sincere thanks and huge hugs to:

Annie McGreevy, my first content editor. Thank you for believing in this project. Your special talent for providing constructive criticism with such a gentle touch was no less than miraculous.

Carolyn Barton, middle-school English teacher for over forty years and crack expert with the red pen, you gave your expert time freely and professionally and somehow made every second fun!

Megan Crowl and the staff at Fulton Books, you got the ball rolling and helped me through each step. Thanks so much for your understanding with my fits and starts and neophyte questions. Your patience was remarkable.

Dean, my husband, you never once complained I was spending too much time at my computer. Perhaps that was because this gave you more time to binge-watch your detective shows, but you also walked the dog, cleaned the kitchen, did the laundry, went to the grocery, and finished other domestic tasks without one word of complaint. Not that I'm sexist, but I promise to take my turn soon (unless you enjoyed all those domestic chores). I am so grateful for your support.

Jayne Hartman, thank you for gently nudging me year after year, for begging to read my story the minute I told you about my idea years ago. Without your frequent gentle "nagging," this project may never have seen the light of day. Your suggestions and help with research were greatly appreciated!

Kathy Brown, your inspiration also kept me going with your pleas to send "just one more section" as you couldn't wait to find out what happened. You made me journey on whenever I began to doubt myself.

Kate and Eva, my youngest editors and readers (who better to judge my work?), you two could have chosen a million other YA/tween novels to read, but you chose mine. Kudos and big hugs for your suggestions, praise, and time.

Mary Nicolls, I can't find the words to thank you, my beautiful mother, may you rest in peace. You never failed to correct my grammar (not so silently). Your love of the English language and fine literature was my inspiration and shaped my life from the beginning. I picture you in your heavenly library in the sky, surrounded by millions of books with Max, the cat, curled up by your side. Read on!

Lindsay Rumple, big smooches and kudos to my lovely daughter for helping me in those areas which are her forte and my downfall—social media and logistics, not to mention giving me the two best. Gifts. Ever. Cam and Ben—you are my two little diamond stars who offer me much-needed breaks from the computer grindstone as well as grounding me and reminding me daily that love, laughter, and hugs are what life is really all about.

I saved my most special thanks for last. To my amazing son, David Kyle Kauffman (1979–2020), ADD artist and partner in (lawful) crime, creative ventures, imagination, and just plain fun for over forty years, your rough draft for the cover design of *Crystal Child* is now one of my most treasured possessions. I envision you on the Diamond Star, dancing your heart out just as you did at your sister's wedding, the best day of my life. "For those who were able to love and love well, for eternity their love will matter." You certainly loved well, my sweet child, and your love will most definitely matter for all time. Thanks for sharing your many creative gifts with the world. May your incredible *sisu* spirit grace the universe forever. See ya later, Sonnily.

Resource Guide

Outer Space

1. *The Inexplicable Universe: Unsolved Mysteries*—Neil deGrasse Tyson
2. Google.com
   - BPM 37093
   - 55 Cancri e
   - Is teleportation possible? Yes, in the quantum world
   - Kepler 452b
   - Wormholes in space

Climate Change and the Future

- Project Drawdown: The world's leading resource for climate solutions. Their mission is to help the world reach "drawdown"—the point at which greenhouse gasses stop climbing and begin to decrease. (Drawdown.org)
- www.drawdown.org
- www.swcoalition.org
- NextGen: www.nextgen.ecovillage.org
- www.treehugger.com
- Girl Effect: video showing the benefits of valuing girls, www.girleffect.org
- www.ouricebergismelting.com
- Youth for Climate Change for Unicef

- Greta Thunberg—a climate activist on the autism spectrum; also diagnosed with OCD (obsessive-compulsive disorder). She calls her so-called disabilities her "superpowers," as they help her persevere in her fervent mission to advocate for climate change remedies. SolarSister.org.
- *Sustainable World Sourcebook*: One of the best guides educators can use in helping students learn about efforts to heal the earth.
- Water.org: Brings water and better sanitation to parts of the world that need it. The charity works with small business loans to carry out their mission. They were rated in the top 10 percent of charities in transparency and fiscal accountability according to Top Charity Navigator. One of the founders is Matt Damon. (Water.org)

Other Resources

- *The Finnish Way*—Katja Pantzar
- *The Hidden Meaning of Birds: A Spiritual Field Guide*—Arin Murphy-Hiscock
- *Crystals for Everyday Living*—Christina Rodenbeck
- *Water Crystal Healing*—Masaru Emoto
- EPIGENETICS: Information about what makes genes switch on or off. Whatisepigenetics.com
- Five-dimensional Penrose tiling (Google.com)
- Lonsdaleite diamond (Google.com)
- Artificial intelligence
- DARPA/memory enhancing medication
- SETI—WOW message
- Nanobots for healing

Developmental Challenges

ADHD/ADD: www.chadd.org
Autism: www.autism-society.org
PTSD: www.ptsd.va.gov
Anxiety disorder: www.nimh.gov>health>topics>anxiety-disorders

CPSIA information can be obtained
at www.ICGtesting.com
Printed in the USA
LVHW041055300623
751251LV00027B/199/J